PURSUED:
TEN KNIGHTS ON THE BARROOM FLOOR

A NOVEL

MEL R. JONES

MEL&MARE™
Publications, LLC

Publishing management by Marian Jones
Assistant publishing management by Mark Jones
Editing by Doris Lora
Cover design and interior character illustrations by Timothy Flatt
Interior maps by Don Ellingsen
Interior layout and formatting by Mark Jones
Author photography by Joseph Szebeni

Library of Congress Control Number: 2018900073
ISBN-13: 978-0-9997651-9-7
ISBN-10: 0-9997651-9-1

Mel & Mare Publications, LLC
Wales, WI

DEDICATION

May this novel be part of the earthly expression of the "Ship From Wales" my mother, Viola Jones Geiger, always hoped would come in for me and my nine siblings (and their families), my beloved wife and helpmate, Marian, my four children, daughters Beth and Grace and sons Mark and Matthew (and their spouses), my seven grandchildren, future generations of my family, and those readers who are drawn to the creative adventure of this novel.

PART 1: DISTURBING DISCOVERIES

PART 2: DIAMETRIC DICHOTOMY

PART 3: DEVASTATING DISASTER

PART 4: DANGEROUS DÉNOUEMENT

ACKNOWLEDGMENTS

Every day that passes we learn about the demise of more and more WW II veterans. Paradoxically, the more their numbers dwindle, the greater the present generation's interest in these veterans' global experiences in the greatest conflict of the twentieth century.

My specific interest in WW II was stirred in 1973. Serving as an U.S. Army public affairs action officer on the news desk at the Pentagon, I was contacted by the Army Mortuary Service about news coverage on a B-24 Liberator bomber shot down in New Guinea in WW II, discovered 30 years later with remains recovered.

This event captured my imagination and inspired the idea for a novel which stayed with me until I finally finished writing my multi-layered manuscript 30-some years later.

My early interest in the downed B-24 was fueled when I was stationed at the U.S. Army Headquarters in Europe, and I was afforded the opportunity to witness the reclamation of a B-24 bomber by the Dutch from the Zuider Zee. I was told the copilot Charles Taylor survived and had visited the site a week prior to my visit. I was able to meet and interview him sometime later.

My eldest son U.S. Air Force Major (retired) Mark R. Jones and I also took a flight in the only B-24 bomber still operational, the Collings Foundation's *Witchcraft*, and we experienced the thrill of a sense of yesteryear in the present. I am also grateful to Mark, a former C-130 pilot, for research on the B-24 at Maxwell Air Force Base in Alabama.

Another writer, Michael J. Cundiff, a U.S. Army veteran and later a firefighter, also was drawn to the same news article of the ill-fated B-24 bomber that crashed in New Guinea in 1943. His nonfiction book, *Ten Knights in a Bar Room: Missing in Action in the Southwest Pacific in 1943*, was published by Iowa State University Press in 1990. He reported a feeling similar to mine in that the story would not let him go. His main interest centered on the ten-man B-24 crew members. He was inspired to interview relatives of the actual ten crew members of the downed aircraft who perished in the crash. My fictional mystery tale was enhanced by reading his detailed reporting of the incident, the lives of the B-24 crew members and the aftermath of 30 years of uncertainty for the families of the pilots involved.

An interview with my neighbor, U.S. Army Air Corps Major (retired) Carl L. Borgstrom, who was a flight engineer on a B-24 Liberator in the Pacific in WW II, including New Guinea, also embellished my research with much first-hand information.

To depict remote and primitive Papua New Guinea accurately required a great deal of research, particularly to create authentic interactions between the civilized and the primitive in my fictional account. These daily contacts and detailed conversations in the novel involve the physical anthropologist and her U.S. Central Identification Laboratory (CIL) team. In 1973 they are assigned to recover the remains of U.S. war dead from the 1943 crash of the "Ten Knights on the Barroom Floor" B-24 bomber near the base of Mount Bosavi in the Southern Highlands District of Papua New Guinea.

In my novel, the CIL team is camped on a mountain between two antagonistic primitive native tribes, one a river tribe and the other mountain dwellers. So the characters must try to bridge the 2000-3000-year cultural gap between their two worlds in order to work cooperatively with the tribes whose help proves essential in conducting the search for remains and determining what happened 30 years previously, notwithstanding the language barrier.

Books by early explorers in New Guinea that were especially helpful were those by Jack Hides and Michael J. Leahy, supplemented by innumerable other authors who visited the land that time forgot. Hair-raising accounts by Joel Kramer in *Beyond Fear* and Kira Salak in *Four Corners* are sure to keep readers up at night to see what happens as these young people relate the stories of their dangerous journeys into the New Guinea jungle environment and their encounters with native dwellers.

In order to understand and demonstrate the mindset and background of my WW II Japanese characters, I also researched a plethora of reference materials regarding Japanese society in the WW II time period. In addition, there was the need for information about a myriad of other subjects, including Johns Hopkins University in Baltimore, Maryland, Tripler Army Hospital in Hawaii, the field of forensic pathology, the U.S. Central Identification Laboratory (CIL) and the field of physical anthropology.

I also gathered detailed information about the B-24 bomber, the Japanese Ki-61 Tony and the deHavilland Beaver aircraft, Australian *kiap* experiences in New Guinea, salt wells, and spine-tingling accounts of coastwatchers in the Southwest Pacific. Extensive map research of New Guinea was required as well.

Heartfelt gratitude goes to my wife Marian Nelson Jones who assisted me in researching these topics in addition to her considerable secretarial help and never-failing enthusiasm for my writing endeavors. One of our most memorable research visits was to Johns Hopkins University in Baltimore in 2000. My friend U.S. Army Lieutenant Colonel (retired) Dale Keller drove Marian and me to Maryland from Washington, D.C. (where we had attended an honors ceremony) to view the sundial in front of Billings Hall, as well as the huge marble 10-foot statue of Jesus inside the building.

My son Matthew and his wife Kim, and family friends Charles and Jill Price were early readers of the finished novel, and I appreciated their enthusiastic response to the work. I also am grateful for the efforts of literary agent Jack Byrne who supplied a helpful critique of the novel, but could not follow up with it due to consolidation of his business to other genres after the passing of his partner Larry Sternig, whom I also had the pleasure of working with. Deep appreciation goes to my late father-in-law Al P. Nelson, University of Wisconsin Extension writing teacher and fellow Raconteur writing club member, for his many years of encouragement and helpful consultation regarding my writing projects.

Finally, I wish to say a word about my vision for this novel, the first of a planned trilogy with the underlying theme of why we go to war. A book concerning political philosophy by John G. Stoessinger entitled *Why Nations Go to War* posed the question and possible considerations. Is it the way we organize ourselves as nations? Or is it how we form alliances with other nations? Or is it inherent in the nature of man? Those of us who have been involved in the military in one way or another have been sent to protect our country by engaging in war to attain peace—a paradox of the human experience that repeats itself generation after generation, century after century.

In the novel, two worlds, civilized and primitive, past and present and four cultures, American, Japanese, Australian and native Papuan, deal with the horrors of war and conflict, but also relate to the connectedness of the human community in a literary mystery filled with this paradox of experience.

Notation: U.S. Army Lt. Colonel (retired) Mel R. Jones passed away in 2010. This novel was completed before his passing and is now published posthumously as an electronic book and a print-on-demand book by his wife Marian N. Jones through Mel & Mare Publications, LLC. Gratitude is due to professional book editor Doris Lora for her insight and copy-editing of the manuscript, to son Mark R. Jones for his formatting expertise, to Timothy Flatt for graphic design of the cover and interior character illustrations, and to Don Ellingsen for illustrating two interior maps. Son Matthew and his wife Kim offered daily support, commentary and encouragement, which was greatly appreciated for this self publishing project.

PURSUED:
TEN KNIGHTS ON THE BARROOM FLOOR

Mel R. Jones

PART ONE:
DISTURBING DISCOVERIES

"One hour alone is in thy hands,
The hour on which the shadow stands."

1 CHANCE DISCOVERY

Papua New Guinea, May 1972
Research Grant Request, Baltimore, Maryland, 1973

PREFACE TO U. S. ARMY CENTRAL IDENTIFICATION
LABORATORY (PROVISIONAL) FINDINGS, CASE NUMBER 316.
DR. DEANN TOLAND'S REPORT.

Mortui Vivis Praecipiant
"Let the dead teach the living."
On a morning in 1973 when forensic pathologist,
Dr. Emerson Stanek, posted this ancient maxim over
the door to his dissecting room at Tripler Army
Hospital in Hawaii, little did he know who wanted him
killed and why. He had to walk in the shoes of
American airmen from a downed World War II B-24
Liberator bomber in New Guinea, named "Ten Knights on
the Barroom Floor," those of Japanese survivors from
their bombing raid, as well as Papuan tribal leaders
to find the answers, as did the rest of us.

DeAnn Toland, Ph.D.
Physical Anthropologist

IN A DOWNPOUR, a search and rescue team fought against the
rapids of the Rentoul River as they paddled their canoes toward
8,000-foot Mount Bosavi, the tallest mountain on the boundary
marking the Southern Highlands District of New Guinea. They
were searching for a Qantas airliner which had disappeared a few
days earlier. The heavyset, red-haired Australian patrol officer or
kiap, leader of the team, signaled the natives to beach the canoes,
since further progress by water was impossible. The river was

1

swollen by rains the government patrol officer thought unusually severe for late May in this region.

The *kiap* directed his lone white assistant with two members of the Papuan constabulary to continue searching for the missing aircraft on foot, upstream along the bank of the raging Rentoul River. As the three-man detachment headed east up the slope of Mount Bosavi, the *kiap* found a safe place for the rest of his patrol to set up camp in a clearing on the north bank. Two days out of Nomad, he had spotted Giambu natives, known for their fierceness, on the opposite shore, dogging his patrol, and he was in no mood for an ambush.

After they unloaded supplies and equipment from the canoes, the *kiap* called a break. The remaining members of his band—two policemen and four carriers—hung their ponchos over the reeds along the bank and huddled under them, sheltered from the downpour. No sooner had they exchanged tobacco and lit their pipes than two shots rang out from upstream. The patrol officer sprang to his feet and lifted his revolver from its holster, firing twice to signal his comrades that help was on its way. He then motioned for the carriers to gather their bundles. With their rifles held at port arms, the seven-man patrol set off quickstep for Mount Bosavi.

They had gone about ten kilometers, following the curve of the Rentoul River on the path the advance party had cut through the jungle foliage, when the lead boy shouted, *"Balus! Balus!"* Aircraft wreckage lay like a crippled bird in a clearing against the northern slope of Mount Bosavi. One wing pointed skyward and the other, in a horizontal position, stretched toward the Rentoul. By its markings and configuration, the Australian patrol officer knew this was not the aircraft they had set out to find. His assistant concurred when he and the two constable scouts rejoined the main party.

"Chief, look at the name the Americans painted on the front of the fuselage."

"Yes, I see," the *kiap* answered. "'Ten Knights on the Barroom Floor'. It's a strange name for an aircraft, even for the Yanks. Oh, well. Must've meant something special for the crew who flew her."

Fearing an attack from hostile tribesmen dogging their patrol, the *kiap* drew his six bearers and four armed native constables into a semi-circle along the outer edge of the aircraft's wing, which lay perpendicular to the river. He instructed the Papuans, again huddled under ponchos, to keep their backs to the mountain wall and their eyes riveted on the tall *kunai* grass on the far bank of the Rentoul. Then, leaving his assistant in charge, the patrol officer took up a position under the wing. He shielded his notebook from the rain with the wide brim of his bush hat as he wrote his report.

Tuesday, May 23, 1972—Our patrol is in an uncharted part of the Southern Highlands District. D'Albertis may have had this area in mind when he said it's easier to cross the Alps than to ascend an ordinary hill in Papua. There's no sign of the Qantas airliner we're searching for. However, two hours before sunset, scouts spotted the wreckage of an American B-24 Liberator bomber, with the name "Ten Knights on the Barroom Floor," painted on the front of its fuselage. It is located on the northern slope of Mount Bosavi along the edge of the Rentoul River, not a good place to crash, or be caught after dark for that matter. I'll knock about inside the fuselage for a look. Then move my team back down the Rentoul to make camp where we left the canoes. Doubt after 30 years we'll find any sign inside the bomber that there were survivors. But even if time and New Guinea have forgotten our brave allies, Australia shall not.

The *kiap* closed his notebook, drew in a deep breath and crawled into the aircraft wreckage through the rear section. Five minutes later he staggered from the tail. He pitched forward into the wet *kunai* grass as if struck in the back with an arrow. His assistant rushed to his side and knelt beside him.

"*Come a gutser!*" the *kiap* exclaimed. He laid his folded poncho on the wet grass and began to peel back the corners of the garment, revealing a severed hand.

"Lord, save us all! Who could've done such a bloody thing," asked the assistant patrol officer.

"Dunno, lad, but the mitt's been severed just above the wrist."

"Ye suppose the same cannibals trailing us done in the Yank, chief?"

"First, we can't be sure the bloke's American. And this is not likely the work of cannibals. The ones I've pinched never left a morsel behind. Especially a dismembered hand. Fingers and hands are usually carried back to the village for the women and children to feast on."

As he spoke, the *kiap* turned the severed hand over, palm down, on the poncho. "By the size and shape of the nails, I figure the victim was white. Hold on! What have we here?"

"Bloody hell, chief! He's got a cig lighter sandwiched betwixt his thumb and forefinger."

"Yes, lad, I see. It's a Zippo—a coveted item during the war. Pull the fingers apart whilst I pry it loose. Zippo's are usually inscribed. There, see beneath the sketch of a sundial—markings!"

"If it's devil's mumbo-jumbo, I don't want to look."

"No, lad. Under the sundial the inscription reads:

One hour alone is in thy hands,
The hour on which the shadow stands.

"Must be a code. What's on the other side of the lighter?"

"Initials, 'OCS'."

"Creepy! All this coded stuff in a severed hand. I'm for getting out of here straightaway."

The *kiap* did not answer. He began rewrapping the evidence in his poncho, and with a quick glance at the line of Papuans guarding them, the middle-aged official took in a deep wheezy breath and rose to his feet.

"Best keep the matter to ourselves for the time being, lad. Once back in Nomad, we'll examine the hand more thoroughly. Its condition suggests a more recent crime rather than one of 30 years ago. Then there's..."

"Dear Lord, don't tell me any more."

"Ye should know the interior of the Liberator looks like a combat zone. Somebody fired shots through the fuselage from the inside—confirmation we've got a crime scene here. War is a ghastly business, lad. It pits souls against one another until the world is aflame, dismembering peace."

After a moment of silence, the big Aussie sighed and added, "It's not for us to conduct a requiem. The Yanks will want to run their own investigation of this crime scene and search for remains, although none were visible I could see, except this mysterious severed hand holding a lighter."

"We've got a more immediate problem, sir. Look! A string of warriors are quickstepping down the mountain slope on our side of the river, heading straight for us. If they're hostile, we're trapped!"

               *   *   *

In the spring of the next year (1973) at Johns Hopkins University Medical Center in Baltimore, Maryland, 38-year-old Dr. Emerson Stanek, youngest member in an entourage of distinguished alumni, bounded past the campus sundial. He hardly glanced at his five colleagues gathered around the icon as he continued up the second tier of steps leading to Billings Hall. About to enter the Queen Anne-style domed building named for the post-Civil War surgeon who had organized the hospital, Stanek stopped when he heard his mentor call.

"Wait, Emerson," Dr. Thomas Haveland, dean of forensic pathology, called to his protégé. "Join us on the terrace, my boy."

Stanek retraced his steps, joining the group around the sundial, his shaven head bent low and his dark Van-dyke style beard throwing a shadow across the sundial's brass plate.

"What's the delay this time?" he demanded snapping his fingers. Haveland pointed to the sundial and Stanek's hard, steel-blue eyes fixed on the faded inscription.

Dr. Haveland read aloud:

One hour alone is in thy hands,
The hour on which the shadow stands.

"So?" Stanek asked.

"So, Emerson, what does the sundial's message say to you?"

"I'd say we're wasting time better spent discussing a grant for my beekeeper cancer study. Or has the committee forgotten why I'm here? Certainly not to indulge in sentimentality."

Haveland shook his white mane. "Come now, my boy, eight years away from campus, and you've already forgotten the traditions of the pathology department. Each time we pass this way, we devise new meanings for the sundial's message, remember? For example, Dr. Corsairs just reminded us one's courage is greatest at the beginning of a journey. My own contribution is the first principle of pathology you may recall from my lectures."

"Yes, I remember. 'Look intently enough at anything, and you'll see something that might otherwise escape you.'"

5

"Well done, Emerson."

Still exasperated by the delay, Stanek shook his head as he eyed the chairman and each colleague in turn. He then walked past the sundial to the edge of the terrace, gripped the iron fence and surveyed the campus like a sea captain on lookout for troubled waters. Instinctively his eyes were drawn to Reed Hall. Surrounded by magnolia trees which stood like sentinels against the gray, spring sky, his old student residence could still be seen across Broadway's double lanes, slightly to the right of the horseshoe drive marking the administration building's entrance.

Far off down the magnolia-lined cobblestone concourse, he looked for the Victorian-style house at the intersection of McElderry and North Caroline Streets. There, at age 11, he had gone to live with the Staneks—Rufus and Patricia and their daughter Catherine.

The house was gone. A naked gray parking lot stood in its place. He remembered the night he and Catherine had shared an innocent kiss under the big magnolia in the front yard upon returning home from her high school prom. He had remembered that night for many years as a student and resident physician, and how it had later unexpectedly led to a nightmarish expulsion from his adoptive family. The incident had scarred his reputation, just as chemicals thrown by his adoptive sister had burned into his cheek, leaving their mark on his face. The old house was gone, just as the family he loved had been torn asunder so many years ago.

"Emerson, the sundial. We're awaiting your impressions," Dr. Haveland prompted. He fluffed his long white hair away from his starched collar. "Please, indulge us," he added.

"Never paid much attention to monuments strewn along the path of scientific progress on this campus," Stanek scoffed.

"Surely, this memorial has special meaning for you," Haveland reminded him. "After all, a gift from the Stanek Foundation maintains the old sundial and other monuments." Haveland extended his arms as if to embrace the entire campus, then continued, "We're grateful for the support and generosity of visionaries like Catherine, and your father before her. Without them, our icons would fall into disrepair. Surely, we can agree on this."

Hearing the names of the father and sister he acquired through his adoption into the Stanek family turned the young pathologist's cheeks crimson. How dare the committee fritter precious time away on campus monuments or raise family relationships which Haveland, at least, knew were estranged. Before he died, Emerson's adoptive father had stripped him of all but the Stanek name. No more than a stone's throw from where he stood, Emerson's adoptive mother languished in a mental institution. And Catherine had stolen the dignity and happiness he once cherished.

"No way!" Stanek replied. "Rufus Stanek threw me out, and Catherine shattered my reputation, leaving Patricia bereft, as well! I've had to find my own way since then."

He started to follow his outburst by asking how much longer his group of peers intended to slight the data he had submitted two months in advance of this meeting. But when he saw Haveland's paper-thin lips glide into a benign smile, he clenched his teeth, bit his own full lips and tried another tack.

"I've hit on an interpretation for your sundial: 'All hours offer opportunities, but wasted ones kill all potential in the end'," he said.

For his part, Haveland turned and pointed at some dark clouds still off in the distance near Baltimore harbor.

"Maybe this afternoon walk down memory lane is not one of my better ideas. Come, gentlemen, we'll chat along the way, while Emerson beguiles us with his statistics."

Stanek's flush subsided, and he smiled, wasting no time launching into the facts he had stored in his memory for this moment. "Well, 84% of the beekeepers surveyed reported no malignancy."

As the group turned to move, Stanek hesitated when he spotted an elderly gentleman hobbling up the stairs and onto the terrace as fast as his age and crutches allowed. The patient, if he was one, paused in front of the sundial to catch his breath. He braced his crutches against the stone pedestal and blinked at the young pathologist as if to apologize for the intrusion.

He was more than half a foot shorter than Stanek's six feet, although had he stood upright, he might have reached five-foot-seven or eight. His eyes, like his shoulder length hair dangling over the open lapels of his sports jacket, had a telltale, yellowish-green hue. As the stranger turned to face Haveland, his eyes became like live coals ready to burst into flames. At one point the man's legs seemed to go out from under him, signaling loss of connective tissue, thought Stanek, a possible malignancy.

"Fibrasarcoma," Stanek whispered under his breath. He watched the intruder's needle-marked hands twitch and tremble with the rubber grips as he struggled to align his wooden crutches with a body as used up as a burnt log. Yet, Stanek noticed deliberateness about the man's manner and his quick movements suggested control.

"Dr. Haveland, Jim Cole, *Honolulu Advertiser*. I've one question to ask you." Cole's voice was surprisingly strong as he stared at the chairman, who looked perplexed.

Stanek studied the reporter's profile. Not the face of a day-to-day working journalist, he surmised.

"Surely you can see I'm busy," Haveland said.

"Aw, c'mon, sir. You're one of the few medicos who'll talk to the press these days."

Haveland shot a quizzical glance at the other dons. Stanek interpreted this as a denial the chairman had ever been chummy with the media. "If you'll be quick about it, I'll take one question," Haveland said.

"Are you going to take the B-24 case?"

"Hmm... B-24... Let me see..."

Stanek noticed America's number one forensic pathologist was, in this exchange at least, as inarticulate as the murderers he had seen Haveland demolish in courtroom testimony. By contrast, Cole seemed indomitable.

"Yes, sir, the bomber shot down in New Guinea 30 years ago. The clock is ticking. General Antonio Bellicosi requested your help identifying crew remains." Cole's eyes were now flaming darts as he pressed his advantage.

Haveland looked away as if to study the sundial. After a brief pause, he resumed eye contact with the reporter.

"At the moment, I don't have time for a new case. Besides, I've told the Pentagon that co-mingled remains make identification extremely difficult. Anyway, they've got a young anthropologist working in New Guinea. I'm proud to say Dr. DeAnn Toland attended my physical evidence seminar in Chicago and is surely capable of handling matters."

The reporter loosened his grip on one of his crutches and swiped a needle-marked hand across his forehead. "Pardon me for

8

saying so, sir, but I don't think you've got all the facts. We're talking more than dead bodies here. I've heard from a reliable source we might be dealing with a crime scene, and a maimed American survivor could be roaming the jungle as we speak."

"I'm sorry, but you asked for one question, Mr. Cole, and I'm going to have to hold you to just one. We've set aside the next hour or two for Dr. Stanek's project, perhaps of more interest to you. You could wait and interview our colleague on his cancer research after we're finished if he's agreeable."

"Maybe I will."

Stanek had already dismissed the possibility of talking to a member of the press, especially a journalist as pesky as Cole came across. The pathologist followed his peers into Billings Hall thinking if Cole knew about him, as he seemed to, the reporter would know better. If asked, Stanek would tell Mr. Cole, "I might critique my colleagues now and then, but I don't grant media interviews, whether here in Baltimore, at Tripler Army Hospital in Hawaii where I work, or anywhere else."

As Haveland's committee walked down the short corridor toward the rotunda, Stanek heard the thump, thump of crutches striking the floor. He looked back to see Cole doing his best to keep pace.

"If you gents don't mind, I'll just have a look around. What an interesting place Major Billings created," the reporter called in a voice amplified by the echo in the corridor. "Won't find any dusty crevices attracting dirt and insects. No, siree, not in the house the major built. Billings did away with corners wherever he could and put easy curves in their place. What a recipe for life, wouldn't you say so, Dr. Stanek?"

Stanek didn't answer. Up ahead in the rotunda, Dr. Haveland paused before the ten-foot Christ statue and rubbed the Carrara-marble feet. One by one the other members of the committee followed the chairman's example. Stanek grimaced. How could these old fools carry on a non-sectarian ritual begun 80 years ago? Surely current medical students had no time for the sentimental religiosity practiced by young Hopkins doctors, students and patients in 1896 when the statue was carried through the north entrance of the hospital and placed in the rotunda.

Stanek felt his throat go dry, and he had to swallow hard to keep from choking. He saw himself at age 17 being dragged by the hair and neck and forced to kneel before the statue, while the sweat of a hovering Rufus Stanek dripped into the long, open chemical burn on his right cheek. He had pleaded to be treated for his injury. But the old man had tightened his grip, demanding his adoptive son confess. Catherine was only defending her honor, he had raged, when she smashed a vial of sulfuric acid against his jaw during a laboratory experiment.

"No, no, father, we didn't do anything wrong," Emerson had pleaded.

But the irate parent shoved Emerson's slightly disfigured face between the statue's massive feet and bellowed, "Tell Christ why my daughter was naked from the waist up if you didn't do anything wrong, you ungrateful little bastard."

Emerson was certain his adoptive father would have suffocated him had not a staff member come by and intervened. After many minutes, which Emerson remembered as pure agony, Dr. Thomas Haveland was able to calm down his mentor and persuade him to release Emerson into his custody so he could be treated in the emergency room. Only later did Emerson learn Rufus had insisted the injury be recorded as a laboratory accident involving "teenage experimentation."

Thereafter, what had been a symbol of compassion and hope for his colleagues and their patients, the huge, Viking-style Christ statue became for Emerson a bitter reminder of his expulsion from the only family he had ever known. Throughout his years at Johns Hopkins as undergraduate, intern and resident, he felt an inner satisfaction he had never succumbed to praying before the stone idol for anything.

Once more, he elected to bypass the figure others associated with forgiveness. He kept his head bent forward as he hurried after Dr. Haveland and the committee. Only when Cole called out from behind him did Stanek look back.

"Hey, Doc, they have bees and beekeepers in New Guinea, too, you know," the reporter shouted. "Only the bees don't sting. They bite!"

2 MISFORTUNATE MOUNTAIN ENCOUNTERS

Papua New Guinea, 1973

U.S. ARMY CENTRAL IDENTIFICATION LABORATORY (PROVISIONAL) FINDINGS, CASE NUMBER 316. DR. DEANN TOLAND'S REPORT.

The moment I descended the rung ladder of Major Frank Yowell's Beaver aircraft on a makeshift airstrip on Mount Bosavi, Southern Highlands District, Papua New Guinea, I was surrounded by a group of Riami women and children. The pervasive humidity intensified the heat. The women were topless and the children were naked. All wore a dumbfounded, albeit excited, expression on their dark faces as they gazed at the first white "misis" I assume they had ever seen.

By evening, after the dancing and singing subsided, I was smeared with stale pig grease and sweat from the enthusiastic embraces of the Riami women and children. I proceeded to move the Central Identification Laboratory (CIL) team further up the mountain. Per agreement with both of the rival Tugaru and Riami tribes, we established our base camp adjacent to the Tugaru, who are the overlords in this district.

In contrast to the female natives, only a trickle of warriors from either the Riami or the Tugaru tribes showed themselves. Their long-time inter-tribal war and fear of the sorcery of white "sky" people kept them at bay. Realizing that our mission, the location and identification of the remains of our young WW II American heroes, turned on cooperation between all parties, we searched within these patriarchal societies for a suitable emissary. He found us instead.

DeAnn Toland, Ph.D.
Physical Anthropologist

A LSO IN ANOTHER particularly wet spring in 1973, Riami tribal leader MilkEye set out for the upper slopes of Mount Bosavi on a honey-gathering mission for his ailing daughter, LikLik, by his favorite wife. LikLik lay dying in the woman's hut. The child refused the yams and pork prepared for her, and MilkEye believed only honey would give LikLik the strength to fight the fever and chills racking her small body.

As he drew closer to the salt well guarded by the feared Tugaru, he paused to feed a taro root to the small pig he carried in the open mesh string bag, or *bilum*, slung over one shoulder. "Eat. No squeal. Noise bring Tugaru. Put you in cooking pot," he whispered. Although a heavy May rain had fallen the previous night, MilkEye was pleased to feel the warm morning sun on his bare back.

The slippery trail under his flat, callused feet was drying fast. Thankful for a drier trail much easier to negotiate should a fast escape become necessary, MilkEye waited until the Tugaru sentry on the west slope of the well made his turn, then he slipped by him. He passed the Tugaru burial rock and then cut his way through the bush until he reached the isolated place where he and his late father Situmu had set their hunting boxes for sniping the flightless cassowary birds.

When he came to a clear ledge, he looked down to make sure he wasn't being followed. Below ran the Rentoul River and on its southern bank, not far from his village, he saw the carcass of the great iron bird that had brought the sky people to Mount Bosavi 30 years earlier. Standing next to the aircraft, was the *kiap*, whom he and his fellow warriors had rescued from the Giambu cannibals last year, just as his father had done for the first white spirits, helping them escape detection by the Tugaru so long ago. MilkEye sighed, anxious about his mission. But his honey-gathering for LikLik was too important to turn back or think about anything else.

The 16 other Riami warriors who had set out in the morning from his village with MilkEye had balked at going beyond the

Tugaru salt well. Their warning rang in his ears as he moved farther up the slope. "Tugaru cross you go up to salt well. No go up mountain. If Tugaru no kill you, evil mountain spirit, Two Face, kill you like he kill papa, Situmu." Seeing the mixture of fear and admiration in his tribesmen's faces, MilkEye had hidden his own fears. He could not even persuade his *one-talk* and *age-mate*, WonTok, to accompany him, even though they had often gone there as youngsters with Situmu, MilkEye's father.

MilkEye, alone with his sacrificial pig-gift, had quickly passed through enemy territory, using the tricks Situmu had taught him, into the mystic realm where Two Face reigned. The mountain spirit would not be as easily fooled as the Tugaru, so MilkEye turned to Situmu for guidance. He sat down on the ledge, began his questions, and then he supplied the answers, as if they came from his father.

"Great Situmu, how MilkEye reach honey Two Face share with Riami when you Riami headman?"

"Hear warning, my son. Two Face no more give golden honey. Two Face cross white people came for his treasure."

"But MilkEye no white! Sky people bring honey down from mountain. Why Two Face cross at MilkEye, but like people of great airplane?"

"Remember tribal mysteries. Two Face one, but has two faces. One face good. Other face evil. Tugaru know this. Tugaru trade salt with Riami. Please good face of Two Face. Tugaru also make sacrifices to evil face of Two Face. But Riami warrior must choose face he follow."

"WonTok tell Tugaru trade salt with Riami, so we no steal Tugaru pigs. No eat Tugaru flesh again. Is cousin wrong?"

"Son, WonTok talk true, but MilkEye ask Situmu about spirits. Make plan if Tugaru war party find you. Give Tugaru pig for salt, but no more search for honey then. WonTok stay away from Tugaru, but MilkEye wise to fear evil Two Face more than Tugaru."

MilkEye trembled. "Papa, me have no plan to fight evil spirit."

"Spirit of Two Face have no body, my son. Two Face fears only stronger spirits. Evil Two Face no care about Riami or Tugaru."

MilkEye shivered again and turned to head back. But like thunder in the distance, he heard the call of a cassowary. It packed courage, like the sound of his father's voice addressing the tribal council before sending out a war party. He sniffed the clean mountain air anticipating the taste of honey awaiting him further up the mountain. He began to climb again, swinging a machete to clear a path.

After a hundred yards or so, he slid the bark straps of the *bilum* with the pig in it down a sweat-drenched arm and set the bundle beside the track he had just cut. He rested next to it in the tall, cool grass. Once his breathing approached normal, he slung the bow, which he had been carrying in his hand since entering Tugaru territory, to the shoulder still aching from the weight of the heavy bag. MilkEye knew he must have both hands free for the ordeal ahead, so he fastened the *bilum* around his forehead. The pig squealed, but then settled down in the bag resting between MilkEye's shoulder blades. MilkEye removed a stone L-shaped axe and balanced it against the shoulder opposite his bow.

As he puffed up the steepest part of the trail, he was again so hot and exhausted that he thought of turning back. He reflected on his comrades waiting among the cool blades of *kunai* grass below the Tugaru salt well. MilkEye scolded himself for such thoughts. His was a desperate mission. LikLik's life depended upon his obtaining Two Face's honey, as it had helped sustain the sky people who had crashed on the mountain in the great airplane.

MilkEye came to the arch formed by limestone and returned the machete to his girdle so he could pass through. The way through the limestone arch was so narrow he had to turn sideways to continue. As he brushed against the low vegetation, he could feel the leeches settling in between his toes. Blood from the leech bites would alert the Tugaru, who, with their sensitive noses, might easily pick up his trail. Nevertheless, MilkEye pressed on.

It was only a short distance to the clearing at the edge of the swamp, MilkEye reminded himself. There a ladder fashioned out of vines cut by his father awaited any Riami brave enough to climb higher for the honey. When he reached the clearing, he cleared the leeches from his toes and reached for the vine ladder. Before ascending, he bowed his head, touched his heart and pointed to the spot where Situmu had been killed by a falling boulder. He used his other hand to reach over his shoulder and cover the snout of the squealing piglet.

It wouldn't do for the mountain god to hear MilkEye's sacrifice before he had adequately prepared it in exchange for the honey.

The pig's now-muffled squeals reminded him of the pitiful sounds LikLik made, lying on a grass mat as she passed the night whimpering for food she was unable to keep down.

Midway up the ladder, MilkEye heard a chopping sound above his head. In his haste to reach his prize, he had forgotten the safer, alternate route he, WonTok and Situmu had discovered and had used to slip into evil Two Face's domain undetected. It was too late now. He gripped the vine with both hands, thinking someone was cutting the ladder he stood on more than halfway up the escarpment. As the sound drew closer, the chopping was interspersed with grunts resembling those of a wild beast gnawing at the sugar cane *pitpit* rungs as it worked its way toward him. But he knew better. In the desolate wilderness, wild men or their wilder spirits were the only beasts he must guard against.

He started to backtrack, but the weight of the squealing piglet pulled him down faster than his feet were able to go. Anchoring himself against the vines, he reached for the small, steel knife in his belt the white *misis* had given his *one-talk* at the carcass of the fallen airplane. He had acquired the knife in a trade with his friend for just such an emergency. Working furiously, he cut the bark fiber straps holding the *bilum* tight against his forehead and heard the string bag and its cargo crash against the limestone outcropping below him. The animal gave a final squeal, then fell silent.

Afraid the pig's dead spirit would become entangled in his own, should Two Face suddenly suck in his great breath to devour his sacrifice, MilkEye looked neither up nor down. Instead he planted his face against the vine ladder and scurried down the rungs as fast as his 33-year-old legs could carry him. He paused only once to gauge whether the strange noise had gained on him.

This time he heard a more ominous sound. Above him steel clanged against stone, and MilkEye felt bits of limestone fall onto his head and face. His flared nostrils caught the scent of wet moss, freshly dug. Certain the beast or wicked spirit was dislodging a boulder to hurl down on him, MilkEye froze again against the vine ladder, his face buried deeper in the *pitpit*. Two Face had many ways of dealing with warriors foolish enough to trespass into his territory. His own father's body had been crushed beneath a boulder only a god could heave.

Fearful lest he meet the same fate, MilkEye shuddered at the consequences to his family. For a son to die in the same manner as his father meant the whole clan was cursed. To keep the evil incident from spreading from one generation to another, Riami tribal law under such circumstances dictated MilkEye's wives and children forfeit their lives as well. Sweat and tears streamed down his dark cheeks at the thought, and in the same instant panic gave way to action.

Although he was still 15 feet above the landing upon which the pig's carcass lay, MilkEye pushed away from the escarpment, grasping his legs behind the knees hoping to land on his wide, flat feet. The fall left him winded and dazed. He also lost his knife, his favorite stone hunting axe and a quiver of bone-tipped arrows. Without the arrows, his bow was useless anyway, so he took it from over his shoulder and flung it aside. He stopped only long enough to shake the dead pig from the *bilum* and wrap the bag around his arm. He waded through the leech-infested swamp toward the limestone arch. Then he made his way hastily along the path he had cut toward the more level part of the trail that passed by the Tugaru salt well. Now, an encounter with the enemy could mean the loss of his head.

MilkEye did not rest until he came in sight of the cane fence that marked the boundary between the living and the spirit world. He lay down in the trail and rolled over on his side to avoid being seen by the Tugaru sentry patrolling the living *pitpit* barrier. The sword-like leaves that protected the enemies' salt well tore at his bare torso, and when MilkEye saw the young Tugaru sniff the air for the scent of blood, a new source of alarm arose.

The enemy drove his three-pronged spear blindly into the *pitpit* barrier. MilkEye dodged the first three or four thrusts. But when an outer point of the trident nicked his arm, he knew it was only a matter of time before the poisoned-tipped middle prong found its mark. MilkEye stood up, climbed out of the *pitpit* and faced his enemy across the path. He laid himself open to attack by extending his hands to show that he concealed no weapons and carried only an empty string bag. He expected the sentry to call in the other Tugaru patrols for help, but the surprised youth hesitated.

MilkEye decided to appeal to the vanity of one so young. He pretended to offer the string bag. He squinted to hide his own fear. "Here. Take my head. Put in *bilum*. Tugaru make *singsing*. Trophy is head of Riami headman, son of Situmu, taken by one man."

The youth smiled triumphantly as he lowered his spear and pointed it at MilkEye's mid-section. The Tugaru charged. MilkEye sidestepped the thrust and allowed the lethal end of the trident to pass by him. Next, with lightning quickness, he caught the neck of the charging youth with the cut bark strap of his *bilum*, and he wrapped it around his opponent's throat.

MilkEye kept pressure on the *bilum* collar. He watched the Tugaru's tongue slip from the side of his mouth as his eyes practically flew out of his head. Still, MilkEye tightened his grip. Only when he saw the bloody froth form at the edges of the young warrior's lips and felt the man's gourd-covered penis grow erect against his own bare thigh, did MilkEye gently lower him to the ground.

The murder had to be concealed. Of this, MilkEye was certain. No one would believe he had acted in self-defense and was reluctant to kill one so young. As he looked at the body, he realized with a start the youth was the brother of *Bikmaus*, or as the whites called him, Loud Mouth, the Tugaru tribal leader. To make matters worse, both brothers were the sons of Salty Meri, the head of the Tugaru salt well operation. If they discovered he had committed the murder, the Tugaru tribe would track MilkEye and his heirs to the end of the earth, never satisfied they had spilled enough blood.

"Papa, help MilkEye," he implored. Then he answered himself, "Hide body where bodies commonplace."

Ten minutes later MilkEye arrived at the Tugaru burial site. He threw the slain warrior and his weapons into the pit between the two giant stones. But when he saw that the body remained visible from the top ledge, he cupped a hand over his nose and mouth and climbed in among the decaying corpses. He began covering his recent kill with other Tugaru bodies, most of which had been reduced to bones.

MilkEye drew back suddenly as his fingers closed over a clothed figure. The white man had been decapitated, and when MilkEye grasped the bones, he slipped and rolled to the bottom of the pit. There the native saw a large bundle wrapped in banana leaves next to the decapitated head on the floor of the cavern. He inspected the bundle and then scraped back the covering. Inside he saw many things belonging to the great airplane, including the sky people's canoe-of-air. MilkEye covered the package again with the banana leaves and rolled from the hole between the rocks.

He got up and crept over the limestone until he could feel it give way to the softer *kunai* grass, long enough to conceal him until he reached his comrades, if they had not scattered. After making his way 100 yards or so through the grass towering over his head, he was relieved to hear the murmur of Riami voices from the clearing where he had left them.

When MilkEye emerged from the tall grass, all but one of MilkEye's companions rendered their customary greeting—a standing embrace in which they swung their muscular arms around each other's waists. After his encounter with the evil mountain spirit and the Tugaru youth, the old warrior was happy for the contact of his fellow Riami tribesmen and paid no attention to the slight of one. WonTok, his closest friend, hailed him. He told the assembled warriors: "MilkEye brave warrior, great spirit. Trick Tugaru, and escape evil Two Face. Came back to Riami." But the recalcitrant member of the group still did not come forward and offer his praise.

MilkEye wondered if WonTok would let the slight pass. He did not. WonTok chided the young man, pointing out his recent induction into warrior status would not excuse him from a warrior's duty. "No greet MilkEye. Make you like Tugaru. Riami no strut like proud, cruel Tugaru," WonTok admonished. "Fierce look no make man warrior."

The others in the group seemed to grasp what was coming next. They formed a semi-circle, their backs to the sun facing MilkEye, his *one-talk* and the chastised warrior. After a nod to WonTok, MilkEye joined the others sitting cross-legged in the luxuriant growth of *kunai* leaving his *age-mate* and his young quarry standing in the center clearing where a blazing morning sun spotlighted them.

WonTok pointed to MilkEye. "Great warrior lose eye when WonTok throw way-ward dart in war game. Now MilkEye's eyelid blink over cloudy socket. MilkEye got one eye. When MilkEye, WonTok ready for initiation, one eye no stop MilkEye from warrior status." WonTok paused and circled the youth like a *kiap* inspecting a line of boys before going on patrol.

"MilkEye take razor-sharp leaves of green *pitpit*, tilt head back, put leaf rolls into nose. MilkEye smile when face bloody. Take away weak mama's blood. Make place for warrior's blood. Honor papa, great warrior Situmu. Situmu turn head aside like cassowary.

Situmu too proud of fledgling to speak, but Riami warriors cheer."

WonTok stopped in front of the quivering boy and threw-up his hands in disgust. "Your papa no teach you customs of Riami warrior. You no sleep in men's hut or learn sacred mysteries if mama's blood still in you. You like woman who see men's trophies, steal magic. Warrior's ways no like woman's ways. Riami cut women who steal magic into pieces. Throw into river."

WonTok paused again. The boy whimpered, but everyone else sat in stony silence. WonTok extended his hands palms-up and turned about on his heel. "Where's your *one-talk*?"

The boy hesitated, then with a shaky hand pointed to a youth so close in age and size to his own, they could have passed for twins. WonTok stepped in front of the *age-mate* indicated. "You, stand up. Tell legend of MilkEye," he commanded.

At this point MilkEye also rose to his feet. He positioned himself between WonTok and the new boy to be interrogated. WonTok seized the moment. "Headman hear first, then talk," WonTok said, as MilkEye cupped a hand behind his ear and circled the standing participants as if to listen first to one and then the other.

In a singsong manner the boy spoke for his reluctant *one-talk*. "MilkEye headman, strong, wily, courageous, got spirit of Riami, bend like river, twist like vine in huts, but then agree. MilkEye learn to speak pidgin from Situmu, who help sky people. First, Situmu work for *Masta* Hides, who give Situmu steel axes, long knives. Situmu bring back to Riami. Then Situmu help white spirits from great airplane."

WonTok held up a grimy hand. "Stop. Speak about MilkEye's legend before Tugaru hear you, come, throw you into river like small fish."

The storyteller waited until the laughter subsided, then, on signal from WonTok, he resumed. "MilkEye tell about spirit in here," the youth pointed to his heart. "No in head." He tugged at a long ringlet greased with fat. "No in mask of warrior." He traced the contours of a discolored bone-ornament in his nose. "Only spirit make warrior fearless."

WonTok held up his hand again. "No more talk. Who finish legend of MilkEye?"

A murmur rose from the seated warriors as the recalcitrant initiate stepped past WonTok and the still circling MilkEye. The youth thrust out his thin chest and in a combination of pantomime and words started to pick up the narrative.

"Sit down," WonTok said to the boy who had slighted MilkEye. "Me finish legend," WonTok said.

"No, let him talk," MilkEye ordered, winking at the youth.

The boy faced his comrades. "MilkEye leaps on shoulders of ancestors who help him defeat enemy. Like white spirits, he smiles and winks. With good eye, MilkEye see, like on top of great mountain. With one eye of great bird, MilkEye see what make enemy quiver."

An iridescent sheen accentuated the lines of MilkEye's face and ran down the sinews of his naked chest, arms, thighs and legs as he led a cheer for the recalcitrant. MilkEye gestured for the boy to come to him. "Why you no greet MilkEye?" he inquired of the young warrior, who had begun administering the traditional Riami greeting, albeit belatedly.

The youth hung his head and muttered, "MilkEye of legend go against evil Two Face. Bring Two Face's anger down on Riami."

The old warrior turned to face his comrades. "Riami men, hear. Spirits have magic medicine, like wind, sometimes blow good, sometimes bad. MilkEye see what way spirit blow. One man go into place of mountain spirit. Find Two Face still wicked, selfish; no like good mountain spirit so long ago. Two Face no give payback to all Riami, but kill MilkEye's daughter, LikLik, instead. LikLik grow weaker each time moon change face. Without sweet honey, LikLik die. Then Two Face get one more sacrifice from clan of Situmu."

A mane of tightly braided hair, long-since laced with gray streaks, swung from shoulder to shoulder as MilkEye shook his head. Then, using his entire body, he reenacted his near fatal encounter with evil Two Face at Situmu's vine ladder, but he did not include the murder of the Tugaru warrior upon his return from the honey expedition. When he had finished, MilkEye embraced the boy standing next to him. At this point MilkEye's *one-talk* broke his silence. "Maybe white *misis* help LikLik," WonTok offered.

"Would white *misis* pit her magic against the mountain spirit's?" MilkEye asked.

"*Misis* give knives and blankets to Riami. Maybe her magic stronger than Two Face's."

"MilkEye no want knives and blankets, but want honey. Sweet food come from gods, who order bees make honey."

"WonTok see white *misis* eat honeycomb her *one-mate* bring from inside bubble face of fallen airplane."

For the first time since coming down from the steep part of the mountain, MilkEye's lips broke into a broad grin.

"Will she, who give you knife, let us get honey from the nose of the airplane for LikLik?" he asked.

"She no like Riami or Tugaru go near airplane, but maybe she trade honey for pig," WonTok replied.

"What white *misis*' name?" MilkEye asked.

The warrior's friend held up two grimy fingers. "Sky people like two names. *Misis* turn head when *Ki-ap* No-ble say 'Dok-tor Tow-land'. Her gold-head *one-talk*, Mah-jah Yow-ell, pilot of small airplane, call 'Dee-Ann,' and she turn head to him."

"Where is two-name *misis* now?"

"Near belly of big airplane looking for bones of lost white people, or tapping her fingers on typewriter."

MilkEye's smile grew so wide the upward tilt of his curved lips met his cheekbones and his flat nose crinkled. Creases spread out from his one good dark beacon glistening in a pool of clear white marble, as well as from the milky white socket that appeared, then disappeared as MilkEye blinked.

"We help Dok-tor Tow-land. Maybe she trade honey for bundle of sky-people-magic MilkEye find. We test. See if Dok-tor Tow-land's magic stop Two Face's curse on LikLik, and bring good Two Face back to LikLik and Riami."

MilkEye called WonTok aside. "Send warriors back to village. We go to Tugaru burial stone. Take away white man's sorcery MilkEye find there. Take back to *misis*."

"Tugaru no like we go sacred place."

"Maybe white *misis* trade honey for work?" MilkEye asked.

"WonTok like *misis*, make me police boy. *Misis* give me *thunderstik*," WonTok replied.

"If *misis* no trade honey for work, then MilkEye take WonTok's bow, quiver, axe and go to Tugaru burial stone for sky-people's-magic. Give to *misis* for honey," MilkEye said.

WonTok wrapped his arm around his *age-mate's* shoulder. "If MilkEye go up mountain to burial stone, this time WonTok go along. Make sure MilkEye no lose weapons again!".

21

3 DIVERTED DUTIES

Baltimore, Maryland, 1973

U.S. ARMY CENTRAL IDENTIFICATION LABORATORY
(PROVISIONAL) FINDINGS, CASE NUMBER 316. DR. DEANN
TOLAND'S REPORT.

Against my better judgment, I acquiesced to
Brigadier General Antonio Bellicosi's request for raw
field data to use in recruiting Dr. Thomas Haveland,
forensic pathologist, to the "Ten Knights on the
Barroom Floor" case. Because of the severed hand
discovered by the Australians and the evidence of
shots fired from the inside of the B-24 through the
fuselage, an investigation was necessary into any
possible criminal activity at the crash site. Sending
this raw field data to General Bellicosi had grave
consequences.

                    DeAnn Toland, Ph.D.
                    Physical Anthropologist

STANDING ERECT AT the foot of the long mahogany table in the
Johns Hopkins Hospital conference room, Dr. Emerson Stanek
glared at the backs of the retreating pathologists. The committee
had rejected funding his proposal in a four-to-one decision. Dr.
Thomas Haveland was the lone dissenter.

Stanek began shuffling copies of his beekeeper cancer study
into a battered brown valise and did not look up as Dr. Haveland
turned back toward him after seeing the other dons out of the
conference room. The chairman walked back to the head of the

table, sighed, then slumped into his high-back, well-cushioned chair.

After a moment, Haveland leaned across the table and tapped his white fingers on the polished surface. "Emerson, I tried to sway the other dons, but there're just no funds available in this time of war."

Stanek continued sorting papers, emitting a few grunts as he did so. Haveland responded by drumming louder. Stanek finally looked up and stroked the crescent-shaped, six-inch scar on his right cheek several times.

"I've been stung more times by the people at this institution than I have in the past year working with bees," he said through clenched teeth. "I can't believe you'd scuttle a whole year's research for the flimsy reasons your board outlined."

"I wouldn't trivialize the Vietnam War. Despite our opulent appearance at Hopkins, we've had to tighten our belts like everyone else in America."

"Since when? Academia never paid much attention to war before."

"Making our wounded boys whole while the guns are firing is priority number one. You know this from your association with the military mortuary in Hawaii."

Stanek emitted a grunt. "By the time I get involved at Tripler Army Hospital, sometimes there's little left to go on but a fingernail for identification purposes."

"Still it siphons money from the government."

"Please, sir. Spare me the poorhouse lectures. I'll bet if that reporter Cole turned up evidence of survivors or war crimes committed in New Guinea, this institution would spend the government's money to investigate."

"Your statement puzzles me, my boy. Are you intimating Cole is connected to Hopkins in any way?"

"Perhaps not. Yet he's quite familiar with the campus and the work going on here and makes it clear he's a Pentagon messenger."

"What's your point, Emerson?"

Stanek tugged at the corners of his dark mustache. "For years, Hopkins has been among the top three or four medical schools in the amount of competitive research grants awarded by the National Institutes of Health. If your committee won't fund my research, use your influence to get a NIH grant or other governmental agency funding. It should be a snap with your connections."

"Not for research unrelated to the war."

"I see. The war *de jour* takes precedence over the battle against cancer. Human beings and societies resort to the cruel solution of war time after time, generation after generation, century after century. When will there ever be a break from war to release funds for cancer research?"

"Be that as it may, Emerson, you yourself told the committee it would take five years to isolate the variable responsible in your cancer cure—whether honey, royal jelly, pollen, even bee stings or some combination. I'm afraid such a long commitment would leave little in the coffers for anything else. Please, my boy, reconsider the three options the committee majority offered—scale back your own research, apply later, or seek a grant from a source able to sustain the kind of commitment you need."

"Number three option—the only one I'd consider—brings us back to government."

"Not necessarily. There are others with deep pockets, unless..."

"Unless what?"

"You're truly unwilling to mix science and business as you've often stated."

"Depends on the business."

"I should think Catherine and Stanek Laboratories would leap at the chance to be the first out with a cancer vaccine, war or no war."

"No way. I'd sooner renew my contract with the army than lift a finger to keep Catherine in diamonds and furs."

Haveland knitted his thick white eyebrows together and shook his head. "Too bad. I thought you aimed most of your grievances at your adoptive father, not your sister. Are you and your mother on good terms or have you severed ties with her as well? Patricia Stanek strikes me as the type who would've provided for you."

For several moments neither man spoke. Stanek rose from the chair and shrugged his broad shoulders. "Call me in Hawaii if you come up with a better suggestion."

Stanek turned heel and headed for the doorway. He called back over his shoulder, "Goodbye, sir. I came on campus for a grant and leave empty-handed as usual."

Haveland rose from his chair and came after him. Stanek continued to move toward the doorway, but when he saw the chairman dragging his steps in his effort to catch up, Stanek hesitated long enough for the older man to close the gap between them.

"Hold on," Haveland said, puffing as he gripped Emerson's forearm. "Cole is out there in the rotunda. I'm sorry I enticed him to wait for you by waving your research under his nose. Neither of us is in the mood for press queries.

"Let me make amends by running interference for you, or at least let me arrange to drop you by your hotel. We've got a Baltimore squall brewing outdoors."

"No thanks. I'm going over to Phipps after I leave here. Cole doesn't bother me. But I do find it strange you'll let a reporter intimidate you, while I'm sent packing with no regrets."

"You're being grossly unfair, Emerson."

Stanek turned away and pretended to clear phlegm from his throat. His face was red when he turned back to speak. "I'll tell you what's unfair. There's only one other member of the Stanek family this esteemed institution has no use for—Patricia Stanek who suffers from schizophrenia over there." Emerson jerked his thumb toward the Henry Phipps Psychiatric Building behind the hospital. "But she's the only Stanek I care about or want to see for the rest of my life. So, please step aside, sir. I hear my mother calling for help."

"One doesn't suffer schizophrenia; one is schizophrenic," Haveland corrected in a professorial manner. "Besides, you'll need Catherine's okay to see Mrs. Stanek."

"What?"

"She's her legal guardian. No one just pops in on a schizophrenic. Those are the rules."

Stanek looked down at the floor and shook his head. Haveland gently squeezed his arm and said more softly, "My boy, I'll call Catherine from my office and see if we can clear you through. By the way, when are you heading back to Hawaii?"

"Day after tomorrow."

"Good, we'd better schedule a visit at Phipps for tomorrow morning, if it fits your plans. I'll catch you later if I can. But I've got a rather lengthy meeting at the Pathology Building this evening. Then I'm off to New York tomorrow evening to do my part in pinning a murder rap on mobster, Filipino Freddie. You might've read about him in the newspapers. He uses a variety of weapons to dispose of rivals and witnesses. At any rate, after I get Catherine's okay, I'll call your hotel tonight."

Stanek nodded. He caught the look in Haveland's eyes. This time it was inexpressibly sad.

"My boy, you have my word that I'll do what I can to generate interest in your beekeeper cancer study. No war can last forever. Once Vietnam winds down, I suspect agencies like NIH will beat a path to your door. Meantime, there's a matter you could help me with, if you've got the time and the inclination."

"More time on my hands than I expected at the moment, and as for inclination, you're more than my favorite instructor; you're my friend."

Haveland reached into his brief case and withdrew a sheaf of yellowed, dog-eared papers held together by a rubber band. He laid the strange bundle on the table.

"You may have heard me refer to Dr. DeAnn Toland during Mr. Cole's inquisition regarding the B-24 shot down in New Guinea 30 years ago."

"A physical anthropologist, or something along those lines."

"Yes. As I said, DeAnn attended my Chicago seminar on physical evidence." Haveland pointed to the package. "Here's her report to General Antonio Bellicosi, including one of the logs they found at the B-24 crash site."

"Bellicosi, you mean the guy Cole mentioned?"

"Yes, you might've come across him in Hawaii. He heads the casualty branch at the Pentagon. The brigadier asked me to give an opinion on Toland's initial findings, whether I take the case or not. And, as you know, other matters have a priority for me. Even if I weren't so busy, I doubt I could ever withstand the rigors of Papua New Guinea at my age. Perhaps General Bellicosi just wants to use my name to authenticate his project."

"Let me guess, sir," Stanek interrupted. "It's conscience-assuaging time. You regret having to thwart the army and want me to render an interim report in your behalf as restitution."

"Exactly."

"As long as I don't have to go to New Guinea, I'd be glad to bail you out. Who gets the report when I've finished—Cole, Toland or Bellicosi?"

"Certainly not the reporter. I thought you could give it back to Bellicosi in Hawaii. He's trying to organize a permanent Central Identification Laboratory there, but doesn't have congressional support for his brainchild yet."

"Not at the Pentagon?"

"No, he flies back and forth between Washington, Hawaii and New Guinea. He had the original documents hand-carried to me a week or so ago, and I'd like to send them back the same way. And Emerson..."

"Yes, sir."

"After I've gone, take a look at the inscription on the Zippo lighter Dr. Toland included in her packet. I'm interested in your take on it."

"With my own plans on hold, I might as well get started here in your conference room this evening. Should I leave a copy of my observations with your secretary when I return in the morning in case we don't connect?"

"Much obliged. Keep in touch, my boy, or I'll call you if something breaks your way on the beekeeper cancer study."

After Haveland left, Stanek removed his suit jacket and resumed his place at the conference table beneath the only skylight in the room. As he lifted Toland's package, he heard what sounded like footsteps overhead. But when he looked up at the skylight, all he could see was a branch from a nearby magnolia tree crashing noisily against the pane, blown by the wind and pelting rain. Carried by the wind, the branch sailed off into the dark sky. "Like me," he thought, "buffeted by the wind and ending the day as just another teaching fellow picking up the loose ends for a professor whose time is considered far more important than mine."

Taking a deep breath, he slid his fingers under the thick rubber band and spread the documents on the table next to his notebook. He picked up the lighter and scanned the inscription: *One hour alone is in thy hands, the hour on which the shadow stands.*

In his usual brisk manner, Stanek discounted Haveland's indirect suggestion there was a connection between the inscription on the pilot's lighter and the same one on the sundial at Johns Hopkins. To link the two items based on shared words would be, it seemed to him, to invite a thought process laced with a thousand lures and deceits. Without physical evidence to bond the two items,

Stanek choose to downplay the significance of the words engraved on the lighter.

In his report, he decided to tell Haveland the identical phrases were probably a mere coincidence. No sense torpedoing the chance his mentor might work out a *quid pro quo* at NIH for his services on the B-24 matter.

Setting the lighter aside and grunting assent for his strategy, Stanek leafed through the documents searching for Dr. Toland's letter to General Bellicosi. Instead he came upon the Missing Crew Report (MCR). He recalled from his brief sojourn in San Francisco as a medical examiner the importance of the MCR and its companion form, the Missing Aircraft Report (MAR). Together they furnished the "who" and "what" of each disaster involving a military aircraft. For the B-24 missing in New Guinea, the crew's names were typed alphabetically on the MCR and identified by position. Someone had penciled a third column containing nicknames:

Sgt. John S. Alexander III	Radio Operator	Signals
2/Lt. Samuel R. Bottorf	Copilot	Toggle Joe
Sgt. Alfred T. Grant	Gunner	U.S.
Sgt. Elijah B. Ingersol	Gunner	Prophet
2/Lt. Mitchell B. Nelson	Navigator	Admiral
Sgt. Timothy K. O'Leary	Gunner	TKO
2/Lt. Philipi I. Patterson	Bombardier	Pip
1/Lt. Oscar C. Sanchez	Pilot	OCS
Sgt. Douglas M. Shipley	Gunner	Sharpshooter
Tech/Sgt. Harlan J. Wells	Engineer	Deep

He placed the MCR face down on the table and, not finding the Missing Aircraft Report, Stanek picked up Dr. Toland's letter in his left hand. With the fingers of his right, he tapped gently at the crescent-shaped scar on his cheek. The anthropologist's cover letter to Brigadier General Antonio Bellicosi was typed on official letterhead in the field using a portable.

Department of the Army
Central Identification Laboratory
(Provisional) Thailand
April 8, 1973, W/Team Alfa, Mount Bosavi,
Papua New Guinea

My Dear General Bellicosi:
  This will confirm the verbal report delivered
by Major Frank Yowell to you last week in Goroka.
CIL Team Alfa recovered a number of remains and
personal items buried near aircraft #2-41009, AKA
"Ten Knights on the Barroom Floor." Unfortunately,
the ensuing fire upon impact, the natural ravishes
of nature over so long a time period and the co-
mingling of remains, probably later when buried,
combined to make identification difficult if not
impossible at this stage. That's the bad news.
  There's also good news. At site marked "X-1"
(see-attached map) we found enough bone fragments
and teeth to account for several persons (perhaps
four crewmembers). The remains were wrapped in an
eroded piece of canvas or rubber material buried
approximately 30 yards southeast of the wreckage.
Buried with them (and this is equally exciting)
was a metal ammunition box containing two logs
written by the pilot and copilot respectively. The
copilot's journal was written after the airplane
crash, as the pilot's log appears to be. Although
the authenticity of the logs hasn't been verified
as yet, they indicate there were survivors!

Stanek's cheek drumming stopped. He turned over the MCR
and located the names Sanchez and Bottorf, noting that they were
at the controls of the ill-fated bomber. He then entered their names
and positions in his notebook. Beside each name he wrote
"possible survivor." He sorted through the papers for the copilot's
log and burial map cited, but he did not find either one, so he
continued with Toland's letter.

  Other items in the ammo box included frames
from a pair of aviator's goggles, a gold pocket
watch initialed "OCS", an officer's cap insignia,
and a Fifth Army Air Force shoulder patch.
  At "X-2", ten yards from "X-1", we found a
single set of remains with a Japanese ceremonial
sword and another metal ammo case buried beside
him. This box contained a decorative geisha's fan,
an inscribed miniature Japanese flag and a
Japanese "senninbari," or a thousand-stitch belt.
Neither burial site turned up any dog tags or
other identifying badges or emblems.
  It's my guess an inexperienced person or group
discovered this site before the Australians

29

stumbled across the B-24 wreckage while searching for a civilian aircraft lost in the vicinity. A professional never places diverse fragments and artifacts together until they have been carefully catalogued as matches. Far better for us if the first person(s)on the scene had left the crews at their individual stations, which would have aided identification by position in the aircraft if nothing else.

The Australian authorities suspect foul play because of the severed hand found and the bullets fired from inside the fuselage. Major Yowell said you were already aware of this. In view of the above, I concur in your decision to call in a forensic pathologist to review this case, providing you still believe a full accounting is necessary under the tenants of Operation Simpatico.

Also, this case is riddled with puzzles. We have only one lead concerning possible remains of six other crewmembers. According to the copilot's log, he and three others tried to make an unsuccessful escape down the Rentoul.

Perhaps another lost aircraft is more suitable for your campaign, given the time constraints you have set for us. We on the CIL team know how much loved ones value individual identification, but sometimes circumstances dictate otherwise.

Unless a survivor turns up to help us in our search, or more evidence is found, this is where we stand. Meantime, I am trying to win the tribesmen over so they can aid us in searching for crewmembers, missing aircraft parts and artifacts they may know about or might have in their possession.

Major Yowell will deliver pertinent documents on his next supply run to Goroka. I've reluctantly enclosed only the pilot's log for now, because you wanted something to show Dr. Haveland. He'll tell you the less handling the better, so we'll keep all other original artifacts and documents here for him. Forgive my old field-portable typewriter and me. Both of us have seen better conditions.

Sincerely,
DeAnn Toland, Ph.D.
Physical Anthropologist

P.S. Good luck in recruiting Dr. Thomas Haveland of Johns Hopkins fame for the criminal aspects raised by our Australian friends. He's the best forensic pathologist in the business. It would be my pleasure to work with him again.

P.P.S. I have enclosed an engraved lighter Kiap Noble found in the aircraft during his initial search and just now surrendered to me. The Zippo seems to bear the pilot's initials, "OCS."

The next two appendices following Toland's cover letter did contain a map of New Guinea marked with the B-24's flight path, and a half dozen black and white photos of the crash site. Stanek glanced at the photos but studied appendix three—a handwritten inventory of B-24 emergency equipment and ration packs. They should have been aboard the B-24 Liberator at the time of the crash, but they were all listed as absent. Included were a 2,500 pound-capacity rubberized life raft (type E-2) complete with pyrotechnic pistol and extra flares, emergency drinking water cans, ten packages type K rations (five dinners, four breakfasts), sea markers, flashlight, knife, and a first aid kit. Also listed were tarpaulins for use as a sail and for catching water, fishing tackle, a rubber raft repair kit, 40-feet of 75-pound cotton cord and a sea anchor. Stanek began jotting down and underlining in his notebook the missing emergency equipment.

Whistling softly under his breath, Stanek wondered why not a single item on the emergency equipment list turned up at the crash site, according to Toland's report. Perhaps crew survivors had deployed the raft and its accessories in an attempt make their way down a river at some point, or the natives had stripped the bomber clean.

Stanek turned to appendix four, a cutaway diagram of a typical B-24 bomber to look for answers. He tallied a hundred items ranging from weapons, gun mounts, extra ammunition, to seats, parachutes, oxygen bottles, plus equipment used exclusively by the bombardier and navigator. Why hadn't any of these items shown up in 30 years' time? Stanek let out another low whistle. And if there were survivors, surely they would have kept emergency gear on hand for contingencies as recommended by most reputable survivor manuals?

He thought the pilot's log might shed more light on the situation, so he picked it up next. But seeing the last document in the pile was also the thickest, he decided to read Sanchez's log in the comfort of his hotel room.

Stanek opened his valise and placed the B-24 materials inside next to his rejected beekeeper cancer study, then headed for the doorway. "A colossal foul-up in both cases, it seems," he muttered softly to himself. "Happens whenever fools get involved with the unknown," Stanek conjectured. As he turned out the light, he thought he heard the sound of scuffling feet above him. He dismissed it as another branch trapped on the roof.

The young pathologist had barely passed through the rotunda on his way out the south entrance when he spotted Cole. The reporter was leaning on his crutches writing in a big ledger placed on a stand in front of the Christ statue. Stanek had often witnessed this act during his years as a medical student and resident. One couldn't pass through Billings Hall without seeing a pilgrim or patient recording his or her life and death experiences in the big book used as a confessional or for a prayer request.

Stanek's spine stiffened. He remembered all too well Catherine's pledge the night following his narrow escape from her father. She had promised to absolve her adoptive brother from blame in the so-called laboratory incident. "My confession will be in the ledger tomorrow for Papa and all the world to see," Catherine had assured Emerson. He had looked for her written testament, but it had never appeared. What's more, the enraged Rufus had destroyed his reputation in the elite circle of pathologists by innuendo.

A few more steps and he would have made it past the back stairway out of Cole's line of sight. But as the reporter called his name from across the rotunda, Stanek came to a standstill.

"Yes, sir," Stanek replied civilly. "What can I do for you?"

"Has Dr. Haveland left?"

"Yes he did, some time ago."

"Oh, he must've given me the slip. I'm sure you're in no mood for palaver, so I'll catch you back at the hotel, or in Hawaii one of these days." Saying no more, Cole braced a crutch against the north entrance door and shuffled out onto the rain-soaked steps. Stanek waited until the reporter's gray head disappeared down the terrace before he crossed the rotunda and examined the guest book. In a rambling, shaky stroke Cole had scribbled, "Oh, Lord, let him be the one to relieve me of this terrible burden before I die."

Stanek grinned. His blue eyes flashed with triumph. Journalist or not, somebody on this day of rejection appreciated what his cancer cure could do in relieving pain and suffering. He set off with short quick steps down the familiar back corridor. Outside, he felt the rain on his shaven head and walked quickly to catch a cab. He reached in his pocket for the visitor's badge and saw it was missing. As he passed the Phipps Psychiatric Clinic building on his way to Wolfe Street where the taxicabs parked, he visualized Patricia Stanek seated, prisoner-like, waiting for death to set her free. Other memories of his adoptive mother swept over him. He tried to toss them aside, but they reappeared by the time he reached the corner and began hailing a taxi.

Regular order was important to Emerson Stanek. It was like an autopsy. A post mortem showed where a disease had been and where it was going. Order and resolve had gotten him this far, and it would carry him through the disappointment of this day. He would find a way to fund his cancer study without Stanek money or assistance.

Now where did he lose his visitor's badge? And how dare Catherine assert her will over him? Irritated, he decided to turn around and march right into Phipps, consent or not. But as the cab pulled up, he hesitated. He hadn't felt such indecision since he'd been a boy in his teens. Haveland was right. One didn't just barge in on a schizophrenic. "Catherine always holds the trump card," he muttered. "I'll come back tomorrow morning, and if she shows up, she'll regret it." He looked at his watch. It was ten past five, but so dark it looked like it was much later. "Nearly a whole day shot and nothing to show for it." He hated talking to himself. It meant he had lost control and was getting out ahead of regular order.

Stanek reached his hotel room, settled in and then ordered some food from room service. Sometime later he began reading the pilot's log when he heard a knock at the door. He set the pilot's log aside and peered through the small opening in the door. At first he thought it was a messenger sent by Haveland to pick up the B-24 papers. But closer inspection revealed a man as large as a Sumo wrestler balancing a tray he kept in front of his face. The interloper held his other hand inside his white jacket, Napoleon style.

Stanek glanced at his watch. It was 11:30. He distinctly remembered reading in the hotel's brochure the kitchen closed at 10 p.m.

"Who is it?" he asked.

"Room service."

"I didn't order any more food," Stanek said. After fastening the safety chain, Stanek opened the door just enough to see the man was not alone. In a blur of painted nails and floral patterns on a long-sleeved blouse, the woman retreated behind her companion before Stanek could see her face.

"Sorry, our mistake, sir. I'll see you're not disturbed. But while I'm here, can I offer you the services of a lady for the evening?" the giant asked.

"Just leave me alone," Stanek replied. He stood at the door for a moment. Then when he heard the elevator down the hall open and close its doors, he walked over to his bed, picked up the telephone and dialed Haveland's number at the Pathology Building.

The night custodian answered, "Dr. Haveland's whole group done left here 'bout an hour ago. The other doctors hadn't been gone 20 minutes before the boss doctor come runnin' out in the vestibule sayin' somethin' 'bout findin' the smokin' gun. He said if anybody wanta get hold of him, he'd be at his office in the Admin Building. You got the number for Billings Hall?"

Stanek said he did and hung up. He started to call Haveland at his office but changed his mind. Haveland was dependable. His mentor had never let him down, especially like the night after the incident with Catherine's father. Taken to the Haveland apartment from the hospital, Emerson had awakened to hear Tom tell his wife Lily he had no choice but to cover up the alleged rape attempt and Emerson's injuries as a laboratory incident gone awry. "The scandal would scuttle the boy's chances of education here at Hopkins. There's nothing else I could do." Stanek had heard him say.

Before he left the Havelands to take up residence in Reed Hall, his mentor presented him with a signed copy of Dr. William Welch's great treatise, but didn't give him the identity of the person addressed. The founding father of pathology at Hopkins had written in the flyleaf:

"H.D., you're a man who keeps his word. So admirable a trait should be passed on. Do Popsy one last favor. Create your own dynasty and pass this book on to your prodigy. How else is an old fool to be remembered?"

"Fret no more," Emerson chided himself. "Tom will call tonight, and we'll get this Catherine business squared away. He'll want a summary of my B-24 findings, too."

Propped in bed, he adjusted a pair of half-moon reading glasses on the bridge of his well-proportioned nose and once again took up the pilot's log. He intently studied the paper stock and the flowing scripted stroke, made, it seemed, with a small brush for painting Chinese characters, on which Lt. Sanchez had written his account. The pilot had decorated his title page with a verse from the Old Testament. Stanek raised his eyebrows, and continued to read.

4 PILOT'S LOG

Papua New Guinea, 1943

U.S. ARMY CENTRAL IDENTIFICATION LABORATORY (PROVISIONAL) FINDINGS, CASE NUMBER 316: EXHIBIT A— PILOT'S LOG. DR. DEANN TOLAND'S REPORT.

> FOR EVERYTHING
> THERE IS A SEASON,
> AND A TIME
> FOR EVERY PURPOSE
> UNDER HEAVEN
> Ecc. 3:1

I'M FIRST LIEUTENANT Oscar Carlos Sanchez from Las Cruces, New Mexico. Friends call me "Ox" for my initials, O.C.S., and because I'm a graduate of Officer Candidate School (OCS) as well.

Shortly after the Japanese bombed Pearl Harbor, my father gave me a gold pocket watch inscribed with the above verse to commemorate my graduation from pilot training at Lubbock Field, Texas. Later, I became the first Spanish-American to command a B-24 in the war. Only my family and my brother aviators may find any of this important.

My crew uses nicknames as a way to skirt the formality of rank that disappears anyway once the shooting starts. The military probably tolerates the practice for individuals and units for this reason. For example, Lieutenant Colonel Arthur H. Rogers took command of our heavy bombardment group in July 1943. Thereafter, the 90th became known as the Jolly Rogers, complete with a skull and crossed-bombs symbol painted on the twin tails of the group's B-24s. A black background behind the white skull designated our squadron as the 400th or the "Black Pirates" as they liked to be called.

At first these changes had no effect on us. We didn't have our own aircraft. Just lots of dead time in New Guinea. Dead time kills the fighting edge. Crews go nuts if they don't keep busy. So we washed clothes, played cards, wrote and re-read letters, listened to New Guinea Ginny's Jap propaganda or drank and fought the aircrews who were doing something meaningful—anything to combat boredom.

Occasionally, we "prostituted" ourselves. As pilot and copilot, Toggle Joe and I flew B-26 reconnaissance missions, and when possible we filled the other slots on this smaller bomber with members from our original B-24 crew. We were glad to get the points awarded for these reconnaissance missions, especially for their impact on our rotation home, but we really just wanted to maintain proficiency until our own B-24 arrived. Rumor had it the B-24 was developed as a seaplane, but when engineers found out how much it leaked, they converted it to a bomber. But to us, the B-24 was the most beautiful bomber ever built.

Less than a month before Christmas 1943, Santa Claus came early for us. General Douglas MacArthur himself directed the "Knights of the Barroom Brawls," as he called us, be given a B-24 and a chance to show "they could fight in the air as well." Colonel Rogers assigned us the first aircraft to come through the pipeline to Port Moresby. No pirate names for us. We painted "Ten Knights on the Barroom Floor" on our lady's fuselage in honor of escapades so notorious even the brass noticed our plight.

There wasn't time for any other nose art, or little else. Colonel Rogers gave us six hours to check out our new B-24, on the ground and in the air. It was strange, but on the first day the "ten knights" were airborne, after months away from B-24s, even Pip stopped joking, and the interphone never clicked on except to talk about aircraft performance. Perform she did during her shakedown. I pushed her to top speed of 303 miles per hour at 25,000 feet, and her four Pratt & Whitney Wasps engines hummed like an angel's choir over the Owen Stanley Range. We could've flown forever, but by noon six other D models came up for shakedown flights. So we came in to give them maneuver room.

In the evening at the pilot's briefing, Colonel Rogers planted his feet on the podium more firmly than usual as he addressed his officers:

"Gentlemen, forget the myth about bomber crews, that 'we work for Uncle Sam en route and over the target, but after bombs away, we're unemployed.' This kind of thinking won't get us back here safely from Wewak, tomorrow's target.

"From the air, Wewak looks harmless enough. But don't be fooled, as many of you have found out. The little spoon-shaped peninsula jutting out into the Bismarck Sea bristles with every anti-aircraft defense imaginable. Artillery, balloon cables and small arms fire will greet you. Even sling shots if they have 'em.

"And expect enemy fighters to outnumber our escorts by a rate of five to one. What's more, since we're coming in low, cloud conditions over the target area almost guarantee some bombers will get separated from the top cover and the rest of the formation. So stay employed! Get back here the best you can. God speed!"

The intelligence officer briefed us next. "Your primary target is Boram Airfield," he said. "Your aiming point is the center of a row of corrugated steel buildings along the northern edge of the base. We believe they house aircraft and engine repair shops. Aircraft from Rabaul and other parts of New Guinea are serviced there. Destroy the facility and we shorten the war."

Pip "midnight-requisitioned" the suit of armor hanging above the bar in the officer's club, and at dawn, ten able-bodied "knights" and one stolen totem crossed the Bismarck Mountain Range in our B-24, headed northwest in a 23-bomber formation led by Colonel Rogers. This time there were 5,000 pounds of bombs on board for Pip to drop over the target area. I told my crew what Colonel Rogers had said to me, "Do us proud and there'll be no more B-26 recon missions over the Southern Highlands' District."

Everyone cheered. Nobody wanted to fly over jungle so uninhabitable not even Hannibal could move an army through it. Pip even made up a ditty he sang repeatedly over the interphone on the way to Wewak. "No more Southern Highlands District for me, I'll take my chances o'er the Bismarck Sea."

As in other recent strikes, fighters protected our formation, but due to cloud conditions near Wewak, the B-24s became separated from the top cover. Once past Boram Airfield, 20 to 30 enemy fighters, mostly Zeroes, jumped our formation.

Matters got worse. A few minutes after dropping most of our ordnance on enemy anti-aircraft emplacements protecting the airfield, we were hit by flak. Number two engine caught fire. "Toggle Joe," my copilot, and I had our hands full getting the wing up, propeller feathered, mixture throttle closed, and ignition, fuel and generator off. We were disappointed neither of us could bring his predominant hand to the flying task. Nicknamed the "agony-wagon" by other pilots, the B-24 was definitely hard to control at such times. But Joe, a natural lefty, and I, having developed a strong right arm through arm-wrestling in bars during all that down time, were able to work the center pedestal situated between us. Each of us handled controls on our respective sides, Joe in the right seat and I in the left.

Initially, a boost of power to our three good engines kept us in tight V formation at number five position, but soon our hopes sailed away as we maneuvered loose and low, ran our emergency checklist, and lost sight of our squadron in the poor visibility. We glimpsed their twin tails disappearing into the soup like a candelabrum missing two candles. No one faulted them for leaving us. The beer always tasted better back at Ward's Airdrome at Port Moresby, or at any other B-24 base in New Guinea or Australia. We were trained to act in the same manner.

Then the interphone erupted with more bad news.

BOMBARDIER PATTERSON (Pip): Ox, we've got a couple 500-pounders lodged in our rear bomb bay. And two Jap fighters, standing on their wing tips, just whizzed past on our left.

NOSE GUNNER O'LEARY (TKO): They got off a few bursts, and I answered 'em and missed. But so did they.

PILOT SANCHEZ (Ox): I saw 'em, Pip. TKO, they came in on your dead spot—a Zero and another aircraft I didn't recognize. Expect 'em to adjust on the next pass. Did anybody get the new guy's license number?

ENGINEER/TOP GUNNER WELLS (Deep): Yeah, Ox. Pulled up so fast I thought I was going to eat for lunch the flaming asshole painted on his fuselage. The little yellow man in the muddy-gray airship is sporting a Kiwasaki 61, or "Tony" to the Allies. [The nickname comes from being modeled along the lines of the Italian Folgore.]

TAIL GUNNER SHIPLEY (Sharpshooter): We're all gonna be "folgore" in a minute, Wells! Three more assholes bearing down on our own rear.

PILOT SANCHEZ: Sharpshooter, go for 'em.

TAIL GUNNER SHIPLEY: I've got the middle guy in my sights, Ox. Maybe Deep on top and Prophet in the belly can get the other two bandits.

BOTTOM GUNNER INGERSOL (Prophet): Roger, Sgt. Shipley. Sgt. Ingersol copies. That makes one Nip for Wells and one each for us bottom-feeders.

PILOT SANCHEZ: Everybody else look for the Tony. Signals, switch to the fighter frequency and wake-up our cavalry escorts.

COPILOT BOTTORF (Toggle Joe): They've more likely headed back with the formation.

PILOT SANCHEZ: You're probably right, Toggle Joe. Oh shit! Sounds like we've been hit! Somebody give a damage report.

RIGHT WAIST GUNNER GRANT (U.S.): Ox, this is Grant. Sharpshooter got a Zeke! But the Tony came from nowhere and got him. He took a shot in the head, although there's not much bleeding. Must've just grazed him. Shipley's wandering around back here talking crazy. I gave him a shot of morphine, so he'll be out of action for awhile. Want me to take Shipley's place in the tail turret?

PILOT SANCHEZ: No, Grant. You stay where you are. Deep, did you see the Tony?

ENGINEER/TOPGUNNER WELLS: He's vanished. Anybody heard from Prophet?

PILOT SANCHEZ: Don't know. Prophet, what's your report? Ingersol, do you read me? Come in, Prophet. Wells, get down there and get Prophet out of the belly turret. TKO, you're to lend a hand, then move over to Sharpshooter's place in the tail. Everybody else stand pat, except Pip who'll man the front guns.

NAVIGATOR NELSON: Ox, Pip's up to his armpits with those two jammed bombs. Want me to take over TKO's spot?

BOMBARDIER PATTERSON: I second that.

PILOT SANCHEZ: Okay, Pip. But I want you back on those twin fifties as soon as possible. Your aim is better than the Admiral's. Signals, any word from the cavalry?

RADIO OPERATOR/LEFT WAIST GUNNER ALEXANDER (Signals): Not a peep since before Wewak.

PILOT SANCHEZ: Deep, TKO, how's Prophet?

ACTING TAIL GUNNER O'LEARY: Wells can tell you. I'm too upset.

ENGINEER/TOP GUNNER WELLS: Ingersol's dead, lads. Hit in the throat and chest. God rest Prophet's soul.

PILOT SANCHEZ: (after long pause) Wells, prop Ingersol's body against the bulkhead. We've lost our first crewmember, a "knight" of our brotherhood. Anyone want to add anything?

ACTING TAIL GUNNER O'LEARY: I'd like to get back at those bastards.

RIGHT WAIST GUNNER GRANT: I'm with TKO, Ox. Prophet was my best friend.

PILOT SANCHEZ: I know, Grant. It hurts like hell to lose one of our own.

BOMBARDIER PATTERSON: Ox, the two bombs are ready. Before we release them, what do you say, fellows, we join together and sing our favorite tension reliever?

PILOT SANCHEZ: Good idea, Pip.

(ALL SINGING): We're gonna find a fella who is yella and beat him red, white and blue.

NAVIGATOR/ACTING NOSE GUNNER NELSON: (solo) To be specific, it's our Pacific.

PILOT SANCHEZ: Pip has the better aim, and Admiral has the better voice.

RADIO OPERATOR/LEFT WAIST GUNNER ALEXANDER: Here's a voice we've all come to love and hate. I'll pipe in New Guinea Ginny. She's playing *Sentimental Journey*. It was Prophet's favorite song.

PILOT SANCHEZ: Okay, but turn her off before she starts blaming everybody but Tojo and Hitler for this war.

BOMBARDIER PATTERSON: Say, lads, let's make Prophet's song Ginny's last.

PILOT SANCHEZ: What's cooking in your thick skull, Pip?

BOMBARDIER PATTERSON: I say we avenge Prophet by dropping our last two 500-pounders straight down Ginny's antenna.

NAVIGATOR/ACTING NOSE GUNNER NELSON: We're pretty close to Angoram where her trash originates.

PILOT SANCHEZ: I don't know. Maybe we ought to hightail it out of here before the Tony comes back.

RIGHT WAIST GUNNER GRANT: Well, then let me parachute down, screw Ginny until she's blind and then slit her throat with Prophet's bayonet.

ACTING TAIL GUNNER O'LEARY: I wouldn't touch a piece of Jap crap with your dick, U.S. She's got to be one ugly bitch.

RIGHT WAIST GUNNER GRANT: You're lucky you've got a girlfriend in Sydney, TKO.

RADIO OPERATOR/LEFT WAIST GUNNER ALEXANDER. With her sexy voice, I'll bet Ginny looks like her namesake, Ginger Rogers, or the dame who played Scarlet in *Gone with the Wind.*

NAVIGATOR/ACTING NOSE GUNNER NELSON: Who cares what she looks like. Like Tokyo Rose, she's bad for morale. Let's shut her up for good.

ENGINEER/TOP GUNNER WELLS: Hadn't we better head home and not look for any more trouble? We're banged up pretty badly.

PILOT SANCHEZ: As usual Deep's is the voice of reason. Okay, everybody, here's my plan. If the Tony or more Zekes close fast, spraying tracers all over the sky, slightly right and below our tail fin, I'll roll the aircraft off to the left out over the Bismarck Sea. If they come from the opposite side, we'll head right, inland along the Sepik River.

ENGINEER/TOP GUNNER WELLS: Too late! The Tony's on top of us!

PILOT SANCHEZ: Can you get him, Deep?

ENGINEER/TOP GUNNER WELLS: He's not giving me much of a target. But he's not firing either. Looks like he's assessing our damage on this run. There! He just peeled off over Toggle Joe's side. Did you see him?

COPILOT BOTTORF: Yeah. The son-of-a-bitch fired a few shots at empty air and blew past us like a fart in the wind. He's playing games. Keep it up, you yellow monkey! Go ahead. Waste all your ammunition!

PILOT SANCHEZ: Easy, Sam. He can't hear you. Aren't Nips a race with defective inner ear tubes and generally myopic? He'll self-destruct. Although, I must say, this guy shows a great sense of balance and swings a mean hammer. Yellow Hammer—a good name for him.

RIGHT WAIST GUNNER GRANT: Sharpshooter's coming out of the morphine. But he's not right in the head. Just keeps repeating what he hears over the interphone.

PILOT SANCHEZ: U.S., is Pip back there with you?

RIGHT WAIST GUNNER GRANT: He's down in the bomb bay and can hear you through the jack connection.

PILOT SANCHEZ: Pip, leave the bombs for now. I want you to take a look at Shipley, then return to your station and relieve Admiral on the fifties. I've a feeling Yellow Hammer wants to come in the front door.

BOMBARDIER PATTERSON: Okay. But why doesn't someone read this Jap the right scenario? This is the point where he's supposed to fold his hands across his stomach and die cheerfully for the glory of the empire.

PILOT SANCHEZ: No time! Yellow Hammer's closing at one o'clock over Toggle Joe with canons blazing. Get em, Deep!

RIGHT WAIST GUNNER GRANT: I'm hit! Good Lord, I think I'm going to die.

COPILOT BOTTORF: I can't see!

PILOT SANCHEZ: Pip, check on Grant in the waist. Wells, help me with Toggle Joe. Part of the instrument panel erupted in his face. He's flopping around and bleeding like a fish gaffed through the eyes. Take him back to the tail section and tend to his wounds with our first aid kit as best you can.

RADIO OPERATOR/LEFT WAIST GUNNER ALEXANDER: The Tony knocked out our radio transmitter. All we've got left is the interphone and New Guinea Ginny.

BOMBARDIER PATTERSON: U.S. Grant's gravely wounded. I've taken him to the back with Toggle Joe and Shipley. O'Leary's trying to stop the bleeding from Grant's wound, and Wells is tending to Toggle Joe's injuries. Shipley's out of it and can't help.

PILOT SANCHEZ: One dead and three wounded, with two tending to their injuries takes out six crewmembers from their positions. Plus, number two engine is out, and we've got no radio transmitter.

BOMBARDIER PATTERSON: Time the "knights" figure out how to "stay employed," as Colonel Rogers would say.

PILOT SANCHEZ: Okay, everybody, listen. We're below 220 knots in airspeed with only three good engines. The Tony can better our speed and match us in ceiling as well. We all know B-24s are notoriously slack on the controls on daylight missions, so we can rule out any slick evasive tactics. Anyone have any suggestions?

BOMBARDIER PATTERSON: If Yellow Hammer attacks us again, let's dive for the heavy cloud cover over the Sepik and follow the river to the southwest, ditch some of our weight, and hope he gives up the chase.

PILOT SANCHEZ: Or runs out of fuel.

BOMBARDIER PATTERSON: Even this washed out pilot remembers what they drilled into us at Lubbock—the larger the tank, the lighter the load, the greater the distance.

NAVIGATOR/ACTING COPILOT: Pip's right, Ox. We could set a southwestern course inland. We can fly over a coastwatcher's station between Aramut and Mendam, on an inlet just northwest of where the Sepik River empties into the Bismarck Sea. The coastwatcher would surely report our situation and last position to anyone up for mounting a rescue mission if we don't return to base.

BOMBARDIER PATTERSON: And while in the vicinity, we'll kill two birds, make our presence known to the coastwatcher and drop our non-essentials. Then we can slip on down to Angoram and put New Guinea Ginny out of business on our way inland over the Sepik River.

ACTING TAIL GUNNER O'LEARY: I don't want to ditch in the sea and become shark bait, or bail out and have the Nip fighter gun us down while we dangle helplessly in our parachutes. Think of my girl in Sydney.

PILOT SANCHEZ: We're not going to ditch or bail out at this point, TKO. Admiral will point our way from Toggle Joe's old seat. Deep, where do you stand? Can we reach Port Moresby with only three engines, using our B-26 recon route through the Southern Highland's District and outlast the Tony's max?

ENGINEER/TOP GUNNER WELLS: Yes, if we don't sustain any more damage, but I'll follow your lead. My hands are full with the wounded back here in the tail section.

BOMBARDIER PATTERSON: Yellow Hammer's coming in for another pass from the rear on our left side. He's aiming for you this time, Ox. Roll off to the right and head for cloud cover ASAP!

PILOT SANCHEZ: Roger, Pip. Signals, man your gun and let 'em have it.

RADIO OPERATOR/LEFT WAIST GUNNER ALEXANDER: Lost him in the clouds, Ox, but I got off a few rounds before we rolled.

PILOT SANCHEZ: Good work, Signals. We can't take any more chances in Yellow Hammer's territory. Admiral, guide us over the coastwatcher's station. God willing, the coastwatcher will spot us, so he'll know we're headed southwest along the Sepik River instead of the usual route home. Pip, get ready to release the bombs when we get to Angoram. With only three engines, we've got to lighten our load.

BOMBARDIER PATTERSON: And avenge our dead and injured!

*   *   *

When we reached Angoram, we unloaded our two 500-pounders. New Guinea Ginny went off the air immediately after the first bomb hit. We cheered until we saw women running out of the buildings, some with children in their arms. All of us wished we could've called back the second bomb. But of course it was impossible.

Bombing a defenseless radio station was hardly anything to cheer about. All it did was allow enough time for the Tony to find us. Yellow Hammer jumped us again with fury.

He bore down on our number one engine this time, our worst case scenario. The B-24 manual directs pilots with a failed engine to avoid unusual maneuvers and make turns toward the two operating engines, in our case, engines three and four, on the right wing.

I alerted the crew that I intended to do the opposite, hoping to confuse our pursuer. I rolled to the left, then yanked back on the yoke to get as much climb as we could muster. The maneuver threw the enemy attack off, and Yellow Hammer had to duck under us, while TKO in the tail hurried him along with some well-placed tracers.

The maneuver bought us enough time to find the Sepik River again and disappear into the cloud cover below us. The closer we hugged the river, the thicker the clouds. After a few minutes, all lookouts reported no sign of the relentless Tony.

So I tried to calm the crew. "Sit back and relax," I said. "At the controls today is a soft-spoken Spanish-American, or New

Mexican, who has been flying since he was six, when most of you were still cradle jockeys."

It was true. Since the day my father brought me a model airplane with a gasoline engine home from his job as aircraft mechanic at the Las Cruces Aero Club, I've loved flying. Later, whenever a barnstormer came to town, Papa would trade engine repairs in return for flying instructions for me. Next to my father, who kindled my desire to fly, I loved best the response of a powerful machine as together we pulled a bit of heaven down to man's level. Papa told strangers he met on the street his son was like Adam in Michelangelo's Sistine Chapel painting, soaring across the sky reaching for the fingers of God.

*   *   *

After following the Sepik River for some distance, we turned south to fly through the Tari Basin area with the Mueller Range on our right and the Central Range on our left as we had done on those B-26 recon flights. Once we cleared Mount Bosavi, we planned to turn east and return to Port Moresby along the southern coast. To take advantage of the time, I reviewed our ditching, emergency landing, and bailout procedures, should I deem any necessary, since many crewmembers were scattered from their regular positions.

Before I finished the review, we were astonished when the Tony reappeared and attacked us again. This time he caused a fuel leak somewhere, necessitating a back-up plan, because the damage wouldn't allow us to return to base. After flying over Mount Bosavi, we'd have to head west instead of east and ditch in the marshy area of the Great Plateau. We kept our fingers crossed we wouldn't have to bail out over the jungle or in mountainous terrain where we were bound to be separated.

I can't speak for the others, but last night before our bombing mission in the B-24, a wave of nausea overtook me. It was similar to the attack I suffered on the college gridiron the day an overzealous tackle came in from the left sideline and separated me from my left shoulder. As I was being knocked out of bounds, I got off a 40-yard zinger and we scored. But that was little consolation for the pain in my arm and my fear that I'd never fly again. I ended the game cradled in the arms of my cheerleader girlfriend. Before the ambulance came, I had vomited twice on Norita Tapia's skirt.

In my dreams last night, I only felt like puking. I was worried about the "ten knights" first foray into combat as a cohesive unit, when both aircraft and crew would get the ultimate test. Papa kept appearing throughout the dream. I'd hand him one broken airplane after another, but he would only shake his head and throw his arms up, indicating that it was beyond his power to repair. Yet, he could fix anything. Here in our crippled airplane, I miss the old man most of all.

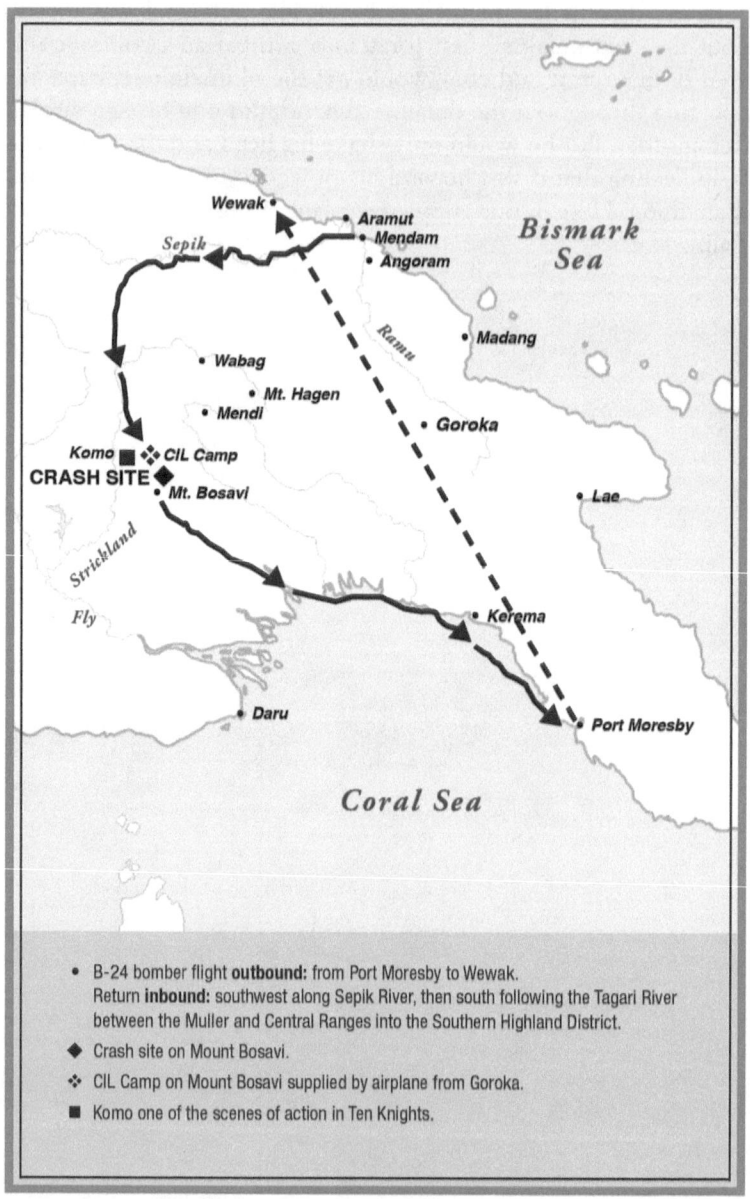

- B-24 bomber flight **outbound:** from Port Moresby to Wewak.
  Return **inbound:** southwest along Sepik River, then south following the Tagari River
  between the Muller and Central Ranges into the Southern Highland District.
- Crash site on Mount Bosavi.
- CIL Camp on Mount Bosavi supplied by airplane from Goroka.
- Komo one of the scenes of action in Ten Knights.

5 B-24 CASE DISCREPANCIES

Baltimore, Maryland, 1973

U.S. ARMY CENTRAL IDENTIFICATION LABORATORY (PROVISIONAL) FINDINGS, CASE NUMBER 316. DR. DEANN TOLAND'S REPORT.

A search of Air Force records revealed several examples of crew survival in the mountainous terrain of New Guinea. The pilot of a B-24 took his aircraft up to 18,000 feet and ordered his crew to bail out. Fourteen days after they had left the plane, seven survivors stumbled into a coastal village and were rescued by friendly natives.

On another occasion, three sergeants were thrown clear as their Liberator split open upon impact. Australians on patrol in the area witnessed the crash, threaded their way through the jungle and got the injured trio to a hospital.

Nowhere in WW II archives are there recovered logs of such length written by survivors, such as in this case. If the logs are authentic, as they appear to be, we can gain valuable clues to help us identify remains.

DeAnn Toland, Ph.D.
Physical Anthropologist

STANEK TURNED TO the last page in the stack. It was a note from Dr. Toland summarizing anthropological clues from the logs to aid in identification of remains and artifacts. She had written:

```
O'Leary (TKO, gunner—remains not recovered)—boxer—
jawbone fracture? (per copilot's log) "Girl in
Sydney." Check to see if she's connected with
Geisha fan and other Japanese mementos.
Patterson (Pip, bombardier—remains not recovered)—
One of three officers—Sanchez, Bottorf and
Patterson—trained at Lubbock Field, Texas, as
pilots. Pip washed out. Greek origins.
Sanchez (OCS or Ox, pilot-copilot's log confirms
as dead—Yes!—old football injury—clavicle or
scapula involvement. See if Norita Tapia still
lives in Las Cruces area and can confirm. Geisha
fan might've been earmarked for her. Inscribed
gold watch and Zippo lighter initialed OCS,
probably both Sanchez's. Cap, goggles, etc.? Too
early to say.
Bottorf (Toggle Joe, copilot—remains not
recovered)—foreign objects embedded in cranial
cavity near optic nerve?
```

Next, Stanek unfolded the only map included in Dr. Toland's packet. She, or someone on her team, had traced the ill-fated bomber's flight path across Papua New Guinea, with two different-colored markers. He located the starting point depicted by a solid red line. It ran from Wewak on the upper eastern coast of the crocodile shaped island, then followed the coastline south to an inlet just northwest of where the Sepik River emptied into the Bismarck Sea. The inlet was labeled as the location of the coastwatcher's station, and it was situated between the villages of Aramut and Mendam, approximately 60 miles south of Wewak.

From this point the red line swerved southwest to Angoram and then west, heading along the contours of the Sepik River. The B-24 left the Sepik and headed south when it reached the turn toward the Tari Basin. Dr. Toland labeled this point on her map, "End of initial B-24 vector."

From there, her blue-dotted line traced the bomber's new vector. It threaded its way between two mountain ranges, following the Tugari River's southerly flow through the Tari highland valley. As the blue line indicated, the B-24 almost cleared Mount Bosavi in the Southern Highlands District in order to make its final turn west along the Rentoul River necessitated by the fuel leak. But it crashed on the northern slope of Mount Bosavi instead.

Stanek opened his notebook and was poised to enter his own observations on the pilot's log and map when the phone next to his bed rang. He picked up the receiver before the second ring, anticipating the call was from Dr. Haveland.

"What loops does 'Saint' Catherine have for me to jump over before I can see my mother?" he asked.

"Sounds rather biblical," the caller remarked.

"Who the hell is this?"

"You've got me placed right, Doc. I'm the damned newspaper fellow from hell, bedeviling souls foredoomed to failure unless they repent."

"Cole!"

"In the flesh, or what's left of me. Just thought I'd check and see if we could move up the timetable for our next meeting. Time's become a dwarf running in place at my side instead of my larger shadow. Each day I shrink closer to this new companion's eye-level, and I can't tell you how it scares the hell out of me."

"I'm sorry."

"Do you think I'm after sympathy, Doc?"

"Mr. Cole, I've got no idea why you're pestering me, unless you're looking for a cure years away from development. Since you seem familiar with my research, you should know the beekeeper cancer study has been placed on the back burner for who knows how long. Now if you'll excuse me, I've got lots of work to do, and, like you, precious little time."

Stanek started to hang up, but when he heard no immediate response, he thought Cole had already done so. Suddenly, the reporter filled the silence with laughter so unsettling Stanek jolted back against the bedstead. He thought Cole had slipped into delirium.

"Pardon me, Doc, but all I want is to be your friend. Meet me in Hawaii like we agreed, and I'll tell you why."

"I don't recall any such..." But Stanek could have saved his breath. This time there was a clicking sound followed by dead silence.

No sooner had he replaced the receiver than the phone sprang to life again. He let it ring three or four times, thinking Cole had not given up for the night.

"I hope this is Dr. Haveland," Stanek said, lingering over the instrument, ready to hang up if it wasn't.

"Emerson, since I got a busy signal on my first try, no need to apologize for waking you. I trust the last caller was Catherine letting you know the visit with your mother is set for 9 a.m. at Phipps. Catherine indicated she wanted to break the news herself."

"I hope you didn't tell her why I came to Johns Hopkins and where to find me."

"Good Lord, my boy, by now everyone in the world knows about your research. Don't you read the papers or watch television?"

"Not when I can help it. Why?"

"The strange reporter from the *Honolulu Advertiser* broke the story on your beekeeper cancer study two weeks before we got your proposal at Johns Hopkins. The AP carried the Cole article as well. Believe me, Catherine would never miss such news unless she was shipwrecked on a deserted island."

"This shouldn't shock you, but I'm sick of hearing about Catherine. Let's keep her out of my life."

"Hold on, my boy. I'm afraid you've got to go through Catherine to see your mother."

"I thought you took care of that."

"I did. But she set conditions..."

"What kind of conditions?"

"Catherine wants to brief you on what to expect. She's got a couple of Patricia's doctors standing by at Phipps tomorrow morning for this purpose."

"I won't have her or any doctors looking over my shoulder while I'm talking to my mother."

"Catherine's not going in with you. She hasn't visited her mother in a couple of months, she told me. It's been hard for her to face Patricia since Rufus' death and your going away eight years ago."

With a furious motion of his fist, Emerson Stanek pounded the air, unintentionally striking the nightstand. "Ouch! My mother's own husband and daughter drove her off the edge into the abyss, and now I'm the one blamed."

"Calm down, my boy. No one's forcing you into an uncomfortable situation. I'll tell Catherine you've declined her offer, and end the difficulty. Meantime, give me a summary on what you've found on the B-24. I don't want to be blind-sided if I run into Cole again, or General Bellicosi calls me. Emerson, are you still there?" Haveland asked.

"Yes, just getting my thoughts in order. Your Dr. Toland made a little progress, but she has gotten herself tangled in an inextricable snarl."

"How so?"

"She missed obvious clues in the supporting documents and in the log."

"Really? How serious are these omissions?"

"Enough to make me question the log's authenticity."

"Give me your observations one by one. Like I said, I don't want to be blind-sided. If it'll save time, I'll sit back and listen, Emerson."

Stanek cleared his throat, signaling he concurred. "Let's start with appearances, beginning with the map. It shows the bomber so far off course, it's hard to imagine experienced aviators, like this crew was, staggering around like drunkards.

"Why risk going inland over uncharted territory in a crippled aircraft when the Bismarck Sea offered the best chance of rescue? I'd want to see better evidence than what is depicted in the pilot's log, or on the map, before concluding they arrived in the crash area by the route indicated. Why weren't there separate confirmations by the coastwatcher, whose position they flew over trying to draw his attention?"

"Good questions, my boy. Go on."

"I would assume Dr. Toland checked the Missing Aircraft Report for this information. I further assume that since the MAR wasn't included or mentioned in her report, this vital document failed to turn up. Are you following this so far?"

"Yes, yes, Emerson, go on."

"Regarding crash site photos, they show an aircraft so damaged I don't see how anyone could've survived the impact. A whole section of the twin stabilizer is missing. The pilot must've lost control when the plane struck the mountain peak.

"Most of the fuselage, especially in the vicinity of the cockpit, is so severely crushed a pygmy couldn't have survived the wreckage. Yet, the log's stated author, an individual the size of a football player was at the controls on impact and survived to write his account.

"This brings us to the appearance of the pilot's log itself. It begins with a verse in brush strokes wielded by a right-handed person. As the regular script commences, the handwriting shifts to a slanting-style consistent with a left-handed writer. You might be wondering what's the connection between the pilot's size and his handwriting?"

"Go on, my boy."

"Here's the link as succinctly as I can make it. We have a left-handed writing pilot, who, when playing high school football runs down the left sideline, and, as he's being knocked out of bounds by an opposing tackle, manages to throw a football with his right hand far enough across and down the field to score a touchdown.

"What's more, this same allegedly left-handed individual, seated in the left seat while flying a bomber during an emergency would use his predominant hand on the yoke while his right hand could manipulate the switches located on the center panel above him and on the copilot's side. This is an ideal setup for him, yet he states he is "disappointed" and having difficulty controlling the bomber. And if the copilot is left-handed, as I suspect most of them nicknamed Toggle Joe were, it makes no sense for a left-handed pilot to transfer flight controls to a lefty copilot who would then have to fly with his non-predominant hand."

"No sense at all, my boy. So, you're saying the log was written by a left-handed person, yet the pilot, who claims to be the author, was right-handed?"

"By his own admission. Do you want me to read you the part from the log where the pilot states he and the copilot used their predominant hands to adjust the instruments situated between them as well as the overhead switches?"

"No, but couldn't the copilot, this Toggle Joe, have written the log?"

"It wouldn't make sense either. Why would he assume the persona of someone else when his own account has turned up in a separate document, according to Dr. Toland? Without comparing the pilot's log to the copilot's, we're admittedly at a disadvantage. But there's another problem with the log, no matter who wrote it."

"And that is?"

"The entire document is written on thick paper over blue contour lines consistent with depth charts used by mariners. I'd think army aviators and navigators might have standard issue brown-lined aeronautical charts on board, depicting various mountain peaks rather than ocean depths."

"Certainly over New Guinea, you'd think so, Emerson." Haveland paused, then continued. "Look, it's awfully late, and though I'm fascinated by your findings, we'd better call it quits. But before we do, did you find anything in Dr. Toland's materials suggesting a crime?"

"Not from any of the scant evidence I've seen. Your anthropologist even appeared reluctant to go that far. I don't see how this case merits any more of our time as pathologists. Nor need anyone else investigate the matter further, other than identifying remains."

"No survivors?"

"If there were, they didn't walk or crawl away from this particular aircraft, as it sits practically demolished. However, there is an intriguing aspect..."

"Yes, yes, go on."

"In the photos, half the B-24's twin tail is missing and according to the pilot's log, the wounded, including the copilot, were moved to this section before impact. I suppose one or more of the wounded could've survived the crash and died later from starvation, from their injuries or at the hands of hostile natives. Doubt they would last long roaming the world's second largest island, a terrain perhaps even more remote and more unforgiving than Greenland."

"Well, at least DeAnn hasn't struck out completely. If I hear you correctly, there's a slight chance for survivors."

"Perhaps, but I'd advise your Dr. Toland to go slow using this log for identifying crew remains. This whole case rests on a tissue of irrelevancies, if you ask me."

"Examples, my boy, give examples."

"We've got a lot of relationships cited without much solid data. For example, those between crewmembers and their contemporaries as well as the relationship between the pilot and his father seem excessively sentimental for men at war. I'm reminded of people of our acquaintance."

"Still smarting over Catherine's conditions for visiting your mother, I see. I don't know what's going on between you two. But for whatever it's worth, my advice is to play out the string and see where it leads. Patricia at least will benefit from a one-day visit, just as I have from seeing you again. But it's your call. I've taken up too much of your time already, and I know how important your schedule is. Thanks for your input. I know DeAnn Toland will also appreciate getting a second opinion on a most unusual case. Maybe I'll see you tomorrow on campus. Good night, my boy."

Strange, Emerson thought after he hung up. Haveland had not mentioned his breakthrough on the Filipino Freddie case. Stranger still, Stanek had forgotten to ask him about the "smoking gun."

6 DECEPTIVE FLIRTATION

Papua New Guinea, 1973

U.S. ARMY CENTRAL IDENTIFICATION LABORATORY (PROVISIONAL) FINDINGS, CASE NUMBER 316. DR. DEANN TOLAND'S REPORT.

In the 1930s, expeditions conducted by Jack Hides, Mick Leahy and the Leahy brothers spread a disease, known as the cargo cult, across the island of New Guinea. In a Stone Age culture still dependent on trading shells for commerce in remote areas, it is easy to see how cargo cult greed took root.

In return for taking sides against one or the other of the island's occupiers, the natives were promised white man's riches. By promising to return from the sky with the expected cargo, the warring civilized nations gave false hopes to a primitive people, who otherwise would have withheld cooperation unless compensated on the spot. Americans, Australians and Japanese (all considered white by the natives) left with their pledges unfulfilled.

Thereafter, every downed aircraft, or "balus," became prey for the Papuans. The wreckages were stripped of everything that could be hauled away. I have no doubt the American bomber on Mount Bosavi was picked clean by Riami and Tugaru warriors before the CIL's arrival, including items valuable to our investigation.

Per General Bellicosi's directive, whites are forbidden to barter or trade with the indigenous population. Since "quid pro quo" arrangements are at

the heart of the cargo cult feeding frenzy, they are
included in the prohibition.
                    DeAnn Toland, Ph.D.
                    Physical Anthropologist

UNDER THE RISING noonday heat, DeAnn Toland shed her
usual fatigue jacket and braced herself for another six hours
of work. The humidity and threatened rain of what old-timers
considered an unusually wet year in the Southern Highlands
District had left no less an authority than *Kiap* Roger Noble, reared
in New Guinea by Australian missionary parents, scratching his
head. Noble, Australian patrol officer for the Southern Highlands
District, had predicted an end to the miserable conditions by late
April. But a month later the rain continued.

Throughout the uncooperative weather, DeAnn maintained her
schedule. She arrived at the B-24 crash site where the aircraft lay on
the slope of Mount Bosavi at sunrise and directed the search for
remains until the sun set again 12 hours later. Her one respite from
work was a sparse lunch followed by letter writing activities.

As she sat at her field desk under the wing of the B-24,
perspiration formed on her forehead. She tried to wipe it away with
a handkerchief, but it soon reappeared. Nor could she keep her
white T-shirt dry in the high heat and humidity. She saw Major
Frank Yowell waving at her from atop the wing of his single-engine
Beaver aircraft parked on the makeshift runway. The pilot had
swapped his flight suit for short trousers and had taken off his
shirt. She thought it was her duty to remind the CIL team's primary
link to the outside world of the dress code. Furthermore, it was
important he refrain from parading his bare, fair skin around in the
noonday sun. He seemed oblivious to the danger.

"Hey, Frank," DeAnn shouted, "Just because you don't feel like
you're burning doesn't mean you aren't."

The army pilot cupped a hand behind his ear pretending he had
not heard her, but his response proved he had. "Reckon I'm
burning alright," he called back placing his hand over his heart,
"burning with desire."

Not taking the bait, she gave a friendly wave, thinking how
particularly small and frail she must look sitting under an awning
attached to the wing of the big bomber. In relating to Yowell, she
found it hard to maintain the "command presence" she worked so
hard to cultivate between the soldiers in her charge and herself.

While the CIL team was in Thailand, her leadership qualities, as a civilian heading a military operation, never came up. But in New Guinea, she sensed erosion. Yowell, intentionally or not, belittled the disciplined manner in which she led by example. "Soldiers need a good kick in the ass to get 'em moving in tough terrain like this," he had told her.

She watched Yowell bend over the wing, flex his muscles and somersault to the tarmac like a gymnast dismounting a pommel horse. It reminded her of her own college field and track prowess. As a cross-country champion, she had developed the stamina and litheness of a young gazelle whose high cheekbones, smiling brown eyes and soft lips never twisted in pain no matter how arduous the course laid out before her, or regardless of the caliber of competition she faced.

DeAnn clapped her hands appreciatively as Yowell bowed in her direction. Then a tinge of envy mixed with sadness came over her. By nightfall Yowell would be back in Goroka amid a bustling white community, while she retreated to a lonely tent on the outskirts of the Tugaru village. Her breasts swelled against the flimsy T-shirt as she remembered how petite she had felt pressed against his massive chest as they said goodbye the night before. There had been other embraces in her life, but none had had the pleasurable effect of Yowell's. She had always seen herself as a runner, somewhat gangly and muscular, towering over the shorter men attracted to her. But in Yowell's arms, she had felt warm, vulnerable and protected as fit her image of femininity. Her thighs trembled and she felt an urgency surge all through her body as the major mounted the aircraft ladder, turned abruptly and blew her a kiss before retreating inside the cabin.

In the same instant she felt a bit nettled. Yowell, like her male colleagues on the college track team, could, whenever the mood struck, escape the insufferable humidity by baring their torsos. For a white woman in New Guinea, even this luxury her black counterparts took for granted was denied her. Once in a playful mood she had donned a Riami grass skirt to cool her loins and a major scandal had erupted bringing a minor reprimand from General Bellicosi.

"I'd rather see you douse yourself with pig grease than bare any part of your body before these heathens," he chided.

She had given serious thought to the general's alternative. Native women smeared their bodies with pig grease and never showed any signs of sweat on their ebony skins, even though their day, like hers, began at dawn and ended at dusk. The women kept the village supplied and tended to much more strenuous tasks than the men did.

Nor did respite for the womenfolk come on those rare nights when a cool breeze stirred through the villages. She had often observed young maidens and married women slip off into the gardens, hand-in-hand with males who had rested all day, anticipating a night of sex.

Perhaps white males were no different. For all she knew, Yowell might already have a girl in his hometown, in Goroka, in Honolulu or in Saigon—all recent ports of call for the handsome Texas bachelor.

DeAnn picked up the B-24 copilot's log next to her typewriter. She wondered how the young, stranded aviators from her own Western culture coped with appetites known to have launched wars in the past. If any of the young aviators had been as flirtatious as Major Yowell was, they must have left behind women who longed for their return. She recalled the copilot's log mentioned one of the missing aviators had a wife and two others mentioned girlfriends. She hoped whatever the circumstances, the B-24 survivors had relatives and friends back home who loved them, as Bottorf had indicated in the series of letters he had written to the next of kin of the fallen.

DeAnn put these thoughts aside and sifted through the papers in the copilot's log in order to select the letters she thought might be useful to Dr. Haveland once he arrived in the country. She began to read once again the letters of sympathy constituting the copilot's log and didn't stop until she got to the end of Bottorf's last letter. She felt a lump of sorrow in her throat as tears cascaded down her rose-colored cheeks. She wiped the tears from her dark brown eyes and cheeks with a handkerchief.

After selecting several of the letters for Dr. Haveland's perusal, she decided to write a letter home, and rolled a blank piece of paper into her portable typewriter.

She had barely begun when *Kiap* Noble appeared under the wing of the B-24 serving as a roof for her crash site office. The Australian patrol officer removed his wide-brimmed bush hat, exposing a thatch of red hair streaked with gray, and settled his bulky frame into the folding chair in front of DeAnn's field desk.

"Sorry to barge in, pretty lassie, but two Riami warriors turned up outside the rope line perimeter askin' to see the white *misis*. They said they wanted to work for ye, but I told 'em we had plenty of Riami men. If they'd been Tugaru, I'd have hired 'em on the spot."

"Have I met them, Roger?"

"One ye had given a knife to, and the other bloke I recognized as the half-blind Riami headman who led his tribe to save our patrol from the Giambu cannibals last year. He's kept his distance from us up until now, but I suspect the dodgy little rascal's working on some scheme to get steel of his own."

"What do you want me to do?" she asked.

"Nothing for the time being. I'll send them both away, but it's important the leader and his *one-mate* see I'm carrying their message to you."

She stood up and looked around Noble's thick frame to take her own measurement of the two men standing with their fingers wrapped around the rope barrier that separated the two worlds.

"They look friendly enough. Here, take them a couple of blankets, get their names and tell them I'll ask for them personally if an opening occurs."

"About those wool blankets," the *kiap* said, "don't ye have another type material?"

"Why?"

"Out here, wool draws maggots like these people are drawn to war, sex, salt or honey."

DeAnn smiled, "Honey we can supply." She picked up a large honeycomb wrapped in a banana leaf from a stool next to her desk and broke it in two. "Well, here, take this to them with the blankets. We don't want to turn any warriors away disappointed."

"I saw Major Yowell pay a boy to go into the aircraft to get the honeycomb for ye. Are you sure ye want to give it away?"

"I've warned Frank not to trade with the natives and start another cargo cult frenzy. Every time he flies in here, they're expecting goods the whites promised them during the war. Maybe the honey will break the cycle."

"I see, lass, Bellicosi's orders. No *quid pro quo*."

61

DeAnn watched as Noble delivered the items to the two Riami men. The warriors showed little emotion when the *kiap* gave them the blankets, but when he passed the honey across the line, their reaction was unexpected. They danced and whooped in jubilant fashion, pausing to bow at the waist in her direction, treating the honey like it was a pot of gold. The one with the bad eye looked straight at her, pointed to his forehead above the cloudy socket and in pidgin called out, "Dok-tor Tow-land know before MilkEye ask. Two Face no guess this. *Misis* sorcery stronger!"

"What does he mean?" she called to Noble who was busy posting a second guard around the wreckage site.

"Ye've got magic," the *kiap* shouted over his shoulder.

DeAnn smiled and clasped her hands together in prayer-like fashion and saluted the grinning old warrior with her fingertips. She held the gesture until the retreating pair reached the footpath to the vine bridge crossing the Rentoul River. Then she saw Major Yowell giving chase.

She watched the panting pilot catch up with the Riami warriors, reach out and grab the one called MilkEye by the shoulder and swing the poor fellow around in the trail like a constable apprehending a poacher. "Oh dear," she mumbled. "Frank, you'll get yourself killed!"

DeAnn fumed. What could've possessed Yowell to sneak up on armed warriors and then start bullying one of them, acting like a Tugaru overlord? She shuddered. If Yowell had waylaid a Tugaru in the manner he did the two Riami men, he'd be greeted with the tip of a poisoned spear. Since she did not know whether Yowell even knew the differences between the warring groups, she hurriedly flung her fatigue jacket over her shoulders as a sun shield and headed for the riverbank.

When she reached a point where the path crossed the airstrip, then narrowed leading to the river, she halted and watched a new drama unfold up ahead. MilkEye and his companion were rubbing their black greasy hands through Yowell's blonde hair and began administering the traditional Riami greeting. All three men squealed like middle-school boys after scoring a touchdown as they slapped and poked each other. Suddenly the half-blind Riami warrior reached into the colorful *bilim* slung over his shoulder. Screwing himself up to appear taller, he handed Yowell what DeAnn guessed was a river stone the size of small fist.

She crept closer. The pilot briefly examined the proffered stone, then sent it skimming far out into the rapids of the Rentoul. Each time MilkEye handed Yowell a stone, the pilot repeated the act. After five or six rejections, Yowell finally accepted one of the stones, which he put in the pocket of his shorts. From the other pocket he withdrew a pack of cigarillos and handed it to MilkEye.

Barter had occurred. DeAnn knew it was her duty as team leader to point out the infraction. She started to announce her presence but instead collapsed in the grass beside the trail wringing her hands. "He'll think I'm a meddler and out to disrupt a relationship only just begun," she whispered to the blade of *kunai* grass brushing against her cheek.

She summoned the spirit of her college track meet days. Then, without further reflection, she rose from the grass, repositioned her long, auburn ponytail over her shoulder, and like a British soldier swinging his arms on parade, stalked toward the river to confront Major Yowell.

By the time DeAnn reached the landing, the Riami men were gone and Yowell stood facing the river flipping an object in his hand and whistling. As she drew near, she recognized the tune from the hit movie *Goldfinger.*

"I see you're a 007 fan," she remarked. "Mind telling me what you're up to, Mr. Bond?"

The pilot, still whistling, whirled around, slipped the object in his pocket and pointed to the top of his head. "Last time I checked 5' 11" even, about three inches taller than you," he said.

"Really, I pegged you as taller." She wondered if the hot sun had made his face red, or whether he was truly embarrassed.

"When I'm around you, sweet stuff, I'm at my Texas best, standing cactus tall and as eager to please as a newly broken colt."

"I hope your best includes following the rules, Frank."

"What's wrong?" he asked leaning toward her and lacing his fingers behind his head signaling surrender. "Take me into custody, sheriff, but do you have to look so forlorn?"

As their eyes met, his narrowed to green slits. She could see he wanted to evade the question, nevertheless she pressed the point.

"Frank, I saw you trading with the Riami."

"Sure, I give 'em smokes from time to time—the Tugaru, too."

"And what do you get in return?"

"Sometimes a little honey."

"Not from the women, I trust."

"Of course not, I meant the stuff I get for you, and you pass off as charity. Hey, boss lady, these cannibals have nothing I want, including their women. If you're talking about the stones, so I'm collecting a couple of arrowheads for a nephew in Dallas. Big deal."

"Well, if arrowheads are the extent of it, there's no harm done. But I wish you wouldn't trade with the natives. They don't understand our values."

"You're the boss, but if I have to close down my dealings with Salty Meri, you'll never get Tugaru cooperation in solving this case."

"Who's Salty Meri, and what's her connection to the B-24?"

"I'm surprised you two haven't met. She's boss lady of the Tugaru salt well operations. Nobody gets near the place unless they go through her."

"How did you meet her? Is she a lady friend?"

Yowell placed his hand over his heart as if an arrow had struck him. "Now your last question really hurts. I'm lonely, but not that lonely. Salty Meri is so ugly, when she fell through the ugly tree, she didn't miss a branch on the way down."

"Frank, how awful!"

"Wait 'til you see her. We're talking major league hag, and mean enough to wear a man's jawbone around her throat for a necklace."

"How do you know it's a man's?"

"Reckon it's too big to be anything else, and the teeth have huge fillings in 'em to boot. You don't have to be an anthropologist to know it belonged to a white man."

"Were they mercury/amalgam fillings?"

"I don't know the chemical makeup. But I figure the original owner is one of my fellow aviators. I've been trying to get the gruesome artifact away from Salty Meri and bring it to you, but she won't let it go. Claims the jawbone was her husband's."

"Why didn't you tell me this before?"

"Afraid you'd react like you did over the stupid arrowheads, I reckon."

"We'll have to report this to General Bellicosi. He'll know what to do. Meantime, I'd like you to point out Salty Meri to me."

"Don't reckon it'll be any time soon. I'm heading to Goroka to pick up my things. From there, it's on down to Port Moresby in the

Beaver to catch a flight to Hawaii where I'm to wait for a VIP and escort him back here."

"Is Dr. Haveland coming back with you?"

"I don't know Haveland from no-land, except I don't cotton to flying in any competition."

"Oh, Frank, Haveland's old enough to be my father."

Yowell swiped a hand across his broad forehead. "Reckon you just gave me the best news I've heard all day."

Aware he was studying her candidly, she tried to see herself through his deep-set and restless green eyes. But when those same eyes swept over her wasp-thin waist, then lingered on her high breasts pressed against her damp, cotton T-shirt, she put her arms through the sleeves in her fatigue jacket and pulled it closed in front of her.

"If you're leaving soon. I really should get a letter ready to send with you," she said.

"As long as it's a letter to your parents and not some other guy, you can call, and I'll haul," he said smiling.

Ordinarily such directness from a man made her uneasy. But the youthful manner with which Yowell flirted stirred an unusual excitement in her and made her respond in kind.

"Sure, like you haven't noticed all my incoming mail bears the same Chicago postmark where my parents happen to live. I suppose more sophisticated women of your acquaintance would never admit as much."

Frank Yowell grinned so broadly he had to remove the unlighted cigarillo from his strong white teeth before he could speak. "You have no idea what a turn-on honesty is, my lady." Suddenly he took her tapered fingers in his hand and kissed them below the smooth white knuckles. "Here's to honesty," he murmured, "something I've been working on all my life." He turned abruptly and went back toward the airstrip, his bare shoulders sagging.

She thought of the other lonely aviators who might have walked this same pathway in the same dejected manner and was about to chase after Yowell when *Kiap* Noble came out of the high grass and took her arm. "Lassie, me and my boys will walk you back to the Liberator. Don't have to tell ye the bush is no place for man or woman to go waltzin' about in unaccompanied."

Hours later, Dr. DeAnn Toland sat alone typing a report for General Bellicosi about the copilot's log in the shade of the B-24 wing. She was unaware of the two Riami warriors who slipped under the rope barrier, then squatted in the tall *kunai* grass, timed to avoid two sentries patrolling the line in front of her. MilkEye and his *one-mate* crept closer on hands and knees. Between them they dragged a large bundle wrapped in banana leaves. They maneuvered so skillfully through the grass, had DeAnn or the sentries detected any movement, it would have been dismissed as nothing more than a small animal foraging.

Within 15 feet of DeAnn's field table under the wing of the fallen *balus*, MilkEye and WonTok stopped, abandoned the package and silently crawled back the way they came into the setting sun. The entire operation took less than five minutes.

7 COPILOT'S LOG

Papua New Guinea, 1944

U.S. ARMY CENTRAL IDENTIFICATION LABORATORY FINDINGS
(PROVISIONAL), CASE NUMBER 316: EXHIBIT B—COPILOT'S
LETTERS TO FAMILY AND FRIENDS OF TEN CREWMEMBERS. DR.
DEANN TOLAND'S REPORT.

To Mr. and Mrs. A. C. Sanchez of Las Cruces, New Mexico
RE: 1/Lt. Oscar Carlos Sanchez, Pilot, B-24

Dear Sanchez family:

If you receive this letter, by now you've received official word
from the War Department that Lt. Oscar Carlos Sanchez, or "Ox"
to those who served with him, is missing in action. I can now
confirm his death. Our hearts sorrow with you. Your son was a
great leader and a pilot without peer. All the gentle virtues came
together in full bloom in Ox. Painful as it may be to recall some of
them here, I know Oscar would've done the same thing for me had
I died in his stead. The rest of the crew of "Ten Knights on the
Barroom Floor" who survived mourn his passing as well and can
only pray a merciful God will keep a bond forged in war intact in a
peace lasting forever.

We sealed this solidarity born of war with a poem. Our
purpose: to express our responsibilities to each other should we
find ourselves in a mishap like the one that has separated us. Here's
what we wrote:

Rise brave knights from the barroom floor,
After a sortie through hell in your B-24.
Now heaven-bound, ten souls doth soar,
Once the last knight out has closed the door.

In battle, soldiers understand mistakes are made. Ours was made because we all wanted to come home. It would be untruthful of me to say war had not hardened our hearts, although Ox's great faith made him least affected by the horrors of combat. Owing to your son's pilot skills, getting the most he could out of a damaged aircraft, and with his faith, Ox almost brought most of us home (except for the two killed by the attack of a Japanese fighter pilot, of course). The four of us (and perhaps one other) surviving here in the jungle attest to his effort to save his crew.

On approach to the swamplands we thought lay beyond Mount Bosavi, where ditching would be safer, Ox read us an excerpt from I Corinthians 2:9. Your son's last words were: "Eye hath not seen, nor ear heard, neither have entered into the heart of man, the things which God hath prepared for them that love Him."

We trust Ox's testimony will bring you the same measure of hope it has given those of us who remain. From all he had told us about his family back home, we know Ox would want us to express the special love he had for flying and for the man who made it possible. "My Dad knew I should've been born with wings, and he sacrificed so much to make it happen," Ox never tired of telling us.

Please, if appropriate, share this letter with Norita Tapia. Perhaps she, too, will find comfort in the knowledge of the affection in which his crew held "OCS." God be with us all.

Yours,

2/Lt. Sam Bottorf, Copilot, "Toggle Joe"

   *   *   *

To Miss Amanda Glenn, Sydney, Australia
RE: Sgt. Timothy K. O'Leary, Nose Gunner, B-24

Dear Amanda:

Your boyfriend, our Army Air Corps buddy whom we call "TKO," is one of the surviving crewmembers of a B-24 bomber, which crashed on a remote mountain in New Guinea. TKO was one of the bravest of the brave of the "ten knights" who survived the crash. The others are Technical Sgt. Wells, ("Deep"), Sgt. Shipley, ("Sharpshooter") and myself, Lt. Sam Bottorf ("Toggle Joe"). I'm certain TKO mentioned all the "knights" by their nicknames in his letters to you, and if this letter reaches you, it means one of us got out of here alive.

A week or so ago, we left our mountain refuge to make our way down the Rentoul River in canoes in the company of some natives whose leader had befriended us. However, it wasn't long before our native escort disappeared, and the four of us found refuge in a cave behind a cascade on the Rentoul River.

We had hoped to use the waterways as an escape route home, connecting with the Strickland and the Fly from the Rentoul. But since our native guides are gone, and our dinghy is back in the B-24, we have had to rethink our plan. We thought of the possibility of air rescue. TKO was a great help in laying out parachute panels for possible air rescuers to see, especially if the coastwatcher whose station we had flown over had noted our heading. Unfortunately these efforts only alerted the fierce Giambu natives in the area to our presence. We had heard from the Riami about the Giambu tribe's appetite for human flesh.

Our daily food gathering forays made us especially vulnerable to detection by the Giambu. Then again, we feared one of our food gatherers might inadvertently bring back poisonous plants from his daily forages and kill us all, so we subsisted chiefly on caterpillars, beetles and maggots. We decided it was too dangerous to remain in the lowlands trying to avoid cannibals and hordes of insects, neither of which gave us any respite night or day.

Wells and TKO were the most able-bodied "knights" standing. Sharpshooter's mental state was precarious, and I am nearly blind. I can only see objects about a foot distance from my eyes, due to injury sustained in a Jap fighter attack on our aircraft. So, three days ago, my three buddies, including TKO, left me here to wait for them. They went to find food and scout the area for safer environs.

TKO and Sharpshooter (his real name is Shipley, but we often call each other by our nicknames) went to find food along the western section of the Rentoul, while Wells headed northeast back to the friendly native village to get help. I have heard from none of them, and I fear that death, the last enemy, has overtaken them. I hope they have not fallen into the hands of cannibals. I write this in haste because without food and unable to venture beyond this cave, I will die if they don't return soon. I have to hold on to the hope they are alive and will come back for me.

Tim, or TKO, is, as you probably know, from Tulsa, Oklahoma, and proud of it. He told us you were against his boxing, but you were not squeamish, except when he was in the ring. Something in his blood made him want to fight. Over here, he boxed to keep from getting madder about the war. (By the way, TKO did quit boxing after he broke his jaw, as he promised you he would.)

As for your love letters to TKO, he spent much time rereading them when in garrison. I suppose, before every mission, he felt he might never see you again. As aliens in New Guinea territory, we were deprived of both love and sex. Perhaps to compensate for this loss, TKO began to play with fire, mentally setting ablaze the love burning in his heart for you. But when he started setting fires willy-nilly, we were afraid he'd give away our position, so we took his matches and lighter away from him until he regained his senses.

Only one of your letters remains, the last one he received from you before we left on our ill-fated mission. TKO took it with him and entrusted it to me each time he went in search of food. Since I have no love to call my own, and no girl at home waiting for my return, perhaps TKO felt your letter might help keep hope alive for the rest of us if anything happened to him. One of the lines in your letter was particularly inspiring, "Could a woman love a man any more than I do you? Not even dreams compare to the love we've shared."

Amanda, Sgt. O'Leary spoke your name as if you were a treasure better than gold. The two of you built a world of happy memories. And those of us privileged to share such dreams can only turn to the Lord for solace. He says: "Because I live, ye shall live also." I'm sure TKO will live in your heart forever.

Your Friend and Fellow Mourner,

2/Lt. Sam Bottorf, Copilot, "Toggle Joe"

*   *   *

To Rabbi Rosenberg, Davenport, Iowa
RE: Sgt. Elijah B. Ingersol, Belly Turret Gunner, B-24

Dear Rabbi Rosenberg:

It is with a heavy heart, but a sense of duty I must inform you of the death of a member of your synagogue, one Elijah B. Ingersol, "Prophet," as we called him. None of us particularly liked war. We all wanted to go home. Unfortunately, Elijah had his life snuffed out in a battle with an enemy fighter while we were on a bombing mission. He was in the belly turret of our aircraft at the time.

Take it from me. This is the least desirable place to be on a B-24 bomber. Yet, kind, quiet and good-natured as anyone could be, Prophet volunteered for this duty. Because he was the shortest member of our crew, he said the belly turret would fit him best. I know it is as hard for you as it was for us to imagine Prophet could kill anybody. But this war in the Pacific has boiled down to the sad state of any war—you either kill or are killed.

I think you should know his best friend on the crew was a Catholic lad, who like Prophet was 21, and was wounded at his station by the same Japanese fighter pilot. Christians and Jews are standing together here in the Pacific as they are in the European Theatre. I think God wanted it that way.

If Prophet had one vanity, it was bragging about his hometown, Davenport, Iowa. I once heard him say if every city in the world was like Davenport, there would be no wars. I'm sure part of his pride was connected to the Jewish community there, which he hoped to serve one day as a teacher like yourself. In his behalf I say to all those who knew this gentle soul, "Shalom."

Faithfully yours,

2/Lt. Sam Bottorf, Copilot, "Toggle Joe"

*   *   *

To Norman Grant, Marion, Alabama
RE: Sgt. Alfred T. Grant, Right Waist Gunner, B-24

Dear Norman:

I bear sad news about your brother, Alfred, whom we called
"U.S." When several Japanese fighters attacked our bomber, U.S.
was critically wounded and died while we were airborne. We were
able to ward off most of them, except for one persistent Jap who
took your brother's life. He also killed his friend Prophet, and he
wounded several others, myself included.

U.S. often spoke about his kid brother back in Marion,
Alabama. He said you were always interested in what it was like to
fly in combat, although he never got around to telling you. (This I
learned from his own lips as I was with him when he lay dying
from his wounds.) I promised him I would write to you and not
glorify battle, lest you believe there is something heroic in killing
another human being.

Once when we were at our air station in Port Moresby, U.S.
gave us a rundown on what it was like to be a waist gunner on a
B-24 over a target at night. He described how the flares burst
around him, turning night into day, aided by searchlights, which
became beams we tried to dodge. Then the ack-ack guns sent up a
terrible roar as the projectiles burst around us. He said at times like
this, and especially when an enemy fighter entered the picture, his
breath came so short and his chest felt so empty of air that he
nearly passed out. There was nothing to do but stay at your station
and hope none of the fire directed against you had your name on it.

After the battle, if you survived, it was like death itself. Every
muscle in your body went flabby and you collapsed over your gun
like a little boy leaning over a fence rail. Your thoughts were of the
missing aircraft in your formation, and the fate of the men who
were able to parachute into enemy territory. I know I speak for the
whole crew. We hope, by the time you grow up into manhood, this
war will be over, and boys like you will never know the horrors of
combat against a relentless enemy.

Your brother fought for peace, and those of us who have lived
long enough to talk about it share his desire. I know your brother
always encouraged you to go into medicine, as I would have done if
I had it to do over again. One must admire a profession that

promises to do no harm. Near the end I think your brother was trying to express the same sentiment.

Sincerely,

2/Lt. Sam Bottorf, Copilot, "Toggle Joe"

*   *   *

To Elliot "Skipper" Young, Toledo, Ohio
RE: 2/Lt. Mitchell B. Nelson, Navigator, B-24

Dear Skip:

I feel like I know you, because our mutual friend Mitchell, whom we called "Admiral," spoke of you and your training together at Lubbock, Texas, so often. I got my pilot's wings there as well. I hope you don't mind my using your nickname, but it's a habit we flight crews have gotten into. We hardly ever refer to one another by rank or given names, because we want to keep any would-be captors guessing as to our rank for awhile, until we're requested to give name, rank and serial number. We went so far as to wear no insignia of rank on our green flight coveralls during combat missions.

Why am I telling you all this? Admiral, which only now do I realize the irony in that name being a rank itself (as well as skipper denoting the top man), told us about your trauma after washing out of flight school. You see, we officers, serving as pilot, copilot, navigator and bombardier, think of ourselves as one entity along with the enlisted men making up our crew. So to switch over to the navigator's position should bear no stigma, especially if you get assigned to a B-24 crew.

Admiral would have told you these things personally, but unfortunately he was killed occupying my old seat as copilot when our plane augered into a mountaintop. He and four others (two of which already had been killed by a Japanese fighter pilot) never survived the crash landing. One is still missing and three of the others, along with myself, miraculously escaped mortal injuries as we were thrown from the tail section. As far as I know, our bombardier (if he's still alive) and I are the only officers surviving. So you see, God doesn't discriminate when it's time to call us home.

I started out this letter hoping to make you feel better about your navigator status, but I'm sure Admiral's death is something we can all mourn, regardless of position or rank.

I understand you and Admiral went to high school together in Toledo, Ohio. From his description of the city, we all "frothed at the mouth" to go there, except for Wells, our engineer, who is married and T.K. O'Leary, who has a girlfriend in Sydney. Admiral said we didn't know what a date was until we dated a girl who lived along the rim of Lake Erie. In high school, the two of you collected garters the girls wore to proms, he told us, and he envied you because your collection was larger than his. Strange how the things we do as kids live with us until the day we die.

But of all the things with lasting value, friendship has to be right at the top. And I know, as his best friend, you would want to hear about Admiral's death from his second best friend, and not some cold, second-hand tale based on a War Department telegram. (They never send out notices to friends. I think this is a flaw in the system.) Trusting this letter has helped ease your sorrow,

I remain yours truly,

2/Lt. Sam Bottorf, Copilot, "Toggle Joe"

     *   *   *

To Mrs. Harlan Wells, Peedee, South Carolina
RE: T/Sgt. Harlan J. Wells, Engineer, B-24

Dear Mrs. Wells:

I struggle with grief and pain to bring these ill tidings to you. Your husband, Harlan, whom we called "Deep," has been missing for three days, and I fear he has met with some misfortune.

Deep was the chief morale raiser on our crew. In addition to being the best engineer and mechanic of all those who have ever serviced a B-24, he understood the sacrifices called for in war. As the senior enlisted man on our bomber, "Ten Knights on the Barroom Floor," Sgt. Wells said his top priority was to build morale, which he reminded us is 90% pride in one's leaders and fellow fighters and 10% desire.

"Don't confuse the two," he said. "Most soldiers like me desire nothing more than to be with our families instead of in a fight, but war leaves us no other choice but to defend our country."

Deep made it clear his choice was to be with you and little Harlan. Neither of you ever left his mind. He bragged more about the two of you than he did his skills as an engineer, renowned all over Port Moresby, and probably Australia as well.

We used to tease him by saying after the war we "ten knights" intended to descend upon Peedee for a reunion just to see the "perfect" family. He laughed and told us if we made good on our promise, we would double the population in his hometown.

As you know, he distributed good-humored chaff whenever the situation got too serious. Between Deep and our bombardier Pip, we didn't have time to feel sorry for ourselves. Still, holed up in a cave, hoping Deep or one of the other two—TKO or Sharpshooter—would return to end my isolation, I must confess it's hard to keep my chin up. But I know, speaking for the rest of us, we would prefer, if only one of us were to get out, it to be Deep, the only member married and raising his own family.

I have a sister in Minnesota to greet me at home. But as much as she cares for me, she herself would say she is no substitute for a little boy with his arms wrapped around your legs, while your loving wife renders a homecoming kiss.

Perhaps my worry is premature. Deep might have met up with Pip and the two of them have gone to bring back help. Wouldn't we share a good laugh and a happy reunion if this were to occur? One way or the other, this letter might not reach you. If Deep arrives, there's no need for it, and if help doesn't come soon, I'm afraid all of my letters of condolence will die with me.

Yet, Deep would be the first to tell you. It is the surviving officer's duty to write and express his deepest sympathy to loved ones of those at whose side he served. Trusting I have rendered my duty to this obligation to your satisfaction, I send my earnest prayers the Almighty may support you and little Harlan.

Your friend,

2/Lt. Sam Bottorf, Copilot, "Toggle Joe"

   *   *   *

To Mr. and Mrs. John S. Alexander I, Seattle, Washington
RE: T/Sgt. John S. Alexander III, Radio Operator, B-24

Dear Mr. and Mrs. Alexander:

Your grandson John, whom we called "Signals," often spoke of his life with you and your wife after his parents were killed in a tragic car accident. He said he was nine when he went to live with you and a wonderful dog, Teddy, his best friend and playmate. He especially liked to romp with Teddy whenever his cousins visited, because their parents would not allow pets in the house. I suppose the other members of my bomber crew heard enough stories about Teddy to last a lifetime. Unfortunately, the senior partner in the John-Teddy relationship was killed by a Japanese fighter pilot, who attacked our B-24 after a bombing mission to Wewak, New Guinea.

Signals had a zest for life and wanted very much to pursue a career in radio. Next to Teddy, he loved electronic gadgets best. When he tackled a job, he tackled it vigorously, as you probably know better than I do. He was a fountain of boundless energy. No doubt this was a carryover from his boyhood days growing up among your acres of apple trees where he and Teddy were in a relentless pursuit of every comic book villain Signals could think of. He knew all their names and regaled us with their nefarious exploits, making us think his collection of comics must have filled one of the rooms in your home. You and his cousins kept him well supplied, we were told. He especially liked any story featuring Rin Tin Tin or the radio show of *The Wonder Dog*.

Beyond these facts, I must confess I did not get a chance to talk to Signals very often, as we were separated by rank when at Port Moresby. Then, once aloft, our duties as radioman and copilot respectively kept us occupied with other matters. Signals shared with us letters from his cousin Danny and those he wrote in reply. We learned John was a man who left no loose ends. Shortly after he went to war, he asked Danny to take care of Teddy should anything happen to him. I hope this has been the case, and I can picture a lonely black lab waiting under an apple tree for the return of his master. There has been so much tragedy in your life already with the loss of a son and daughter-in-law, and now a grandson, I deeply regret having to add to your grief. I only pray these few words may somehow cheer saddened hearts.

Though my personal situation grows dimmer as I write, I'm buttressed through prayer, believing that in the light of another morning, our Lord may not only soften our sorrows but lift our hearts as well.

Sincerely yours,

2/Lt. Sam Bottorf, Copilot, "Toggle Joe"

      *   *   *

To Messieurs Giovanni and Guglielmo Sirica, Brooklyn, N.Y.
RE: Sgt. Douglas M. Shipley, Tail Gunner, B-24

Dear Sirs:

I am writing to you because I don't know who else to write to about the probable death of one of my crewmates, Sgt. Douglas J. Shipley. As you may know, he was a gunner on our B-24. He has been missing for nearly a week, and I believe he and his companion, Sgt. T.K. O'Leary are lost in the jungle of New Guinea. When it comes down to it, I'm in the same fix.

"Sharpshooter," as we named Doug, partly because he talked loud and continuously, shooting down anyone within earshot, and partly because of his prowess at his tail gunner's position, never tired of relating stories about life with "Uncle" Johnny and "Uncle" Willie as he referred to you. He said you took him in after his parents split and moved away. As far as I know, he never told anyone how old he was when this occurred. But I figure it must have been in his early teens, because he often spoke of a girl he had met at school. After he swept up at the barbershop in the mornings and served as a busboy at Uncle Willie's Italian restaurant during the afternoons, he told us he still had time on non-school days to visit East 7th Street where the young lady lived.

Despite his propensity to order everybody around, including officers, he failed to work up the nerve to ask the girl for a date. We teased him about sitting outside her door on the curb in the summer and never knocking at her door. Sharpshooter hit back with a string of cuss words in both English and Italian, but most often a mixture. Please don't get the wrong impression. We did not think of him as a smart aleck. He just liked to talk big, being from New York and all. But if he gave you his word, he stuck by it.

He loved Brooklyn and the Dodgers. He used to say, "Where else but Brooklyn can my two Italian uncles, not long off the boat, serve consecutive terms as president of the O'Brien club. As for the Dodgers, after the war he planned to join the club in some capacity, "even if it meant being the oldest batboy in the National League."

Regretfully, Sharpshooter's dreams have turned to nightmares. You see, he suffered a head injury at the hands of a Japanese fighter pilot that dogged our bomber after we bombed Wewak. His injuries weren't fatal, but amnesia, or whatever it's called, set in, and we can't be sure he understands a word said to him. One of us always has to be at his side, because he can't function on his own.

We speak about the times he lived with you, and sometimes he smiles at the mention of Uncle Johnny and Uncle Willie. Even when dirty, he pretends to adjust a tie he said you gave him to help break the ice with the girl on East 7th Street. He is still a ruggedly handsome fellow, and if he pulls out of this and the girl is still around after the war, he might still break the ice.

Forgive the intrusion if none of this information is of interest to you, or put it down as the ramblings of a dying man if you like. But from what Sharpshooter told us about his honorary uncles, I believe you would want to know the influence you had on him and how much he respected you, especially if he can't tell you himself.

"Sirica, president of the O'Brien Club." What a good one to save for my children, if I ever live to have any.

I am in your service,

2/Lt. Sam Bottorf, Copilot, "Toggle Joe"

  *   *   *

To Whom It May Concern
RE: 2/Lt. Philipi I. Patterson, Bombardier, B-24

Dear Sir or Madam:

No doubt this is the hardest letter of condolence I've had to write of the eight others already completed. "Pip," as we called our bombardier, was orphaned at 12 when his parents were lost in a storm off the coast of Kavala, Greece. Since he had no surviving relatives, he was put up for adoption and taken to America by a young couple, who turned him over to an orphanage after only two months in their care. The official reason for abandoning him was, and here I quote from Pip himself: "His adoptive parents considered him a Sphinx whose riddle they could not read."

Indeed, much of Pip's life was shrouded in mystery. As close as we were, one could even say like brothers, he never spoke about his past. Except once he said he hoped to return to Kavala and place a wreath on the spot in the water where his parents were said to have perished in their small fishing boat. We, the other officers, our crew and I, thought he might have been in the boat and was the only survivor, since it is not unusual for boys of 12 to work the nets with their parents. One thing is certain. He loved the beach at Kavala and spoke about finding a place of his own near the sea.

One would think, having lost loved ones at sea, he would go in the other direction. But it was part of his mystery. Ox, our pilot, and I threatened to go to Greece and backpack from Athens to Kavala in order to see what drew Pip to the area. Admiral, our navigator, said we'd never find the place without his help, so we could count him in on the journey.

As I grow weaker from lack of food, unless help comes soon, I'm afraid Pip will be the only officer left, if he still survives, and will have to make the journey to Kavala alone, since both Ox and Admiral are dead. I pray when Pip finally reaches his Kavala, he'll discover it exceeds all his expectations, and he finds someone to share it with.

I have not done Pip justice in this letter. It is far too short because of my limitations, since I have one more to write and must conserve my energy. If this should find its way into the hands of someone who cares for Pip the way we all did, I would remind them, as it says in Romans 8:23, "love covers all sins."

Brothers to the end and beyond,

2/Lt. Sam Bottorf, Copilot, "Toggle Joe"

* * *

To Priscilla Bottorf, Lakeland, Minnesota
RE: 2/Lt. Samuel J. Bottorf, Copilot, B-24

Dear Prissy,

Odd a brother should send his own obituary to his sister. But you must admit that you have been no ordinary sister to me. We were always great friends and would have been even if we weren't related. As I lay dying, I want you to know I appreciated all those times you tossed aside your dolls and trailed after me with a fishing pole so I would not have to go alone. How many guys have such a great sister?

Earlier, I had hoped help might be on its way, but my luck seems to have run out, like the string on that old reel you made me throw away. You said you were saving up to buy me a new reel when I come home from the war to celebrate my homecoming. Had I survived, I really wanted to ask a bigger favor, since I was partially blinded when we were attacked by a Japanese fighter pilot shortly after leaving Wewak. Since my eyesight has gotten worse, I was going to ask you to be my eyes and lead me to all those fishing holes we went to before. Without your help, I would not make it. Ironic, though, I would be the one tagging after you this time.

I have no doubt you would have fulfilled this dream for me, although it is a selfish one. Surely you would want to marry and have children of your own and teach them how to catch fish, clean them and serve them up with heaps of fried potatoes. How many times have I thought of such a delicious meal in these last days. I know. Why should I tempt myself with thoughts of food? Forgive me. I find myself rambling.

Before I go any further, let me thank you for the letters, and for the ones you pressed your girlfriends into writing. Next to T.K. O'Leary, who has a girl in Sydney, I'm the second best champion letter receiver. I really must end this letter, as it's not making any sense to me, and I'm afraid I'll pass on before it's finished.

Furthermore, before I go, I want to relieve you of your promise to name your first-born son after me. It's a nice gesture, but I wouldn't want him to inherit my bad luck along with the... No, I haven't had bad luck, for I can say I've died the death of one who has been loved by so many. Farewell, Prissy. May they keep bitin'.

Your loving brother,
Sammy, Copilot, "Toggle Joe"

8 FORETHOUGHT FLIRTATION

Baltimore, Maryland, 1973

```
U.S.   ARMY   CENTRAL   IDENTIFICATION   LABORATORY
(PROVISIONAL) FINDINGS, CASE NUMBER 316. DR. DEANN
TOLAND'S REPORT.

   Reared  in  Papua  New  Guinea  by  Australian
missionaries, Kiap Roger Noble deserves special
mention here. More so than any other member of the
CIL  team,  this  patrol  officer  had  the  mental,
physical and emotional stability to deal with the
vagaries of jungle life. I asked him once how he
coped with the distractions and detractors plaguing
our mission. He laughed and quoted the placard hung
in his tent in remembrance of his parents, "No matter
how  awful  circumstances  appear,  we're  only  one
thought away from happiness." Many of us come late to
such a philosophy.
                    DeAnn Toland, Ph.D.
                    Physical Anthropologist
```

WHEN DR. EMERSON STANEK spotted Catherine, flanked by two physicians, blocking the entrance to the Phipps Psychiatric Clinic on the Johns Hopkins campus, he cursed under his breath. Three-on-one, he thought. He watched his adoptive sister tap her shoe against the cobblestone, then glance at her wrist. Her cohorts followed her lead and consulted their watches as well. Stanek pulled his worn fedora down across his forehead and steered straight for Catherine.

"You're late," she scolded.

"Tom Haveland had me up late working on a project," he said.

He waited. His eyes, as did those of her attendants, followed Catherine who advanced toward him. Her hips swayed, as if caught in the rhythm of the siren's song she had sung to him on her prom night so long ago. Catherine slid a blue shawl, as pale as her eyes in color, down from her hair. As she shook her tresses free from the shawl and let them fall against her bare shoulders, her hair shimmered like gold inlaid in alabaster. And the small sprigs of Indian jasmine worn over one ear and purple lilac over the other not only accentuated features so delicate they reminded him of Meissen china, but also their flowered message was unmistakable.

He remembered Catherine's whispered words the night he pinned the corsage to her gown. "Jasmine means I attach myself to you, and lilac stands for the first emotion of love." The memory of her voice as she had spoken those words came wispy and soft like threads of silver unwound from the heart.

Emerson shuddered. The two psychiatrists eyed him with puzzled curiosity. Catherine came closer, their lips nearly touching as she brushed one ear then the other close to his nose. "Smell the language," she said. "Flowers pierce the coldest heart and like Cupid's arrows linger there for all time. I promised long ago I'd only wear lilacs and jasmine for you."

He watched her re-adjust the shawl so that it now outlined the contours of breasts so delicately shaped they pressed against her thin blouse like pears curved upward and beckoning to be held. He fought the urge to tell her that although she was 36 and divorced, beauty had not deserted her. Instead, he took in a deep breath to quiet the pounding in his chest.

"Primordial tactics won't work this time," he said.

"Don't you have any regrets about how we've drifted apart since father died and mother fell ill?"

"I do have one," he said.

"Oh, please, Emerson, tell me."

Stanek looked down at his sun-bronzed hands. "On the Hawaii to San Francisco leg of my flight, I tossed aside a magazine cover story featuring you, dear sister."

"Yes, I know the one. The headline's clever, don't you think? 'Our April Profile's No Bitter Pill—Meet Pharmaceutical's Most

Comely Chief Executive.' Imagine. The writer compared me to Helen of Troy!"

"I skimmed over the article and went directly to your celebrity ex-husband's sidebar piece accompanying the piece. Shall I quote the famous yachtsman for you?"

"Emerson, don't do this unless you're going to take Charles to task for humiliating me in public."

"Why, sister, my only regret is I didn't join Charles in warning the world what living with Catherine Stanek was like. Quote: 'Unless you're capable of casting a blind eye on classic beauty and a beguilingly sensuous mien that wins at any cost, prepare yourself for life among the shoals and hard places commensurate with a shipwreck.' End of quote."

"How awful."

Emerson lowered his head. "Well, give the old boy credit. If I read Charles right, he seems to be saying, Helen launched ships with her beauty, but you destroy them with yours."

"Why don't you look at me when you're talking," she chided.

Emerson kept his head down and made his eyes into slits. "I'm trying to avoid a hypnotic spell lacking the serenity and passion of your mother's. Under her gaze I felt like I had been struck by crystals from heaven, clear and blue. When you look at me, the blue is there, but there's nothing heavenly about the calculations going on in your mind as reflected in your eyes."

"How dare you dissect me like a specimen under one of your microscopes, or a defendant you're trying to badger into a confession," she said tightening her lips as though ready to pout. Instead she leaned forward, tilted her head and kissed Emerson's cheek at the point where the crescent-shaped scar faded into his beard. Her scent of lilacs and jasmine drifted across his face and lingered under the rim of his hat. He jerked the fedora from his head.

"Oh dear," Catherine cried as she stepped back a single pace, "I know men who would've killed for hair like yours—dark, wavy and gorgeous like a movie star's."

The corner of his lips turned down. "Amazing! Eight years apart and a fashion statement is all you can offer," he said.

Sensing the shift in advantage, he pranced like a proud stallion, inclining his shaven head indulgently toward her. He rubbed his fingers across his scalp almost lovingly. "Take this old thing. It's a throwback to the Japanese tradition immigrants to the islands brought with them. *Samurai* believed a bald warrior had the upper hand in close encounters. With no hair to grab, his enemy groped at a billiard ball, you see. Wish I had known about this tactic the night your father forced me to kneel at the Christ statue. But I'm prepared now."

She retreated farther from him. "Emerson, please. This is not the place to parade your grievances against father. We're here to discuss mother's condition with her attending physicians. I'd like you to meet psychiatric specialists..."

He ignored the extended hands. "Thanks, but no thanks. I don't need the advice of your minions. If you don't allow me to pass, I'm prepared to call Jim Cole, a reporter from Hawaii who's been covering my beekeeper cancer study, and give him an exclusive on those I hold responsible for Patricia Stanek's mental collapse."

Her face took on the deep color of an autumn maple. "Would you drag our whole family through the mud for revenge on father, or me?"

His own cheeks swelled so his dark mustache and beard felt tight and uncomfortable against his face. "What do you think?" he asked.

Catherine averted her eyes and glanced down at her long fair legs. He raised his eyebrows as she suddenly raised her head and smiled at him. Lips as pink as rose buds and as full as peonies in bloom quivered when she said. "I only know in a world where truth is elusive and nearly impossible to find, you're the one person incapable of lying, dear brother."

Emerson blinked. "Agreed. But remember I'm your 'a-d-o-p-t-e-d brother,' and didn't suffer as long as you did under the brutal hand of Rufus Stanek."

This time she moved into the opening he had served up to her.

"How sweet," she said. "You remembered the night at the prom when I spelled out our relationship so my girlfriends would quit pestering me for a dance with my handsome 'brother'. You don't know the number of times I've defended you in public ever since."

"Then why do we need these intermediaries?" he asked, pointing at the two psychiatrists who huddled by her side like bodyguards.

"We don't. And I've already advised good Doctors Lieberman and Cohn to retire at the first rumbling of opposition from you. I've been briefed sufficiently by both gentlemen on mother's condition and can cover the important points, if you'll at least grant me time to do so."

Emerson nodded. "Where shall we meet?" he asked.

Catherine thanked the residents for 'standing by in her hour of need.' She waited until the two doctors disappeared behind the clinic doors before answering him.

"Certainly not in there. The place is crawling with shrinks," she said. "Let's find a bench in the lovely U-shaped garden court out back between the clinic's two wings. Remember how we used to play around the fountain, among the boxwood and trees as we waited while mother allegedly visited Zelda Fitzgerald?"

"What do you mean 'allegedly'?" he asked.

"The Zelda stuff sprang from mother's imagination. Father said it couldn't have happened the way mother described it to us in 1945. Zelda Fitzgerald had left Phipps in the spring of 1934, never to return. Those idyllic summer afternoons we spent in the garden together occurred 11 years later."

"Well, who was your mother visiting at the clinic then?"

"Father would never tell me. But I've got my ideas."

"No more speculation," he said.

"Alright, then we'll go to the garden and you can up-date me on your wonderful beekeeper cancer research. It has the scientific world abuzz. Pardon the awful pun. For my part, I'll tell you about the thousands of times I've knelt on our spot overlooking Fells Point, and prayed for your return and mother's recovery. One prayer answered—one to go," she said clapping her hands in rhythmic style like a high school cheerleader.

"Our spot? I don't recall any such place."

She moved closer and caressed his lapels with her fingers. "You've become so comfortable with dead tissue, you hardly ever take time for vibrant things. You've forgotten the fragrance of a flower in full bloom, the golden hue of a rainbow after a storm, a smile, a tear or two, shed upon a favorite spot once shared with a lover. Take time to listen to the echoes in life. Many of them are benign, you know."

She was so close her teeth showed white and even behind lips parted and poised. He felt like he was a plum she was about to devour.

He wrinkled his nose. "Your fantasy world doesn't exist for your mother and me. Your father and you saw to it when you broke your vows to us."

"Oh, Emerson, you are cruel." She sobbed. She threw his hat aside. Then taking both of his hands in hers she spread one against his chest and laid the other across her own breasts. "Is there so little room for emotional ties in a heart hardened by scientific methodology? Can't the flame of love be rekindled instead?" she asked. Before he could respond, she covered his lips with her own.

His knees buckled as he tried to pull back from the double bridge she had fashioned between hands and lips. But she held firm and brought their frames closer still. An overwhelming tremor ran down his body. Her thighs quivered against his at this third point of contact, and her breasts felt warm and soft under his fingers. She slid his hand from one breast to the other and each grew firmer as his hand was drawn across them in turn. He felt faint and closed his eyes. Lost in her sensuality, his intellect ebbed away.

Each time he tried to untangle from her and reinstate his will, Catherine resisted. The slightest movement only intensified the contact between their bodies, so he fell back on his mental agility to free himself. All he could think of was the warning from Dr. William Welch, handed down from one generation of pathologists to another on how they were "to deal with those trifling excitements known to derail pure genius."

Emerson relaxed his facial muscles and in the next instant Welch's dictum rang through his mind: "Shock is the pathologist's only refuge when confronted with emotions run amuck."

Holding Catherine by the wrists, Emerson lifted her hands and raised them until they were level with his eyes. "I see you're still ruled by your hormones, little sister. Dr. Welch would've advised treatment, as do I."

She broke his grip and covered her face with her hands and her shoulders shook. "Oh, how cruel for you to throw the name of Popsy in my face. You know how father despised William Welch."

Emerson raised his eyebrows and his jaw went slack. "I don't know what you're talking about," he confessed.

It seemed the anger in her tone dissipated as fast as it had risen. "If you weren't so intent on getting your way, you'd let me brief you on mother and how she's become fixated on William Welch."

"Who cares? Popsy, as his students called Welch behind his back, has been dead since 1938."

"A true Stanek should care. Welch tried to ruin father's career by promoting, to put it politely, the illegitimate H. Douglas Addison to the pathology chair earmarked for Daddy. And now when mother goes into one of her spells, in addition to Zelda fantasies, it's Popsy this and Popsy that. Now you know why I haven't gone to see her as often as I should. I can't stand seeing her that way."

He retrieved his fedora from the sidewalk. "Why torture yourself?" he asked. "You can't make sense out of the ravings of someone who's out of touch with reality."

"Right there's the difference between us," she said, depressing the corners of her mouth. "You're not curious about emotional issues. You'd think mother would have our late father on her mind, or me, or you, for that matter. But that old reprobate Welch! Something about the man has driven mother mad. And until we get to the bottom of it, perhaps she won't be cured."

"Okay, have it your way. Turn everyone's life into a soap opera, and while you're at it, why not make Zelda the secret daughter of Welch, the villain? This is how you can explain the Popsy business. Your mother copes better in Zelda's persona than in her own because, like the celebrity, she too has been wronged. Only not by a father, but by her husband. Therefore, in order to keep secret her husband's role, Welch, or Popsy, becomes a convenient substitute."

"How smug you are. And how unfair of you to make fun of me, Emerson. If I had your research skills, I wouldn't rest until I followed every lead. Yet, you've blocked out your own origins. Lord knows. There're plenty of ways to trace birth parents in this modern era. Why don't you do something about it?"

"No, thanks. One soap opera is enough for me."

Her demeanor softened suddenly. "I'll accept your answer as meaning you've no time at present, busy as you are with the cancer research project."

"My project's in the past as well. I'm sure you've heard Haveland's committee rejected my proposal."

"I can only speak for Stanek Laboratories, and we like what we've seen so far in the press. I've been authorized by the board to make you an offer."

"Oh yeah," he said. "How do we circumvent the fact it's illegal for us to work together, and I've been stripped of everything but the Stanek name? You, your heirs and all Stanek corporate entities are prohibited from engaging in business with me. Or have you forgotten?"

"My lawyers could work through Johns Hopkins and not you directly. Perhaps, it's as simple as giving the school your research and having Stanek Laboratories underwrite the cost as the final beneficiary."

"Nice try. But first clear my name of all the mud attached to it. Have your lawyers draw up a statement absolving me of the attempted rape charges your father believed I was guilty of to his dying day. You both wronged me, not the other way around."

"What would you do with such a statement? Destroy my life?" she asked.

"Well, you'd have something to worry about for a change. Better yet, go over to Billings Hall and place your confession in the prayer book beside the Christ statue in the rotunda like you promised. If you can't trust me, at least trust something."

"You're asking a preposterous thing after 20 years!"

"Well, there you have it, Catherine. Nothing's changed."

She repositioned the shawl on her head so it covered the flowers over her ears. "Can't we talk about this after you've seen mother?"

"Sure, call me when you've met my conditions."

Catherine's tone softened. "Meanwhile, you won't mind if I get with Tom Haveland and see what he might suggest regarding funding for your cancer study?"

"Take your time. Dr. Haveland has me working on another project. It's top priority for him at the moment."

"Lord no! Don't tell me Tom's got you assisting on the Filipino Freddie murders. The mobster has already killed two district attorneys and nobody knows how many witnesses."

"No. Sorry. Nothing so challenging. Stanek Laboratories wouldn't be interested in a B-24 lost in New Guinea during WW II. Then again, one never knows how far the arms of a multinational corporation may stretch if there's any money to be made."

She tapped her shoe against the cobblestone. "B-24s don't sound like the kind of 'Bs' you or Tom should be wasting your time on."

"Clever. Well, my part's pretty much completed anyway. Now, if you'll excuse me, I'd like to get back on schedule."

"Wait, I see you're not displaying your photo ID. If you've misplaced it, they'll let you into Phipps on my authorization, but you'll have to get new credentials before going anywhere else on the campus."

"Thanks for the advice."

"Please give me a call before you leave with your assessment of mother's condition."

"I'd prefer to give my observations to Dr. Haveland. He expressed interest in your mother's care as well, and since he seems willing to act as an intermediary between us, maybe we should keep it that way."

"For now, Emerson, but I'll never give up on you. Do kiss mother for me and please don't do or say anything to upset her."

She started past him, then whirled around smiling. "But like a 'stinging bee in hottest summer's day, led by her master to the flowered fields,' I'll find recompense."

"Whatever do you mean?"

She laughed. "It's from Shakespeare. But, I forgot. Artistic *savoir faire* doesn't come in a test tube. Hand me your pen and a blank page from your notebook, and I'll try something else."

When she finished writing, she folded the paper and stuffed it in the breast pocket of his jacket. "Please read this after I've gone so we can avoid another argument. And don't forget to kiss mother for me."

Catherine did not turn around again until she reached the corner of Wolfe Street where a liveried chauffeur waited beside a Rolls Royce. How fitting the car was royal blue, he thought. Before stepping into the limousine, Catherine blew him a kiss and sent another flying toward an upper window in the Phipps Psychiatric Clinic. Only then did he unfold her note.

Emerson, forgive me. There, I've said it in writing! Now please meet me at the Maryland Club for cocktails at six, followed by dinner with a few selected board members interested in your beekeeper cancer project. I'll send my chauffeur to pick you up at 5:30 at your hotel. Until then.

Love, Catherine

As Dr. Stanek passed through the outer portals of the clinic, a cacophony of sirens erupted behind him. He paused to pinpoint the wails and whines he heard converging on the hospital campus from both ends of Wolfe Street and more faintly along North Broadway. Except for their number and intensity, there was little else unusual about the sounds. So, chalking them up to a mass casualty drill, he went inside the psychiatric wing of the hospital. On second thought, what if an actual incident had occurred requiring so much attention? In which case, it was a bad time to misplace an ID badge, as there was sure to be a lockdown of all facilities.

9 PENTAGON PROPOSITION

Washington, D.C., 1973

U.S. ARMY CENTRAL IDENTIFICATION LABORATORY (PROVISIONAL) FINDINGS, CASE NUMBER 316. DR. DEANN TOLAND'S REPORT.

It was obvious from the outset that General Bellicosi and Mr. Cole had forged some sort of alliance. We were certain it had something to do with the B-24 story. But it was so unusual to see the military and press working together during the Vietnam War era, we missed valuable clues to solving the mystery—clues hidden in the motivation behind their collaboration.

DeAnn Toland, Ph.D.
Physical Anthropologist

O N THE SAME BALMY MORNING Dr. Stanek confronted his adoptive sister Catherine, Jim Cole's taxi pulled up in front of the Pentagon's river entrance. The crippled reporter was met by a young officer, who identified himself as General Bellicosi's aide. The lieutenant invited Cole to stow his crutches in the back seat and hop aboard the battery-powered vehicle parked at the top of the stairs.

"How thoughtful of your boss," Cole said taking a seat beside the lieutenant. "My senior editor back at the *Honolulu Advertiser* warned me about wandering around the Pentagon on my own. He claimed he entered the world's largest office building as a second lieutenant and before they found him he'd been promoted to colonel! Thanks to you and General Bellicosi, I won't experience the same fate, even if I could last so long."

As they glided along the E-ring, Cole studied the soldiers and civilians who stepped aside to let the vehicle pass. They reminded him of the workers on his uncle's bee farm who darted from one hive to another at harvest time, always in a hurry. Only, the Pentagon masses seemed friendlier. If they were perturbed by his intrusion into their sanctuary, it didn't show. Cole smiled back at the nods and smiles and an occasional, "How's it going today"? Buoyed by this unexpected courtesy, he felt a sense of exhilaration shoot through his cancer-ridden body. Perhaps on this second meeting with the brigadier, he would finally pry loose the evidence of B-24 survivors he had been promised. Meantime, he vowed to hold Bellicosi to their pact. In exchange for the *Advertiser's* cooperation, the B-24 story was Cole's as an exclusive.

As Cole entered the E-ring office, leaning on the aide's arm, General Bellicosi faced the ceiling-high window and did not turn around. The brigadier was dressing down a captain who stood hunched over behind him, Bellicosi's voice ricocheting off the walls like canon fire.

"I can't look at you. A West Pointer with less sense than God gave a piss-ant," he roared. "I ask for a background profile on Dr. Toland. What do I get? A character right out of Dickens!" Without turning, Bellicosi held up a paper clutched in his pudgy fist.

"Listen to what you wrote: 'DeAnn loves wayfarers, the deformed, the half-witted, the abandoned, and the so-called misunderstood!' What does it tell me about the woman, except she's a bleeding heart liberal? Hell, the country's crawling with 'em. If Toland loves half-wits, as you said she does, she'd go wild over the idiot who submitted this report."

The aide standing next to Cole leaned over and whispered, "Except for his stature, General Bellicosi isn't known for his brevity. This may take awhile, sir."

Cole watched the stout little man with his back to his audience settle into a rambling rut.

"What I want to know about Dr. Toland isn't in your report. Tell me how she reacted when her sister Daphne drowned? Did she start stuttering after the tragedy when she was five years old? Or did it come from getting laid in her sophomore year at the

University of Chicago by a hippie boyfriend? This kind of stuff is helpful for assessing someone's breaking point under stress. Not the liberal claptrap you've given me. Damn it! I want to know if she's missed any periods while in Thailand or New Guinea. Then we'll know whether she's fit 'Operation Simpatico' material for the long haul, or is just screwing around."

Cole's jaw went slack and his feet felt heavy under him. In a weak and thin voice he stammered, "Perhaps, I should come back at another time."

Bellicosi emitted a roar of indignation as he pivoted. "Who dares to...!" He spotted Cole and his demeanor shifted. "Thanks for coming, Jim. I'll be right with you as soon as I get rid of this asshole."

Despite his short legs, Bellicosi covered the distance between the windowsill and his desk in one or two strides. He leaned across the top, gathered a handful of pencils, and began hurling them one by one at the subordinate who fled the room under the fusillade. Cole witnessed a second impaling when the lieutenant, acting as his escort, did not move fast enough to clear away the crutches Cole had leaned against the front of the general's desk. Then, before Cole took the proffered chair, a third aide was speared for daring to serve coffee too cold for the general's palate.

"Jim, no doubt you've come to garner our secrets. Well, you won't leave here disappointed." As he spoke, Bellicosi picked up another pencil from his stockpile. Cole instinctively ducked seeing all the other targets had fled. Bellicosi erupted with a roar of laughter betraying his Mediterranean roots. "I never fire at civilians," he said. "Hell, I work for one." With the pencil, he pointed to a huge photo of President Nixon hanging on the wall.

"Jim, can you see how the President signed the portrait he gave me? He wrote 'illegitma non-carborandum' above his signature."

"Don't let the bastards drag you down." Cole translated.

"Good, I like a man who understands Latin."

"A little Italian is all."

"'Poco' is like lovemaking. A little is better than none. Ever come across the term 'simpatico?'" Bellicosi asked.

"I did a moment ago while waiting for you to finish with the captain."

"Do you know what it means?"

"Something to do with sympathy, I suppose."

"You're half right, Jim. It's an Italian word implying solidarity as well as sympathy." Bellicosi's face lit up with enthusiasm and his bulging eyes brightened.

"Solidarity is at the heart of Operation Simpatico. In order to get Congress, the American people, and Hanoi for that matter, to take seriously our oath, our commitment to the fallen, we created Simpatico. We demand to know the fate of the missing, including 'Killed in Action/Body Not Recovered.' We'll use the B-24 matter to this advantage."

"Then give me some facts to build a story around."

The general's thick eyebrows furrowed. "First, let's look at the big picture. During the recent release of POWs from North Vietnamese prisons, note there was no mention of MIAs or KIA/BNRs. Yet, they're our only trump card in the final peace agreement. Hanoi won't get a dime from us for the reparations promised by Henry Kissinger until they give us a full accounting. Of course, the Democrats are content with peace at any price after denying the President any military options to use as a big stick. And his fellow Republicans will never agree to reward North Vietnam for its intransigence. Unfortunately, it leaves our fallen comrades as pawns in this political struggle."

"How awful," Cole said.

Bellicosi paused and asked Cole if he had any questions. The reporter replied, "Not at the moment." So the general continued.

"Nixon devised a plan, and I came up with the name, 'Operation Simpatico'. I haven't told you this before I knew I could trust you with politically sensitive material."

"What is it?"

"Simpatico's real objective is to garner support and get the public's mind off the Watergate fiasco. By equating Vietnam MIAs, KIA/BNRs with their more popular counterparts from WW II, it'll trigger sympathy for our policy *vis-à-vis* accountability. Ingenious wouldn't you say?"

"So this is where the lost B-24 fits in."

"You're too smart for me, Jim. But I've got to ask you to treat everything you hear in this office as embargoed information for the time being."

"But we agreed."

"I know—your exclusive. I'll get to it in a moment. For now, tell me what you think of Simpatico's campaign slogan. I wrote it myself, but it might need a wordsmith's touch."

Bellicosi handed his guest a slip of paper, took a cigar from his desk, lit it and threw his head back against the chair and closed his eyes. "Read it to me, Jim."

"The saddest state no matter the war, a soldier lost or unaccounted for."

"Catchy, don't you think?"

"When do I get to run it?" Cole asked.

Bellicosi leaned forward and blew a smoke ring that sailed over Cole's head. "Sorry, you'll have to wait. Until B-24 crew remains are sorted by a physical anthropologist and certified by a pathologist, we'd be crazy to tip our hand. Congress doesn't know we've diverted a provisional CIL team from Thailand to New Guinea for this purpose. Those assholes on the hill are hell-bent for impeachment. If our real objective for Operation Simpatico was discovered during the current crisis, Congress would find a way to hang it on to Watergate and by extension on to the President.

"You see our ultimate goal is to establish a permanent Central Identification Laboratory, which is in the inception stage at the moment. Working out of Honolulu, they'd have the authority and funding to proceed anywhere at any time for any war to account for our fallen heroes. As the war in Vietnam winds down, I fear the enthusiasm for a Central Identification Laboratory will diminish. With a forensic pathologist backing us..."

Cole interrupted, "But as I told you on the phone, I failed to get Dr. Haveland to sign on like you asked me to do."

"True. Yet, you reached the same conclusion I had reached several months ago. Haveland's not the man for the job. Besides being a dotard, he's physically unfit to squirrel around New Guinea looking for lost airmen. Young Dr. Stanek's our man."

"Let me see if I've got this straight. You sent me to approach Haveland when it was Stanek you were after all along."

"Of course. You and the young pathologist both work in Hawaii. You broke his beekeeper cancer study story, and you said yourself he impressed you. Stanek strikes me as a man we can do business with. You'll get your exclusive on the lost bomber, and I'll get someone who'll win Congress's trust. Everybody wins."

Cole attempted to interrupt again, but Bellicosi waved him off with a flick of the cigar. "Before we go further, perhaps you need some background on how things work in the Nixon Administration. Ever hear of 'mushroom management'?" Bellicosi did not wait for an answer.

"Mushroom management's a style of leadership for keeping your subordinates in place. 'Keep 'em in the dark and feed 'em shit'. This Watergate business is an example. The President plays the game better than Congress does."

"Am I the only one connected with this project who knows the real intent is not to locate the missing B-24 crew, but to score a propaganda victory and pull the wool over Congress's eyes at the same time?"

Bellicosi chuckled. "Think mushrooms, Mr. Cole. Of course, our fighting men are important. But if word leaks out their sacrifices also serve a greater glory, your news colleagues would be the first to rush to judgment, searching for phantom causes to make us look heartless. Then all we'll be doing is putting out fires instead of gaining the offensive in a war the other side is winning with their blatant propaganda, although nobody calls them on it."

"What about the staff in the field? Have those searching for remains or survivors been informed of this greater cause they serve?"

"They know all they need to know about Operation Simpatico for the moment."

Cole squirmed in his chair. "Noble cause, General, but the tactics seem a bit over the top, if you ask me."

Bellicosi squashed his cigar in an ashtray, picked up another pencil and drummed it on the desktop. "I believe this concludes our interview, Jim. Your next task, if you still want the exclusive, is to go back to Hawaii and await further instructions."

"When do I get to see the bomber crew documents you promised to show me on background?"

"I'm afraid there's been a snag. What's not in Dr. Haveland's possession is being retained in New Guinea awaiting the arrival of a pathologist. Unless you're willing to travel there, I don't see how I can make them available to you until our specialist, preferably Dr. Stanek, completes his investigation."

Cole knew the general was not only stalling but was bluffing. Either he hoped the reporter would die of cancer before he got his story, or believed his illness precluded an arduous journey into New Guinea's highland bush country. Cole sat upright in his chair and replied in a voice surprising him with its volume and strength. "Let me know the next time you head for the crash site, and I'll go along with you."

As Cole expected, Bellicosi did not respond directly, except to say, "I'll take it under consideration."

On his way out the door, Cole fired a parting shot. It landed on the general's desk like one of Bellicosi's pencils. "For what it's worth, General, I have a hunch Dr. Stanek won't quietly play your little mushroom game."

Bellicosi met him at the door: "We're already working on that, Mr. Cole. Again, stand by. I may call on you to close the deal with him at any moment."

"How will I know where to find Stanek?"

"Don't worry. We're keeping tabs on the good doctor's movements. At the moment, he's visiting his sick mother at Johns Hopkins. But I see no need for you to go back there."

They shook hands and parted. Cole sighed as he took his seat beside the escort officer in the electric scooter.

The lieutenant bent over Cole and whispered, "Sir, for what it's worth, don't piss off or cross General Bellicosi. He's lined a whole section of the Pentagon basement with secret background files on people he wants to keep tabs on. I'll bet J. Edgar Hoover's collection at the FBI is smaller than the general's. Strange, though. Most of my boss's dossiers are on civilians like you, people not affiliated with the Department of Defense."

"Thanks for the tip, Lieutenant. But I can't see why a reporter like me would generate special attention from anybody."

"Maybe so, sir. But were you always a reporter?"

Cole let the question slide, considering it too obvious to answer. Still, it lingered in his mind all the way to the river entrance. He gripped the foam under his fingers and was surprised his hands dripped with sweat the sponge-like handles of his crutches failed to absorb.

"Now I know how a mushroom must feel," he told himself, before getting into the taxi the lieutenant had hailed for him. Cole turned to the lieutenant, who handed him his crutches. "In answer to your question, young man, I've been other things than a reporter; some would say a bastard. But your boss is right about one thing; we shouldn't let it grind us down. Damn it, souls are not mushrooms!"

10 DISTRACTED BY DELUSION

Baltimore, Maryland, 1973

U.S. ARMY CENTRAL IDENTIFICATION LABORATORY
(PROVISIONAL) FINDINGS, CASE NUMBER 316. DR. DEANN
TOLAND'S REPORT.

Two contingencies out of our control forced us to
expedite this project. Papua New Guinea was to become
independent in 1975 from Australian Trusteeship. This
could mean we would have to start from scratch with a
new government. In addition, the Vietnam War was
winding down. Some, like General Bellicosi, believed
it would be settled by the time Papua gained its
independence, and that would mean the end of
Operation Simpatico.

These two factors placed considerable strain on
psyches steeped in science. They limited us on the
time needed to reach conclusions based on proven
data.

DeAnn Toland, Ph.D.
Physical Anthropologist

EMERGENCY VEHICLE SIRENS on Wolfe Street continued to
screech their particular tone of horror as Stanek followed the
attendant down the narrow corridors of the Phipps building into
the part of the clinic forming the bend in the horseshoe. Beyond
the large windows he could see Fells Point. A police boat and a
fireboat pulled up to the landing and disgorged a dozen or so
armed men in uniform. After forming teams, they fanned out

across the Johns Hopkins campus. One squad headed south in the direction of the Pathology Building.

"You certainly take drills more seriously than when I was here at the hospital," Stanek commented.

"I've been here 14 years myself and never saw a mass casualty simulation this authentic," said the attendant.

"I hope this nonsense doesn't interfere with my visit."

"No. I'll get you settled in Mrs. Stanek's room before I go to my emergency station. Usually patients and visitors are excluded from these exercises."

Stanek nodded. Resolved to be free of the matter, his thoughts turned nostalgic. Each time he passed one of the ceiling length windows and looked down on the antebellum garden, his throat went dry. At ages 11 and nine respectively, he and Catherine had played around the fountain and pink dogwood trees behind the clinic. "Pirates" was their favorite game and the children competed for the highest perch wanting to be the first to spot a white sail beyond the roofs, spires and domes of Baltimore, far out into the harbor Francis Scott Key had immortalized in his anthem. Patricia Stanek used the game to remind her children they were at Phipps, not for play alone, but to visit Mrs. Zelda Fitzgerald whose husband, F. Scott, was a descendent of the composer.

Stanek smiled as he reflected on the gentle admonition he and Catherine received, "Zelda was hardly a lady who cavorted with pirates," their mother had told them, sandwiched between reminisces of her own childhood in Alabama.

As the attendant began unbolting the huge oaken door, Emerson trembled. Had his 71-year-old mother become so imprisoned by her own mind she had to invent the Zelda stories as a way of coping? Let Catherine find the answer, he decided. She was interested in this kind of intrigue. His concern centered on the current mental and physical state of the patient he had come to visit.

The young man in the white jacket hesitated before opening the door to Mrs. Stanek's room, "I've got to ask you to surrender any notepads or pens on your person. Patients seem to clam up whenever they see us taking notes. And before we go inside, Dr. Stanek, there're a few things your sister wants you to know that are peculiar to your mother."

"Go on."

"Mrs. Stanek has sudden switches in midstream."

"Yes."

"Sometimes her sentences are long and peculiarly involved. On other occasions they break off without warning. It has the doctors baffled."

"How so?"

"She seems torn between opening herself up and shutting herself in behind someone else's mask."

"Like Zelda Fitzgerald? It's not unusual for someone in my mother's condition to hide behind another's persona, real or imagined."

"I'm afraid it's much worse, Dr. Stanek."

"Out with it. What are you trying to say?"

The attendant looked away and shook his head. "Your mother's evasive and unproductive, sir. For her, doctor's calls are mere social visits. She retreats from serious inquiry by repeating some ditty about Popsy."

"I've heard about it."

"Then you know about the spells after she keeps repeating the ditty?"

Stanek nodded and asked a question of his own. "How do I summon you when I've finished?"

"Ring the red buzzer inside the door jam."

Stanek entered his mother's quarters. There was no sound or movement in the room proper. At the window a swarm of yellow butterflies beat silently against the pane between the bars, obviously disturbed by the sirens of the emergency vehicles racing up and down the street below.

If his mother heard the commotion outside, she gave no evidence of it. Patricia Stanek sat gaunt and bareheaded at an easel in the center of the room. Her face and hands were coated in a rainbow of colors, no doubt picked up from the palette and inadvertently rubbed across her skin. She held a brush in her hand, but it, like the pendulum on the clock by the window, hung motionless. Emerson stepped closer. He rustled the change in his pocket, hoping to draw her attention without startling her. No response came. He then tapped gently on the easel with the tips of his fingers. Still there was no answer. But from the adjacent room he heard the faint echo of someone tapping.

Suddenly, Patricia Stanek threw her head back and stared at the wall. Addressing the point of the tapping, she cried out, "Not now, Meredith. I have a visitor. You'll see our painting when I'm finished."

Before he could speak she stood up, extended one hand and settled a bonnet on her head with the other.

"You're a doctor, aren't you?"

"How'd you know?

"Your sagging shoulders gave you away, young man."

"I never realized my shoulders sagged."

"You doctors can reconstruct an entire person from one bone, but you've never learned what a woman learns instinctively."

"Can you tell me about it?"

She touched the sides of her wide bonnet. "Our posture and our dress tell us more about a person than their words sometimes."

"Incredible."

"Not if you think like a woman and see with your heart."

"And what does this particular bonnet say about its wearer?"

She turned pale and then blushed. He saw traces of her former beauty as the color returned to her face and her shy smile made her face appear more rounded.

Almost singing, she began, "The misshapen contours and worn condition of this old hat shows a young woman on the move, unafraid to put her head down and march into the wind on occasion. And the artificial yellow acacia flowers embroidered around the brim suggest a maiden familiar with needlework and flowers—the secret languages of love."

"And what does the pink ribbon dangling from the bonnet tell us about the woman who wore it?" He was afraid the sudden sag in her features meant his question was too direct.

She clapped her hands. "How observant you are, doctor! Just like a woman would, you spotted the frayed ends of the ribbon where our maiden nervously twirled the fabric around her fingers like other women do their curls."

He nodded. "The wearer had anxieties then?"

"Oh, yes, they too are present in this old blue bonnet. But there is more joy than sorrow connected with it. Mostly happy times—a stroll along the harbor, a picnic under the box elders, her lover's hand caressing her blonde tresses and a kiss concealed behind the wide brim."

She turned the hat over and over. "Finally, from the spilled paint across the length and breadth of the bonnet we see the artist dons it before seating herself in front of the easel. No doubt, it inspires her and drives away the demons within. You're a doctor aren't you?"

Although he was startled she had retreated to their earlier conversation, he decided to play along with her.

"How'd you guess?"

"I asked myself when I saw you, where else did I see shoulders with so much sag?"

"Really noticeable, huh?"

"My husband and son and their colleagues were all getting round-shouldered from bending over, peering into microscopes. We ladies pleaded with them to stand up straight. To no avail I'm afraid. Doctors Welch and Addison were the worst."

Like a person overcome by sudden fear, she fell face down against the easel and assumed the semi-paralyzed state she was in when he entered the room. With arms spread, she lay against the canvas like a still life model. He felt her pulse and was relieved to note her heart rate was normal for a woman of her age.

Since further conversation seemed out of the question, Emerson turned and surveyed the rooms in her clinic living quarters. There were two. He merely glanced into the bedchamber furnished with a four-poster bed and a Windsor chair. He recognized both antiques, and his heart grew light with nostalgia for the old home at the intersection of McElderry and North Caroline Streets.

Emerson turned back to the anteroom doubling as a studio and studied it more carefully. He saw three portraits overlooked on his entry. On the far wall opposite his mother, three faces peered at him. The portrait on the left was unmistakably Rufus Stanek. His pig-like eyes squinted from beneath bushy eyebrows. And his trademark mutton chop sideburns and dark beard, interwoven with silver threads, did little to soften his countenance.

The middle portrait was a three-quarter profile of Catherine. She seemed to be fixated on the portrait hanging to her right of a young man in uniform. Emerson searched the walls for his own likeness, but it was not in sight. Yet, he recalled the day his mother had sketched him.

Catherine, as usual, was to sit first, but she fidgeted so much, their mother moved his appointment forward. The pattern continued. Consequently, his portrait was finished months before Catherine had hers unveiled. Now, an unknown cavalier stood in place of his own portraiture.

"How is it you're hung with honor, and I've been excluded, soldier?" he asked in a jovial manner. Then he remembered. He and Catherine had been playing in the cellar where they found the handsome officer's portrait wrapped in brown paper. They took the painting to their mother. Patricia Stanek ordered it returned to its hiding place and made them promise not to tell their father about its existence.

"Who are you?" Stanek tapped his fingers against the gold frame.

He heard his mother stir and turned to see her sitting up in her chair: "Honestly, Meredith! You can tap and pound until your fingers bleed, but I told you I have a visitor."

Emerson hurried to her side and stood in the exact spot he had vacated earlier. "Someone had a little nap," he said.

"No, I heard the voices mocking me again."

"Mocking you?"

"Yes, the voices read my thoughts before I even think them. They came the other day and told me I would die during the night. The next morning they came and laughed and told me it was only a rehearsal."

"Other than the voices, are you treated well here?"

She giggled quietly, "I suppose you're doing your best. Must not be easy dealing with a full-grown bird unable to break out of her shell. I feel like a nestling, you know. No wings to flap and fly away like the others."

"Where have the others gone?"

"All the fledglings and mature birds have left—Zelda, Meredith, and my husband. He was imprisoned too, you know. Rufus' work became his tomb. Every man in my life, save one, pushed the heart aside. For them, intellect stood supreme!

"Is this why you became an artist?"

"Yes. To clear my heart and soul and make room for the sunshine stolen from me."

"By these men?"

"Yes."

"Could you tell me about them?"

"Why should I?"

"Because I want to avoid their mistakes."

"You're more clever than your clumsy colleagues who try to coerce answers from me. Perhaps, I'll make an exception just this once providing..."

"Yes, go on."

"Providing you keep no record of our conversation in your little notebook."

"As you can see, Mrs. Stanek, I've come here empty-handed, no notebook, recorder, not even paper or pen. Therefore, if you choose to tell me about the men in your life, or share other thoughts with me, it will not go beyond this room."

He thought he saw a slight smile cross her thin, pale lips, but in a flash it turned to a tremor. "There now," he said in as soft a tone as he could muster. "Think of me as a friend stopping by for a social chat." The hint of a smile returned. She picked up at the point of her earlier philosophical statement.

"My husband, Dr. Rufus Stanek, the noted Johns Hopkins pathologist, always placed intellect above heart. This sent him about with a fitful curiosity, probing, observing and noting everything related to death.

"This obsession with dead tissue and specimens, 'alive' only under a microscope, rendered him incapable of seeing most people lived in a world invisible to pathology. And, when his family needed an emotional anchor, Rufus left them adrift. While his wife and children floundered in uncharted waters, he sailed on, accomplishing great deeds for science."

"You mentioned family. May I inquire about them?"

"Certainly," she said pointing proudly to the portrait of Catherine. "There's my daughter. Of course, no artist is capable of capturing such natural beauty. People say she favors me when I was her age. But I know they are just being kind. God applied the brush and man came up with the term 'gorgeous' to describe Catherine."

"Do you see her often?"

"Oh, no, neither of my children visit me. After their father died, they, too, withdrew. Wait! I take that back! My son stopped visiting many years before Rufus' death."

"Does his portrait hang next to Catherine's?"

"There's no painting next to Catherine's, except her father's."

"Sorry, my mistake," he said. Then he quickly added, "But you did paint your son, didn't you?

"Yes, when Emerson was 11, the year he came to live with us in the big house astride McElderry and North Caroline Streets. Are you familiar with this part of the campus?"

"Indeed, I am."

"Then you know what a charming setting it is for raising children, although Rufus never thought so. My husband turned on the boy for one reason or another. He cursed me and said we had made a mistake in adopting a child whose parents we didn't know.

"'They could be molesters or maniacs for all we know,'" he argued. "Then Rufus took my hand in his and said, 'Patricia, you're a gardener and should know better. The tree withers when its roots are watered with corrosives.'

"But I did know better. For I had secretly nurtured this little acorn long before I convinced my husband we should adopt him and start what Rufus always wanted—a dynasty in pathology under the Stanek name."

"Why was a dynasty important?"

"Due to some quirk in nature, pathologists' offspring are almost universally female, and with a daughter already in the home, we decided to beat the odds through adopting Emerson. Rufus thought it'd give him a leg-up on his rivals and insure continuity amongst his wealthy patrons."

"How did you know the lad was intellectually capable of such promise?"

"At first, we didn't."

"We?"

In 1934, when Zelda was back at Phipps again, I took her for an outing over to the orphanage, and we saw this adorable little boy who had just been brought in by an iceman who found the infant in front of Emerson Hall during a delivery. Led by our hearts, we both wanted to adopt him immediately.

"But of course, being ill, Zelda couldn't. And since I knew Rufus wouldn't agree at the time, I promised Zelda I would take care of him until she got better. She had things to work out in her own marriage with Scott."

"Emerson Hall? I don't recall it."

"Why, it's the library at Johns Hopkins. Hmm...I think I'm right."

The only library Emerson knew was named for William Welch. But he decided not to challenge his mother on this point, or her credibility with regard to Zelda Fitzgerald's role in his adoption. Forewarned by Catherine and the attendant about triggers, which plunged his mother into the depths of irrationality, he decided to avoid them now and probe later, if necessary.

"What was little Emerson like?"

"A sweet and intelligent child, if ever there was one. It didn't take long for me to agree with the staff at the orphanage about this precocious child's parents, who must've been educated people enrolled in the college. Who else would leave a child on the library steps wrapped in a dormitory blanket? Zelda thought Emerson's parents were students, or maybe a professor and a student who couldn't keep a child born out of wedlock."

"So, you took him into your home?"

"Goodness, no, not until he was 11, three years before Zelda died in 1948. I knew she'd never come back for him because of her illness. But even from the beginning, I knew I could never give up Emerson to anybody. I paid for his keep and visited him daily through the week.

"Following my confinement with Catherine, I was only able to visit the orphanage on weekends. Emerson called me 'mother', you know, and clapped his hands whenever I came into his room. Did I tell you how brilliant he was? During tutoring, he caught on to science so quickly, it gave me an idea."

"You convinced your husband to adopt him and create the Stanek dynasty."

"Oh, dear, I must've mentioned it already." She slapped an open palm against her forehead. "What's wrong with me? I can't think straight anymore."

"This precocious nature you spoke about, how was it apparent in one so young?"

"One way was through his inquisitiveness. Young Emerson never abandoned a puzzle, but returned to it again and again until it was cleared up. And never did he think he had grasped any part of a subject until he understood the whole. It was all I could do to keep one step ahead of him. Such a persevering child! There's only one other person I've ever met with such a mind. God rest his soul."

"What happened to Emerson after he grew up?"

"I don't remember, because after he became a young man I never saw him again, although I never stopped loving him. He might've been lost in the war, like so many sons. They come to me in dreams, all these boys who lost their loved ones; some are still in uniform."

"Like the young officer in the portrait hanging across from your easel?"

"I don't know what you're talking about," she interrupted, lowering her head as if refusing to gaze at the portrait. Her voice had been strong, but now became a whisper. "My portraits consist of family members, no one else. It's Emerson, you see."

He was about to correct her by pointing out the son in her story would have been too young for WW II. But when he saw her face contort in pain like a stroke victim, he knew he had tread too close to the fragile part of her mind wherein the voices dwelt.

"You mentioned a daughter. Tell me more about her."

Her jaw went slack as she looked past him. "You mean Scottie, my beautiful golden-haired little Scottie. She doesn't come to see me either. Scott won't let her. They both stopped coming here. Now it's like I'm buried alive, smothered under grief. It weighs me down and deprives me of life-giving air. Everyone I loved disappeared and left poor Zelda alone in the world."

Patricia Stanek laid her stained hands across the tilted easel and, cradling her head in her arms upon the still wet canvas, she entered her own world. He knew by the look in her unfocused eyes the door was about to close to all but Zelda Fitzgerald and whom ever else roamed a tortured mind.

He went over and gently lifted her head from the canvas. She resisted by shaking herself free. He stood for a moment fingering the scar on his cheek.

"Please, Mrs. Stanek, before I go, may I see the magnificent work you have in progress? I'm intrigued by the brush strokes and color you're hiding from me."

She threw back her shoulders and reached for his arm. Her voice gained strength as she spoke. "Let's trace the contours together, shall we? You'll get a feel for the work in this way."

"Fine," he said, surprised her skin was as soft as swan's down as she draped his hand over hers and guided it across the canvas. Unlike the detailed portraits hung on the wall, the painting under his fingers consisted of lines and blotches incapable of being fathomed.

"As you can see, this silver and black line in the middle is an airplane breaking apart in mid-air." She pointed out several blue dots standing alone. "These are crewmembers falling from the wreckage."

"And the silver bellows around them?"

"Parachutes."

"Ah, yes, I see. There are four of them."

"Wrong."

He thought he heard her giggle as if to say I fooled you. She then guided their hands to the vanishing point on the painting where a barely discernible silver bellow appeared.

"Five," she said turning to face the wall and the portrait of the uniformed man whose existence she had earlier denied.

"Oh, he must be the one man in your life who listened to his heart?"

The words were barely out of his mouth before Mrs. Stanek rose and flew into a rage, terrible for its intensity. In that instant he saw in her flashing eyes the very center of her anger. As she moved to strike him with her raised fist, he retreated toward the door.

"Run, coward! Like all of Popsy's spies, you've no stomach for a fight," she screeched.

He tapped lightly on the door hoping she would think it was Meredith and snap the spell.

Suddenly she broke off the attack and fell back into her chair. Her head was tilted towards him, but her eyes were focused in space. Her chant fluctuated between audible and inaudible with each repetition:

> No one knows where Popsy eats;
> No one knows where Popsy sleeps;
> No one knows whom Popsy keeps, but Popsy!

Only once did she make eye contact while chanting. But in that brief moment his heart sank. To see her once lovely face and hair framed by a perfect coiffure now besmirched in paint was unbearable. Her eyes remained dry, and she looked like a clown who had donned makeup without the benefit of a mirror.

Shaken, Emerson buried his head in the crock of his arm and beat his fist against the heavy oak door. Unlike the awful moment when his adoptive father pushed his face into Christ's marble feet, this time his anguish was for his mother.

By the time the attendant swung the door open, Stanek had regained his composure. "Sorry about the noise," he said lowering his eyes.

"We're used to it, Doc. Lots of people can't find the buzzer on the first try, so they panic. I see your mother has gone into one of her spells again. It'll probably last for the next week or so."

"Will she remain in a comatose state?"

"If it's bad enough, sometimes we're forced to use the feeding tube."

"I'm sorry," he said again.

"Don't blame yourself, Doc. Nobody can stop Mrs. Stanek once she gets this Popsy stuff in her head. Oh, before I forget, there's a cop waiting for you downstairs. Introduced himself as Lt. Sam Dunbar.

"Police?"

"Yeah, all those sirens were for real. There's been a double murder on campus, and the whole area's been cordoned off while they hunt down suspects."

"What possible assistance could I be to the police?"

"All I know, Doc, is that one murder took place in the Pathology Building and the other inside Billings Hall."

Emerson swallowed hard. This news, like his mother's outbursts, set him shaking again. With a modicum of composure, he pressed the question uppermost in his mind, although he feared the answer.

"The victims—do you know who they are?"

"I've heard that one was the night custodian at the Pathology Building."

"And the other?"

"Dr. Thomas Haveland."

11 DISINTERRED EVIDENCE

Papua New Guinea, 1973

U.S. ARMY CENTRAL IDENTIFICATION LABORATORY (PROVISIONAL) FINDINGS, CASE NUMBER 316. DR. DEANN TOLAND'S REPORT.

Our main mode of communicating with the native populations rested on pantomime. Through this game of charades, we learned names of villages, rivers and mountains by pointing to the object. We found out the names of people in the same manner. Whenever a villager learned enough pidgin by our naming the object in English, he became a "turnim-talk," or interpreter. Unfortunately, no amount of pantomime was useful in getting our "turnim-talks" to understand that we wanted more information on the remains discovered in burial site X-2 with the Japanese artifacts.

In the end, we relied on our CIL linguist, Erik. He had studied in Japan and knew the culture. He was a great help in deciphering the slogan painted on the miniature flag, and explained the meaning of the fan and "senninbari" found with the Japanese remains of a man in his late twenties. How his remains got buried near the bomber crew remained a mystery until fortune again smiled on us, this time from an unexpected source.

DeAnn Toland, Ph.D.
Physical Anthropologist

D R. DEANN TOLAND HAD no sooner reached the vine bridge stretching across the Rentoul River than *Kiap* Noble caught up with her. The big Australian tilted his bush hat against the setting sun and sat cross-legged in the trail panting. The constables with him followed suit, as did Toland's two armed escorts.

DeAnn noticed Noble's wheeze and asked, "Are you unwell, Roger?"

Noble shook his head.

"Are you just out of breath?"

Kiap Noble nodded his head, wheezed again and held up a finger to indicate he needed a moment more. He rose to his feet.

"*Come a gutser*, lass, we've struck the mother lode! Right under our noses it was—the B-24 inflatable dinghy, emergency equipment, a weapon and, by the looks of it, another journal, six volumes no less."

"Six! How wonderful!" DeAnn clapped her hands and danced a jig in front of the astonished constables.

In as few words as possible, Noble told of how he had stumbled on a large bundle while posting the night watch around the fallen bomber. He explained the find had not been there in the morning nor that afternoon just before Major Yowell took off in the Beaver for Goroka.

"The lads and I always sweep the area before a landing or a take-off. Never know who's lurking about, planning a sneak attack."

"It's a miracle!" she cried, failing to see the huge, gray-haired, beet-red *kiap* let his shoulders sag. "I want to see for myself; but first tell me, how do you think the stuff got there?"

Roger Noble moistened his lips and continued, "I figure those two Riami men who came here earlier, MilkEye and his *one-mate*, sneaked back with the cache and left it on your doorstep as payment for the honeycomb you gave them."

"Oh, I could kiss them if they were the ones who left the cache! So, I'll kiss you instead."

This time she read the signs as he forced a smile and extended a wooly cheek to collect his reward. "I'm sorry, Roger. I can see you're upset. Was it something I did or said?"

"No, lass. It has more to do with a memory, triggered by this latest find and yer exuberant reaction. It reminded me of me poor wife, Liz, and daughter, Rosie, gone so long ago. Nothing else."

"We're not taking another step, cache or no cache, until you tell me why my enthusiasm triggered an upsetting memory. Maybe it would help if you told me what happened to your wife and daughter." DeAnn took his hand, and they both sat down on the trail and faced each other cross-legged.

"I'm worried, lass. Getting too chummy with the natives and all. Ye can't trust 'em, darlin'. One moment things are all kissy and in the next, they revert to ambush and bloody raid."

"So, now I know why you're so protective of me. Wouldn't it help to talk it out?"

"I suppose if I'm gonna tell anyone, it would be ye, lass. Sure ye don't want to do this another time? Didn't mean to throw a damp blanket over yer parade."

"The cache you found isn't going anywhere. You need a friend to talk to, and I'm here to listen. Nothing's more important at the moment."

Noble heaved a heavy sigh. "It's not a pretty story. But if it can alert a sympathetic soul like ye to the dangers of dealing with natives, here 'tis. As I might've told ye, one of my government posts was at Kanganaman, a village built over a swamp just off the Sepik River. At one point during the last war, it had been occupied by Japanese soldiers who infiltrated overland from Wewak. The Japanese poisoned the natives' minds against us. They told 'em the government people had disrupted the goods promised 'em as part of the cargo cult. They warned the natives if we ever came back, we should be treated as enemies."

The *kiap* paused as he looked at the constables surrounding them on the grassy trail. "Rest easy, lads," he said. Then he looked back at DeAnn and continued. "Have ye ever heard the pidgin expression, 'Man is no good unless he kill 'nother man'?"

"No, I can't say I have."

The *kiap* paused again. He saw the constables nod knowingly to each other.

"Well, lass," Noble continued. "It means if a man hasn't killed another, he's no man, or next to nothing."

"How awful!"

"Whilst in Kanganaman, we took in a little lad named Sotameri to help Liz with the chores and to be a playmate for Rosie, seeing she and the boy were *age-mates*. He was about nine at the time, so he was with us until a few years later when he would have to face initiation into the men's cult with its requirement of killing another. I was away on patrol at the time, but witnesses told me what had happened. Sotameri was led to the clearing in front of the spirit house where the important men were gathered. My Liz and Rosie were the bound captives on whom Sotameri was forced to perform the ritual murder."

DeAnn was aghast. "Why a woman and child?"

"Any age and either sex would do. My girls were chosen because of the alleged cargo confiscation, and because they were too weak to put up any fight when I was gone. As it happened, Sotameri couldn't perform the required deed, so a relative was chosen to guide the steel or bamboo blade into the breasts of my dear girls."

DeAnn's eyes welled up with tears, and she could see tears also wetting the *kiap's* beard. She leaned forward, took his hand in hers and kissed his fingers. "Oh, Roger! I'm so sorry!"

The *kiap* quickly regained his composure so the constables would not see his distress. "Of course, this act of betrayal has been hard to live with, but I've never taken any revenge. Raised by missionaries, I was not about to go against the teachings I grew up with. Still, I promised God I'd never be caught off guard again in this primitive world."

"I'm so glad to have you as a friend and protector, Roger. Thanks for telling me a story so hard to relate, but at least I have two names to add to my prayer list."

"Make it three, if ye don't mind, lass. I need 'em as well, 'cause if I ever come across Sotameri, or any members of his tribe, I'm afraid of what I might do."

He stood up. "Now back to the business at hand," Noble said as he helped her to her feet. We got sidetracked right after your congratulations."

"Yes, thanks to you, this new find may help us bust this case before Dr. Haveland gets here," she said as she shook his hand.

"I should be thanking ye, lass. Ye've made it happen with yer gift of honey."

Ten minutes later DeAnn walked up and down the rows of equipment that Noble had laid out for her. She nodded as she checked off items whose absence had previously puzzled her. In this category she placed the 2,500-pound capacity rubberized life raft (type E-2) which seemed intact with pyrotechnic pistol, extra flares, K rations, fishing tackle, sea markers and water cans. She frowned when she could not find the 40 feet of 75-pound cord to complete the inventory of emergency equipment.

What had happened to the rope? What was the crew saving the other items for, and how did they manage to keep them out of the hands of the Tugaru and Riami natives? Other vital questions swept through Toland's mind. Who had kept the items hidden and for how long? And how much did the person who brought them to her know about their origins? Noble said there was a diary found in the materials. It might give her answers to many of the questions she posed.

The *kiap* was wiping down the barrel of a .50-caliber machine gun when DeAnn queried him about the journals. He pointed to her field desk. "I put the tablets over there for safekeeping. At first glance it looks like the work of a Japanese lass. Calls herself Kioko. Hard to believe she was aboard an American bomber during WW II, eh?"

"Where else would it have come from if you found it among the other things from the bomber?"

"I expect ye'll be telling yer mates the answer, lass, once ye've read it through. But ye'll have to take the tablets back to base camp with ye. After dark my Riami lads are edgy about passing through Tugaru territory."

"Maybe she came here with a Japanese team searching for the remains of their WW II comrades, like we're doing for our boys," DeAnn said.

"Maybe. But one thing I've noted, this Kioko lass had her fingers 'round gold at one time or another."

"How do you know, Roger?"

The *kiap* held up the .50 caliber barrel for her inspection. "See there, the fine powder. It's all over the journal and the other items found in the bundle."

Dr. Toland frowned, "Are you sure?"

Noble's gaze focused on the gun barrel. He found a spot he had not cleaned and ran his tongue across it.

"Yep, gold dust," he said. "Ever since Jack Hides opened up this territory nearly 40 years ago, patrol officers have learned the taste, smell and feel of gold. A few of 'em made fortunes and retired."

Toland shook her head. "Oh, no, we don't need a bunch of prospectors and mining officials coming in here disrupting the natives even more. Please, Roger, don't say anything about the gold, or Kioko's log, until we've sorted things out for ourselves."

"Not even Bellicosi?"

"Most of all not the general," she said.

"I'll keep it to myself, lass. I've never been one for *fossicking*. Once gold fever takes hold, there's never enough."

"You're a dear friend, Roger."

"So was Mackelwaite."

"Mackelwaite?"

"Yes, I'll tell you about him whilst we make our way back to camp. We'll have the constables gather the B-24 equipment and take it back to the CIL camp with us."

She went over to the aircraft, found Kioko's six-volume diary and put the tablets in her backpack. If she hurried, she thought, they'd pass through the Riami and Tugaru villages during the slackest part of the day, after the workers and warriors had returned home for the evening meal, and before they left again seeking the pleasures the night offered.

How she wished Frank Yowell would hurry back. He would be as excited as she was about the new discoveries. She couldn't wait to tell him.

12 INEXPLICABLE CASUALTY

Baltimore, Maryland, 1973

U.S. ARMY CENTRAL IDENTIFICATION LABORATORY (PROVISIONAL) FINDINGS, CASE NUMBER 316. DR. DEANN TOLAND'S REPORT.

Recovered bones provide an abundance of information for determining sex, race, age, height and muscularity of victims. Teeth are almost indestructible and offer more precise identification. If dental charts obtained from service records are available, they can be matched against remains, especially when evidence of fillings, crowns, extractions or other dental restorations exist.

In our case, only seven out of ten crewmembers on the ill-fated B-24 had dental records on file. Since records kept by the army in the 1940's lacked the thoroughness expected today, they are questionable for use as evidence.

DeAnn Toland, Ph.D.
Physical Anthropologist

COMING SO SHORTLY after his mother's emotional breakdown, the sight of Haveland's lifeless body next to the conference table in Billings Hall drained the last ounce of enthusiasm for Stanek's mission at Hopkins. The grief he felt sickened his heart even more. He followed the police lieutenant past his slain mentor into the office off the conference room Haveland shared with his secretary. Stanek walked like a man caught in a nightmare. He

116

wanted to bolt from the place and forget this scene of chaos—file drawers flung open and papers scattered everywhere. Instead, he leaned against the door and closed his eyes.

After he collected his thoughts, Stanek took a seat across the desk from Lt. Dunbar. The detective got down to business at once. He asked Stanek how long he had known Dr. Haveland and whether he knew anyone who had threatened the pathologist lately.

Stanek answered perfunctorily, not even aware of what he was saying. His thoughts were on Patricia Stanek and Tom Haveland. Life without the woman who had nurtured him from infancy was unthinkable. And life without Haveland's steady guiding hand and kindness, always present like a gentle breeze in summer, was devastating.

Dunbar persisted. "Mind telling me what you were doing in Dr. Haveland's offices yesterday evening? We found your security badge next to his body. The photo above the signature had been torn away. Got any idea why the murderer wanted your picture?"

Stanek's eyebrows shot up and his mouth flew open. "None whatsoever! Surely Haveland's secretary told you about the B-24 case I was working on for Tom."

"Did you begin this work in the presence of Dr. Haveland?"

"No, he had left, and I stayed awhile to look over the material he had given me."

"What time did you leave?"

"Five-ten p.m."

"A pretty precise answer. How do you know?"

"I had intended to keep another appointment and checked my watch. It was 5:10."

"Where was your other appointment to take place?"

"Phipps Clinic. It's the building behind this one."

"Do you know your name didn't appear on the sign-in sheet at Phipps until this morning?"

"After I lost my badge, I knew I couldn't get past security. So, I went to my hotel, intending to come back here this morning to keep an appointment with my mother, a patient at Phipps, and then to deliver my findings on the B-24 case to Dr. Haveland. In fact I was on my way over there when..."

The dark-skinned officer's eyes held a merry twinkle as he placed a thin hand on Stanek's shoulder. "Easy, Doc. You're not a suspect. We already checked the phone log. Haveland called you at your hotel at 11:45 p.m. Postmortem lividness began sometime after midnight, according to the medical examiner. Anything we should know about your lengthy phone conversation? Did Dr. Haveland mention Filipino Freddie?"

The switch in the lieutenant's demeanor came as a surprise to Emerson Stanek. He was used to detectives and inspectors who maintained the saturnine expression of an inquisitor. This was a man open to bargaining.

"Tell you what, Lieutenant. Make me a part of this investigation, and I'll not only tell you all I know, but I'll give you the analysis of a forensic scientist, for what it's worth, free of charge. Tom Haveland was my best friend."

Dunbar clasped his hands together and formed a steeple with his index fingers. He placed the spire under his dilated nostrils. "Hmm, sounds like a winner to me. What do you say we get back out there in the conference room and get crackin'?"

Haveland's body lay near his chair at the head of the conference table. He was in a prone position with both hands beneath him at lower chest level. Except for the slight smear of blood staining the collar under the white mane at the nape of his neck and another spot around the lips of his open mouth, there were no signs of struggle.

"Looks like Haveland was about to cry out when he got zapped," Dunbar said.

Stanek shook his head. "I don't think so. He seems to have been surprised from behind." He knelt beside Haveland's body and pointed to the sheet partially covering it. "May I?"

"Examine away. Our coroner's finished, and we've got all the photos we need. As you can see, we cut the decedent's shirt away to get pictures of the wound."

Haveland's body was cool to the touch. He had an entrance stab wound in the lower neck between the shoulder blades. Non-consistent bloodstains around the wound indicated a sharp instrument, possibly a sword, had been driven into Haveland's back and pushed downward in line with his spinal column. The impression put Stanek in mind of the *coup de grâce* delivered by a matador. The blood splatter on Haveland's shirt confirmed as much. Here the patterns on the fabric were consistent with a blade withdrawn from the same tear in which it had entered.

Stanek relayed to Lt. Dunbar the events which had transpired since he had left Haveland's office. Then he added, "Thanks to methodology developed by Dr. Haveland, your medical examiner can actually reproduce the weapon's blade by pouring a hot wax-like substance into the wound. All he has to do is wait for the substance to cool; then you have a replica to shop among sellers and collectors of swords."

"Thanks, it's worth a try. Got anything else, Doc?"

"Yes, I'd like to look into Dr. Haveland's mouth."

"Go right ahead."

"You might want to see for yourself." Stanek waited for Dunbar to kneel down beside him before continuing. "The blow dealt Haveland was designed to keep him from crying out. A blade inserted between the shoulder blades would collapse the lungs and leave the victim gasping for air. No way could he have expelled air or blood through an open mouth. No, Haveland's mouth was opened and suffered the trauma producing blood and bruising around the lips sometime after he was fatally struck and fell to the floor."

Stanek paused. He ran a finger inside and along the upper jaw of his murdered mentor. "There were five teeth connected by a gold bridge. It's missing. Haveland often joked in class about the dentist charging him so much for the bridge he was sure the gold stock at Fort Knox had been cut in half."

The lieutenant's eyes widened. "What kind of man besides Hitler would rob a corpse of its gold teeth!?"

Several moments passed before Stanek was able to detach his emotions and offer an opinion. "This is probably a very greedy one, or perhaps you're dealing with a psychopathic killer who wanted a souvenir from his victim. If the mob's involved, maybe somebody wanted proof the hit had been carried out."

Lt. Dunbar remarked that he was puzzled at the amount of moisture he found on the carpet and on the conference table proper. "I'm even more amazed," he added, "that after a quick inventory, Haveland's secretary reported none of the doctor's important papers missing, My stars! If this doesn't beat all, the assailant didn't even take the manila folder containing Filipino Freddie's file Haveland had been working on. It was tucked under the decedent's right elbow just as you see it there."

119

The lieutenant scratched his head. "What do you make of it, Doc?"

"Haveland might've been working on the Freddie file in this office, but it's not the 'smoking gun' folder he may have brought with him from the Pathology Department."

"How do you know?"

"Because folders from pathology are color-coded purple in order to keep track of them, so they find their way home eventually. I'm sure you've already packed up a lot of stuff to haul down to the station for analysis. Look for a purple folder, and it may lead you to what Haveland's murderers were searching for, but never found."

"You've been a great help, Doc. Now what can I do for you?"

Stanek asked to see the initial crime report submitted by the first law enforcement officer on the scene. Dunbar called over a Johns Hopkins security guard and directed him to give an oral report. Stanek recognized the officer. He was known as Joe to students and faculty and had spent 30 years at his post in the administration building. Haveland treated Joe like he did all staff on campus, like a member of the family.

Joe extended his hand. "Well if it isn't young Dr. Stanek. It's great to see you, but not under these trying circumstances." Joe turned toward the lieutenant. "Dr. Stanek will find out who did this horrible thing to as gentle a soul as ever walked these corridors."

"Joe, I haven't much time. Can you tell me what happened after you were called?" Stanek asked.

"Mary Lou, you know, Dr. Haveland's secretary, telephoned this morning about eight o'clock and said Dr. Haveland had given her the morning off, but she felt guilty about it. Said she tried to call him to say she was coming in anyway. Got no answer, so, she asked me to go by his office and check on him."

"Yes, go on, Joe."

"I knocked on the conference room door, but he didn't respond."

"What time did you knock?"

"About 8:15."

"Go on."

"I knew Doc Haveland often locked himself in to keep from being disturbed, so I went back to my desk and got the master key."

"How long were you gone?"

"Not more than 15 minutes. Stopped to take a another call from Mary Lou who was mighty worried."

"Go on."

"As soon as I got the door open and went inside the conference room, I saw Dr. Haveland sprawled on the floor. My first thought was he'd had a stroke or heart attack. But the files and papers strewn about the conference room and adjacent office made me think it was burglars."

"Did you call for help?"

"Not immediately. I first wanted to see if I could help Dr. Haveland. I knew he kept an old stethoscope in his desk, so I went in there and got it. When I came back into the conference room, I applied it to my ears and to his heart. You don't work around a hospital as long as I have and not know the techniques."

"Joe, did you move the body to get the stethoscope under him?"

"Yes sir, slightly I'd say. But it didn't make any difference. He was dead all right. I applied the scope to his neck to make sure, and then I saw the blood oozing out between the shoulder blades. Stabbed, I hear."

"Joe, I need to know what you saw and did, not what you've heard."

"I can't think of anything else, Dr. Stanek. I called the Baltimore Police and was told to stay at the scene and await the arrival of detectives. On orders from Lt. Dunbar (he was the first to arrive), I went back to the front entrance on North Broadway and stood beside the old sundial on the terrace and kept everybody back from the scene."

The lieutenant told Joe he had done well to protect the area from intruders and dismissed the guard for the time being. Dunbar then turned to Stanek.

"Does any of this make sense or fit into the timeline you gave me? For example, the telephone call to the custodian at the Pathology Building who turned out to be a victim as well. And what about the suspicious couple you saw at your hotel. Any ideas on how they fit into this case?"

"Not at the moment, but you might turn up a link during your analysis of the evidence sweep you conducted at both murder sites," Stanek replied.

"Yeah, I only wish you weren't leaving for Hawaii tomorrow. Your expert opinion would be invaluable once the evidence comes back from the lab. I don't have to tell you there's no evidence more perishable than what's collected at a crime scene. I appreciate your thoroughness, Doc."

Stanek's cheeks reddened as he stroked the crescent-shaped scar. "Sorry, but I've got to go back to Hawaii. Feel free to send me a report on anything that you'd like me to look over though. Meantime, I'll give you my gut reaction, if you think it would be helpful from someone especially close to one of the victims."

"Please do, Dr. Stanek."

Emerson took in a deep breath. Again it was hard to think of Tom Haveland in the cold, detached analytical terms used in discussing a murder case. His mentor's oft-repeated dictum, indeed only recently expressed at the sundial, came to mind, "Look intently enough at anything, and you'll see something that would otherwise escape you." Good advice, he thought. But Haveland wouldn't expect him to abandon his beekeeper cancer research to go chasing after murder suspects. Besides, the police already had their sights set on Filipino Freddie who packed the most motive.

"I can't think of anyone in the hospital or on campus with the motive to commit such a heinous crime against Dr. Haveland. Except for criminals, he befriended everyone."

"I've heard as much," said Dunbar.

"Yet, we're faced with these facts," Stanek continued. "Someone entered his office, although the doors were locked from the inside. The assailant, or assailants, whom Haveland might've admitted, drove a sharp instrument between his shoulders at the back of the throat, thereby insuring he couldn't scream out or otherwise call attention to his plight."

Stanek paused. "This, and the fact his offices were ransacked, points to a professional job planned in advance. And the murder weapon used in conjunction with how Tom was slain—impaled as it were—suggests an African or Asian technique. Filipino Freddie certainly fits that profile. He runs a worldwide operation and could've imported a couple of hit men.

"I don't know, lieutenant, this Freddie seems too convenient a suspect. Haveland didn't mention the breakthrough he had achieved in his case, nor did he give any indication he considered

Freddie a personal threat—at least not in my last conversation with him."

"Well, how do you think this went down?"

"I believe when I heard the noise in the skylight over the conference table last night, it was someone on the roof checking to see if I was Haveland. After I closed out the B-24 report I was working on, they must've left when I did, exiting by ladder, because they certainly weren't on the stairway or in the rotunda where I encountered Mr. Cole, the reporter."

"Do you think there was more than one perpetrator?"

"Yes, possibly as many as four."

"Why so many?"

"It's only an assumption at this point. But let's assume the man and woman who came to my hotel room at 11:30 p.m. were accomplices. They might've followed me after I left Billings Hall. They were looking for something and maybe they thought I might have it.

"Meantime, their accomplices, already on campus, possibly another man and woman team, tailed Dr. Haveland to the Pathology Building and then back to this spot where he was murdered."

"Any thoughts on how they got in through a locked door and bolted windows?"

Stanek looked up at the skylight. "My guess is one of them came in through the skylight. And the sounds I heard on the roof the night before, which I mistook for a branch blowing against the pane, could've been someone cutting the glass in order to unlock the window."

"But it was stormy yesterday."

"What better time to divert attention and prepare the site than during a storm when it disguises your activities."

"Let's see if I've got this straight, Doc. The murderer, or his accomplice, came here, cut the pane, waited until you left, then removed it and reached in to unbolt the skylight. Later, when Dr. Haveland came back to his office, our intruder opened the skylight and then slid down a rope into the conference room while Haveland was in his inner office."

"Yes, it's a fair assumption at this point. You can check to verify if the glass was cut and then replaced."

"My stars. We can check it. But how or when did they get back out?"

"Here it gets more sketchy, but you said the carpet was wet when you arrived, Lieutenant, indicating the skylight had been opened. Let's say a petite woman climbed down a rope or cable, then opened the door for her accomplice to enter, and possibly he exited the same way."

"I don't quite follow you."

"Joe gives us a possibility there. After knocking on Haveland's door and getting no response, Joe left for 15 minutes to go get the master key and take a call from Mary Lou. It was time enough for an acrobatic woman to scurry up the rope leaving her stronger partner to handle Joe. But when Joe went into Dr. Haveland's inner office to get the stethoscope, the murderer saw his chance to slip out the front door. Lucky for Joe."

"Now, as to our acrobatic woman. Having already left the murder room up the rope and through the skylight, on her way she propped an ice cube between the bolt and latch. Once melted, the bolt, spring driven, slams into the latch and the skylight window is locked, as if from the inside."

"The opening and closing of the skylight would account for the water on the conference table and carpet, directly underneath it," said Dunbar. "My stars! You think the assailants hung around the murder scene from after midnight to early morning?"

"Yes, I do."

"But why?"

"Because, again, they didn't find what they were looking for, which means it wasn't in Dr. Haveland's office, or on him at the time he was murdered. The manila folder with Filipino Freddie's documents inside could've been moved by Joe when he shifted Dr. Haveland to check his heartbeat, or it could've been planted there by the assailants to throw us off. At any rate, they weren't after Freddie's dossier."

"Then what was important enough to murder two men over?"

"Find the key motivation, lieutenant, and you'll break this case. But the killers thought their other victim—the custodian at the Pathology Building—knew what Haveland had discovered in one of the purple folders containing evidence from unsolved cases. Maybe they overheard the custodian tell me about the 'smoking gun' when I called from my hotel."

"Then you're marked as a target as well, Dr. Stanek."

"Yes, if my theory holds, unfortunately your assumption follows, Lt. Dunbar."

*   *   *

It was well past time for the rendezvous Catherine had unilaterally scheduled at the Maryland Club when Emerson started to insert the key into the lock and saw that the door to his hotel room stood ajar. In the dark Stanek could see the telephone message light blinking near his bed. "Catherine never gives up," he thought as he switched on the overhead light. His room looked as if a tornado had entered the open window, scattering clothes and articles in its path. He replayed the events of the day over in his mind and decided he had had enough.

Stanek called the front desk and asked the clerk to have a cab standing by out front to take him to Washington National Airport.

"There's a message for you from Catherine Stanek," the clerk said.

"Cancel it. There's been a change in plans. I'm leaving for the airport tonight," he said. Then he added for no particular reason. "Nothing more I can do here."

Two hours later, Stanek looked out the window of his San Francisco bound flight and saw the Washington Monument piercing the horizon like a candle in the dark. As the lights in tourist class were dimmed, he propped a pillow against the window and leaned against it, hoping to catch four hours of sleep before changing planes in San Francisco for Hawaii.

He thought he had spotted Jim Cole in the seat across from his, and a few seats down the aisle from the reporter he had seen a heavy-set man and a petite woman huddled together in conversation, keeping their heads down. Across from them sat two men with close-cropped hair who looked like the military types he worked with at Tripler. Since he was too tired to investigate, he dismissed the idea people were following him as paranoia brought on by the events of one hellish day. Nonetheless, he took his valise containing the beekeeper cancer study and the B-24 report Haveland had asked him to deliver to General Bellicosi from under his seat and cradled it in his lap.

13 RIVER MISSION FOR MEDICINE

Papua New Guinea, 1973

U.S. ARMY CENTRAL IDENTIFICATION LABORATORY (PROVISIONAL) FINDINGS, CASE NUMBER 316. DR. DEANN TOLAND'S REPORT.

Natives selected to work with the Central Identification Laboratory team went through a simple induction ceremony. We outfitted them with a "laplap" to put over their native dress, a small backpack to replace the "bilum," and if approved by Kiap Noble, a rifle designating a "constable."
DeAnn Toland, Ph.D.
Physical Anthropologist

A S MILKEYE STEPPED from the men's house, the rim of the sun was visible over the eastern slope of Mount Bosavi. He walked to the edge of the fence and looked down the empty street littered with refuge from the last evening's meal. He continued past the pigs rummaging in the garbage strewn in front of the row of rectangular-shaped houses. A mist, which floated up from the Rentoul River, settled in the ravines below the level of the houses and hid some of the squalor.

Even to a one-eyed warrior, the filth was offensive, MilkEye thought. He looked up. The overburdened clouds would unleash a cleansing rain by mid-afternoon, but the village would be a pigsty again by dusk. MilkEye shook his fist at the rectangular houses he passed. Could Wontok have been right after all? His *one-mate* had urged Riami elders to be like the Tugaru and build roundhouses that were easier to keep clean.

But then MilkEye remembered the problem at hand. He told himself, "LikLik very sick. Need more honey. MilkEye help LikLik. No more think of village garbage, or Wontok who have no children." He said aloud, "WonTok no worry 'bout children. His *meris* no got any. WonTok got small penis. At initiation, MilkEye put own seed on banana leaf for WonTok, so he pass warrior's first test. Situmu no like if he find out."

The spirit voice of his father had been silent since the murder of the Tugaru youth. Nevertheless, MilkEye asked Situmu for help. "Papa, how MilkEye get more honey for LikLik?"

When Situmu didn't answer, MilkEye thought, "Make path like waterfall, but change to fit what day bring."

MilkEye pressed on until he reached the front gate of a hut larger than the others clustered around it. He called. A young woman emerged from a narrow doorway fastened with planks. She rubbed her eyes as she stood beneath the trimmed eaves. He called again. In a single bound she cleared the *pitpit* fence MilkEye had built to keep the village pigs away from the garden next to his wives' hut. MilkEye marveled at her agility. He made a mental note to come back at nightfall and see firsthand if her friskiness waned or not when he crawled on top of her in the garden.

She greeted her husband cordially. But MilkEye showed LikLik's mother his filed teeth and waved a hand away from his body in a patting motion.

"Goodbye? Where you go?" she asked.

"To great *balus*," MilkEye said.

"You come back at night?"

"Yes. We go to garden," he said.

She turned to leave. But he called her back with a low whistle. "Give me LikLik and pig from Wontok," he commanded.

"Pig for *singsing* to honor Situmu," she said.

"Me take pig to two-name *misis* at great *balus*."

MilkEye's wife rolled her eyes, "White *misis* no need pig."

"*Misis* trade plenty honey for pig. LikLik die without more honey. Bring LikLik and pig to MilkEye!"

The woman stroked his bare chin with her hand. "Look out. Tugaru salt train go to Nomad today. Bearded warriors cross.

Yesterday, Tugaru find body of Salty Meri's youngest son in burial stone. Find bits of Riami *bilum* around his neck!"

"Hurry up. No time for talk," MilkEye said.

"Me make you new *bilum* for lost one. Me bring you new *bilum* with LikLik and pig," she said.

With the squirming pig in the *bilum* and a listless LikLik in his arms, MilkEye headed back to the men's hut to call for his *one-mate*. A sleepy elder came out and told him WonTok had left the men's hut shortly after MilkEye had gone out and didn't say where he was going.

MilkEye released the pig, which joined some others feeding in the garden provided for them. He laid LikLik on the porch-like structure and sat cross-legged next to her with his loincloth folded modestly between his thighs. Hands resting on his knees, craning his neck and hoping to spot WonTok among the villagers who began to pass by the men's hut, he sat for a long time.

"Me need WonTok," he thought. "Two-name *misis* like Wontok. Give WonTok knife me lose. *Misis* help MilkEye if me with WonTok," MilkEye reasoned. Then he got an idea.

"Send up smoke. Wontok find you," he said to himself.

MilkEye took the new string bag from his shoulder and laid it across his lap. He rummaged inside the *bilum* until his fingers closed over the pack of cigarillos the little *balus masta* the whites called Mah-jah Yow-ell had traded him for a yellow stone. He preferred the black tobacco of the sky people, as did WonTok. The wad of raw native leaf inserted into a bamboo tube did not compare with the smooth aroma of cigarettes brought in on the small *balus*.

He drew a match across the serrated surface of the brass wristband another sky person had given him long ago. He inhaled deeply, holding the smoke in his lungs and releasing it slowly, convinced Wontok would catch the scent and come running. When his *age-mate* did not appear, MilkEye readied LikLik for the journey down to the great *balus*.

MilkEye took the *bilum* on his lap and lined it with a mat of bleached pandanus leaves he found stacked beside the porch. Once LikLik's bed was completed, he placed her in it and swung the *bilum* up to the top of his head, securing it with the bark strap. Next he chased down the pig. With the pig under his arm, he joined the flow of natives walking in the village. He looked for WonTok most of the morning, but he was not to be found.

Because of the delays, he did not reach the rope barrier in front of the great *balus* until noon. Not a drop of rain had fallen. Hot, hungry and thirsty, he waited patiently while the constable delivered his message to the white men. When he did not see Doctor Tow-land at the typewriter, MilkEye began to worry.

MilkEye sank down in the grass as the sentry returned without a honeycomb. He put his hand to his lowered forehead when he was told the white *misis* was still in the camp above the Tugaru village and would not be at the *balus* today.

"*Misis* calm Tugaru. Want to make war with Riami over slain warrior," the constable said. "Give me pig. Take to *misis*."

MilkEye was reluctant to surrender his trade item, but realized he didn't have the energy to lug it and LikLik back up the slope to his village in the heat. Besides, he could see the natives going on the Tugaru salt train cross the vine bridge over the Rentoul and assemble for their journey on to Nomad in canoes furnished by the Riami. So he gave the pig to the constable.

MilkEye told himself, "Tugaru no find out MilkEye kill *Bikmaus'* brother at salt well, or no more peace between tribes. Me stay away from Tugaru."

Suddenly WonTok appeared at his side.

"Me look for you. No find," MilkEye said.

"WonTok at camp of two-name *misis*. *Misis* make me constable."

"Why you got *thunderstik* and no rifle for me?" MilkEye demanded.

"Need two eyes make stick roar. Dee-Ann like you work for her instead. *Misis* happy with sky people things we give her."

"How she know?"

"WonTok tell *misis*. Go up to white people camp after you go out. Me like to bring back surprise."

MilkEye cupped his hands over his ears. "No like surprise. Like LikLik better."

"WonTok tell white *misis* about LikLik. *Misis* say you take LikLik on salt train to Nomad. Missionary with powerful medicine live there. Make LikLik better."

"But Tugaru guards look for Riami warrior who kill son of Tugaru sow sky people name Salty Meri," protested MilkEye.

"Tugaru no know who kill warrior. We be boatsmen. Hide LikLik with salt bundles."

"Salty Meri know me. She think me kill her husband," MilkEye said.

"Salty Meri no look at Riami paddlers. Too busy with Tugaru *meri* salt bearers and warrior guards."

"Maybe. Me think about plan."

"No time. Bring LikLik. Me leave *thunderstik* with Riami constable. We change places with two Riami paddlers."

The old Tugaru woman sat motionless on a throne of salt bundles. She was no larger in girth than the natives who swirled about her—Tugaru warriors wearing their traditional headdress and *meris* with banana-covered packages on their heads. Riami men, armed only with paddles, and each, wet from wading across the Rentoul River in a rush to join Salty Meri's expedition, stood by their canoes.

Since they had used the vine bridge to cross the rapids behind the Tugaru, MilkEye and Wontok splashed water on each other's bodies in order to blend in with the Riami paddlers. They waited. Then as Salty Meri left her perch to supervise the portage of the ten-canoe convoy, MilkEye and Wontok darted out onto the trail behind the last boat.

MilkEye negotiated a quick trade with the two Riami men walking under the canoe balanced over their heads. For their places in line, he gave the two Riami men all of his tobacco. But the swap raised the suspicion of a Tugaru warrior moving along the line prodding malingerers—whether carriers or paddlers.

"*Throwim way leg*! Tugaru come," MilkEye called as he hoisted the aft section of the canoe over his head.

From the prow, WonTok answered. "Me hurry up. Long walk about ahead,"

MilkEye called on Situmu for guidance, "Papa, help MilkEye talk to Tugaru." But the spirit voice of Situmu did not respond.

MilkEye checked LikLik. She was asleep in the *bilum*. He pulled the pandanus leaf blanket over his daughter's face moments before *Bikmaus*, the Tugaru headman, barred their path with his trident.

"You two no same Riami carry canoe before," said the Tugaru headman.

MilkEye peeked out from under the canoe. *Bikmaus'* dark beard and sideburns framed pig's tusks tilting upward from his pierced nasal septum. Holes in his nose contained heads of rhinoceros beetles and his yellow, bird-of-paradise headdress all marked him as a Tugaru of great status—the headman.

"Riami *age-mates* got fever. We take places." MilkEye said.

"See you no lag behind. Me get Tugaru *meris*, stronger than Riami warriors, in your places," *Bikmaus* threatened.

WonTok started to respond to the retreating Tugaru warrior, but MilkEye shook his head at his *one-talk*. They walked on in silence until the canoes were put in the water beyond the rapids.

Seated in the last canoe with three Tugaru women perched on salt bundles between them, MilkEye and Wontok paddled out from shore. After they had traveled some distance, LikLik in the *bilum* bed between MilkEye's legs began to whimper. To drown out her cries and draw the Tugaru women's attention away from his daughter, MilkEye pointed with the handle of his paddle and called out to WonTok, "Soon we come to Lower Falls. Find bones of sky people there."

"No like place. Giambu attack us there."

MilkEye started to reply, but LikLik stirred at his feet and began to whimper for food. He dared not offer her the yams he had brought along, knowing his daughter couldn't keep them down. He increased his paddle stroke, hoping to draw attention away from her cries growing louder. But the woman closest to him inclined her head toward LikLik, now kicking at her string bag cradle. She bent over the child.

"Child hungry," the Tugaru woman said.

"She need sweet food for fever," MilkEye said. He blew out his breath, relieved the woman had not called out to her companions in the canoe, or alerted the warrior's canoe following, about the length of a couple of boats behind them.

Before he could react, the woman rose slightly from the salt bundle upon which she sat. She scooped LikLik from the *bilum* and cradled the child against her long, pendulous breasts, which looked like those of Liklik's mother. He wondered how long his wife would wait in the garden before she realized he wasn't coming tonight. Worse, what would the younger men in the village do to her once they discovered her alone?

The Tugaru woman offered LikLik her nipple and the child took it between her teeth, emitting a loud smacking sound. It brought MilkEye out of his reminiscence, and drew the attention of the other women in the boat. The Tugaru salt carriers made no attempt to chastise the woman for feeding the enemy's child as MilkEye expected they would. He saw only sympathy in their faces.

"Riami your enemy. Why you help child?" MilkEye asked the woman holding LikLik.

She smiled. "You have gentle look of papa, no look of warrior. No fear you, but hate Riami who kill husband at salt well," she replied.

MilkEye turned away momentarily. The Tugaru widow had probably signed on to carry salt to Nomad in order to feed her family until another man took her as his wife. She was young and no doubt strong, for when he turned back to hand her two salt bundles to rest LikLik on, he was surprised how easily she handled the heavier of the two.

"Salt bundles same, but why one heavy like fat pig and other light like possum cub?" he asked, hoping to steer the conversation away from the murder.

"Me no know. Me first trip to Nomad."

"Me too," said MilkEye. "Go get medicine for child from missionaries. Me give you my share of trade goods. You help child."

"Husband's spirit no rest 'til Riami warrior who kill my man die. Yet, you give me your trade goods?" she asked.

"Me glad you give milk to child. Husband's spirit leave at last with blood of warrior who kill your man. In this, Riami and Tugaru agree," said MilkEye.

MilkEye knew the law of the mysteries applied equally. As the Tugaru war canoe with its eight warriors swept by, MilkEye lowered his head and dipped his paddle in the Rentoul River. If only he could wash away his troubles as easily as the water fell from the short, broad blade of the oar, he thought.

14 AUTOPSY ASSAULT

Tripler Army Medical Center, Hawaii, 1973

U.S. ARMY CENTRAL IDENTIFICATION LABORATORY
(PROVISIONAL) FINDINGS, CASE NUMBER 316. DR. DEANN
TOLAND'S REPORT.

I've been asked why we civilians threw ourselves
behind Operation Simpatico with so much zeal. My
personal answer as to why I wanted to see the task
through to completion had less to do with the clock
per se than it did with the nature of war. Each time
I read the copilot's condolence letters from WW II, I
could not help but equate his sentiments with those
of so many young soldiers killed in Vietnam and the
families they left behind to reconstruct lives
shattered by war and conflict.
                    DeAnn Toland, Ph.D.
                    Physical Anthropologist

WHILE THE DIENERS prepared the basement dissecting room
for his next post mortem, Emerson Stanek made his way
along the dark corridor and onto the terrace at Tripler Army
Hospital. Wisps of salmon-pink clouds drifted by overhead, and
from higher up the Moanalua hillside, he could hear the brassy
blare of a bugle sounding retreat. A wind from Diamond Head, or
maybe the Pali Lookout, swept across the terrace and set the
rubber apron Stanek wore flapping against his thighs. He steadied
the apron with a gloved hand and realized again how far outside his

routine things had gotten in the week following his return from Baltimore.

Only Catherine had been uncharacteristically silent. Meantime, phone messages from Jim Cole of the *Honolulu Advertiser* piled up. All week the reporter had been asking to see the B-24 documents Stanek still had in his possession. This set off a whole series of questions Stanek couldn't answer. How did the reporter know he was tasked by Haveland to deliver Dr. Toland's packet to General Bellicosi? More importantly, did Cole have him under surveillance? He suspected he was being tailed. Is this how the reporter knew the B-24 documents remained undelivered? But most disturbing of all was Cole's last message. It contained a blunt warning. "Leave Hawaii immediately! The army's got a spot in New Guinea safe for you to hide out until things cool down. Give me a few minutes of your time, and I'll explain."

Stanek stared thoughtfully at the apron in his hands. He could not recall the last time he had appeared outdoors in his green dissecting clothes.

He retreated inside the basement area designated for post mortems. But his thoughts shifted to the incidents he had experienced at Johns Hopkins, especially Haveland's murder. He had disrupted his routine morning jog along the section of Waikiki beside his apartment at Ft. DeRussy when he had tried to outrun his own shadow, as if physical exertion would rid his mind of all the wounds the Baltimore trip had opened. He felt like a pilot flying blind through a patchwork of mist and cloud from which he could not break free.

His mind throbbed with questions regarding his mentor's murder. Who could've done such a thing and why? Had he acted too hastily leaving town before the old man's funeral? Should he have stayed and helped Lt. Dunbar with the investigation? And what business did Cole have in all this?

Since he had not taken time to hand deliver the B-24 documents to General Bellicosi's office as Haveland had requested, Stanek wondered if much of his self-questioning sprang from this delay. He vowed to drop the documents off at the general's office in the morning, as Haveland had wanted him to do. It might lift a part of the burden off his shoulders and place it on Dr. Toland and General Bellicosi where it belonged, he decided.

As he strode down the corridor with new resolve, two dieners, also dressed in green, passed him from behind pushing a gurney bearing a lifeless form covered with a sheet. He could see by the outline that it was the body of a young woman. The mortuary assistants told him this was his next autopsy. Stanek paused inside a doorway to check his schedule, but before he entered the room, he heard the soldier at the head of the cart call to his trailing companion, "The S.O.B.'s been in a foul mood since he returned from the mainland."

"Yeah, I heard Hopkins wouldn't give him a grant for his cancer study. And wouldn't you know it? Tonight, we've got University of Hawaii premeds standing in on the next case. Are they gonna catch hell!"

"Stanek hates that shit—people gawking over his shoulder."

"Ever notice, those frat boys never show up for his autopsies on infants or old farts?"

The trailing diener whipped back the sheet and partially unzipped the body bag, exposing the woman's upper torso, "Can't blame 'em. Big tits will pack the gallery every time," he said.

Stanek had heard enough. He stepped back into the corridor to make his presence known in time to hear one of them sound the alert.

"Man, cover her quick! Stanek's coming back. If he saw you disrespecting the dead, he'd bust your ass."

Stanek waited until his assistants passed into the dissecting room and then followed them into the room. Once inside, he pointed to his left. The two attendants immediately wheeled the gurney containing the young woman's body to the table indicated. They eased the corpse on to the stainless steel examining surface, removed the top sheet and lowered the zipper on the protective plastic bag.

Stanek's steel-blue eyes flashed at the two dieners. "Tell me why the zipper on the bag has already been halfway lowered?" he demanded.

Like green snakes caught in the garden, the two attendants slithered toward the anonymity of the pale green wall. The dozen or so students already gathered there shuffled nervously. Ignoring them, Stanek pulled on a new set of rubber gloves and squared around as if to address an imaginary point on the floor. He made no attempt for eye contact with his audience.

"It's bothersome for me to have you here," he said. "Whether you stay or not depends on your conduct. Listen and learn. Don't talk. I'll not answer questions, so you shouldn't ask any. Save your questions for your professors. Now let's see what this young woman's death can tell us about her life."

In quick, agile movements he turned the vertical lifting screw on the pedestal. The table groaned, then came to rest at a slight pitch. "You want the blood and other fluids to drain off the end of the table into a gutter on the yellow tiled floor," Stanek explained. Someone in the crowd guffawed. Stanek's eyes immediately singled out an observer larger and older than the rest. Next to him was a petite woman. She too did not fit the student profile. Stanek was certain they were the pair he had seen on his return flight from Baltimore.

"One more outburst, and I'll throw you all out," Stanek said. He touched the scar on his cheek, then added, "Tomorrow night's post mortem will yield more scientific substance. Raise your hand and one of my assistants will arrange for you to come back for the old beekeeper."

As he expected, there were no takers. He selected a clipboard off an overhanging rack and began reading from the clinical abstract in a strong, clear voice in order to trigger the audio pickup system for recording dictation.

"Single, 19-year-old female, Caucasian. Admitted 10 May 1973 as an emergency case. No known habits such as alcohol, tobacco or narcotics. Father, Navy Captain deceased at 56 from cardiac arrest following surgery for wounds received in Vietnam. Mother, medical history and whereabouts unknown. Previous personal history indicates normal childhood diseases and injuries. X-rays show multiple fractures of the jawbone and right clavicle. These seem to fit the profile of a battered woman. Died, Tripler Army Medical Center at 0200 hours, 12 May 1973, presumably from gunshot-induced trauma, right side of the cranium, above mastoid process." Stanek paused and the only sound heard in the room was the recording device clicking off.

He vaguely remembered a similar case. And in a flash the answer came to him. Dr. Toland's report on the B-24 indicated a crewmember's injuries consistent with the broken bones the young woman suffered. With a thoughtful stroke of his beard, he resumed the examination.

"Permission for post mortem has been granted by a surviving sister who suspects foul play. We shall see."

He parted the shoulder length strawberry blond hair on the woman to uncover the dried blood around the gunshot wound, and in an unguarded moment, saw instead the image of Haveland's silver mane in his hands. Death had not yet robbed the woman's body of its supple beauty. As he turned the pale sleeping mask from side to side, observing lips the color of lilacs, he was reminded of Catherine's face. Stanek elevated the woman's eyelids and held his breath. Under the lids, he half expected to see large, unreflecting pools of blue like those of his mother's eyes on that last day at Hopkins when she slipped into delusion. He slowly exhaled. The sockets surrounding the victim's pupils bore a yellow tint.

"Possible jaundice," he said as the voice-activated recorder clicked on.

Moments later, as his fingers moved over and under the woman's breasts, then searched the aurora around the rigid nipples for tumors, one of the observers nudged another and whispered, "He has all the fun."

The recorder automatically clicked on.

Stanek bolted upright and whirled to face his audience. "Out! Everybody out!" he demanded.

He glared at the two dieners. "It was one of you wasn't it? I don't even have to hit the playback to find out. I heard your lewd remarks earlier in the corridor."

"Whose gonna take a civilian's word over a soldier's?" the heavier assistant asked.

"I want you two out of here stat!" He picked up a scalpel from the tray and pointed it at the insubordinate soldier. "Haul ass, soldier, even if, in your case, it takes two trips."

"The general's gonna hear about this threat," the overweight diener shot back over his shoulder. He rushed to catch up with the students who had fled into the adjacent morgue and escaped out the back door.

Stanek was about to resume the post mortem when an emergency page summoned him to pick up line three. He turned off the tape recorder, strode over to the wall phone and punched the blinking light.

"Doc, sorry to bother you at work. Can we talk?"

"Lt. Dunbar?" Stanek asked.

"Yeah, I should've identified myself. Sorry."

"What's going on, Lieutenant?"

"We've tracked down the two thugs who appeared outside your hotel door in Baltimore the night Dr. Haveland was murdered. They're working for Filipino Freddie. We were able to trace the fingerprints they left smeared all over your ransacked room. But we need you to press charges before we can pick 'em up for questioning."

"I can save you the trouble, Lieutenant. They were here tonight posing as students."

"Followed you to Hawaii?"

"It would seem so. I spotted them on my flight back."

"Doc, before doing anything else, get down to the Honolulu police and get these guys under lock and key. You're a marked man."

"Thanks for the warning. But involving the police here won't do much good. Both your suspects look Hawaiian to me which probably means they have friends on the force."

"Then get the hell out of Hawaii and come back to Baltimore under my protection."

"Thanks, again, Lieutenant. But Dr. Haveland would want me to carry on with my research here, and I intend to do so. Yet, there is something that you could safeguard for me."

"What is it?"

"My beekeeper cancer study. I have the original here, but a copy was among Dr. Haveland's papers when we searched his office. I'd appreciate it if you would place the study under your custody until we find out whether or not this is what our friends are after."

"Sure, Doc. Consider it done, but call me if you change your mind about the protection."

"Will do."

After he hung up, the message signal continued to blink. He lifted the receiver and again pressed the button, "You have another call, and someone's here to see you," the operator said. "Catherine Stanek is on hold and says it's urgent. Also, a Mr. Jim Cole wants to come down to see you. He insists on meeting with you, something about a B-24 case. Security has detained him. Please advise."

"Keep Cole away from here," Stanek snapped.

"And Miss Stanek?"

"Put her call through."

Don't let them rattle you. Maintain regular order, Stanek thought as he fingered the scar on his cheek while he waited for Catherine to come on the line.

She launched into what appeared to be a well-rehearsed diatribe. It was no doubt designed to make him feel guilty about standing her up, leaving Baltimore without attending Dr. Haveland's funeral (or no notice for that matter) and saddling her with the responsibility for telling their mother why he never came by any more.

"Then you saw her, and she remembered I was there?" he asked.

"Not as her adopted son. Only as a 'nice young doctor who understood her paintings'."

"Oh."

Her tone softened. "Dear Emerson, I'm afraid it hurts you to hear mother didn't recognize you. But it serves you right for the way you treat me."

"Are you finished?"

"No, there's more. I went to mother's room to check on her after your visit and her Popsy episode. There on the wall next to father's and my portraits was the bastard H. Douglas Addison glaring down at me with a smug expression."

"So, the guy in uniform has set you off?"

"He's not just any guy. He was father's rival at Hopkins before he left to serve as a doctor in Spain and was killed in an air crash there."

"Fine, forget him. Hardly seems worth the trouble for either of us. Now, if you'll excuse me I've got a post mortem underway."

"Wait! I took his portrait down from mother's wall and would've had it burned, except mother stipulated in her will you were to get all her paintings. I hope you'll let me burn it. You know how father hated him and how mother made us promise to hide his painting from father."

"Yes, I remember," replied Stanek.

"Well, I conducted my own 'post mortem' and found out why mother wanted to keep Addison's picture hidden in the basement. The bastard married mother's best friend, Meredith, but he was mother's lover before the marriage. She painted Addison's portrait from a photograph Meredith had given her, before Meredith herself had a breakdown and was committed to Phipps for a while."

"Did you call me just to relate another one of your soap operas?"

"No, I wanted to get your permission to burn the darn thing. Who knows, mother's condition might improve if she didn't hang on to the past so tightly. And I want you to know I don't appreciate you going behind my back where mother's concerned."

"Now what in the hell are you talking about?"

"Taking the Addison portrait to mother's room and hanging it without checking with me first."

"What the..."

"Well, if you didn't, who did?"

"I have no idea how it got there. I didn't even know who the subject of the painting was until you just told me, remember?"

"Well, it must've been Dr. Haveland. He's the only other person who knew our family history."

"What difference does it make? If it's bequeathed to me, I don't want it burned, which is probably what you did with my portrait, since I didn't see it in your mother's rooms."

"No, mister-know-it-all. I have it in my penthouse. You can come and get it anytime. Or, if you like, I'm coming to Hawaii next week, and I'll bring it with me. We can talk some more about your beekeeper cancer study after a moonlight swim."

"You know my terms, so save yourself the corporate jet fuel. Meantime, keep my paintings safe. Seems like I have one Stanek legacy your father can't steal from me."

As she began to sob, he hung up, wondering if her tears were for not getting her way, or whether she was truly upset about the one thing they shared—loneliness. In a sense, they were both orphans.

He lifted the full section knife from the silver tray and pierced the young woman's body just below the clavicle above the armpit on the left shoulder. Blood oozed from the incision as he cut down under each breast and up toward the right clavicle.

In the reflection of the overhead light on the stainless steel table, Stanek caught sight of his image glaring back at him. He was surprised at how weary he looked. His untrimmed beard and scowling eyes bore evidence of the fitful nights he had spent since returning from Baltimore.

In the next instant, to the right and left of his visage, two other faces appeared, distorted by the diffused light. He heard the vertical lifting screw turning on the pedestal. He tried to spin around but was held against the table by a pair of arms as thick and powerful as his own thighs.

"How dare you?" he gasped, hoping to trigger the device and record the voices of his assailants. Only when the lights in the dissecting room dimmed and the room fell into total darkness did he realize his mistake. After taking the calls from Lt. Dunbar and Catherine, he had forgotten to reactivate the automatic voice recording system. On the chance the intruders were the embarrassed dieners come back to exact retribution for being summarily dismissed, Stanek asked, "Okay, fellows, haven't we carried this prank far enough? What do you say we get back to work?"

From all around came familiar sounds—a cart being wheeled into position and the rustle of sheets indicating the transfer of a body. With silence came fear. In a flash, Stanek found himself gagged and strapped to the dissecting table in place of the corpse he had been working on. He felt the young victim's blood soaking into the clothing on his arms and legs from where she had lain on the table.

Stanek began to feel the room moving. As the dead woman's blood pooled around his neck and ears, he realized what was happening to him. His assailants had tilted the dissecting table so that his head now hung over the drain. Slowly the room began to spin.

"Don't let the *haole* pass out on us." The sound of the voice came from his right where a woman knelt beside him. Her dialect was unmistakably Polynesian.

"Not before we're finished," her companion replied from Stanek's opposite side. He also bore the marks of a native Hawaiian, only his voice was deeper and thicker in tone.

"Haveland passed information to you," the male voice said. "Give it to us, and you won't get hurt."

Stanek shook his head.

"He can't talk with the gag on," the women said. Then she leaned over and whispered in Stanek's ear, "Don't look to your left or right, or cry out, or I'll slit your throat." She showed him the clavicle knife while her companion removed the gag.

"Now, about the 'smoking gun' evidence. Where can we find it?" she asked.

Stanek gulped in huge breaths. His head throbbed. His legs and feet went numb. He tried to speak, but the pressure of the swelling in his throat made it impossible. The woman dug her nails into his neck and lifted his head slightly, crooning into his ear, "Is that better? Come on, sweetheart, tell us what you did with Haveland's papers, and this will all be over."

"Haveland didn't...give me anything...on Filipino Freddie." The splitting tightness in his temples was so severe Stanek wondered if the words lay trapped in his head or were actually spoken aloud.

Whatever he had managed to get out brought a titter from each assailant in turn.

The woman shook the knife at Stanek and made a clucking noise with her tongue, while her companion tightened the gag across his lips. "Afraid that won't do, darling," she said.

It was too dark in the room to see, but Stanek felt a tug on his apron bib and heard the knife slice through the rubber, and then rip through the thin fabric of his scrubs. The woman drew soft fingers across his exposed chest and, at first, her teasing touch seemed no more sinister than had Catherine's the morning they met outside the Phipps Clinic in Baltimore. But then, as the knifepoint pierced his skin, pain like an electrical arc shot across his chest and into his armpit. Like a lump of highly charged energy, the pain formed itself in a ball and rolled toward his throat. Choking, he closed his eyes and shook his head from side to side, then nodded.

"Remove the gag," the woman said. "He's ready to..."

Suddenly, the double steel doors of the dissecting room flew open and light from the hall split the room in half. Stanek opened his eyes. From his inverted position, he saw a phenomenon unfold so quickly he hardly had time to gather his impressions into thought.

Cole, or someone else who had the same shaggy appearance of the reporter, came out of the light, flailing away at the large front wheels that propelled the prone cart upon which he lay headfirst. Like a ghost riding a strong wind, Cole could not, or did not, stop until the cart veered slightly and crashed into a supply cabinet, sending it careening along the wall into a couple of stands. Amidst shattering glass, instruments and steel basins clattering across the tile floor, Cole maneuvered his cart through the clutter and wheeled about to face the assailants. Stanek stared horrified. After their initial shock, his attackers now moved in on the crippled reporter.

"Not so fast, you black guards!" Cole said. "The cavalry's coming straightaway and not far behind. Listen!"

Sounds of heavy breathing and leather boots striking the rubber runner in the hallway might not have been convincing enough, but the voice of the first of three security guards to reach the open doorway was enough to send the felons scurrying toward the mortuary and out the back door.

One of the guards raised his baton, "Stand fast, Cole."

"There's bigger quarry afoot than me, officer," Cole said pointing to the part of the room in the dark.

As the military police gave chase, Cole wheeled the cart over to the dissecting table, set his crutches under him and climbed down. With great effort, he turned the crank to raise the table to the horizontal position. Next he removed Stanek's gag.

"They told me upstairs you were tied up, Doc. But I thought it was just a ruse to get rid of me. Oh, my, I see you've got a nasty cut. Tell me what to do, and we'll get you patched up."

Stanek pointed to a roll of gauze displaced by Cole's wild ride and gasped, "Wrap it...all the way...torso...tight."

"I get the picture, Doc. You save your strength. Who knows where or when those guys will strike next."

As he worked, Cole explained how he had managed to get away from security and make such a grand entrance into the dissecting room.

"Whilst I was being held in the duty officer's office, two corpsmen came in demanding to see the Officer of the Day. They said they had been threatened by a civilian doctor and demanded he be fired. As they were making their complaint, I asked to be excused to go to the lavatory. Outside the john was the empty chariot I used to give the guards the slip. It enabled me to get here in the nick of time. The Lord sure does work in mysterious ways."

"But what about the warning you gave me? If you knew I was being followed, tell me by whom?"

"The guys working for the brigadier were tracking you, but they came across the man and woman who were also keeping tabs on you. All Bellicosi's guys were instructed to do was to let me know where you were, so I could invite you to go to New Guinea."

"The B-24 case, I take it."

"Yeah. Seems like with all the troubles you've got piling up, you might be persuaded to leave town for a while, but we'll talk about it once you're up and about."

Stanek fell silent. Cole's interest in him, after all, did not center on finding a cure for the cancer that riddled the old reporter's body. Perhaps he was just a super patriot who wanted to do all he could for his countrymen. Even without knowing Catherine was about to breeze into town, adding to his troubles, Cole had offered him a temporary escape route. Stanek knew enough about the B-24 case to solve the mystery in a week or two on site in New Guinea. There couldn't be that much more to it, he reasoned.

"Mr. Cole?" he said.

"Yeah, Doc?"

"Didn't you once tell me there were beekeepers in New Guinea?

"I don't know how many beekeepers there are, but I know for sure you'll find some bities."

"Bities?"

"Bees that bite."

Stanek reflected for a moment. "Then, here are my terms. You get your general to plug in some extra time for me to study these creatures, and I'll go to New Guinea to solve his mystery for him."

MEMORANDUM FOR RECORD
SUBJECT: Second Thoughts

The following information was furnished by Jim Cole to General Bellicosi:

With all due respect, General, you know I wholeheartedly agree with the goal of "Operation Simpatico." Gaining congressional support in establishing a permanent American government agency for finding, identifying and returning remains of soldiers who die in America's wars is essential. But featuring the downed WW II B-24 bomber discovered in New Guinea as your example to garner sympathy and support for remains recovery has taken an ugly turn. As eager as I am to get an exclusive for my newspaper on remains recovery and also help you publicize your project, the murder of Dr. Thomas Haveland and interrupted assault of Dr. Emerson Stanek weigh heavily on my conscience. How can we be sure these macabre incidents aren't related to the B-24 case? Can we call it a coincidence that both pathologists, who, granted could give prestige and validation to the Operation Simpatico, each have initial ties to the case. I'm having second thoughts about it. I'm almost sorry I helped persuade Dr. Stanek to go to New Guinea!

The following is General Bellicosi's reply to Jim Cole:

Nonsense, Jim! We can't base our decisions on "what ifs." Certainly we have sympathy for Dr. Haveland's demise and Dr. Stanek's assault. But the two pathologists certainly have had other cases that could have come into play in these incidents. Good job helping get Stanek on board. Our timeline is too important to hold up with second thoughts. Besides, I have my sources keeping tabs on the situation. Not to worry!

> Antonio Bellicosi
> Brigadier General, USA
> Casualty Operations Branch,
> Pentagon

PURSUED:
TEN KNIGHTS ON THE BARROOM FLOOR

Mel R. Jones

PART TWO:
DIAMETRIC DICHOTOMY

"One fella road, dassall"
(There is only one road for all of us)

15 MOUNTAIN KNIGHT-SIGHTING/MAY DAY ALERT

Mount Bosavi, Papua New Guinea, 1973

EMERSON STANEK LOOKED out the aircraft window down at Mount Bosavi and gasped in disbelief. Below him, on the 8,000-foot peak, a "knight-in-armor" shepherded a dozen natives or so across a sea of volcanic limestone. A golden bird-of-paradise plume adorned the knight's gray helmet, which, like the silver breastplate, glistened in the early afternoon sun. The figure wore khaki trousers cutaway at the knees. The knight's legs, thin but muscular and bronze-colored, seemed weighted down by the need to support the body armor. Yet, the knight, now brandishing a sword, drove his charges on.

When the last native in line slipped and the leafy bundle he had been carrying toppled over the mountainside, the knight stood over the fallen man, raised his sword and beheaded the native carrier. No doubt, seeing what had befallen their comrade, the other carriers dashed behind an outcropping of limestone and disappeared into the face of the mountain.

Mouth agape, steel blue eyes unblinking, Stanek strained for a look beyond the open visor at the murderer's face. But unexpectedly, Major Frank Yowell banked left, sending the U.S. Army de Havilland Beaver away from the peak toward the western slope of Mount Bosavi. Stanek pushed his forehead against the window. He did manage one final sighting. In what appeared a

147

defiant gesture, the butcher snapped the visor shut, turned away from the aircraft and then headed for the same outcropping of limestone behind which the natives had taken refuge. Trailing a wisp of long, dark, unkempt hair beneath the helmet and golden plume, the knight, too, vanished into the mountain.

In the next instant, Stanek saw a sliver of silver shimmering in the sunlight. Unlike the previous phenomenon, which had shaken a well-ordered mind steeped in scientific verity, the silver object was not totally out of place. Stanek thought over the possibilities. He had either seen a waterfall or a piece of wreckage from an aircraft.

The pilot put the nose of the plane down slowly and the curve of the descent carried them into a cloud formation. Stanek realized they were flying blind now, too close to the mountain for comfort. All he could see out his side were gray vapors streaming past the window like smoke from a locomotive. Stanek felt the muscles beneath his Van-dyke style beard, sideburns and mustache twitch slightly. He turned to see Major Yowell indicate that an opening lay ahead.

"Spooky place, eh, Doc?" the pilot asked.

"No more so than any other jungle habitat."

"Oh yeah, then how come a moment ago you looked paler than my first flight instructor? 'Yowell's flying leaves me breathless and bug-eyed,' the S.O.B. wrote in my evaluation. Hope my flyin' doesn't affect you the same way, Doc."

"No, no, I was just trying to get a fix on our position."

"Check your map. New Guinea's a crocodile-shaped island, and we've just come up on part of the croc's rugged backbone in the Southern Highlands District. Did you know the mountains betwixt here and the eastern coast have swallowed up more aircraft than any other place on earth? Yes, sir. Regular graveyard for twisted metal. Bet fellows in your line of work have lots of traffic with graveyards and spooky goings on, eh?"

Stanek pretended to study the map spread across his tropical shorts and tan muscular thighs. He did not want to reveal the "knight" sighting and open the conversation to the kind of superstitious dabble Yowell and his ilk probably hitched to every unexplained phenomenon in the universe. Stanek had learned from Haveland long ago, "Keep the inexplicable to yourself until validation becomes possible."

Major Yowell tapped the corner of Stanek's map, then pointed his gloved finger toward the left side of the cockpit as he banked the aircraft to the left. The pilot was a man approaching Stanek's age and height, although his uniform and clean-shaven chin made him look younger and slightly more muscular.

"We'll break through this soup in a moment, and you'll see the Rentoul River. It flows north off the mountain, then takes a sharp westward turn toward Nomad, cannibal territory." Yowell's drawl placed his origins far south and west of Stanek's native Baltimore, Maryland.

Stanek nodded. Without consulting the map or the major, he set arrival at the B-24 wreckage site for ten minutes or less. As a former medical examiner in San Francisco, he was used to flitting around the county in a helicopter, hopping from one crime scene to another, one step ahead of the news hounds. Accurately gauging the time allotted each case allowed him to escape the scene before the press spun everything out of control with its penchant to chase false leads.

He wondered if the "knight" on the mountain was part of a hoax. Yowell and his friends could easily have perpetrated the stunt to scare off or initiate new arrivals. He had heard of similar pranks and assorted rituals employed by fraternities for controlling pledges. Still, Stanek thought, the slaying of the native by the knight was too authentic and too disturbing to ignore. Yet, it was no matter for discussion with Yowell.

Ten minutes into the aerial search for the Rentoul, they had flown further west of the mountain. Stanek saw dark rain clouds, trailing a white mist, begin to drift in from the south. He decided to break a self-imposed silence.

"Look here, Major, we've crisscrossed six rivers. One of those silver ribbons in the yellow marsh plains below has to be the Rentoul. General Bellicosi told me you've flown this route many times."

By invoking the name of the U.S. Army general in charge of joint casualty recovery operations for the entire Pacific, Stanek hoped to speed things along. But, except for a nervous shift of an unlighted cigarillo from one side of his mouth to the other, Yowell appeared oblivious to the ploy.

"Why, me and General Bee are on a first name basis. He calls me 'Frank' and I call him 'sir'," the major said, adding a chuckle.

"After I drop you off at the crash site, it's up over the great limestone barrier to Goroka for me. And the next time you'll see me is when I bring the general and some VIPs back here on my 12th or 13th trip. Damn! Sure hope this flight isn't unlucky number 13, seeing I've never come up from the south following the crocodile's tail before."

"You mean we're lost?"

"Nothing so drastic, Doc. Like I was saying, I usually approach Mount Bosavi from the northeast out of Goroka, not directly from Port Moresby like we did. They told me you requested this routing. Mind telling me why?"

"A direct route saves time so I can arrive and accomplish the job as soon as possible. Your friend General Bellicosi approved my itinerary."

"Fair enough, Doc. You know there aren't but two airstrips in these wild parts for us to land—a refueling point at Nomad and the CIL makeshift airstrip on a slope of Mount Bosavi. These are our only choices in the immediate area, unless you care to go on to Goroka in the Eastern Highlands District with me. I thought we'd be stopping there first. Better quarters there. And I know a couple of Missionary Air Force stewardesses who'll put us up."

"Mount Bosavi will do."

"No sweat then. You'll be kicking back your feet and sippin' herbal tea with Dr. Toland and her crew in five minutes tops. Although I'll envy you, I'll have fulfilled my instructions."

"Who gave instructions to deviate from my itinerary?" Stanek demanded, shifting his tall, lean body sideways to relieve pressure on his spine.

"Why Bosavi's boss lady, DeAnn the delightful. Wait 'til she bats those pretty brown eyes at you, or plays you like a triangle with her soft, tinkling words vibrating inside your head until you can't refuse any request.

"Remember the WAC on the WW II recruiting poster? DeAnn's the spittin' image of the girl Ernie Pyle wrote about in one of his WW II dispatches. Pyle called her the most soldierly of all WACS and said, 'She is so good-looking it makes you hurt.' DeAnn's the same way. She'll make you wonder how God packed so much beauty, brains, perkiness and freshness into one person. A smile from DeAnn is the same as having a plate of biscuits, gravy and grits piled in front of you. Your mouth starts watering, and you hurt all over from anticipated joy."

"Nonsense! I believe we're lost, and you improvised this meandering route to cover up your mistake. Admit it. You have no instructions."

"Oh yeah, there were instructions alright. DeAnn made me repeat them 'til I got 'em straight. 'When you pass over the Rentoul River, let him drink in the scenic beauty of this place and don't leave out a thing. Like most Johns Hopkins grads, Dr. Stanek is bound to be a stickler for detail'."

"There, I've caught you, Major. If only General Bellicosi, you and I knew we were taking the southern route, how did Dr. Toland know we'd pass over the Rentoul?"

Yowell chuckled. "She gave me instructions before I left. When I called the CIL on Mount Bosavi by radio-telephone while you were being briefed at Port Moresby, I gave the information to Erik, her interpreter, to pass on. Told him to tell her we'd be comin' in over the Rentoul, just like she asked me to."

Stanek decided further banter with Major Yowell was non-productive. The pilot had pestered him with irrelevant information throughout the three-hour flight from Moresby, and on the Pan Am trans-Pacific flight from Hawaii to New Guinea. In each case, Yowell's attempts to engage in small talk cut into valuable analytical time.

If military authorities were interested enough to go to the extremes they had, enticing him to tackle a 30-year-old mystery, why not give him more thoughtful team members to work with, Stanek reasoned. Why hamper a scientific mission with a roué for a pilot and an anthropologist who, like a British matron, hosts tea parties in the jungle of all places? And what was Jim Cole's role in what so far had become a grand charade?

Hoax or not, he was glad he kept the "knight" sighting to himself. Unscientific minds like Yowell's were best left unburdened with unusual occurrences. For Stanek, no experience was more wholly wasteful and stultifying than to try to explain the difference between scientific data and the nonsense one might choose to believe.

He was reminded of his brief sojourn in San Francisco and the incident terminating his career there as chief medical examiner. San Francisco tabloids tried to pass off a chimpanzee's remains as those of a missing child kidnapped and held for ransom. Stanek had debunked the cruel hoax by pointing out that each human body contained 206 bones—no more, no less. In addition to other differences, Stanek took pains to explain chimpanzees usually have one extra rib, making 13 pairs, while a human only has 12 pairs.

At the time he had chastised the news media for this blunder, he also ridiculed reporters for a series of photographs featuring a suit of armor they claimed haunted a local museum. "There's a difference between you and the empty suit in the museum," he told a national TV anchor. "You have the right number of bones, if not brains, to qualify as human." Shortly thereafter, Stanek left the Golden Gate area to take the job at Tripler where he no longer dealt with the news media.

Yowell's aircraft was now low enough that Stanek could see the Rentoul as it swerved west away from Mount Bosavi's foothills. The river smoothed out and grew wider as it meandered across an enormous plain toward the Fly River. The Fly, 700 miles in length, was one of New Guinea's longest navigable waterways.

If, according to the pilot's log, the B-24 crew was headed toward the Fly because the fuel leak made it necessary to ditch in a swampy area, then surely one out of ten might have succeeded in navigating the escape route. Assuming no mental or physical impairment of any of the survivors, they would have had a chance to make the journey in an inflatable rubber dinghy down the great river and across the Gulf of Papua to Port Moresby.

Yet, as intriguing as this scenario appeared, Stanek chose to stick with the conclusion he had drawn the night Dr. Haveland was murdered. Despite the evidence presented in the pilot's log, Stanek believed no one inside the aircraft could have survived when it crashed, much less attempt to reach the Fly. He allotted himself two weeks to prove or disprove the case for survivors, without which the B-24 was just another wreckage in Yowell's metallic graveyard.

Turning the aircraft east to follow the Rentoul back to Mount Bosavi, Yowell swung the Beaver from side to side through a thin mist rising up from the rapids like steam from a cauldron. On and on they advanced up the Rentoul, over rapids, followed by pools of calm water, repeating the pattern until they came near the mountain.

Suddenly, Yowell swung west away from the mountain as Stanek saw they were too close to the trees along the Rentoul.

"You just pulled one hell of a maneuver!"

"Sorry 'bout it." Yowell bit nervously on his cigarillo. "We were coming in too low. Better to go back out, get some altitude and try again." Then in a nonchalant tone, he continued what Stanek considered incessant chatter. "You know, Doc, this country reminds me of Vietnam. Mountains, rivers, streams, and as far as the eye can see, green everywhere else. 'The land that time forgot', the Leahy brothers called it. Ever hear of them? Or Jack Hides, the first white man in here?"

Stanek's patience had gone beyond his normal limits. So he calmed himself by looking at his watch and reminding Yowell they had far exceeded the five minutes promised earlier. "How long before we land?" Stanek asked.

"Bet the Leahys posed the same question when they prospected New Guinea territory in a rickety Ford tri-motor back in the thirties. And Lord knows what those "ten knights" in the B-24 were thinking when they came down here only eight years after Hides patrolled this area. Damn sure our guys weren't exploring or looking for gold. Though we can't be sure once they got on the ground, I suppose."

"Water, food and shelter would've been their first priorities, if they had any sense," said Stanek with no attempt to hide his irritation.

"Yep, no doubt at first they had to be concerned with strange people and their crashed aircraft, but sometime or other, it must've dawned on any American survivors there's probably more undiscovered gold in New Guinea than in the fields of California and Alaska combined. Although in New Guinea, the gold is generally found in highly inaccessible tribal areas. But you probably heard all about this from the "ten knights" briefer in Port Moresby.

"Major, I've got no interest in gold exploration."

Stanek and Yowell suddenly focused on the shoreline. In a clearing a few yards offshore, they saw a small aircraft overgrown with jungle vegetation. On the wreckage sat a warrior smoking a pipe. Yowell eased off the throttle and swung the aircraft in line with the man. As they drew overhead, Stanek saw the native dive for cover under the heap of metal.

All at once, from a half dozen points from within the aircraft graveyard, puffs of blue smoke dotted the wreckage. In the next instant, Stanek heard what sounded like pellets fired into a tin can at close range strike the fuselage behind his seat. One bullet hit under the wing of the unarmed aircraft, and Stanek saw a small piece of metal streak past his window. He glanced over at Yowell. Sweat poured from the pilot's forehead.

"God Almighty!" Yowell shouted, struggling to put altitude and distance between his aircraft and the shooters. Simultaneously, he tried to raise the CIL base camp on the radio. "Bosavi Base—Army One Niner. Mayday! Mayday! We're taking ground fire! Then, turning to his passenger he exclaimed again, "God Almighty! Never happened before, except for this time! Who gave the natives rifles?"

Stanek said nothing. Every alarm bell in his brain and heart called for action, but he could do little more at first than blame Yowell for putting their lives in jeopardy. Yet, if Yowell was just following instructions as he had claimed, then perhaps others had been tipped off somehow, or at least had guessed Stanek's destination, setting a trap for him.

Taken with Haveland's murder, the incidents at his hotel in Baltimore and the attempt on his own life in Hawaii, this latest attack fit the pattern of hired assassins determined to score a hit. Perhaps he, not Haveland was their primary target. The fear of attack was unpleasant. But the thought his stalker was someone cunning enough to plan his murder without revealing his motive was unbearable. As more bullets were fired at the slow-flying Beaver, Stanek began to question his decision to flee Hawaii.

16 A CHILDHOOD CALAMITY REMEMBERED

Mount Bosavi, Papua New Guinea, 1973

A N HOUR BEFORE Yowell's estimated time of arrival at Mount Bosavi, DeAnn Toland strolled along the path down the hillside to the Tugaru gardens marking the boundary between her tent city and the native huts. She chose a spot under a clump of bamboo, sat down, sipped water from her canteen and loosened her blouse.

The slight movement of air, cooled by the bamboo spears overhead, served as a ventilation shaft against heat and humidity severe enough to cause constant concern about dehydration. Behind her, tents erected by the army for the Central Identification Lab team soaked the light so thirstily from the early afternoon sun that their canvas walls glistened, saturated in a liquid brilliance of olive drab.

From her vantage place on the slope, she watched the activities unfold below her. Tugaru women and children began to leave the gardens where they had been working since shortly after sunrise and sought what little shade their porches afforded. Here and there next to the roundhouses, Tugaru men too old to work or keep pace with the younger warriors kept silent vigil from the comfort of their hammocks. In between dozes, the elders looked past her to check out activities in the white settlement.

DeAnn switched her attention to the grove of casuarina trees sandwiched between the round huts of the Tugaru and the Riami settlement with its rectangular-shaped houses. On the northern edge of the stand, a Tugaru warrior mounted a watchtower atop the tallest tree. The sentinel had the best view of the westerly flowing Rentoul River by which Yowell always approached the airstrip. In the time she had observed this action, the sentinel never once failed in his duty. Three times he would call out "*balus*" to announce the major's arrival. On this signal, Tugaru and Riami women and children already near the airstrip waited to stream onto the sparsely covered field in search of handouts and discarded items Yowell often distributed from his Beaver.

By agreement, no warrior from either tribe dare set foot on this no-man's-land of casuarina trees unless it was to fight, change the guards in the watchtowers or escort the Tugaru-run salt train through the Riami village. The tribes did come together again along the banks of the Rentoul, but only to prepare the salt train for its journey to Nomad in Riami canoes under escort by Tugaru warriors. DeAnn was convinced, and General Bellicosi concurred, they could use the compromises forged for security and transportation to expand cooperation between the warring parties.

This was not a day to worry about treaties, DeAnn reminded herself, as she inspected her fatigues, spotted with sweat stains and faded from hours exposed to sun and rain. Yowell had promised to bring back a couple of new sets for her from Hawaii. She could almost feel the new fabric against her skin, dry and clean, repelling moisture the fatigues were designed to do.

She had also heard the army treated its utility uniforms to make them insect resistant. "But someone forgot to tell the bugs in New Guinea," the soldiers in her charge never tired of reminding her. They insisted Papuan flies, ants, bees, beetles and other vermin had armor piercing qualities. "Nothing keeps them away," the troops griped. DeAnn encouraged hygiene and cleanliness as a method of coping. But even more than the heat and humidity, pests drew the most complaints, second only to isolation.

She glanced at the watchtower a second time. Yowell would bring in a sack of mail, lifting morale on the mountain. No matter how late the Beaver arrived, she, the CIL's mail clerk, and the native women and children would be there to greet it. She couldn't wait to see Yowell's reaction when told about the new discovery and the love story it revealed.

"Won't he be surprised," she thought, "to learn two people could find love in the midst of war on a remote mountain." She wondered if she could get through the story without crying again. With a twinge of anxiety at having Frank Yowell and the new pathologist coming in with him find her too emotional, she switched her plans. She would first write a letter to her parents. Then, if time permitted, she'd reread only the first of Kioko's journals for discussion with Yowell later when they were alone. Besides, after a long absence, Frank would be anxious to take outgoing mail with him to Goroka.

Dear Mom and Dad,
    We just got word of the terrible murder of Dr. Thomas Haveland in his offices at Johns Hopkins three weeks ago. I learned so much at his physical evidence seminar in Chicago last year. His was a gentle soul dedicated to helping others. All here anticipated his help on our project. Please send me any news clippings you might've saved. My information came via radio-telephone from a colleague just returning from Hawaii to New Guinea. Haveland, (God rest his soul) will be replaced by a Dr. Emerson Stanek. Any info on the new pathologist would be appreciated as well.
    Meantime, every passing day, I've a growing sense of confidence in our mission. Sure there are hardships. Imagine! I've survived six full weeks in New Guinea sans oatmeal and strawberries. But it helps one cope if both parents are prominent Chicago psychiatrists.
    Yesterday would've been Daphne's 29th birthday. As I recall, she was six and I was five when she drowned in our neighbor's pool. I'm always grateful for the way you transformed my worry and fear, evinced by my stuttering following this tragedy, into an untrammeled voice. You taught me to always be the same person who was happy on those many spring mornings at play with my dear sister. "There'll be other playmates," you advised, "but only one happy DeAnn to greet them." Now, even my frustration in not winning the Tugaru over to our side fails to evoke a stutter. There is but "one happy DeAnn" to greet these holdouts.

Mom, you asked for a sketch of the area so you could follow my progress. I made one for Haveland's replacement and have enclosed a copy for you. Most of the information was contained in my previous letters, but the sketch will help pull it all together for you.

Dad, you wanted to know if I'm holding my own on what you dubbed "masculine-mountain." Kiap Roger Noble has taken me under his wing. He's your age and has been reared to respect women. Major Frank Yowell is a bit of a flirt, but Noble's disapproval keeps him from getting out of line. Although I'm perfectly capable of fending for myself, Noble's fatherly concern for my welfare and safety is uplifting. The enlisted men in my charge are no problem. I'm too much like an officer (i.e., too bossy) for any of them to harbor romantic notions. To keep things on an even keel, Major Yowell and I have decided not to date until we've left this mountain.

Native men present a different problem. Most of the time they treat all women, including their wives, with indifference. However, Kiap Noble told me a great number of Riami, a few warriors included, poured ashes over their heads after learning I was moving further up the mountain away from their compounds. Noble said this method of grieving is a sign of great respect. The Riami do this only for people of good nature, patience and a serene personality. I suspect they first saw these qualities in a Japanese woman who lived among them long ago and left a six-volume account of her experiences. I may have benefited from the good will she established with the Riami.

The Tugaru overlords in this district, however, maintain their indifference. Whatever charm worked on the Riami has failed to win over their fierce neighbors.

Until we gain cooperation from all parties on this mountain, our mission to identify and catalog the lives of our young WW II American heroes remains in doubt. Perhaps Dr. Stanek has a magic solution for creating harmony.

There's no more news this week. I'll write again after I've read your letters Frank Yowell is flying in with. Can't wait!

As always, I remain your loving daughter,
DeAnn

She smiled. Her parents would have a field day with the last line in her letter. They'd interpret the two words "can't wait" the way her subconscious mind intended. Her longing for Yowell had grown deeper and stronger during his prolonged absence. She smiled again. "Psychiatrist parents," she thought, "how they love to connect the dots."

Seeing there was no one in the immediate vicinity except her two native bodyguards—a Tugaru constable and his Riami counterpart—DeAnn unbuttoned her blouse down to the navel to try to find some measure of relief from the oppressive heat. The Tugaru man paid her no mind. His eyes were on the women resting in the shade of their porches. The Riami constable straightened up and turned toward her. She recognized him, but gave the hand signal for him to stay away. New recruits to Noble's constable corps were only too anxious to respond to the slightest movement DeAnn made.

"There's nothing going on here you have to fear, WonTok. Get some rest."

She made a mental note to ask WonTok why MilkEye had not come to see her since his return from Nomad with his sick daughter. Oh well. She would have to wait to find out. Yowell would be landing soon, and there was so much to share with him. She picked up Kioko's tablet marked number one and began to read.

17 KIOKO'S JOURNAL #1, BOMBING'S AFTERMATH

Angoram, Papua New Guinea, 1943

U.S. ARMY CENTRAL IDENTIFICATION LABORATORY (PROVISIONAL) FINDINGS, CASE NUMBER 316, EXHIBIT 3a, KIOKO TANAKA'S FIRST JOURNAL. DR. DEANN TOLAND'S REPORT.

MY BELOVED HUSBAND is my enemy. So I, Kioko, writer of this diary, beseech the possessor of these documents to keep its secrets hidden from him. For if my husband learned of my transgressions against his brothers-in-arms, he would kill me. My greatest fear is for our son. What will happen to Kazuo when I'm gone? Must his blood, too, be spilled for our sins? Was not God's own hand responsible for bringing his father and me together after the awful bombing raid at Angoram?

It was 1:25 p.m., and I had just completed the musical portion of our noon to 2 p.m. broadcast. Lt. Michio Mori, the camp commandant and propaganda officer, plopped down in the desk next to mine beneath the Imperial Portrait and began his critique.

"Ginny," he said addressing me in the name the Americans in New Guinea despised, "You forgot to close the American segment with a voice over as *Sentimental Journey* fades out."

I forced a smile, practiced at my mother's knee, for use in deflecting male anger. "Forgive me, sir. When we sign back on air

160

to remind our Japanese listeners that theirs is a great crusade, I'll correct my mistake."

From behind his tinted glasses, Lt. Mori's strange eyes impaled me with their haughty glare, and like a peasant swept from the path of a *samurai*, I felt small and insignificant. Mother had advised me on dealing with men trained in the ancient tradition of the warrior. She warned, "*Samurai* are more touchy than other men on the most trivial of matters, your father and brothers included."

Mori tapped the script on the desk. "While we have a few minutes I want you to read the piece to me the way it was written."

I began, "We are 100,000,000 Asians tyrannized by 3,000 whites, yet every morning our brave pilots leave Imperial Navy carriers to do battle with an enemy who'd rather surrender than fight."

Lt. Mori brought both fists down on the desk. "Stop! What I've just heard was Kioko-san reading, not New Guinea Ginny. Your performance lacks emotion. You call yourself an actor?!"

In order to be polite, I averted my eyes and turned my lips down at the corners. He didn't speak for a while, but when he did, he shifted to a tone more wistful than brusque.

"Kioko-san, use your natural lilt. Bring the listener to the sentimental moment on board the carrier *Shoho* plowing through the Coral Sea to attack Port Moresby. Paint with words a picture of *Gyokusai*—men choosing to die heroically in battle rather than surrender."

I thought the sinking of the *Shoho*, with nearly three-quarters of her crew of 900 lost, was a wrongheaded example to set before our listeners, but I dared not say so. Only a soldier whose moods and dispositions had yielded to the vagaries of war could turn such a defeat into victory. While threat and fear made Lt. Mori unable to distinguish between the two, it was not a woman's place to tell him. My silent acquiescence fueled his enthusiasm. He spoke with even greater passion.

"Carry your listener to the moment the aircrews are aroused from their bunks and began donning their 1,000-stitch, good-luck belts. Let him see in his mind's eye how you, Kioko-san, and 999 other women each added a stitch, symbolically joining the men as they strapped on the *senninbari*, willing to sacrifice their lives for the Emperor. Close with a word snapshot of the pilots penning farewell letters bulging with ritual clips of hair and fingernails to be delivered to their families and lovers."

I took in a deep breath to disguise my anxiety. "Excuse me, sir. Taro said American torpedo bombers sank the *Shoho*."

"Your brother betrays Imperial secrets with such prattle. Ginny's listeners don't know what Taro knows, and we don't want to tell them either."

Lt. Mori hesitated again. He removed his tinted glasses and wiped at eyes scarred albino white around the edges. Never before had he revealed, in my presence at least, the wounds he suffered on the flight deck of the burning *Shoho*. Afterwards, he was ordered to command our small garrison in Angoram where other wounded awaited transport home, many never to see combat again. Able-bodied soldiers who did visit our compound came for sensual favors bestowed by young girls forced to provide such comforts.

Mori leaned toward me with scrunched up pink splotches for eyebrows. His lips parted almost in pain. "I hate Americans more than I love life," he said.

My heart sank. For the first time, I wanted to touch the wounds of this once proud and handsome *samurai* and tell him I understood. As a girl, I had stood hand-in-hand with my proud parents while my brothers, Taro and Jiro, each won the right to wear the two swords of the warrior—highest of the four classes into which the people of Japan were once divided. How hard it must be for one steeped in this tradition to run a combination rest camp, brothel and propaganda station so far removed from battle.

I was about to apologize to Lt. Mori when an old man we recognized as the gardener, Mr. Hanzo, leaned in the window. "I don't think I've seen one of those so low before," Hanzo said.

The officer and I rushed to the window to see what the gardener was pointing to. Across the sky came a single bomber, roaring in low and fast.

"*Ajapa!* Everybody get down, for heaven's sake," Lt. Mori bellowed, but instead he made a dash for the Imperial Portrait. I hesitated. The old man remained transfixed, so I leaped through the window and tackled the gardener to the ground. We both looked up and saw the aircraft bank steeply. Then a bomb fell away from it and soon after exploded near enough to unleash the force of 1,000 typhoons. The roof of the radio station collapsed. Part of it struck an adjacent infirmary.

My older brother Taro, a technician at the station, usually sat at the desk next to mine. But he had gone to the canteen in the infirmary to buy a bean-paste sweet. On his return, he heard the officer's warning and dove down the steps to the only below ground shelter in our building. Even so, Taro was abruptly blown some distance by the explosion. He wiped the soot from his eyes and staggered through the clouds of dust searching for me. Under one of the desks, Taro found the propaganda officer. Lt. Mori lay trapped beneath a roof support clutching the Imperial Portrait.

"Sergeant, this will have to serve as a ritual transfer. Take the portrait to a safe place, then come back with some stout lads to lift this plank off me."

"Have you seen my sister, sir?"

"Secure the Imperial Portrait first, then come back for her if you must. The American cowards never drop just one bomb. Now go before they come back, or land an invasion force."

I had stepped back into the building through the gaping hole where once there had been a window. Taro was startled to discover me standing directly above him as he knelt beside the propaganda officer.

"I'm all right, Taro. Do as Lt. Mori ordered. I'll tend to him while you go for help. Take the old gardener with you. He twisted his knee in our fall."

Lt. Mori nodded. "But take Kioko along, too. I don't need your sister clucking over me like riverbank folk panicked by the annual floods, which turn their theaters into sampans. Now's the time for the harsh discipline of *Bushido*."

"But we're so few in number and many of our comrades have unhealed wounds. How can we make a stand against an invasion force?" Taro asked.

"What about our radio equipment? Can we still use it to contact Wewak headquarters?"

Taro looked over to the rubble where our radio transmitter/receiver was located. "It looks like it has been smashed by the fallen roof, sir."

"Then we must gather the remnants of those who follow the warrior's code and leave for Wewak immediately. There, we'll regroup and return to repel the invaders." Lt. Mori paused for a moment hiding his injuries behind a face contorted in pain.

He shifted his upper body and spoke in the most sober and

solemn tone I had ever heard him use. It was as if he stood before a squadron of fliers rather than the two pitiful, dust-covered figures kneeling at his side.

"We're trained to fight to the death for our Emperor. This is the coin by which we purchase family honor and for ourselves salvation. Keep in mind, capture means you not only disgrace yourself, but your parents and family as well. Never will they be able to hold up their heads again. A soldier taken prisoner has erased his own existence. His name's stricken from the register of his village or town. Better he die than surrender. Why do you suppose we regard Americans as subhuman, worthy only of contempt and treatment as slaves? They'll surrender over a broken toenail rather than die nobly."

Lt. Mori paused again, and I thought he would faint. But from some reservoir unknown to me, he summoned the energy to continue.

"Go. First, find those who have survived the bombing. Then tell my brothers to start preparing the motor launches for our escape to Wewak up the Sepik River. We'll probably have to pull some rafts behind the boats to carry the fuel and supplies needed for the journey, especially if we have a large group of survivors to transport in the launches."

"How far do you plan to follow the Sepik to the west, sir? At some point, we'll have to be able to supply our troops as they travel by foot overland to Wewak on the north coast."

We'll make camp at Moim tonight. If we don't see any Japanese airplanes overhead or any of our patrol boats on the Sepik as we journey, we'll have to assume the worst. We'll proceed as far as Marui and then trek north from there on the Maprik Road. In case an enemy invasion force has overrun Wewak, we'll approach cautiously from the west until we know it's still in Japanese hands."

Finally Lt. Mori's lengthy address got the better of him. He fell back across the debris and closed his eyes. As I saw him there in the rubble, I realized how tall he was and how dark his hair remained for a man in his 30s. Taro had said Lt. Mori's skin was so smooth it was rumored he had never taken a razor to it.

Moments later, as Taro and I laid the gardener down beside a tree next to the infirmary where a medic was already tending to the wounded, my brother related how his sweet tooth had saved his life.

As we headed back with some hastily gathered natives towards the headquarters and radio station of our small community, the American bomber appeared overhead once again and dropped another bomb. This one struck the women's quarters two buildings east of the station. Splinters of bamboo shot throughout the compound like deadly missiles cutting down anyone caught in their path. Fortunately, our group had ducked behind the infirmary which was damaged but still standing after the first bomb attack.

After the plane disappeared into a cloud, Taro ordered the group of native rescuers to follow us into the radio station. As they proceeded to aid Lt. Mori, Taro went off to find a secure place for the Imperial Portrait and then to round up survivors as his superior had instructed.

After the natives freed Lt. Mori, he tried to hide his burns by rubbing his hands over his eyes. I had found his special glasses lying beside him intact and placed them in his hand. He did not thank me, but instead ambled off a few paces to test his legs. Before long Taro returned with some garrison soldiers.

"What was hit hardest?" he asked.

"The comfort girls' quarters, sir," Taro replied.

"The bulk of our combat soldiers were taking the first of their three night's bivouac there. Bring these soldiers you've rounded up, Taro, and let's get over there."

At first Lt. Mori refused to let me accompany the group, saying I would see devastation of all kinds to haunt my nightmares. But I persisted by offering my services to help any comfort girls who had survived the blast. Reluctantly, Lt. Mori gave me permission to go along.

We entered the women's quarters through dense clouds of dust. Every glass window had been shattered. The bomb blast had wholly or partially stripped the clothing away from all the bodies we encountered. Some girls wore only stockings from which slivers of glass protruded like daggers shot from a cannon. On a bed a soldier lay astride one of the comfort girls, his trousers barely clinging to legs, now bloody stumps. A remnant of the girl's dress mercifully covered her head crushed by a fallen roof support. Nothing could be done for either of them.

We moved through the debris listening for the low, persistent moaning which seemed to come from everywhere. Whenever we located bodies with any life in them at all, we called for a stretcher.

Most of the time it proved fruitless. The casualties were beyond first aid. When the supply of stretchers ran out, Lt. Mori ordered us to leave the girls and concentrate on the soldiers who had been caught in the brothel. But even here, there was little to do but carry the men outside where medics administered morphine to ease their passage through time to the handless clock of eternity. What madness drove men to war and such senseless slaughter?

The hours passed swiftly and our losses mounted. Lt. Mori and the other men stripped down to their loincloths to give them relief from the heat and humidity as they buried the dead in a mass grave. I noticed only the lieutenant and Taro wore the red cotton *mons*. Red undergarments helped ward off demons, according to *samurai* superstition.

By 6:00 p.m., shaken and exhausted, Lt. Mori posted the casualty list on a bamboo tree in the center of the compound. He had changed into army khaki half breeches gathered below the knee with cotton puttees extending to the ankle. He wore the *tabi* boot split at the toe and fastened at the heel for getting around in the jungle. Except for his dark blue, wool junior officer's cap with its distinctive naval insignia and the parade saber and scabbard which hung at his side, Lt. Mori might have passed for an ordinary army officer instead of a naval aviator.

Lt. Mori stood before a mound of equipment, parade flags and other personal items collected from the dead. One by one, seven able-bodied soldiers who had come to Angoram for rest and recuperation, including two who had been jailed for killing a fellow soldier in a fight over a comfort girl, filed by. Seven of our garrison soldiers, including Taro, followed them. They bowed to honor comrades either killed or too badly wounded to make the journey to Wewak. He instructed each of the 14 survivors to take a flag or other memento from the pile, or handed to them by a wounded comrade, so they would have something to give to their family back home.

He called the dead the "fallen 30," while he decreed the 20 wounded left behind, including 12 soldiers who represented more than half of our garrison force, "heroes of the Imperial Army."

"This duty carries a special stipulation," he said. "I've given every other man, save one, a pistol with two bullets. To avoid capture, those who have a pistol must kill one comrade, bury him, then turn the gun on oneself. One soldier, known only to me, will remain hidden until none of his comrades are left standing. He has orders to kill any coward who remains and would humiliate us all by surrendering. Once he has buried his last comrade, the lone survivor will find a natural grave and commit *seppuku*, knowing neither he nor any of his comrades bear the shame of leaving an exposed corpse behind like a common criminal."

Done with this grisly business, Lt. Mori turned away.

I called after him, "What about the comfort girls and other civilians, like the old gardener? Who will care for them?"

He whirled around. "Do any harlots yet live?"

"Two girls, a Korean and a Filipino. Sun-Hi and the one called Butterfly are injured, but can walk."

"Then I place them in your care, Kioko. Do what you would with them. But remember, if rations run short, their portion will come from your plate. If it were me, I'd kill them, or if they prefer, leave them to find pleasure in the arms of the Yankee dogs."

"And the gardener?"

"Go to him. Inquire whether his old legs can sustain him on the river trip and overland walk to Wewak. If not, leave him. He's a farmer by birth and became a calligraphy master in his youth. Now in his dotage, he contemplates an actor's life. You riverbank folk bring all but the warrior down in status."

I fumed at his use of ancient terminology no longer applicable. He knew theaters were built in areas other than run down waterfront districts. But Lt. Mori did not want, nor did he wait, for my answer.

"Oh, well. Since the warrior code doesn't apply to gardeners or actors, who cares if one more old fool dies in his sleep or is taken captive?"

"I care."

"Then take him on as your charge as well, but make it quick. Out of 65 fighters, we have only 15, including myself, remaining for the trip to Wewak. Only seven are battle-tested, transient soldiers now under my command, including the two who were jailed. The other seven come from our garrison force."

I sent Taro to fetch Sun-Hi and Butterfly while I went to the old gardener's hut. He was resting in a hammock and rose to greet me. His pink scalp gleamed under a twist of towel tied around his head, and but for the towel, a scanty white cotton loincloth and straw sandals, he was naked. He bowed, turned, and hurried into his hut as quickly as his sore knee would allow.

Moments later he reappeared dressed in a robe of sheer purple over white with a golden stole. Now it was my turn for embarrassment. No doubt this was his best theatrical costume, and there I stood like a peasant girl in short jacket and trousers.

"Kioko, please come in. I had given up hope you would stop by so I could properly thank you and your brother for saving my life when the bombs fell."

"Lt. Mori sent me. He wants to know if you will be going with us by motor launch on the Sepik, perhaps as far as the Maprik Road, and then overland to Wewak on the northern coast."

"Thank his Excellency for his kindness, but he'll have to find another calligraphy tutor in Wewak. I can only go as far as the gardens, and even such a short distance leaves me panting and wheezing like an old midwife instructing a woman in her care."

He bowed and led me inside his hut. At the door, I stepped out of my hot shoes and into the cool slippers he had laid out for me. We had barely seated ourselves on rice-straw mats before a table set for tea when his inquiries began. He spoke calmly as if the harrowing experience we had just been through had never happened, or had already been forgotten.

"Tell me about yourself, daughter. Where do you come from, what brought you here and where are you headed tomorrow and beyond? Fill these grandfather ears with tales of home, of your ancestors and the youth who take their places."

He listened politely as I began with my dynasty of a grandfather many generations past who was given a small inn for his loyal service as *samurai* to one of the Shogun's ministers. I related how Grandfather Tanaka had turned this Fifteenth Century fiefdom into a dynasty carried through to my father, the 20th Earl of Tanaka-ya.

"Our family inn sits below Satta Mountain where the Takaido Road bends close to Suraga Bay..."

"I know the area well, daughter. Many times as a youth I passed through this little paradise of yours on my way from Tokyo to Osaka. Doesn't Satta's peak stretch toward the bay like the prow of a ship about to set sail?"

"Yes. In the shadow of the mountain stands Tanaka-ya. You would have to wade through the bay to miss it."

The gardener nodded and bid me continue with my story.

I began anew, relating how shortly after my birth, when there was no Tanaka male heir to succeed my father, he adopted Taro, a farmer's son, and Jiro, from a merchant's family, as his successors. We were raised as sister and brothers just as if the same blood coursed through our veins. Taro reluctantly trained in the *samurai* ways. He preferred the harmony of life on the farm. On the other hand, Jiro took to his training so eagerly he kept pace with his older brother and the two of them graduated at the same ceremony. But Jiro, before he joined the air force and learned to fly, hired himself out as a bodyguard and troubleshooter for a rich merchant, displaying little interest in our humble inn.

The old man grinned, "In traditional times Jiro would've been branded a *ronin*—a masterless *samurai*, who abandons one allegiance for another. I'm sure your father was disappointed, knowing a family is responsible for the conduct of all its members."

The old gardener must have sensed I, too, had gone against my father's wishes and entered theater life as a dancer. His next question caught me off guard.

"Then how is it you've turned up in such an out-of-the-way place as Angoram? First answer this question, daughter. Then, if there's time, we will again take up the life of your brothers."

I told him how I was sent by my father to locate Taro and Jiro, whom we hadn't heard from in some time. My father agreed to give his blessing to an acting career if I would go to New Guinea as part of an entertainment troupe, which was bound for Rabaul where last we heard from Jiro.

The old gardener's lips curved into a smile. The few yellow teeth he still possessed were exposed. He seemed to sense my hesitation to go forward.

"I can keep your secret. Besides, after you've gone, I'll have no one to talk to."

Reluctantly, I proceeded to tell how I had set sail from Tokyo on a military supply ship, which carried wounded soldiers back to the front for limited duty, dependent upon their infirmities.

"On board I met Lt. Michio Mori..."

The old man interrupted. "Michio,'man with the strength of 3,000.' How well his name suits the commander of our meager band. But he'll need ten times the strength of 3,000 if he hopes to reach Wewak by taking such a circuitous route. I suppose he wishes to avoid a possible American invasion force. But on with your story, daughter."

It was hard to admit I had been tricked into diverting to Angoram where Lt. Mori told me my brother Taro had been posted.

"But, wasn't this true, daughter?"

"Yes, the part about Taro was true. But as soon as Lt. Mori learned I was fluent in English, he promised me if I would accompany him to Angoram, he would relieve Taro of his broadcast duties and allow the two of us to search for Jiro. But instead, once here, he told me if I did not do his propaganda broadcasts, he would have me sent from New Guinea and have Taro posted to one of the islands where he was sure to be killed by advancing U.S. Marines."

"Ah, so like the poor comfort girls, you have been pressed into a service which steals your dignity. Better for you to stay here and await the Americans. I'm sure the enemy will treat you better."

Neither of us had heard Lt. Mori until he was already inside the small hut. He rattled the sword that hung at his side. "What nonsense is this?"

The old man stood firm in the face of this threat. "We're only passing a few moments together, your Excellency. Nothing to chop off our heads about."

"Kioko! Your time is up! Leave the old fool. Can't you see he thinks the Americans will respect his age?"

Encouraged by the gardener's grit, I attempted some of my own. "I'll stay behind with him and see he's respected. You can leave Sun-Hi and Butterfly with us as well."

Lt. Mori laughed so loud it rattled the rafters. "The Americans will kill all of you, but only on you, Kioko, will they perform unspeakable tortures. Rape will not be enough for the woman whose voice has taunted them this past year. Whether you consent or not, you're coming with me. I cannot allow the daughter of one *samurai* and the sister of two others to fall into enemy hands."

The old man who had been silent bowed to Lt. Mori. "You are right, Excellency. Before this war, Americans never caused us any trouble, except to complain we closed the shutters at night before retiring. But if their grievance against Kioko is more severe than the closing of shutters, perhaps she is better off with you, her brother and your soldiers. But, begging your indulgence for a moment more, may I give this woman and her brother farewell gifts for saving my life when the bombs fell?"

Not waiting for an answer, the old man limped over to a rickety cabinet and removed what I recognized as a Japanese officer's leather map case. "Take this, Kioko," he said. "Inside are paints to make you even more beautiful when you dance. For Taro, there are calligraphy brushes, writing tablets and pencils. They're of great importance to a *samurai* in his continuing study of Confucian ethics."

Here the old man paused and looked straight at Lt. Mori. "His Excellency can vouchsafe my claim regarding the importance of calligraphy."

"And what can my brother and I give you in parting?"

The gardener bowed. "Perhaps one of you will return to Angoram to dance for me, or bring me a poem after the war."

Lt. Mori rattled his saber again. "Why would you want to lug that stuff around? Throw it back in this old fool's face. I assure you, none of my men will help you carry it, Kioko. Our hands will be full with the bare essentials."

I slung the map case over my shoulder as Lt. Mori took my arm and led me from the hut. I blew the old man a kiss, never expecting to set eyes on him or Angoram again.

On the riverbank of the Sepik, I began to feel the horror of the day's events. I was oblivious to the soldiers who came in line behind me to board the two motor launches until a commotion brought them into full view. They brought before me a young native woman whom I recognized as the gardener's housekeeper. She pleaded for my protection, and once I stepped out of line, she handed me a note from her master.

> Kioko, Lt. Mori has ordered the wounded soldiers he has left behind to burn the village after your party has gone and is out of sight. The natives won't understand the scorched earth policy to deny Angoram's resources to the American invaders. The warriors will kill those Japanese responsible, if they haven't committed "seppuku" first. I believe the natives will continue to trust me because I am not a soldier, but an elderly gardener. As one who shares their fate, I shall survive. But please, do not come back to Angoram whatever you do! Yours truly, Hanzo.

171

18 NATIVE WAR PREPARATIONS

Mount Bosavi, Papua New Guinea, 1973

A MIST FELL in the clearing about the same time Major Yowell, fighting a crosswind, centered the nose of the small aircraft over the narrow runway on Mount Bosavi. Stanek was impressed. Maneuvering the Army Beaver over water and finding a makeshift airstrip on a slope 2,000 feet up on a mountain covered in vegetation required special skill. He was about to admit as much, but fearing more banality from the pilot, he said nothing.

Yowell shut down the engine and opened the air vent. "Well, would you look at that? They've rolled out the welcome wagon. Got our Mayday all right. The boss lady turned out to greet us as usual, but she's looking mighty concerned this time 'round."

Stanek followed the major's gaze, but all he could see were bodies, dark and naked, mostly women and children, pouring out of the grass along the riverbank. Despite the efforts of black males armed with rifles to keep them back, the horde encircled the aircraft.

"Give *Kiap* Noble and his boys a minute or two to clear a path for us. Might as well sit back and enjoy the scenery, Doc. You've entered the free-swinging zone. Bra-less as far as the eye can see, except for DeAnn, of course."

At this point a white woman appeared on Yowell's side of the aircraft. Under her arm she carried tablets or a book wrapped in cellophane. She shouted through the open vent, "Glad you made it safely, Frank. What's this about being shot at?"

"Must've been poachers after crocodile skins. We scared them more than they did us. Far as I can see, not any major damage to the aircraft. Still, I want to check the aircraft and make a quick turn around as soon as I drop my passenger off. A storm followed us in, and I'm hankering to head out of here for Goroka before it hits."

The woman held up the package. "Shucks. I've brought you something beautiful and poetic."

"Yourself?"

"Better."

"What could be better?"

"A love story."

"You're kidding."

"Stick around and read it with me. You'll see."

"I would, sweetheart, except duty calls. General Bellicosi wants me in Goroka tonight. He's lined up a reporter for me to fly in. If it were up to me, I'd like nothing better than to have you model your new fatigues, then afterward join you in a spot of tea while you read love passages to me."

Stanek felt forgotten. He stroked his beard two or three times. "The man is incorrigible." He quickly amended the thought. Yowell was like Catherine, only, instead of ovaries, he marched wherever his gonads led him. Obviously, DeAnn Toland, judging from her banter, followed the same drumbeat. If they weren't serious about this case, why should he make haste to solve it?

He answered himself. The sooner he wrapped up matters involving survivors, atrocities and identification of bomber crew remains, the earlier he could get on with his beekeeper cancer study. Furthermore, what if Yowell was right about the shots fired at the aircraft over the Rentoul being the work of poachers. If the B-24 case did no more than keep Stanek temporarily out of the reach of would-be assassins, it was worth postponement of his research. Not so coincidentally, New Guinea was half a world away from Catherine Stanek.

The thought he had once more thwarted his adoptive sister forced the crescent-shaped scar on the right side of his face to retreat in the folds of a smile. He turned towards Yowell. "Major I'm anxious to get started. I've only scheduled a week or so on this project."

A crack of thunder sounded in the distance. "I'm as anxious as you are, Doc. It looks like Noble's cleared a path through the heathen. Here, I'll get the door open for you."

Before he dismounted, Stanek stood for a moment on the Beaver's one rung ladder and surveyed the grassy spur serving as a tarmac. Off against the western slope of a flat ridge on Mount Bosavi, a large section of the ill-fated B-24's twin tail assembly pointed to the threatening sky like a totem pole. A floodlight fastened to the top of the tail cast an eerie shadow on a grinning white skull and crossed bombs insignia painted on the right vertical stabilizer.

From his reading of pilot Sanchez's log, augmented by the Air Force briefings at Port Moresby, Stanek recognized the Jolly Rogers' symbol denoting an aircraft assigned to the 90th Bombardment Group. He noted the distinct tail pattern. Just as Lt. Sanchez had described it, the white skull and crossed bombs were set against a black background designating the aircraft as belonging to the 400th Squadron, nicknamed "The Black Pirates."

The Port Moresby briefer had specifically mentioned the 90th's heavy bombers descended on the Japanese forces in the Pacific like "marauding pirates," establishing for themselves the best bombing record in theater. The briefer had added, "Unfortunately, since the Jolly Rogers fought virtually the whole Japanese Air Force, their losses were heavy as well."

As Yowell began tossing bags out the hatch, the pathologist moved to the front of the Beaver for a better view of the wreckage. Five or six yards from the bomber's single tail section lay the rest of the Liberator's fuselage reduced to a crumpled heap of rusting metal overgrown with reeds, vines and *kunai* grass. Stanek fumbled in his backpack for a pair of binoculars.

He scanned the wreckage. Intrigued by a humming sound coming from behind the bomber, he sought its source. Without visual confirmation, Stanek decided the unusual noise came from a portable generator. After a few moments, he turned to the woman who had come around the aircraft to greet him.

"I assume lights strung along the wreckage are for night recovery operations?"

"Oh, no, we keep the lights powered around the clock. The corridor we have to work in is too dark otherwise."

"And the floodlight atop the tail?"

"Other than a beacon for Major Yowell's aircraft, the searchlight's there to keep superstitious natives at bay."

"Really? And how does it keep them away?"

"Something about the skull and crossed bombs insignia painted on the tail frightens them."

"Well, in due time we'll have to find out why these primitives stand in awe of this particular part of the wreckage. Also worth exploring is whether they connect the emblem on the B-24 tail fin with its identical mate, presumed lost."

Stanek passed over the woman's attempt to speak and pressed on. "Before I hear any more, I'll want to inspect the wreckage close-up."

He could see by the way she retreated toward Yowell, who now stood by her side, he had caught both of them off guard. Business came first as far as Stanek was concerned. Introductions could wait. Yowell obviously disagreed. The major stepped between Stanek and the woman dressed from head to foot in a predominantly civilian version of faded green army fatigues. He gave an exaggerated bow and announced, "Dr. Toland, meet Dr. Stanek, a man of so few words, he's even chintzy with his first name."

"Emerson."

"Well then, my dear Emerson. Meet DeAnn. You don't have to be a doctor to see she's a woman whose beauty of mind and body is in full flower. Don't like leaving you two alone, except I know her character's above reproach."

She looked down at her canvas boots, and Stanek recognized her attempt to conceal her embarrassment. She turned slowly and stood quietly for a moment looking up at him. When she spoke, her voice trembled. "D-Doctor, there's a storm brewing, and we should find shelter. Wouldn't you like to meet the rest of the team and get settled in your tent before we get down to business?"

Stanek felt a sudden chill of dread, wondering if it showed. He stood transfixed, drawn by an unaccustomed alertness to this woman's slightest movement. She tilted her head, framed by auburn hair. The imploring look in her eyes, predominately brown but with flecks of yellow like a goldenwave, captured his attention.

The woman, like the flower, had an iridescent and translucent rush about her. Her beauty sprang from a radiant depth, both strong and vulnerable, which he had sensed only one time before.

175

Yowell had been right in comparing her to a flower in bloom. Indeed, DeAnn Toland exuded the same innocent wholesomeness, yet strange elixir, which had drawn him to Catherine in their youth. In the second before he answered, he cleared his mind of all these thoughts.

"Dr. Toland, I'm not asking you to arrange a tea party for me, only a few minutes at the crash site."

She stepped around Yowell and squared off to face him. "Whoever gave you the impression we're s-slackers, d-doctor, was wrong."

"Good. After a quick on site overview, perhaps then you can tell me what happened to the other part of the twin tail—more precisely, the left vertical stabilizer. Surely you've searched the whole mountain for it." He looked directly into her face for a reaction.

She avoided his eyes and glanced over at the major. "Frank will tell you. We aren't allowed to venture beyond a native salt well further up the mountain."

"Why not?"

"Everything above the s-salt well is off limits to us—t-tribal holy ground. In other words, t-taboo to whites."

"Really? I was assured you were Bosavi's boss lady."

This time her pale cheeks blushed crimson under her floppy hat while her dark eyes, streaked with those flecks of yellow, scorched Yowell.

She turned on Stanek. "It's not a matter of control, D-Doctor Stanek. Feuds come easily in this part of New Guinea. Every single object is staked out and jealously d-defended. Each inch of this territory belongs to someone. You're standing on an invisible 'no trespassing' sign right now. If we don't abide by the native's rules, then we're not welcome here."

"My mistake. I thought we all worked for the Pentagon," Stanek replied.

"Not the natives. They're three years away from independence, and very sensitive about whether the white man will keep his promises. If you want to take this up with General Bellicosi, then do so. I'm sure Frank would like your company on his trip to Goroka. Otherwise, you can stay, and we can go over our findings at our camp. Under the circumstances, I think you'll find we've done a pretty thorough job. What's it going to b-be?"

Yowell spoke up before Stanek could answer. "I'm out of here. I'll be back in a day or two with General Bee. He's the guy to referee such matters. You surprise me, though, Emerson. You're a lot sharper than I thought. Many of my brother pilots don't even know the B-24 had twin vertical stabilizers, but DeAnn does."

Stanek called after the retreating pilot. "Don't forget the high Davis wing, making the B-24 a 'bitch to ditch'." He then turned to Toland. "Get me over to the crash site. I'll take it from there."

Even though the constables had cleared a path, pushing back a sea of outstretched hands, it took Stanek and Toland about ten minutes to reach the B-24. He paused at the rope perimeter, removed his bush hat, and began wiping sweat from his brow. In that instant the beam of the circling floodlight mounted on the bomber's tail swept over his shaven head. In the reflected light from his head, native women and children, who had dared go as far as the rope barrier, backed off cautiously, then broke into full retreat.

Under the bomber's wing, two white men and four native constables greeted them. All were armed. Dr. Toland hurried through introductions. Stanek was only able to catch the first name of the Central Identification Laboratories' linguistic specialist—a young man named Erik, although he asked the woman to repeat the patrol officer's last name.

"Noble," she said.

"Ah, yes, the *kiap*. You discovered the B-24 bomber while you and your team searched the area for a downed airliner a year ago, right?"

Noble drew in a deep breath followed by a wheeze. It shook the patrol officer's short, stocky frame all the way to the belt line of his khaki mufti. "Sorry, mate, I've got a bit of a *blow-in-the-bag*. Asthma I'm told. Maybe you'd best start with Erik."

Stanek was tempted to object, but changed his mind and began grilling the interpreter. Had any natives ever spoken about seeing whites other than CIL personnel come in or out of the wreckage? Erik didn't know of any, nor did he know whether any natives had ventured inside. Had he asked them? No, he had not. Did the natives report seeing any other parts of the airplane—say on top of the mountain? No, but the Riami reported a *balus*, as they call it, further down the Rentoul River. Was the plane small or large? It seemed large to them. How many engines did the plane have? They didn't know. How far away from the bomber is this other wreckage? For natives, two days' walk, one by canoe. For whites, four days walk or two by canoe.

Stanek paused and stroked the scar on his cheek. "One more question, young man."

"You can call me Erik, sir."

"Well, Erik, I may lean on your linguistic expertise later, but for now can you tell me if any of the natives have seen any human bones, expended rounds of ammunition or anything else pertaining to whites at either crash site?"

"We've offered gold-lipped shells, a prize in these parts, to any native who brings us the kinds of items you described."

"And has the bounty system worked?"

"Two natives brought us emergency equipment and the inflatable dinghy from the B-24 recently, but none others have come forward yet."

"Really!"

The *kiap* broke in. "There's a storm afoot. If we want to beat it, we'd best get humpin' up the trail. Shall I go through?"

Stanek pulled at his goatee. "Hold on a moment. I've two more questions. Both are for you, *Kiap* Noble."

"Okay, but don't expect a lot of *yabber* from me."

"Is the wreckage, as it sits now, the way you found it last spring?"

"For the most part."

"Nothing's been removed?"

Noble glanced at Toland. Stanek saw her shake her head before she answered for the patrol officer. "I'm in charge there. *Kiap* Noble is here to provide security and represent the Australian government."

Stanek ignored her. He pressed the issue with Noble. "Let's say nothing's been removed. Then when I look inside the bomber, I should find the same evidence that led your government to consider this a crime scene, right?"

Noble again looked at the woman for guidance. Once more she answered for him demanding, "Who misled you with such information?"

"Why you, Dr. Toland, in your cover letter to General Bellicosi. I quote, 'Australian authorities suspect foul play.' It triggered the *raison d'être* for a forensic pathologist to enter this case, or have you forgotten?"

This time the *kiap* came to the woman's aid. He twisted the edges of his turned-up mustache as he spoke. "No need to *throw a wobbly*, lad. Ye can knock my government, Erik or me. But nobody on this site will stand by whilst ye criticize she who embodies the spirit of this operation."

Stanek refused to yield. "My charter is different than yours. I must first determine if there were survivors, next whether they engaged in atrocities, or were merely victims. Finally, my job is to assist the CIL in identification of remains. My questions may sound critical, but I assure you this is only because Dr. Toland's first priority, identification, is last on my list.

"Understood, mate," the *kiap* said. "Now I'll go through, and the rest of ye come after." He excused himself and left with the interpreter to answer a summons from one of the constables guarding the rope line.

"We have their logs. How can anyone d-doubt there were survivors?" DeAnn asked.

"The one you sent Dr. Haveland was a forgery."

"You d-deny it was found with crew remains?"

"No, but I'm skeptical about the authenticity of the author. If the pilot went down with his aircraft, there's no way he, or any others on board at the time of impact, could've survived such a crash."

"You deduced as much without even visiting the site?"

"The photos in your packet led me to suspect a forgery, but now I've gotten confirmation."

"B-but we have other journals and native accounts."

"I've only seen one—the pilot's. And didn't your interpreter just say natives report no whites entering or exiting the aircraft?"

"Erik said he hadn't asked them."

"You're right Dr. Toland. But here's the deal. I'll postpone my on-site inspection in exchange for inquiries among the natives at a later date. Give me Erik for a few days, and together we'll get to the bottom of the questions I've raised."

She nodded. "I'll match your cooperation. Tonight, I'll have all the evidence we've cataloged so far d-delivered to your tent."

Stanek reached down to pick up his bags.

"L-leave them. Just bring your backpack. I've brought two boys along to carry the rest of your equipment. We've got a lot of rough terrain ahead, and we'd better cross the Rentoul before the bridge is underwater."

The Australian patrol officer and the interpreter stood at the rope perimeter. Both appeared extremely agitated. The Aussie drew the party of whites aside, addressing his remarks to Dr. Toland.

"I've gotten a report the bloody Riami and Tugaru are *having a blue*. Both tribes are armed to the teeth, itching for a fight."

"Is it about the murdered Tugaru youth?" she asked.

The Aussie pointed at Stanek, "No, it's about him."

"Me?" Stanek threw up his hands in disbelief.

19 COVERT COALITION CONTEMPLATED

Goroka, Papua New Guinea, 1973

JAMES COLE LEANED against an army jeep parked near a coffee shed at the margin of the Goroka airstrip. It was half past 12. Brigadier General Anthony Bellicosi had not yet emerged from the District office where he had gone to receive a call shortly after their aircraft had touched down at noon. Exhausted, Cole rocked forward on his crutches, wishing he had accepted the wheelchair offered by the airline.

Above his head he heard a soft hum. It was a single bee. Cole whispered, "If you've come to bite me or lead me to your honey, you've got the wrong bloke on both counts. They've pumped me full of chemicals to kill the cancer. Can you imagine what a lethal morsel I'd make? As for the honey, it's more Dr. Stanek's bailiwick. You'll find him in the Southern Highlands, not the Eastern."

The reporter chuckled. With so much left undone, conversing with insects was about as useful as an ashtray on a motorbike, he thought.

Cole leaned back and surveyed Goroka, trying to get a fix on how the settlement had changed since his father's and his own earlier stays in the Eastern Highlands District. Sure to be his last visit to the area, he wondered what significance it held for his current quest. The best he could hope to uncover from the once dusty trails of the pre-war settlement, now marked out in neat streets for its inhabitants, was some evidence one or more of the B-24 survivors had made it as far as the edge of civilization.

Cheered by this prospect, Cole continued his survey of Goroka. Along the streets on the suburban squares of lawn encircling the airstrip, bungalows rose up like box statues. The buildings put him in mind of his own family homestead in Adelaide. He remembered the day his father had left Australia for New Guinea during the war to help plan the airstrip at Goroka, which was the brainchild of American Army engineer, Colonel L.J. Sverdrup. Cole wondered if the colonel still lived. He wondered too, if he had enough time before his own death to look up Colonel Sverdrup and tell him how his brainchild had developed into one of the busiest airports in New Guinea, shipping passion fruit and, more recently, coffee throughout the world.

Cole was about to make a mental note to enlist General Bellicosi's help in tracking down the colonel when a white cockatoo called from a nearby patch of scrub. Another bird's cry followed, but this time it was a hornbill. Then a distressing sound came from a bird-of-paradise. It fell at the reporter's feet with a small arrow in its side.

In the next instant, several native youths dressed in semi-European clothes emerged from the bushes. A brawl settled sole rights to the feathers of the fallen bird. Were these lads aware of the impediments Papuan independence, promised by the white man, would bring to them, Cole wondered. In centers of civilization like Goroka, backward people had to adapt to white man's rules or stay in the bush.

Cole began to admonish the miscreants in pidgin when a jeep pulled up alongside of his and sent them scurrying. General Bellicosi was not on board. The single occupant was an Australian patrol officer who spoke to Cole's driver, turned and saluted the reporter. He handed Cole a note written on the flag officer's stationery.

```
Jim,
    Excuse the delay. I'm up to my armpits getting
things  set  up  for  the  arrival  of  another  VIP,
who'll  be  joining  us  on  Major  Yowell's  flight  to
Mount  Bosavi  tomorrow.  Meantime,  you  should  use
this  dead  time  to  rest  up.  You  really  looked  drawn
on  the  flight  across  the  big  pond  to  Port  Moresby
and  again  into  Goroka.  There's  a  doctor  on  call  at
the   Goroka   Lodge   should   you   desire   a   more
professional   opinion.   If   you   were   one   of   my
```

soldiers, I'd put you on immediate bed rest. I've
ordered an early dinner sent to your room for each
of us. I'll join you then, and we'll have time to
talk.
    Tony B.

In the late afternoon, as soon as the dinner table had been cleared, General Bellicosi stood and lit a cigar. Amidst a swirl of smoke, he crossed the narrow room and stopped before a doorway.

"Fresh air will fix you up, Jim. Grab your crutches and join me on the verandah. I've been in monasteries with more space and a helluva lot less musty. But for now, these are the best accommodations New Guinea has to offer. Neither is it suited for our next guest, due into Goroka before nightfall."

Cole waited. Other than in his note, Bellicosi had not referred to the person who would be joining them on the flight to Mount Bosavi.

"I suppose your other so-called VIP prefers anonymity. Must be a member of Congress on a junket," Cole said.

Bellicosi chuckled. "No, just a private citizen like you—secretive, but with a keen interest for getting to the bottom of this B-24 business as soon as possible. You know, in 'simpatico' with our mission."

"Remember, you promised me an exclusive on this story."

"I brought you here to New Guinea, didn't I? Rest assured, Jim, I intend to keep my promise. I certainly appreciate your help in getting Stanek on board. Without the personal risk you took in Hawaii, we'd still be looking for a pathologist."

"Then you know what happened?"

"Every detail."

"Through the spies you had tailing Dr. Stanek?"

"Those and other sources."

"Stanek believes the attack on him was related to Dr. Haveland's murder at Johns Hopkins. Then, if your men were tailing Stanek, they must've crossed paths with his and Haveland's assailants as well."

"Whenever my sources deemed information pertinent to the two attacks you mentioned, they shared it with the Baltimore Police Department. I suggest you direct any further queries to Detective

Lt. Sam Dunbar. He's running the investigation. But I don't see where any of this affects Operation Simpatico."

"Don't you think Dr. Stanek would like to know who almost dissected him back in Hawaii?"

Even before Bellicosi had nearly bitten his cigar in half, Cole knew he had pressed too far. The general snuffed the cigar out between his thumb and forefingers and threw it over the rail of the verandah.

"It's been a long day, my dear Cole. We're apt to get sidetracked. Fatigue often affects a man this way. But let me leave you with this thought on Dr. Stanek. He's an intellectual ostrich who's got his head up his ass on matters unrelated to science. No 'knight in shining armor', I'll tell you. What business is it of ours if there're people in his past gunning for him for stepping on their toes, or worse. It's not for me to spread rumors, but you'd be horrified to hear one of the allegations made against him by a member of his own family."

"If he's so awful, why bring him into your project?"

"Because we need his skills and, to a greater extent, the credibility he brings to the table during the identification process. No congressman will lock horns with the findings of a forensic pathologist. After he's done his job, who cares what he does, or who he does it to."

"But Stanek thinks he's here to solve a crime—his real expertise."

"Not on your life, Jim, old boy! We don't have time for that shit. Besides, what kind of fool would I be to send one alleged felon after other criminals? Who'd believe him under those circumstances? He's here to certify identifications before we run out of money, or Nixon's impeached, whatever comes first."

"What happens to his cancer study?"

"We'll keep our promise there. If Stanek gets the B-24 crew remains identified in a timely matter, and to my satisfaction, we'll give him a week to chase bees around New Guinea on our nickel."

"I believe he expects more."

"Don't we all. You want your exclusive and more strength, but you may have to give up one to get the other. Tradeoffs—it's life in a nutshell. You've got some time in the morning before our flight to Mount Bosavi leaves. The driver will take you in the army jeep to look around Goroka if you like. It should be like old home week for an old New Guinea hand like you."

After the general left, Cole stood for a long moment at the rail. The wind from the night came down from the mountains and whistled through the thin needles of the trees, shaking the frailest ones to the ground. He was reminded of the fallen bird-of-paradise, crying out against the darkness with its last breath as it fell at his feet. Cole wondered. Did death come to man in the same manner?

Summoning his last reserves of strength, he forced his inner debate away from death toward other matters requiring resolution. He must forge an alliance with Dr. Stanek. The pathologist, like himself, whatever his other faults, wanted to get at the truth surrounding the B-24 mystery. General Bellicosi would not tolerate any such coalition, since he did not control it. Cole knew he and Stanek must move with caution and stealth, like 'mushrooms growing in the dark', in order to avoid detection of their alliance by General Bellicosi. Everything could be laid face-up at the end.

Bellicosi had already dropped one of his cards with the comment to him about his stay in Goroka being old home week. So, the general knew. The question remained, how much did he know?

20 PASSIONATE PLEA IN A DOWNPOUR

Mount Bosavi, Papua New Guinea, 1973

STANEK FLUNG THE KNAPSACK over his shoulder, set his bush hat square on his head and addressed Noble. "Mind telling me what there is about my appearance to cause such a ruckus? The women and children have fled from the B-24 site, when only a moment ago they were jubilant. And now you tell me warriors have taken up arms."

"Ye best leave an explanation for a more appropriate time," the *kiap* replied. "Right now there's another type of storm kicking up her heels and headed our way."

DeAnn Toland inclined her head. "Roger's right. Once the rain comes down, the vine bridge you'll have to cross over the Rentoul River will be under water."

"So much for the scenic tour," he mumbled to himself. He wanted to press the point on why his presence had stirred things up among the natives, since as a forensic pathologist, he knew every event and nuance was germane, especially during a criminal investigation. Ideas, assumptions and superstitions which made no sense still had to be followed up.

The *kiap*, interpreter and two armed constables took the lead. Stanek fell in step behind DeAnn Toland. She led him down a well-used track where the Rentoul River, running beside the airstrip, narrowed to a big stream, already swollen even before the rain fell. Toland halted beside a vine suspension bridge anchored to trees on each side of the runnel. She gestured, indicating she should cross

186

first. Unsure the bridge could carry his weight, he waved her on and proceeded to inspect the crude structure. He saw the vines tied to the handrails and matted footway were held together with cord ropes resembling parachute shrouds. So far, so good.

By the time his boot touched the footway, he saw the bridge was little more than a tightrope. From across the bridge, Toland, who had been joined by two native constables on the far bank, called, "We'll hold it steady on this end. The constables with you will keep it from wavering on your side."

How had she gotten across so fast, he wondered, as he eased his 175 pounds onto the bridge? It creaked and groaned with each step he took. To make matters worse, the noise of Yowell's aircraft lifting off behind him startled a great number of parrots and other birds, which screeched and took wing from the trees. Then lightning cracked high up on the mountain, and when the thunder rolled down on him, he froze in his tracks.

"Come on," Toland urged. "Major Yowell outweighs you by ten or more pounds, and he's made it across many times. Hurry! It won't be long before the rain begins. Can't you see the river's already running faster?"

Stanek looked down at the surging water weaving in and out of jagged stones. Since he was now at the midway point, he had two choices, backtrack or plunge ahead on the bridge, which swayed violently despite the efforts of his cohorts to steady it from both banks. Several times he fell through the matting to his hips, saved only by vines and parachute cord caught between his legs. One strand caught him across the chest and set his knife wound bleeding.

"You've got to get your weight in the middle and lean forward for balance. It also works better if you carry your knapsack in front of you, so it doesn't catch on the upper vines."

He followed Toland's shouted instructions. After 30 feet or so, he collapsed on the other side out of breath. Sweat poured down into his eyes under the rim of his bush hat. Splotches of perspiration formed at the edge of his short sleeves, along his knee-length trousers and began to show through his jacket. Worst of all was the tightening sensation in his legs. He immediately recognized it as cramps, and grabbed both calves, beginning to knead at the pain.

"Here, let me help you," Toland said as she lifted his right leg and with surprising strength bent his toes back.

She spoke without a trace of panic, "Now you can see why General Bellicosi prefers the flat plains down at Nomad or the Goroka highlands. When he's here, he never ventures beyond the crash site or airstrip. Just think, when Major Yowell returns with the general, you've got to do this again, over and back." She smiled, and he interpreted it as a tease.

"Expect to see me at the wreckage site early tomorrow," he retorted.

She gave the same smile with a twinkle in her eyes. "We'll see."

As the pain subsided, he remarked in his own sly way, "Glad I wasn't wearing a suit of armor while crossing the bridge." He looked in her brown eyes for any kind of reaction. She gave no particular shift in demeanor save a quiescence matching the gentle way she lowered his leg to the *kunai* grass, and started administering to the other cramp.

"Any more high-wire crossings like this ahead?" he asked.

"No, but we've got two native villages to go through and two tiers of mountain to climb before we reach the CIL encampment."

"Why so far from the wreckage site?" he asked.

She hesitated. "Two good reasons."

"And they are?"

"One, if you read my report, you know the Tugaru are the dominant tribe in this area. They decided on the spot for our camp. Here, you can see for yourself." She paused from the kneading and handed him a waterproofed sketch of the area. "Where visitors stay on their land is up to the Tugaru. Otherwise, an uninvited intrusion is an invasion."

He interrupted, "Couldn't you work out a better deal so you wouldn't have to haul everything up the side of a mountain? Hardly seems an efficient way to conduct recovery operations."

She worked on the cramp in silence for a while, then she replied, "By forcing us to a higher elevation, the Papuans actually did us a favor. We're 1,000 feet or more above the mosquito zone, so there's less chance of contacting malaria, the biggest killer around here. There, the kneading should hold you for awhile. If you're feeling better, we really should get started, unless you want me to dress your chest injury. It looks like it's bleeding."

He touched his chest. "No, thanks, it's already bandaged."

188

As they neared the crest of a plateau, the Australian patrol officer who had gone ahead to scout the area signaled for them to halt.

"I don't think the Tugaru intend to let us pass," Noble said.

Stanek thought this was the right time to raise the question on his mind since they had left the B-24 wreckage. "Now, do you mind telling what I've done to cause this ruckus?"

Noble answered. "It started with the Tugaru. Those bloody buggers said the mountain spirits told 'em a white man with powerful magic was comin' in with the storm. This white sorcerer was goin' to align himself with their enemies—the river people—so together they could capture the salt well and drive the Tugaru off the mountain."

"Such superstitious nonsense," said Dr. Toland. "We've been here six weeks and nothing bad has happened to them yet, except the slain Tugaru boy hidden in their burial site."

"What I want to know is how they knew I was arriving today?" Stanek asked.

"Yes, Dr. Stanek has raised a good question, Roger. Any ideas?"

Noble twirled the ends of his red mustache before he answered. "Word travels fast among these people, as ye know, DeAnn. Superstitious talk is their way of life. Anyway, the Riami like the idea, since Dr. Stanek is supposed to be on their side. They're all decked out in their Sunday best, includin' ceremonial axes, to welcome him with a *singsing* like they did for ye. Of course, this made the Tugaru madder, so they armed themselves as well."

"I see," said Toland.

"Look, here. I don't know a Riami from a ravioli," said Stanek. "Somebody's got to get these people under control. You have the guns. It ought to be easy."

"They're 300 against 24 of us, including our carriers and police boys, many of whom are related to one tribe or the other. Unless we want a mutiny, we'll have to find a better solution," she said.

The woman huddled with the Australian *kiap* and the interpreter, leaving Stanek alone with the four native policemen who eyed him suspiciously. After a few moments, Dr. Toland rejoined Stanek and briefed him on her plan to avoid trouble with the natives.

She told him they probably could proceed safely through the Riami settlement, first in their path to the CIL camp, as it was unlikely these river nomads would attack her or him if they viewed Stanek as an ally. Once on the outskirts of the last Riami hut, they would stop, assess the threat from the Tugaru encampment located above the river people and proceed accordingly. By then, the storm probably would have dispersed the Tugaru and sent them scurrying for their shelters. If not, her party would be in position to signal the rest of their comrades—five white assistants and 12 native carriers—to clear a line through to the CIL encampment, only a few minutes walk up from the last Tugaru compound.

"What about the two natives you left with my equipment down on the airstrip?" Stanek asked.

The woman smiled. "One's a Riami, and the other is a Tugaru. They'll be able to talk their way out of any scrape." She added, "The best piece of advice I can offer you is never go anywhere around here without an interpreter and escort from each tribe."

"I wonder if the same rule applied to your B-24 survivors. How do you suppose they made it on their own out here?"

"Maybe they learned to coexist with primitive peoples."

"Anything's possible, but probability is a different matter altogether," he said.

They filed past a grove of casuarina trees with the patrol officer and two rifle bearing natives in the lead, followed by Dr. Toland, then Stanek. Behind the pathologist came the CIL specialist and two more native constables who formed a rear guard. As the party neared the point where they heard the loudest singing, Stanek had the feeling they were being watched. He leaned forward, tense with excitement, and tapped Dr. Toland on the shoulder. When she turned, he pointed to the top of a large casuarina tree beside the trail.

She nodded and whispered, "It's a Tugaru watchtower. Pay the sentry no mind. He's there to announce our arrival."

The words had barely escaped her lips when the naked warrior in the tree let fly a series of yodels. Stanek heard answering calls from further up the trail and after three or four of these yodels, the singing ahead abruptly stopped. Except for the birds and the rain, which had started to fall, the forest fell silent.

As they emerged from the tree line, Noble raised his rifle horizontally over his head, and the column stopped. Following a brief exchange with Dr. Toland, the stocky *kiap* with his two boys in tow resumed the march at a quickened pace until they halted again on the upper plateau of an elliptical mound. Stanek moved close to the woman whose eyes were glued on the trio up ahead. The *kiap* questioned a warrior who had come forward to greet them. Seeing no signs of panic in her eyes, Stanek said nothing. Instead, he looked at the diagram she had given him earlier.

The sketch of the area was well drawn, he thought. The airstrip was clearly marked and ran along the bottom of the map in an east-west direction. At the western end of the runway, a large "X" marked the B-24 crash site. Next to it were two smaller "X's" indicating burial grounds. He was about to ask Dr. Toland whether she had positively identified any crewmember's remains from the graves when Noble returned with his two constables in tow.

The Aussie's ruddy features were drenched in sweat, while his two dark-skinned assistants showed no signs of exertion. Stanek inched close enough to eavesdrop on Noble's report directed to Dr. Toland. After the Tugaru yodeling stopped, the warrior had said the Riami *meries* and their children fled the *singsing* grounds.

DeAnn Toland agreed the absence of women and children usually meant the men were gearing up for a fight. She asked Noble if he had seen any encouraging signs. He replied the one Riami warrior, he pointed to the solitary figure waiting on the mound, had broken ranks to greet them.

Noble rolled his large green eyes in the direction of the man. "It's the chap, MilkEye. He's back from the salt train trip to Nomad where he tried to get medicine from the missionaries for his sick child. Evidently, whatever they gave him for his daughter has worn off. He fears she's near death. MilkEye said the storm sweepin' down the mountain from the Tugaru settlement was the mountain spirit comin' for his daughter, and he wanted to know if we could help."

"What about the rest of the Riami?"

"MilkEye says they've gone indoors. Afraid they'll ruin their fancy dress in the approachin' storm, or get caught between a vengeful spirit and his quarry. He claims our problem is the Tugaru. They show no sign of relentin' and are paradin' about in the rain as big as ye please."

"The Tugaru might yet provoke a confrontation with the Riami, Roger. We'll have to delay our original plan and stand pat here until somebody budges, even if it means getting soaked ourselves."

Toland then turned to Stanek. "I don't suppose you have any rain gear in your kit?"

"No. It's back there with my other things."

"Well, I've got a shelter-half we can share. But you're taller than I am. I don't know how we're going to manage this."

"I can hold it over both of us, since I take it we're not going to be moving," he said.

She turned back to Noble and directed the Australian to return to the mound and signal whenever it was safe for them to proceed.

Stanek interrupted. "Wait just a minute before you go, *Kiap* Noble. I know you told me the natives prepared for war because each tribe thought I would give the advantage to one side or the other. But can you tell me what spooked the Riami back at the wreckage and now seems to have triggered all the Tugaru yodeling we heard?"

"You go on ahead, Roger. I think I can answer Dr. Stanek's question," she said.

"Finally!" exclaimed Stanek.

Toland took the tarpaulin from her belt and handed it to Stanek. "Here comes the rain." She nudged closer to him. "Please don't be offended, but your appearance evidently caused consternation among the tribes. At first glance, the sentries on the watchtowers described you to a tee, or should I say 'goatee.' I should've thought of it earlier. Your beard and mustache are similar in style to a Tugaru warrior's. Riami men, or river people, on the other hand, pluck their facial hairs."

"So my facial hair scared the Riami. What made the Tugaru change their minds?"

"The sentry we passed got a closer look as you gaped at his watchtower. He described you as a Two Face look-alike. Two Face is the name both tribes give their god with two faces. The evil spirit of the Tugaru lives on the peak of Mount Bosavi, and the good spirit resides with the Riami. The Tugaru can't be certain whether you'll turn on them or the Riami."

"Unbelievable. I've gone from potential ally to potential foe in a matter of minutes."

"Believe me, in this strange land, tribes war over less. Like us, they're organized in political societies which spawn war, only on a smaller scale."

"Interesting. And I always thought we go to war because we're born mean."

Before she could respond, a gust of wind awash with a torrent of rain pushed her against him, and it took all his strength to keep them both from toppling backward. As the canvas covering whipped back and forth over their heads, he lost his grip. Their only shelter flapped free in the wind, taking with it her floppy cap and his bush hat. His broad forehead and shaven pate took the brunt of the drumming rain as he buried his face in her hair to protect his eyes from the downpour and flying debris. He could feel her arms tighten around his rib cage. Her fingers gripped his jacket with every surge of wind.

Something stirred within him as a sweet aroma floated from her hair and caressed his face. If he but surrendered to it, he feared it would envelop his senses and his world as well. Reminded of the earlier experience he had blocked out of his mind for 21 years, he shook his head, clearing away this innocent encounter with DeAnn Toland and a painful memory of Catherine Stanek.

Toland tugged at his jacket. "Is it over?"

"The wind has died down a little. But Noble and company are nowhere in sight. We've got another visitor though," he said.

She pulled away from Stanek as he pointed to the elliptical mound where sheets of lightning illuminated the warrior headed directly toward them. In a calm voice, she directed the CIL assistant, Erik, and the two constables, crouched together with him in the grass under a single poncho, to intercept the native. They moved out in the heavy rain at a brisk pace.

"Erik will get to the bottom of this," she reassured Stanek. "He speaks fluent pidgin."

She smiled as she turned her head slightly upward and to the side, grasping a thick strand of auburn hair from which she wrung the rainwater. "Our government boys speak to the tribes in their mother tongue when necessary, then give Erik a pidgin translation which he feeds to us in English. Like everything else out here, communication is a slow process."

"There is nothing slow about the gale. Makes one wonder how anyone not born and bred in this harsh environment can survive for any length of time," he said.

"Oh, I don't know. I've learned 'necessity is the mother of invention,' cliché or not. Because we were able to withstand one of the worst winds I've ever been through in my life says something about human adaptability. If you hadn't been my anchor, someone would be picking my body out of the branches of a casuarina tree, along with our hats and shelter-half by now."

He was about to turn his face down and away when Erik and the Riami warrior, flanked by the two native policemen, approached them. Although the CIL sergeant gestured for the warrior to come forward, the Riami man hung back, his rain and grease streaked face set in an expression both stony and sullen.

Without speaking, the Riami man took an L-shaped stone axe wrapped in taro leaves from his vine belt and squatting in the wet grass laid the weapon in front of the pathologist. Leaning forward, he pointed first at the axe, then toward Stanek, whose own eyes were on the child slumped across the warrior's shoulders, her small head quivering against his naked wet torso.

Erik started to speak, but DeAnn Toland startled him into silence as she snatched the poncho from the CIL specialist's head and spread it across the trail.

"Tell MilkEye to place the child here," she said tapping the rain gear.

Erik spoke in pidgin English. But the warrior blinked his blind eye at the interpreter and turned to face Stanek instead. He removed a bamboo ornament from his nasal septum and untied what appeared to be a pig's scrotum band wrapped around his right biceps. Both items were carefully placed beside the ceremonial axe.

Sizing up the situation, Stanek inched toward the middle-aged warrior. "And what do you want from me in return?" he asked.

The unmistakable look of solicitude on the tribesman's face further emboldened the pathologist. Stanek's next move might have caught the others by surprise, but it was calculated. In one continuous motion, Stanek lifted the child's body from the warrior's shoulders letting his fingers brush against the man's wristband in the process. Only then did he cradle the little girl in his white arms.

"Oh, *Masta*," the Riami man began in halting pidgin. "Child belongs to me. Got fever."

"MilkEye says she has a fever," Erik interjected.

Stanek ran his hand across the girl's chest and forehead. "Even in this cold rain, she's on fire. Malaria has probably broken down her heat regulating centers."

"Oh, dear, is it too late to save her?" Toland cried.

"I don't know. If the parasites, spreading like cancer, have reached the red cells in the small capillaries of her brain, starving it of oxygen, she's in real trouble. Ask her father if she's had any of these symptoms." Stanek ticked them off one after the other—slight nausea, pains in the shoulders, arms and legs, headache and lassitude.

After a pause for translation, Erik explained MilkEye said his daughter had all the symptoms listed, although he did not understand 'lassitude.'

"How long has she been limp, practically comatose, in a languor state, like a rag doll?" Stanek snapped.

Again, the pathologist paused, listening as his question was translated to pidgin and then the answer back to English, after which Erik announced, "One day."

"Good. There's a slight chance if we get my nostrum in her stat, we can slow the disease's progress."

"A homemade remedy? Are you sure it's safe?"

Stanek handed the child to Toland and began rummaging through his pack while trying to shelter its contents from the rain. "Experimental, but harmless. I've tried it myself. We'll supplement the bee formula injections with quinine tablets. I have a syringe and tablets in here somewhere."

The anthropologist bent over and whispered in his ear. "A word of caution, Dr. Stanek. In this timeless land, a day or two means nothing. His child might've been like this for a week or more. If someone they consider a medical demigod treats them, they expect a cure. This could backfire if your homemade remedy and the quinine fail."

"Yes, but if we do nothing, she's sure to die." The pathologist then proceeded to explain the dosage, but the woman again interrupted him.

"Her father will never get it straight. I'll have to stay with her in his wives' hut for the next 24 hours, or at least until she's been given the second injection you recommend."

"Are you sure you want to take such a risk?" he protested.

"It's more a risk for you than for me, but I think both of us will be okay," she replied, smiling as she saw Noble and his constables return.

"While ye were examinin' the child, the Riami stayed in their huts and the Tugaru have taken shelter as well, thanks to those gale-force winds," the relieved *kiap* reported.

"What good news, Roger! But MilkEye's child is very sick. I'm afraid I'll have to go back with him and take his daughter to the child's mother. Natives can't properly administer the medicine Dr. Stanek brought with him and prescribed for her, so I'll have to help. Please go ahead and make sure Dr. Stanek has safe passage the rest of the way to our camp. Then instruct my staff to get him settled comfortably in CIL tent city."

"Will do, lass. But just be sure yer constables stand guard outside the hut through the night. Erik will have to go along as well."

Stanek protested. "I had planned to review the material on the B-24 case with you, Dr. Toland, especially the other survivor's log mentioned in your cover letter to General Bellicosi."

"Roger, have my staff send over copilot Bottorf's papers and other materials to Dr. Stanek with his dinner tonight. Dr. Stanek, you'll want to change into dry clothes, so I'll have the extra flight suit Yowell leaves behind for rainy days such as this delivered to your tent as well. Do you have any other concerns?"

"Yes, there is one, as a matter of fact."

"Well?"

"I take it the axe and other disgusting items are payment for my services."

"You'll insult MilkEye if you reject his gifts."

"Tell the Riami man my medicine costs more."

"What?"

"Tell him through Erik, if his child lives, I want him to bring me the brass wristband inlaid with cowry shells he's wearing. Nothing else will serve as payment for my services."

"Your request is preposterous! Next to his wives and pigs, you're asking for perhaps his most prized possession."

"Well, then, he can keep the cowry shells. I'll settle for the piece used to deflect the bowstring from his wrist. If you look closely, you'll see it's made of flattened brass. There're only three ways he could've obtained a cartridge casing so large. Someone could've given it to him off a B-24 .50 caliber machine gun, or maybe he swiped it, or got it some other way."

He smiled when he saw the surprise in Toland's face. He had finally gotten the reaction he was looking for, although it was missing earlier when he had probed for information about the bomber's missing tail fin, followed by his comment about negotiating the bridge in a suit of armor. Her astonishment indicated she hadn't noticed the native's wristband was made of brass. Like the rest of her party, she had realized his powers of observation were never switched off. Whether she intended it or not, he took her quiet withdrawal as a sign of capitulation by someone outmatched.

He wrapped a plastic bag around the vial of bee extract, syringe and quinine tablets and handed it to her. Dr. Toland remained silent. With still no word, she departed, the child hanging limp in her arms. He watched MilkEye and two native constables, plod after her and her interpreter in the rain, their bare feet splashing through the tall grass. He had never felt more alone.

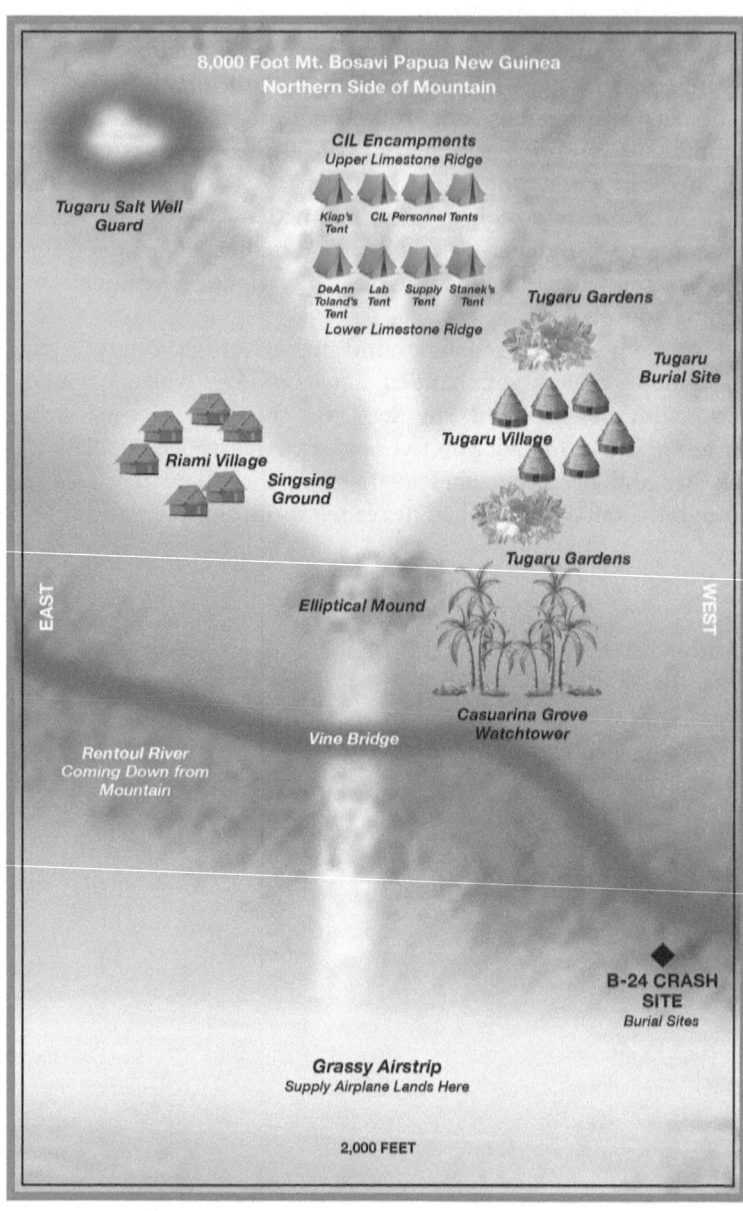

8,000 Foot Mt. Bosavi Papua New Guinea
Northern Side of Mountain

CIL Encampments
Upper Limestone Ridge

Tugaru Salt Well
Guard

Kiap's
Tent

CIL Personnel Tents

DeAnn
Toland's
Tent

Lab
Tent

Supply
Tent

Stanek's
Tent

Lower Limestone Ridge

Tugaru Gardens

Tugaru
Burial Site

Tugaru Village

Riami Village

Singsing
Ground

Tugaru Gardens

EAST

WEST

Elliptical Mound

Rentoul River
Coming Down from
Mountain

Vine Bridge

Casuarina Grove
Watchtower

B-24 CRASH
SITE
Burial Sites

Grassy Airstrip
Supply Airplane Lands Here

2,000 FEET

21 FATHER/DAUGHTER VIGIL

Riami Village, Mount Bosavi, Papua New Guinea, 1973

IT WAS LATE when MilkEye set out in the rain for the men's clubhouse at the eastern edge of the Riami village. As he followed the path along the ridge, he kept a palm-like pandanus leaf over the mesh bag looped across his right arm like a cloak. Dry tobacco was essential on this first night of planning the greatest of Riami *singsings*.

MilkEye's immediate responsibility was to help the elders of his clan establish a timeline for a competitive exchange of wealth held every five years among the Riami. He had already made up his mind to persuade his *age-mates* to postpone the great festival until the Tugaru slackened in their search for the murderer of the young warrior at the salt well. Since LikLik's status as a future bride hinged on how congenial his *age-mates* were to his plan, MilkEye halted within a few yards of the clubhouse to appeal to Situmu for last minute guidance, if not for his sake, for his father's granddaughter.

"Oh, Situmu, Riami would like me to surrender to Tugaru so enemy not disrupt *singsing*. You no speak. Tell me if brothers fill mouths with tobacco, then open eyes to MilkEye's plan. Me would like Riami to put off big *singsing*. Set LikLik's bride price later time."

MilkEye cocked his head and waited. Raindrops momentarily clung to his ringlets greased with fat, then fell across his eyebrows and dust-covered face with the circular bone ornament in his nose and finally came to rest in the almost invisible hairs of his chest. He hoped the rain would not wash clean the "mask of sorrow" he had intended to portray. But the only sound came from the clubhouse. From within the wooden walls, the low voices of his *age-mates* weighed security arrangements for the great festival.

Some wanted to cancel the event altogether in light of the unsolved murder of the Tugaru youth. "Tugaru attack when Riami off guard celebrating." MilkEye heard the leader of this faction press his point.

The opposition countered, "MilkEye have plan."

MilkEye sank down on the porch where only a few weeks ago he had sat with LikLik while he blew smoke rings waiting for WonTok to show up. A sudden throb coursed through his body and one knee began to bang against the other. He dismissed the tremor as a delayed reaction to a rain-chilled night in which there was no moon and no shadows against the darkness. Could this be the cloud of fear Two Face had placed over his head since the day he had tried to steal the mountain spirit's honey for LikLik? MilkEye counted his sorrows. His daughter lay dying in the women's hut, tended by the white *misis*, his friend WonTok had become all but a white lackey and Situmu hid his face from him. But there was more.

Although MilkEye looked skyward, he pointed to the brass wristband he wore. "Please, Situmu. Tell MilkEye if sky spirit come to take away wristband he make me."

When for a second time the spirit of Situmu failed to answer, MilkEye fell back upon the porch and waited for the cloud of despair to drag his own spirit down the trail of loneliness. Several minutes must have passed before he heard footsteps coming from the direction of the village. The sound of his name spoken by WonTok brought MilkEye upright.

"We go inside?" WonTok asked.

"Me wear mask of sorrow."

"LikLik die?"

"No. But white sorcerer take away LikLik if me no give back wristband."

"Situmu talk to you?"

"No. Papa no speak since murder."

WonTok held a finger against his friend's lips. "Shh, no good you talk. Tugaru constable at gate hear you."

MilkEye reached for his bow. "Me take away Tugaru."

"No can take away Tugaru patrol constable. He carry *thunderstick*. Constables go in Riami and Tugaru villages together. No stop them."

A deeper sadness came over MilkEye, and he sat up on the porch and lowered his head between his legs and muttered. "Warrior nowhere to go. Friend loyal to enemy."

WonTok took no notice of the complaint. "*Masta* Stan-neck not same sky spirit that give you wristband long ago."

MilkEye raised his head. "You know sorcerer's name?"

WonTok pointed to the Tugaru at the gate. "Tugaru and Riami constables take ruksaks to tent, then guard Stan-neck. Tell that *masta* no same *masta* from time long ago."

"*Masta* no like ceremonial axe. Tell MilkEye trade wristband for LikLik's life."

"*Masta* use magic. Take away wristband. You no stop."

"Yes. Sky people and spirits have great power."

"WonTok take what white people give others—tobacco, *laplaps*, *thundersticks*. WonTok find *misis* hat. Carry back. Where *misis*?"

"*Misis* with LikLik in house of MilkEye's *meris*. Me carry to Dok-tor Tow-land. No you."

"You no go to big *singsing* meeting?"

"No, WonTok. Head thinking."

He stood and embraced his friend. He realized how typical WonTok was of his clan. Most Riami warriors were five feet three inches tall and had to look up at the average Tugaru. But when it came to battle scars, neither side had the advantage. Like his own body, WonTok's had a dozen or more healed lacerations and indentations where spears, arrows, axes and clubs had left their mark. Most of their wounds had been obtained while fighting alongside each other and their *age-mates*.

Mollified because his complaints had found a sympathetic ear, MilkEye offered WonTok a handful of tobacco, "Go inside spirit house. Carry to brothers. Keep some for you."

"WonTok go inside. Tell others you no come. Brothers not decide on big *singsing* until MilkEye, son of Situmu, speak."

At the gate to the men's hut, the Tugaru constable glowered at MilkEye who loosened his bowstring in a gesture of peace. In a further sign of submission he clenched his fists and laid them against his stomach. The Tugaru did not challenge him, but at the

201

hut of his wives when he repeated the acts, the Riami and Tugaru on duty guarding DeAnn Toland questioned him.

"What you like?" the Riami asked. "Only white *misis* let go inside."

MilkEye dropped his hands to his sides and bit his lip to control his emotion. Since when does a warrior need permission to visit his wives, he wondered.

"Me no go away. See sick child. Give hat to Dok-tor Tow-land."

"Give hat to me. Me give to *misis* in morning."

"No. WonTok find hat. Like me give to *misis*."

At this point, DeAnn Toland appeared wrapped in a blanket in the doorway. MilkEye could tell she was annoyed at the disturbance by her tone. She spoke to another figure under the eve beside her. MilkEye recognized Erik, the interpreter.

"Let MilkEye pass," the interpreter said to the guards. He then addressed MilkEye, "*Misis* thanks you for returning her hat and asks if you'll come in and warm yourself by the fire. She has a surprise for you as well."

MilkEye felt strange following a white woman into a house he had built from the ground up with his own hands. But as he closed the door behind him, which was the only opening in the walls, he realized how her presence shone like the moon in a hut otherwise impervious to both light and rain.

The woman switched on a light stick and ushered him to a spot beside the circle of stones he had laid down as a hearth. Since it was too wet to cook outside, his wives had kindled a fire he thought was for the morning meal. Through the interpreter, the *misis* told him the fire was to keep LikLik warm when the chills struck. MilkEye asked to see his daughter.

"She's too weak to come to you, but if you'll go over there, she wants to tell you something."

Careful to step around his wives asleep in the front part of the room, MilkEye followed the beam of light to the rear portion, raised a foot or so above the ground. There sat LikLik chewing on a roasted pig's snout.

She called to her father, "Me eat pig."

MilkEye shook with joy. He leaned back against the thatch to steady himself. Overcome by the sight of his daughter awake and taking solid food for the first time in weeks, he brushed aside his tears and asked, "You like food?"

LikLik nodded and laid her head back down on the mat.

"She's not out of the woods yet," he was told, "and needs more medicine before she can leave her bed."

MilkEye slid the brass band from his wrist. "Please give to Stan-neck. *Masta's* sorcery save LikLik."

The *misis* and the interpreter exchanged glances. Then the woman did a strange thing. She laughed. "I'm sure Dr. Stan-neck (she laughed again) will show up to gloat and collect his fee. You keep it until then. He'll appreciate it more coming from you."

MilkEye understood and said he would come back in the morning to check on LikLik and give the sorcerer his due. He asked if he could sleep under the eve with Erik, and he was told he could. As he turned to leave, the white *misis* took his arm gently in her hand and asked, "How is it a Riami warrior of great status shows such great affection for a girl child?"

MilkEye was eager to tell his story. To make the translation flow easier without interruption, he told his tale in the manner of a Riami headman addressing the council on a serious matter. MilkEye asked and answered a series of questions. He paused only long enough for Erik to translate.

"LikLik sick because of curse?"

"Yes, sorcerer put curse on Situmu's clan."

"Who is sorcerer?"

"Two Face, the mountain spirit."

"Two Face kill papa, great Situmu?"

"Yes."

"Two Face take away curse then?"

"No. LikLik born on day Situmu die."

"Then Situmu's wisdom, spirit, curse pass to LikLik, is it not so?"

"Yes, and more."

"More?"

"LikLik is Situmu's chosen granddaughter, exalted above brothers and *age-mates*. Way she acts in village tell us so."

"How will this end?"

"With death of LikLik, unless..."

"Yes?"

"Unless Two Face's curse broken by more powerful sorcerer."

"But what sorcerer risk magic to save girl child?"

The white *misis* excused herself after his series of questions and answers. When she returned, her eyes were red and swollen, no doubt irritated by the dirt and smoke that filled the hut from below the timbers of the roof to the ground floor. He was ashamed of the dirt and dust left on his mask of sorrow and wished he had washed before he entered. She would think he, like Riami women, never bathed. Again, MilkEye started to leave and again the white *misis* took his arm, "Tell us, did you know a woman named Kioko-san?"

When he heard her speak the name known in so many dreams, his heart filled with emotion. As DeAnn produced the tablets of Kioko-san and held them under the light, he could feel his eyes water.

She patted his arm. "I can tell by your reaction you knew her," the *misis* said.

MilkEye looked at the interpreter and said, "Kioko-san Mama of Riami people."

"I thought as much, MilkEye. Cheer up. Did you know the spirit of Kioko-san lives in the pages of her book?" Maybe someday we can have a long chat about her."

He gave the sign for goodnight, and she returned the hand movement by drawing the book across her breasts and away from her heart.

As he closed the door, MilkEye sneaked a peek back into the hut. Dr. Toland sat cross-legged next to the hearth her head bent over the words of Kioko-san.

Moments later as he slipped under the poncho the interpreter had given him for bedding, he asked Erik, "All white two-names inside book with Kioko-san's spirit?"

"Whose name do you have in mind, MilkEye?"

"Two Face in book?"

"No, I don't suppose so. It's not about mountain spirits."

"Oh. But Kioko-san can put Two Face's name in book?"

"Sure, along with you and the other Riami as well."

MilkEye fell back against the wooden beams and smiled. The day hadn't been so horrible after all. LikLik had survived and gained strength. And the mother of the Riami people had sent her white spirit as comfort at a time when Situmu was so angry he hid his face.

The old warrior looked in on DeAnn Toland a second time. How the *misis* reminded him of Kioko-san who had often read aloud to him the words from her ancestors contained in the same tablets Dr. Toland now held under the light.

True, he did not understand all the words, which echoed in his head since Kioko-san left so long ago. But there was no mistake about the power in one oft-repeated verse she had sung to him:

The lonely last leaf,
Bridging heaven and the earth.
Carry on, brave knight!

Ennobled by the magic of words Kioko-san said were intended to warm the heart of the warrior of peace, MilkEye felt his own spirit lifted. With new zeal he planned his next move. Tomorrow he would return the brass wristband to the sky spirit, who now wanted it in exchange for LikLik's life. Fair enough. Then he would appoint WonTok the father/guardian for LikLik, and ask the white people to find Kioko-san. When he found her, he would ask Kioko-san to trap the sorcery of Two Face inside her book so the curse might end. Then he could save his family and return to his people.

As he drifted off to sleep, MilkEye laid his plan before Situmu and asked, "Papa, you tell MilkEye story of sky people. You help white people, but you warn me. More come. Then MilkEye decide if he help them. Once decide, no go back. But you no speak now. You no tell MilkEye if white spirits who come now are true like Kioko-san?"

MilkEye was not surprised his query met a dreadful silence. Spirits hated to be rushed. Until Situmu spoke again, or he found Kioko-san, he was sure Doc-tor Tow-land would find the spirit of Kioko-san in her books and be moved to help him find her in the days ahead.

22 KIOKO'S JOURNAL #2, SEPIK RIVER ESCAPE

Papua New Guinea, 1943

U.S. ARMY CENTRAL IDENTIFICATION LABORATORY (PROVISIONAL) FINDINGS, CASE NUMBER 316. EXHIBIT 3b, KIOKO TANAKA'S SECOND JOURNAL. DR. DEANN TOLAND'S REPORT.

OUR COMPANY OF bombing survivors motored up the Sepik River, camping in native villages at night. After leaving Angoram, we traveled many hours to Moim, arriving late in the evening. Moonlight illuminated our way on the final leg of the journey as clouds of mosquitoes mercilessly attacked us, making us miserable. Crocodiles here and there slipped silently into the shimmering water. The next day we traversed long stretches of river in the heat and humidity with nothing but jungle on either side, stopping at the village of Kanduanam for the night.

On the third night out from Angoram, we camped at Tanduanam, where we saw unusually large native huts. The massive log structures were built on 15-foot stilts, housing several families. They were completely enclosed with high arching roofs.

After we set up camp there, my brother Taro came to the tent I shared with the comfort women who had been placed in my care. It was raining again, and Taro hastened to get inside the flap I held open for him. There had been a time when such a downpour had sent Taro and our little brother Jiro racing for the creek on Satto

Mountain where they tested the sails on their small wooden boats against the storm. But it was obvious by the way Taro pursed his lips in a face still pink and as unlined as in his youth he had more than sailing in mind this day.

"Kioko, one of the soldiers died from wounds suffered in the bombing at Angoram, and Lt. Mori has sent me to ask you to participate in the funeral service tomorrow."

"What does he want me to do?"

"Scatter banana leaves and ginger over Cpl. Akatsu before the soldiers fill in the earth."

"I'll get Sun-Hi and Butterfly to help."

"No, the lieutenant said it wouldn't be proper."

Sadness infused my whole body. I wanted to speak but the words didn't come. How could I tell Taro how I felt about what the war had done to all of us—bombing and burning villages, and treating others as outcasts, unfit for one reason or another, or in extreme cases as subhuman. Instead tears sprang to my eyes. Ever sensitive, Taro drew a handkerchief from the pocket of his uniform and handed it to me.

"Kioko-san, you must steel yourself against matters over which you have no control. You've not gotten over the burning of Angoram, have you?"

I nodded. "What an evil thing to do. And the man who ordered it done has yet to lift a finger in the search for our brother Jiro, which brought me to New Guinea in the first place."

Taro, mercifully aware of the longing each shared for days spent in happier moments at the family inn overlooking Suruga Bay, changed the subject away from Lt. Mori. "What was the saying the Christian missionaries taught you while you were learning English, and Jiro and I were practicing to become *samurai*?" he asked.

"You mean the verse I sang at my confirmation?"

"Yes, that's the one!"

"All good men are free. All bad men are slaves..."

Taro clapped his hands. "You must not think of Lt. Mori as a bad man, but as a good man with a tough and sometimes bad job on his hands aggravated by the war. Evil acts can enslave a good person. Try to see Lt. Mori in this light as both of our faiths encourage us to do."

"I'll try. But what's to become of us?"

"See, Kioko-san, this is what I mean. You're not to fret about such things. Lt. Mori is a trained leader. His experience as a naval officer and aviator will get us to Wewak, even with the deviation to the west to shake off any American pursuers. However, the death of Cpl. Akatsu is a setback."

"Why?"

"Akatsu was a medical corpsman. Our doctor's duties will be much heavier without his assistant's help. The risk of disease, infections and injuries on this long journey are great, not to mention the danger if we run into unfriendly natives or become the victims of nature's fury in this wild, untamed land. Then, too, we face the danger of getting lost on this wide, meandering river, which has many tributaries and even some dangerous whirlpools and floating islands we must avoid."

I threw my hands to my mouth. "Oh, dear, I hope we'll survive this ordeal so we can find our brother Jiro and together return to our home."

I knotted the handkerchief around my finger several times. Taro took it from my hand and placed it in his pocket. "Don't worry, Kioko. We must have faith in our leader. Lt. Mori will see us through."

The next morning before the funeral procession left our campsite, Taro was placed in charge of half our number including my two female companions, Sun-Hi and Butterfly, while the rest of us set out to the south of the river under a clear sky over rolling downs country. About an hour's march from our camp we stopped where Lt. Mori had decided to bury Akatsu. He choose the site, he told us, thinking it far enough away from any signs of civilization so that no one could find the body, dig it up and subject Akatsu to humiliation.

Lt. Mori bent over the body and collected photographs and flags. "We're sorry to bury you so far from home," he said. "But rest assured, we will see the Akatsu family in Japan gets a lock of your hair." The lieutenant stepped aside while the others rolled up their comrade in banana leaves with the rest of his belongings and placed him in a deep hole. Lt. Mori waved me forward. The two of us bowed in unison as I dropped the banana and ginger leaves on the bier, while the others piled on earth with their bare hands.

When the hole was filled in, Lt. Mori carved Akatsu's name and Tokyo for his home city on a stake and drove it into the ground as a headstone.

As we got ready to return to camp, Lt. Mori saw smoke in the far distance and decided to investigate the source.

Our instructions were to keep an eye out for food in order to augment the meager rations we had taken with us from Angoram. As we proceeded inland, our route took us along a lake with a large native settlement on its banks. We marveled at the mathematical precision by which these primitive people laid out gardens fenced in by cane grass to protect their crops from numerous pigs milling about the village. The neat rows of sweet potatoes, sugar cane, yams, and other crops would have done Mr. Hanzo proud, or any other Japanese gardener for that matter.

As we stood in the center of the main village, natives crowded around us. Since we had brought no trade goods, I began to feel uneasy. One of the soldiers pointed to the weapons the warriors brandished. There were no banana leaf sheaths around their weapons. The sheaths would have been in place if they were peaceful. I knew we had no chance against a sudden attack on us by hundreds of warriors armed with stone axes and glaring at us from behind painted faces and bone ornaments hanging from their nostrils and ears.

Lt. Mori did not wait to learn whether their intentions were hostile or not. He ordered one of the soldiers to shoot a bird to demonstrate our firepower. Before the bird fell from its perch in a nearby tree, the warriors had scattered, leaving their crops and pigs at our mercy. After we had filled our pockets and pouches with yams, sugar cane and sweet potatoes, Lt. Mori shot a pig, and the soldiers hauled it onto Akatsu's now empty stretcher.

Thereupon, in the first and only words spoken to me directly the whole day, he asked, "Kioko, what is it you write in those tablets and keep hidden in the map case old Hanzo gave you?" But instead of waiting for my answer, Lt. Mori emptied his pockets of yams and cane stalks, tossing them on the stretcher with the slain pig. The soldiers followed his lead, placing their bounty on the platform they would take turns carrying back to camp. When it came my turn to surrender rations, Lt. Mori eyed my meager contribution of four sweet potatoes.

"You'll have to do much better if you intend to feed yourself and the two whores you brought along. Next time, throw out those writing tablets and stuff the map case with food," he said.

The soldiers within earshot laughed. Perhaps it was their attempt to relieve the tension on a stress-filled day. But I saw nothing to laugh about in remarks unbefitting an officer of *samurai* status. I was both ashamed and saddened for Lt. Mori. How far would he stoop to be accepted by the rank and file? Could Taro have been mistaken? Didn't Michio Mori know leaders have no peers except other leaders?

It was raining again by the time we straggled into camp. Taro had a fire going and soon the stolen pig was roasting over it. Lt. Mori supervised food distribution and told Taro my share was one serving of pork and four sweet potatoes. I was too tired to plead for more. All I could think about was how to force my body up before daylight and into clothes still damp and cold in time to move out at first light.

Butterfly came to my rescue. The Filipino girl had heated water for the perforated tin Taro had suspended from the tent ridgepole to serve as a showerhead. Butterfly also motioned me inside where she had a hot cup of tea waiting. I collapsed beside Sun-Hi's mat and began removing my heavy, wet boots. I inquired about the Korean girl.

"Sun-Hi velly, velly sick. No eat. No drink all day," said Butterfly.

"Help me lift her up. Maybe we can get her to take a little tea and nibble on a freshly roasted sweet potato."

Each taking an arm, we propped Sun-Hi against the tent wall. My 90-year-old grandmother had more color in her cheeks than this girl of only 18. But most alarming of all was the high fever. Heat radiated from Sun-Hi's thin body and hung about her like a vapor in the cool tent.

"Did you dress her wounds while I was gone?"

"Sure, Kioko-san. Me no forget this time."

I lifted Sun-Hi's blouse to check for myself. Blood had seeped through the bandage under her left breast and had formed a stagnant stain. This is where we figured a fragment from the American bomb or debris from the comfort women's hut had lodged in her body. Fever indicated that some kind of poison had entered her blood stream as well. I touched the edges of the wound and confirmed the diagnosis. As I withdrew my fingers, they were covered in a pus-like, sticky substance, which gave off a putrid odor.

"It's infected. Go find my brother, Sgt. Taro, and bring him here with the doctor."

Butterfly smiled, no doubt eager to escape into the fresh air. "I go. Chop, chop."

While I waited for Taro and the doctor, I combed Sun-Hi's hair, darker and longer than my own. She did not stir in the slightest as I laid her back on the mat. Unlike the other times when we had ministered to her, she kept her eyes closed. I told her about the day's march. The trace of a smile crossed her lips when I asked rhetorically, "Why can't we be like native women? They never consider tomorrow. There are no tomorrows in New Guinea. Only today matters. What do you say we get you better tonight?"

At this point Butterfly poked her head inside and told me Taro was waiting with the doctor. I bowed a greeting, and while Taro, Butterfly and I stood outside in the rain, the medical man went inside to examine Sun-Hi.

Taro moved closer to me and whispered, "Not a word about this house call to the lieutenant." At the same moment he pressed his handkerchief into my hand. I could feel the pork still warm wrapped inside it.

I protested. "But it's your portion."

He chuckled. "No, only half. I figured you'd give your share to the girls and starve yourself. Now there's enough for all of you to keep up your strength."

"More than enough. Sun-Hi won't eat."

I was about to kiss Taro's cheek to thank him when the doctor came out of the tent shaking his head. He lowered his spectacles so they rested on the point of his nose as if to punctuate the grave prognosis he bore.

"Even if Lt. Mori authorized me to give the comfort woman any medicine from our meager stores, it wouldn't help. She's too far gone. The infection has spread, and she's bleeding internally as well. Besides her wounds, she's hemorrhaging from a miscarriage. I'm surprised she made it this far."

In a feeble voice, I asked, "Nothing we can do?"

"Nothing except to keep her comfortable." The doctor seemed to grasp the irony in his words, because he quickly added, "She's

MEL R. JONES

comatose and is as comfortable as any of us can hope for before dying—comfort woman or soldier. It makes no difference."

Taro and I bowed as the doctor departed and Butterfly went inside to tidy up after him. Taro took me in his arms.

"Dear, gentle Kioko. Is there anything a brother can say to console you? I wish mother or father were here. They'd know what to do. Even Jiro is better at this sort of thing than a farm boy like myself."

I looked up at him and asked through my tears, "How can you say such a thing? Jiro ran away and hid his emotions behind his pouting. You and I stayed put, cried and faced the consequences."

Taro drew apart, but the remembrance brought a smile to his face. "I meant Jiro is like Lt. Mori, a born leader."

I saw my chance to tell Taro how the lieutenant had made fun of me in front of the soldiers after a day of the silent treatment. "Why did he show me disrespect?" I asked.

"Did you attempt to speak to him?"

"No, there was nothing to say after he refused to allow Sun-Hi and Butterfly to attend Cpl. Akatsu's funeral."

"Well, there, you answered yourself. Lt. Mori was right. Sun-Hi would not have survived such a long and arduous journey. She'll join Akatsu soon enough as it is."

"But none of us knew how sick she was when we set out this morning. And what about Butterfly?"

"In this situation I'm sorry to say, you are the pouter, unlike the old Kioko-san. Let me tell you what our leader is up against."

In his soft, boyish manner, Taro gave me a primer on the Japanese Army. Orders must come from a direct superior, such as a company commander. Lt. Mori's case was further complicated. As a naval officer, he could lead the men, but he could command only those eight, now seven since Cpl. Akatsu died, assigned to the Angoram garrison. The other seven marched to orders issued by an immediate superior—God knows where.

Taro continued with his explanation. Deployment does not take precedence over orders. Lt. Mori can tell soldiers how he thinks the thing can be done, and explain the consequences for not doing it his way, but it is up to an immediate superior to decide whether the action contravened his orders.

Taro drew in a deep breath, and I knew he was about to reach his main point. "This lack of authority has turned out to be a terrible encumbrance to Lt. Mori and in a lesser sense me. Seven of these men are combat fit. We, on the other hand, are rear area 'commandos' in their eyes. And if we go against their orders—say to make it back to their own units whatever the cost—their disdain will turn to mutiny."

At this point, Butterfly interrupted to say the hot water she had prepared for me was getting cold. Taro helped me rig the outer curtain into a shower stall, and then he left.

The water was warm against my skin and revived me enough to tackle my own hair neglected for these last four days. The grass mat had a luxurious effect on feet tired from a long day's march in the heat and humidity. I lingered in the stall long after the tin had emptied. Soon I began to shiver in the rain. Butterfly came to my rescue again. She led me inside where she patted me dry with a towel and drew a cloak over my shoulders. She handed me the tea, which was now only lukewarm.

"You're too kind to me," I said.

She blushed. "You like beautiful sister to me and Sun-Hi. All time bring food. Make pretty, same you."

It was my turn to blush. "Did you eat the pork Taro gave us?"

Butterfly shook her head.

"And the sweet potato?"

She shook it again. "Eat now, same, same you."

She was right. I had not eaten since morning, so the two of us sat and ate in silence. After dinner we took rainwater and gave Sun-Hi a sponge bath, hoping to reduce her fever, but it didn't help. It was then I saw the hemorrhage the doctor had discovered earlier.

"How long has she bled like this?"

Butterfly pointed to her own womanly parts and explained, "Every time you go away, Sun-Hi jab stick here. She say soldier no more want her where baby make too loose."

"Dear God! Neither of you has to go back to being comfort girls. You're free now."

Butterfly shook her finger at me. "Never free. All soldiers same, same. Want only slave girl for pump, pump."

Butterfly, her hips gyrating, continued. "Pump, pump, or die. Death only way to free comfort girl. Same, same for geisha in your country."

I saw the futility in upbraiding a Filipino girl on her coarse language acquired in a brothel, or in addressing the false comparison she made between her situation and a geisha's. I was too tired to find words simple enough to tell her a comfort woman once freed was better off spiritually than the geisha, who offered her body and other favors to her patron for profit. So I dropped the matter.

More in sorrow than pique, I grabbed the shoulders of Butterfly and shook them gently. "If I thought it would help, I'd dress her in my kimono and style her hair to make her beautiful like a geisha, if only to lift her spirit. But better to pray for our sister Sun-Hi. Tell me, is Sun-Hi Christian like you and me?"

Butterfly shook her head and threw her hand to her mouth as if suppressing an uncomfortable cough. "Not know. Never speak same." Therewith she fled the tent with tears of grief, leaving me alone with the Korean girl.

In my frustration to find some way of comforting Sun-Hi, I waited a moment or two, then held an ear against her lips as would a priest hearing a last confession. But the gesture met with silence. So, I took a bolder step, if in violation of the church's teaching, I ask forgiveness as a recent convert. I laid Sun-Hi upon the mat, bent over her and kissed her forehead, belly and breasts, making the sign of the cross, as if to enshrine her mind and heart in the divine spirit of Christ.

Imagine my surprise when Sun-Hi opened her eyes, inclined her lips toward my ear and whispered, "*Namu Ami Dabutsu.*" I recognized the chant. As a child I had heard an uncle cry out these words with his last breath and had myself offered it as solace to another dying relative.

"I believe in Buddha," Sun-Hi repeated. I nodded. She closed her eyes and fell back on the mat. She died in her sleep during the night—peacefully, as far as we knew.

At dawn I found Taro and begged him to intercede with Lt. Mori to allow us to pay last respects to Sun-Hi before the motor launches set out for the next campsite at Timbunke. Taro got permission for two soldiers to accompany me to a nearby hill, spotted yesterday on our march, where Sun-Hi's body was to be thrown into a small ravine. I must have looked aghast at the treatment, because Taro took my hand and said softly, "We can't expect any more under the circumstances."

214

Quickly, I traded some paint from the leather map case Mr. Hanzo had given me with a native for a carved wooden mask to take along for marking a spot on the hill for Sun-Hi. I scratched her name in the wood with a small knife. The climb up the hill with Sun-Hi's body was hard going, especially for the disgruntled solders who bore the burden of carrying her body. When we reached the top, there were only five minutes left before we had to descend again in order to meet the schedule Lt. Mori had set for us. On the summit the soldiers began swinging Sun-Hi's body back and forth to gain momentum for heaving it into the ravine.

"Wait! She must have a prayer to carry her into the next world."

The two soldiers set Sun-Hi's body down, looked at me and laughed. "We didn't know she had any religion. Certainly she doesn't practice Shinto," one of them said.

"No, but she's Buddhist, so I'll start there."

I remembered a prayer that my father had given before the name-tablets of his ancestors when his brother, who was estranged from the family, died.

Trying to think like a girl of 18, I began to address Sun-Hi's ancestors for her. "Forgive me of any dishonor I have brought on this house. There have been changes in my life I've been powerless to oppose; others, for which I must acknowledge guilt. If I have offended any of you, or failed our family, I am humbly sorry for myself and for the child I carry. As I pray for the peace of your souls, I ask only for someone to pray daily for the peace of our souls as well."

Feeling my own inadequacy to speak for a stranger, I closed the prayer by intoning the sound of the bell in the tower atop Satta Mountain overlooking Surago Bay. Since 1314 it has been struck 18 times at dawn and dusk, and at midnight on New Year's Eve 108 times, for that is the number of the sins of man. Surely, one as young as Sun-Hi deserved at least six intonations for herself and three for the unborn child. Then I placed the carved native mask in between a nest of rocks as a headstone.

The two soldiers grew tired of the delay. They picked up Sun-Hi's body, carried it to the precipice and hurled it into the ravine below.

"Too bad it had to be Sun-Hi to croak," said one.

His comrade answered. "Yeah, I know what you mean. There goes the tightest *manko* in Angoram, except for Ginny's of course."

215

"Ha. You can bet the bastard Mori's saving little miss peach-ass Kioko for himself."

They both leered at me.

Disgusted, I brought my hands up to shield my ears from the vulgar talk. The soldier who spoke last caught my wrist.

"Come here, *momojiri*. Give us a sample of what Mori's been hiding."

I broke loose and ran down the hill. When I had gotten far enough away, I called back through my tears, "Shame on you. Back home such comments in the presence of a good family girl would have been punished severely."

Later, the soldiers on the burial detail sent several of their comrades to my tent as I was packing to beg me not to tell Lt. Mori about the incident, but I refused. In the evening, after we had set up our new camp at Timbunke, Lt. Mori ordered the foul-mouthed offenders stripped to the waist and tied to a tree. He then stepped back and removed his sword from the scabbard. My brother Taro and I looked on in horror, as did the soldiers' comrades. We wondered if Lt. Mori had gone mad. Would he summarily execute these two, reducing our numbers further? The punishment seemed hardly appropriate for the meager crime committed. But Lt. Mori had no such intention. He handed the empty scabbard to Taro, "Sergeant, deliver one stroke across the back of each culprit, then pass the scabbard to a comrade who will do the same, down to the last man."

Afterward, the two soldiers were released and Butterfly administered to their wounds while Lt. Mori took me aside. "Kioko, stay close where I can watch you. Since your words condemned them, the men will blame you for their punishments. Who knows how they will seek revenge when my back is turned."

He started to leave, but came back. He stood before me with scarred eyes looking more hurt than even the first time I had seen them exposed. He twisted the glasses in his hand. "Maybe I'm to blame. I shouldn't have dressed you down in front of the men after Cpl. Akatsu's burial. They must've thought they could take liberties with you."

It was the closest thing to an apology I had ever received from Michio Mori.

After the canning incident, I could not stay asleep in the shelter I shared with Butterfly. At intervals I awakened to every footstep outside our lean-to, because I feared that a soldier had come to slit my throat. Shortly before midnight, Lt. Mori came to our shelter and announced himself. He ducked inside and pointed at Butterfly who was just awakening. "Get the Filipino whore fixed up to sleep with the men tonight."

I shook my head vigorously. "Please don't make me! You placed her under my care and protection. You gave your word."

He grabbed Butterfly's arm. I'll take her as she is."

"Against her will?"

"On my oath as a *samurai*, I'd never take a woman against her will."

"But shouldn't the same oath prevent you from allowing others to do what you know is wrong?"

Lt. Mori drew back his other hand, and I thought he might have slapped me, had not Butterfly pressed her lips against the hand holding her.

She spoke in English, all the while kissing his knuckles. "Kioko, no speak to Commandante. I go with him. Better for us. Better them. Make soldier *chinchin* go limp again."

I burst into tears as Lt. Mori led the Filipino girl from the shelter. Sadness ringed her eyes, as Butterfly looked back at me and smiled. "It okay, Kioko. One week maybe soldier no more like Filipino *manko*. Butterfly come back, happy place—you."

All I could do was scream silently at Lt. Mori's back as he retreated with Butterfly, "Taro will never participate in your orgy."

Lt. Mori whirled around to face me as if he had read my mind. "Check with your brother. He knows what must be done." I started to plead once more for Butterfly's release, but he held up one hand and swung Butterfly around in front of him with the other. He continued, "Taro and I feel some of the troops are about to mutiny. Here is the prize we must offer to deter them. The men are in no mood to dicker. If it should come to the worst, and they kill me and Taro, they'll come for you next."

But Lt. Mori's plan was only a temporary deterrent. Butterfly did not satisfy their lust for long. The seven combat soldiers did mutiny. Led by the two previously jailed soldiers, they left at dawn in one of the motor launches and took the Imperial Portrait with them. Lt. Mori was furious and insisted we pursue the renegade soldiers. He told us they must be punished and the Imperial Portrait recovered at all costs.

We proceeded west up the Sepik from Timbunke. Just before we reached the place where the Karawari River joins the Sepik, we stopped at a small village. Our interpreter asked some natives if they had seen another motor launch like ours. They nodded enthusiastically and led us in their canoes to the junction of the two rivers. They pointed up the Karawari River. Either the mutineers were trying to lose us, or they had taken a wrong turn. Lt. Mori chose to believe the natives, and we turned south up the Karawari, away from Wewak to the north, into the interior of New Guinea in pursuit of them.

My misgivings about veering off course made me tremble within, not only because of the physical hardships and risks ahead, but also because of a premonition of my soul. I sensed danger lay ahead for my heart—a danger making me more vulnerable, but also requiring more forgiveness of my own people and the American we encountered than I felt capable of giving.

23 PATHOLOGIST'S PERIL

Tugaru Village, Mount Bosavi, Papua New Guinea, 1973

EMERSON STANEK PUSHED aside the mosquito netting and swung his legs over the frame of the canvas cot, being careful to keep his feet above the damp pallet used for a floorboard. He felt around for his socks and boots. They were dry, so he put them on, checking the illuminated dial of his watch as he laced his boots. It was four a.m. He scolded himself for having frittered away 10 of the past 14 hours in sleep. Not since his medical internship at Walter Reed Army Hospital had he crashed so long out of sheer exhaustion. Nor had his mind been so foggy. To make matters worse, his stomach churned in a delayed reaction to the tin of cold beef and biscuits Dr. Toland had her staff send to his shelter last evening.

Pelted by wind and rain, the sides of the tent lifted and sagged as he made his way toward the dimmed lantern hanging on the center post. His mood was further dampened as he realized the uncooperative weather scuttled any chance of an early morning survey of the B-24 crash site, or a planned foray up Mount Bosavi to investigate the armor-clad killer he had sighted from the aircraft the day before. Stanek vented his frustration on DeAnn Toland.

Had she not had Yowell parade him along the Rentoul, only to rush him away from the crash site and finally desert him to trot off like some missionary administering to the sick and afflicted, perhaps he could have resolved part of the B-24 mystery by now. DeAnn Toland's delaying tactics confounded the problem. Worst

219

of all, Toland and the others were deliberately withholding information. Yowell, Noble, and the translator Erik no doubt followed their leader. Until he could ferret out their motives for obstructing the investigation, he decided to keep the knight sighting under wraps.

Stanek turned up the lantern, pulled the small wooden folding chair out from under the army field desk, sat down and leafed through the additional documents and physical evidence Toland had provided him. His first duty was to discover whether a crime, or crimes, had occurred on Mount Bosavi by or against American servicemen.

On his flight in, someone dressed as a medieval knight beheaded an unarmed man. Murder was a crime, whether brutally committed in a primitive society like New Guinea or on the campus of Johns Hopkins. But he could not recall a single modern incident where the killer wore western-style armor. The recent murder on Mount Bosavi was one thing. But there may have been others. The official documents Stanek had seen at Port Moresby listed another atrocity which had occurred in the vicinity of the Rentoul River as early as 1951. Who knows how many more there were, and when and where they took place, or who was responsible? More importantly, Stanek thought, the criminal must be brought to justice before he strikes again. The question boiled down to "who done it"? And in this sense, his and Dr. Toland's investigation dovetailed.

Should her probe divulge survivors from the B-24, the murder on the mountain cast possible suspicion on a member of the American bomber crew who might still be alive. According to Pilot Sanchez's log, out of war and violence this brotherhood had forged a persona for themselves. The "ten knights" even carried a suit of armor into combat with them as their totem.

Stanek decided an outline summary of the known facts, which had preceded and followed his entry in the case, was the best approach. He began with the correspondence Dr. Toland had sent through General Bellicosi to Dr. Haveland and which Haveland had subsequently passed to him the night before his mentor was murdered. All the items in Toland's original packet had remained in Stanek's possession, including the engraved lighter. He added the copilot's letters to the next of kin and the list of emergency equipment recently discovered by Toland to the maps and photographs sent with Pilot Sanchez's log.

Before retiring, he had already read the copilot's account and checked the missing emergency equipment against his own notes written in Baltimore. As far as he could determine, only the 40-foot cord, part of the B-24's emergency raft package, remained unaccounted for in Dr. Toland's recent find. Even more remarkable were the incongruities the latest facts revealed. Dr. Toland had caught most of them. Her most recent summary so nearly matched his own thoughts on the matter that he decided another outline was unnecessary at this point. Toland anticipated many of his questions when she wrote:

Pilot's log—I've changed my mind about its authenticity. No way Lt. Sanchez could've written this after impact. Crash damage, especially around the cockpit area, is simply too severe to emit survivors. Initialed lighter—"OCS"—found in fuselage (by Noble) linked to buried remains tentatively identified as belonging to Oscar Carlos Sanchez.

Copilot's log—i.e. letters to next of kin appears authentic. But Sam (Toggle Joe) Bottorf accounts for only four of five initial possible survivors. Toggle Joe leaves lots of loose ends. For example, we learn there were Americans on the ground. But without physical evidence, we don't know their fate. Bottorf says those crewmembers in the separated tail section—Wells, O'Leary, Shipley and himself—initially survived, except perhaps for the critically wounded Grant who was near death before impact. What happened to bombardier Patterson? Neither the log attributed to Sanchez, nor Bottorf's letters account for Pip in any detail.

Casualty dispositions—from pilot's log, two members of crew—Ingersoll and Grant—were killed or wounded in fighter attack on bomber before impact. Four sets of remains were buried at Site #1. These most likely include Sanchez, Nelson and Alexander, who sustained injuries commensurate with impact. The fourth is probably Ingersoll, because the wounded Grant had been moved to the back. Six others of the ten-member crew are missing. According to the copilot's log, four of the surviving crewmembers tried to escape down the Rentoul River, but their Riami escorts

```
disappeared. Left with a struggle to survive,
three went out to look for food, leaving Bottorf
in a cave behind a cascade on the river. Their
final end is in question. Grant might've been
buried near the missing tail section on the
mountain.
```

Stanek studied the anthropologist's notes and reviewed in detail the questions she had raised. Suddenly a new thought struck the pathologist. Had he and Toland overlooked the significance of one of the clues?

Where was the cigarette lighter? He removed the engraved Zippo from his briefcase and read aloud the inscription his colleagues at Johns Hopkins were so fond of quoting: "One hour alone is in thy hands, the hour on which the shadow stands."

Stanek's thoughts focused on how inappropriate the message inscribed on the lighter seemed when compared to the religious expression on the pocket watch given Lt. Sanchez by his father. Stanek fumbled through the items Toland had had delivered to his tent and gave a sigh of relief when he located the watch. He laid it next to the lighter on the table. Not only were the inscriptions different, as one was biblical, but so were the initials. O.C.S. was engraved on the watch. The lighter had no periods inserted between the letters. This raised the possibility the lighter belonged to someone other than OCS graduate, Oscar Carlos Sanchez, perhaps someone with a tie to the sundial at Johns Hopkins.

With an eye to uncovering more information, Stanek turned the lighter over and over in his hand, inspecting every detail. He flipped the cover open. The carbon deposits inside the lid indicated the lighter was usually tipped on its side after the flame got started. This was a technique used by pipe smokers to get the flame down into the bowl. Who among the crew smoked a pipe?

Stanek leaned back in his chair. Despite the rain, these early morning observations brought a measure of enthusiasm for the case. Outside his tent he heard voices speaking in pidgin.

Stanek jumped to his feet. "Who's there?"

"Roger Noble and the mornin' watch. Might I come through?"

Stanek unzipped the front tent flap and the *kiap* stepped inside shaking water from the hood of a poncho he slid across his bushy red head.

"Spotted a light blazing away under the tent and wanted to make sure everything's ship-shape in here like DeAnn asked me to."

"Is Dr. Toland with you?"

"Naw, just me and a couple of boys on patrol. Tugaru warriors have been sneaking around the perimeter of the camp all night. Probably wanted to get a closer gander at ye."

Stanek offered the big Australian a chair. Noble waved it off, explaining he didn't want to keep his boys standing in the rain too long.

"No time to answer a few questions?" Stanek asked.

"Only if the subject is New Guinea or security. Otherwise, I try to keep my big nose out of other people's business."

"Well, yours is exactly the type of expertise I'm looking for at the moment, *Kiap* Noble."

The Aussie stroked his mustache thoughtfully. "Tell ye what. Drop the formality, and I'll send the boys over to DeAnn's tent to stand under her awning whilst we chat."

Stanek nodded his approval. "I wouldn't want to disturb her at this hour though," he said.

"No problem there. DeAnn's still down with the Riami tending the sick child, I hear. Word was sent up to us she'd be there for a couple more days. Emerson, isn't it?"

Stanek nodded again. As the *kiap* dismissed his constables, the pathologist spread several maps across the desk. One showed a section of the Southern Highlands District with Mount Bosavi prominently marked. Stanek pointed to the section on the map and asked, "What do you know about this area?"

The patrol officer sat down and bent over the table. "As ye can see, Mount Bosavi is a natural barrier between Lake Kutubu to the east and the plains around Nomad to the west, separating some of the fiercest tribes in New Guinea."

"What about the southern slopes?"

This time the *kiap* studied the map more carefully, pointing as he spoke. "The mountain isn't accessible from the south because of sheer cliffs."

"Have you ever scaled the peak of Mount Bosavi?"

The Australian shocked the American when he threw his head back and roared. "*Come a gutser!* I don't know of any way up or around, Emerson, even if ye could get past the Tugaru guards. This mountainous area is known for its limestone caves and waterfalls, but I've only gone up as far as the Tugaru salt well on the Lake Kutubu side. Nothing of interest higher up for whites I'm aware of."

"What about the tail section of the B-24 which struck there first and broke off?"

"The only way to find out is by whirlybird, and the brigadier is too tightfisted to hire one."

"I'm certain the peak can be reached by foot. How else did the surviving crew members get down from there?"

Noble stifled a chuckle. "Well, then perhaps ye'll show me the way up sometime, Doc. From the salt well on a clear day, ye can see the lake and some of the taller mountains to the northeast and northwest. The bomber flew through the Tari Basin to avoid these mountain ranges on either side."

"Yes. The pilot's log described their route."

"Ye might see the landscape I'm jabbering about if ye go to the salt well. If nothing else ye'll come away impressed by how the Tugaru women gather salt from briny pools at the 4,000-foot level and haul it back down here, then by river to Nomad. There the salt is traded for the small tambu shell, which remains the currency for this part of New Guinea."

"I'd like to see it, Roger."

"Ye should've spoken up earlier. The salt train leaves at noon today on its bi-monthly run."

"Maybe I could join them?"

"Small chance."

"Why not? I can't do much more with these documents until Dr. Toland gets back."

"Ye'll need DeAnn's okay, which she could give by radio. But you'll need approval from Salty Meri as well."

"Salty Meri?"

"Yes, sir. She's the Tugaru hag who forms up the salt train and guides it to Nomad. Salty Meri's the only Tugaru woman the warriors have granted such shaman status to. She's exalted by her claim to be the widow of a white man."

"Could you get her to let me tag along?"

"A bribe of ten or more gold lip shells might sway her. But it'll cost ye another ten to hire a Riami canoe and paddlers, and maybe five more to keep the Tugaru guards from harassing ye on the expedition. Anyway, the armed escorts ye'd require would come courtesy of the Australian Territorial Government. Hell, I could guide ye myself after I've gone off duty."

"What time?"

"Eight a.m., but I'll come by for ye before noon. Need to slip in a couple more hours of sleep. Not as spry as I used to be. Meanwhile, here, take this." Noble laid a black revolver on the desk.

"What's the gun for?"

"For yer protection if any Tugaru warriors should break in here after the boys and I are gone."

"I've never shot anyone."

"No need to shoot 'em. Just scare 'em off with a shot or two. But aim at the floorboard, or else ye'll put a hole in the tent. Sometimes ye need to take yer courage in both hands, lad. Any other questions? I'd better get crackin' myself."

"Two more quick ones."

"Sure, Emerson."

"Have you heard of ghosts or spirits haunting this mountain?"

Noble roared and threw his head back so hard this time, it struck the tent pole, nearly dislodging the lantern.

"Awfully sorry for the outburst, mate. But ghosts or magic images are a way of life amongst these heathens. Just like their superstitious talk. Why, if ye went outside yer tent right now and pissed in the grass, ye'd not only draw an audience, but a chap would collect every drop from your *donker* on a leaf to dispense as magic water to his mates.

"And *meris* are worse. They've been known to sleep with a white man only to catch his sperm in the old *Mappa Tassie* and carry it back for their husbands, fathers or brothers to brood over. This way, the clan schemes to turn our powerful magic against us. I don't mean to sound like a *yobbo*. Yet, mind where ye *catch a naughty* 'round here, though ye don't strike me as the type to *give it a burl*." The stocky Aussie slapped his knees, bent over and laughed.

Stanek waited until the *kiap* regained his composure. "Roger, my interest is more along the lines of an apparition, say a spirit clad in a suit of armor."

Noble twirled the corners of his mustache. "Ye must mean Steiner, the German *fossiker* murdered near Finschafen at the turn of the century. He forged himself an armor breastplate, thinking he could defend himself against the cannibal's spears and arrows. But he didn't know how to make hinges, so his legs were left unprotected. The fuzzies figured out his vulnerable spots, probably with the help of the *meri* Fritz was bedding, chopped his legs off below the knee with their stone axes, then roasted the rest of him alive."

"Was he alone?"

"Yes, as far as whites go. A Gahuku boy witnessed the killing, and after he accepted Christ, confessed to a Lutheran missionary."

"Could a white man or a small group survive out here on their own?"

"If they knew what to do, like Mick Leahy or Jack Hides did. The natives feared the whites as spirits who came down from the sky. The whites told 'em if they tried to attack and kill, our spirits would come back and kill 'em all. But Hides and Leahy were seasoned explorers. They knew how to trap fish and eels and live off the land. But even they needed native help to carry supplies, show 'em where to go and supplement their food supplies from native gardens."

"What about possible survivors of the B-24 crew?"

"Ye know Leahy advised the Yanks during the war. He taught survival classes to the 90th Bomb Group after the Australians refused him a commission. I'm sure they've got his lesson plans on file down at Moresby. Leahy's a legend to us *kiaps*, although he never was a government man, officially speaking. My mate, now there was a patrol officer for you—a real *bushie*. God bless Angus Mackelwaite's bones, wherever they rest."

"Mackelwaite?"

"Some years back, Mackelwaite disappeared near this very mountain. Angus came up here from Nomad following a new lead on six Japanese mortuary workers lost while searching for their own war dead in 1951. He was the *kiap* assigned to this original Japanese party allowed by U.S. and Australian authorities to search the Southern Highlands. Since the Japanese remained the hated enemy for both blacks and whites for a long time after the war, the civilian search team was attacked."

"So, what happened to Mackelwaite?"

"He escaped. In his report filed at Nomad, Angus allowed as how Giambu warriors had ambushed them. Reluctant to kill a *kiap*, the bushmen let him flee. But his Papuan boys were slain on the spot. And the Japanese prisoners were never heard from again."

"The Rentoul massacre?"

"Yes, it's in the record book. Anyway, Mackelwaite roamed these parts long before I found the B-24. Angus had heard white men had been spotted in this area, and since tribal clans make no distinction between us and the Japanese, as far as color is concerned, he came up here with a small force expecting to find survivors from the earlier Japanese expedition."

"Then he must've come across the B-24 wreckage?"

"If he did, he didn't live to report about it. Some say the Giambu, fearing Angus had come back for revenge, set an ambush along the Rentoul. His constables must've fallen in the bush, or run off, which my lads are going to do if I don't get back to 'em."

"So, Mackelwaite's body was never found?"

The *kiap* pulled the poncho hood over his head. "No, but I haven't given up. Angus was as tough as they come. Once he got his nose pointed in a certain direction, he was like a bull elephant headed for a water hole. Nothing could stop him from reaching trail's end, except when he got a gutful of piss. Then he was *off his face* by 9 p.m."

"Drunk, you mean?"

"Rotten!"

"Why wasn't he sacked?"

"Everybody suffered from *troppo* back then. It came from drinking with the flies—alone I mean—in the bush as we Aussie's like to say. But Angus had the worst case of tropical madness I've ever heard of."

"Too long alone can make one lose the veneer of civilization," Stanek offered.

"Yeah, Doc, but have ye noticed white men behave better whilst in the company of white women? Angus had another fault. He preferred his women black and was as cross as a frog in a sock if he couldn't take two or three *meris* along on patrol for *fossicking* along the way."

"Prospecting for gold, was he?"

"Right. Angus taught his bush girls how to pan for it. I'm convinced he wanted to get back here one more time and strike it rich. The Japanese search opened the door for him. When I found the B-24, I hoped my government would have a go at looking for

Angus. I got approval and came to work with you Yanks on Mount Bosavi."

Stanek picked up the Zippo lighter from the field desk and flipped open the cap. "Maybe we can help each other. Macklewaite smoked a pipe, didn't he?"

"How did you know?"

"From the burn patterns on the lighter, we can assume the Zippo's owner turned it sideways to get the flame down into the bowel."

"Ye'll need more evidence to peg the lighter to Angus."

"Agreed, but tell me, what do the initials 'OCS' stand for on your collar insignia?

"Why, 'Officer Constabulary Service'—a *kiap*."

Stanek handed Noble the lighter. "The letters match those on your insignia, wouldn't you say?"

The patrol officer laid the lighter on the desk, rose to his feet, placed his hands behind his back and clasped and unclasped them in unison to the swaying lantern. After a moment, he bent over the table and gazed into Stanek's face. "Yer theory might be the right one. I don't know. But from the day I found the bomber, I've feared Angus was mixed up in this business somehow."

"Is this why you didn't surrender the lighter at the outset but held it until Dr. Toland arrived?"

"During the war, Angus was district officer for the Southern Highlands. I became his *offsider* shortly after hostilities ended. He treated me like a mate, not an assistant."

Noble drew in a deep breath, then added, "I owed Angus me life. He passed the techniques learned from Hides and Leahy on to me—the same basic survival tips any of yer Yankee mates who didn't *cark it* must've known."

"What're these tips?"

"Vigilance, fearlessness and innovativeness. Never turn yer back on a native. Keep yer eye on 'em so ye can read their intentions. They've endowed all whites with supernatural powers. Use these powers to thwart all challenges fueled by primitive braggadocio. Shoot to scatter at first, then, if they don't run, pick off a few of the leaders."

The big Aussie heaved another great sigh, wheezed, and then continued. "I part company with my mentors on the use of force. Most of the time, it's unnecessary. I'd never sleep again at night if my body count tallied over 40 like Leahy's did during his time in the bush. I try not to kill a bushman except in self-defense. I found superstition packs more power than a rifle out here. All things about the white man and in his possession have sorcery behind them. The lot."

Stanek stood up. "I know you're pressed for time, but at some point it would be helpful to learn if indeed the crew got its survival techniques from Hides and company, or from some other source."

"Yeah. I see what ye mean, Doc. On the other hand, yer chaps could've picked up jungle lore from the Japanese woman who lived with 'em. Now there was an expert. From what little I've read from Kioko's diary, she spent years living and surviving amongst the savages."

"Kioko? A diary!"

"Yeah. Check the documents DeAnn had sent over to ye."

Stanek sifted through the papers on his desk. "It's not here."

"Then DeAnn must still have the six volumes. I gave 'em to her with the emergency raft and other items found right under our noses. I'll tell DeAnn ye asked for it."

"Thanks, but I'll ask her myself. But I'd like you to get me on that salt train."

"Ye help me find Angus Macklewaite, and it's a deal."

As they shook hands, Stanek asked, "Did your friend ever visit a college campus in Baltimore, Maryland, called Johns Hopkins?"

"No, Angus never left the bush I know of."

"Thank you, Roger. You've been a great help."

After the *kiap* left, Stanek went back to his desk and held the first page of copilot Bottorf's log close to the lantern. He noted a left-handed person wrote it in blue ink. Then he held pilot Sanchez's alleged log next to the copilot's. The latter was written on paper slightly thicker than the paper Bottorf had used. Borttorf's script was written over brown contour lines similar to those used by a map or chart maker to denote various elevations. The Sanchez document had all the earmarks of a mariner's chart. It measured sea depths. Useful on a submarine but not usually found in an aircraft.

He was anxious to see what type of paper Kioko's diary had been written on, and whether its timeline bridged the gap between the pilot and copilot's accounts. A Japanese perspective might shed light on other incongruities in the case, Stanek thought.

To follow up this lead, he turned next to the hand-stitched belt, decorative fan, cap insignia and personalized flag found with the male remains at burial site number two. Certainly all but the fan were typical items carried by Japanese Imperial forces. Perhaps the fan belonged to Kioko. But here was an assumption Stanek did not accept *prima facie*. Unlike in America, where the fan is considered an effeminate article, Japanese culture places no such gender bias on its use. He set the fan aside on the table with the stitched belt and cap insignia. These items, including Bottorf's log, required further study.

He picked up the cigarette lighter, pilot Sanchez's log and the personalized flag. He secured them in the deep side pocket of his bush jacket, which hung over his bed where it had been set to dry. Toland had requested he return these items when finished. The personalized flag was an add-on as his reminder to ask Toland to have the Japanese characters on the flag translated, if she had not already done so.

He had barely sat down at the table when he heard a high-pitched squealing sound outside his tent followed by bare feet sloshing through the mud. Stanek reached for the revolver Noble had left behind. By the time he got his hand around the grip, the two sounds moved off together in the direction of the abandoned garden separating the CIL camp from the Tugaru village.

"Kids chasing a pig," Stanek thought. Stanek laid the weapon aside. Except for the disturbance outdoors, a measure of tranquility resumed within. However, the pig squeals returned and soon reached the pitch of animals terror stricken or in pain. Stanek could no longer ignore the commotion. He slipped the revolver into the knee pocket of the flight suit borrowed from Yowell, grabbed a flashlight and stepped outside the tent.

The cold, damp morning air blew over his face. The rain had given way to light drizzle forming droplets on his shaven head. Stanek inched his way along the front canvas to a point where the tent angled right, running beside a limestone ledge. At the corner he hesitated, listening. The pig-like squeals had diminished in both volume and intensity. Instead there now was a tone so pitiful it resembled a child's gurgle.

Aware a beam of light might draw Tugaru arrows and spears down on him from natives Noble had reported earlier as roaming the area for a glimpse of him, he switched on the torch anyway.

Within a few yards of the tent fly, two pigs, dyed white and smeared with black grease, were lying on the grass tethered to a pole by vines attached to each animal's hind legs.

Stanek prodded the beasts with his boot. Blood squirted from arrows stuck in the pigs' throats and stained his flight suit up to the waistline. He felt the texture of the liquid, and when he drew his fingers under the flashlight beam, confirmed blood so thick and dark red it could have only come from a major artery or the jugular. He had little doubt the animals were sacrificed in a manner designed to prolong agony in order to maximize bleeding. As they thrashed about and squealed the blood flowed faster. This was commensurate with a ritual act. But what kind of message did the natives intend? Who was responsible?

Noble would know what to make of it, Stanek decided. But first he had to locate the *kiap's* quarters among the four identical tents clustered above his own on the second level of the CIL compound.

Stanek backed down the mountain a few paces. He searched first for signs of activity within or around the other three tents on his level of the limestone ledge. DeAnn Toland's tent, the lab tent, the supply tent and his quarters constituted the lower level. Except for his, the rest were dark against the mountain wall. But as he stepped back a little farther, he caught a glimpse of light reflected off the limestone. Maybe it was Noble's tent, or the watch quarters above him.

He thought the Tugaru hamlet on a rise beyond the clearing offered a better perspective of the upper CIL encampment. He switched off the flashlight. It wouldn't do for the Tugaru to spot him alone so close to their village. Without an interpreter, how could he explain his presence?

From his trek up the mountain yesterday, he remembered beyond the clearing there were blind spots along the narrow path as it meandered past the huts and gardens. Careful not to bump into someone coming from the opposite direction, he paused at each curve. He occasionally stopped, turned around and scanned for signs to indicate the *kiap's* tent or guardhouse. The upper reaches of Mount Bosavi were a dark blur in the distance. Now, because of the tall *kunai* encompassing him, he lost sight of his own quarters as well. He felt for the heavy revolver and walked on.

Stanek checked his watch. Dawn would break in less than an hour. He had to hurry before the natives stirred. If he ran into a

Tugaru patrol, the folly of his naiveté would have placed him in a jam he couldn't talk his way out of. A few more yards and he should reach the rise where he could view the entire CIL encampment and get a bearing.

He came to a straight unfamiliar strip of trail. Directly ahead he could make out the round, grass silhouettes marking the outskirts of the main Tugaru village. Five hundred yards beyond the last Tugaru structure further down the slope, he could see flames from a dozen cooking fires casting their own shadows against the rectangular huts of the Riami, clustered around each other like ships at anchor. He thought of DeAnn Toland inside one of those huts. "Five hundred yards and thousands of years of science separate us," he murmured, unaware he had veered off the main trail and into a Tugaru garden.

By the time he saw the three-foot fence of living *pitpit*, the grass tassels and sword-like leaves of the cane had entangled his boots. He stumbled and fell headfirst into a sweet potato bed. The wet scent of mud mixed with pig excrement drove him to his feet. His legs began to cramp. He leaned back against the *pitpit* hedge and stretched one calf, then the other. To get his bearings, he switched on the flashlight he still held in his hand.

No more than five yards in front of Stanek stood a man, his bare buttocks faced the pathologist and his black legs were sunk up to his knees in an irrigation ditch. The native's body gyrated between a woman's thighs floating below his hips like wings of pure ebony—smooth and shiny. In a delayed reaction, the man froze for a moment, then turned his head toward Stanek. He hid his face behind his hand. In the next instant, the native leaped from the ditch and headed for the pig barrier to the right of Stanek. As he fled, he wrapped a khaki *laplap* around his middle. Stanek marveled at how easily he cleared the fence.

The woman moved slower. But with the beam now turned on her, Stanek could see she was too startled to cover her face as her paramour had done. Her dark eyes peered at him from curved lids, over which hung plaits freshly oiled for a nuptial night. The grease and soot covering the woman's face, the assortment of colored feathers stuck in the fleshy parts of her wide-flat nose, flared at the nostrils, and the ringlets of dark hair framing her cheeks all revealed her status. In preparation for this assignment, he had combed dozens of photographs of New Guinea ceremonies, including weddings.

Like a child hypnotized by the flames from a campfire, the Tugaru bride stood motionless before Stanek's light. He was about to switch off the torch out of respect for her privacy when she made a sudden move toward the ground as if to retrieve a weapon. Instead, she reached down and pulled a grass skirt of colored leaves over her genitals. Her bare breasts swung from side to side as she fastened it around her hips with string aprons. More deliberately, she bent down a second time and produced a string bag and tied it around her forehead. As she turned to flee, Stanek recognized the largest item carried in the *bilum*. She had his bush hat.

"Halt! Halt!" he yelled. But the young woman never looked back as she cleared the *pitpit* fence at almost the exact spot her male companion had exited moments earlier. Stanek shuttered at his own stupidity. Surely, if there were armed Tugaru warriors on watch around the settlement, by now they had seen his light or heard him call out.

A babble of voices came from the direction where the man and woman had fled. His fears confirmed, he switched off the flashlight, sidled backward until he made contact with the sword-like *pitpit* leaves. He rolled over the fence, scrambled to his feet and ran up the wet and sloppy *pitpit* walled track. Spurred on by shouts, grunts and heavy panting heard behind and on both sides of the path, he picked up the pace.

He had only gone a short distance when his breath deserted him, and sweat poured from every pore. Up ahead he had to clear two blind corners before he could see his pursuers, and more importantly, show them he was armed. The revolver! Now might be a good time to fire a warning shot, he thought. He reached into the knee pocket, but came up empty. He must have lost the *kiap's* gun back in the garden where he fell. "Now what, you clumsy fool," he chided himself. "Keep running."

As the tall pathologist approached the first blind spot in the pathway, he devised a new stratagem against an ambush. Rather than take the chance of a headlong plunge into a spear point held by a Tugaru advancing from the opposite direction, Stanek would drop to his knees and crawl until he got safely around the blind corner. Arrows fitted to bows at such close quarters would also be nullified by this maneuver. But, if the Tugaru warriors were armed with axes, like the one MilkEye had offered him, then crawling was out. It could invite a well-placed blow to his head or neck.

Stanek asked himself, "What would Hides, Leahy or the B-24 survivors do in this situation?" Then he recalled Noble's admonition given earlier, "Let the natives see you as a white spirit come down from the sky."

Stanek stopped, stroked the scar on his cheek, then moved his fingers over his shaven pate. He positioned the flashlight against his chin so the beam illuminated his entire face and head. He grimaced. It wasn't a grin like the skull painted on the tail fin of the wrecked B-24 bomber wore. Yet he hoped it was a good enough imitation to buy him some time.

24 TUGARU TROUBLE REPORTED

Riami Village, Mount Bosavi, Papua New Guinea, 1973

SUNBEAMS PEEKED THROUGH the cracks in the crude hut MilkEye had built for his wives when DeAnn Toland awoke from a troubled sleep. Kioko's tablets were still strewn about the hearth, so she secured the six volume diary in her knapsack before stoking the fire. For an instant, the anthropologist saw in the embers the images from her dreams. Kioko, like a Greek goddess from mythology, bent over the bomber crews' remains and with her breath transformed them from once shattered bones into ten glorious knights. MilkEye stood to the left of the Americans and on their right was the silhouette of another man. Just as in her sleep, DeAnn could not identify the shadow, but she had narrowed down the possibilities to Major Yowell, *Kiap* Noble, Lt. Mori, or Dr. Stanek.

"Please, God, must this pathologist invade my dreams as well?" she asked herself.

Just then a cry came from the child Dr. Stanek had placed in her care. DeAnn looked over her shoulder. LikLik lay naked on the straw mat and her body shook by fits and starts with each cry and gasp for breath.

DeAnn hurried to the child and cooed, "Poor dear, we've got to keep you warm until you stop shivering."

Carrying LikLik over to the hearth might induce nausea, as would any movement in this stage of the disease, DeAnn thought. Stripping to her underwear, she laid the little girl across the exposed part of her own body and pulled the wool blanket around them both. But again she did not sleep.

Her mind was filled with observations eliciting questions and strong feelings. The contrasts between the mother's lack of tenderness toward LikLik when compared to MilkEye's recent display stirred her anthropological interest. Why had LikLik's mother welcomed a stranger into the women's quarters, yet written off her own daughter as so near death nothing could save her? The mother's attitude, Erik had agreed, seemed bereft of the hope MilkEye placed in Dr. Stanek's cure.

In addition, DeAnn forced herself to admit she had mixed feelings about Stanek's intervention in LikLik's illness. True, his medical oath required him to treat the sick, but if LikLik died, the simplistic reasoning of the Riami natives would see the white man's medicine as weak, and place further cooperation in jeopardy. Nonetheless, in fairness to Stanek, she decided it was MilkEye who had laid this dilemma at their feet.

She heard bare feet shuffling across the room and turned to look. Riami women moved in and out of the small entranceway, carrying what looked like porridge for their children. LikLik's mother was not among them. One of MilkEye's other wives held a bowl of the pungent mixture under LikLik's nose. LikLik stirred against her belly and rose on one elbow. Through sign language, DeAnn managed to convince the native woman that the child was still too sick to eat at the moment. As the woman exited the hut, DeAnn got the impression she had hurried away to report to MilkEye, who slept outside the entrance.

LikLik stirred again, and this time the movement released a horde of maggots. They crawled from the edges of DeAnn's bra in clusters as thick as steamed rice. DeAnn jumped to her feet brushing the larvae off her with one hand while she cradled the child in the other.

"H-help us," she cried.

Two of MilkEye's wives sprang into action. One took LikLik out of DeAnn's arms, and the other shook the wool blanket vigorously. As DeAnn lowered her head to unfasten her bra, she saw more of the disgusting creatures emerge from the edges of her panties as well. Trying not to show panic, she removed her underwear, slapped them against her legs until all the maggots fell free. Then she flung the white bra and matching briefs across a vine where her outer garments had been hung to dry.

Alerted by the disturbance in their hut, the remaining Riami women stopped their chores and giggled, muffling the sound with a hand across their mouths. The object of their interest, DeAnn realized, were her bare, firm, white breasts. She leaned forward to brush larvae off LikLik, and her audience leaned with her. At first, Toland covered herself with one arm, then located her T-shirt on the line and slipped it over her head. Her fatigue trousers felt like a damp washcloth. She pleaded, "Honestly, ladies. Your husband's going to march in here in a few minutes. Won't one of you please bring me something to cover myself?" She made a gesture of wrapping a skirt around her middle.

MilkEye's oldest wife took off her grass skirt and handed it to DeAnn. The woman then helped her fasten the garment around her waist with a bark belt. She thanked the woman, then extended her arms, indicating LikLik should be returned to her. The woman who held LikLik seemed relieved to be rid of her burden, so she could join her sisters whose curiosity focused on what DeAnn assumed was the never-before-seen bra. With their working sticks, each took a turn poking the garment as if it were a living organism emanating great magical powers.

The Riami women grew tired of the game, however, and not a moment too soon, for MilkEye ducked through the entranceway. Close on his heels were Erik and two of DeAnn's bodyguards. The rifle bearers restrained MilkEye, while the CIL sergeant shouldered the old warrior aside to confront Dr. Toland.

Erik jerked his head toward MilkEye. "He's worried about his daughter, but we've got a bigger mess up at the Tugaru campground."

"What?"

"A massacre in the making!"

"Dear Lord! Not *Kiap* Noble?"

"No, he's trying to stop the Tugaru from killing Dr. Stanek. The rest of us are next, I suppose."

"S-Stanek. W-what did he do?"

"Raped a Tugaru *meri* early this morning. Their headman, *Bikmaus*—we know him as Loud Mouth—is broadcasting the charge all across the mountain. Seems his latest bride was the victim. Loud Mouth and his mother Salty Meri have rallied a sizable audience of hotheads bent on revenge for the rape."

"Rape? How preposterous!"

"I'm only repeating what the *kiap* sent word that I should tell you."

"Where's he now?"

"*Kiap* Noble?"

"No, Dr. Stanek."

"He was last seen surrounded by Tugaru warriors out in front of his tent. Somehow or other he's worked the situation into a stalemate—they're afraid to attack until they test the strength of the Doc's medicine—at least according to *Kiap* Noble."

"And what's Noble's plan?"

"He sent word he's assembled every available armed boy on the limestone ledge separating the two parts of our camp. They've got their guns trained on the Tugaru awaiting further instructions."

"We'd better get up there right away. Give me a few minutes to get some things together."

She saw him hesitate, so she asked, "There's more, Erik, isn't there?"

"I was going to wait 'til one problem was settled before I brought up the other."

"Nothing could be more horrible than what you've just told me, so let's hear it."

"The same messenger brought a radio message from Major Yowell. He's due to land in the next hour or so with General Bellicosi, a reporter named Jim Cole and a Catherine Stanek."

"Great. We've got a war underway, and our own reporter to cover it. Who's Catherine Stanek?"

"Major Yowell didn't say, but I guess she's the doc's wife."

"Did anyone tell the major how unsafe it is to land on Mount Bosavi at the moment?"

"No, Ma'am. Interference ended the transmission before Noble could even roger the major's message."

DeAnn pressed the child closer to her as she contemplated the problems in the calm manner her parents had taught her. Foremost was the safety of all those in her charge, including Stanek. Best take one thing at a time, starting with the most urgent and working down to MilkEye's concerns and her own personal problem regarding her disheveled appearance. She turned to the sergeant.

"Here's what we'll do, Erik. Send my Riami bodyguard down to the airstrip. Tell him if he hears any shooting to send up a red flare to wave off General Bellicosi and his party. We'll take the Tugaru rifle bearer and head up the mountain. But, before you go, tell MilkEye we need to take his daughter LikLik to our campsite for stronger medicine. Don't mention Dr. Stanek's troubles to MilkEye. We might need the old warrior and his Riami people if this soap opera turns into a full-fledged war."

"Yes, Ma'am," Erik said, motioning for the others to follow him as he left.

DeAnn delayed only long enough to throw the rest of her garments into her knapsack. Then, with LikLik in her arms and the grass skirt pulled tight around her middle, she ducked through the doorway where Erik, MilkEye and the Tugaru policeman waited. MilkEye pointed to the Riami houses grouped closely together in the barricaded village. Beside the smoke of numerous cooking fires smoldering in the morning sunlight, Riami warriors scurried to arm themselves, as had MilkEye. In a split second before Erik could interpret the scene, DeAnn understood why. From higher up the slope came the beat of Tugaru drums accompanied by yodeling. And the echo bore an ominous sound—gro–broom, gro–broom, gro–broom, sha–sha–sha. The drums and yodeling sent shivers along her spine.

Erik called DeAnn aside. "MilkEye insists that he go with us. He wants to see Dr. Stanek and give him the wristband, so he'll make his magic powerful again to save LikLik."

"Tell him it's out of the question. His presence would only outrage the Tugaru more. Can't he hear the drums?"

"MilkEye thought you might refuse him, so he said to remind you his *one-mate* WonTok had brought the messages from the CIL camp. He is determined to return with him, because the Tugaru can't be trusted. We might need his help, as your Tugaru body guard left when he heard the Tugaru drums."

"Where is the Tugaru constable who is paired with WonTok?"

Erik shook his head. "WonTok said he looked for his Tugaru constable partner early this morning, but couldn't find him. Perhaps he went back to the Tugaru side once the ruckus started."

"Any recommendations, Erik?"

"Given these circumstances, I don't see how we can stop MilkEye from forming a raiding party of his own. It would be far better for us to take him along under your influence."

"Very well. Let's get moving."

As Dr. Toland and her small group threaded their way up the narrow pathway leading to the Tugaru compound, she relinquished LikLik to her father, mainly to fill the old warrior's hands, lest he let fly the bone-tipped arrows he carried in his quiver. She tried not to think of anything else but what lay ahead of them. Recalling *Kiap* Noble had cautioned her about the attraction flies had for wool in New Guinea, she realized she should have taken precautions in line with his warning.

"Unless ye want maggots in bed with ye, best keep the blow flies away from the wool by rolling it up in a cotton or canvas covering when not used. Otherwise, they'll deposit their eggs in the wool to hatch in the first glimpse of the sun or warmth from body heat."

Noble's advice was similar to what she had read when boning up on New Guinea. "Like everything else out here," one of the early explorers had written, "eternal vigilance is the price of survival."

She looked back at MilkEye. He had wrapped his daughter in pandanus leaves, and placed her in the string bag that hung from his shoulder. Behind MilkEye trotted WonTok.

As DeAnn and her small party entered the outskirts of the first Tugaru compound on the northern slope of Mount Bosavi, a large group of natives ran away at their approach. Dr. Toland noted those left behind were mostly old women and children. Uncertain whether MilkEye might use the occasion to pursue his fleeing enemies to extract payback for some never forgotten feud, she turned to look back at the old Riami warrior. He seemed to ignore the Tugaru and gave no signs he was more interested in them than in his daughter's welfare. She admired him for his restraint. In this matter, MilkEye showed better judgment than had Dr. Stanek, who had initiated this crisis.

After crossing over an irrigation ditch, they followed the path as it wove between the tidy gardens that the Tugaru had cultivated in contrast to the helter-skelter fields passing for gardens in the Riami village. They encountered another group of Tugaru, again women and children, peering at them from the window ledges of rounded houses, sturdier in every respect than the oblong, mostly grass houses of their Riami neighbors just below them on the mountain.

DeAnn slowed her pace to negotiate the sharp turns through rugged, thick bush. Here the population had noticeably thinned out, and she could no longer see the Tugaru huts strung along the ridge, marking the village boundaries. Whenever there was a straight stretch of trail, she looked back to see MilkEye struggling along. Although the path seemed too steep for both him and his burden, MilkEye somehow managed to stay on his feet.

Suddenly, out of the grass behind the old Riami warrior and WonTok, there appeared four Tugaru warriors, hurrying to close the gap between themselves and DeAnn's party. MilkEye must have sensed their presence, for without looking back, he lowered LikLik to the ground and began stringing his bow. DeAnn maneuvered past MilkEye and WonTok to confront the pursuers.

The Tugaru men reminded her of the subjects of an anthropological study she had conducted on the American Indian for a seminar on battle dress held at her university. Not one, from Sitting Bull to Geronimo, had ever set forth for battle in more garish paint, or gaudy finery, than the Tugaru warriors who strode toward her now. Although their headdress bobbed menacingly with every step, it had the opposite effect on DeAnn. She was captivated by the ornamentation, especially the 18-inch long wing feathers protruding from the headdress. A brilliant blue round spot the size of a silver dollar adorned each feather. She recognized the symbol from which one of New Guinea's rarest birds derived its name. Only when the lead Tugaru pointed his ten-foot-long, trident-shaped spear inches from her breasts did the spell of the dollar bird's feathers lose its hypnotic effect.

Behind her, she heard WonTok chamber a round in his rifle. To a man, the warriors in front of her knelt behind their wooden shields, each bearing the carved mask of bug-eyed talisman. Strange, she thought, the Tugaru war deity depicted on the shield wore a plumed helmet, rather than the headdress she had been captivated by moments ago.

She turned her head slowly toward Erik behind her and whispered, "Tell the Tugaru we come in peace."

But it was MilkEye who responded. The Riami man sidled up next to her on the right side of the trail. She was surprised to see that the old warrior had discarded his bow and axe. Instead, he waved green branches he must have gathered from the bushes at the side of the trail. He moved them in a crisscross manner across his chest while he called out, "*Shean-ee! Shean-ee!*"

Aware that they had no common language except pidgin, she prayed MilkEye's words and gestures had a peaceful intent. She looked to Erik for help.

He threw up his hands. "I'm not familiar with the phrase, but the gesture indicates peace."

"Then perhaps we should join the chorus."

"*Shean-ee! Shean-ee!*" the three of them called out in unison.

From the tops of their wooden shields, also decorated with cassowary plumes attached to sticks came the full headdresses, then Tugaru eyes encircled in an assortment of colored pigments appeared. Finally four bodies bathed in grease stood upright and lowered their spears. The Tugaru warriors took up the chant, and on each side of the path, unseen warriors repeated the magic word "*Shean-ee.*" DeAnn was certain the message was loud enough to have reached the CIL encampment along the limestone ledge overlooking Stanek's tent. When the cry fell to a dim echo, the drums also stopped beating. Without any urging, MilkEye faced his foe-men and said, "*One fella road—dassall.*"

Again DeAnn looked to Erik for interpretation.

"I know this phrase. It's the most eloquent heard in pidgin, rivaling anything uttered in a civilized lecture hall," he said.

"Well, what does it mean?"

"There is only one road for all of us."

Then turning to MilkEye, she patted the old warrior on the arm. "Thank you," she said.

As MilkEye hoisted LikLik to his shoulder, he blinked his good eye toward the morning sun. He handed DeAnn the green shrubs and motioned for her to lead on.

Two Tugaru men placed themselves in front and two behind the little band. Like prisoners, DeAnn and her cohorts were led up the mountainside. DeAnn turned to Erik and asked, "Where do you suppose they're leading us?"

"To the clearing where Dr Stanek's trial is underway, would be my guess."

25 NATIVE ALLEGED RAPE TRIAL

CIL Encampment, Mount Bosavi, Papua New Guinea, 1973

A DEEP ALARM arose in Stanek as he arrived at the clearing from the twisted path where the Tugaru were in hot pursuit. He wished he had heeded DeAnn Toland's advice not to venture into the territory of one native tribe or the other except in the company of an escort from both and an interpreter. His early morning wanderings beyond the outside boundaries of the CIL encampment had placed him in a very precarious situation, for Tugaru warriors had arrived ahead of him and were now assembled in large numbers in front of his tent, successfully blocking his escape.

He had been certain that when the sun rose, it would bring a much clearer picture of why the Tugaru had pursued him in the dark all the way to the CIL encampment. But as dawn broke, the flashlight ruse became ineffective because the light was no longer concentrated under his chin, illuminating his features to make his head resemble the skull painted on the tail of the B-24.

Exhausted, he staggered into the clearing. Six Tugaru men left the main force and crept forward to within 20 yards of the pathologist. It was then Stanek spotted Noble. The *kiap* and several armed constables had taken positions atop the limestone outcropping above the Tugaru main force.

Relieved, Stanek called, "Any ideas, Roger?"

Noble lowered his rifle and answered. "This calls for a bold stroke. Stand fast, lad, my boys and I have 'em in our sights. Those

243

breaking for ye just now are the advanced party. They want a closer look and maybe do some ear bashing. Hear them out, but if they get too close, better show 'em ye're armed. Wave that pistol I gave ye under their bloody noses. If ye have to, fire off a couple of rounds in the air."

"Can't. I lost the gun."

"Ye what?"

"It's gone. I don't know where."

"*Come a gutser!* Any minute DeAnn's likely to come marching in here, unaware there's a pistol-toting Tugaru amongst that mob. We'll have to search and disarm the lot. Think of a bluff to buy some time whilst I make my way down there."

Stanek turned his back on the advancing warriors and bent over. He kept the Tugaru in sight between his legs as he hurriedly removed the six batteries from the extended flashlight. Next he ripped off his bootlaces and tied the ends of one lace to two batteries and the ends of the other to two more. He hung one set of makeshift bolos around his neck and stuffed it inside his flight suit, so that the batteries dangled undetected against the sides of his sternum.

The warriors advanced another five yards before he got the flight suit open far enough to loop the other lace around his waist with its attached batteries, which formed a shield over his crotch. He dropped the two remaining batteries into the thigh pockets of the borrowed flight suit, stood upright and turned to face his adversaries. The Tugaru were now close enough that he could smell their skins coated with human sweat and pig grease.

It had taken Stanek little more than a minute to don his own protective shield of batteries, such as it was, but already he could feel his own sweat sticking to his body. Sweat or blood, he wondered, thinking the battery rubbing against his wound had reopened the site where the clavicle knife had pierced his chest in Hawaii.

The next thing he knew, something struck a glancing blow on the right side of his pocket where he had just placed one of the batteries. He looked down and saw a stone rolling away harmlessly, obviously thrown by one of the warriors. He picked it up and pounded it hard against the battery covering the wound still not completely healed and grimaced. Stanek grimaced again as he shifted the blows to the other battery and on down to his crotch and each thigh in turn.

The warriors screamed and jerked from side to side, halting behind their shields. Astonished that he had tricked them into thinking he wore armor, Stanek pitched the rock aside.

In the deepest tone he could muster, he taunted. "Your stones, clubs, arrows or spears can do no more harm than the blows I strike against myself."

He knew the Tugaru could not understand his words, but he repeated them again along with another demonstration, this time using the empty flashlight case, careful to strike only the batteries concealed below his waistline.

He turned away to show disdain. But out of the corner of his eye, he saw five warriors fall to their knees and crouch behind their shields. The sixth and the most hideous looking of the group, stood his ground and even edged closer. Stanek whirled around to face this adversary with the distinctive yellow bird-of-paradise feathers on his headdress and shield, and beetles stuffed in his nose and ears. The warrior pointed his trident-shaped spear at Stanek's chest. Stanek had only the flashlight case to counter the weapon, yet he stood his ground.

Not since that awful night in the mortuary where he had nearly been sliced open, or again, when shots had been fired on the unarmed Beaver as he and Yowell passed over the foothills of Mount Bosavi was he so frightened, outraged and confused at the same time. How could all this be happening on a case so benign and routine as the discovery of a lost B-24 bomber and its crew?

Someone sidled up next to him. He looked over to see MilkEye grinning back at him.

"*Masta*, we take yella fella; turn him red, white and blue."

Stanek couldn't believe his ears. If he was going to die, at least it was with an ally at his side, someone familiar enough with the American bomber crew to repeat one of their slang catch phrases.

The Tugaru warrior must've been as astonished as Stanek was by the sudden appearance of a sworn enemy. Just then DeAnn Toland approached, took Stanek's arm and gently moved him aside. She shifted MilkEye's child to her other arm as she spoke.

"Stay calm," she said. "*Kiap* Noble's right behind our escorts with his constables. He won't let any fighting break out. But you're not excused from the mess you've gotten us into."

245

Stanek jerked his thumb toward MilkEye. "I haven't done anything, except try to help this man's sick child. At least he's grateful."

"Rape is taken very seriously among these people."

"Rape?"

"Yes, Dr. Stanek, and you couldn't have picked a worse victim than the bride-to-be of the Tugaru leader, Loud Mouth, whom you've shamed," she said.

"So, I'm accused of rape! I happened upon the man who cuckolded our ugly friend here." This time Stanek pointed to the Tugaru warrior in front of him. "And now I'm the one blamed. I can tell you it wasn't me."

"We can sort it out later. Right now we've got to defuse this situation," she said. Then she turned to Noble as he came up next to her. "Roger, do you have any gold lipped shells in your bag of tricks?" she asked.

"Sure do, lass. There're some in my haversack. Maybe ye should reach in and get 'em so I can keep me rifle ready."

She produced the shells the natives of New Guinea cherished as their highest currency and offered them to Dr. Stanek. "Here. Pay off your accuser with these, and we can get on with our business."

Stanek turned his palms down. "I'll do nothing of the sort. Erik or Noble can tell Loud Mouth I want to face my accuser. At least let his bride-to-be show herself."

"Roger, please tell Dr. Stanek we're not in a position to make any demands, will you?"

"Wait a minute, lassie. Let's stay cool. Emerson has a point. The Tugaru wouldn't be pursuing this matter if they didn't have some evidence as proof. I'll ask *Bikmaus* to show his hand, and let's see where it goes."

"And if Loud Mouth refuses?"

"Then there'll be no compensation."

Stanek smiled at Noble. "Good idea, and while you're explaining our terms, I've a question for Dr. Toland."

She nodded, and the *kiap* made his case loud enough in pidgin for the entire assembly to hear.

"What's on your mind?" DeAnn asked Stanek.

"Did you hear what friend MilkEye said to me when he came to my aid just now? It was pidgin mixed in with English, but clear enough for me to make out the phraseology. I caught something about a 'yella fella' and 'red, white and blue.' DeAnn, don't you see? According to the pilot's log, the bomber crew used to sing this going into battle with the Japanese!"

He surprised himself blurting out her first name in his excitement. Then he continued, "MilkEye not only received the wristband he wears from an American, but also the phrase as well. Don't you see? This means he must've had long-term contact with possibly one or more members of the bomber crew!"

"So, I was right. There had to have been one or more survivors," she said.

Her reaction was unexpected. She seemed much less astonished than he had been when MilkEye uttered the phrase. There could only be one reason for this, he decided. She had more information than she had shared with him. He guessed it had something to do with the diary he hadn't seen. He was about to question her about this when *Kiap* Noble returned.

"*Bikmaus* has agreed to bring your accuser forward along with the evidence. You're not going to believe what she's got though."

"Your pistol I lost?" Stanek looked at DeAnn again for her reaction. Her face registered utter disgust at his further endangering the mission.

"No," the *kiap* continued. "*Bikmaus* surrendered the pistol. Said one of his warriors had found it. What the *meri* has produced is even more damaging. She's got yer bloody bush hat. Claims it was given in exchange for her favors."

Noble had no sooner related the Tugaru side of the story than a young woman and perhaps her grandmother together made their way to the center of the clearing. Except in age, the pair was indistinguishable. Each had a coating of grease soot on her face. Their broad noses, made wider by the assortment of colored feathers stuck in the fleshy part of their nostrils, reminded Stanek of his encounter with Loud Mouth who had disgusting beetles in his nose. Their hair, arranged in ringlets, swung against each ear almost in cadence with their cracked and callused feet as they drew closer.

"Stand fast, lad," Noble said, restraining Stanek.

The pathologist cupped a hand over his mouth so only Noble could hear his reply. "I'm amazed anyone could find the pair attractive," he said.

The younger woman laid Stanek's hat in the dust, and stepped back. Then the older woman stomped on the hat with such force her wrinkled and sagging breasts flapped against her abdomen like deflated inner tubes. Stanek's eyes were not on the actions of her feet or her breasts. Instead, he focused on the jawbone hanging about the woman's neck on a string of bark.

DeAnn, too, seemed fixed on the object, and Stanek heard her utter, "Salty Meri."

The anthropologist handed MilkEye's daughter to the Riami warrior. Then taking Stanek by one arm and Noble by the other, she ushered them to where the woman continued her attack on the hat.

"Roger, tell Salty Meri I was with Dr. Stanek when his hat was blown away by the wind. Neither of us was close to the Tugaru village at the time. Indeed, my own cap flew off with his. But mine was returned later by MilkEye in behalf of his friend WonTok, who had recovered it."

"Sure, lassie."

Stanek waited while the *kiap* interpreted DeAnn's message. He was pleased she had come to his defense, but discouraged she had wrested control of the situation away from him. All he could do now was sit back and watch the developments unfold. They came sooner than expected.

Noble frowned. "This is going to get nasty. Salty Meri wants us to bring WonTok forward so she can question him directly." The *kiap* stroked his red beard, then continued. "No Riami warrior is going to allow himself to be dressed down by a Tugaru woman no matter how exhalted her status."

Stanek noticed WonTok had discerned he was the center of attention. He was surprised to see the Riami warrior trembling and taking frail steps toward the big Australian. Noble had to bend over to hear WonTok who spoke in a whisper.

When WonTok had finished, Noble stroked his beard again and said, "Ah. We've got a new twist. This good lad was on duty with his Tugaru counterpart. Together they found the hats the wind had blown toward the Riami village. WonTok agreed to take your floppy cap to you, DeAnn, and the Tugaru constable said he'd get the bush hat back to Dr. Stanek."

"What does it prove except they found the hats?" DeAnn asked.

"Ah, but wait, lassie. There's more. WonTok says he saw the Tugaru give Stanek's hat to the young bride-to-be standing over there. Payment in return for a romp in the garden with her, as it were."

"Could WonTok point out the Tugaru man to us?" DeAnn asked.

"I'm sure he could, lassie, except the Tugaru man surrendered his rifle, deserted the constable corps, he did. For all I know, he's part of the mob stirring up all this trouble."

"Can't we tell Salty Meri what really happened and see if she can get the real culprit to come forward?"

"DeAnn, I doubt we'll get a fair hearing. The Tugaru might already know what happened. They're hell bent on extracting something from Dr. Stanek. He's got more material goods to offer 'em than if they settled on a couple of pigs as compensation from one of their own tribal families."

Stanek broke his silence. "Speaking of pigs, there were two sacrificed outside of my tent right after you left, Roger."

The *kiap* bolted upright. "Ye don't say!"

"Yes, the squealing of the pigs sent me outside to investigate. I was looking for your tent when I inadvertently stumbled into the garden where the alleged sexual assault took place."

"These pigs, sacrificed ye say?"

"Arrows in their throats, I think. But what difference does that make?"

"Well, if their throats were slit with a knife, it's a good omen. But, if they're pierced by an arrow to keep them squealing 'til their last breath, it's an ominous sign. One is meant as an offering. The other is devised to instill fear. I'd be interested in seeing those arrows. But it can wait 'til we settle the business at hand."

DeAnn pressed into the opening. "Back to WonTok. What do we do to get out of this if the Tugaru won't accept his explanation?"

Noble rubbed his hand across the stock of his rifle. "We can't shoot 'em all. I recommend Stanek pass 'em those gold lipped shells. Maybe we can buy our way out of this situation as suggested earlier."

"Good. Propose compensation to Salty Meri," DeAnn said.

"Wait. I protest. I'm not going to admit to a crime I didn't commit!"

"I don't think you have much say in the matter, Dr. Stanek. I'm in charge here."

"Oh, yeah, the 'boss lady'. You're about as easy to reason with as the other bossy lady out there with her mind made up."

Stanek was too late. *Kiap* Noble was already explaining the terms of compensation to Salty Meri. But from the way she continued her foot attack on his hat, she was holding out for something more. Stanek noticed that Roger's face was redder than usual when he began to interpret. He also noted MilkEye drew back and shielded his daughter in his arms as if LikLik, too, was in jeopardy.

Kiap Noble shook his head. "The old hag has us over a barrel. She wants the Riami man WonTok to be turned over, or she'll up the ante. If we don't turn over WonTok, she insists Dr. Stanek marry the woman he violated and thus become a Tugaru and use his sorcery powers to find the killer of her youngest son who was slain at the salt well."

"What would they do to WonTok?" DeAnn asked.

"They'd torture the bugger before they killed him, adding to the blood feud these people can't shake off."

Stanek took the *kiap's* arm.

"Surely, Roger, we can't have an innocent man lose his life when all I've got is my pride and reputation on the line. Tell the old witch we'll agree to part of her terms. I'll not admit to doing something I didn't do. I won't marry a native girl, but I'll help Salty Meri find the killer of her son after this B-24 case is over. Now tell her my answer, or I'll drag Erik up here and tell her myself."

Noble looked at DeAnn. She nodded. Only then did the *kiap* set off on his mission once more. In a minute or two he came back and told them Salty Meri had added her own amendment. Stanek would not have to marry the Tugaru girl, but WonTok must prove he was not involved in this incident by undergoing a trial by fire against Loud Mouth, her oldest son, one-on-one in deadly combat.

Noble planted his feet apart. "Here's where we stand. Salty Meri suspects WonTok is the rapist. Since *Bikmaus* is not only the brother of the slain warrior, but the aggrieved bridegroom as well, he must have his revenge. Salty Meri accepts the Doc's offer to track down her youngest son's murderer. But she believes the trail will lead to WonTok or another Riami in the end."

Stanek threw up his hands. "Well, I really think this is getting ridiculous. We're talking about these people without their knowing what's going on. I think WonTok and MilkEye deserve to know what their enemies are saying about them, and as with me, given an opportunity to confront their accusers."

He was surprised to see DeAnn nod again. "I agree with Dr. Stanek, Roger. Please tell WonTok and MilkEye what you just told us."

When the *kiap* had finished, all but MilkEye cringed. He calmly handed LikLik over to DeAnn. Then he took WonTok by the arm and led him front and center. Stanek, DeAnn and Noble followed close at heel.

"I'll interpret what MilkEye has to say to the Tugaru, but don't worry. We're ready if things get out of hand," said Noble.

Thus spoke MilkEye, as translated by Noble, "Tugaru people, you charge WonTok with rape. He did not and could not commit this crime. See what only I have known since we were boys. WonTok was not born like other warriors. He has a warrior's mind, but not the body. As a friend, I shared some of my seed, so that he could present it to our elders at our initiation ceremony and produce evidence of his manhood. If you will not believe me, believe your own eyes."

In a flash, MilkEye ripped the *laplap* from WonTok's waist and threw it to the ground. He then grasped his friend by the shoulders and turned him slowly around full circle. When WonTok's tear-streaked face came in front of Stanek, he could see why the man was so distraught. His genitals were no larger than a three-year-old's. There was no way this man could ever be a rapist. Sorrow for WonTok welled up inside of Stanek. But for the Tugaru warriors who jeered from the sidelines, some even tossing their penis gourds at WonTok's feet, he had nothing but disdain. He stepped in front of MilkEye and WonTok and picked up the fallen *laplap*, handing it to WonTok, who wrapped it around himself and fled.

Stanek found himself face-to-face with Salty Meri who waved a grimy finger under his nose. He grabbed her hand and spun it away from him.

"No, you should be ashamed," he shouted. His face was so distorted in anger that the scar on his cheek stood out like a fresh razor cut. She brought her hand to his face again, and this time the look in her eyes was one of astonishment. She caressed the scar with two fingers as if she were drawing a line along the stem of a delicate flower. Tears whelmed up in her eyes, no longer swollen with bitterness.

"My husband," she said in close to perfect English. "You've come back to me."

She then lifted both hands and must have repeated in Tugaru language what she had said to him. The warriors cheered as Salty Meri cupped her hands around the tips of her breasts and tilted them up toward him.

Stanek looked at Noble for an explanation. "I'm afraid ye're going to have to kiss them twigs, as distasteful as it may be, me lad."

"You're out of your mind!" Stanek exclaimed.

Noble shrugged. "Maybe so. But a symbolic tug at the tribal mother's breast will afford ye Tugaru protection."

The Aussie stifled a chuckle. "Look at them hideous things as tribal welcome mats."

Stanek hesitated. Still Noble urged him on. "Go on, lad. If ye want to go on the salt train, or secure the cooperation of the Tugaru, there's no better ticket than by this simple gesture."

In the end, Stanek forced himself to press his lips against the old matriarch's bosom. The assembled Tugaru cheered. As Stanek began to raise his head, Salty Meri removed the jawbone ornament from her neck and gently guided it over his shaven pate. She kissed the scar on his cheek, picked his hat up from the dust and brushed it off with a stroke one would use on a cat and set it upon his head. Then, she took her would-be daughter-in-law in hand, turned to announce the salt train would be delayed and departed through the crowd. In a moment or two, most of the Tugaru trailed after them.

"What caused Salty Meri's change of heart?" Stanek asked.

"Obviously she thinks ye're her lost husband come back to her in spirit." The *kiap* paused and slapped his thigh. "*Come a gutser!* Why didn't I think of it before? Mackelwaite was bald, had a beard, much fuller than yours, and a scar from a bar fight. A broken bottle slashed against his right cheek. Well, I'm a bloody fool, I am! Salty Meri is Mackelwaite's woman, left in his wake!"

Stanek wanted to hear more, but he sensed that MilkEye was displeased with the ritual just performed, turning him from MilkEye's ally into an honorary Tugaru.

"Roger, please tell MilkEye I don't consider myself a Tugaru in any way and want us to remain friends."

DeAnn interposed. "It won't be necessary. MilkEye trusts you. Otherwise he wouldn't have brought his daughter all this way for further treatment. Another magic injection, I suppose. On the way up, we discussed long-term hospital treatment for LikLik, and MilkEye agreed to give it a try if you approved."

"Well, it won't hurt to reassure him about my allegiance. MilkEye is critical to unraveling this B-24 mystery." Stanek was about to add he would like to have MilkEye assigned as his aide, but thought this wasn't the time, and so he said to Noble, "Go ahead and give him the assurance."

"Straight away," said Noble.

Out of breath, Erik joined the group. The interpreter spoke directly to DeAnn. "General Bellicosi just radioed in. He and his party are about to land. He insists we all gather at the runway with every available document and piece of evidence. He's got a couple of VIPs with him and wants to dazzle them with our progress."

"Oh, dear. The General's arrival is even earlier than I had anticipated. No time to get ready. We can't even stop to change clothes," DeAnn said.

"What about me? As Noble would say, I'm a bloody mess in this flight suit covered with mud, blood and pig excrement. And after what I've just been through, nobody could begrudge me a mouthwash," Stanek protested.

"Later. The General spends a limited amount of time on the ground, especially when he's got VIPs in tow. He'll want your input as well. Go to your tent and gather all the documents and other items I gave you and report back here."

"What about LikLik's serum injection? I'm sure there's time for it."

"Just do it, but hurry. We all have to make sacrifices. Do you think I'd go down there in this grass skirt and T-shirt if it weren't urgent?"

"And if I can't move fast enough for you, Dr. Toland?"

"Then you'll have to go down the mountain alone. And I know you don't want to try it again," she snapped.

He hurried into the tent and remembered he had put most of the items from the B-24 in his bush jacket along with notes he had written to Lt. Dunbar of the Baltimore police and the widow of the murdered Dr. Haveland. He grabbed the jacket, picked up the items on the table and headed for the tent fly. He came face-to-face with MilkEye at the exit.

"Make child better," the old warrior pleaded and tried to thrust his daughter into Stanek's arms. But the pathologist directed him to lay her on the bed.

Stanek found his medical bag, took out the syringe with the experimental bee serum in it and injected the child's buttocks. Sometime during the procedure, MilkEye left.

When Stanek emerged with LikLik, he found the old warrior standing next to *Kiap* Noble. The two stood over the fallen pigs examining the arrow tips they must have removed from the animals' throats.

Noble scratched his beard, tilting his head toward Stanek. "Just as I suspected and MilkEye confirms. These are neither Riami nor Tugaru arrowheads. Looks like Giambu craftsmanship to us. Now what in God's heaven do ye think Giambu from the plains and marshes towards Nomad are doing so far up this mountain?"

The question was left unanswered as DeAnn called, "Hurry up!"

The trio left the tent and moved out into the clearing. Stanek started to hand LikLik back to her father when Noble intervened. "I'll see the little lass gets down to the runway so DeAnn can petition General Bellicosi to take her back to Goroka with him."

While Stanek switched the child from his arms to Noble's, MilkEye took the occasion to remove the band from his wrist. He handed the metal object to Stanek. The pathologist clasped his hands in front of him in a gesture orientals use to signify they are saying thank you.

Stanek smiled. Despite the missteps and the turmoil, this hadn't been a wasted morning after all. The jawbone given him by Salty Meri dangled around his neck, and it was obvious it had at least two amalgam fillings visible in the worn teeth. This placed a white suspect, if not a survivor, on the mountain at some time in the past. Either the lower jawbone belonged to patrol officer Mackelwaite or one of the B-24 survivors. Obviously, the possessor of the jawbone had died, but perhaps others might still be living and hiding among these people.

What's more, he had won MilkEye's friendship, for not only did the Riami warrior come to his aid against the Tugaru threat, but he had used phraseology revealing he had been exposed to American slang. Finally, MilkEye had forfeited the wristband forged out of a .50-caliber shell casing by a white man who had befriended him.

However speculative the case remained at this point, the progress in solving the puzzle was significant. Despite DeAnn Toland's intransigence, he had won the cooperation of Salty Meri, the real boss lady on Mount Bosavi it seemed. Information about a Giambu presence made it imperative for him to go down the Rentoul River aboard Salty Meri's salt train.

As for the Giambu connection, he'd have to find a way to enlist government protection in order to investigate this tribe in its home territory. The Giambu might have information on the missing American remains and the massacre of the Japanese search party along the Rentoul in 1951. This fierce tribe might have tracked down the B-24 survivors as well. And it certainly was plausible they fired on the Beaver upon his arrival with Yowell. If the Giambu had orchestrated the pig sacrifice at his tent in an attempt to frighten him off the case, as Noble surmised, he had to determine their motive.

Stanek outlined in his mind four logical, if not chronological, steps to follow next in the B-24 investigation:

* Persuade Salty Meri to allow him to accompany the next scheduled salt train to Nomad. Meantime, win the approval and support from General Bellicosi for such an expedition.

* Ask everyone to lay their cards on the table to reveal what they know about this case, including any knight sightings on the peak of Mount Bosavi.

* Request Kioko's diary evidence from DeAnn Toland.

* Use his new relationship with the Tugaru, i.e. as the chief investigator into the murder of Salty Meri's youngest son, to persuade his adopted tribe to allow him to expand his search further up the mountain beyond the salt well into land considered off limits except to spirits. Somewhere near the peak, he expected to find the missing twin vertical stabilizer of the B-24 and any human remains buried nearby. Of equal importance, he wanted to determine the identity of the murderer masquerading as a medieval knight and why such a *modus operandi* was necessary.

* All of this hinged on learning MilkEye's language to glean every bit of information from him firsthand and help pull the other elements and facts together.

Only the white team members and natives in khaki *laplaps* in DeAnn's contingent were in the clearing by the time he, Noble and MilkEye rejoined them.

"Got everything?" she asked.

Stanek smirked. "Yes, I'm sure I do. Enough to get me back to my bee keeper cancer research sooner than anticipated."

"I'm happy for you," she said half-heartedly. "MilkEye won't be going down the mountain with us. He's insisted he has to go find his friend WonTok. Just as well. He might frighten General Bellicosi's guests. By the way, there's a reporter named Jim Cole coming in with General Bellicosi and someone named Catherine Stanek."

"Oh, no!" Stanek exclaimed.

This time he detected DeAnn's smirk. "Sorry I didn't give you time to clean up for your wife."

"Oh, no!" Stanek repeated. "I can't believe it! Catherine followed me here?"

26 FRIENDSHIP ESTRANGEMENT

Riami Village, Mount Bosavi, Papua New Guinea, 1973

THE WHOLE VALLEY glowed with a golden light as MilkEye reached the Riami burial grounds. Did WonTok come here to seek guidance from his own ancestors, he wondered. He passed the bleached bones of once proud warriors laid against a plank keeping them upright, as if guarding the area from intruders. When he came to Situmu's place among the elders, he pleaded with his father to show him how to bring WonTok back to the bond they shared. But Situmu didn't answer his son. Perhaps Situmu had not forgiven him for the tainted incident at the initiation ground, now revealed to the Tugaru to the shame of all Riami. He had given WonTok his sperm to save him from becoming an outcast. Without proof of manhood, WonTok could expect no more than woman's work among the cooking pots instead of fighting alongside his *age-mates*. MilkEye knew how angry Situmu would have been if he had known his own son had violated his edict to keep the ceremony pure.

Now MilkEye stood before the bones of Situmu, as white as the skin of the sky people from years of exposure to the sun, and asked his father for forgiveness. Then he added, "Devil twin, Two Face give MilkEye troubles, but Situmu no speak. MilkEye need WonTok to find Kioko-san. Two Face know Kioko-san can use magic to stop his curse."

MilkEye spent no more than a couple of minutes at the burial site before he dashed off to the ceremonial ground where his daughter LikLik would choose her future husband if she lived to carry on the seed of the great Situmu. A childless WonTok had little to celebrate, MilkEye realized, and chided himself for wasting time seeking his friend in such a place.

"Where me go if me WonTok?" he asked himself. He thought the first place would be the men's hut. He might have consulted the mysteries that brought so much spiritual guidance to the Riami.

MilkEye stopped at the gate to the men's hut to catch his breath. Before turning in, he spotted two girls approaching. They swayed in unison, arms encircling each other's waists as they came up the path. MilkEye wondered if LikLik would live long enough to display her own friendships to the world in such a fashion, but for the moment his mind was on WonTok. He sensed his friend faced a great peril, so he did what a man of his status almost never did—question two giggling girls.

"You see WonTok, the warrior?" he asked. The taller of the two girls stuck her tongue out at her companion, and MilkEye could not help but think how remarkably pink it was, like LikLik's was before she fell ill.

Her gesture silenced her *age-mate*, and the taller girl turned her head in the direction of the great *balus* against the mountain on the south shore of the Rentoul. The smaller girl giggled again.

"Stop," her friend admonished. "MilkEye's *one-mate* like to kill self on stones."

"WonTok? Where?" cried MilkEye.

"Swaying bridge. *Meris* and children on *balus* side of river, but warriors on village side. WonTok in middle, shake bridge. WonTok jump into river if any come near. Many go to small *balus*, get gifts, but WonTok stop. Many people no like to see WonTok die on sunny day, so they look for white *misis*. Maybe *misis* give gifts."

MilkEye's expressed his fear. "WonTok die?" he asked.

"WonTok no jump yet," the girl said.

"MilkEye give you pig on wedding day," MilkEye promised.

The girls smiled at MilkEye as they moved off with hips and shoulders touching and giggling once more.

MilkEye thought it was a good sign the girls were not so distraught they couldn't dwell on happy times together.

The Riami warrior quickened his pace and again called on Situmu for help. "WonTok no die," he cried out. "Papa no speak, but help me hurry up to stop WonTok." MilkEye drove his fists into his stomach as he spoke, showing Situmu the thought of WonTok dying was killing him inside.

He continued with his soliloquy. "Riami blame me if WonTok die. Clan of Situmu bear shame." But his father's spirit would not be goaded into answering.

Yet a thought, rather than a voice, filled MilkEye's mind. He alone could save WonTok. He would go out on the bridge and coax him back to safety, or die with him on the jagged rocks below the bridge. In this manner WonTok could take his revenge, if he chose, for the humiliation he had suffered. They would both fall to their deaths, or live to find a way to bring their friendship together again. Either way, the choice to live or die was in his *one-mate's* hands. Not once since they were young boys had WonTok been at the helm. Always MilkEye guided the pair in their shared adventures.

MilkEye formulated his thoughts as to what he would say to WonTok, even as he ran faster down the mountainside.

Now you are in charge, my friend. But before you decide our joint fate, think on this. Only you would miss this murderous fiend if I should die. But this is not possible, because you would die, too, and take the secret of the slain Tugaru with you. Think of our tribe's grief if the Tugaru killed our people off one by one until their lust for revenge is satisfied. If you should throw yourself upon the rocks, you leave behind no greater person to grieve for you than MilkEye, who has been like a brother to you, and so must die along with you.

I have a solution from Situmu, although he did not speak it directly, but put it in my mind. I must place my life in your hands and beg you to live on until the day when you want your revenge for my betrayal and turn me over to the Tugaru as the murderer at the salt well. But if we die now, all this will die with us and many Riami as well, as the Tugaru take their revenge.

MilkEye looked back up the trail and saw DeAnn and her party crossing no man's land between the Tugaru and Riami settlements. He would have to hurry to tell WonTok his plan before the sky people got to the bridge. Otherwise, in order to greet their brothers who come in the small *balus*, they might shoot WonTok with their *thundersticks* if he blocks their way.

259

He would urge WonTok to choose and choose quickly whether they lived or died. If WonTok chose to live, MilkEye must try to enlist his aid in finding Kioko-san, but if WonTok ran away to hide his shame, he had the right to come forward at any time to identify MilkEye as the murderer of the Tugaru youth.

If WonTok chose to live but would not help him, MilkEye turned his thoughts to what he would do next. His only hope was to hook up with Stan-neck, whose magic had already proven strong. But what if Stan-neck, as he had promised Salty Meri he would do, discovered he was the one who killed the Tugaru youth at the salt well? If this happened before he had contacted Kioko-san, he could never erase Two Face, the troublemaker, from his life and save his tribe. No, he must go with Stan-neck and lead him to the bones of his brothers from the *balus*. This would lure him away from the investigation of the murder at the salt well.

MilkEye shook his head from side to side like a dog shaking off a bothersome fly. Should Stan-neck interfere with his quest to find Kioko-san, even though he didn't want another murder on his hands, MilkEye resolved to kill the man whose magic helped save LikLik.

27 VINE BRIDGE BLOCKADE

Mount Bosavi, Papua New Guinea, 1973

EVEN BEFORE SHE reached the vine bridge that crossed the Rentoul and led to the airstrip and bomber wreckage site, DeAnn Toland heard the commotion ahead. She sent *Kiap* Noble to investigate what sounded like the high whine of a distant siren coming from both sides of the river.

Meanwhile, Stanek paced back and forth behind her. The pathologist's feet made little sound on the narrow part of the path except when his legs brushed against a creeper or fern on the edges of the track. He had not been in the country long enough to realize the trails between the Tugaru and Riami were generally overgrown and difficult to follow because the tribes were not on good terms. Occasionally his pacing set to flight a pigeon or some other bird. DeAnn wondered why it bothered her. She thought it was because Stanek's movements, combined with the sound of the bird protesting this invasion, reinforced her own feeling of uncertain anticipation. What news would Roger bring back with him?

In a matter of minutes the *kiap* returned shaking his head and cursing in Australian. He motioned for all the whites in DeAnn's party to close ranks around him.

"*Come a gutser!* It won't do for some of our boys to learn their wives are trapped on the other side of the bridge. I think General Bellicosi's party has scared 'em."

"Oh, dear, what's going on, Roger?"

"Our bloody WonTok's got the bridge blocked. The women and children who came out to meet Yowell's aircraft are caught on the bomber side, whilst their warrior husbands and fathers are raising hell on the other."

"Why would WonTok do such a thing?"

"Probably had something to do with his humiliation in front of the Tugaru," Stanek volunteered.

"Please, Dr. Stanek, stay out of this. Haven't you done enough?" She saw that her words had stung and decided to soften them a bit. He had only volunteered an opinion, perhaps trying to be helpful. She quickly added, "Sorry to be so sharp-tongued, but this has been a horrible day for me, and I doubt it's over. Roger, tell us what WonTok wants to do."

"As I said, lassie, WonTok's out in the middle. Threatening to dash his brains on the rocks below, he is. Says he'll chop the bridge in half with his axe if anyone approaches. I don't know where we can go from here to avoid bloodshed."

MilkEye came out of nowhere and joined the circle of whites. The Riami headman pulled Erik aside and spoke to the interpreter in pidgin. "*Masta, Masta,* no kill me friend."

DeAnn heard him and understood the old warrior was pleading for the life of his friend WonTok. "Erik, tell MilkEye no harm will come to him or WonTok once the bridge is cleared."

She could imagine the scene on the other side where the general must be fuming because she had not been there to greet him and the VIPs as directed. No doubt the women and children clamoring to reach their warrior husbands and fathers on the northern side of the bridge created an unsettled situation. So did the warriors of the Riami and Tugaru tribes yelling what must have been obscenities at WonTok for keeping them away from their kinsmen.

She thought their wail could probably be heard as far north as the elliptical mound and to the southern riverbank where their families waited to cross. She knew the Tugaru sentries in the watchtowers set among the casuarina grove would be severely agitated as they picked up the whining sound. Now as she drew closer, the sound was more like one made by a flock of cassowary birds in distress rather than a siren. The mob scene certainly lacked the discipline of a military operation. To understand the native tribes on the mountain, one had to have patience. She was certain the general had little forbearance.

Another thought crossed her mind. Bellicosi and his party might be as frightened as the women and children by the commotion and decide to board Yowell's aircraft and hightail it back to Goroka. In which case, she could expect a reprimand so severe it would put her job in jeopardy the next time she faced the general.

"We can't waste any more time," she said. "We've got to get over to the bridge immediately. Erik, if MilkEye has given you any ideas, please let's hear them as we press on."

It calmed her a bit to see that neither Erik nor MilkEye seemed alarmed as they fell in step beside her.

Erik spoke first. "MilkEye says he knows what's going on and only he can persuade his brother warrior to surrender the bridge."

"And how can he accomplish it without getting himself killed?" DeAnn asked.

"I don't know," Erik replied. "He won't discuss it with any sky people except Kioko-san, and she's not here."

DeAnn shot a glance at Stanek who followed behind her. She saw by his expression he knew about the diary, but her explanation about it could wait.

She turned to face Erik and said, "Tell MilkEye I cannot let him go alone on the bridge. Ask him if I can fill in for Kioko-san just this once, since I'm white like her and have tried to be kind to his people like she was."

She waited for Erik to translate and heard MilkEye mention Dr. Stanek. The interpreter shook his head. "MilkEye says the only sky person who can go on the bridge with him is Dr. Stanek, the man who saved his daughter."

"Impossible. He could hardly get across the bridge on the first attempt, and besides, if WonTok carries through on his threat, both he and Dr. Stanek could be injured or killed."

Erik smiled. "Seems like the sly old fox has got it covered. He said Dr. Stanek is our passage through the warriors on this side, for no Tugaru dare raise an axe to him after the man he calls Stan-neck had been made a full-fledged member of the tribe by Salty Meri. As for the Riami, MilkEye says his people remain uncertain about the powerful magic the doctor has, and they don't want it turned against them, like the evil twin face of Two Face has done." Dr. Stanek need only go to the edge of the bridge, so WonTok can see

MilkEye has great magic on his side. This will make everything turn out all right."

"Two Face?" Stanek asked from behind the interpreter. "Did I hear you say 'Two Face'?"

Erik turned and addressed Stanek, "Yeah, Doc. He's the mountain spirit both tribes recognize. Or I should say 'spirits' since Two Face has two faces, one good and one evil."

Stanek waited until the path widened before he caught up with the trio and fell in step next to MilkEye. "I also heard this man speak my name, and I'd like to know what it's all about."

"Go ahead, Erik, tell Dr. Stanek what's in the cards if we accept MilkEye's offer."

Erik briefed Dr. Stanek as *Kiap* Noble listened, but when Erik finished, Noble pulled Stanek aside. "Emerson, I've been in the bush for a long time, and I can tell ye, these people are craftier than we give them credit for being. MilkEye may be yer friend today and yer enemy tomorrow if given the slightest cause to slit yer throat."

The *kiap* then turned to DeAnn and continued, "I don't think we should send Dr. Stanek and MilkEye down there alone, but if ye decide to chance it, me and the boys will find some high ground where we can cover them with our rifles. Don't worry. I'll take LikLik with me and keep her safe."

DeAnn bit her lip. "It's Dr. Stanek's call, not mine. If he wants to risk it, and MilkEye's plan works, then perhaps this will atone for the trouble he caused this morning."

"Oh, I see. We're going to play 'blame Stanek,'" the pathologist said.

"How else did this mess start?" she asked.

"I've nothing to do with what's going on at that bridge at the moment, or any responsibility if MilkEye's mission fails. I trust him more than I do those who've been withholding information from me, so let's get on with it."

DeAnn dropped her chin. "I suppose I deserve your criticism, and promise you, Dr. Stanek, as soon as General Bellicosi's party leaves, I'll turn over Kioko's six volume diary to you for examination."

"Good. Then we've got a deal. I'll go down there with my friend MilkEye, and we'll get you guys across the bridge."

"I still have bloody misgivings, lad," said Noble.

Stanek stroked his goatee. "Thanks, Roger. The constables under your command are excellent marksmen, I'm sure. You and your men backing me up is all the insurance I need."

As Emerson Stanek started out with MilkEye, DeAnn took his arm. "Do be careful, Dr. Stanek. I really mean it. Your wife awaits your safe arrival."

For the first time since they had met, DeAnn saw Stanek throw back his head and heard him laugh so hard that everyone jumped. She wondered what he had found so funny in her remark.

DeAnn felt helpless after the two left, since all she could do was sit on the side of the trail and hope MilkEye succeeded in his quest for all their sakes. She thought it strange that Stanek would put so much trust in a native he hardly knew, but then she remembered how MilkEye doted over his daughter during her illness and displayed tears when told about Kioko-san's writings. MilkEye's public display of affection—a rarity in New Guinea—still puzzled her.

Perhaps, she admitted to herself, she had underestimated Stanek. He might be a better judge of a person such as MilkEye than she. But if so, why would he be so cavalier responding to her remark about his wife? Something was amiss. Still she couldn't put her finger on it. Maybe the doctor and his wife were estranged, and she was coming to collect some alimony due her. DeAnn could not suppress a chuckle herself at the thought of Stanek's wife, probably matronly in appearance, coming so far to get her settlement.

"If he were my man, I'd send him packing and say 'good riddance'," she said to herself. "Better yet, after the Tugaru incident today, speaking for myself, I'd like nothing better than to send Dr. Stanek back to Hawaii with a swift kick strategically placed to get him airborne."

Then her thoughts turned to Major Yowell, and she found herself comparing the two men who had invaded her life, albeit uninvited. Yowell was charming and fun to be around. Stanek was what her dad used to call "an old sourpuss," while her mother designated those who couldn't see all the good around them as "prune faces." But, she decided, this might be unfair, for she hardly knew Stanek, while Yowell had been around for weeks. But it would serve Stanek right if his wife fit either parent's description.

"Get these frivolous thoughts out of your mind," she chided herself, "I've got a serious crisis going on and should be praying it ends well." But this thought, too, left her unsatisfied. There was only one thing to do. Get down to that bridge and lend a hand to Stanek and MilkEye as they tried to diffuse the crisis. After all, Bellicosi held her responsible for the small contingent on Mount Bosavi. She signaled Noble so he would know what she was doing, then hurried down the trail after Stanek and MilkEye.

By the time she caught up with them, MilkEye was already on the bridge approaching WonTok who threatened him with an axe raised over his head. She saw MilkEye had shed his own weapons. She was able to see what was going on because Stanek's presence had evidently split the Riami and the Tugaru warriors right down the middle. Neither party made a made a move against the other for fear they would displease their newly crowned shaman. In this way, Stanek's luck was better than hers, she decided. There was no way she would shave off her hair and try to resemble the image on the tail of the B-24, which both tribes referred to as Two Face, as if the image was some kind of spiritual icon.

She could see the surprise in Stanek's face as she approached alone. "I thought you guys could use some help," she said, trying to create a matter-of-fact impression, when inside her heart pounded and her stomach knotted in fear. There must have been 20 fully-armed warriors from each tribe facing each other across the pathway Stanek and MilkEye had created on their arrival. MilkEye was right in this respect. Dr. Stanek was the safe passage he needed to pass through the two lines of warriors. Maybe the second part of MilkEye's plan to prevail upon his friend to desist might work as well. All they could do was wait.

She felt Stanek wanted to ignore her presence, but she was determined to get his attention. "Any idea how MilkEye's progressing out there?" she asked.

"None whatsoever."

"What's your guess?"

"He'll persuade his friend to leave the bridge, and we'll get across."

"I hope you're right," she said.

"But if one of us knew the language, we wouldn't have to rely on hope, or Erik, would we? By the way, where is your interpreter?"

"He went with *Kiap* Noble as an extra marksman if needed."

"Dr. Toland, this is the last time I want to be cut off from communication with any of your assistants or indigenous personnel involved in this case."

"Certainly I'm not equipped to teach you the local language even if I had the time."

"No, but after this is over, as part of our deal, I want you to lend me Erik for as long as it takes for me to speak pidgin."

"Why do you want to learn pidgin? I thought you weren't going to be here long?"

"Well, things have changed."

"I see, Dr. Stanek, you want to question MilkEye about his use of the slang phrase 'yellow' something-or-other.

"It's part of the reason."

"And the other?"

He held up the human jawbone Salty Meri had placed around his neck. "This, and what I've already seen with my own eyes makes me certain one or more crimes have been committed on this mountain."

"And so you need the language to question the native population about these crimes, right?

"Exactly."

"You wouldn't classify the two pigs slaughtered outside your tent as criminal behavior, would you?"

"No, but if Noble's right and the pig sacrifice was meant to scare me off this case, the incident outside my tent could've been connected with the beheading I saw for myself."

"The what?"

"Murder!"

"When, where, who?"

"You'll get the answers to some of your questions later at the briefing for the general, but now, shouldn't we focus our attention on MilkEye who has nearly reached WonTok?" he asked.

"Yes, but if his mission fails, and we can't cross the bridge, the briefing is out. General Bellicosi won't wait around very long."

"We'll just have do what those natives are doing down there." She followed his pointed finger. "They seem to be able to climb over the rocks below and wade across what must be the shallowest part of the river without too much difficulty."

"Oh dear! The general will have them shot, or he'll get his party out of there. We've got to stop them."

"Well, why didn't you bring Erik along so he could shout instructions down to them? See how important it is to know the language? And didn't you caution me not to venture forth without an interpreter and escort from both tribes?"

"*Touché*," she said. "But if you'll break off a branch from that tanget shrub next to you, I'll try something."

She could see the skeptical look in his eyes as he handed her the branch. Breaking the branch in half, she hurried to the edge of the bridge and waved the branches over her head in a crisscross motion and shouted, "*Shean-ee. Shean-ee.*" She repeated the phrase over and over.

She knew the warriors heard her down below. To a man, they halted in midstream and turned their heads up at her. She saw the shocked look on their faces. Then they did the unexpected. They retreated back to the shoreline and squatted in the grass.

"How in the hell did you do that?"

"Remember, doctor, I've been here a lot longer than you and have picked up a few tricks."

"*Touché* back to you. Amazing! If only all the world's problems could be settled with the wave of a branch and a single word. What does it mean, anyway?"

"*Shean-ee?*"

"Yes."

"Something to do with peace in conjunction with the waving of a branch. I saw and heard MilkEye use it to the same effect."

"Speaking of MilkEye," Stanek said, "It would appear our mutual friend has done his job, for he's coming this way with a disarmed WonTok right on his heels. Maybe when you shouted, WonTok threw his axe over the bridge. Like I said, it's one powerful word and the first thing I want Erik to teach me."

"I'm sorry, but we'll have to wait to cross until the traffic clears, because the women and children are pouring across on the heels of MilkEye and WonTok. General Bellicosi must've really scared them. He scares me sometimes."

"Really?"

"Haven't you heard the rumor?"

"No."

"Would you like to know?"

"If it's got anything to do with our mission, yes. If not, no."

"Indirectly it does."

"Then I suppose I should be kept informed."

"The general has a secret file on all of us who work for him. I've heard he uses it wherever someone crosses him."

"Well, I don't have to worry. I don't intend to cross him."

"Yeah, but you can't tell. This secret file could hold something to destroy one's reputation. I hear for every star Bellicosi achieves, 40 of his underlings have their careers ruined."

"Then neither of us has to worry."

"Why?"

"We're civilian contracted personnel and not directly in his chain of command."

"I hope you're right, but Bellicosi is said to have the ear of the President."

"I still don't intend to stay here long enough for anybody to dig up any dirt on me, unless..."

"Yes."

"Unless you're going to report the alleged rape of the native girl."

The concerned look on his face showed his anxiety, and if it weren't enough, the way he drummed his fingers against the scar on his cheek indicated how disturbed he was. He'd irritated her by acting as though theirs was a professor/student relationship. Yet, this was no reason to possibly ruin his marriage and soil his reputation. After all, he had been cleared of any wrongdoing. DeAnn decided to allay his fear. "I don't expect the matter to ever come up again," she said.

His drumming ceased immediately. "Thanks. I'll hold you to it."

She and Stanek made way as MilkEye reached the edge of the suspended vine bridge a step or two ahead of WonTok. They brushed past without a word. No sooner had they reached the shoreline than the two natives separated. WonTok practically dove into the underbrush lining the trail. DeAnn could see MilkEye's face bore the look of sorrow, and she didn't appreciate it when Stanek quipped, "Whatever agreement they reached on the bridge didn't last long."

White people didn't take time to understand native culture, she thought. For the second time in one morning, MilkEye had shamed his closest friend—first in front of the Tugaru and now on the bridge where every Riami could see WonTok had easily been thwarted from taking his own life.

DeAnn was surprised to see the one-eyed warrior return to the bridge, this time carrying his weapons. He shoved his axe inside his bark belt on one side and on the other he attached his quiver of arrows. Before he put his bow over his shoulders, he set his string bag on the ground and removed a head ornament, opossum's fur tails, other bits of fur and five pig's tusks. DeAnn watched as MilkEye pulled the ornament composed of tambu and cowrie shells down over his head almost to his ears and slipped on a bark wristband to replace the metal one which Stanek now wore. He put the fur tails through holes in his ears, and stuffed the pig tusks in five different places in his nostrils.

Snuffling from the weight of the pigs' tusks suspended from his septum, MilkEye turned to Stanek and drew his hand around to show he included DeAnn, saying, "We altogether go meet big *Masta* at small *balus*."

DeAnn immediately grasped his intent. "Oh Lord," she said. "He wants to go with us to the airstrip to meet General Bellicosi!"

Stanek replied, "Yes, I think he means he wants all of us to go together to meet the 'top man'. He must've seen the general coming and going at the airstrip, although he never showed himself to him. Now he's got a reason."

"What is it?"

"You're sending his daughter back with the '*bikmasta*'. Evidently MilkEye has made himself presentable for the occasion."

"He certainly looks fierce. I'm going to ask Roger on his return if he can persuade MilkEye to stay on this side of the bridge."

"We're really in no position to criticize his appearance, seeing we didn't have time to make ourselves presentable."

Stanek's remark reminded DeAnn of her own problem. The immediate one dealt with getting across the swaying vine bridge in a grass skirt. Although in a hurry to meet General Bellicosi, she decided the best way to maintain her modesty was to cross last, putting all the males in front of her should a gust of wind distract them at her expense.

When *Kiap* Noble, Erik and the constables returned, the patrol officer was still holding LikLik. DeAnn whispered to Roger about MilkEye's desire to go with them, but she didn't think it was a good idea. Then in a lower tone she added an explanation of why she wanted to cross last.

"Lass, I think ye're forgetting this is MilkEye's turf. We can keep him outside the rope barrier, but I don't think we can stop him from crossing the bridge. As to yer second problem, I agree ye'd draw a crowd in the nuddy. We've had enough side shows for one day."

The *kiap* pointed to Stanek. "Why don't ye lead the way followed by MilkEye? My boys will cross next, then me and Erik whilst DeAnn brings up the rear."

DeAnn looked at Roger and furrowed her brow. "Couldn't you have put it a little more delicately, *Kiap*?" she said teasing him.

She watched Stanek shift his rucksack so none of the frame stuck out to be caught by the vegetation covering the bridge. He was a quick learner, she thought. She scowled as MilkEye fell in step behind Stanek.

"Roger, how do you suppose Bellicosi will react to being so close to a former cannibal?" asked DeAnn.

"I haven't seen the general except when he's been as cross as a frog in a sock, lassie. All we can do is *give it a burl*. Look how close MilkEye follows Emerson. My old *bluey*, the best working dog in Australia never heeled as well."

"What are you saying, Roger?"

"I'm saying we've underestimated MilkEye. He's as cunning as a *dunny rat*. Dr. Stanek's got something he wants, and he'll stick to Emerson 'til he gets it. Likewise, Emerson needs MilkEye. They'll be inseparable mates here out, 'til one or the other discovers he no longer needs a partner. The doc is at greater risk. He doesn't know how to play by jungle rules."

28 JUNGLE VIP BRIEFING

Mount Bosavi, Papua New Guinea, 1973

DEANN STRUGGLED on the bridge. She had not realized how hard it was to keep her grass skirt in place while gripping the vine railing. As a result, she fell several spaces behind the men and reached Bellicosi's party standing in the shade beneath the wing of the B-24 just in time to hear the woman dress down Dr. Stanek.

"Really, Emerson. I've heard of white men degenerating in the tropics, but you take the cake. You look like Robinson Crusoe, and I suppose it's your man Friday on your heels. Now look. How nice. Here comes your Jane. You've brought her along to greet us as well."

DeAnn blushed. The contrast in the two women was almost unbearable. She had never seen someone so beautiful or immaculately attired. Her suit included a pith helmet with a trailing ribbon like one she had seen in a store window on 5th Avenue advertising safari outfits for the discerning lady.

But she had little time to dwell on the woman, for General Bellicosi threw his cigar to the ground, stomped it out, looked at her as if she were in line for inspection and demanded, "Egad, DeAnn, where're your clothes?"

If his comment didn't hurt enough, Major Yowell turned on her. "How could you, DeAnn? Stanek's wearing my flight suit, or whatever's left of it!"

The older man in the group stood hunched over a pair of crutches, and DeAnn felt his voice had a soft tone to it, although he spoke almost in a whisper. "My, My. What an interesting couple we have here," he remarked.

The General whirled to face his older guest. "Damnit, Jim, I hope you're not intending to print any of this. I don't want it to get out we've got scientific personnel running around in the jungle like savages and wearing their ornaments no less. And I must say, in DeAnn's case, scantily clad as well. And what in the hell is the foul odor I smell?"

Yowell blurted, "It's pig shit, sir, and he's got it all over my flight suit!"

"Major, stow the barracks talk in the presence of ladies," admonished General Bellicosi.

Yowell's jaw dropped as he looked at DeAnn and repeated his previous question, "How could you, DeAnn?"

Try as she might to control her stuttering, DeAnn had no better response than, "E-e-e-events s-s-s-sort of g-g-g-got out of c-c-c-control."

The late arrivals were still standing in the sun as they faced this inquisition, yet DeAnn started shivering. Catherine, although more heavily dressed than any of the others, seemed unfazed by the heat and humidity. But what happened next surprised DeAnn most of all. Stanek set his medical bag down in the grass, unfolded his bush jacket from over his arm and draped it over DeAnn's shoulders. She immediately pulled it across the front of her sweat-soaked T-shirt.

The woman drummed her fingernails against the desktop. "My, my, how gallant, brother, dear. I see you still haven't lost your charm."

DeAnn searched Stanek's face and exclaimed, "B-b-b-brother?"

He smiled, "Oh, I'm sorry. Let me introduce my jungle companions. Catherine, this is Dr. DeAnn Toland, field leader of our expedition, and this gentleman with the pig tusks through his nose is MilkEye, headman for one of the tribes. I'm sure General Bellicosi has told you about *Kiap* Noble and his constables, who keep us safe as we go about our work, and our interpreter, Erik. DeAnn, Roger, Erik, MilkEye, meet my adoptive sister, Catherine Stanek, CEO of Stanek Pharmaceutical Laboratories, Inc. But I question why Catherine has come to this remote spot. Surely she's not after big game, although dressed for it, since the largest animal

I've seen has been a pig, two as a matter of a fact, but they were dying."

"Yeah, but I bet they lived long enough to squirt blood and shit all over my flight suit," Yowell protested.

General Bellicosi took out another cigar and lit it.

"Stow it, Major. As for you, DeAnn, if there were time, I'd allow you and Dr. Stanek to clean up, but we want to get out of here. We've already missed some valuable time waiting for you and listening to the chants of those damn natives yelling and screaming."

Yowell offered to go to his plane and retrieve a blanket for DeAnn to cover her shoulders and grass skirt.

She pulled Stanek's jacket tighter around her body and replied, "I'll be fine in this 'til we get through the briefing."

She could see Yowell was hurt by her refusal of his help. But in a flash the major had turned his gaze on Catherine, as did all the males present, including MilkEye, as she spoke. "Before we get down to your business, General, I want to respond to Dr. Stanek's question relative to why I'm here. One is professional and the other is personal. The personal can wait until we get a moment alone. My professional interest is in seeing my brother doesn't fritter his time away in this hideous place, but gets back to his cancer research as soon as possible."

"Stanek Laboratories won't get the results, as I've told you, Catherine."

"So what? The world will be better without cancer."

In that instant, DeAnn's eyes met Catherine's. Although the woman's features were somewhat concealed by a very thin veil, almost a mosquito net attached to her safari, turban-like helmet, to DeAnn she appeared Aphrodite-like, as if rising from the sea. Instead of perspiration, femininity, if possible in anyone, seemed to exude from every curve in her body. When Catherine tilted her head so she did not have to face DeAnn directly, DeAnn was reminded of an exquisite model she had seen in a fashion show in Chicago. Even Catherine's pleated khaki blouse and jodhpurs and brown boots accentuated her figure, rather than concealed it, as one would expect.

Catherine turned back, lifted her veil and faced DeAnn straight on. "Well, I hope your assistance, Dr. Toland, expedites Emerson's return to his beekeeper cancer study."

DeAnn replied, "I understand when Dr. Stanek finishes this case, he's been given time to pursue his research."

"Well, I want all of you to know this is the most preposterous thing Emerson has ever done—leaving a promising cure for cancer hanging in the balance. You most of all, General, ought to be ashamed for taking him away from such important research!"

"But we have a contract," Bellicosi protested.

"Fine. I'll buy it out and pay you double what it's worth to get him back on his cancer project."

"I've got some say in this," Stanek interjected.

The man with the crutches spoke up in what DeAnn saw as an attempt to tone down the bickering. "Pardon me for butting in. My name is Jim Cole. I'm a reporter and, as you can see, unwell. My frailties limit the time I can be up and about, especially in such an arduous environment. May I ask we get on with the briefing I was promised, and the rest of you postpone these matters for a more cordial setting?"

Bellicosi slapped Cole on the back. "Well spoken, my journalist friend. Let's all sit down in the shade and focus on the plight of our fallen comrades, which is the real purpose for us being here. Dr. Stanek, you go first."

Stanek took DeAnn's arm and gently guided her under the wing of the aircraft. "If Dr. Toland will be so kind as to retrieve the evidence from the pockets of my bush jacket, I think we can move things along more quickly."

Catherine looked away toward Mount Bosavi. "I certainly hope so. I'm like Mr. Cole. I want to get out of here."

"I think you'll find this boring anyway, Catherine. But the others should know that my initial reaction is we're dealing with survivors. But as to whom, or how long, one or more of them survived, we are only left with a document I suspect was not written by any member of the crew during the emergency situation or immediately after the crash."

He paused, cleared his throat and continued. "In other words, the pilot's log wasn't written by the pilot whose remains are identifiable in gravesite one. Even more perplexing is the lighter *Kiap* Noble found in a hand severed not too long ago, decades after the B-24 reportedly went down on this spot."

A hush fell over the group, except Jim Cole rose unsteadily from the chair he had taken next to General Bellicosi and spoke to Emerson Stanek. "May I see your evidence, Doctor?"

Stanek looked to Bellicosi and received a nod of approval. He placed the pilot's log in one of Cole's hands as the reporter leaned forward on his crutches, and the Zippo lighter in the other. The reporter perused one and examined the other of the items. Then with a look of horror on his face, he fell back into his chair.

"Good Lord, he's fainted!" Bellicosi cried. "You're a doctor. Do something, Stanek!"

"This man suffers from a rare form of cancer. It's important to keep him from entering a possible comatose stage, but we don't have anything available to bring him around, except, perhaps..."

DeAnn offered, "Except the drug you used on LikLik, MilkEye's daughter. I recall you saying at the time malaria had the same properties as cancer cells, and it certainly worked on her. I saw her come out of her stupor myself."

"Really!" Catherine exclaimed. "Then, Emerson, you must've tried your experimental bee serum on one human at least and gotten results. Do you know what this means?"

"You're wrong, Catherine. I've used it on two people, LikLik and myself; in my case as an inoculation against malaria, but it's hardly scientific proof it works."

"Use it on Cole, man. If it saves his life, or at the very least prevents him from becoming comatose, what will he or we care about scientific verification? If it's a legal situation making you hesitate, I can tell you Cole gave me power of attorney to act in his behalf should a medical emergency occur on this trip. So, do it. I'll cover your back. Cole's as essential to Operation Simpatico as any one of us."

After Stanek had given Cole the injection, DeAnn whispered to him, "Why do you suppose just a glance at the document, or the lighter, or both, caused enough stress to make him faint?"

Stanek answered, "A good question, DeAnn. Perhaps somewhere down the line, one of us should inquire about it if he survives." Out of the corner of her eye, DeAnn could see Catherine was displeased at her *tête-à-tête* with Stanek.

"May I assume the little girl who got the serum is the very one being held by the patrol officer?" Catherine asked.

"Indeed she is, Miss Stanek," replied Noble. He held the child up so all could see that she was conscious and alert.

"What's a child doing down here anyway?" Bellicosi asked.

DeAnn brushed a hand across her auburn hair, leaving a spot of grease on her forehead. "Sir, she was brought along at my request. She's the daughter of this very powerful chieftain in the Riami tribe, and needs long-term care at Goroka. It'll benefit our mission here if you take her back with you. Her father has agreed."

"Absolutely not. These people have their witch doctors, or shamans. Let them treat her."

MilkEye snorted and reached into his string bag. He held out a *kina* shell to General Bellicosi. "How much payment for trip in *balus*?" he asked in pidgin.

"Someone interpret this gibberish for me!"

Erik, who had been pacing back and forth in the background, came forward to participate. "General, he wants to know how much a flight to Goroka would cost, and offers to buy a ticket for LikLik with the shell he's offering."

"Tell him it's no deal, Erik. How do we know his daughter won't subject us all to a disease in the close confines of an aircraft, to say nothing of the putrid odor of pig grease and sweat she bears, as her father does. If we dismiss those two natives, we'll cut the odors down by half."

Catherine Stanek took off her pith helmet and gently set it on the desk in front of the general. She shook her head and every blond curl seemed to fall in place. DeAnn noticed she glanced at Stanek to see if he was watching, although she spoke to Bellicosi, "Let's not act too hastily, Tony. This child carries Dr. Stanek's possible cancer cure in her blood stream."

"What about it, my dear?" Bellicosi asked.

"With Emerson's okay, we could give his research an assist by taking the child back with us and analyzing both the blood taken from her and Cole, and see if we can help my brother isolate the element in his serum which could destroy cancer cells."

Stanek touched the scar on his cheek. "If it means the child gets medical attention, I've no objection. True, I don't know whether it's the royal jelly, the honey, the venom from the sting, the combination, or what it is arresting her disease."

"A blood sample may provide a start in finding an answer. What's more, Emerson, I'd have the professionals at Johns

Hopkins conduct a better analysis than you could obtain anywhere in this God-forsaken country."

"But let me remind you, Catherine, I've filed a patent for all discoveries related to my research. And Stanek Laboratories, or any of your other subsidiaries, better not violate or interfere with any of my work in progress."

"Understood," Catherine said.

"But who will to take care of the little urchin?" Bellicosi asked.

Catherine replied, "Until we get to Goroka, she'll be under my care. After we arrive, I'll hire a nursemaid or nanny to look after her."

"Great! Finally we agree on something," said Bellicosi. Put the child on board and tell her ugly father I don't want his payment."

Noble cautioned, "If you don't take the shell, General, he'll just toss in more items to meet the price."

"Nonsense," said Bellicosi, "I'm not going to put the damn shell in my nose like he has done! Tell him I have no use for it."

MilkEye reached into his bag again. This time he pulled out a gold nugget and offered it to Yowell, indicating the major should intercede for him. Yowell backed away holding his hands in front of him as if he had just been offered poison.

"No, no," he said. "Put it back!"

MilkEye turned toward the river, swung his arm holding the nugget in a motion like one would use in skimming a rock across the water and looked at Yowell.

Bellicosi rose, reached for the gold nugget and snatched it away from MilkEye. "Let's not have him throw it away. Noble, if the Australian government recognizes his right to the gold, tell the native he's come up with payment to buy a plane ticket to Goroka for his daughter and care for her treatment at the hospital as well."

Noble inched toward General Bellicosi, "Better let me take possession of the nugget, sir. Belongs to the Papuans, it does. My government will keep it in trust 'til they get their independence," said the *kiap*. General Bellicosi relinquished the gold nugget to him

From this exchange DeAnn noticed MilkEye understood more than they had credited him for, and Noble must have realized it as well, because she had seen him raise an eyebrow. If it registered with Stanek, he showed no outward sign. More importantly, she realized Yowell had indeed betrayed her trust by encouraging the cargo cult when caught trading with MilkEye. "Arrowheads for a nephew in Dallas, my eye," she thought.

General Bellicosi returned to his chair. "Ah, I see our man Cole is coming around nicely. Now, continue your briefing, Dr. Stanek."

DeAnn watched Stanek shift uneasily from side to side as if deeply disturbed. The golden-haired woman must have seen the same thing, because she said, "Oh, Tony, give Emerson a moment to gather his thoughts. He reflects on everything and every word."

"My dear, I thought you were in as much of a hurry to get out of here as we are," replied the general. "I want to know if we've made any progress in identifying remains," he added.

Emerson removed the necklace Salty Meri had given him and laid it on the desk. "This is all we've turned up since yesterday, and even this may not be what you're looking for."

"What do you mean?" asked Bellicosi.

"I mean this might not be the lower jaw bone of a crew member on the B-24, but rather of an Australian patrol officer who came to this area and has been missing for many years."

Yowell shouted, "How'd you get the jawbone away from Salty Meri?"

DeAnn interceded, "Frank, please wait until later. Let's not waste the general's time with details."

Catherine turned her head aside. "Dear Lord, don't tell me he's frolicking with another woman on this mountain. Emerson, what's gotten into you?"

"Well, I want my flight suit cleaned and returned," said Yowell.

General Bellicosi grabbed a handful of pencils from DeAnn's desk drawer and speared one right into Yowell's chest. "Damnit, Major, and everybody else, keep quiet and let the man speak."

Emerson removed his battered and dust covered bush hat and waved it at those seated. "I'm afraid we're all working at cross purposes. We can settle the jawbone question by having it shipped to Australia where they might have dental records of a *kiap* named Angus Mackelwaite. If we get a match, we know it's not one of the crewmen."

How do we know it's the jawbone of a white man?" General Bellicosi asked.

"Because of the fillings," Stanek replied.

"But if it turns out to be the jawbone of one of the B-24 crewmen, do you have any idea yet which one it might be?" Bellicosi inquired.

"Taken with the information I've given you about the pilot's log, we can rule out the four crewmen tentatively identified in burial site X-1. They were probably killed on impact. Here I'm referring to the pilot, the navigator, who was in the copilot's seat at the time, the radio man and the body of one gunner killed in combat before the crash, according to the pilot's log."

"But I thought you said the pilot's log was a hoax." interrupted Bellicosi.

"No, I said it was not written by the pilot," replied Stanek.

General Bellicosi raised his eyebrows. "Then how did it get in the X-1 burial site?"

"One of the other crewmen still unaccounted for might've put it there as a record of his recollection sometime later."

Stanek paused to wait for Jim Cole, who struggled to get back up on his crutches. "I believe Mr. Cole has a question," he said.

"How do you know any of the other six unaccounted for crewmembers survived, Dr. Stanek?" the reporter asked.

General Bellicosi interjected, "We concluded as much from the copilot's letters of condolence which were written sometime later, Jim."

Stanek added, "It, too, was found in burial site X-1 with the pilot's log, although it's a mystery how either one of them got there."

"A second document! When do I get to see it?" asked Cole.

"Later, Jim," said Bellicosi. "It's really just a bunch of letters written home to the next of kin. It might be too personal for publication."

"You told me I'd have a free hand to examine all the evidence."

"Yes, you will, Jim, but first let's hear what else Dr. Stanek has to report. Continue, doctor."

Stanek cleared his throat and began. "The six crew members unaccounted for may include the copilot, bombardier, engineer and three gunners."

"Two officers and four enlisted men," Yowell interjected.

Bellicosi raised a pencil and gave the major a stern look. "Go on, doctor," he said.

"I think our best chances of recovering their remains are to go down the Rentoul River and up to the top of Mount Bosavi."

DeAnn winced. "Neither the Riami nor the Tugaru, especially, will allow an expedition to the top of the mountain where the spirit Two Face, dwells. Why do you think we'll find any remains up there anyway?"

"Because there's where one of the airplane's twin stabilizers broke off at the initial point of impact with the mountain. Some of the crewmembers in the back fell out or were thrown out of the airplane as the stabilizer was ripped off with part of the tail section, and the pilot subsequently lost control. The bomber then plunged down the western slope of the mountain where it crashed beside the river, killing the three previously mentioned (not to mention the fourth already deceased) who were still in the aircraft. It's possible there were some fatalities on top of the mountain as well, when probably the other six were ejected, and we might find some remains there."

"But you aren't certain?" asked DeAnn.

"No, Dr. Toland, I can't say for certain this was the case, except from the copilot's log we learn one of the gunners was dying of wounds in the back of the aircraft before it crashed. We might find his remains on the mountaintop and possibly those of another. At some point at least, four of the remaining crewmembers left the mountain to go down river toward Nomad. I want to make these two trips to search for the missing remains and possibly more evidence about what occurred at these places."

"I don't like this 'down the river and up the mountain' nonsense. Don't you realize how important it is to complete this mission as soon as possible?" asked the general.

DeAnn watched, astonished at Stanek's next move. The pathologist leaned across the desk and faced General Bellicosi eye to eye. "General, I'm certain what I'm about to say will upset your timetable as it has mine."

"Come to the point, Doctor!"

Stanek continued. "As we agreed from the outset, my charter is to go beyond merely searching for and identifying remains. Dr. Toland and her team are fully equipped to do this job. I'm here to determine if crimes were committed, by whom and with what motive. In other words, conduct a criminal investigation. Why else would you call in a forensic pathologist?"

The general twirled the pencil, and DeAnn was afraid he was going to hurl it at Stanek as he had done to Yowell. She was relieved to see he drew it back and tapped the eraser against the desk. "What is it you're driving at? We proposed the same deal to Dr. Haveland before his untimely murder."

"Yes, but I know Dr. Haveland wouldn't have taken this case unless he would've been given free rein to follow the investigation wherever it took him."

"You sound so certain a crime has been committed. You've only been here 24 hours. Egad, your sister's right. You're a genius."

"No, General, just an observer. On the day I arrived, from the cockpit of Major Yowell's aircraft, I saw a murder committed. It happened as we passed by the peak of Mount Bosavi approaching from the south."

A hush descended on the group. Then DeAnn whispered to *Kiap* Noble, "Roger, how is this possible?"

The *kiap* patted her on the shoulder, and then he stepped up beside Stanek who stood almost at attention in front of the desk. "Lad, ye know I'm in yer corner, but I must say I'd be daf to back ye up on this one. The southern top of Mount Bosavi is nothing but a large, volcanic crater, inaccessible from any direction, except on the north side. Yer murderer would either have had to parachute in or go through the mountain to reach the area."

Bellicosi laid down his pencil and clapped his hands together. "There, you see. Things are not always as they appear, especially after a long flight. Yowell, you were there. Did you see any murder take place, or did Dr. Stanek tell you what he had seen?"

"No, sir. Though he did look pale at one point, I dropped the matter, thinking my talk about cannibals had spooked him like a long horn caught in a stampede."

"And you, DeAnn? Did Doctor Stanek fill you in?"

"No, General, not at the time, but he did mention it later and said details would follow at this briefing."

Even before Stanek pounded a fist into the palm of his hand, DeAnn sensed he had mistaken her testimony as piling on. She started to amend her statement, but Stanek had already launched a counterattack.

"I didn't say anything to Major Yowell because we were already past the point where he could've verified the sighting, and since the clouds were closing in, I didn't think it safe to circle the mountain another time. Once on the ground, I found out how hesitant your people were to cooperate with me, so I kept quiet until Noble verified there was at least one other incident in New Guinea in which a murder was committed involving a victim wearing medieval style armor."

General Bellicosi flipped the pencil into the air and took up his cigar. "Armor! What in the hell does armor have to do with anything?"

"The bomber crew had a suit of armor on board taken from the officer's club at Port Moresby as a totem or good luck charm. The person I saw commit the crime was at least partially clad in a breastplate and visor."

Noble twirled the corners of his mustache. "I remember our conversation, lad," said Noble. "But I had no idea what ye were getting at. I'm sure the general and the rest of us would like to know what ye saw on the mountaintop yesterday afternoon."

"As I said, someone dressed as a knight brandished a sword and brought it down with enough force to behead a native carrier. Then the murderer drove several more bearers into the mountainside where there must've been an opening, because they disappeared."

DeAnn wondered if Catherine had heard enough. She didn't have to wait long. "All this is getting too gruesome for me. Can't we all pack up and just leave this place?" Catherine asked.

The general stood up from the desk. "I'm afraid it's not that simple, my dear. Operation Simpatico is President Nixon's pet project. What will it take to speed things up?"

Stanek was the first to answer the general. "Cooperation from everyone here, a little more time and your authority to go where the leads take us."

The general puffed savagely at his cigar. "How do you propose to proceed?"

"First down the Rentoul, then to the top of Mount Bosavi," Stanek said.

"Why the river first?"

"Yowell and I were attacked as we flew over the Rentoul. I'm sure it was reported to you. What's more, I believe the river attack was related to the knight sighting."

"Isn't your assumption a huge stretch of imagination in such a primitive land with poor communication to say the least?" Bellicosi asked.

"Perhaps. We shall see. But I believe our best chance of finding remains lies down river where the copilot indicates the crewmen had to find refuge on their way to Nomad when their native escorts disappeared. They were left to forage for food on their own," replied Stanek.

Cole glared at Bellicosi, "Then this second document has more to it than just a series of letters!"

General Bellicosi frowned at Cole. "As I said, Jim, you'll get to see the document in due time, but you'll just have to be content with the redacted version after I've looked it over in order to retain the dignity of these soldiers who served us so well. Right now I want to ask Dr. Stanek why he needs to go up the mountain at this point?"

"Because, General, someone on the mountaintop committed murder. We need to rule out a crewmember as the killer."

Bellicosi looked straight at DeAnn. "Do you approve of this plan?"

"No, sir. With the Tugaru on a war footing due to the slaying of a young warrior at their salt well, I can't spare any of our resources to accompany Dr. Stanek on either venture. The risks far outweigh the gains."

Stanek pounded his fist into his hand again. "What risks? I'll go alone, if I have to, or at least with a few of Noble's constables. Roger, ask MilkEye if he'll go along with me."

DeAnn was shocked to see that the old warrior nodded enthusiastically after the translation.

"What's this about being shot at, Emerson?" Catherine asked. She stomped her foot and continued. "I won't allow this expedition. You're too valuable to science to risk your life on something, which doesn't mean a hill of beans to anybody but the President and Tony. I gave a $100,000 contribution to Nixon's re-election campaign, and I'll match it for your Simpatico operation to buy Emerson out of this awful contract."

Stanek drew in a deep breath. "You don't know my life is already on the line. Someone wants me off this case as much as you do, but they were willing to slice me open back in Hawaii."

Catherine came back with the question on DeAnn's mind. "Did you know about these attempts on my brother's life, General, or did you read about it in the newspaper like I did?" she asked.

Bellicosi looked over at Cole, who was now up on his crutches. "All I got was bits and pieces from our reporter friend here. He can tell you what happened. He was there at the time and saved Dr. Stanek."

In the same, calm voice he had used earlier, Cole asked, "May I suggest a compromise? Why don't we let these people get back to their work and see they have the resources to finish the job?" He turned to Catherine. "Miss Stanek, why don't you use your $100,000 to hire a helicopter and fly Dr. Stanek to wherever he needs to go to wrap up this investigation and search for survivors?"

DeAnn wondered what stake Mr. Cole had in all this. Why was he so anxious to have the mystery solved and for what purpose?

Catherine Stanek took out her checkbook. "Emerson, here, take the money I've offered General Bellicosi. Hire a helicopter and go wherever you need. Just wind this business up, come back safely and get on with your cancer research."

"Good try, Catherine, but it's not so easy. I can't search for bones and other clues in triple canopy jungle from the seat of a helicopter. Besides, I've already arranged to go down river with the salt train, courtesy of Salty Meri."

DeAnn saw Yowell wince.

Bellicosi rubbed his hands together. "I've got the solution. With Miss Stanek's generous offer, we'll hire more constables to keep control here while Dr. Stanek takes a small force and follows his first lead. We'll also hire a helicopter to be on standby in case they run into any trouble down river."

"And later up the mountain as well?" Stanek asked.

"First things first, Dr. Stanek. Let's see what you find down river before we make any further decisions."

DeAnn started to protest. "General there's something you should..."

"Oh, come on, DeAnn. Don't be a spoiler. You can go with Dr. Stanek so he doesn't do anything to upset your precious natives."

Catherine interjected, "Is this wise?"

"What do you mean, my dear?"

"I mean, if it's so dangerous, why would you send a woman along?"

Noble slapped a hand against his hip. "Don't worry, Miss Stanek. Two or three of my boys and I'll protect 'em."

285

"I'd feel a damn sight better if we had a least one more white man in the mix to communicate with backup security in the helicopter," said Bellicosi.

Major Yowell snapped to attention, "Count me in, sir.

Never got to see river country up close and in living color." He winked at DeAnn as he spoke, but she was watching for Stanek's reaction.

"General, this is getting out of hand," Stanek said.

Give me Noble and his men and the Riami man called MilkEye to act as guide and interpreter and forget about the rest."

Bellicosi stood up to leave. "No, Dr. Stanek, I must insist that DeAnn and Major Yowell accompany you on your expedition. She knows the natives, and the major knows ground to air communications. I expect you to keep in touch with backup security by radio, which will be Yowell's job. And to allay your concerns, Miss Stanek, I assure you, we'll make a quick extraction by helicopter if it becomes necessary."

"Thanks, Tony, I'd never forgive myself if my support for Emerson's project brought any harm to him."

"Overkill, if you ask me. But you can waste your money if you want to, Catherine. I don't care," said Stanek.

"Emerson, may I have a moment in private with you?"

"No, say it here in front of witnesses."

From their body movements and the way they talked to each other, DeAnn could see the strain in their relationship. Though Catherine seemed to brush it off lightly, Stanek appeared apprehensive. Catherine simply reached into her purse and brought out two envelopes.

"One of these letters is from Lt. Dunbar from the Baltimore Police. His letter contains a clipping informing you of the murder of Filipino Freddie, his chief suspect in Tom Haveland's murder. The lieutenant wants me to ask you where to go next."

"Thanks. I just happen to have a note addressed to him and another letter of condolence for Dr. Haveland's widow in my bush jacket. DeAnn, you'll find two letters in the left inside pocket. Please pass them to Catherine."

"Do you need your jacket?" she asked. "Yowell can bring me a blanket from the plane."

"No, all I want is for Catherine to give me the other message she mentioned."

For the first time, DeAnn noticed Catherine seemed uncomfortable. "Really, Emerson, I'm not sure I should tell you the contents of the second letter in front of these people," Catherine said.

"Go ahead. I've nothing to hide."

"Well, if you insist. I've done some research on your birth parents, and the results will startle you like they did me. You're the son of the woman named Meredith mother is always chatting with in her imagination. As to who your father is, I haven't found out yet."

"I'm sure you'll keep searching," Stanek snapped.

Bellicosi broke in to round up his party. "Let's get cracking, people. Yowell's got to fly us back to Goroka and then fly back here to join Stanek's expedition. By the way, when do you plan to start the first leg down river, Dr. Stanek?"

"Week after next when the Tugaru salt train leaves for Nomad."

"Good. We'll fly in reinforcements by then. They'll take care of things here while the rest of you are gone. What else do you need to get this project back on a fast track?" the general asked.

"I need to remind Dr. Toland she promised to loan Erik to me."

"What for?"

"So I can learn pidgin and do my own interpretations," Stanek replied.

"Erik, we'll make time for you to instruct Dr. Stanek in pidgin English in addition to your other duties."

Erik nodded. "I think Dr. Stanek will pick it up quickly."

Bellicosi put the pencils back in DeAnn's desk. "More time wasted. How long does it take to learn the language anyway?" Bellicosi asked.

"About a month for most people," Cole replied.

DeAnn wondered why Cole, not Erik, or Noble, had been the first to reply to the general's question.

"Well, a week should be long enough for me," said Stanek.

"See, I told you he was a genius, general, but like Einstein, he forgets the little important things in life, like sending his little sister away with a hug and kiss."

As Stanek stuffed one letter in the flight suit, he took out the clipping from the other, read it, and then tossed it on the desk Bellicosi had vacated. Meantime, Catherine drew along side of

Stanek and touched two fingers to her pink lips. "So I won't soil my outfit with your unique jungle cologne, this will have to do for a goodbye," she said, tracing the scar on his cheek with her two fingers even more tenderly than Salty Meri had done.

DeAnn was surprised to hear her say as she turned to leave, "Darling, I do believe your scar is growing fainter and fainter."

What mystic power did the scar possess, DeAnn wondered? Two women from diverse cultures had been drawn to it in a single day. After she got better acquainted with Stanek, she might ask him how he got it.

As soon as the Beaver took off with General Bellicosi, his party and LikLik, Stanek looked at DeAnn and said, "I believe we've got some unfinished business."

"And what is it?"

"The Japanese woman's journal." Stanek replied.

"I tried to tell General Bellicosi about Kioko's log when I said there's something else he should know, but no one gave me the chance." DeAnn set her knapsack on the desk, pulled out the six volumes containing Kioko's journal and handed them to Stanek. "Really I meant to turn them over earlier, but had no opportunity to summarize them for you."

"I'll draw my own conclusions, thank you," he said turning to leave. "I'll read these while I'm learning pidgin."

"Before you go, Dr. Stanek, I've got a question for you. The newspaper clipping you tossed on my desk. Did you want me to read it?"

He nodded. "Doctor Haveland was your mentor. He told me so himself the night of his murder. I thought you might like to read about the chief suspect in the case."

She lingered behind as Stanek left with Erik, MilkEye and a couple of Noble's armed constables. The *kiap* waited for her at the rope barrier drawn around the site. She picked up the clipping and read:

```
SUSPECT FOUND STABBED TO DEATH IN CREEK
    The chief suspect in the murder of Dr. Thomas
Haveland, a well-known forensic pathologist and
professor at Johns Hopkins Medical Center, was
found dead in a creek near Bowie, Maryland,
Saturday. Enrico F. Marcos, 51, also known as
Filipino Freddie, died of suffocation and multiple
stab wounds, according to the medical examiner.
```

Marcos had failed to show up at the court hearing of a case in which Dr. Haveland was to testify as an expert for the prosecution. Filipino Freddie was discovered face down in the water behind the parking lot near Bowie Racetrack. Lt. Sam Dunbar of the Baltimore Police said, "We'll find out who did this, and we are dedicated to bringing to justice the person or persons responsible."

The police are calling on the community to provide them with any information leading to the double murders of Dr. Haveland and Emanuel Morris, a custodian who worked at the pathology lab at Johns Hopkins, as well as the murder of Filipino Freddie.

Born in Manila, Marcos was known to deal in drug trafficking and smuggling in his native country during WW II. He was also alleged to have collaborated with Japanese occupation forces during this time. More recently, he had also been brought up on murder charges in three cases in which the prosecutors were murdered before the case came to trial. Dr. Haveland had testified in each of these cases, but was unable to provide convincing evidence to link Freddie to the murders.

Lt. Dunbar would not discuss the case beyond saying he had a well-known forensic pathologist on his team, and together they would solve the murders in due time. However, sources on the defense attorney's team said they thought Freddie was murdered in order to keep him quiet about who was involved in the Haveland/Morris murders three weeks ago on the Johns Hopkins campus.

Marcos, AKA Filipino Freddie, was married and had two children. He immigrated to the United States from the Philippines when he was 28 with his father who was a jeweler. He had dropped out of school at an early age and fell in with "the wrong crowd" in the Philippines, according to an aunt who did not wish to be identified. "You name it, and Freddie found a way to smuggle it into or out of the country," she said when interviewed at her Brooklyn home.

In line with the unsolved murders, Lt. Dunbar refused to name the pathologist who is working with him on the case. But speculation centers on Dr. Emerson Stanek, a former student of Haveland's and a close friend. Dr. Stanek is out of the

```
country and could not be reached. But it was
learned that he nearly became a stabbing victim
himself in Hawaii. Other district attorneys and
the pathologists testifying for them have been the
target of violence in the past.
```

DeAnn folded the newspaper clipping and placed it inside her desk drawer. She did not know why she wanted to save it.

With everyone gone except *Kiap* Noble and two escorts, DeAnn sat at her desk and reflected on the impact Catherine Stanek had on her brother. Convinced the Stanek siblings had a brother-sister relationship in name only, she decided this would account for Catherine's rejected flirtations with the pathologist. Sometime or other, they had to have been lovers, or close to it. For only a woman in love would keep trying when so little progress was made.

Early on she had pegged Stanek as a loner, and nothing she had seen or heard had changed her impression. She wondered if he was an orphan, or someone born out of wedlock, then adopted. Now she knew why he had laughed at her remark about getting him safely across the bridge to a waiting wife. What's more, she had just seen theirs was not even a real brother-sister relationship. Therefore, it must have been his promising scientific discoveries keeping them together.

But then she thought of Kioko and her life, on this very ground. DeAnn prayed that Emerson Stanek would find some solace in the pages of this remarkable Japanese woman's chronicle. Kioko had her life threatened, yet found love amidst the terror.

MEMORANDUM FOR RECORD
SUBJECT: Timeline Concerns

The following information was furnished by Catherine
Stanek to General Bellicosi:

Tony, you witnessed my attempts to try every angle
I could think of to extricate Emerson from such a
risky assignment in New Guinea, but failed in the
face of his resolve. You are aware that my interest
in his cancer research project is blocked while he
dallies with DeAnn Toland and the natives. And what
will it do to your timeline if his investigation into
the crime scene inside the 30-year-old bomber
distracts the CIL team from the recovery of remains?
I infused my own funds into the investigation to
speed things up, but can't we join forces to call a
halt to the project if no positive results are
achieved soon?

The following is General Bellicosi's reply to
Catherine Stanek:

I certainly appreciate your monetary support,
Catherine. Personally, I think the proposed trip down
the Rentoul River and another to the top of Mount
Bosavi are fraught with potential disaster. Without
your support and the need to find more than 4 sets of
remains of the ten man crew, I would never have given
my consent. Unforeseen complications arise at every
turn, but I'm determined to stick to my timeline,
regardless of anyone's resolve. The sooner the team
is out of there with a substantial number of remains
recovered, the better for everyone concerned, crime
or no crime.

                    Antonio Bellicosi
                    Brigadier General, USA
                    Casualty Operations Branch,
                    Pentagon

PURSUED:
TEN KNIGHTS ON THE BARROOM FLOOR

Mel R. Jones

PART THREE:
DEVASTATING DISASTER

"The lonely last leaf
Bridging heaven and earth
Carry on, Brave Knight."

29 KIOKO'S JOURNAL #3, MUTINEERS' ESCAPE TRAIL

Papua New Guinea, 1943

U.S. ARMY CENTRAL IDENTIFICATION LABORATORY (PROVISIONAL) FINDINGS, CASE NUMBER 316, EXHIBIT 3c, KIOKO TANAKYA'S THIRD JOURNAL. DR. DEANN TOLAND'S REPORT.

I AM ALONE now. Butterfly, the Filipino comfort girl, spends her nights with the garrison soldiers who take out their frustrations with Lt. Mori on the body of this poor soul. Butterfly eats very little, and when our eyes meet across the evening fire, I see she is an unhappy child. I fear she will not make it as we travel farther south each day in search of the renegade soldiers. Lt. Mori consults a map, inadequate as it is, and uses a compass to help us on our way. He was certain, without such aids, the mutineers would be hopelessly lost and were relegated to following the rivers for the time being.

Just as he predicted, Lt. Mori found the bodies of two of the seven renegades up the Karawari River near Amboin. They had killed several natives, perhaps in an unsuccessful attempt to barter for food or canoes, causing the villagers to turn on them. The remaining five renegades had escaped in native canoes, leaving the motor launch behind.

When we arrived at Amboin, the natives had scattered, perhaps fearing we were the government coming to punish them for the murders. We could feel their eyes watching us from the bush as we searched for the Imperial Portrait. We came up empty. So, Lt. Mori, in his anger, ordered the two deserters buried without military honors. He did, however, mark their gravesites with stakes.

Before we left the village, Lt. Mori scuttled both motor launches. He said he didn't want the Americans to spot them from the sky should they fly over. While the soldiers proceeded to disassemble the canoes from the attached platforms we had towed on the Sepik, Butterfly and I helped repack our supplies and place them into the long canoes we would use in pursuit of the remaining renegades. With our preparations complete, Lt. Mori, the seven soldiers still under his command, including Taro, my brother, and in addition, Butterfly and I, made our way south up the Karawari River toward the shallower Arafundi River.

In the week since we had left Angoram for Wewak, I've only been alone with Taro on two occasions. The first was when he brought me some extra rations and reinstalled the makeshift shower outside my shelter at Tanduanam. The second time, Taro came to see me when we camped at Imboin on the Arafundi River. From this point on, we would have to walk, carrying what supplies we could manage, as we headed toward the Central Range in pursuit of the renegades. Taro had tears in his eyes, so I knew it had something to do with our brother Jiro.

"Is he dead?" I asked, surprised at my own question, which could have been taken as callousness.

"The lieutenant will be here in a moment. He will explain."

Lt. Mori did not come to my tent. It was hard to sit across the evening fire from our leader. Finally, Lt. Mori apologized for the delay in speaking to me, especially since he had sent Taro earlier as his emissary to say he was coming. "I would've told you sooner, Kioko-san, but I didn't want to add to your worry."

"If something's happened to Jiro, I don't want to hear about it!" I blurted.

He took my hands in his. "When I told you I'd help you find both your brothers if you'd broadcast propaganda over the radio, I already knew none of us would see Jiro again. He and his squadron left Rabaul to escort bombers on a raid to Port Moresby. Of the 28 pilots in the formation, only one, Saburo Sakai, our great ace, returned."

If I had been a man, I would have struck the sympathetic look from Lt. Mori's face. How dare he attempt to console me after his lies! Of course, slapping his face was out of the question. It would only earn me a beating. But I wondered why Taro, when told about Jiro, did not defend the family honor and request the items Jiro must have bequeathed to us for his proper burial—a lock of hair, a fingernail, any small remembrance. All I could do was hold my hands over my ears as Lt. Mori spoke. This in itself was a defiant gesture deserving punishment.

Mori appeared not to notice I had withdrawn my hands as he continued. "The bodies of some like Lt. Jiro Tanaka might never be recovered, but how dare any of us think they, including your brother, died in vain? We find our solace in the famous verse from the *Manyoshu*."

I knew the verse well since it was part of my military dance routine, but Lt. Mori began reciting it anyway:

Across the sea, corpses soaking in the water; across the mountains, corpses heaped upon the grass. We shall die by the side of our lord. We shall never look back.

I could hold my tongue no longer. "Then why, please, sir, do we pursue these soldiers when certainly they, like Jiro and the rest of us, will die and never be recovered?"

He surprised me by smiling at my plea. "Don't you see, Kioko? We must save our men from shaming themselves, their families and their villages if the Imperial Portrait were to fall into enemy hands. Once we find the renegades and retrieve the portrait of our beloved Emperor, I'll offer them *seppuku*, or I'll have them shot. Then we'll take a lock of their hair for their relatives back home."

My voice shook and tears streamed from my eyes. "Why have you chosen to tell us about Jiro's death now?"

"To help you bury the past. What we can't do for Jiro, we must press on to accomplish for our countrymen, who so foolishly have chosen to mutiny. They must know by now, as the *garamut* drums continue to track our progress, we are in pursuit of them. Why else would they attempt to cross the mountains? We can't return to Wewak without the Imperial Portrait." My early training helped me understand this explanation, but I remained angry, overcome with grief, and was exhausted to the point of despair.

We were so far off our course to Wewak that I had no idea
what small village we were in on any given day. Lt. Mori and our
interpreter found a native who guided us along a difficult trail he
said the renegades had taken from Imboin to Maramuni. It took us
five days. I was glad for the help of the dark-skinned villager with
tightly curled hair, which protected his head from direct sunlight.
Our pink and sallow skin with little pigment worked against us in
the tropical jungle areas where the soggy humidity dampened
everything including our spirits. My blouse stuck to my body
shortly after putting it on.

Whenever we stopped along the trail cut by the men with their
machetes, Butterfly showed no outward signs the heat bothered
her. At first I thought this was because she was raised in the
Philippines, but then I saw how she stayed close to the *kunai* grass
where it grew to a height of six or seven feet, casting a shadow in
some areas. I started doing the same and immediately cooled
somewhat. My temper, however, was anything but cool.

When we reached Maramuni in the highlands, our native guide
would go no further, and as he turned back carrying the trade
goods we had given him, I wished Taro and I could go back with
him, then on to Wewak and back to Japan.

The natives at Maramuni hid from us in the bush, as at
Amboin, and we could see their gardens had been stripped of food
and the village torched. The renegades had taken what they wanted
and had made sure no native attackers would follow them for fear
of further devastation. Nor did they want to leave anything with
which we could re-supply ourselves.

Onward we trekked, further into the highlands, following the
Sui River valley to Wailep high in the Central Range. The natives
there, fearing the whites who had come before us, and uncertain as
to what we might do, gave us food and offered to guide us through
the mountains to the Lagaip River valley, perhaps glad to be rid of
all of us.

The mountains were especially cold at night, unbearable when it
rained, and the limestone outcroppings tore our hands, clothing
and boots. Moss hung from the trees in the forests. Food was
scarce. What, but the thought of getting caught, shot or forced to
commit *seppuku*, could have possessed the renegades to endure
such hardships as we, too, suffered in pursuing them. I began to
see what a loss Cpl. Akatsu, the medic, had been to our group,

when our doctor's burden became ever heavier as we progressed and our ills mounted.

At Kasap near the Lagaip River, we followed the renegade soldiers on the trail west to Porgera where two of our number fell ill and died of pneumonia, including our doctor and a garrison soldier. The look in the eyes of the thin and ragged soldiers on burial duty reflected their belief death would soon follow for them as well. The trail of the fugitives led through the most rugged and isolated areas yet to be encountered. We all feared for our survival for we went days without food.

Finally, we turned south and descended into a highland valley, following the Paru River. Upon entering the village of Pari on the outskirts of the southern highlands, Lt. Mori caught up with two of the five renegades. Cannibals had already killed the soldiers. Their headless, handless torsos without legs were stuck on a pike at the edge of the compound. We wondered if they were the two prisoners who had shot a fellow soldier back at Angoram. The garrison soldiers buried what was left of the two renegades in the ground at the foot of the pikes. Perhaps to counter the fear of cannibalism permeating our group, Lt. Mori shot five warriors and razed every hut in retribution, although he had no proof this particular settlement was responsible for the murders.

Thereafter, the wigmen we encountered yodeled to each other to warn of our approach in each subsequent village as we pursued the three remaining deserters. The villages had been cleared of pigs, stores and people well in advance of our arrival. My anger at Lt. Mori bordered on hatred. This man had not only kidnapped me, but now, out of some foolish sense of duty, honor and pride, was going to get us all killed. Whenever we got word there were white men in the area, this monster whom I had once pitied, drove us further south, ever away from Wewak. It took all of Mori's skills to keep his small band together.

It was not hard to track the renegades for they left devastating destruction in their wake. Whole villages were stripped of food, their neat cultivated gardens laid waste. And they forced local natives, as did we, to lead them to the next village. More and more desperate for food, the mutineers blazed a trail of hostility into the Tari Basin. From this point on, all the natives we encountered were in full war mode. With wigs decorated with opossum fur, the fierce warriors yodeled wildly as they dogged our path, waiting for an opportunity to pounce on our small group. Sometimes the noise was deafening and we could hardly stand it, but Lt. Mori paid them no mind. He had utter disdain for their spears, bows and arrows and stone axes, because to be effective, the natives had to be on top of us.

After another forced march, we caught up with two of the three remaining deserters at a place named Tari. As fate would have it, they were the two soldiers who had tried to molest me at Sun-Hi's funeral. Both had been stricken with malaria and lay near death in a village, deserted except for them.

Lt. Mori gave out a cheer when he saw that these men had the precious Imperial Portrait. Now it was once again in his possession. The renegades told us the last deserter had probably died in the bush on a scouting mission for food. Before he left, however, he had given them his headband to take back to Japan in case he didn't come back. He had been gone three or four days. We knew the villagers were somewhere in the bush waiting for the soldiers to die so they could reclaim their huts. Unfortunately, Lt. Mori got there first.

Despite his jubilant mood at recovering the Imperial Portrait, Lt. Mori had the two sick soldiers hauled to the center of the village where he offered each of them a dagger. "*Seppuku* is the only way to overcome your shame," he said. Scooping water from a bowl and pouring it over both sides of his *samurai* sword, Lt. Mori turned to me and added, "Kioko, you must watch this from start to finish and learn how the true soldier dies. You might include this act in your military dance routine. I, myself, will render the *coup de grâce*."

I glanced at the two prisoners, and they seemed prepared. One even caught my gaze, and in his eyes I saw an apology for his treatment of me at Sun-Hi's funeral site. The other man looked first at the grass, then at the mountains, and finally at me. He, too, wore an expression of contriteness as he lowered his head in unison with his partner. Together they drew the daggers across their emaciated stomachs and spilled their entrails on the muddy, street. Lt. Mori steadied himself, spread his legs apart and drove the *samurai* sword through the back of the neck of one man and then the other.

One head rolled within a foot of me, while the poor soldier's blood spurted up in two fountains from his trunk. I saw his eyes half shut like a puppet in the theater trying to appear sly. Soon the bodies were left with not a drop of blood in them. The severed heads on the ground turned my stomach in circles. My head began to spin as well when I heard the three garrison soldiers standing next to me make light of the executions.

"What a story to tell my children," whispered one soldier.

"Ho. Even if you get back home alive, you'll never remember exactly how it happened," replied another.

The third suggested, "Write it down so Kioko can turn it into a dance."

It took several minutes after this appalling episode for me to catch my breath. Only after Taro and the others buried the renegades did I feel I could breathe normally. Lt. Mori seemed unfazed that he had taken the life of his own soldiers, mutineers though they were. He wiped his sword clean of their blood with a lock of their hair, which he labeled with each man's name, and placed it in his kit. Then he did something strange, even for Lt. Mori. He hid his *samurai* sword in a hollow tree overlooking their burial site.

"After we've won this war, I'll come back to this spot and gather these remains and those of the others who started out with us and return them to Japan so their families will have more than a lock of hair or headband to bury. Only then can I reclaim my sword," he said.

Taro came forward and offered to place his sword in the same tree, but Lt. Mori would not allow it.

"This is my duty, Sergeant. Yours might come at another time, perhaps in defense of your sister."

Before leaving the village, Lt. Mori had his men round up three native warriors who were questioned through our interpreter as to where the final deserter might be found. They pointed to a mountain off in the distance and repeated the word "Bosavi." There was no question they were telling us there was a white man in the vicinity of the high mountain.

Although it was dusk and we were wet and tired from trudging through the mud, we pushed on south for another two hours before making camp near the Tagari River. Lt. Mori seemed more pleased than ever that his quest was almost over.

"Let's celebrate the return of the Imperial Portrait, Kioko. Take out those paints old Hanzo gave you before we left Angoram, and we shall get a military-style dance from you under the mess tent tonight. Tomorrow we'll track down the last soldier and bury him as well."

The soldiers cheered at the prospect they would have a night of entertainment before another trek through bush country. I asked if Butterfly could help me with my wardrobe and makeup. Lt. Mori agreed, adding, "If you need any other props, tell us."

"Taro's *samurai* sword will be enough," I said.

The lieutenant laughed. "Here, take my ceremonial sword as well. I'm sure you can find a place for it in your dance, only don't wield it too close to my head."

I was taking my bow after the first act when a shot rang out, and I saw a soldier sitting next to Lt. Mori slump to his knees, then plummet face down in the mud. In the next instant, there was a whirl of naked bodies armed with stone axes. They advanced into our camp and surrounded us. Taro sprang to my side. His *samurai* sword leaned against one of the tent poles, as it was to be used in the second act. I looked for Lt. Mori and could not see him at first. Then I saw two husky warriors spring from the darkness, lifting Lt. Mori from the mud. They pinned his arms behind him so he could not reach his pistol or the short dagger in his belt.

I waited to die as the natives hovered around me. Strangely, they fell back when they looked into my white, painted face. From the edge of the jungle stepped a tall white man wearing an American aviator's jacket. He said something to the natives in a language I didn't understand. He turned toward me chuckling and said in English, "They won't hurt you in your get-up with a white face. They think you're one of their ancestors."

He appeared stunned when I replied in his language, "I'm Kioko, and this is my brother Taro. I suppose we're your prisoners."

I had barely tendered our surrender when Lt. Mori broke free from his captors and shouted, "No surrender." He drew his gun, shot one native and drove his dagger through the other. With the sound of the pistol, the other natives disappeared into the bush. The lieutenant turned his gun on the English-speaking white man and would have shot him had I not stood between them.

"Please, sir," I pleaded, "must there be more bloodshed?"

"Move aside, woman. You're aiding the enemy. He must pay for his evil deeds before his friends come back."

The American pointed his weapon at Lt. Mori. "Go ahead and shoot, you yella son-of-a-bitch. Let's see who gets whom first."

I saw Taro easing his way toward his sword, and once he had grasped it, he started to swing it at the American's head. But Butterfly pushed him aside and he missed. When the American turned to shoot Taro, I knocked the gun from his hand, careful to keep myself between him and Lt. Mori.

"There, he's now an unarmed prisoner of war. Shouldn't you and Taro treat him that way?" I asked as our soldiers moved quickly to take the American into custody.

Lt. Mori looked down at his boots, then straight at me. "Good thinking, Kioko. We'd best keep him alive for now. Perhaps a hostage is what we need to keep his native friends at bay."

He turned his gaze on my brother who was just now recovering from the shock of the attack. "Taro, bring me my ceremonial sword. Then get some rope so our soldiers can bind this devil's hands. In a few days, we'll hold a trial with you and me as judges. We'll find him guilty of war crimes and then execute him. Since he is an American aviator, you know he has dropped bombs on civilians. This is the bestial nature of our enemy."

"What about the body of the last deserter?" Taro asked.

"We have his headband, and after the war, when we come back for the others, we'll search for his remains as well. For the moment, it's too dangerous to press ahead. This devil has evidently befriended the natives who were with him. At any rate, it's been a good day. We've got the Imperial Portrait and have captured an American prisoner. After we bury our comrade shot by the American, we can head into Wewak with our heads held high."

"But at what cost?" I wanted to ask. We had now lost a total of four of our eight garrison soldiers searching for the Imperial Portrait of our Emperor, who was deemed a god, and we had buried six of the seven renegade soldiers who had stolen the portrait. I drove this thought from my mind, because if we did get back to Japan, my whole family might be killed because a daughter had blasphemed Japan's living god.

I truly dreaded the day of the American's execution. He was about my age, but his dark hair, tied pig-style in the Chinese fashion, dangled between his broad shoulders and made him look older, as did his heavy, unkempt beard. His eyes were hazel in color and seemed as sad as those of Lt. Mori. The scars across his sculptured upper torso showed him, like Mori, to be a man of war. There the similarity stopped. Even without his disfigured and burned face, Lt. Mori would not have been as pleasing to look at as the American. Perhaps Mori's wounded soul had borne a greater brunt of war than had the American's, and it showed in his visage.

None of us could get any information from the Yank, the name I had used to taunt the Americans over the radio. He only confided in Butterfly. Over the next few days, the Filipino girl brought the Yank food and water and tended to the wounds Mori heaped upon him almost nightly. Yet, the lieutenant could not even get his captive to part with his name, rank and serial number, which Taro said was customary. Of course, the American's silence just made Lt. Mori angrier, and none of the heavy beatings even brought a scream of pain from the Yank's lips in the presence of his Japanese tormentors.

Butterfly gave him the only tender care he received. She bathed his wounds in the tea she had saved from her evening meal. And to cover the deepest cuts, she made bandages from strips of her clothes. For whatever reason, I made her promise not to tell him I was once New Guinea Ginny.

The American's trial and execution were postponed as we made our way north up the Tari Basin. Lt. Mori was determined to break the man, using me as an interpreter. He wanted to know the disposition of other American troops, the types of weapons they carried and whether he had been part of the attack on Angoram.

Every evening ended the same. Mori got nothing, and took out his frustration on the American. He slapped him, beat him with heavy bamboo rods and raised stripes across his back and legs with the flat side of the ceremonial sword or its scabbard. All the while he bated and taunted the American.

Mori shouted at him, "I don't beat you because I hate you, although I do. I beat you because I want you to beg me to kill you, so you can die like a soldier."

It got so bad even Taro pleaded for me to urge the American to give his name, rank and serial number, as all the combatants agreed the prisoners of war must answer.

Frustrated with his failures, Mori announced there would be no more postponement of the execution. He would kill the American tomorrow. I told the American he must provide the requested information this very night, if for no other reason than to avoid any more beatings before he died. In response to my translation, the American spat on the ground in front of Lt. Mori. The lieutenant drew his ceremonial sword and pointed it at the American's bare chest while the enemy looked toward the sky. He then let his head fall forward, exposing his neck. However, he could only hold this position for a short time. A stake fastened him to the ground and made any movement difficult. His arms extended to the side and were lashed to a bamboo stalk crossbeam.

"Tomorrow at dawn, you die!" Lt. Mori proclaimed.

On our journey north, the American had remained attached to the crossbeam. Each night, Mori and Taro had bound the Yank's ankles and had slipped the horizontal bar over the long stake forming an inverted cross. I alone, being a Christian, even without knowing the captive's faith, found significance in the symbol presented by this procedure, once again demonstrating man's inhumanity to man.

Almost immediately an idea to buy more time for the American sprang up in my soul. I shored up enough courage to try my idea on Lt. Mori. In the evening after more interrogation and beatings of the American, Mori gave me an opening.

"It's no use, Kioko. The American either has no intelligence or is too stubborn to part with what he knows, even in the face of imminent death. No matter. He dies at dawn, as I have proclaimed. No sense feeding him from our meager stores any longer."

"There might be another way to get the information you seek," I said. "Gentleness sometimes works where threats fail."

"Don't tell me you'll dance for him?"

"No, sir. But he probably shares my Christian faith, and if I pray for him in English, he might feel inclined to converse with me the way he does with Butterfly."

"Why don't I just beat the information out of the whore and be done with it?"

I had unintentionally involved Butterfly and had to think fast, lest any harm befall her. "Lieutenant, Butterfly's English is poor and her Japanese even poorer, because it comes from the gutter expressions of the soldiers she's slept with. I doubt she could provide any enlightenment, even if the American told her his secrets."

"Then, tell me, Kioko, what scheme are you hatching in your pretty head?"

"Let me administer to the American instead of Butterfly. Perhaps he'll open up and see we're a more friendly people than this war has made us out to be."

"No, the American dog is not worthy of your tender care. He'll spit on you as he does me."

"Then let Butterfly bring him food and water and tend his wounds, while I set some distance from him but in listening range as if in prayer."

Lt. Mori grasped his chin between his forefinger and thumb. "Hmm. Promise me you won't touch the dog, only listen."

"Not unless he spits on me. Then I'll smack his face."

Mori laughed at the prospect. "Very well. I'll suspend the beatings and set the execution in a week's time. If your eavesdropping doesn't work, maybe New Guinea Ginny will help me lop off the American's head."

I dared not say more. But Lt. Mori had not emptied his quiver of barbs. "I wonder if it would loosen the American's tongue if I told him yours was the hated voice he and his comrades heard so often over the radio? Oh, well, I suppose he'd just spit on both of us, Kioko, although it might be worth the effort to see you slap his face. Best save it for later just before he dies."

30 BUSH-HAT HOMICIDE

CIL Encampment, Mount Bosavi, Papua New Guinea, 1973

STANEK CLOSED VOLUME THREE of Kioko's log and was about to begin reading the fourth tablet when someone lifted the fly to his tent and called, "Morning, *Masta*." He recognized the voice of MilkEye and invited the old warrior inside. "How are you?" he asked in pidgin.

"Me good." MilkEye replied and grinned. "*Misis* say give this to Stan-neck. Bring back answer." He handed Emerson a folded letter. The old warrior's one good eye never veered from the pathologist's face. Stanek hesitated, then opened the letter.

```
Dear Dr. Stanek:
    I have not forgotten our conversation last
evening relative to safeguarding the complete set
of Kioko's journals in one person's custody. Since
we are only a day away from the river expedition,
may I offer a compromise? You return to me those
volumes you've read by way of MilkEye. Keep
whatever you need to finish in your custody.
Although it's been nearly two weeks since I gave
them to you, I'll wait longer until you have
completed your examination. Please waterproof the
documents in your possession and don't allow them
out of your sight.
    On another matter, since I need Erik, our
interpreter, to pass on instructions to the
constables going with us down the Rentoul, he'll
not be available for your morning lesson before we
```

leave for Nomad. Erik tells me your progress in
learning pidgin has been so remarkable his
services are no longer required. But as a courtesy
to you, he wants to meet one last time and
suggests this evening after dusk.

Erik also said you and Kiap Noble planned to
examine the bomber wreckage today, so this change
should not unduly upset your schedule. Erik looks
forward to celebrating your "graduation." He tells
me you won't attend the evening meal tonight. I've
no objections to your absence, but I must insist
you release Erik shortly after sundown. He is
needed at the mess tent to brief the newcomers who
will be taking up our duties while we are gone.
They're scheduled to arrive this afternoon with
Frank Yowell and another pilot who will fly in
supplies to Mount Bosavi while the major is with
us. No doubt you will cross paths with the new
arrivals at the airstrip.

Sincerely, DeAnn Toland

Stanek looked up into MilkEye's gaze. "I do have a reply. Give
me a minute," he said in pidgin. Stanek tore a sheet from his
notebook and wrote his response.

Dear Dr. Toland:

Your terms are agreeable. The reason I insist
on holding on to Kioko's journals four, five and
six is to check them against the copilot's report
as we proceed down river. I'm particularly
interested in Kioko's mention of the massacre in
diary number six, which, along with numbers four
and five, I've only had time to skim.

As for my delay in reading them, I've looked
upon these past two weeks as down time, except for
Erik's lessons, of course. You might like to know,
I was promised two or more weeks in New Guinea to
pursue my cancer research study. Whether I take
the time now or later was left up to me. Meantime,
I'm returning journals one through three for your
safekeeping as you requested.

Cordially, Emerson Stanek

Piqued at her inference he was negligent in reading the journals
or might mishandle critical evidence, Stanek wanted to chastise her
for entrusting MilkEye as an intermediary. But he thought better of
it. She, like Catherine, pouted whenever things didn't go her way.

He had won approval for the trip down river over her objection, and no doubt this had interrupted Toland's precious timetable. He thought back to the day of his arrival. Time had been less important to her then. She even discussed with Yowell about taking a moment to share "love on the mountain," while ignoring him. In the end he committed none of these thoughts to writing. Instead he handed his terse reply to MilkEye. The old warrior turned to leave. Stanek caught him at the tent fly. "Come back at dusk, and we'll have a long talk in your language," Stanek said.

MilkEye shook his head. *Misis* say me can look for WonTok before we go down river."

"Fine. But I expect you here at dusk. In two days you start work for me, not *misis*."

MilkEye nodded, passed through the fly and started to close the flap after him.

"Leave it open. The *kiap* will be here soon," Stanek said in pidgin.

After MilkEye had gone and before Noble arrived, Stanek updated the entries in his journal to include information summarized from Kioko's journals one through three:

Volume I—Kioko's Journal 1943
- Two bombs fall on Angoram. By 10K B-24?
- Old gardener Hanzo eyewitness. See if he's still alive.
- Calligraphy set and stage-makeup given to Kioko by Hanzo. Check if they have turned up anywhere.
- Escape from Angoram on Sepik (Lt. Mori, Taro, Kioko).

Volume II—Kioko's Journal—to validate her entries, must locate:
- Burial site for Cpl. Akatsu and Sun-Hi. Search for remains.
- Check route of Japanese party on inland journey and note burial sites.
- Japanese "senninbari" belt, flag, fan and ceremonial sword found at burial site X-2—Taro's or Lt. Mori's? Imperial Portrait—where?
- Pursue leads on Japanese mutineers. If possible, recover their remains in order to rule out as murder suspects.

Volume III—Kioko's Journal
- One of seven mutineers unaccounted for. Others

reportedly killed by cannibals or beheaded by Lt. Mori and buried.

- Lt. Mori's "samurai" sword hidden in tree trunk. What happened to Taro's "samurai" sword? Could his sword be the weapon used by armored knight on mountain?
- Was the American aviator a survivor from the "ten knight's" crew?

On the page opposite his observations on Kioko's tablets, the pathologist wrote, "Regarding the murderer on the mountain". Under this heading, he drew three columns and labeled them as follows:

Suspect	Motive	Opportunity
Mackelwaite	gold	to be determined
Lt. Mori	hatred	TBD
Bomber's crew	schizophrenia	TBD
Kioko (unlikely)	guilt	TBD
Taro	protection	TBD
Japanese renegade	revenge	TBD
Native suspects	preservation	TBD

Stanek closed his notebook. He had set aside the rest of the day for inspection of the B-24 site with *Kiap* Roger Noble. When Noble failed to show up at the arranged time, Stanek figured he would find him at the supply tent next to his own quarters. He heard the burly Australian before he saw him.

"*Come a gutser!*" Noble exclaimed as he mounted a packing crate to address the constables and carriers circling him. "Put the film equipment back. We're not luggin' such heavy stuff 84 miles down the river." The *kiap* paused, caught his breath and continued, reading from a list. He ticked off the items. "Make sure ye pack the tape recorder, three sleeping bags and three air mattresses for the *misis*, Dr. Stanek and the major. I won't need any. We need to take along a tarpaulin for each canoe, a half-pound sack of salt, since we can't expect Salty Meri to share any of hers. I see ye've got four or five steel axes and knives for trade goods. Good.

"Don't forget the tobacco and a bundle of newspapers for rollin' cigarettes. We'll need the papers for barter should we encounter any Giambu people. Pack those cookin' and eatin' utensils separately and be sure to bring along sweet potatoes and sugar cane which ye'll need for the three day journey down and four days back, unless ye want to pay Nomad prices for the return trip. Whites will take their own food from the tins we've already got packed. But we'll share with ye any edible stuff found along the way, like long beans and wild pigs."

Noble got down from the makeshift platform and hailed Stanek. "Doc, ye'd think they'd learn by now to travel light. My boys would take the whole kit and caboodle if I let 'em."

"Why?" Stanek asked.

"It's the damn cargo cult. Every trip's the same."

"What do you mean?"

"Natives want to go along and as far as they can in search of goods the white man promised 'em during the war."

"You'd think after 30 years..."

Noble chuckled. "Not on yer life. Ye couldn't beat the notion out of their heads even if ye tried. They're born with the idea we're goin' to make 'em rich like us. Fancy that."

Stanek drew the straps of his backpack over his shoulders. "Interesting. But shouldn't we get to the wreckage?" he asked.

"Ye don't have enough in yer kit to keep me back."

"You're sure my work won't bore you?"

"Hey, Doc, remember our deal?"

"Mackelwaite?"

"Yep. If it's old Angus' severed mitt found in the B-24 wreckage last year, I want to know if he's still alive."

"An inspection on site won't tell us whether he's dead or alive. There's lots of lab..."

The *kiap* interrupted. "The lads at Walter Reed Army Hospital in Washington took charge of what was left of Angus, I'm told, if it be his. They probably have the mitt under a microscope right now. D.C.'s where the lab rats in Brisbane packed it off to, they did."

"Wish I'd known earlier the hand was in Washington, Roger. To think I was 36 miles away in Baltimore from an important piece of evidence and didn't know it."

"My bet's still on ye, Emerson. An itch in my gut tells me ye already know more about this case than any of us do. Ye'll have solved the mystery before we know it. Let's get crackin'."

"You lead, and I'll follow," Stanek said.

With the sun on their right as they threaded their way through the Tugaru village, Noble remarked they should have encountered more warriors up and about, sharpening their spears and doing other men's work. A small group of young boys approached and stood back as if in awe of Stanek. They told Noble the warriors had left for the great *balus* to collect the trade goods promised them by the white men and foretold by Stanek's arrival on the mountain.

"Today, Stan-neck, great sorcerer, give goods," the boys said.

Noble took Stanek by the arm. "Ordinarily we could share a good laugh at this, but I'm concerned the rumor has worked its way through both the Tugaru and Riami villages. It doesn't speak well for our mission if warriors from both tribes are lurkin' about the B-24 wreckage."

"Shall we turn back?" Stanek asked.

"No tellin' what we've got ahead, lads," Noble said, addressing Stanek as well as the armed constables he brought along. The *kiap* then took one of the two pistols from his belt and handed it to Stanek. "We'll press on, but try not to lose yer weapon this time. We'll know whether or not firearms are needed once we reach the vine bridge. Look for warriors to come out of the shadows like buck deer."

The sun was still not at its peak when they reached the bridge. Except for a few swampy patches where Stanek sank up to his knees in mud and slush, he felt the walk down the mountain had not been too unpleasant. Across the river where the crumpled B-24 bomber laid at rest, Stanek saw a frightful sight. Massed around the rope barrier were 30 or more spear-carrying Tugaru warriors matched in number by Riami bowmen. They had formed a semi-circle around the site, separated by the narrow strip of white-man's land in between them. *Kiap* Noble chambered his rifle and instructed the two armed constables to do likewise.

"Luckily, they haven't crossed the rope barrier and pulled the aircraft apart to divvy up the booty. Guess they're waitin' for ye to distribute the goods as predicted by the cargo cult."

"Why me?" Stanek asked.

"Because, as the youngsters back there said, both tribes see ye as a great sorcerer deservin' their respect."

"What did I do to earn it?"

"Ye brought LikLik back to life from near death and stood yer ground with the Tugaru. Yer devilish trick with the batteries fooled the Tugaru. They think ye're invincible. But better let me and the boys handle 'em this time. Just keep yer pistol ready in case things get out of hand and we need backup."

They crossed the vine bridge and at the crash site Stanek watched Noble put his words into action. He and his armed constables politely drove the silent crowd of sightseers away from the wreckage to a respectable distance. Careful to keep the two warrior groups separated, Noble then requested all spears and arrows be laid on the ground in front of their owners if they chose to stay. The Riami complied immediately. But the Tugaru hesitated since they had the advantage over the Riami in their choice of weapons. Their spears were better suited for close-in combat where one jab could cripple a man before he got an arrow fitted to a bow.

Noble asked again in a calm voice for the Tugaru to disarm as the Riami had done. Still they made no effort to do so. Loud Mouth, in his yellow headdress as the Tugaru leader, stepped front and center. In one hand he held his long trident and in the other he held up a small leafy branch Stanek had come to recognize as the universal symbol for peace among the tribes. But Loud Mouth did not hold the branch in his hand long. Instead, he threw it to the ground in front of Noble and stomped on it with his bare feet.

Stanek watched as Noble drew close enough to Loud Mouth for his bush hat to brush against the warrior's headdress. The pathologist's hand shook as he closed it around the handle of the revolver. Loud Mouth started to speak, but the *kiap* drove the barrel of his rifle into one of Loud Mouth's flaring nostrils.

"*Bikmaus*, tell yer people to lay down their spears, or I'm goin' to blow one of those beetles in yer nose so far into yer head, in the next life all ye'll hear is buzzin'."

The change was electric. Loud Mouth retreated, and Stanek could see the sight on the tip of Noble's rifle barrel had drawn blood. The Tugaru headman swept a hand across his nose, looked at the blood, then laid down his spear. His followers backed down as well. Stanek was certain he had seen WonTok trying to hide among the retreating Tugaru. He looked at Noble for confirmation.

Noble tugged at his beard. His own gaze fixed on WonTok who slipped behind the second row of Tugaru warriors. "Lucky his kinsmen didn't see him. Traitors aren't tolerated by either tribe unless..."

"Unless what, Roger?"

The *kiap* held up the rope barrier for Stanek to duck under. "Unless WonTok's got information he can sell for his life."

"Well, I'm sure we can't do anything about WonTok's

311

defection, except keep it to ourselves. More pressing is what happens when we emerge from the wreckage without the expected cargo to give the natives?"

"Ye can speak to 'em in pidgin. Tell 'em, as the great spirit sorcerer, ye're displeased with their actions today. We'll toss 'em a few honeycombs and send 'em packing to await a more handsome reward at another time."

"And where do we get the honey?" Stanek asked.

Noble chuckled. "From where it's always been—in the nose of the B-24, under the navigator's wooden table. There's a hive there, but we're too big to get at it. I'll have to send one of my police boys in."

Stanek rubbed the scar on his cheek. "If I ever get back to my beekeeper cancer study, I'd like to examine this hive, even if it means moving a section of the wreckage to get to it."

"I trust Mackelwaite's fate comes before yer study, eh, mate?"

"Maybe we can do these projects simultaneously. Now excuse me while I take some measurements," Stanek said.

"Go right ahead, Doc. I'll keep my eye on *Bikmaus* and his mates, squattin' peacefully in the grass over there, now they are. As I've told ye before, don't let 'em see too much of your back, or back 'em down like I did *Bikmaus*, drawin' his blood. Shame, like plain murder, calls for revenge and requires payback. *Bikmaus* might take years to close the unsettled account he has with each of us."

Stanek looked at his boots. "With any luck, I'll be far from this place by the time Loud Mouth gets around to me. And you wouldn't have survived this long if you couldn't handle these situations as a *kiap*, Roger."

Stanek began stepping off the crash site from north to south where the severed wing lay against the slope of the mountain in a vertical position. He estimated the distance as 50 yards from where the wing closest to the river buttressed the fuselage to where the wing against the mountain lay. He then stepped off going from east to west—tail to nose. In his notebook he wrote "about 185 yards from east to west".

At this point Roger Noble joined him. "What's yer purpose in takin' all those measurements, Doc? DeAnn's already laid out the crash site perimeter. I thought ye wanted to look inside, and the only way we can enter is through the tail."

Stanek did not look up from his notebook immediately. Finally he answered, "By using a little triangulation, my guess is the aircraft's tail initially struck the mountain higher up near the peak. The wing standing vertical must've broken away during a second contact with the mountain. Of course, the aircraft would then have been completely out of control and must have fallen toward the 2,000-foot level where it now sits."

"How can ye tell from just pacin' about?" asked Noble.

"Well, we can see one of the twin stabilizers and part of the tail rudder is missing along with a good section of the aft fuselage. I think we'll find part of the aircraft near the peak of Mount Bosavi."

"I don't quite follow ye, Doc."

"Think of it this way, Roger. When you were a kid, did you have one of those little, wooden, toy airplanes you could wind up with a rubber band?"

"Yep, my father made me one out of soft wood."

"Remember how, when the propeller stopped turning, the airplane descended completely out of control? Sometimes it crash landed on one of its tails and another time on a wing tip? Occasionally it struck the ground simultaneously on tail and wing tip."

The *kiap* leaned forward, "Yep, I follow ye."

"Well, as we know from the pilot's log, the number two engine was already shut down, or should I say, shot out, before the aircraft reached Mount Bosavi. We also know, because of the fuel leak, they had to plan on a heading from east to west toward the soft marshes between here and Nomad once they cleared Mount Bosavi. However, a belly-up landing in the swamp isn't the easiest of approaches because the Davis wing is so high.

"The rest we can speculate on our own. Perhaps, blinded by the mist, or having used up most of their fuel, they were a split second from clearing the top of the mountain. But when the left tail section with the left vertical stabilizer impacted and ripped off, the pilot lost part of the aircraft's control surfaces. With structural damage to the aircraft, it stalled and departed controlled flight. Losing air speed, the aircraft's wings dipped and it plummeted downward and crashed. And like our little, wooden model, the port wing struck the mountain, broke, but initially did not tear off completely. As the aircraft fell, the part to strike the mountain at impact was the front section of the fuselage. This would account for its condition. Unfortunately, those who were in and around the cockpit at the time had no chance of survival.

Roger took his flashlight from his knapsack. "Amazin'! Let's go see what ye uncover inside."

As the two men ducked under the tail section of the damaged B-24, Noble asked, "What do ye expect to find in here we haven't already turned up?" Again, Stanek did not answer immediately. He had dropped to his knees and began patting the ground where the bottom of the fuselage had rusted away. He stopped. He turned his head slightly and asked Noble to shine the flashlight beam in front of the spot where his hands rested.

"Is this about where you found the severed hand and Zippo lighter?" the pathologist asked.

The *kiap* peered over Stanek's shoulder. "Damn, if ye didn't find the exact spot. How did ye know?"

Stanek smiled. "Your knee prints and those of the victim before you are embedded in the mold. My guess is rain had soaked the ground on the days both you and the victim knelt at this spot, and the mold has preserved the imprints. Of course, now I've added my own, and we can't be sure someone else hasn't visited this spot before or after you. But we've yet to discover our chief concern. We know why you knelt here, but what was the victim after when he lost his hand?"

Noble scratched his beard. "He must've been lookin' for something under the moss."

"Good. My thoughts exactly. But what?"

Noble shrugged his shoulders. "I'll leave the answer to ye."

Stanek found a dry spot and sat down in the sparse grass. He gazed up at the gaping hole in the roof of the fuselage where sunlight began to filter in as the sun broke through a cloud and bathed the area in light.

"Let's assume the victim came here at night and used the lighter to find his way to this spot." Stanek demonstrated by holding his right hand up like one would grasp a torch. "From the small caliber bullet holes shot from an angle inside the aircraft, we might further assume the victim was armed and fired at least three shots at his assailant. But were they fired before or after he lost his hand?"

Noble shrugged again.

Stanek continued, "After, because our victim was left-handed and held the gun in his predominant hand."

Noble slapped his thigh. "Of course, the lighter he used for a torch was in his right hand."

"Which attracted the assailant..."

"Whilst the bloke laid the gun nearby to dig with his left hand. But what was he lookin' for?"

Stanek scooped a handful of dirt and let it slip through his fingers. "Let me ask you, Roger. What would make a man take such risks digging at night in hostile territory?"

"Gold?"

"Possibly."

The *kiap* hung his head. "Then, someone diggin' for gold and the initials on the lighter points to my mate, Angus, the *kiap* turned *fossiker*."

"Not so fast, Roger. We already know the initials on the lighter do match the collar insignia for the constabulary, but can you think of any other organization during the war using OCS as an identifier?"

The *kiap* twisted the corners of his mustache. "Only one—those serving in official coastwatcher's service."

"Well, there, you see. We can't jump to conclusions, especially if dental forensics shows it was Mackelwaite's jawbone Salty Meri gave me. It would clear him of the murder I saw committed on the mountain, but unfortunately the obvious conclusion would be your friend's demise."

"*Come a gutser*, lad, ye caught us all by surprise with yer account of the murder on the mountain. But, is there any way at this point ye can clear or exclude Angus of the massacre down river in 1951?"

"Afraid not until we see for ourselves in the next few days on the Rentoul."

"Damn pity, damn pity." Noble said.

Stanek stood up and placed a hand on the patrol officer's shoulder. "We've got all the information this site will yield for now. We'll know more after the river trip."

As they exited the wreckage, they heard the drone of an aircraft engine followed by another. "Major Yowell and another plane with the new lads are comin' in for a landin'. Suppose I'd better stay to greet 'em. I'll send ye back with two police boys."

"Go ahead, Roger. I'll take a few minutes at DeAnn's desk to tidy up my notes."

The *kiap* reached into the deepest drawer of the desk and withdrew a brand new bush hat. "Don't look at this as a bribe to steer ye away from Angus, but I'd like ye to take this gift to replace yer battered old hat."

"Thanks, Roger. I'm comfortable with the old one. Still, if you don't mind, there's someone I'd like to pass this hat on to."

"And who might it be?"

"My language tutor, Erik."

"Splendid choice." Noble added, "Well, would ye look around, Doc? *Bikmaus* didn't wait for his reward. The sight of the two airplanes comin' in must've scared him and his warriors off."

*   *   *

Later, Erik's cheerful "good evening" in pidgin pushed the events down at the B-24 site onto the back burner in Stanek's mind. It was graduation day, and Erik reminded his pupil he had come to celebrate.

The interpreter beamed. "Your pidgin is better than mine! Not to say, however, we could hold a conversation in the 700 plus languages spoken in New Guinea."

"Thanks. I'm anxious to try it on MilkEye. I've got lots of questions for him. He should be here soon."

"Strange, Doc. I saw the grizzled old warrior a few moments ago. He was lurking outside your tent, but when I called to him, he turned and left."

"You must've been mistaken."

"No, it was MilkEye all right."

"Then he must've spotted WonTok. He's been looking for him."

"Maybe so, but the Riami have spread a rumor about MilkEye. They say he no longer attends Riami tribal counsels 'cause he thinks he's a white man and can sit down all day and do nothing. It might explain why he's giving us wide berth."

Stanek grinned. "Do nothings! Now we know what the natives really think of us. When they saw the gaggle of VIPs General Bellicosi brought with him the other day, they must've thought the same thing. They may have a point. Anyway, I'll bet MilkEye won't act so strange once he and WonTok renew their friendship."

"WonTok never reported for duty after the incident involving you and the Tugaru."

"I saw WonTok no more than three hours ago at the B-24 site. He was with Loud Mouth and his mob."

"MilkEye will kill WonTok if he finds out he has gone over to the enemy," said Erik.

"I don't plan on telling him. Neither does *Kiap* Noble. We believe the Riami at the site couldn't spot WonTok as he remained hidden in the ranks of the Tugaru."

Erik drew three imaginary circles in the air with his finger. "MilkEye, WonTok and *Bikmaus* in the same orbit spells trouble."

"Don't worry. MilkEye's going down river in my canoe tomorrow. I'll keep him occupied and out of trouble."

Erik cocked his eyebrow. "Is this river trip really necessary at this time, Doc? If you postpone it a week, I could go."

"Sorry, I'm on a tight schedule from here on out. What you could do for me, though..."

"Name it."

"Did I hear someone say you studied language in Japan?"

"Yes, sir."

"Then could you tell me what it says on the flag found at burial site X-2 with the Japanese remains."

"Sure. The soldier penned a personal note to his family back home, promising never to disgrace them."

"No signature anywhere?"

"No, sir. The family would've known who it was from."

"Thanks, Erik. By the way, what's Dr. Toland's plan for you while we're gone?"

"I'm assigned nursemaid duties to the new cadre. You must've seen them come in?"

"I heard them arrive. *Kiap* Noble and Major Yowell had them in tow before I left. Surely they've reached the main camp by now and are sipping tea with your boss lady. Have you missed them?"

Erik put a finger to his lips. "Shh... Don't tell Dr. Toland I found a quiet spot on this side of the escarpment where I can catch a few winks, or daydream of home. I'll see the newcomers at the mess tent shortly when I have to brief them."

Stanek drew his thumb and forefinger across his lips, indicating "zipped."

"Before you go, Erik, please take this hat as my thanks for all your help." He set the bush hat Noble had given him on Erik's head and stepped back. "There, wear it proudly. A man in a brand new hat shouldn't have to answer to anybody. An old woman very dear to me once said, 'You can tell a lot about a person's character from the appearance of one's hat.'"

They shook hands, and Stanek followed his guest through the tent fly. "It's a grand night. The moon is high, and tomorrow should be good for a canoe trip down the Rentoul," he said. Then he added almost to himself as he turned to go inside, "Wonder what's keeping MilkEye?"

No more than ten minutes had passed before he got his answer. MilkEye tore through the tent fly, his one good eye wide open and etched with horror. "*Masta, throwim way leg! Bikmaus* kill Er-ik!"

"What! Where?"

MilkEye indicated Stanek should follow him. Stanek found the interpreter's body at the bottom of the slope dividing the CIL camp into two sections. The killer had timed the attack to occur when Erik reached the blind spot, which obscured the view of anyone from either section of the camp from seeing the murder. Stanek stared in dismay. Why, he wondered, didn't Erik call out, and why weren't there any signs of struggle?

The first clue was the position of the interpreter's body. He had fallen forward with his face buried in the bush hat Stanek had given him. Seeing the assailant had struck his victim from behind, Stanek began his examination at the back of Erik's neck, expecting to see an axe or knife wound. When he spotted blood oozing from between the shoulder blades and pooling around the stake driven down through the neckline of Erik's tunic, he recoiled and murmured, "Oh, no! Not again!"

Erik had been killed in the same manner Dr. Haveland at Johns Hopkins had been slain. No one could've heard Erik scream. Like Tom Haveland, a sigh was the most he could manage as his lungs collapsed.

Under ordinary conditions, Stanek would have left the weapon intact until photographed and dusted for fingerprints, but the jungle afforded no such luxuries. He pulled the murder weapon from the body, expecting to find a sword or long knife. Instead, he saw the killer had used the leg bone of an animal, sharpened and pointed like a spear, to take Erik's life.

"Cassowary leg bone," MilkEye said.

Stanek suspected the murderer had gotten the wrong man. The bush hat must have confused him in the dark. He turned to MilkEye. "You know this was intended for me," he said in pidgin.

"*Masta* no die. Stan-neck great sorcerer. Like magic in Kioko-san book. *Bikmaus*, or Two Face, no kill."

"Did you see *Bikmaus* do this?"

MilkEye nodded as he pointed to the ledge. "Me see him go up here. Leave place Er-ik die. We follow him."

"No. We must go down river first," Stanek said in pidgin.

Stanek's mind was swirling. The unsolved murders and incidents, which had occurred since he became involved in this B-24 case, were increasing. First, there were the murders of Haveland and the custodian in Baltimore. Next the attack on him in Hawaii occurred, which Cole had foiled. Then the beheading on the mountaintop, followed by the shots fired at the aircraft as he approached Mount Bosavi. Once on the ground, there was the warning implicit in the pig sacrifice and the slaying of Salty Meri's son, which he had promised to investigate. Nor could he forget Filippino Freddie's death, so untimely for the chief suspect in the Haveland murder. Finally, Erik was killed at approximately the time the pathologist himself left each day for the mess tent.

Stanek was convinced there was a link between the ten knights case and events so bizarre they seemed to defy explanation. Haveland had inferred a connection when he had asked him to look at the B-24 matter with his suggestion to pay particular attention to the inscription on the lighter found in the severed hand. The verse matched the words on the sundial at Johns Hopkins. Was this a coincidence, or was there a link? The inscription was the only visible connection between New Guinea and Baltimore, other than his presence in these places and now the murder weapons involved.

He walked up the hill path to inform DeAnn and the others of Erik's murder. The immediate task was to convince DeAnn and the rest of his party the river trip must go on as planned, since they would lose several weeks if they waited for the next salt train to Nomad. On his return from Nomad, he wanted to take a side trip to the hospital at Goroka where he could speak to Jim Cole, who might shed some light on these matters. The reporter had an unusual familiarity with all three of the trouble spots Stanek had encountered—Johns Hopkins, Hawaii and New Guinea.

At least it was another lead to follow before another murder occurred, perhaps his. He suspected someone had mistaken Erik for himself and had committed murder to prevent him from joining the salt train, or to stop any criminal investigation of these murders.

31 REPORTER'S MISSING LETTER

Goroka, Papua New Guinea, 1973

A T THE HOSPITAL in Goroka, Jim Cole wheeled himself down the corridor toward the children's ward. The reporter felt an ache in his mind matching the pain in his cancer-riddled body. Rain struck the windows on this overcast mid-morning. It added to his mood of despair.

He prayed LikLik's cheerful smile would once again pull him back from the abyss into which his mind, plagued with remorse, had thrust him. He understood the sooner he purged the guilt from his soul, and let go of the charade he had built in this life, the easier the crossing into the next.

Cole turned the wheelchair and faced the window. He wondered what Doctors Toland and Stanek made of his fainting spell on Mount Bosavi. Did they attribute it to his cancer, or did they suspect his interest went deeper than the opportunity to get a story scoop? He wavered between emotions. On one hand, the thought of American survivors lifted his spirits. On the other, it troubled him to think they suffered so long, never to see their families. He set his mind on a course of action. After his visit with LikLik, he would send word to Stanek and ask for a meeting between the two. But he realized his note to the pathologist must await Stanek's return from the river trip.

The decision to take action settled his mind, and he again wheeled toward LikLik's room. At the door to the children's ward, the day nurse stopped him.

"Mr. Cole, I'm sorry. LikLik had a late appointment and hasn't gotten back yet."

"How much blood does Stanek Laboratories need? At this rate, they'll drain the life out of the lass like they've already done to me."

"Oh, Mr. Cole, you know the body..."

"Yeah, yeah, I know the body replenishes every drop taken. Not if you're already half dead."

"I do have some good news for you, sir."

"About time."

"Starting today, you're going to get a roommate."

"Anybody but General Bellicosi. He can talk a magpie into the ground—only a magpie makes more sense."

The nurse offered a weak smile. "Now, now, you've got to be nicer to others. Give Mr. Waiola a chance. Like you, he's from Hawaii."

"Don't tell me he's a preacher connected with the Waiola Church in Maui. The only thing worse than non-stop pontificating from General Bellicosi would be non-stop preaching to a dying man."

"No, I believe our Mr. Waiola is a wrestler from the main island."

"Never heard of him, but maybe his professional name is "Hawaiian Punch," or something similar."

"Good! You're joking again, Mr. Cole. Let's have more of it."

"Give me a push, and we'll go meet the guy."

"He's still registering, but I'll take you past there so you can see what he looks like."

Mr. Waiola sat in a cubbyhole across from the admissions clerk. His bulk was so large Cole noticed it filled up most of the space so the clerk could barely be seen. The giant turned his head, one side to the other in quick movements, as if to be leery of someone coming upon him unexpectedly. During one of the turns, Cole saw a pockmarked face. He had seen his visage before, and it wasn't inside a ring. But for the life of him, he couldn't remember where and under what circumstances. Cole decided to check with the sports editor at the *Honolulu Advertiser*. He would know if Mr. Waiola fought under an alias.

Cole turned to the nurse and said, "Sister, if you don't mind, I'd like you to take me back to my room. I'm exhausted and still have a letter I need to write. I wonder if you would be so kind as to come back later after you drop me off and see it gets on the next available flight to the American CIL team on Mount Bosavi. It's for Dr. Emerson Stanek."

"Sure, Mr. Cole. But by the looks of you, I'd be surprised if you get around to writing it before the pain medicine kicks in and you fall asleep."

Back in his bed, Cole realized how hard it was to write a simple letter. It had been wise to leave General Bellicosi's party to remain at Goroka. He could never have made the trip back with the general and Miss Stanek, no matter how luxurious the accommodations in her private jet. His condition had reached the point of 24-hour nursing care if he expected to live long enough to write about the downed aircraft, "Ten Knights on the Barroom Floor", and its crew. Such a name shows how low all we "knights" must fall until we are lifted up and taken home to God, he thought.

Just in case he lacked the strength to complete his assignment, he wanted to hear from Dr. Stanek what befell those ill-fated young airmen. Only then could he tell his side of the story. He took paper, pen and envelope from the drawer at the side of his bed. First he addressed the envelope—"Confidential to Dr. Emerson Stanek." Then he wrote:

```
Dear Dr. Stanek:
    I trust this note will be waiting for you, and
I'm still alive when you get back from your trip
down the Rentoul. It's urgent we meet here in
Goroka where, as you've probably heard, I'm in the
hospital with LikLik. MilkEye's daughter is doing
very    well,    and    we're    both    grateful    your
experimental bee serum bought us more time—she to
recover and me to linger a little longer. You have
information I need to know before I die, and I
have    information    in    exchange    to    aid    your
investigation into the ten knights case. Please
hurry and do not confide in General Bellicosi or
any of the others, as I trust you alone.
    Yours truly, Jim Cole
```

After he'd finished the letter, he sealed the envelope and placed it on his serving tray for the day nurse to take with her when she went off duty. His last thoughts as he drifted off to sleep were not of the aborted visit to LikLik. Instead, he thought of the men he might have betrayed.

32 SALT WELL SIDE TRIP

Tugaru Village, Mount Bosavi, Papua New Guinea, 1973

STANEK FELT A DEEP sorrow as he made his way to the CIL main camp where the other members of the expedition had gathered to pay last respects to the interpreter. Erik had been his tutor and he had developed genuine respect and affection for him. Now he was gone.

In contrast to the mood among Erik's mourners, the day had broken like a warm summer morning in Baltimore. Stanek paused at the spot beneath the outcropping where the interpreter had been murdered. Below lay the Tugaru and Riami villages. Hundreds of cooking fires sent up clouds of smoke, which hung like the mist over a river, or like the fog rolling in at Fells Point. Strange he should think of Baltimore now. It seemed so long ago he and Catherine had romped among the dogwood trees as children while they waited for their mother to visit her friend at Phipps. The harbor in Baltimore with its smell of the sea could never match the scent of sweet potatoes roasted in ashes. Nor was there anything in the civilized world to compare with cooked green bamboo shoots, except possibly asparagus. Erik had regarded them as a delicacy, and the natives devoured them at breakfast.

In addition to pidgin, he had learned much more from the interpreter in the week they had spent together. Instructed by Erik on how to forage in the jungle, Stanek had gained insight into survival in New Guinea. Essentials included knowing where to find potable water, how to cook green bamboo shoots, roast sweet

323

potatoes and the rudiments of building a shelter. The shelter need not be as elaborate as the CIL encampment. A simple lean-to along with a mosquito net would suffice.

Stanek arrived at the main camp just as Erik's comrades were carrying the interpreter's body to the airstrip for the funeral and shipment to the United States via Goroka and Port Moresby. He saw DeAnn Toland lower her head, perhaps in prayer, as she followed behind the body bag carried by four soldiers.

The imagined struggle with DeAnn on whether to proceed down river or not under the circumstances had not materialized. He wanted to thank her for agreeing the river trip with the salt train should continue as scheduled, except for the hour of departure. The evening he and MilkEye had delivered the interpreter's body to her, she had asked in honor of Erik they delay the morning departure until early afternoon. Noble had received Salty Meri's consent for the change. What surprised him most was DeAnn's suggestion Stanek might want to visit the salt well with Noble in the morning to see how the commodity was produced and packaged.

This plan to send him off with Noble to the salt well during Erik's funeral made him suspicious of DeAnn's motive. Was this her way of avoiding him further, or did she understand funerals and the preachments during the service made him uncomfortable? He had eschewed Dr. Haveland's funeral for this reason. Whatever her motive, he dared not interrupt her grieving. So instead of disturbing her, he stood erect and in silence as Erik's body passed by him.

        *   *   *

Through her tears, DeAnn Toland glanced at her colleague. He stood rigid at the side of the path. The only emotion he had shown was to remove his hat as the interpreter's body passed him. That hat! That stupid hat, which had cost Erik his life! By his own admission, Stanek took responsibility for giving Erik the gift. She hoped her tears hid her desire to strike out at the man who had caused so much turmoil since his arrival. Now another murder had occurred!

The interpreter's death had thrown the entire expedition into shock, disbelief and disarray. The natives considered the slaying a curse, and in their fear they blamed white man's sorcery at work. Three carriers quit and two constables said they were afraid to sleep at night lest the sorcerer who took Erik come to steal their souls as well. Friends of Erik's, like the good soldiers they were, showed anger, but vowed to continue the mission. Even her resolve had been shaken. She had confided to Noble one of them should always be at Stanek's side. Trouble followed him like a shadow. Noble had encouraged her patience. Stanek would complete his investigations and move on.

"Leave him to me," the *kiap* had promised her. "I'll keep the bloke occupied and out of yer pretty hair, if ye want me to?"

"At least through the morning hours," she had answered. "Take MilkEye with you and Stanek to the salt well," she had insisted. "Maybe, if we're lucky, the old warrior will lead you to the place he found the dinghy and the other items, including Kioko's journals. Did WonTok tell you where he and MilkEye had found them?"

"Yep. The little bugger did so after I made him a constable. Now he's been seen hobnobbing with the Tugaru. MilkEye will be furious if he finds out."

"MilkEye and Stanek seem to be getting on well together," she had said.

"Too well, if you ask me," Noble had replied. "Ye hardly see one without the other. Why do ye suppose the old warrior sticks so close to Emerson?"

DeAnn had not answered the *kiap*, but in the back of her mind she had wondered if it had something to do with MilkEye wanting Stanek to use his magical powers to bring back the spirit of Kioko.

As the funeral procession reached the outskirts of the Tugaru village, Major Frank Yowell fell in step beside her. He took her hand in his.

"I looked for you last evening, but could see you were busy preparing a proper send off for Erik. I'll miss him. He was a good fellow. He deserved better than he got in the end. I'd hate to die in this place. I suppose the river trip is off."

"No. Just delayed until early afternoon. The interpreter you brought with you to help Erik will have to carry on here, so we can proceed as planned."

"Does Bellicosi know the river trip is still on?"

"He's been informed by radio."

"No objections?"

"We don't know whether he got the message, but we informed his staff."

"It's not the same."

"I know. Generals hate surprises," she said. Then she added, "What good would it do to cancel at this point? It won't bring Erik back, and it'll only complicate matters with the helicopter and other security arrangements."

"Bet Stanek's got a hand in this."

"Yes, he wanted to go ahead, but it was my decision to do so. Let's not talk about him. You heard Erik's killer might've really been after Dr. Stanek?"

"Yeah. The news has probably reached my home state of Texas by now. If this guy causes any more trouble, you'll have my support in getting the general to send him back to Hawaii."

"Thanks, but let's hope it doesn't go that far. Maybe the river trip will hasten the day when we can all leave."

"Don't bet on it, sweetheart. There're crocodiles in the river, and people who might as well be crocs themselves. I promise to stick to you like a leaf on a turnip. Nothing is going to happen to you on my watch."

*   *   *

The last 500 feet to the salt well was a steep climb up the eastern wall of Mount Bosavi. Several times Stanek nearly fell down navigating rocks as slippery as ice. He guessed they were made soggy from the banana plants dripping pulp onto the ground as the Tugaru women transported them from the salt well to their village.

They came to a clearing. Stanek motioned to Noble, MilkEye and the two constables escorting them he wished to stop and survey the mountain above them. From his vantage point, he could see Mount Bosavi was riddled with caves and caverns on its upper levels. Canyons split the limestone, probably created by earthquakes and volcanic eruption.

In the clearing itself, near the 4,000-foot level, a dozen or so Tugaru women sat in silence beside pools of brine in which banana tree segments soaked. All the women except Salty Meri jabbed at the soaking segments with sticks. The Tugaru matriarch caught all of them off guard as she charged at MilkEye with her digging stick held like a javelin.

"No deal. He no come here," she said.

Kiap Noble sprang into action. He stepped between the old adversaries and caught Salty Meri's stick before she could jab it into MilkEye's one good eye.

Noble's tone was conciliatory. "Come on, old girl. Let's not get angry. MilkEye's here to help the great Stan-neck find the murderer of yer son."

The *kiap* wheezed a few times, then continued in pidgin, "Now, if I let go, promise me ye won't strike the Riami man with yer stick."

Salty Meri looked at Stanek, then back at Noble. "No kill boy here. Other side of mountain happen." She pointed to the west. "Place papa and all Tugaru warriors go when they die."

Noble faced Stanek and whispered, "She means the ceremonial Tugaru burial rock. Play along with me before she calls the salt well guard over here."

Stanek nodded. Still he felt uncomfortable. The old woman might think his failure to speak up meant a change of heart. He wanted to reassure her he would find the murderer of her youngster once the B-24 case had been settled. He hoped whatever Noble planned to do, it would not interfere with their getting permission to search the burial site where MilkEye and WonTok had found the rubber dinghy loaded with evidence.

Noble's tone grew even softer. "Come now, Meri, me darlin'. Ye've got to cooperate. Ye know to kill yer young'in, the murderer would've had to pass by the salt well at some point. There's no other way to get to the burial grounds. He might've left some tracks MilkEye might recognize as Riami, and Stanek can confirm, ye see."

Emerson found his voice and spoke. "We need your permission to go to the burial stone after we're finished here. Send along a sentry to watch us if you like. But we need the man called MilkEye, for he has learned a white man lies beneath the split between your sacred stone."

Salty Meri glowered at MilkEye. "How Riami man know white man's bones in burial stone?"

Stanek saw Noble and MilkEye were as dumbfounded as he was at a question with no answer, unless it was to implicate WonTok and MilkEye in the crime.

Noble cupped his hand and whispered to his companion. "Perhaps ye'd best answer her question, Doc."

"Thanks, Roger. You get the softballs and I get the hardballs. Are you being fair?"

"Baseball's not an Aussie sport."

Emerson drew himself up to his greatest height. He spoke in pidgin. "Mother of the Tugaru, I speak as one of your children. None of us can answer your question until we visit the burial site and see what is hidden there among my Tugaru brothers' bones. I'm also a white man, and we need to find my white brothers as well. Now please tell us about the operations here. Are they getting the salt ready for our trip down river?"

The old woman let fly a cackle that Stanek interpreted as a laugh. "You good sorcerer and son of Tugaru. No good make salt. Leave to *meri*," she said.

"Then you must teach me, so I can understand the process."

The women working at their task so deliberately only moments ago now clapped their hands together. He smiled at them. Salty Meri smiled as well, showing the gaps between teeth worn down from years of chewing raw bark to make string for the net bags both women and men carried. Aware Salty Meri had played to the audience of women, he decided to press his advantage while everyone seemed delighted at the prospect of his learning to make salt.

"Tell me, Mother of the Tugaru, why do you laugh when asked if this salt made today will go down river with us?"

Salty Meri cackled again, softer this time. "Many get salt today, but wait long time before go down river. Must dry many days."

Stanek then asked her to describe the process and in his notebook under the heading of "salt" wrote:

```
Absorbent material is prepared before salt is
collected. Outer sheaths of a banana tree trunk
are peeled, leaving the trunks. Trunk is then cut
into three-foot segments. Remaining sap is pressed
from the banana tree using the digging stick as a
rolling pin, to make the trunk more flexible and
absorbent. Then segments weighing anywhere from
50-100 pounds are hauled up the steep path to the
salt well. It's all business here. The women
neither tarry nor gossip, but they concentrate on
soaking the banana tree segments in the brine
pools. Next day they are collected and taken back
to village to dry. Several days later pulp is
burned to ash, which is wrapped in banana leaves
and shaped into hard balls. Two or three in a
package shipped to Nomad for trade. Important to
note the salt packages are left unattended during
```

parts of the process and others, including
warriors, might have access.

Stanek was about to close his notebook when indeed a Tugaru
warrior came to the well. The man dipped a long bamboo
container shaped like a straw into the pool and filled three gourds
with enough brine perhaps for a single family. Then he left. Stanek
noted warriors came to the well unannounced. By mid morning,
work at the well ceased. The women gathered the segments into
their string bags and headed home.

Emerson closed his book. Salty Meri seemed pleased with his
interest in the one activity which gave her status among the Tugaru.

She smiled and said, "Spirit of husband, before now you no talk
about salt, only look for gold stone. Now you go where you like.
Go up sacred mountain. Speak to sky people there, or Two Face,
like before."

Stanek opened his notebook again and scribbled:

```
* Yellow stones—gold?
* Sky people—Mackelwaite must have had company.
* Two Face—same deity for Tugaru as Riami.
```

He dared not question Salty Meri about these matters, for she
would expect him to know about them as the "spiritual form" of
Mackelwaite. No, there was an even better source. Milkeye held the
answers to these and other clues. First, Stanek must find a way to
win his confidence and then loosen the old warrior's tongue. For
starters, he decided to enlist the Riami in his search for the killer of
Salty Meri's youngest son, as Noble had suggested. If he could clear
WonTok and MilkEye, or other Riami, of any involvement in the
crime, perhaps they would show gratitude through greater
cooperation in the ten knights case.

*   *   *

MilkEye watched Stanek and the *kiap* circle the clearing. They
kept their backs to the few remaining salt workers as they searched
the *pitpit* perimeter. Stanek stopped at the very spot where MilkEye
had strangled the young boy. The sorcerer then called for the old
warrior to join them.

"What do you make of this?" he asked in pidgin.

MilkEye felt the sweat roll down his cheeks. He shrugged his shoulders and grunted. He feared speaking might betray his anxiety.

Kiap Noble filled the void. "*Come a gutser!* I'd say one hell of a brawl took place 'neath our feet. Look how the ground is chewed up and how the *pitpit* is squashed down in one spot."

"And see the depth of the footprints and one set of handprints in the soggy moss. What does that suggest, Roger?"

"A struggle between two men. And just like ye found inside the bomber, one fell to his hands and knees."

"Very good. And friend MilkEye, are the prints Tugaru, Riami or both?"

MilkEye dared not take another step while they watched. Or had they already seen one set of footprints matched his? He needed Situmu's advice more than ever. In his mind he called on the spirit of his father, but as before he heard nothing. Situmu was still angry with him. Then it came to him on his own. He must divert their attention.

"*Masta*, we *throwim way leg.* Go burial stone now. Sun here. Light way down cavern of bones."

"You're right. This investigation can wait. Lead the way, MilkEye. The *kiap* and I will follow."

"No good. You go first. If snake in path, *masta, kiap* kill with boot. Snake no bite MilkEye's foot. Path go one place—to burial stone."

"How far must we go up the trail?" Stanek asked.

Kiap Noble held up both hands. "Ten minutes tops. I know the way. I'll take the point as ye Yanks say. But MilkEye is wrong. There're two trails—the one leadin' up the mountain intersects with the one we're going to follow to the burial site. White men and strangers aren't allowed to take the upper path since it leads to the home of the mountain spirit."

Noble chuckled and then continued. "I'd say Salty Meri gave ye a free pass, seein' she thinks yer're the spirit of ole Angus."

MilkEye paid little attention to this banter. He knew he must kill the sorcerer before Stan-neck could write his name as the murderer in the book he carried, like Kioko-san's. Situmu would agree that not to act would place his kinsmen in the hands of the Tugaru who had never shown any mercy when it was time for payback. The Tugaru burial ground was not the right place to strike. He must get Stan-neck alone and make it look like an accident. The crocodiles on the banks of the Rentoul might help him.

He agonized whether he must kill WonTok, too, if he did not close his mouth. His friend had told the sky people too much—things to point to MilkEye as the killer. How much longer could he fool a great sorcerer like Stan-neck, who even now was calling for him to come see what he had found beside the trail.

"What is this, MilkEye?" Stanek asked in pidgin.

MilkEye pointed to his genital area. "Tugaru warrior wear. Make look fierce."

Stanek called the *kiap* back to see the penis gourd. They spoke in English and MilkEye did not know what they were saying. He only knew it was not good for him. When he dragged the body up the trail, he must've dislodged the Tugaru sign of manhood.

Stan-neck acted strange. He took a small, cotton-tipped stick from his bag and stirred it around inside the penis gourd. Then he took the little stick and put it inside a small jar. Now MilkEye understood what the *kiap* and Stanek were talking about. Stanek was truly a great sorcerer. He would know by the semen inside the gourd the youth had been strangled. MilkEye must get the small jar away from him before he could study it and learn more about the murder and the killer.

As they drew close to the Tugaru burial rock, Stanek noticed MilkEye again lagged behind. He asked Noble for an explanation as to why the Riami man kept his distance from him. The *kiap* twirled a finger to the side of his head.

"He's either addle-brained, or he's dissatisfied with his employment status. Ye'd better call him up and make it clear he's yer boss-boy now and for the river trip. Throw an extra gold-lipped shell in the mix."

"Good idea. He's worth much more to my investigation than a gold-lipped shell," Stanek replied.

"Only if he cooperates, Emerson. Want me to signal him to get his arse up here?"

"No, I'll do it. MilkEye's much more savvy than the others. Maybe I should return his brass wristband."

"Whatever it takes to buy him off," the *kiap* said.

The pathologist found these bribes distasteful, but decided it was the way people conducted business in the wild. Again he summoned MilkEye to join them. The old warrior shuffled slowly up the trail. He kept his head down and shook it from side to side as Stanek offered him first a gold-lipped shell, then the brass wristband.

"What makes you tarry so? If it's not payment for your services, or the return of your keepsake I only meant to borrow, is there something in your mind or heart that makes your feet heavy? Or are you afraid of the Tugaru spirits who linger here? You're my boss-boy and the *kiap* says you're not acting like one," Stanek said in pidgin.

MilkEye shook his head to each question, then spoke, "No, *Masta*. You good to me. Save LikLik and WonTok."

MilkEye paused. He spat on the ground, then continued. Only now did he face Stanek directly. There was anger in his eye. "No fear Tugaru. Fight many time."

"Then why don't you keep up?"

"No good hurry up now, *Masta*. Souls no time to keep up. Tugaru can steal. No good, *Masta*"

Noble remarked, "He's right there. Mustn't outrun our souls, or allow 'em to be stolen."

The air spiraling up between the split rock at the Tugaru burial site brought with it a stench the likes of which Stanek had never encountered. Perhaps 1,000 corpses over who knows how many years had been dumped into the crevice and left to decompose in the heat and humidity. His interest centered on finding two sets of remains—Mackelwaite's and those of Salty Meri's son.

Mackelwaite, of course, was of the highest priority. Certain Noble's fellow *kiap*, dead or alive, remained a key to unraveling the ten knights mystery, Stanek pursued his distasteful task. Even as his companions balked at his plan to descend into "hell," as Noble called it, the pathologist dangled his feet over the hole and called out to Noble and MilkEye.

"Come now, gents, you don't expect me to climb down there alone."

MilkEye made the first move, but he took a step back from the entrance, and Stanek heard the Riami warrior mutter something about Tugaru spirits rising from the stone and floating around his head like feathers blinding him for life.

Noble explained MilkEye's protest was completely accurate. Tugaru grouped their dead together in this haphazard manner so when the last warrior died, they could all rise up as one spirit "body." Only then would they have the strength to reach the mountaintop and dwell with Two Face, their god.

"Until then it was taboo for any Tugaru or other person to climb the mountain beyond the burial site, except to bring sacrifices to Two Face. MilkEye's father, Situmu, tried it and died in the attempt," Noble said.

At the mention of his father, MilkEye's movement was so quick, it caught Stanek off guard. The Riami warrior snatched the pathologist's knapsack from beside Stanek at the hole.

"Me take ruksak down. Help *masta*. Wait you come out."

Before Stanek could reply, MilkEye scurried next to the rock and disappeared on the trail running beside it. Noble started after MilkEye. The *kiap* took a step or two toward the hole, sniffed and turned away, cupping a hand over his mouth and nose.

Stanek called out again. "Come now, Roger, don't you go superstitious on me, too. I need you to identify Mackelwaite, if indeed we find enough of his remains intact to do so."

Noble kept a tight grip on his nose and spoke through clenched teeth. "It's not demons in the sky bothering me, but that ghastly aroma. Beats dingo, bat shit and pig shit combined."

"I've got the cure."

"Out with it, Emerson. I'm about to puke."

"Come here and sit by the hole with me for just three minutes."

"Not on yer life. Vomit will only add to the odor."

"Trust me. Three minutes. Your olfactory nerves will go numb. Then you'll be able to tolerate the odor."

"Even so, I don't fancy crawling in amongst corpses."

"There're notches carved on the sides of the hole. I suppose they're there for the shaman to climb down and make his recantations over the bones on special holidays. You don't have to touch anything but the wall, Roger, and hold the light to free up my hands."

Three minutes later, after having instructed Noble's two native constables to remain on guard at the entrance, the two white men descended. Inside, Stanek batted away flies circling around a semi-decayed body seething with maggots. It hadn't decomposed enough to be Mackelwaite's remains, but the corpse was about the right stage to be that of Salty Meri's youngest son, still bloated and oozing fluids.

Noble's right. Ghastly business, Stanek thought as he reached over from his notched side of the rock to separate the first corpse on the pyramid-shaped pile of skeletons. "Wouldn't surprise me if this latest fellow wasn't Salty Meri's son," he called to his companion on the other side of the pile.

Noble swatted at the flies swarming around his face, and Stanek saw the part of the *kiap's* face not covered by his red whiskers had taken on a tinge of pale green.

"There's an exit beneath us. See the light, Roger? MilkEye's probably waiting there. Maybe you should go on ahead and get some fresh air. I'll finish in a moment."

Noble passed Stanek the flashlight and asked, "What about Mackelwaite?"

"He'll be down further in the pile. I don't expect after a number of years in this heat and humidity we'll find much more of him than skeletal remains. Certainly his skull is gone if indeed your friend's lower jawbone is the one Salty Meri gave to me. Our best hope is to find some long bones to examine. From these we can tell whether it's a white man or not. But it can be done in the fresh air."

Noble again cupped his hand over his nose and mouth and scurried down his side of the wall to the exit. Stanek could follow his progress by the muffled wheezing and coughing sounds. Alone now, Stanek brushed aside the maggots from the corpse's neck. He ran his fingers over the cartilage. The thyroid and cricoid were all displaced, indicating the youth had been strangled. He had surmised as much from the evidence gathered from the penis gourd earlier, if indeed it had belonged to the victim. As he drew his fingers over the length of the young man's neck, he found remnants of a bark strap used as part of a net bag the natives carried. He had the victim, the mode and now the murder weapon. The killer had been in too much of a hurry to hide the bark strap from the string bag used to throttle his victim. Next, when time permitted, he must determine if the killer or killers were, as Salty Meri alleged, from the Riami tribe.

As he made his way down the side of the rock, Stanek flashed his light on the decaying flesh and bones. It saddened him to think the evidence thus far pointed to MilkEye or WonTok. Both had visited the burial ground to retrieve the B-24 dinghy. But if the Tugaru youth was murdered at the salt well, then his body must have been dragged to the split rock and tossed on top of the pile. He needed to check with the two suspects to see if either one had an alibi. Any questioning of MilkEye must wait until after he had learned all he could from the native he thought knew more about the ten knights case than anyone else living on the mountain. The trick was not to let MilkEye know he was a suspect.

Finding what were possibly Mackelwaite's remains turned out to be much easier than he expected. Had someone tried to hide the corpse by heaping old bones on it? He found the pelvic bone and several long bones from both the leg and forearm, each distinguished by a bit of khaki cloth with spots of dried blood. Stanek knew he had found the remains of a white man, although the hands and ankles appeared to have been severed and missing. Filipino Freddie used to mutilate his victims in the same manner to make identification more difficult. The skull was also missing, so there was no way to link the lower jawbone in his possession with the remains discovered in the Tugaru burial site. Nonetheless, he gathered up what he could find and made his way to the exit.

DeAnn Toland would have to work her magic to determine whether the remains he had found were those of one of the B-24 crew members unaccounted for or were those of Noble's friend. He also decided to turn the jawbone over to her and hoped dental records were available on Mackelwaite.

Outside he took a deep breath of the thin, mountain air and signaled to MilkEye to bring him his knapsack. "We'll store these bones out of the sun for the time being."

Noble had a puzzled look on his face. "Are those the bones of Angus?"

"We don't know," Stanek replied. He was sorry he couldn't give Noble a clear answer.

"Then we're back where we started."

"Not quite."

"Run it by again, Doc."

"Whoever these remains belong to was murdered, beheaded and mutilated."

"If ye mean head, hands and feet cut off, some tribes do that as a matter of convenience. It's how cannibals lighten their load if they need to haul body parts over a long distance or rough terrain."

"Maybe so, Roger, but the cuts made on this fellow are consistent with a sharp blade, probably a sword."

"Where do we go from here?"

"Down river as planned. Who knows how many other murders we'll uncover to add to our slate of victims?"

"What about the Tugaru lad? How did he die?"

"Strangled."

As Stanek placed the bones in his knapsack, he saw the specimen vial he had collected at the salt well was not in the side pocket in which he had placed it. Although he looked straight at MilkEye, who had retreated to the tall grass where he sat cross-legged, Stanek did not mention the missing vial as he called MilkEye forward.

"Tell me, Riami friend, what do you make of these burnt ashes and footprints around the exit? Also, the smudge marks on the stone?" Stanek asked in pidgin.

Noble reached down and picked up a handful of ashes, "I can answer yer question. Once a year, the Tugaru shaman comes here and lights a fire so the smoke will spiral up the rock and blow away any demons that might've infiltrated the burial site."

"Thanks, Roger, but I wonder if MilkEye could step over here and show me where he and WonTok found the dinghy from the B-24."

MilkEye hesitated. He knew his footprints in the ashes would leave a telltale mark the sorcerer had searched for at the salt well. He called on Situmu for an answer. Silence came back. He took his knife from his girdle and chopped a large branch from a nearby tree. MilkEye dragged the branch behind him as he made his way toward the exit, pleased the leaves obliterated his footprints. At the exit he tucked his head inside where erosion had formed a concealed pocket.

"Sky people canoe in this place. Me fall in hole when me hunt cassowary like old time. See sky people canoe. Take to *misis*. Give me honey for LikLik. Save child. Same you."

Stanek spoke in hushed tones as he passed MilkEye. Still, his voice had a strange echo once inside the exit. MilkEye saw his opportunity and seized the moment. He turned away from the cavern, and dragged the branch behind him until he reached the tall grass. He spoke to Noble, "*Kiap*, we take canoe from stone like me pull branch. You tell Stan-neck. Me go find WonTok before go down river."

336

Confident he had covered his tracks, so Two Face himself could not see them, MilkEye went off in search of his friend.

"Now, where did that sly devil get off to?" Stanek asked as he emerged from the shadow of the exit. Noble told him and added, "Sly devil is right. He's been actin' more peculiar than usual. How much help do ye expect to get from a man who has mastered the act of disappearin'? Better than any magician I've ever seen."

"Roger, I beg your indulgence. Let me handle MilkEye in my own way. Something hangs heavy over his head, and I believe I know what it is, but I can't say at the moment. So, please bear with me."

"Sure, Doc, but, again, let me warn ye. Don't turn yer back on MilkEye unless ye've got someone coverin' yer rear. I'll do the best I can to be there, but as ye know DeAnn's safety is my major concern."

"How long before we go down river?" Stanek asked.

"If we're on schedule, about two hours."

"Good. I'll have enough time to go over another segment of Kioko's journal. Can you suggest a quiet place?"

"Sure. At DeAnn's desk down at the crash site. Everyone else will be packin' up for the river trip."

Noble summoned his constables and the party of four started down the trail when out of the tall grass sprang Loud Mouth with a dozen warriors backing him up. He brushed by the two constables to confront the two white men. He leveled his spear at Noble's chest, then moved it within six inches of Stanek's throat.

Loud Mouth spoke. "No take bones from sacred stone. Leave here, or me kill you. No Tugaru take bones like me see you do."

Stanek stood his ground. "We'll make a trade, Tugaru man to Tugaru man. You hand over the murderer of Erik, and I'll give you the bones."

"How you know Tugaru man kill Erik?"

"A witness saw the killer."

"No good. You give back Tugaru bones."

Out of the side of his mouth, Noble ordered his boys to unlock their weapons. The Tugaru constable hesitated. Stanek figured he did not want to fire on his own tribesmen, much less a renowned leader like Loud Mouth.

"Hold on, Roger. Let's not go to war. The evidence can tell me no more than we already know, except for exact measurements. Maybe there's another way to get at them later."

Stanek laid his knapsack in the trail and took out the bones, fingering them as he did so in order to get a better feel for the height of the victim. This information would aid Toland in her search for missing crewmen.

While still crouching, he laid the bones at Loud Mouth's feet. "Here is what you want. Now let us go in peace. Mother of the Tugaru would be very sad to see us quarreling over what I think belongs to white man."

Loud Mouth kept his spear pointed at Stanek. "We go to mama. She tell us if bones are white or Tugaru. Mama down by river. Make ready salt train."

Noble whispered, "I don't like this idea. They may be lurin' us into a spot between here and the river where they could dispose of our bodies, and they might never be found. After all, if MilkEye is correct, Loud Mouth murdered Erik, and as ye know, we believe he mistook him for ye because of the hat. Damn if I'll stand by and give him another chance. I'll dismiss the Tugaru constable and have him hand over his weapon to ye. We can't afford anyone to go *wobbly* if there's a fight."

"Let's try another tactic first, Roger. You're the one who told me how superstitious these people are. Perhaps we can use it to our advantage."

Stanek then stood up to face Loud Mouth. "Why trouble your mother? You can have the bones to take back to the sacred stone and to the place they belong where they can wait for the shaman to release their spirit."

Loud Mouth pulled back his spear. "No good me go. Only shaman go inside sacred stone."

Stanek smiled. "Well, then, I'll just gather them up and take them back to where I found them. All your people, and Riami as well, know I am a medicine man with great sorcery," Stanek said.

Loud Mouth conferred with whom Stanek guessed was his fierce man, or second in command. They both nodded and pointed to the sacred stone. Stanek gathered the bones, walked back to the burial site, and, instead of laying them on the general pile, placed them in the pocket where MilkEye said he had found the dinghy. Since he had not allowed himself time enough to prepare for the stench, he waited inside the cavern rather than go outside and throw up in front of Loud Mouth. This would brand him a sham in the eyes of the Tugaru. After the allotted time, he returned to the edge of the clearing.

He turned up his palms. "There, it's done. Now let us be on our way."

Loud Mouth signaled to his fierce man to clear a path for Stanek and his party.

Noble pulled up beside the pathologist and whispered, "They're sure to follow us to make sure we don't backtrack and steal the bones. So, instead of headin' directly to the river, we'll veer off at the CIL encampment."

"Good plan, Roger. Let me borrow a couple of your constables to stand guard outside, and I'll read Kioko's log in the comfort of my own tent."

"Better use mine. There are more people on our side hangin' about."

No more than 20 minutes later, Stanek went inside his tent and retrieved volumes four, five and six of Kioko's journal. Five minutes more and he was sitting at the desk in Noble's quarters, glad to put the nightmare at the Tugaru burial site behind him. He was anxious to learn what had happened to the American WW II aviator scheduled for execution. He picked up volume four and began to read.

33 KIOKO'S JOURNAL #4, TABLES TURNED

Komo, Papua New Guinea, 1943

U.S. ARMY CENTRAL IDENTIFICATION LABORATORY (PROVISIONAL) FINDINGS, CASE NUMBER 316, EXHIBIT 3d, KIOKO TANAKA'S FOURTH JOURNAL. DR. DEANN TOLAND'S REPORT.

HERE, I, KIOKO, relate the love story borne on the wings of tragedy. My ruse to save the American aviator did not succeed, so Lt. Mori announced to the assembled survivors the American's execution would take place at dawn the next day in a village called Tadei, which we had sighted.

It was already mid-day when we spotted the smoke from the village. We had another half day's march to reach it since it was below the ridge upon which we stood. We were low on supplies and needed food badly, yet I still felt a deep sorrow that this was where the American would die.

From the times I had sat a short distance from him praying in English and listening to his conversations with Butterfly, I envied the Filipino girl because she heard close at hand the rich baritone in which he spoke. I tried to make myself believe this envy came because he had selected someone to share his thoughts with whose mastery of English was so inferior to mine. But in truth, I'd grown accustomed to the soft tones he so patiently spoke to the Filipino girl.

How could he be so kind and gentle after the beating he suffered every night at the hands of my fellow sojourners? I wondered if he would make it to the next village, even though helped by Butterfly. Each day his energy seemed to ebb away to the point of exhaustion. Where would he summon enough strength to make it through the high saw grass and bracken fern stretching between our party and the village? We would have to hack our way through since the path had run out. The crossbeam to which he was tied made the journey more arduous for him, since he had to turn sideways to negotiate the newly cut path.

I dropped back to the end of our column to eavesdrop on his conversation with Butterfly. To my surprise, they were discussing the terrain. With tremendous effort, the American lifted his face above the bar tied across his back at the shoulders. It amazed me to see his once handsome face was barely visible underneath the cuts and bruises rained down on him by Lt. Mori. Still, he smiled at Butterfly. He addressed her by her Christian name I had not known.

I heard him say, "Maria, the absence of paths between us and the next village is good for us, but bad news for the Japs."

His voice was as strong as it had been since the first day of his captivity, and I realized he wanted me to hear what he was saying. Was it a warning, or meant to strike fear? I had hoped Butterfly would speak his name when she replied, but either she didn't know it, or was told by him to keep it secret.

In essence she inquired, "Won't the lack of a clear path make it more difficult for us as well as the soldiers?"

He almost laughed. "Ah, the Japs in their stupid, arrogant fashion don't realize the absence of paths to any village is a sure sign it is at war with its neighbors. It's the same as if they hung out a sign reading, 'Approach at your own risk'."

When the American saw me draw closer, he said no more. I hurried to the front of the column and told Lt. Mori all I had overheard.

He did laugh. "Kioko, the Yankee dog's lies have frightened you. I'll end his shame for surrendering at dawn tomorrow."

Then Lt. Mori took off his special glasses and glared at me with those eyes, pink and scarred. "I'll make him pay for what his countrymen have done to me," he continued, "but just in case he's trying to save his own skin, knowing you heard him, we'll set up

341

camp in an open space above the village. We'll have a clear view from there."

I fell back to my regular place in the column behind Lt. Mori and the two soldiers, between my brother Taro and the American captive.

Taro stiffened. "What's all this pacing back and forth about, Kioko?" You'll wear yourself out."

He was right. I was already breathing hard, yet still managed to give him the warning I had given to Lt. Mori. He fell silent, so I asked, "Aren't you scared?"

"I'm a soldier. We're not supposed to get scared. What frightens you so about the American?"

"The silence."

"Silence? Because he won't spread his lies to you?"

"His warning might be true."

"What do you mean?"

"After he spoke this last time, the yodeling stopped. Haven't you noticed, Taro?"

My brother shrugged. "What of it?"

"They've always yodeled to each other when we approached a village."

Taro stiffened again. "Maybe they're the ones scared and have abandoned their cooking pots for us to feast on."

The evening before the scheduled execution of our prisoner, it was cool in the highland valley and the dampness was penetrating. After Lt. Mori and the others settled in for one of their brief naps, I made my way to the center of our camp where the American was tethered in the usual manner. Butterfly attended him. I heard them whispering together. On my approach, they stopped. Butterfly intercepted me before I reached my usual prayer position ten yards from the prisoner as allowed by Lt. Mori.

"Kioko-san, tonight the American asked for you to come closer," the Filipino girl said in the clearest English I had ever heard her speak. She continued, "He wants to see your face up close. I tell him how beautiful you are. He say me beautiful, too. And beauty he like look on before he die."

She didn't finish. She wept instead. I took her in my arms, surprised at how frail a creature could find the strength to aid the injured American over so many tortuous miles. I patted the skin covering her ribs, alarmed at how thin she was. "Go tell him I'll pray beside the two of you, but we must whisper, for if Lt. Mori hears us, we'll all be punished."

She smiled through her tears. "I told Yankee soldier you would come. Butterfly can see how you look at each other. I know same-same look in Manila before I become comfort girl. He knows you would help if you could. Kioko not like others, he tell me."

My voice deserted me, but there came an ache in my heart. I could not let this man die and have his blood on my hands. I loosened the knife from my girdle of bark and cut the bark straps holding him to the crossbeam. Through bruised lips, he muttered, "Thank you, beautiful."

I urged him to hurry out of the clearing and into the bush, but it was obvious he could not make it on his own. Butterfly slipped her arm under his on one side and I did the same on the other. Together we started toward the thicket at a crawl more than a walk. At the edge of the *kunai*, we left him on his own and turned to go back. Butterfly wanted to stay with him, but I told her it was too dangerous. She relented. We crawled back a few paces only to find Lt. Mori, feet spread apart blocking our way. He pulled me up by the hair.

"Foolish child," he said in a hushed voice. "You mustn't tell the others what you've done, or to save your family shame, I'll be forced to kill you and your brother Taro."

I started to protest, but he clamped a hand over my mouth. "Stay here, quietly, while I go bring back the prisoner," he commanded.

Butterfly and I wept so loudly we awoke the others. By the time they realized what had happened, Lt. Mori had dragged the young soldier from the bush.

Taro was the first to speak. "Kioko, are you alright? Did the American overpower you and try to escape?"

Lt. Mori answered before anyone else had a chance to speak. "The Filipino whore tried to free her ally, but Kioko sounded the alarm, or else all of our throats might've been slit while we slept. At dawn tomorrow, we'll have two executions. The girl will be shot, and the Yankee dog beheaded. He doesn't deserve the death of a soldier."

By the light of the moon, I pleaded with my eyes for Lt. Mori to show mercy, but he only removed his glasses and glared at me with those pink circles I had come to loath. Throughout the night I cried and could hear Butterfly weeping as well. This dear, sweet, innocent girl who had known so much suffering was tied back to back with the American who tried to comfort her.

The following day brought sunshine but little hope to the condemned or any solace for the anguish I felt. I had forgotten to eat something in the night to prevent a reaction from the quinine and aspirin. So when Lt. Mori ordered me into the center of the village, I shook like one with the fever.

"Are you sick, woman?" the commandant asked.

I shook my head and replied, "It's only an empty stomach, but my heart is filled with sorrow."

"Not for the Yankee dog?"

"No, for Butterfly."

"Pray for her. Like you've been taught by the Christians."

"May I ask one last favor, Sir?"

"You may ask, but I'll decide whether to grant it, not your God."

"Let me pray with Butterfly and hear her confession."

"Kioko, the priestess. What do you make of it, Taro?"

Taro hung his head and mumbled, "Don't push too far, little sister."

I turned to leave. "Wait!" Lt. Mori shouted. "I don't want you pouting about all day. You may have 15 minutes with the whore. But do not speak to the other prisoner or let your eyes meet his."

I bowed and in quick step made my way past the two soldiers to kneel at Butterfly's side. She had picked up bits and pieces of my conversation with Lt. Mori and asked me to listen to her story. My impression was she wanted to set the record straight as much for the American as for my ears. A summary of her last words follows.

She was born Maria Arroyo in a small provincial town in the Philippines, a good family girl. When Manila fell, Maria was visiting an older sister, and both were captured by Japanese soldiers after her brother-in-law and two nephews were killed. The soldiers raped her sister and made Maria watch. When they were finished, one rammed his bayonet into the woman's vagina while the others stabbed her to death.

Then they turned their lust on Maria, who was only 15. As they tore her clothes away, she fainted and awoke in the arms of a young Japanese officer who had thrown his cloak around her. She later learned that the sub-lieutenant told the soldiers one so young and beautiful must be shared. He would make her a comfort woman for all to enjoy.

They left together, but instead of loading her on a truck crowded with other girls kidnapped into sexual slavery, the sub-lieutenant took her to a safe house run by Spanish medical missionaries. While she had been unconscious, someone had raped her, the doctor told her. "Please, God," she cried. "If I have a child, let it be by the one who saved me." Butterfly could never hate him.

The lieutenant came to the center each week and brought her flowers and warned her never to leave the compound. He told her after the war, they would marry and live in the beautiful countryside in Japan. For security reasons, he gave no one his name. Then one day he told her he had to leave. They kissed in the garden, and before he left he gave her a beautiful fan as a keepsake.

As it happened the missionary center was two blocks from the main well where the girls went to draw water at night when the Japanese soldiers were asleep. Because of her near captivity, Maria was exempted from this duty. But one night, the girl who was supposed to take the bucket to the well fell ill and Maria took her place. Unfortunately, she was recognized by one of the soldiers who had raped her sister, and she was recaptured. To save her life, she pretended to be a comfort girl who had fallen from the truck taking her and others to the port for shipment to Rabaul. The soldiers insisted on escorting her to the waterfront, not wanting to soil goods earmarked for the brass at the Japanese headquarters. They named her Butterfly since they thought she hopped from flower to flower. From Rabaul she came to Angoram, never to see her sub-lieutenant again.

When Butterfly came to the end of her story, the American tied to her muttered, "Sons-of-bitches. They deserved what they got at Angoram, and not entirely for Jap atrocities alone."

Shocked to learn of his familiarity with the bombing of our radio station, yet enraged at what Butterfly had gone through, I didn't know on whom to direct my anger. But Butterfly needed consolation.

"I'm sorry you must die, because I don't have your courage," I whispered in her ear as I kissed her cheek.

She forced a smile. "Kioko, in my bag I have fan. You take back home with you. Give to sub-lieutenant's family. He, you, only Japanese kind to Butterfly."

Lt. Mori signaled my time was up. Then Butterfly kissed me goodbye and added, "Don't cry, Kioko-san. Butterfly glad to go to well. Draw water for you, my sister."

Lt. Mori pulled me aside, and I jumped when I heard the report from his pistol. Maria "Butterfly" Arroyo had found peace. Blood trickled behind her ear and on the bare shoulder of the American where her head rested.

As Lt. Mori cut him free from Butterfly, the Yank shook with rage or sorrow, or maybe both. Our eyes met. Mine must have betrayed my fear, for his softened and he said, "I don't blame you, doll. You just come from a wacky system. It's not your fault."

"No talk!" Lt. Mori shouted. He took Taro's sword, stood off to the side and ladled water across the blade to purify it in the name of the Emperor. He ordered one soldier to cut the prisoner loose from the crossbar, tie his hands behind his back and set him in a kneeling position with his neck exposed. He directed the other soldier to prop the Imperial Portrait in front of the prisoner.

"Let the dog's last gaze be on him under whose authority this punishment is delivered."

The moment Mori raised the blade to strike, out from what had seemed to be abandoned huts and from the *pitpit* tracks around the perimeter of the village poured 100 or more natives. Some carried large wooden shields behind which came others armed with bows and arrows, the arrows nocked and pointed at us. Lt. Mori pulled back the sword and drew his pistol. He then ordered the soldiers to load their rifles, but I could see the natives kept coming forward, crab-like in their movements.

The short kangaroo grass around the execution site gave them a clear shot at us from a dozen angles. There was no way we could fend off so many with our meager firearms. The natives pointed their arrows in our direction, and the stacks of extra ones in net bags on their backs were positioned so they need only reach over their shoulders to reload. They kept coming, yodeling in unison, and this fearful sound, in a language I'd never heard, was most likely a call to war.

Out of the massed center appeared a warrior, taller than any of the others, and more decorated with shells around his head and neck. He raised his hand and spoke to the American, who translated his message for me. In turn, I translated his words into Japanese.

"He comes for the American," I told my companions. "If we set him free, we can go in peace."

"Not on your life," Lt. Mori snapped.

I had to find a way to break the stalemate and convince Mori it would be folly to put up any resistance and make our last stand where no one would ever find our bodies or any trace of us to take home to our families. Then it struck me. The lieutenant valued the Imperial Portrait over his own life. If we were murdered, it would be dragged through the jungle and subject to defamation. I tried to sound serene.

"Sir, these people must be those who attacked us earlier with the American as their leader. He must be as important to them as the Emperor's portrait is to us. Perhaps they hold him in a god-like status. Maybe it's not worth giving up everything for one who means so little to us."

Taro and the other two soldiers allied themselves with my cause; Taro, no doubt, out of concern for my safety. Lt. Mori relented.

"Tell the American the natives can have him, since he'll probably die before they can carry him to their camp anyway. But surrender for the rest of us is out of the question."

I passed Lt. Mori's terms to the American, who turned and ordered a reclining chair brought forward. They laid him against the back, and with great effort he raised his head and spoke from his makeshift ambulance.

"Tell your four-eyed monster his terms are unacceptable unless he frees you to go with us and gives me the Filipino girl's body to bury. I'll order the natives to kill the lot of you, leaving Lt. Mori last so he can watch me burn the portrait of his Emperor he's been lugging around."

I hesitated. "Why do you want me?"

"To save your life, since you tried to save mine."

"How do you know I'll die?"

"Because you'll never make it to wherever you're headed, since you've left a trail of hatred in the villages you've sacked. Believe me, they'll find a way to pay you back."

Lt. Mori grew impatient. "What is he saying to you, and what are you saying to him?" he demanded.

"The Yank wants me to go with him."

"What!"

"Otherwise, he'll have the rest of you killed, burn the Imperial Portrait and take me by force if he has to."

"And what was your answer?"

"I haven't answered, but I intend to tell him I won't go anywhere unless Taro is freed."

"No! It would be surrender!"

"Not if you and your two soldiers are free to go."

"I can't allow one trained as a *samurai*, as Taro was, to surrender his sword to this Yankee dog."

"Then you keep my brother's sword and return it to him after the war, or if we don't make it, give it to the Tanaka family."

"You sound like you want to go with the enemy."

"If it will avoid more bloodshed, yes. And Taro would not be surrendering, since he'd go only to protect me."

"But the American will violate you."

"I hope not, but if he does, it wouldn't be any worse than what our soldiers have done to young girls like Butterfly."

Now the American grew impatient. "Enough chatter between you two. Give me your answer."

I told him I could not leave my brother, and he agreed to make Taro part of the deal. Still, I had to convince Lt. Mori this was his only chance to take the Imperial Portrait with him to Wewak and have them celebrate the sacrifices he had made to safeguard it since his carrier, the *Shoho*, was sunk.

I was about to tell him the American had agreed when Lt. Mori took my hand in his and said, "I suppose Taro will watch over you until I can find a place to secure the Imperial Portrait, then come back for you. I promise I'll come back, and together we'll go home to Japan."

The pity I once felt for this man returned, and it seemed to me in his awkward way, he was proposing. Yet, I did not want to give him any encouragement, because the wounds he inflicted on me cut into my very soul. In the end, I simply said, "Take care of yourself and forget me."

"Never!" he said.

Those were the last words I ever heard him speak directly to me. He traded his ceremonial sword with Taro for my brother's *samurai* sword.

As Mori handed over his ceremonial sword to Taro, he said, "Use this sword, such as it is, to protect your sister. I'll be back for both of you, and we can make another swap." He thrust Taro's *samurai* sword in his belt, cradled the Imperial Portrait under his arm and marched out of the clearing with the two soldiers on his heels.

Before Lt. Mori had reached the tall grass, the American rose from his litter and directed his followers to lay the body of Butterfly in his place. As they did so, her little ragged bag fell to the ground, revealing the fan she had bequeathed to me. I picked it up and opened it, astonished to find it bore the peony emblem used as a crest for the Tanaka family. I tucked it inside my shirt, reminding myself to ask Taro if our brother Jiro had ever been posted to Manila.

Oblivious to my actions, the American silently walked beside the bier, helped by two natives upon whom he leaned. At the edge of the village rose the highest elevation in the immediate highland area. The American instructed the natives to carry the bier to the summit, dig a hole, cover it with bamboo leaves, and place the Filipino girl in her grave. They were then to pile on some more leaves and dirt to form a mound. The American further directed the natives to take wood and bark from the stretcher and fashion a cross to be placed at the head of the mound.

The Yank turned to me and said, "Before they leave to bury Butterfly at the peak, we must speak some parting tribute for her. She has been so kind to each of us. I've heard you pray, Kioko. I know your words would be more appropriate than mine."

He had spoken my name for the first time and I knew I had nothing to fear from this stranger. Unless, of course, he ever found out mine was the voice of "New Guinea Ginny."

34 AMBUSHED

Rentoul River, Papua New Guinea, 1973

BEFORE HE CLOSED the fourth journal, Stanek pondered its contents. Here, in Kioko's words, was an alleged link between the bombing at Angoram described in the pilot's log and a possible survivor from the raid. To make any sense of all this, Stanek decided someone must verify the writings of the Japanese woman. He shuddered at the thought of how this would entail site-by-site confirmation of the burial places mentioned by Kioko. Backtrack. A trip through the jungle from Mount Bosavi to Angoram wouldn't be feasible. They'd have to fly to airstrips near the sites if available. Even so, it would delay his beekeeper cancer research, further shattering his timetable. He had no choice unless he could persuade DeAnn Toland to check out these places after they returned from the river trip, while he concentrated on the search up the mountain. Returning volume four to DeAnn might help his cause. Better yet, maybe he would return both volumes five and six to her by way of Noble.

The *kiap* stuck his head inside the tent and wheezed as he exhaled. "Pardon the intrusion, Doc. But, as yer wild-west heroes used to say in the flickers, 'It's time to saddle up and head down river. We've got a salt train to catch.'"

Stanek smiled at Noble's tangled metaphors. "Time to shove off, is it? We'll proceed full speed ahead. But first, do you mind taking Kioko's last two volumes back to Dr. Toland? Tell her I'll read volumes five and six on our return, as I'm confident she's digested enough of the material to aid our down-river search as need be."

"Sure, lad, and I'll be bearin' ye a gift as well."

"From whom?"

"DeAnn. Come out and see. Over there, between my constables outside the men's tent."

Stanek looked in the direction Noble pointed. "WonTok?"

"In the flesh."

"I don't understand."

"DeAnn found WonTok cringin' in the bush. Tryin' to hide his whereabouts from us and MilkEye, I'd say. Knows his *age-mates* and MilkEye might kill him if they knew he went over to the Tugaru."

"I thought WonTok did defect."

"Not exactly. It was a ruse."

"I still don't understand."

Noble wheezed and then took in a deep breath. "Here's what the boss lady and I pieced together. After WonTok was humiliated, he went to the Tugaru. Cheeky devil he is, he asked 'em for protection from his own people."

"Why would he need protection?"

"'Cause death is the Riami penalty for violatin' the rites of passage for a warrior."

"How awful! What did WonTok do to deserve such punishment?"

"He told me he'd substituted MilkEye's sperm for his own at the initiation ceremony when they were boys."

"Then why would MilkEye want to kill him?"

"To keep him quiet. As an accomplice, MilkEye faces the same penalty."

"There must be more to the story."

"'Tis true, laddie. WonTok figured *Bikmaus* would give him protection if he showed the Tugaru headman how ye fooled him."

"Fooled him. What do you mean?"

"The batteries stuck in your breeches. WonTok saw ye pull off yer trick." Noble paused, took in another breath and continued. "And, in his confused state, he spilled his guts. Perhaps he never dreamed Loud Mouth would challenge ye again, since the rape was no longer an issue."

Stanek frowned. "We're all glad it's over with."

"Wrong. It's never finished with these people 'til they come out ahead. They call it payback."

"Illogical nonsense. If followed to its logical conclusion—one payback following another—it could go on infinitum. Never mind. Tell me why WonTok came back to us."

"Not us—ye, Emerson."

Stanek rubbed his cheek. "Me? Why am I always the one singled out?"

"Erik's murder must've scared WonTok. He realized ye were more powerful than *Bikmaus*. Only a great sorcerer or a god could send someone in yer place to die for ye."

"But, I never intended..."

"We know. None of us wanted any harm to come to Erik, but ye've got to see it from the standpoint of these people. Now WonTok thinks ye'll send Erik's spirit back for payback to dog him night and day. I've seen natives die from lack of sleep, thinkin' some lost spirit is goin' to creep up on 'em and take revenge."

Stanek tapped the scar on his cheek. "I'm beginning to get the picture. After Erik's murder, WonTok escaped from the Tugaru, and now he's back here to beg my forgiveness."

"And entreat ye not to tell MilkEye he'd gone over to the enemy. He knows MilkEye would have one more reason to kill him if he ever found out."

"Even if you and DeAnn are right about WonTok, I don't have time to play nursemaid to him. As for Loud Mouth, he'll have to get in line, as I believe there are others who want me dead as well. But it's another story, Roger."

Noble pulled himself upright and thrust his thumbs inside his bandoleers. "WonTok wants to sign on yer canoe as one of the paddlers. DeAnn thinks ye should let him, and so do I."

"Why?"

"Because the other paddler is MilkEye, who'll be aft with you and Major Yowell sitting between him and WonTok. DeAnn thinks these friends will eventually reconcile if given the opportunity when pressed to work together."

"And where will you be?"

"Why, in the canoe straight ahead of ye with DeAnn, of course. Nothin' is gonna happen to our dear lassie. Not under my eye."

*   *   *

By the time the lead canoe in the 12-dugout salt train reached the portage at Lower Falls where the Rentoul narrowed to 70 yards across, daylight was fading. Stanek, seated in the last craft, shielded his eyes from the last rays of the sun by cupping his hand under the brim of his bush hat. Save for the splash of water against paddles wielded by WonTok and MilkEye, kneeling forward and aft respectively, and the occasional crack of static coming over the radio operated by Major Yowell, all was quiet.

Stanek thought about prodding MilkEye and WonTok to quicken the pace. He was worried they had fallen too far back from the boat ahead of them, which bore *Kiap* Noble, his constables and DeAnn Toland. Just then the stillness of the late afternoon was broken by the strokes of a dozen or more paddles coming alongside the canoe. Stanek tapped Yowell on the shoulder and the two white men looked over to see as many as 14 strange warriors standing one behind the other as they paddled in unison.

MilkEye pointed to the long orange-colored oars whose upper section had the carved heads of the black King Cockatoo. "Giambu, no good! Bad talk people," he said.

Before anyone could react, the Giambu war canoe swept past the smaller Riami craft, then turned broadside about ten yards downstream. Again, MilkEye responded first. "Giambu like us stop, but no good hear bad talk people, *Masta*."

The old warrior used his paddle as a tiller and swung his dugout right and set course for the north shore of the Rentoul above Lower Falls. While this maneuver avoided a collision, it brought the two craft broadside to broadside. Seated in the place of honor, Stanek came face to face with his bushman counterpart in the war canoe.

He observed the Giambu chieftain in an attempt to discern his intentions. Unlike either the Riami or the Tugaru, the Giambu had sparse hair, which started way back on their forehead as it clung tight to the skin of the scalp. Through their nasal spectrum, they wore a single piece of bamboo instead of the pig's tusk and shells preferred by both the Tugaru and the Riami as marks of manhood beauty.

Stanek raised his hand, palm out. "We come in peace. Riami men with us, know this is true," he said in pidgin.

Either the chieftain did not understand pidgin, or he ignored the pathologist's gesture, for in the next instant Stanek faced the barrel of a rifle. "Duck," he shouted to his comrades. WonTok struck the other canoe with his paddle, pushing it away. It was just enough movement to throw off the assailant's aim. Stanek felt a sharp pain in his right shoulder just above his previous wound made by the clavicle knife attack in Hawaii. A dark veil began to close over his eyes.

For a brief moment, he found himself sailing across Fells Point with 15-year-old Catherine at the tiller. Propped against her knees, his hand touched the tiller where it made contact with her thighs. He tasted and smelled the salt spray and his cheeks tingled with its coldness. They both listened to the toll of the bell buoy and the rustle of the cordage.

"Those are my two favorite sounds in the world," Catherine said. "Whenever I hear the bell toll or the rigging tap against the spar, it makes me want to kiss you a million times and thank you for teaching me to sail. Oh, say you feel the same way, too, Emerson."

In the next instant, Stanek became conscious of the contraction of his muscles and movements of his wrist and elbow joints as he fought to wrestle control of the tiller from Charles, the playboy yachtsman and ex-husband of Catherine. In his mind's eye, dead ahead, he saw the waves foam white as they broke upon a reef.

He abandoned the struggle with Charles, and the two of them tugged at the sheet and jammed the tiller hard over in an attempt to pass to the windward of the peril. It was too late. The craft struck the edge of the reef where the rocks were sharpest. He heard the crunch of her keel and felt the deck rise up under his feet. He reached for Catherine, but he slipped. The chill of the water closed over him. Charles disappeared. As the dark veil continued its descent, he saw Catherine astride the broken deck. He called out her name as he swam toward her, but his arms and legs grew heavy as though they had anchors attached pulling him down.

Up ahead, DeAnn heard the shot and watched Noble and his constables spring into action. They fired at the alien craft but, as far as she could determine, they missed hitting the occupants. The hostile canoe, brought about so it presented the narrowest of targets, slithered into one of the many tributaries along the Rentoul like a giant python.

Stanek awoke to find himself in the lap of DeAnn Toland, but it was Yowell's voice he heard. The major pointed to his shoulder. "He was struck about here. Then quicker than you could rope a steer, he sailed clean over the side. 'Twas all I could do but grip his arm and hold him tight against the dugout. He kept callin' for Catherine before he passed out. MilkEye and WonTok got us ashore."

"You did well, Frank. Now press down on this gauze while I tape the wound. Then I need you to check in Dr. Stanek's medical bag. There should be a syringe with some morphine in it for his pain."

Kiap Noble bent over Stanek. "We've called the chopper in for ye, mate. Yer sister showed a lot of forethought having the cavalry in reserve."

Stanek protested. "I'm all right. Let's keep going."

DeAnn dabbed at his forehead with a cool cloth. "I can't allow it. You're a doctor. You know the dangers of infection. You're going to the hospital at Goroka. The rest of us can finish the mission."

Noble stood up and stamped his feet. "It's not going to happen, lassie. You're going back to Mount Bosavi with Dr. Stanek and then to Goroka by fixed wing aircraft if ye decide to do so. With this shootin' goin' on, I'll not put yer life at risk. Major Yowell, MilkEye, WonTok, me and me lads will continue to search for remains. We'll camp here and take a good look around after ye've been safely evacuated. The salt train has to stop for the night anyway."

"Now, wait a minute. I've got some say in this matter," said Yowell, handing DeAnn the morphine syringe. "I'll go back with DeAnn and Stanek."

"Let's all calm down for a moment while Dr. Stanek gives me instructions on how to administer this painkiller," admonished DeAnn.

With great effort, Stanek held out his arm. "Make a tourniquet above the site and insert the needle in a prominent vein for best results," he said.

When she finished the task, she looked at Major Yowell and replied, "Best we stick to the original plan, Frank. I want you to go on down river with Roger to Nomad. Then fly him back to Mount Bosavi in the aircraft pre-positioned at Nomad and bring whatever skeletal remains you find along the river to us in Goroka."

"None of us knows what in the Sam Houston we're looking for," Yowell protested.

"Roger, see if MilkEye and WonTok know anything about white people's bones we might find along the Rentoul. According to the copilot's log, four of the B-24 crewmembers tried to escape down the river with Riami escorts. Whatever you bring back, we'll sort out in Goroka, or when I return to Mount Bosavi."

Yowell tried to protest again. "But..."

"No 'buts'. This is the best we can do to salvage the river expedition."

Yowell shook his head. "You're the boss lady, but you should know this area is pretty damn close to where Stanek and I almost bought the farm on his arrival. Must've been a dozen of them shooting at us as we came in low in the Beaver."

"Meaning?"

"Meaning, Roger might be prepared, but I'm not dead set on another shootout at the 'O.K. corral.' For heavens sake, DeAnn. We should all hop on the chopper and get the hell out of here. I mean us whites. This place is hotter than a fire-base under attack in 'Nam!"

Stanek stirred. "As expedition leader, I..."

DeAnn put a finger to his lips. "Shhhh... Too much exertion."

He gave a weak smile and looked up at her. "While we wait, do me and yourself a favor, DeAnn. Quiz MilkEye and WonTok about Lower Falls. WonTok insists it's a cascade, not a waterfall. He said you explained the difference to him. It was clear from their conversations as we progressed down river, MilkEye and WonTok have a special interest in Lower Falls." He paused to catch his breath and then continued. "If Noble and Yowell press them hard enough, I wouldn't be surprised if the two Riami men don't spill a little more than they've told us so far."

Again she put a finger to his lips. "Shhh... No more talk."

He gave another weak smile. "Let me finish. In case I don't make it back, I've got to entrust my findings to someone I can count on. After the river search, you've got to look in two other locations. If there's a Lower Falls, then there must be an Upper Falls—a cascade high up on the mountain hiding a cave or a passageway through the limestone. So a search up there might prove profitable, especially if some of the B-24 crewmembers fell out when part of the tail section broke off. But don't go without adequate protection for there's a murderer or other killers stalking about. I've seen one of them. I'd prefer you hold off on the mountain excursion until my return."

Stanek paused again as the morphine began to take effect. "Kioko's journals must be verified. This means using them as a guide to retrace her journey as far as Angoram. Feel free to consult my notes when you get a chance."

She nodded. "Save the rest for when we get to Goroka and can report to General Bellicosi who's flying in from Hawaii."

Stanek looked at MilkEye, who seemed to be straining to fathom the conversation and perked up when Kioko's name was mentioned. The pathologist's voice sank to a whisper. "As to who wants me dead, I've no idea. I'd appreciate any help you could give me in bringing your expertise to bear in this matter should you uncover something I need to know."

She touched his lips for a third time, and spoke even more softly. "Shhh... Now that's enough. You've got to get some rest."

He lay back against her thighs and dreamed as the morphine took full effect. This time the dream carried him back to Fells Point and his own first sailing lesson under the tutelage of the man he so desperately wanted to call father—Dr. Rufus Stanek, Catherine's father.

35 EVACUATION

Goroka, Papua New Guinea, 1973

JAMES COLE WAITED by the bedside in his wheelchair for the pathologist to awaken. When he saw Stanek change position, the reporter wheeled closer. "Caution," he told himself. "Don't sound too eager. You've waited more than a year for information on the B-24 mystery. What's a few more hours?" Cole's heart thumped in his chest. He wondered if a physician as skilled as Dr. Stanek might read the signs of anxiety by observation alone. Just in case, with hands shaking, Cole drew the robe across his middle. The veins in his hands, swollen by needle pricks, were as blue as the garments he wore.

He cracked a smile. "The human pin cushion welcomes you to Goroka General, the best infirmary north of Port Moresby."

Stanek looked at him but did not comment. "Give him a minute to clear out the cobwebs," Cole thought. "Patience." If Stanek learned anything about survivors, let it come out voluntarily. Then he'd be more apt to open up to a reporter.

"Glad you got my message, Doc. But we've got to stop meeting in hospitals. They brought you in yesterday. DeAnn Toland said you took a bullet in the shoulder down river on the Rentoul. The surgeon dug it out, but both of us are to be evacuated to Johns Hopkins for follow-up, courtesy of your sister. LikLik's going, too. Suppose they want to study her further. We're to leave as soon as the beautiful lady so interested in your serum arranges our

358

transport. Anyway, I'm glad you got my message I needed to see you."

Stanek winced as he propped an extra pillow under his head. "What message?"

Cole wheeled over to the bed stand and held up two pieces of stationery. "On a letterhead like this in a thick envelope marked confidential for you. Sent about a week ago."

"Never got it."

"Wait a minute. Now I remember. I left it on my tray for the day nurse to send it out. She's here today. Stand by whilst I get to the bottom of this."

A few minutes later a nurse pushed Cole back into the room and left. "She didn't see any letter either. Has this cancer reached my brain already? Wait! I'll wager that new roommate I was supposed to get pilfered it."

"Roommate?"

"Yeah. He's a wrestler. Calls himself Waiola, you know, like the church in Maui, an alias no doubt. This big lug never saw the inside of a church. But I saw his pock-marked puss somewhere before."

Stanek sat up in bed. "You've just described one of the assailants who followed me from Baltimore to Hawaii. He and a woman tried to kill me. You saved me, remember?"

"Can't easily forget it. I was on wheels then, too, Doc. Everything happened so fast that I didn't get a good look at them in the mortuary, or whatever you call the place. So they were the couple on our flight to Hawaii, too? Only I could forget that ugly mug. But the woman, now there's a looker, but the guy would've scared the ghost of Al Capone."

Stanek sank back against the pillow. "In your letter to me, did you mention my plans or my location?"

"I wrote it was urgent I see you after you got back from the trip down..."

"River."

"Where DeAnn said you were bushwhacked. Sorry, Emerson, I didn't mean to lead them to you."

Stanek stroked the crescent shaped scar on the side of his cheek. "Don't blame yourself. Could've been someone else who knew about the river trip. You've actually been helpful again."

"In what way."

"We know whoever wants me dead has not given up, and he or she has high speed communication and a far-flung network and knows how to use them."

Cole wheeled his chair around. "I've got to get help. Dr. Toland should notify the District Commissioner to post constables outside this room straight away."

"Hold on, Jim. What was so urgent you sent a confidential letter to me at Mount Bosavi?"

Cole reflected. "It can wait. The urgent matter at hand is your safety."

The hospital sat on a hill overlooking the airstrip north of Goroka. DeAnn Toland and two policemen jostled about in a jeep supplied by the district commissioner on their way to the hospital. Looking at the moonlight reflecting off the windshield, DeAnn couldn't shake her uneasy feeling about Jim Cole's phone call to her hotel. Stanek was, after all, like all the CIL members, her responsibility. She should have anticipated the danger he was in without being prompted. Danger seemed to shadow the pathologist.

Her thoughts turned to the seriousness of Stanek's wound. She wondered if physicians treating a fellow physician looked him in the eye and leveled with him about how close he had come to dying. The European medical assistant had called before Cole rang and told her Stanek had hemorrhaged and could not be moved again for three weeks, as the risk of bleeding to death outweighed the benefits of a quick evacuation to better facilities. Since a portion of the shoulder had been damaged, Dr. Stanek would need up to three months in the care of an orthopedic surgeon for a full recovery. The assistant said he had passed this information on by phone to Catherine Stanek.

In that same call, Catherine had asked the doctor if the physical anthropologist was with her brother at the hospital. When he answered in the affirmative, Catherine requested Dr. Toland stand in for her, as next of kin for Emerson, to be consulted relative to his treatment until it was safe to evacuate him. Meantime, Catherine had informed the doctor she was sending her own physician to assist in her brother's treatment and to accompany him to the Johns Hopkins Medical Center.

How strange of Catherine, DeAnn mused. Why would this woman, who, until now, had shown her nothing but disdain, assign this position of trust to her?

The jeep skipped over a pothole. The bump reminded her of the rocky road all of them had experienced since Dr. Emerson Stanek had sped into their lives. In a month or less, he had been accused of rape, shot at twice, in the air and later with Yowell on the river, and nearly killed when someone mistook Erik for him.

She knew she must confront him with the fact he would have to be evacuated, probably never to return to New Guinea. Would he acquiesce, or would he display the stubbornness with which he had greeted most of her requests? Perhaps she could avoid a confrontation by dropping the matter in the lap of General Bellicosi who was flying in with the physician Catherine had sent.

What would the general do? This worried her. He might cancel Operation Simpatico and send them all home. She wanted to finish the job and hoped to persuade the general they had invested too much time, prestige and the taxpayers' money to abandon the project at this juncture. Bellicosi would most likely ask Emerson Stanek to resign in either case. The general was never too keen on the criminal aspects of the ten knights case. Any crimes committed by American survivors would not sit well with his plans to link the New Guinea fallen with their comrades killed in action in Vietnam, bodies not recovered or missing, a link designed to convince the North Vietnamese of our resolve regarding accountability.

As the jeep continued its climb, a new thought came to her mind. She realized how many people wanted Stanek out of New Guinea. First were those who wanted him dead, next was Bellicosi, then Catherine and perhaps herself. In his defense, he had made a great deal of progress on the case, and before he left, she would have to garner all the information she could and tell him all she knew. She took the fifth volume of Kioko's journal out of her knapsack and clutched it to her breast. In a moment of weakness, she had let down her own defenses and convinced herself he deserved a chance to close this chapter in a very difficult case.

"How silly of me," she told herself, as she transferred the tablet back into her knapsack. "He probably doesn't want to see me, much less the story about love. I'll bet he's grateful to cut his losses and leave his horrifying experiences in New Guinea behind him."

Then, again, there was his dogged determination. Stanek was not beyond digging in his heels on this investigation until the entangled ten knights case with the murder on the mountaintop, Erik's death and the attempts on his life were revealed and dealt with. Whatever he decided, he had three weeks. Then Catherine and Bellicosi were sure to get their way.

Cole met DeAnn at the hospital entrance, and the reporter led her and the two constables down the long corridor.

"The Doc's room isn't hard to find, being only one of two private rooms here. And thanks to Miss Catherine's largess, Stanek occupies one and our little LikLik, the other."

He stopped his chair and wheeled about to face DeAnn. "You did tell the District Commissioner to arrest and question the patient assigned to my semi-private room?" he asked.

She held her hands with palms up, and bit her lower lip. "I did indeed."

"And is he going to do it as I requested over the telephone?"

Before she answered, she bit down harder. "The commissioner said he can't arrest someone for not showing up but he did send two constables as guards."

Cole tapped his finger against the side of the wheelchair. "What a fool! He let a thief and perhaps an assassin slip through his fingers."

She thought a moment, then answered. "Why do I have the feeling all this has something to do with Dr. Stanek?"

Cole told her about the assault in Hawaii. He was sure the man he had seen registering for the bed next to his was part of the team that had attacked Dr. Stanek. Cole had no doubt Waiolo, the wrestler, would try again. "It's the reason I called you to bring in reinforcements." Cole clasped his hands together and looked toward heaven. "Dear Lord, what can a dying old man in a wheelchair do to save the man I helped bring into this woebegone mystery?"

DeAnn patted the reporter's shoulder. "There, then. You've had enough excitement for the day. Why don't you go to your room for a rest while I look in on Dr. Stanek? As the physician ordered, you've got three weeks until you, our pathologist, and MilkEye's daughter find safety in Baltimore, finally out of this business. As you might know, Catherine Stanek has made the arrangements."

The reporter nodded and pointed to the constables. "I suppose you're right, but make sure you post one of these fellows at the door and the other inside to keep an eye on the window. The vermin after the Doc are slippery and will strike wherever they find a weak spot." They proceeded down the corridor until Cole swung to the right and went into his room.

Except for a nightlight, Stanek's room was dark. At first DeAnn thought he was asleep, but then he sat up in bed and turned on the lamp. "Ah, Dr. Toland, I presume."

She took it as a cheerful sign. After all he had been through, he could still make a joke, using that old saw about Stanley and Dr. Livingston. She smiled as the guards took up their positions. "Just an added precaution in case your friends from Hawaii pay you another visit."

"Ah, you've heard about the run-in. Cole saved my life, you know. Where is he, by the way?"

"Resting."

"Yes, even a watchdog needs some rest. How long will you stay, assuming you are his replacement?"

She sat in the chair beside his bed and laid her knapsack across her knees. "As long as you want me to. I thought this might be a good time for you to read another one of Kioko's logs, which I brought along."

He grimaced as he changed positions so that he could face her more squarely. "I'm unable to read comprehensively at the moment. The painkillers seem to have blurred my vision."

DeAnn took one of the Japanese woman's tablets out of her knapsack. "Would you like me to read journal five to you?" She felt the flush begin in her neck and sweep up to her hairline. She raised a hand above her eyebrow to conceal the redness brought on by embarrassment. "But maybe I should just leave the book for you to read at your leisure when you can see more clearly."

He did not make it any easier for her as he took her wrist and gently pulled her hand away from her face. "Let me assure you, Dr. Toland, I can handle the love story you wanted to share with Major Yowell the first day we met."

She turned away and murmured, "I thought you paid no attention to anything I did at the time."

"I'd be a poor forensic pathologist if I didn't register and file in my mind the slightest observation, because it might prove useful later."

"So now I'm to be used?"

"Only as a neutral reader, not in the manner you and Yowell had in mind."

The fire in her cheeks reached the fever point. She wanted him to discover what she had found in Kioko's journals—love emancipates us from sorrow. Why? She had no answer. His hair had reached the crew cut stage, and he seemed more handsome, but it was something else. She sensed his soul cried out for freedom. And if she were to release it, she must set aside her misgivings about sharing Kioko's intimate love scenes in journal five with someone who in the end might ridicule her effort. Nevertheless, she had opened the door, and now she could find no compelling reason for shutting him out. Still, she decided to make one more attempt to extricate herself.

"It's been a long day for both of us, Dr. Stanek, and I'm certain Catherine would find me derelict if I denied you rest."

"What does my adoptive sister have to do with any of this?"

DeAnn wanted to take the words back the minute she spoke them. "Catherine has, in a sense, appointed me your caretaker in her stead for the next three weeks until you, Cole and LikLik are evacuated to Johns Hopkins."

Stanek stabbed the air with his good hand. "Cole told me about the evacuation, but who in the world gave either Catherine or you the right to make decisions for me?"

"We're both acting in your best interests, but I'm as surprised as you are that Catherine asked me to make the arrangements on this end. I would've thought she'd have turned to General Bellicosi."

"Catherine knows I've never quit a case until it was completed, and this one is no different. She's just using you to get her way. Her interest is and always has been in my beekeeper cancer study.

"Well, I don't relish being caught between two people who refuse to work together."

"I know you're thinking how like Lt. Mori I am, or have become."

She didn't know whether he intended the remark in humor, but she found herself laughing at the comparison with the stubborn

Japanese officer in Kioko's story. Stanek smiled, and she knew her attempt to thwart him from the reading had been deflected.

"What do you want me to do?"

"Read from the log and dismiss any notion I'd quit the B-24 case. Even if I'm evacuated, I'll come back, complete this investigation, and then do my beekeeper cancer research as promised. You could help me in this regard by sharing all the information you know about the ten knights or anyone who might've come in contact with them. So, if you please, let's begin with Kioko's next journal."

The flush in her face subsided as she started to read what was to her a compelling love story.

36 KIOKO'S JOURNAL #5, A LOVE STORY

Komo, Papua New Guinea, 1944

U.S. CENTRAL IDENTIFICATION LABORATORY (PROVISIONAL)
FINDINGS, CASE NUMBER 316, EXHIBIT 3e, KIOKO TANAKA'S
FIFTH JOURNAL. DR. DEANN TOLAND'S REPORT.

A YEAR HAS come and gone since Lt. Mori left Taro and me at the mercy of the American and his band of native followers. We had turned south and proceeded back through the Tari basin to the village of Komo near the place where we had first encountered the American and his native followers, the Chiami, who were now our hosts.

No prisoners have ever been treated more fairly than my brother and I. Except for lunch, we are invited to join our captor at the table set by his loyal followers. He never fails to ask after our needs for the next day and apologizes for his absence during the day. I've learned he spends this time searching for signs of his lost comrades among the villages nearby.

Each day he and a dozen or more Chiami depart on this quest. At first, I thought these excursions were an attempt to track down Lt. Mori and kill him and the two Japanese soldiers with him. I steeled my courage and confronted the Yank on this point. He laughed. "Kioko, you jest. It has been a month. Your Lt. Mori and those foolish enough to follow him have long since ended up in someone's cooking pot."

It took another three months for me to question him further, since Taro was sure he had sighted Mori and the others while hunting with the villagers. "If it's not Lt. Mori you seek, then what do you hope to find after you leave us from morning until dusk each day? If, as I've learned, you are looking for your friends, why wouldn't the same fate befall them as you predicted for Lt. Mori?"

He rested his forefinger against his prominent chin and tilted his head forward. "Hmm... Let's see. Should I give you the short answer or the long one? Maybe both will do. The short answer is we Americans are smarter. The longer explanation is based on how we cultivate friendships among indigenous populations, rather than intimidate them as your countrymen do."

As New Guinea Ginny, I had often used idioms to express myself in a manner peculiar to the way American soldiers spoke to each other. "I see. We go haywire, and you don't."

He furrowed his brow. "The last time I heard the expression 'haywire' was over the radio during a card game with my buddies in Port Moresby. New Guinea Ginny used it to describe one of our bombing missions. What did I care? I had just won a huge pot."

I realized I had gone too far in revealing my past and had to regroup. "Pot? I don't know this expression."

"Sure you do. It's the money all the players have tossed in during a game of poker."

"What's at stake, you mean."

"Yes. Like my daily searches. The stakes are high. I'm in a race against the clock. Got to get crackin'. I must find my buddies, or die in the attempt. They wouldn't throw in their hands if our roles were reversed."

I tried not to, but I compared this man's approach and concern to Lt. Mori's methods. The American pursued his comrades in order to save them. Mori tracked down his own countrymen in order to punish them. I was ashamed for my country and for the system placing death over life.

With head lowered, I whispered to my captor. "Please be careful."

He reached out as if he were going to lift my head so he could look into my eyes, but his hand stopped short and fell to his side. "Why, Kioko, if I didn't know better, I'd say you miss me when I'm gone."

It was true. The flush in my cheeks confirmed as much. I had never met such a man. He had the same strength I had seen in my

367

father, the 20th Earl of *Tanaka-ya*, quiet, masculine and undemanding. What's more, he had traits cherished in my mentor the priest who had taught me English—a sensitive, patient and gentle soul if there ever was one.

Added to this combined attraction, he was to me handsome beyond description. He moved about us like Apollo with muscles bronze in color, yet supple in texture, always it seemed on the verge of enveloping me. Though he was careful not to touch me out of respect, inside I felt he already had.

During one absence covering several weeks, I sought Taro's guidance. He expressed both our fears. "Brace yourself, Kioko. The American must've been killed. Now we're at the mercy of these savages, unless..."

"Unless?"

"Unless Lt. Mori makes good on his promise to come back for us. There, then, don't you cry, little sister. Neither Mori nor I will let anyone harm you."

How could I tell my brother my tears were not for him, Lt. Mori or myself, but for the enemy who treated us far more decently than we deserved? I let my silence speak for me. Later, when the American returned in a jubilant mood, I was glad I had concealed my secret yearning from Taro.

At dinner, a week after his return, the American shared the source of his happiness. His eyes shone like amber in the light of the campfire as he spoke. "Each day I've searched in vain for some sign my buddies made it like I did. Now I know one or more survived. I've traded with some natives to the north for a cartridge belt with bayonet. The last name of one of my crewmates is stenciled on the back of the webbing. Wells must've been on his way to the coastwatcher's station to get help. I only hope Deep made it there unharmed."

"Deep?"

"Our engineer. It's his nickname."

He gave me an opening to ask why he had not surrendered his own name to us.

He looked off into the distance and then answered. "Just call me 'G.I. Joe' if you like. I'll reclaim my identity once all my buddies are accounted for."

I wanted to ask if he and his colleagues had bombed Angoram as Lt. Mori suspected, but decided against probing any further.

What good would it do to know? He might have bombed the radio station facilities, but it was Mori and my own people who had destroyed the village by fire. Besides, asking such a question of G.I. Joe would only inflame his curiosity to ask what I was doing in Angoram. Taro agreed. We must never tell the enemy we practiced war's blackest art, deception through propaganda.

One day, during the dry season of the year, when the Chiami held their festivals under clear skies and all social activity reached a heightened pitch, I heard the bamboo door of the thatch hut I shared with Taro being drawn back. My brother was away tending to a small shrine he had erected to celebrate the Emperor's birthday. I had used Taro's absence to remove my bra and under garments to mend them for the umpteenth time since leaving Angoram.

Usually G.I. Joe hesitated at the threshold before entering our hut and called for us by name. This day he did not. In what appeared an uncalculated moment, he glimpsed my nakedness, but quickly averted his eyes. I covered my face with my bra and swung about, trying to hide among the folds of the mosquito net Lt. Mori had left with me.

With a mixture of embarrassment and self-conscious confusion, I began to cry. "Please go."

"Sorry, I didn't mean to barge in."

"Don't explain. Just go."

"My exuberance got the best of me."

"Can't you go and make your apologies on the other side of the bamboo?"

Still he did not leave. "Not until you hear me out."

I felt his eyes on me and peeked out from a corner of the bra to see him remove his shirt.

"Oh, dear, he's going to rape me," I thought.

I was about to scream for Taro when the American tossed the shirt to me. "Cover yourself with this. But no garment can conceal your beauty, Kioko."

I draped the shirt across my shoulders so that it covered me like an apron. "Why did you invade my privacy? You've never..."

"Right. Never done such a thing before. Exuberance carried me away this time."

"Over what?"

"You and Taro are free to go back to your people!"

"You've come to terms with Lt. Mori?"

The American laughed in his hearty manner I had come to know. "Mori's dead as far as I know, dealing with the devil. No, I mean you're free to stay here with the Chiami, who have promised you no harm, or you and your brother can link up with the Japanese colony at Wewak."

"How would we get there?"

"With me and a couple dozen of my Chiami friends to guide you."

"But the soldiers at Wewak will shoot you on sight as spies."

"I don't intend to give them a chance to earn any sharpshooter medals at my expense. I'll take you as far as the coastwatcher's station near Mendam and set you on the trail to Wewak with native escorts. The Chiami headman and I have worked it out. We leave in a week from today if you decide to go."

He said no more and left. Like a child swept up in a fairy tale, even before dressing, I found my comb and stroked my hair. It had grown long, black and thick. How could G.I. Joe see beauty in such a tangled mess?

For three days Taro and I weighed the pros and cons of another journey into the wild with an American leading us instead of Lt. Mori. Taro did not trust G.I. Joe. He suspected the American wanted to use us as bait in a trap designed to draw out rescue troops from Wewak in order to slaughter them. My brother wanted to stay in the Chiami village and wait for the return of Mori.

Although I didn't relish another long and arduous journey through the heart of New Guinea, I wanted to get back to Japan. I could not wait to see my family again, put the war behind me, get married and start a family of my own. Taro discarded this as a womanly thing driven by emotion.

He asked, "Where is the old Kioko—feisty and strong?"

I countered with our father's wisdom spoken to his three children after a quarrel. He had told us, "Once you've plunged into fears and doubts, it's hard to escape the old self and the old way. But look at your unrest, doubt and confusion as an opportunity to start anew. Seek a better way to work out your problems and see how the slightest change in attitude brings new life."

In the end Taro and I did reach a compromise. We agreed if Mori were still alive, he would follow us to Wewak. Short of our destination, however, we would slip away from the American and his followers and hide in the jungle, hoping Lt. Mori would find us. If, after three days, the lieutenant did not show up, we would make our way to Wewak on our own.

I started to point out the American had already freed us. So why did we not ask to leave whenever we wanted to without all the deception? But it was obvious Taro would not accept any plan if it did not allow him to save face as a proud *samurai*. In other words, my brother could not get away from the old self and the old way so easily.

While G.I. Joe loaded supplies for our journey north, I climbed a high hill south of the Chiami village in search of flowers and to say goodbye to this primitive place Taro and I would soon leave. At the summit I gathered some orchids. The view across the valley was breathtaking. Further south and west of our position rose the forested, extinct volcano the Chiami called Mount Bosavi. G.I. Joe had told me the Riami river people, related by marriage to the Chiami valley dwellers, lived on Mount Bosavi.

For several minutes I drank in the new grandeur with which I now viewed the New Guinea territory. G.I. Joe had become my tutor on the landscape. He knew all the mountain ranges and rivers by name as only someone could, who had studied them on a map and had flown over them.

As I gathered my flowers and turned to leave, G.I. Joe, not even breathing hard from the climb, intercepted me. "Beautiful, eh? I saw you looking south towards Mount Bosavi. After I leave you and Taro near Mendam, I intend to come back here and search the mountain, as well as the Southern Highlands District where our aircraft was headed. Would've done it sooner, but for two reasons."

He paused, and I knew he wanted to ask me to guess why he had delayed his search. So I did.

He answered, "First, I couldn't get the Chiami to budge, because they're afraid of the Tugaru who control the upper half of the mountain. Below them, the Riami, the Chiami's cousins, have settled. Tugaru are mean S.O.B.s; they won't allow any relatives of the Riami to enter the area. This would tip the balance of power, I'm told. So I've had to cool my heels here; would be suicide to go there alone."

He hesitated again. "Now take a guess at my second reason for abandoning the search around Mount Bosavi at this time."

I scratched my head. "After you found the cartridge belt and bayonet, you reasoned your colleagues had gone north, not south."

G.I. Joe smiled. "Not entirely. The evidence points only to Wells."

"What then?"

He took my hand in his, touching me for the first time. "I'd hoped to convince you to join my search before going to Wewak, but I see you're set on leaving, so I'll honor my word."

I slipped my hand from under his. I wanted to remind him we were enemies. Instead I said something even more foolish. "Like you, I've enjoyed having someone to talk to in English, but we must think of our families."

He turned aside and murmured, "I'm an orphan. I have no wife or girlfriend to go back to. My buddies are my only family."

"But you said yourself they might be dead."

"Dead or alive, scattered across New Guinea, I won't leave this country 'til I find out which."

Neither of us spoke for what seemed like minutes. I was only too happy when he changed the subject.

"See there, off in the distance toward the northwest, the dim outline? It's the Muller Range with the Central Range on the northeast. We'll make our way between them through the Tari Basin, but then we'll have to cross part of the Central Range on our way to the Sepik River and on to Mendam on the north coast. You and Taro will be on your own from there westward to Wewak."

I remembered the route he described only too well from the journey southward with Lt. Mori. Now the northward trek loomed in my mind. "We'll pass the place where Butterfly was shot and then buried on the mountain by the Chiami. Neither she nor Sun-Hi deserved to die as they did."

"Sun-Hi?"

"A friend like Butterfly, only a Korean girl taken captive by my people."

I don't know why, but I held up the flowers I had gathered for his inspection and asked, "Will there be time to visit the site and pay homage to Butterfly?"

He nodded, but I could sense the irritation in his voice when I remained resolute about my intention to leave. "You're a free woman. Do as you wish. It'll take us two months to reach the north coast of New Guinea. Longer if we have to avoid Japanese patrols along the way. If all your people are like Lt. Mori, I think you'll agree that the Chiami and I make better traveling companions."

This was the last conversation of any length or contact between us until later when we reached the valley below Butterfly's mountain.

The next morning we set off from Komo with a large contingent of Chiami people. Those Chiami not going with us for the entire journey had agreed to help ferry our supplies up a branch of the Tagari River, then onto the river itself. From there we hired a new group of natives friendly to the Chiami to carry our supplies to Tari, where we engaged some Huri wigmen to take over as far as Tadei, near the territory of the Duna wigmen. With the help of native guides, G.I. Joe led us through the river valley, keeping the Muller Range on our left and the Central Range on our right.

I was sad to leave Komo and those who stayed behind. For over a year, these people had been part of my life. Although I yearned for the quiet inn in Japan run by my beloved parents, I must confess, under the care of G.I. Joe and the Chiami people, I flourished in strength, health, knowledge, and dare I say, happiness.

G.I. Joe had a knack for making friends, and unlike Lt. Mori, he never forced the natives to do his bidding. When necessary, he traded with them for goods and services. On most occasions, however, they voluntarily offered food, lodging and labor, no doubt out of respect for the white man who shared their burdens.

In this manner, the legend of G.I. Joe, the white sorcerer, spread, and other villages brought their elders, women and children to Komo to marvel at how he had improved the status of the Chiami. G.I. Joe helped cure the sick and wounded, built pedal-powered irrigation wheels, dug ditches beside the warriors and became their best friend. He also taught pidgin in a makeshift school which Taro and I attended.

All these good deeds did not go unnoticed, and on the journey north, we stopped at villages friendly to us and to the Chiami, and avoided the hostile ones. This was another departure from Lt. Mori's tactics. Along our route among tribes of wigmen known for fighting each other at the least provocation, friendly villagers were only too happy to share their food, offer their services as carriers, or anything else "GeeJo", as they called him, requested.

They even offered wives and brides, but GeeJo would point to me and joke, "One is enough, even for a sorcerer." Taro did not like the reference to me. I found it amusing, and though I blushed like a bride every time GeeJo used the line, I was flattered by the attention. But, as previously reported, our conversation was sparse since the strained moment on the hill overlooking Komo village when I told him I wanted to go home.

GeeJo knew the customs and habits of the native tribes we met along the trail. When in doubt about whether a tribe was hostile or friendly, he relied on his Chiami escorts for advice.

One day on a trail close to a river, we came upon a native bathing his wound in the cool waters. An arrow had pierced his abdomen just above the right hip. Part of the shaft had broken off, and we could see a splintered fragment protruding from his side. He must have been unable to dislodge the arrow, which caused him to bend over the water in some agony.

After an exchange of words with the wounded warrior, the Chiami with us fell to their knees and began to wail. It was obvious to all they knew or had heard of the fallen man and looked upon him as a person of high standing. The stranger was taller than the average Chiami, and though in pain, he still bore a regal bearing. To our surprise, he spoke pidgin. He told us he was a Riami elder sent by his headman, Situmu, with a small party to search for a white man reported to be in the Tari Basin. They had been following up on the reports when Duna tribesmen, fierce and temperamental natives given to fighting, attacked them.

GeeJo spoke to the man, and after getting his consent for treatment, he gave him a bamboo stick to bite down on. "This'll help you bear the pain," GeeJo said to the man in pidgin,

Then with his knife, GeeJo began to probe the wound. He began to remove the broken shaft, hollowed out a piece of bamboo and inserted it deep in the man's wound. GeeJo spoke to the native again. "It will drain off the poison while you recover." Then he said, "Tell me about the white man you are tracking."

With some effort, the warrior rose on one elbow and removed the bamboo stick from his clenched teeth, not even flinching as GeeJo probed deeper with his knife. "Situmu, great leader of Riami, help white man Jack Hides into highlands. First time Riami see white man. Situmu hear talk about another white man, like help him too; send Riami men look for white spirit."

Taro turned to me and shrugged. "Who's Jack Hides?"

Although my brother had spoken to me in Japanese, GeeJo answered before I could respond. "Like the Riami man said, Hides was the first white explorer to enter this country. I believe it was in 1933. Hides came in here mapping unknown territory."

Then the American spoke to his patient. "I'll have four Chiami scouts carry you back to their village. With the Duna on the prowl, this place is not safe for any of us."

"Wait," I said. "I have a needle and strong thread. Let me close the wound around the drain." I tore off a length of fabric from the hem of my blouse, already tattered in places. "Use this cloth as a bandage to place over the wound. I also have something in my bag that will provide pressure and keep the drain in place while he is jostled about on the long trail back to Komo."

When I returned with Lt. Mori's 1,000-stitch belt, Taro's face contorted and his rage was so fierce, he had trouble getting out the words. "Kioko. I'll not allow you to defame the *senninbari* in this manner. Lt. Mori placed it in your trust to take home. You must obey."

My brother tried to snatch the belt from my hand, but GeeJo intervened. The American winked at me and smiled. "This is not the time, nor place for a sibling spat. Kioko, do as you wish with the belt. Believe me, saving this man's life will pay dividends down the road." Then he turned to the Riami warrior and asked, "What happened to the rest of your party, and how many were there?"

"Seven die or hide.

"How did you get away?"

"Hide on mountain. Me come to river when Duna look for friends."

We could see the Riami warrior was exhausted and the Chiami scouts were anxious to begin the return trip to Komo. GeeJo wanted to question the wounded warrior further, but he still had an infuriated Taro to deal with. As the Chiami left with the Riami elder, his wound bound with Lt. Mori's *senninbari*, Taro demanded to know why GeeJo treated the savages like civilized people. I softened the question in my translation.

The American drew in a deep breath and said, "How can you call them savages? They've survived for God knows how long in a primitive and hostile environment. No creature on earth did so much with so little. Had their land been blessed with beasts of burden, like oxen and horses to pull plows, or other livestock larger

375

than the tree kangaroo, this island jungle by now would be one of the cradles of civilization. Not a lack of intelligence of its peoples, but only an accident of geography rendered it otherwise."

Taro scoffed at GeeJo's explanation. For my brother and the generation of young men he represented, there was only one superior race divined by the sun goddess, who bestowed power on the emperor to lead the Japanese people. All others were in an inferior position.

For myself, I marveled at how much love a soul must contain to look past our primitive natures to see what GeeJo had seen. Where did he come by such thoughts? Surely it wasn't in the military. Although I believed his search for his lost comrades had something to do with such a benevolent viewpoint, I had heard such kind words before from the Christian missionaries, especially the priest who taught me English. I know GeeJo wouldn't have revealed so much of himself but for Taro's outburst. Although Taro remained furious because I had offered Mori's 1,000-stitch belt to help the Riami native, I was glad for the conversation with GeeJo. I longed for our talks of old, if for no other reason than to gain insight into the manners and values of the Americans, or so I convinced myself at the time.

We were not far from the foothills of Butterfly's mountain near Tadai. The heat of the highland grasslands had receded and the trees along the river now dripped with dew in anticipation of the autumn rains. The mountain air was cool and pleasant, but none of us were prepared for the chill which swept up from the river we crossed.

It was afternoon when we made camp on the crest of a hill below Butterfly's mountain. Above us a clump of tall trees raised their branches, saluting a cloudless sky in every direction. Near one of the bush shelters the local inhabitants had carved out at regular intervals along the trail, we cooked our lunch over the leaping flames of our campfire.

GeeJo sat in silence. Taro tended to his swollen feet and bruised knees damaged by the slippery stones we had had to negotiate. The American rubbed some kind of native oil on his knees and his feet, then offered the substance to Taro and me. My wounds were minor, so I applied the oil on Taro's wounds, realizing he would need a day of rest before we pressed on. This meant he would not be able to go with me up the mountain to where Butterfly was buried. My only hope was to get my brother to consent to having GeeJo alone accompany me if willing.

"Brother, you'll not make 500 meters, much less all the way to Wewak until you rest your knees, ankles and feet. I will ask GeeJo to take me up Butterfly's mountain. The Chiami will look after you while we're gone."

Taro winced as he pulled a leg away from me and wobbled to his feet. "Absolutely not! First you give away Lt. Mori's *senninbari*, and now you would shame yourself and your family by cavorting with the enemy."

I had to stand firm. "Look at you. You can barely stand. As for the 1,000-stitch belt, we'll come back after the war and collect it with all the other trophies left along our trail of misery. Even our first casualty, Cpl. Akutsu, will not be forgotten."

"Ha! Like the American fool, you treat these people as humans. You'll never see the belt again. The Riami man will trade it for something else. Maybe an axe to kill us with."

"You heard GeeJo say kindness is repaid. We must trust him. He has gotten us this far."

"Not with your honor, we won't. What if you're alone with him and he violates you? How could you protect yourself?"

"If GeeJo had wanted to, he could've done so anytime this past year."

To this Taro had no reply, since he knew he could not have defended me against the American and those who served him. Still, I offered him something to think about. "If, as you believe, Lt. Mori will come back for us, why not stay here to greet him. Then the two of you and any other of our soldiers who survived can come for me."

Taro sat down and put his head in his hands. "Now you're beginning to make sense, Kioko. With the American gone, Lt. Mori can easily overpower the followers the American leaves behind. But what if you run into the Duna and how can you get him to go alone with you?"

"I'll tell him I've gotten your consent."

"I doubt my consent will sway him."

"Then I'll have to appeal to his debt to Butterfly. She tended him when he was Lt. Mori's prisoner."

"What does our enemy know of honor? Even if he agrees, I'm still worried about the Duna warriors."

"You've seen how clever GeeJo is on the trail. No harm will come to us. You might be in more jeopardy. Once we reach the mountaintop, we can spot the enemy and come to your aid if necessary."

Across the fire, Taro looked at me with the eyes I had seen so many times when we played in the garden at our father's inn. "Promise you'll be careful, little sister."

"Promise."

I dared not tell Taro what was really racing through my mind. Lt. Mori would not come back. And if he did, I would show him I preferred the company of GeeJo. "Lord, forgive me if you find this deceitful," I whispered under my breath.

GeeJo agreed to take me to Butterfly's burial site. I had no need to ask to go alone with him. GeeJo brought up the matter himself.

"Because we must stay hidden from the Duna, no more than two at a time can climb the footpaths and cross the bridges, in some places over rivers swollen from the autumn rains. With just two of us, we'll be able to move faster to reach our destination. Pack light but take a jacket. You'll need it higher up. Got anything warmer than those pajamas, or whatever you call them?"

I shook my head. "Just a kimono used in my performances, but I can't walk very well in it."

"Pack it anyway. We can't build a fire up on the mountain. The Duna will see the smoke, and it'll lead them straight to us."

I told GeeJo I understood the difficulty ahead of us, and when he went off to pack his haversack, I entrusted my tablets and writing materials to Taro for safekeeping.

After we had completed our preparations, we set off together with GeeJo leading the way. We had climbed no more than a kilometer or so when we came to a vine bridge. It was so narrow, we had to move crab-like, one behind the other. GeeJo demonstrated the technique and said, "If you think this is tight, you should try threading your way between the bomb racks in a B-24 bomber aircraft."

He smiled at his quip, perhaps meant to relieve the tension, but it had a different effect on me. Lt. Mori's admonishment flashed in my mind. The American he wanted to kill was in all probability one of the renegades who bombed our radio station and the village of Angoram. I could not reconcile the dilemma. This man who treated us so kindly was part of a band of murderers. He, like Mori, had turned my world upside down. Still upset, I nearly slipped and fell to the rocks below and a certain death.

GeeJo reached for my hand. "Here, let me help you."

I pulled it away from him and gripped the vine railing tighter. "I'll be all right."

"You've got spirit, Kioko. There's one more tricky bridge to cross higher up. It's a single span, no more than a log really, eight to ten inches in diameter. We'll have to cross rapids like we're on a tight rope. Fall there, and we'll be swept into the rocks downstream. I'm not trying to frighten you, but if you want to turn back, I'll understand."

I shook my head and repeated, "If the Chiami made it with Butterfly's body, I'll be all right as well." But I wasn't convinced. Instead, I wondered what it would matter if I lived or died.

When we reached the final bridge, I knew the crossing was even more treacherous than GeeJo had imagined. I saw the worried expression on GeeJo's face. About 30 feet below the native structure, a spray was thrown up when the current hit a mixture of mud and branches caught in the river, sandwiched between shorelines ragged with rocks.

GeeJo wet a finger and held it in the air. "Bad news. We'll have a crosswind to contend with as well, and from the spray kicked up, I'd say the water is even colder than the air temperature."

He reached down and touched the beam. "Watch your footing. It's wet and slippery. I'll be right behind you."

My Japanese boots with their worn flat soles were not fit for this kind of obstacle. I thought for a moment about crossing barefooted, but vanity and the chill in the air kept me from doing so. Then, too, a Japanese maiden did not present uncovered feet to a stranger. In hindsight, I should have reconsidered.

At the halfway point, my lead foot slid along the beam. My trailing foot was not planted well enough to anchor me, so my legs split apart. Before I could regain my balance and pull myself up by the single vine railing, I lost my hold. In the next moment I was in the swift current, and the cold water swirled around my submerged head. When I broke through to the surface, I saw GeeJo dive from the bridge. Just as I was about to go under again, I felt his arm laid across my chest with his hand under my armpit. I thought I would lose consciousness, but I gripped his arm with my two hands and lifted my chin like one might do on a crossbar.

After a fierce struggle in the strong current, we finally reached the shore, but we were so cold we could not speak or form words because our teeth chattered so. GeeJo removed his jacket and put it over me, but the cold, wet leather made me shiver more. He reached into one of the pockets of his web belt and took out a little container wrapped in rubber-like material.

D-ry matches," he said. "W-e'll have to risk starting a fire or perish from hypothermia in these wet clothes. "T-ake your clothes off while I find something to start a fire."

"W-hat if I put on my kimono?"

"T-oo wet to do any good, like everything else in our bags."

Talk had ended. He swung into action. He found some dry driftwood and soon had a fire going. He then cut some pandanas leaves and placed them next to the fire like a bed. He cut some more to cover them and then put our clothes on the rocks to dry.

"W-e must get warm to survive! K-ioko, make haste!

S-lide in between these leaves next to the fire with me.

W-e'll use our bodies to warm each other."

The chill from the river had already transformed my nipples, once the size of buttons, small, pink and flat, into acorns, like those which dance among the branches of a spreading oak. Then, as he engulfed me in his arms under the pandanas leaves and his fingers interlocked across my mid-section, there came a new sensation. My breasts stretched out and expanded until they touched his wrists. Against the back of my thighs just below the buttocks, I felt his manhood expand as well. I squirmed ever closer to absorb the warmth engulfing our two bodies. Soon my whole body was like a blossom opening every petal wherever the sunlight of his warmth made contact with me. I felt as though I would swoon when my breath came and went so rapidly, and I knew he could take me as his virginal prize if he had wanted to.

But after a short space of silence, he made it clear he had no intention to deflower me. He whispered through the wet strands of my hair, "Kioko, you are the loveliest creature to come into my life. Only when I'm certain you love me, as I've loved you since the evening you saved me from death, dare I lay claim to any of your possessions—body, mind or soul."

I cried in silence. Thoughts of the bombing at Angoram vanished. Would he feel the same if he really knew who I was? New Guinea Ginny would always stand between us. But I could not bring myself to mar so tender a sentiment, one I shared as well. So I replied, "Yes, GeeJo. You're right. Give us more time."

GeeJo left our bed of leaves twice to turn our clothes on the spit he had erected near the fire to hasten drying. Each time he returned to gather me in his arms, I could feel his body quivering from the cold. Neither of us spoke until he got up a third time and returned with my kimono. "Put this on, Kioko. We've been here too long already."

"What about my blouse and slacks?"

"Not dry enough. You'll have to carry them."

He turned around to allow us both to dress in private. When he was done, he laid his jacket on the fire to smother it. Then he took my hand. "The path through the wood widens a bit once we reach the crest of the slope. We can travel side by side from here on. It'll help us get us there faster. "

I began to think how foolish it was to risk our lives for the diversion up Butterfly's mountain. Yet we had come too far to turn back. Having lain close to a man for the first time in my life, my mind was on the unborn child who had died by the hand of the Korean comfort woman. How hard the mother's life must have been to choose death over life. Sun-Hi deserved better, as did Butterfly, and in their behalf my pilgrimage was to ask forgiveness through the grace of the Lord, not only for the women who were like sisters to me, but for the rest of us caught in this war.

We had reached a point where the path veered downhill, then rose again on the other side where we could see over the top of the trees. I knew we were near the summit. Suddenly GeeJo started. He motioned for me to get behind him. A few yards in front of us baring the way stood a warrior, his hand gripping a bent bow. In dress and bearing, the warrior bore a resemblance to the man whose life GeeJo had saved. The American spoke to the man in pidgin, and I was relieved to see he returned the arrow to his quiver.

GeeJo turned to me. "What luck! He's Riami. Another escapee from the Duna warriors."

"Looking for his friend?" I asked.

"Appears so."

"What happens now?"

"I'll ask him to stay here and watch for the Duna until we come back down. Then we'll take him back with us."

"Can't we just leave?"

"Not today."

"Then when?"

"Tomorrow before dawn at the earliest."

"Oh, dear."

GeeJo spoke to the Riami man at length. "He saw the smoke from our fire and is sure the Duna are combing the area by now, thinking ours was a fire made by a Riami. He also says he is carrying back what he believes are the remains of the white man his chief Situmu sent him to find. A friendly native showed him where a white man had died in their village."

"Oh, dear. Could the bones be those of one of your buddies?"

"I'm afraid they might very well be those of Wells. When he died, the natives would've traded any of his personal items to other natives and so on down the line. Perhaps it's how I came by Wells' cartridge belt and bayonet. The Riami warrior is grateful we helped his fellow tribesman and has agreed to bury the white man's remains at Komo before he and his friend return to their clan."

"Will the Duna come here after the Riami warrior?"

"No chance. He left a false trail. He's agreed to watch the approach and warn us if the enemy shows up."

"What if they come a different way?"

"Let me handle the tactics, Kioko. You get your chores done. Because we dare not make another fire to keep warm tonight, we'll have to snuggle together again. My clothes are still damp. Have you enough room in that kimono for two?"

We found the place where Butterfly was buried marked by the cross made with wood from GeeJo's stretcher. I hurried through the service for Butterfly, my mind filled more with ways to find alternatives to the sleeping arrangements GeeJo had proposed. Could I refuse and let him sleep in the cold when he had risked his life to save mine? Only a selfish child would do so. Damp or not, I decided to wear my peasant's outfit inside the kimono to keep our bare skin from direct contact again.

My plan fell apart ten minutes after the sun left the sky. I pulled the kimono over my shirt and blouse when GeeJo wasn't looking, but it made matters worse. The flimsy silk, still damp from the river drew the warmth from my body with my kimono sealing in the chill.

GeeJo settled my dilemma. "No sense both of us freezing. Go

ahead and get out of those pajamas and use your kimono as a blanket. I'll try to make due with my wet jacket."

He sat a few feet away, but I could see his body shake and hear his teeth chatter. When I could stand it no longer, I whispered for him to join me. He slid down next to me and whispered back. "Are you sure, Kioko? I'll have to take off my damp clothes to make it work."

I felt foolish, but I asked anyway. "Like the last time?"

"Yes, but you'll have to keep the kimono over your shoulders, and I'll have to fit inside. We'll be face to face."

"Oh, dear."

He kissed my cheek. I could feel the hair on his chest against my breasts. My nipples, like grapes on a vine, stretched out to draw him closer. My head spun when he draped his outer leg over mine. His erect penis danced above my mound of venus, and the inside of my thighs dripped with moisture. I tilted my pelvis and parted my legs, drawing him closer to the source of the moisture as intense longing washed over me in waves. I found his lips with mine and kissed him, thinking this would take my mind off the fire between my legs. When our lips parted, he whispered, "Kioko, I love you."

At last the dam burst and I poured out my feelings. "I love you, dear GeeJo. Oh, I do love you!"

We kissed again while I guided him into the harbor our love had created. I winced slightly as the last vestige of my virginity parted from me. He drew back as if afraid to hurt me. But the moisture flooding my inner lips bathed us both in its warmth as the pain passed and turned to ecstasy. Tears of joy rolled down my cheeks as he probed the secret recesses of my inner being. And when he burst forth showering me inside with the seeds of life, something, some mechanism I never knew I had, from the depth of my being, held him in its grasp as if never to let go.

I slept in his arms through the night. The nectars of our bodies intermingled, providing all the warmth we ever needed, warmth fueled by love and blessed by God. I became a woman and a bride in the same night. I had felt our spirits join as did our bodies, despite the world at war labeling us enemies, and no one will ever convince me otherwise.

Dear gentle Taro, however, would see it differently. And for the first time ever, I feared my brother's wrath.

37 ASSASSINATION ATTEMPT

Goroka, Papua New Guinea, 1973

DEANN TOLAND CLOSED Kioko's fifth journal and hung her head to hide her tears from Emerson Stanek. She was afraid to say more than "sorry." She feared her emotion would trigger a bout of stuttering if she attempted a lengthy explanation for her reaction to Kioko and GeeJo's love story, which she had expected to share with Frank Yowell.

Stanek coughed a couple of times as if to clear his throat. "Please," he said. "No need to apologize. You've given me a great deal to think about. Now, if you don't mind, would you jot down some notes so I can plug the new information into what we already know about the ten knights case?"

In one sense, DeAnn was relieved he appeared to treat the intimate parts of Kioko's journal so clinically. Yet, in another sense, she wondered how anyone could be so objective about such a beautiful love story. He must have been deeply hurt in matters of the heart, she decided. Still, this was not the time nor place for psychoanalysis.

She took up a pen and pad from the nightstand and asked, "Where do you want to begin?"

He coughed again and fingered the scar on his cheek with his free hand. "Let's start at the end and work back through the Japanese woman's account. She had an intimate relationship with an American, who might very well have been a member of the B-24 bomber crew. But now we must ask, 'What was he doing so

384

far north of the crash site, and how did he become separated from the others, as it appears was the case?'"

DeAnn touched her lips with the shaft of the pen when she finished writing, a trick she had learned to make her slow down and not stutter. "Perhaps the one called GeeJo was not in the B-24 when it crashed."

"Possibly," Stanek replied.

"If he was one of the B-24 bomber crewmembers, then he would have to be one of the six missing—Toggle Joe, Pip, Sharpshooter, TKO, Wells and Grant," DeAnn surmised.

"We'll be better able to narrow it down when we've recovered and identified as many of the missing remains as we can. Have Noble and company had any success in their search along the river in my absence?"

"Yes, indeed. They've located three sets of remains buried in the Lower Falls area."

Stanek threw up his good arm. "What exciting news!"

She tilted her head slightly and brushed aside an auburn strand of hair back from her forehead. "*Kiap* Noble said MilkEye and WonTok knew the location of this burial site and led them to it. We'll certainly have to question the natives further about this." DeAnn thought she detected a twinkle in his eyes as she related the story.

"Were the remains buried together like those in burial site X-1?" he asked.

"Yes. They were wrapped in an eroded parachute along with a handgun, but it appears two individuals had been beheaded. And, like the jawbone you got from Salty Meri, there were fillings in the teeth of all, but the remains could be Japanese or Australian as well as American. The CIL team will have to do further testing."

"Mmm... Wrapped in a parachute. Toggle Joe mentioned the parachute in his condolence letters, and we know he had a handgun with him when the others went out to forage for food," Stanek said.

"Speaking of Toggle Joe, if his remains are in this new burial site we've listed as X-3, it's a mystery how his log came to be buried back at site X-1 near the bomber," DeAnn noted.

Stanek stroked his cheek and she made ready to jot down his observations. "Both burial sites have similar characteristics. Since the remains have been buried together, rather than separately, with the bones wrapped in canvas in one site and in a parachute in the other, we know they were moved by someone."

"Are you suggesting the same person could've buried the remains in both sites?" she asked.

"Possibly. It could explain how the copilot's log turned up in burial site X-1."

DeAnn tapped her pencil on her notepad. "I suppose you suspect GeeJo is responsible for the burials in both places."

"We can't be certain at this point." Stanek replied.

"We do have evidence Kioko lived on Mount Bosavi. MilkEye told me, when I was caring for LikLik in the Riami village, Kioko was like a mother to the Riami. What's more, WonTok told *Kiap* Noble the two *age-mates* discovered her logs, supposedly by accident, in the Tugaru burial site along with the raft and emergency supplies."

Stanek joined in. "And it's a fair assumption GeeJo and probably Taro, as well as Kioko and GeeJo's son were with her as well. But until we know GeeJo's name, we don't have conclusive evidence he was one of the ten knights, and the question remains, if so, which one was he?"

"Let's not forget GeeJo asked the Riami warrior to take back remains he thought might've been those of his buddy Wells to the village of Komo and bury them there. Kioko writes he mentioned Wells' nickname—Deep—a sure connection between GeeJo and the B-24 crew."

"Very good, DeAnn. But because our mysterious friend GeeJo asked the Riami warrior to bury Wells' remains (if indeed they belonged to Wells) at Komo, this set may prove to be the most difficult to find and identify with any degree of certainty."

"It would mean a search in Komo on foot. Perhaps we'll need the help of the Chiami to locate the burial site there," DeAnn added.

"Yes, and for obvious reasons, I'm not up to it. Maybe this is something you can follow up on."

I doubt if General Bellicosi would approve my taking my CIL team so far afoot from the crash site unless we fly there."

"Well, the only way we can verify the written documentation is to match the account against the physical evidence, at least following Kioko's trail as far as Komo, if not Angoram." Stanek paused. "Not alone, of course."

"MilkEye might be anxious to join an expedition to the north by way of Komo. He told Erik, who was standing watch for me at the Riami village, he was keen to find Kioko to entreat her to use her magic to erase Two Face's curse on his daughter LikLik from her books."

"Noble will no doubt join you and MilkEye, and possibly WonTok, as our *kiap* won't let you out of his sight. Until all the crewmembers are accounted for, we really can't rule out any of them as our murderer. Because the new burial site reveals two individuals were beheaded, I may have two more murders to solve. The question is, did the same person or persons responsible for the recent slayings commit these earlier murders as well? Are these killings connected? If so, what is the motive for these murders?"

DeAnn lowered her eyes. "I don't believe General Bellicosi supports your criminal investigation if it'll delay the identification process."

Stanek reached out for her hand. "I don't see why we can't work together from here on out. In fact, I'd like to ask a favor of you since it'll be some time before I'm well enough to get back on the case."

"What do you want me to do?" she asked as she felt her hand grow warm in his.

"I'd like you to approach Noble to enlist the aid of MilkEye and WonTok to see if they can surreptitiously follow the Tugaru salt bundles to their final destination."

DeAnn retrieved her hand from his grip and asked, "Why on earth would you want to get involved in Tugaru business?"

"Because I noticed some bundles appeared heavier than others. Although the Riami canoes carried the identical loads and number of passengers, some of them displaced more water than their counterparts. I mentioned this to MilkEye, and he told me when he was on the salt train once, he handled two of the bundles and found they were of different weights. He questioned the Tugaru woman, who used them to prop up LikLik so she could feed her, but she didn't have the answer."

"Might I ask what you hope to determine?"

"Whether something's being smuggled from Mount Bosavi to Nomad and perhaps beyond," Stanek replied.

DeAnn frowned. "I hope you aren't talking about what I fear would bring chaos to our operation if word got out."

"We need evidence, DeAnn, or it's only a supposition. So you can see why I need your cooperation."

"I'll be in touch with Roger tomorrow by radio relay. I plan to ask him to return here with MilkEye and WonTok in the aircraft Yowell pre-positioned in Nomad to fly us all back once we have completed the river expedition. And I need to talk to MilkEye. Your sister's wishes notwithstanding, I won't send LikLik to the United States without her father's consent."

"Fair enough. But could you give Noble and company a day or two more to follow up on my request?" Stanek asked.

"Since you're not leaving right away, I think we can spare a few extra days and have them report discretely to you on the matter after they deliver to me the remains they've found."

DeAnn stood up and prepared to leave. "We've accomplished more than enough for now on the ten knight's case. You need your rest, Emerson. By the way, there's one more volume in Kioko's set. Would you like me to come back tomorrow and read it to you?"

"Yes, and if you come early, I'll treat you to breakfast."

"No problem. I'll leave your notes and Kioko's sixth journal here on the table. But we mustn't tell General Bellicosi about this arrangement. I haven't had a chance to tell him about Kioko's six volumes yet. He's a stickler when it comes to the chain of custody, except when he bends his own rules. But I'm taxing you too much. You're looking paler than the day you arrived in New Guinea, if I might say so."

"So much has happened since then."

"Yes, and not all of it good, like the murder of dear Erik. Oh, dear, my eyes are watering again. The last thing you want is a weepy woman at your side."

He rose up to draw closer to her and said in a hushed voice, "Not really. You've been a great comfort to me, DeAnn."

She smiled and then turned away to leave, but stopped, leaned down and whispered, "The guard posted at the veranda window is gone. Something's amiss. Don't be alarmed. I'm going to wheel your bed over to the corner and call for the guard posted at the door."

DeAnn had no sooner put her plan into action than a shot rang out. The plaster on the wall behind the place where Stanek's bed had been seconds ago shattered when the bullet struck. The constable at the door tore into the room. DeAnn was too shocked to speak and pointed to the window. The guard left and came back shortly to announce his partner was unconscious but still breathing, and the assailant had fled. "I must fetch a doctor," he said.

"No, you don't!" DeAnn responded sharply. "You must stay here and guard Dr. Stanek, who is obviously in danger. He's a prominent patient, and it'll go bad for you and your colleagues if anything happens to him while he's under your protection. The doctors and nurses on duty must've heard the shot and will be here shortly to tend to Dr. Stanek and your friend."

DeAnn turned to Stanek. He looked shaken and even paler, but no fear showed in his steel-blue eyes. "I'm going to call the commissioner," she declared, "and have him send more constables to this room immediately. I want one every two feet if necessary."

Stanek replied, "It looks like someone wanted to finish the job thwarted on the Rentoul. Thanks to your alertness and fast action, I've escaped the murderous intent of a relentless foe yet again." His eyes softened. "How can I thank you enough for saving my life? Perhaps one day I can return the favor. But I hope your life hasn't been placed in danger as well because of your association with me, or your involvement in this case through the information I've shared with you."

She patted his hand. "I don't seem to be the target of the murderer, at least so far. I'm so glad I was here to help, Emerson."

DeAnn looked up to see hospital personnel, cleared by the guard, enter the room in an anxious state. After she briefed them on what had occurred, she excused herself to go call the commissioner. Before she left, she spoke to Stanek, "I know I'm not a doctor in the physician sense of the word, but I know enough medicine to see you're badly in need of rest. I'll insist your doctor give you something to slow your racing thoughts and help you sleep."

38 CRIMINAL INVESTIGATION TERMINATED

Goroka, Papua New Guinea, 1973

JIM COLE ENGAGED the attendant in small talk as he was pushed down the hall toward the hospital conference room where General Bellicosi had sent word he wanted to meet with the reporter. Could this be the breakthrough he had been looking for in the ten knights case? Would Bellicosi finally give him the go-ahead to examine the evidence collected and write his exclusive story for the *Honolulu Advertiser*?

As he entered the conference room, these thoughts disappeared. It wasn't a private meeting. Bellicosi stood at the window with his back toward Dr. DeAnn Toland, *Kiap* Roger Noble and Major Frank Yowell seated at the table. Surely General Bellicosi, as he had come to know him, would keep his cards close to the vest in front of so many witnesses.

The general wheeled around, bit the tip off of his cigar and spat it into a wastebasket. "Ah, Jim's here. Now we can start. Before I do, however, I want you all to know what I say in this room stays here and is not to be shared with anyone else without my permission. For you, Jim, this is all on deep background, so you're obligated not to run with it."

Cole saw by the expression on their faces that the others were as surprised as he was. "I haven't failed you yet, General, and you can count on me the rest of the way."

390

"Good. As of this moment, Dr. Emerson Stanek is relieved of all his duties relative to the ten knights case and Operation Simpatico. From here on out, none of you are to give him any information, nor have any contact with him regarding this matter unless authorized by me to do so."

Cole watched DeAnn recoil in her chair, and she looked as if she was searching as to how to reply. So he interjected. "Pretty drastic move, sir. May we ask why?"

General Bellicosi broke the cigar in half and tossed it away without lighting it. "Damn right you can ask. But don't expect me to tell you everything I know about Dr. Stanek. First, his sister wants him out of here pronto so he can get back to work as soon as possible on his cancer research project.

"Second, but more importantly, the man's a human dartboard for mayhem and murder. Or as we might say in the barracks, he draws more trouble than a turd draws flies on a hot day. His hotel room was ransacked in Baltimore, and he was damn nearly killed in Hawaii. He was shot at flying in to land at Mount Bosavi with Major Yowell, and he was targeted for death at the CIL campsite where Erik was mistakenly murdered in his place. Now he's been seriously wounded on that river expedition I should never have approved. And even here in the hospital, where we've got an army guarding him, he's been shot at again!"

Cole saw DeAnn still struggling to express herself. This time Noble spoke up. "*Come a gutser*, General. We can't blame Dr. Stanek for everythin' he's encountered on and 'round the mountain. After all, we were all there when he told us about the murder on the peak by a bloke dressed in medieval armor."

Bellicosi picked up a pencil, broke it in half and sent the pieces in the wake of the cigar. "Yeah, and maybe it was his imagination. There's no denying the man's a menace, whatever his scientific skills may be. I can't afford for all this stuff to get out and jeopardize our operation linked to building a bridge between our heroes of WW II and those still missing or bodies not recovered in Vietnam today. If Congress gets word of this, they'll pull the plug on our funds and kill the opportunity to establish a permanent CIL laboratory for locating the remains from all our wars. Then, too, there's the president. Nixon's critics would jump at another chance to hammer another nail in his coffin."

DeAnn finally found her voice. "B-b-but what about all his work on the crime scene? Dr. Stanek told me he's reached some preliminary conclusions. Who's going to follow up on his findings?"

Bellicosi picked up a pencil, and Cole was certain he was going to hurl it at DeAnn as was his custom when he did not like being challenged by subordinates. But he gripped the pencil in both hands instead. "Nobody! We're done with all the investigation we're going to do, except as it's related to finding and identifying the remains of our war dead, which is your department, DeAnn, and I want you to stick to it until you're satisfied you've completed your task."

Cole tapped the table with fingers colored purple from the bruising caused by needles and blood thinners. "How do we know Dr. Stanek will cooperate? Seems to me he's got to find the murderer, or he's a dead man. And what about the murder of your team's interpreter?"

Bellicosi paused as if to reflect on the matter. "Good question, Jim. Perhaps Dr. Stanek will be safer back in Baltimore. Surely his sister will provide security measures for him there. As for Erik, we'll send the FBI in here if needed once our job is completed. Right now it's essential we keep a lid on these matters. If Stanek refuses to cooperate, he'll force my hand. In order to discredit any disclosures he might make compromising our operation, I'll have to tell the world he's alleged to have attempted one rape and succeeded in another right under our noses. Cole saw DeAnn and the *kiap* shoot a glance at Major Yowell.

DeAnn did not hesitate to speak this time. "General, you didn't hear the full story from your informant. Dr. Stanek was exonerated in the case of the Tugaru girl."

"Please enlighten me, dear."

"The perpetrator was one of the Tugaru constables who left Dr. Stanek's bush hat at the scene."

"And how did he get it?"

"It blew off his head the same time I lost mine when we huddled together against a gale force wind."

"Huddled, hey?"

"M-m-maybe I should've said 'braced' ourselves."

"Well, suppose I told you the man you braced yourself with in the wind—and I don't doubt you—allegedly molested his adoptive sister."

"I-I-I find the allegation s-s-slanderous and hard to believe."

"Believe what you like. It turned up on his background check we conduct on all those involved with Defense Department business. But again, I don't want this or any other information leaving this room. But I must tell you, DeAnn, I'm disappointed you didn't inform me of the alleged rape on the mountain involving Dr. Stanek and the native girl."

"Sir, I told you he was exonerated by the Tugaru. They caught the man responsible and dealt with him in their own manner. I thought it best to leave the matter there."

"Well, I'm thinking of your own safety, my dear. Anybody who causes so much trouble cannot be trusted."

Noble twisted the corners of his mustache. "And who'll be telling the lad he's been canned? I don't think this is a matter for the Australian government to deal with."

Bellicosi cracked his first smile. "I agree, Noble. This is not a matter for the law. We'll have DeAnn tell Dr. Stanek his services are no longer required. His sister Catherine suggested this approach as a way of softening the blow, and I concurred."

"B-b-but she asked me to provide care for him 'til he leaves for Johns Hopkins."

"Exactly. I'm sure you'll find a tender way to break the news. And now the rest of you are excused, except I want Major Yowell and Mr. Cole to stay for a few minutes longer."

*   *   *

Cole wondered why he had been singled out with Major Yowell, who had said nothing throughout the meeting. He did not have long to wait for an answer.

"I've asked you two to stay because I don't want the others to hear your answer to one simple question. What do either of you know about gold on Mount Bosavi?"

Now Cole knew for certain that Bellicosi had discovered the secret he had hidden for so long and expected to take to the grave with him. Since Yowell spoke first, he was spared giving an answer.

The major fished in his pocket and produced a pebble-sized nugget. "Sir, it's not what you think. I trade tobacco to the natives from time to time, and they show their appreciation in this way."

393

"Which is against my policy, as I'm sure DeAnn has told you: no *quid pro quo*. Does she know about these transactions?

"No, sir. I told her I was collecting arrowheads for a nephew in Dallas."

"And she believed you? Well, I want it stopped or you'll find your ass back in Vietnam faster than you can zip up your fly. And whatever other pieces of the yellow metal you've got, I want them turned over to *Kiap* Noble to give to the Australian government. You know it's illegal to take gold out of Papua without a mining permit."

The general walked down to the end of the table and patted Cole's shoulder. "Jim, my boy, I'm finished with you. But remember all this information remains embargoed. And, by the way, I want both of you to know I'm not foolish enough to allow things to take place on or off Mount Bosavi to discredit my mission. My informants are out of sight and unidentified, but they're there."

Cole wheeled out of the room, caught an attendant and asked for a push down to Dr. Stanek's room. He wanted to be there when DeAnn told the pathologist he is off the case.

*   *   *

Stanek rose up in his hospital bed and greeted DeAnn and the *kiap*.

"I was hoping you two would stop by. Roger, I'm especially anxious to hear what you found regarding the salt train, specifically, the differences in weight among the bundles, and whether the two were separated at one point or another."

The *kiap* looked at DeAnn as if seeking guidance. Stanek watched her shake her head, and he wondered if they were back to keeping secrets from him again. "DeAnn, you did ask for this information, didn't you?"

She nodded. "Y-y-yes, but I'm not at liberty to d-d-discuss the case with you any further."

Stanek fell back against his pillow. "And why might I ask?"

"As of just a few minutes ago, General Bellicosi relieved you of any responsibility to the U.S. government on matters concerning the ten knights case."

"Oh, he did, did he? Well, we'll see about..."

Just then Cole wheeled into the room. "Have you told him yet he's been sacked?"

394

DeAnn nodded.

"What was his reaction?"

"He was just about to tell us."

Cole brushed back his neck-length hair. "Well, go ahead, but I've got some ideas on the subject when you've finished."

Stanek waited for DeAnn to speak. "There's more than just a firing from the project. We're no longer free to discuss any aspect of this case with you. S-s-sorry, but those are our orders."

Stanek could see they did not expect him to take the news cheerily, but he grinned. "Oh, my, I see the hand of Catherine, the puppet master, pulling strings from behind the curtain."

DeAnn replied, "Yes, Catherine does want you back on your cancer study, for your own safety I presume."

"She might've added 'for her own profit' as well," Stanek retorted. "Nonetheless, let's look at Bellicosi's rationale for giving me the bum's rush. No, better yet, let me save you, my friends, from any further agony. After all, it's a physician's sworn duty to do no harm. All this has to do with the attempts on my life and the general disarray before, during and since my arrival in New Guinea. You can't really fault the general for seeing matters that way.

"I only wish it were easy to let go of this case. But let's not forget my involvement started some weeks before I came to New Guinea. And if these incidents are connected as I suspect, whoever wants me out of the way doesn't have a simple firing in mind. He, she or they want me dead!"

Cole slapped his thigh. You're very perceptive, Dr. Stanek, and no matter what Bellicosi says, you're still my personal physician. And as we travel to Baltimore together and in the days ahead, I intend to place full confidence in you."

"Here, here," said *Kiap* Noble. "And as a representative of the Australian Trustee Government, I'm not bound by any instructions or limitations placed on me by a foreign officer, especially when people have been slain on my watch."

"And what about you, DeAnn? I suppose you'll be asking me to return volume six of the Japanese woman's journal I was going to read in detail during my recovery at Johns Hopkins."

"Not so fast, Doc," said Cole. "When did DeAnn give you this new evidence?"

"Three days ago when she pushed me out of the way of a bullet meant for my head."

"Well, then, she gave it to you before we were instructed not to exchange information with you on this case."

Kiap Noble scratched the side of his head. "Yer thinkin' like a youngster, Mr. Cole. We all heard the Brigadier say, 'as of this minute,' meanin' a few minutes ago. So, DeAnn, if ye want to let Dr. Stanek keep Kioko's log, I think ye've got a right to do so. *A priori*, as my dear, sainted mother used to say when she was philosophizin'."

"I-I-I suppose you can keep the log for the time being, Emerson. But I must have it back as soon as you've extracted what you need from it, hopefully before you leave Goroka."

Cole interjected, "By the way, DeAnn, does General Bellicosi know about the Japanese woman's journals? I'd like to get his permission to examine them myself."

"I haven't told him about the six journals yet. I wanted to summarize the important information in them first."

"Perhaps Emerson can help you with his notes on the sixth log if *Kiap* Noble is willing to be a go between. "Now what about Roger's report on the salt train? Surely, since this is a New Guinea matter, his investigation was carried out under the auspices of the Australian government, and it's nobody else's business what he does with the information collected."

Noble clapped his hands. "Bravo! I rather like this game. 'Puttin'-One-Over-On-The-Brigadier' let's call it."

"Well, let's have it, Roger," Cole insisted.

Noble took a chair beside DeAnn. "The salt train stopped at the junction of the Rentoul and Strickland Rivers where the heavier bundles were separated from the others. At this point, the credit really belongs to our cheeky devil, MilkEye. MilkEye and WonTok talked to a Riami man who had been hired along with other carriers to take the heavier bundles by canoe to an island down the Strickland River where they were off loaded. The rest of the salt train proceeded up the Strickland, leavin' it to travel up the Nomad River to Nomad. Major Yowell kept watch with me over the main supply, the lighter bundles deposited in Nomad and distributed in exchange for trade goods."

The *kiap* paused and took in a deep breath, giving out a wheeze as he did so. "The Riami man told his kinsman sometimes he earned extra currency by taking the heavier salt bundles from the island on board a steamer from the Strickland into the Fly River, thence on to Daru, where the salt bundles were unloaded."

Another wheeze and Noble continued. "One day, the Riami man was asked to stay overnight in the port of Daru and help load the salt onto a big ship. I assume it was an ocean goin' vessel in port. Someone had written down the name so the carriers would know where to report the next mornin'. Our Riami informant gave MilkEye the paper, and MilkEye passed it to me as he finished his story."

The *kiap* reached in his breast pocket and took out a folded paper and handed it to Stanek.

Emerson said aloud, "The *D'Albertis*."

"I've been on board her myself as part of my constabulary duties. We took Japanese prisoners to Manila for shipment home after the war. Nowadays, she's a tramp ship with Filipino registry. Makes a regular run from Daru through the Torridor Straits to Manila."

Cole wheeled closer to the group. "Why do you suppose someone would ship salt from the mountains where it's scarce to the coast where it's already there by the tubful, much less all the way to Manila?"

Stanek replied, "You've raised the crucial question, Jim. My guess is the bundles contain more than salt."

"Say gold?" asked Cole.

"Exactly what I was thinking," Stanek replied.

"My guess, too, Noble chimed in. "I just hope Angus Mackelwaite isn't involved. It's illegal to ship minerals out of New Guinea whilst the Papuans wait for their independence."

Cole saw an opportunity to add his concern about the gold. "Strange we should be talking about gold. Only a few minutes ago in my presence, General Bellicosi berated Major Yowell for trading tobacco with the natives for some small nuggets. Bellicosi ordered it stopped immediately."

DeAnn put a finger to her lips. "Arrowheads, my eye. Please don't let this word get out. We'll have prospectors by the boatload coming up the Rentoul and interfering with our efforts to recover remains. Not to say how agitated it might make the Riami and Tugaru. They're already on the verge of tribal war over the slain boy at the Tugaru burial site."

Stanek patted DeAnn's hand. "Don't fret, DeAnn. I think I've solved the native murder case. But since you and the rest of us need the suspect's cooperation in this matter, I think we'd best keep mum about his identity as well. What I'd like is for you to follow through on the matter we discussed earlier."

"What are you referring to?"

"Backtracking over the trail Kioko first took with Lt. Mori and later with her common-law spouse. See if you can find American remains in Komo. If you're able to check any of the other burial sites listed in her logs for remains, it'll authenticate her journals as well."

"I'm afraid General Bellicosi's edict forbids it. He won't allow me to venture so far afield from Mount Bosavi with my CIL team, especially if he knew it was your request, Emerson."

Cole pushed himself up from the wheelchair and leaned on the foot of the bed. "Now, Dr. Toland, let's not act too hastily. I'm a reporter, and I've been taught to listen carefully to what people say. I distinctly heard General Bellicosi say your job was to track down the remains until you were satisfied you had completed the investigation. Seems like this trip Dr. Stanek outlined is well within your charter."

"Mine, perhaps, but not with resources from the CIL team needed on Mount Bosavi."

Stanek encouraged Cole to take his seat again in the wheelchair, as he looked unsteady. "I didn't envision you taking the CIL team, DeAnn. And you don't need to go as far as Mendam where the coastwatcher's station was located."

Stanek paused as Cole practically collapsed back into the wheelchair. Then the pathologist continued. "Major Yowell can fly you to the burial sites. Most are located in areas where airstrips have now been built. If nothing else, you must check out the site in Komo where Kioko wrote the remains of Wells were buried. It would also be helpful to interview Mister Hanzo in Angoram if he is still living. You might take *Kiap* Noble, MilkEye and WonTok with you for protection."

DeAnn clapped her hands. "Yes, we must make the trip to Komo to recover the remains reported to be those of Wells. I'm sure I can get authorization to go there, and maybe farther if time allows."

"MilkEye will be very helpful to your team in making contact with his cousins, the Chiami, at Komo," Stanek said. "And, by the way, I wonder if you could send MilkEye around to see me. There're a few questions I think he can answer. Since he doesn't come under General Bellicosi's embargo, you won't be violating any rules."

DeAnn smiled. "I'll tell him you want to see him, Emerson. And it won't be too difficult to persuade MilkEye to go north with us. Noble can explain we're looking for the remains of our people and the people of Kioko. She was like a mother to his tribe. WonTok will go if MilkEye does." She looked down at her hands. "As I mentioned to you before, the night MilkEye returned my cap, I understood from Erik's translation MilkEye needed to find Kioko-san to erase a bad spirit from his life."

Stanek lifted her chin and looked into her eyes. "Let's hope Kioko-san can help us as well."

39 FATHER/DAUGHTER'S LAST VISIT

Goroka, Papua New Guinea, 1973

THE WALK TO THE children's day room took but a few minutes.
Yet MilkEye, accompanied by WonTok, felt like he and his
companion set a pace so slow it was not unlike crossing the
Rentoul River against the wind on the vine bridge back home. He
said as much to WonTok. His friend replied with a grunt as he
planted another flat foot ever so gingerly on the tile surface.
MilkEye assumed they walked on glazed ice *Masta* Hides had told
Situmu about. But after a ride in the small *balus* with wings lifting
them higher than the mountains where ice formed into the sky
people's realm, he expected more white magic once they arrived at
the hospital in Goroka.

What he didn't expect was the laughter he and WonTok
provoked as they stepped into an alien world. Here the people did
not paint their faces, grease their bodies or adorn their nostrils with
pig tusks. The only thing MilkEye had in common with these dark
people in white man's clothes was their color.

As he drew nearer to a room where children's laughter could be
heard, he wondered if LikLik had joined this culture and was one
of those snickering behind the half opened doors. At the threshold
of the children's room, however, a black man dressed in white
halted their progress. He spoke to them in pidgin. "Please, so as
not to terrify the children and fill their nightmares with
cannibalism, don these gowns I have for you."

MilkEye wanted to tell him he had never, and as far as he knew, neither had WonTok, engaged in the taboo practice of eating another's flesh. After a brief reflection, he agreed to the conditions laid down by the attendant, which included no physical contact with any child other than LikLik. If it would speed up his meeting with his daughter, MilkEye decided he would put on a cloak like the evil Two Face's messenger, who wore a steel one, if need be.

Once inside, the old warrior saw LikLik before she saw him. Pleased to learn she stood aloof from the magpies at the door, he studied her face for some clue as to how well she accepted her new circumstances. When their eyes finally met, LikLik pulled the white gown up to her nose and ran over to hide among the other children. They withdrew from her. He squatted and stretched out his arms toward LikLik, who stood alone and seemed frail and slighter of figure than her *age-mates*.

"You got plenty food?" he asked. "Me go kill pig for you."

She lowered the gown to her chin. "Food good, Papa. LikLik like go back to Riami."

He kept his arms outstretched and finally LikLik ran into them. She buried her face against his chest. He could feel her tears seep through the cloth. "Papa, me no like hospital. Carry LikLik back to mama."

"LikLik in 'river' of white people's place. But medicine take away fever. Also time evil Two Face no kill Stan-neck. Me think Situmu like him. Magic of Stan-neck bring us together one more time." He lifted her into his arms and stood up, then continued. "White *misis*, Dok-tor Tow-land, tell papa you go on big *balus* with Stan-neck over plenty water to big hospital with plenty medicine in place of sky people. Then you come back to Riami. Papa go on small *balus* with white people to see Chiami cousins. When papa gone, mama find another man to make baby to take place of LikLik."

LikLik broke into tears again. "Mama no like LikLik when me come back to Riami."

MilkEye motioned for WonTok to join them. WonTok smiled at LikLik when MilkEye said, "WonTok be your new papa if Two Face kill MilkEye. Situmu, LikLik's grandfather, watches over you."

An hour after they had arrived at the children's area, MilkEye and WonTok were back on the unfrozen "ice", as the two Riami men referred to the tile floor. MilkEye put his arm around his *age-mate.* "Before night come, me go to Stan-neck, who like see me. Then we slip outside this place. Stan-neck help us when Situmu still cross with MilkEye and no speak."

*   *   *

Before darkness fell, MilkEye appeared in the doorway to Stanek's hospital room. The policeman on duty ran his hands over the Riami man's borrowed gown. Stanek called from his bed. "He's clean, Sergeant. Let him in. He's an old friend."

MilkEye was escorted to a chair beside the bed, but did not take it right away. "Stan-neck good?" he asked in pidgin.

The pathologist replied he was getting stronger with each passing day. "Please sit down, MilkEye. I have some questions only you can answer, perhaps easier in your native tongue."

Stanek watched him lower himself in the chair like it was covered with a bed of prickly pears. "Questions, *Masta?* Me know nothing about who kill Tugaru at salt well."

The pathologist shook his head. "No, friend, the murder no longer sizzles in my mind and will have to wait until I come back from the home of the sky people with your daughter LikLik."

Stanek saw MilkEye's body go limp, as if a great weight had been lifted from the old warrior's shoulders. "You make me happy man, *Masta.* Me know you no help Tugaru and turn against me. You know who kill Tugaru, but no speak. Take MilkEye long time make things good for LikLik."

"Who taught you to speak pidgin?"

"Papa, Situmu."

"And where did he learn the white people's language?"

"Situmu help Jack Hides. Later, sky people from great *balus* talk pidgin."

"What else did Situmu teach you?"

"Legend of Riami warriors." MilkEye then launched into a lengthy recital of the legend passed from father to son and repeated by every Riami man since. Stanek listened patiently to how the Riami outsmarted the Tugaru and sent hunting parties around the salt well into the upper reaches of Mount Bosavi.

Stanek then asked, "What else did Situmu learn from the white man?"

MilkEye pointed up. "About god."

"What god?"

"Two Face who fall on mountain with great *balus.*"

402

"Twin gods?"

"No, *Masta*. One god with two faces—one face good, one face evil. Kioko-san come and tell me God has three faces, all good. Confuse MilkEye."

"Have you seen the god of Situmu?"

"Plenty time. His face on great *balus*, like Stan-neck's face when you first come to Riami village with no hair on head."

Stanek murmured so low that MilkEye could not hear him. "Of course, the vertical stabilizer on the bomber."

"Tell me. Do the Tugaru worship Two Face?"

MilkEye pointed up again. "Yes, the evil Two Face who lives on big mountain."

"Have you ever seen the Two Face of the Tugaru?"

"Plenty time when me hunt cassowary with Situmu. But evil Two Face got cross, kill papa."

Stanek wished he had asked DeAnn Toland to sit in on this meeting and take notes for him. But translating back and forth would only have slowed the pace further. He would just have to memorize all he learned.

"Just a few more questions. Who gave you the brass wristband?"

"Kioko-san's man."

"The husband, describe him for me."

MilkEye held one hand over his head and swept the other across his chest. "Big fellow, wide, same you, *Masta*."

"Did the white people walk among the Tugaru?"

"No. Live with Riami. Stay away from Tugaru."

"Did the white people go up to the top of the mountain?"

"No go to Upper Falls. Evil Two Face live there. Situmu go to big mountain to bring honey for sick Riami 'til evil Two Face kill papa, like he try to kill me."

"This Upper Falls, is it the twin of Lower Falls, only bigger?"

MilkEye's eyes widened and his mouth fell open. "You see Upper Falls, *Masta*?"

Stanek chuckled. "No, not close up, but even sorcerers can make good guesses once in a while. I'll bet the bigger falls I saw from the small *balus* is like the lower one we call a cascade."

"Cascade. WonTok tell me lesson he got from Dok-tor Towland. Cascade fly out from stones like spit from mouth. No touch lips. Hollow cave behind.'"

Stanek saw MilkEye had more to say on the subject, so he encouraged him with a nod. MilkEye picked up the cue. "Inside cave at Lower Falls, WonTok, me and Kioko-san's man find sky people bones. Bury with bones of two more white people. This time down river after you go away, WonTok and me show *kiap* burial place. Make *kiap* happy."

Another group burial would make individual identification more difficult, Stanek thought, but at least GeeJo had found three more of his buddies and buried them.

"Did you find a sky people book in the cave?"

"Yes. Bring back book to mountain. Find small *thunderstik* in cave too. WonTok like, but me know fallen warrior need for battle in next life if evil face of Two Face block way. Bury small *thunderstik* with bones."

"One more question, then you can go. The yellow stones you trade Major Yowell for tobacco. Where do they come from?"

"On big mountain, near Two Face of Tugaru, but no more go there. No like evil face or bad-talk people."

"Bad-talk people?"

"Giambu who shoot you with big *thunderstik*."

"The plateau bushmen who also left the pig sacrifice in my honor?"

"Same people, *Masta*.

"What are they doing on sacred mountain of Tugaru and Riami?"

MilkEye shook his head. "No got answer, *Masta*, but bad-talk people make bad omen so you go away from big mountain."

Stanek said under his breath. "If it were only so simple." Then he said to MilkEye, "Thanks for your help, and I'll come back when I'm better and go up the big mountain to see what the Giambu are doing there. Until then, is there anything I can do for my friend, MilkEye?"

MilkEye held up two fingers. "Take care of LikLik in land of sky people, then bring LikLik back to papa with fever gone." He dropped one of his fingers and then continued. "MilkEye and WonTok friends again. But at mountain, please let WonTok stay with sky people. Riami make payback if know of spoiled ritual. You tell Dok-tor Tow-land. Make place for WonTok with white people."

Stanek told MilkEye he would make arrangements with Dr. Toland and *Kiap* Noble to see to WonTok's safety. He expressed regret for having to leave and told MilkEye he had been a great help. He asked the Riami headman not to discuss these matters with anyone except Dr. Toland.

He closed the meeting by urging MilkEye to take back the wristband he had given him. "In the land of my people," Stanek said, "I have other magic to protect me. Keep it with you while you help the white *misis* find your Kioko-san, or her bones. Don't worry. The evil Two Face is no match for Tow-land's magic." Stanek put his hand over his heart and then went on. "Her strength, like Kioko-san's, comes from here."

40 TO TRUST OR NOT TO TRUST

Goroka, Papua New Guinea, 1973

EMERSON STANEK FOUND himself looking forward to DeAnn Toland's daily visit to his room at the Goroka Hospital. Cognizant he should not ask her to breech the embargo General Bellicosi had pressed on her and the others, he avoided any discussion of the ten knights case. Instead the two passed the afternoons huddled over some aspect of their various sciences.

But whenever Jim Cole joined them, arriving an hour before the daily session broke up, the conversation took a whimsical and often philosophical twist. "Beats me," the reporter said three days before he, Stanek and LikLik were to depart for America. "Beats me," he repeated, "how two young people can spend so much time on the laws of statistics and the function of the human brain. Enough of this physiological nonsense. It's making my head split!"

Stanek rose to the challenge. "Okay, Jim. What would you have us put on the agenda today?"

Cole flashed what Stanek interpreted as a sly grin. "'Love' and 'soul' for starters," said the reporter.

"Not my cup of tea, old man."

"Mine either," chimed in DeAnn.

"Too philosophical for scientists like yourselves, I gather. But listen to a dying old man. There is no person in the world who can do without the love and the confidence of his or her fellows. Nor does matter fly very far without a soul in the cockpit. Despite Bellicosi's dictum, I'm going to say it anyway!" Cole brought his

406

hand down hard on the wheelchair. "The ten knights, especially the survivors, know what I'm talking about."

Stanek leaned closer. "What do you mean?"

"Our physical bodies fail us, as does strength and vitality from time to time, but the soul, if we let it, lifts us above the biological laws of human nature you two youngsters are so fascinated with."

Stanek tried not to sound harsh. "Perhaps at your age, Jim, the passionate desire for truth has been tempered by how you'd like things to be rather than how they are?"

"I'm no match for your cranial gymnastics, Doc. But I've got a hunch that one day the judge in your own heart will settle the case."

"Please, guys, can we change the subject? We're all friends."

Cole offered his hand, and Stanek took it. "DeAnn's right. Forgive an old man whose guilt has made him lonely." Cole wheeled about and left the room.

DeAnn looked at Emerson. "What do you suppose is upsetting Jim?"

"Anxiety."

"Oh, the cancer."

"No, Cole's done something and it's gnawing away at him, leaving him with the fear of discovery."

"What could it be? He seems like a sweet old soul."

"I'm not sure yet. But I believe we might get a clue from his reaction when we gave him the inscribed Zippo lighter and pilot's log back on Mount Bosavi and again the other day when he heard we had found Kioko's journals. One or the other, or both, triggered or reawakened a recollection he'd sooner forget."

She touched his hand with her fingers. "Can you help him?"

"Neither psychology nor psychiatry are my specialties, but there's an excellent facility at Johns Hopkins. My mother, or Catherine's mother, is being treated there for schizophrenia."

"Hope Jim's problem is not so serious. Oh, I'm sorry."

"It's okay. I've come to terms with my adoptive mother's condition. Maybe in our time together at Hopkins, Cole will open up to me without psychological intervention. I hope so, because I'm certain his guilt is tied into the case we're not supposed to discuss."

She drew a finger across her lips. "Gotcha."

His mind was on the warmth her other hand generated as it lingered across his. But the mention of his adoptive mother caused his thoughts to flash back to Johns Hopkins and her plight. What condition would he find Patricia Stanek in? Could she hold on so he could visit her one last time?

He remembered when Catherine had waved his orphan status in front of General Bellicosi, DeAnn and company on Mount Bosavi. He had not let on at the time her comments bothered him, but now as DeAnn rose to her feet to leave, he feared the latest intimate contact between them—her hand lingering over his—sprang from pity. He decided it was his duty to set the matter straight.

"Those things Catherine said about me before we left on the river trip were not true. Her own mother assured me I was not a bastard, only a child abandoned by parents out of necessity. Patricia Stanek never explained what the necessity was, and I didn't bother to ask."

"Why are you telling me this, Emerson? Is there something else you'd like me to know?"

The clock on the wall struck six. "They'll be bringing my dinner soon. Will you come again tomorrow afternoon?"

"No, I'll be leaving with Roger, Major Yowell, MilkEye and WonTok bound for Mount Bosavi."

"Two days before Cole, LikLik and I depart? Fishy enough to sound like a schedule arranged by Bellicosi or Catherine, or both. At any rate I'll miss our talks."

"As will I."

"I suppose writing to me directly would be out of the question."

"Yes, I dare not cross the general."

But if you find anything interesting on your journey north with MilkEye in search of Kioko, should you agree to take it, you could pass it on by letter to Cole."

"I suppose I could."

"Splendid."

"But it's not to say I should or would."

"Why the reservations? Technically, you're not breaking the rules."

"There's more to it."

"Then what?"

"You've caused a great deal of anguish since entering my life almost two months ago..."

Reminded of the passage of time, Emerson shook his head. "Don't tell me you still have misgivings about the crazy rape accusation on the mountain?"

"Believe me, I wish it were easy to erase from my mind, as I'm sure there are things you'd like to forget as well."

He felt his face grow hot. "Someone other than Catherine is spreading lies in order to sow mistrust between us. It's Bellicosi, isn't it? Cole says the general's got a dossier on each of us."

She did not answer. He took her silence as confirmation she knew about the adolescent incident with Catherine. "Believe me, DeAnn, I'll not let slander or another attempt on my life or more delay on my beekeeper cancer study deter me from solving the ten knights mystery. It will either be with or without your help. It's your call."

DeAnn hung her head and left the room. He had the urge to call her back. The words died in his throat. He had wanted to discuss Kioko's number five tablet with her, not for just the scientific harvest reaped from it, but how the love story unfolded so beautifully and naturally as it flowed from DeAnn's lips like a ballad. He had wanted to compliment her on the reading and tell her he knew how difficult it must have been for a single woman to impart such emotion to a single man. He had wanted to say Yowell would have been far less appreciative of Kioko's narrative than he, yet he could not explain why. DeAnn, Kioko, or the combination, had rekindled a passion he had long stifled. Only one other woman in his life had shown such tenderness of spirit. Patricia Stanek's motherly attentions and nurturing had kept him from turning out like his adoptive father—self-centered and arrogant.

"I'm a fool," he told himself. "DeAnn wanted to hear from my own lips she could trust me, that I'm not a sex offender." He should have used Kioko's reasoning when she defended GeeJoe and pointed out that if it was rape he had in mind, he had plenty of time and opportunity to do so.

He heard a cough and the mess orderly appeared in the open doorway. "Eat food, grow strong. *Misis* same everywhere. Like strong man."

He paid little attention to the Papuan. Already his mind grappled with a theory relative to the ten knights case. Kioko had supplied many valuable clues, and he was certain volume six would reveal even more.

*   *   *

As DeAnn reached the outside of the hospital, she was struck anew at how awkward her meeting with Emerson had ended. Through the reading of Kioko's journal, she felt they had struck a bond, silent to be sure and in its early stages, yet nonetheless much like Kioko and her GeeJo.

Perhaps she should retrace her steps and apologize to Emerson for leaving so abruptly. Cordiality was a hallmark of the Tolands.

But with Stanek's assailant on the loose, she quickened her pace. It would be best not to dally as already darkness had fallen. Uncertain as to whether Roger Noble still waited for her in the jeep parked a block away, her heart leaped in her chest as someone approached. She was relieved to see the *kiap's* bulky form turn toward the entrance.

"Ah, lass, why didn't ye wait for me to come fetch ye like we agreed? Be more careful. There's an assassin still at large."

"Sorry, Roger."

"Ah, well, whilst I was waiting, the commissioner's message-runner brought mail from the last flight in. There's a letter for ye and two addressed to Dr. Stanek. Wait here in sight whilst I duck inside and give these letters to an orderly. I'll only be a minute."

"If it's all the same to you, Roger, could I take the letters? Dr. Stanek needs someone to read to him until his vision improves, and he can manage on his own."

"Sure, lass. I'll come with ye. There's something I've been itching to ask the Doc myself."

"Just don't overtax him. They've just gotten his condition stabilized."

At the door, the *kiap* spoke to the two young constables on guard, and one of them escorted the pair to Stanek's bedside. DeAnn noticed a remarkable change in the patient she had only recently left. Gone from his eyes was the look of loneliness she saw when she had left, now replaced with a merry twinkle when she stepped back into his room. She knew he was glad to see her again after her hasty exit. Or had Roger's presence lifted his spirits so? She did not have long to wait to clear away the doubt.

"DeAnn, you came back. Thanks. I was just about ready to spring from this bed and come after you. We shouldn't have parted on such a sour note. I didn't mean what I said about going it alone. We all have a stake in the outcome of this case, Roger included."

Noble twirled the corners of his red mustache. "Dashed funny ye should bring it up, Emerson. I've got..."

DeAnn interrupted. "Please, Roger, Maybe he'd like to go over his mail before we fire a barrage of questions at him."

"Letters? Who from?"

"Your sister Catherine and Lt. Dunbar."

"Read Dunbar's letter first, if you would, DeAnn."

Patrol officer Noble turned to leave. "I suppose ye'll want to digest the letter in private, mate."

"No, Roger, you can stay. Have a seat. When DeAnn's finished, I'll take your questions as long as my energy lasts."

"Fair enough, Doc."

Before sitting down, Noble took the envelopes from DeAnn. He slit them open with his bush knife and then handed them back to her. She began to read Lt. Dunbar's letter:

```
Dear  Dr.  Stanek:  (I  don't  feel  comfortable
addressing  someone  so  distinguished  by  your  first
name.)
     Heard  from  your  sister  you  were  shot.  My  stars!
I  hope  this  finds  you  on  the  road  to  recovery.
Miss  Stanek  agreed  to  get  this  to  you  post  haste
with  her  letter  by  chartered  flight,  no  less.
     Briefly,  here's  the  situation.  We  found  the
purple  folder  Dr.  Haveland  had  used  in  the
pathology  lab  before  he  was  murdered.  Haveland's
widow  said  he  would've  placed  them  in  the  return
bin  before  he  left.  Thanks  for  the  lead.  We  were
able  to  track  down  the  one  he  used.  Truth  is,  I
can't  make  heads  or  tails  out  of  the  photographs,
sketches  and  dental  files  contained  in  the
folders.  The  photos  are  of  folks  the  late  Filipino
Freddie  hacked  to  pieces  over  his  career.
     Speaking  of  Freddie,  you  might  like  to  know  the
results  of  his  autopsy.  The  Medical  Examiner  says
he  died  from  asphyxiation  before  he  was  stabbed
multiple  times.  Not  your  pillow-over-the-face  type
of  asphyxiation.  No,  those  responsible  for
Freddie's  death  poured  molten  pyrite  (fool's  gold)
down  Freddie's  gullet  and  into  his  stomach.  The
Medical  Examiner  said  in  the  process,  the  hot  iron
sulfide  melted  all  of  Freddie's  extensive
bridgework.
```

I don't know what to make of all this. Hope we
can get our heads together once you get back. We
need a couple of hours to go over the evidence,
including any pertinent facts you might uncover in
the purple folder. Of course, none of this was
released to the press. We don't want Freddie's
killers to know what we know, or think we know.

Signed, Sam Dunbar, Detective Lieutenant
Baltimore Police Department

DeAnn thought she saw the twinkle in Stanek's eyes grow even brighter. "DeAnn, I could kiss you! You don't know how helpful this information is regarding Dr. Haveland's murder."

"All I did was read a..."

"Yes, but you brought it to me personally. Who knows how long it would've taken to get this information, if ever. Cole told me his letter to me was stolen. I've got a reply to Dunbar, if you would care to take dictation."

"Sure, but won't you be seeing him?"

"Yes, but unlike here, I doubt if I'll be allowed visitors until the Hopkins surgeons finish their patch work on me. Catherine will see to it. Meantime, I want to give Lt. Dunbar a heads up, so he can clear his own calendar for follow up in a subsequent meeting. This could be an important breakthrough in the case. I don't trust Catherine to deliver my message to him with the urgency required. Furthermore, she's likely to leak it to the press if she sees an opportunity to garner publicity for Stanek Laboratories."

DeAnn set her pad and pen aside. "Perhaps I should read you Catherine's letter before we answer Dunbar. There might be..."

"Something to aid the investigation? Unlikely. I can predict the contents of Catherine's letter. She'll justify her meddling and portray herself as a candidate for Miss Congeniality."

DeAnn retrieved the writing materials. "Go ahead. I'm ready when you are."

With Noble's assistance, Stanek rolled over on the side opposite his wound. This brought him closer to DeAnn."

"Thanks, Roger," he said.

"'Tis nothing, mate. I should leave ye two alone to catch up on yer correspondence. I'll be back in 30 minutes with a question or two of my own."

Before the *kiap* left the room, Stanek began to dictate:

Dear Sam:
    Your letter was most timely. My wounds allow me
to chatter on, but not write. Therefore, this
letter is being dictated to a colleague here whose
trustworthiness I cannot only vouch for, but who
has saved my life. It helps Dr. Toland's
countenance is pleasing to look upon, and I'm
tempted to stretch this reply longer than
customary in order to prolong the vision of her
loveliness and enjoy her kindness to me as I
continue to heal.
    But, alas, we have murders to solve. Can't wait
to see what information you've uncovered. Good
sleuthing, friend, finding the purple folder. Now
I wonder if I could ask another favor? Could you
have Interpol check the bill of lading on a vessel
called the "D'Albertis"? It has a Philippine
registry and operates between the port of Daru in
New Guinea and Manila Bay. Specifically, I'm
interested to know if any illegal gold shipments
transit the two ports. Filipino police or customs
officials might be the place to start. The gold
would most likely be wrapped in banana leaves.
Perhaps you'll have something on this shortly
after my return. If, for any reason, I'm
indisposed, Dr. DeAnn Toland, the aforementioned,
is your point of contact, although at the moment,
she's working on another case from which I've been
removed.
    Take care, Emerson Stanek

DeAnn tried to cover her blush in her cheeks and control her
stutter. "T-T-Thanks for the undeserved compliments. Is there
anything else you want to tell me about Dr. Haveland's murder?"

He leaned back against the pillow. That can wait until you've
read me Catherine's letter. She hesitated, then began:

Dearest Emerson,
    Your last escapade frightened us to death. I
dare not tell mother you were almost killed. The
shock would send her over the edge, as it has me.
I fear mother is near the end as it is. If your
doctor hadn't insisted you stay put to regain
enough strength to travel, I would've had Charles
send one of his charter planes to pick you up
earlier. Lord knows, he's got enough of them,

413

since he got the airlines as a part of our divorce settlement.

Enough about Charles. Your safety is uppermost in my mind. I'd never forgive myself if something happened to you, and your wonderful gifts to the world were lost. Remember I was against your going on that river trip with all those strange people. Please hurry home. It would be nice if you could see mother one last time before she dies. She still wonders whatever happened to the delightful, young man who was interested in her paintings. Strange, she remembers bits of chitchat, but can't sort out the people in her life. Another visit from you might help.

Ask Miss What's-Her-Name, Toland, if she's incurred any out-of-pocket expenses on your behalf. If so, I'll be glad to take care of them. You know me, always the businesswoman never expecting anyone to provide free services.

I hope you're satisfied with the care you're getting. We've already lined up a team of surgeons and other specialists to take care of you once you return home. If this horrible incident brings us closer together, something good will have come out of it. If so, nothing could make me happier. Despite our differences, you must know I do love you, and not entirely as an adoptive brother.

Signed, Love, Catherine

DeAnn tilted her head sideways and tapped the pen against the blank sheet of paper, waiting to see if he wanted to dictate a reply to Catherine. He read the sign language and shook his head. "Catherine is a hopeless task. Love is as alien to her as it has been to me, except for my work. She, on the other hand, cherishes money, prestige, and social position, not necessarily in that order. I'm only a passport to more of the same in her eyes."

For a brief moment, DeAnn thought he edged up to the question begged by the information General Bellicosi had given the group about the alleged molestation. Had he indeed assaulted his adoptive sister?

To her disappointment, Stanek avoided the subject by reverting back to the Haveland murder. "You know I was with Tom the afternoon before he was killed?"

"No, I didn't."

"Dr. Haveland and his colleagues at Johns Hopkins had just rejected a grant for my beekeeper cancer research project."

"No, I wasn't aware of that either."

"Since my lost ID badge was found at the murder scene, I know I was initially a suspect. Lt. Dunbar interrogated me the morning Haveland's body was found."

"Might I ask what changed his mind?"

"Phone records placed me at the hotel at the approximate time the murder was committed. But even more than this, there is a natural trust between us."

"Trust? Did you two know each other before the murder?"

"No. We were complete strangers, except he had followed some of my cases as a medical examiner. Yet we had a common goal each recognized in the other. We wanted to, and still do, bring Tom Haveland's killers to justice."

DeAnn swallowed hard. Was Emerson trying to win her trust through this account? How could she ask for his side of the story relative to the alleged molestation without compromising her pledge to General Bellicosi to keep silent? Why did it matter? Chances are, she would never see Dr. Emerson Stanek again once he left Goroka. His wounds were too severe to allow a return to New Guinea, even if he wanted to go against his firing by General Bellicosi. Then, too, there was Catherine Stanek. She, like the general, held something over his head. Otherwise, why would he dangle like a puppet on strings, dancing to the tune she set? Finally, DeAnn's own practical side took control, and she decided none of this was her business anyway. So why should she care? But then his next words gave her a jolt.

"I'll let you in on a little secret, DeAnn."

She leaned closer.

"Never has anything moved me more than when you read those love passages from Kioko's story. Talk about trust! GeeJo and Kioko placed theirs, not in the numerals on a sundial, but in time eternal—the hour in which love abides."

His eloquence caught her off guard. He had suddenly displayed such a thought perhaps never shared with another woman. Was there a reason to continue to probe the depths of this man's mind and discover what his heart and soul contained?

Left speechless, she listened as he went on. "There's an old sundial at Hopkins. You've seen its inscription found on the lighter in the B-24 wreckage."

"Yes, I sent it to Dr. Haveland with the pilot's log and report. Whoops. We're not supposed to be discussing it."

"What I'm about to say touches the ten knights case only tangentially at this point. We're talking about the message on the lighter. Do you remember how it goes?"

"The inscription? I'm afraid not."

He began to recite. "One hour alone is in thy hands, the hour on which the shadow stands."

"What about it intrigues you so?"

"Back at Hopkins, we played a game. We, I mean the pathologists. Every time we passed the sundial's inscription, we tried to guess at its meaning, or come up with a new one. But as you read the love story of Kioko and GeeJo, the meaning struck home. I'm almost certain they were aware of the answer to the riddle posed by the inscription."

"What is it?"

"I'll repeat what I've already said about the relationship between GeeJo and Kioko. The hour in our hands is the one in which love abides."

She wanted to tell him her heart hung on every word. The truth he spoke had brought them one step closer in their relationship. But she let doubt cast down another barrier.

"Who are you?" she asked.

"What do you mean?"

"Scientist, pathologist, philosopher or poet? What you've just told me fits more with a poet."

He laughed. "I've never been accused of being a poet before. I honestly couldn't tell you at this moment how or where these thoughts came from. I didn't think I was capable of thinking in such a manner, much less speaking these thoughts aloud. Just carried away by circumstance and timing, I suppose. Or perhaps the painkillers have left me slightly delirious."

For what seemed like a minute she waited in silence. Then he went on slowly. He paused in between words as if they were steps he had to measure carefully before crossing the vine bridge over the Rentoul River the first day he had come to Mount Bosavi.

"Delirious…that's got to be it. Fever…it comes and goes between the chills."

She laid a hand over his forehead palm up. "You're on fire. Is there anything I can do? Call somebody?" The heat from his body traveled up her arm and she felt his head grow cooler.

"You have the healing touch," he said.

Her own cheeks flushed at the compliment. "There's an ice bag on the bed stand. Should I get it for you?"

"Put it under my neck, if you would. Ironic, isn't it? An old knife wound near the heart, neglected too long has caused the fever. But for this, I might've been out of this bed by now. The bullet shattered bone in my shoulder, but two or three operations at Hopkins will clean up the injury, along with some weeks of rehab after it heals."

DeAnn slid a hand with the ice bag under his neck and with the other set it in place, aware her lips inadvertently brushed against his cheek in the process. He turned slightly and their lips touched. She trembled and her long lashes fluttered against the crescent-shaped scar on his cheek. He pulled her closer with his good arm and their bodies came in contact. As her breasts barely touched his chest, she unexpectedly came alive with what she felt in her heart was the beauty of being. It was being enveloped in a source once believed unfathomable.

Then reason returned. DeAnn pulled away, and what moments ago had been incomprehensible now became comprehensible. She, too, for a brief moment must have been caught up in the glow of the love story of GeeJo and Kioko. Nothing more, she told herself.

Emerson lay back against the ice bag. She searched his face in an attempt to read his emotions. She thought he looked as confused as she felt. "Mine isn't really a healing touch, Emerson," she said. "If so, I would've been able to hold on to my sister a year older than me the afternoon she slipped and fell into a neighbor's pool. Instead, as we both tottered on the edge, I had to let go of her to save myself. Before Daphne went under, she uttered 'plu,' the sound which water makes when a stone is thrown into it. I ran to get my mother shouting Daphne's last word over and over again. 'What are you saying, child,' mother scolded. 'You're nearly five and can speak more clearly.'

"Finally, through my frantic gestures, stuttering and tears, she understood Daphne was in trouble. At the pool, my mother dove into the water, scooped Daphne up in her arms and laid her on the grass. She tried desperately to get water out and air into a figure as limp as a rag doll. It was too late. We were left to mourn. Daphne's sudden and tragic passing had left us numb, and my stuttering began then."

Emerson touched her face and brushed aside her tears with his thumb. "I'm sorry for your loss, DeAnn. I regret I didn't know about your sister's tragedy when you had to read the part of Kioko's log where she fell in the river and almost drowned."

"You couldn't have known. You're the first person outside of my family I've told this to."

"I wish there were something I could do or say to ease your anguish. I'm not a religious person as you may have guessed, but as a physician, I'm struck by how you got through your difficult story just now without once tripping over a single word. Surely, you can no longer think of yourself as a person who stutters." He paused, then went on. "May I ask you the same question you posed to me after I introduced my sister Catherine into the conversation?"

"Okay."

"What prompted you to share such a personal story with me?"

She thought carefully. How should she answer? Did she fully understand her motive? Maybe it was the simple fact they would never see each other again, so why should it matter what he knows? Or perhaps, like him, it was tied to some chord resonating from the Kioko and GeeJo story. Yet, if he had left book six unread, how could he know about the tragedy of the two lovers? Perhaps relating Daphne's drowning was merely a trigger to get him to throw open the tragedies in his life, particularly as to what had occurred between Emerson and Catherine in their youth. DeAnn rejected all these potential responses and settled on a less intimate answer.

"If I had this healing touch as you say, as head of the CIL team, I should've been able to prevent Erik's death and secure the safety of the rest of my team, including yours."

As Noble came into the room, she quickly kissed Stanek's cheek. "Goodbye, Emerson. I wish you the best in your recovery. Please don't forget our agreement. Return Kioko's book six as soon as you've read it."

"I've got little more than two hours before lights out. Sure you couldn't stay and finish reading Kioko's log to me? Then I could leave it with you."

"It would be a violation..."

"I know, the Bellicosi edict."

Noble plopped down in a chair. "What's this about Bellicosi's edict?"

"We're trying to figure out a way to thwart the general and have someone read the Japanese woman's last journal to me."

Noble slapped a hand against his thigh. "I could do it after I drop DeAnn off at her quarters. There might be somethin' in the book relatin' to Mackelwaite. Might answer the question I wanted to ask ye."

"I'm sorry, Roger, but your friend isn't mentioned in Kioko's sixth account," she said.

"No mind, lass. I'm glad to help out anyway. Let's get goin'. Later, I'll pop back here, and nobody will be the wiser. I could be readin' Emerson a bedtime story as far as anyone knows."

As DeAnn left the room, she could feel Stanek's eyes following her to the doorway. She stopped and turned to hear him say, "Goodbye, DeAnn. Remember my pledge."

"What pledge?" Noble asked as he and DeAnn passed into the corridor.

"He plans to stay with the case until the mystery is resolved."

"Good for him. And there's nothin' to keep me from passin' on his observations to ye, like Cole and I agreed."

"Thanks, Roger. You can start by keeping me informed of Dr. Stanek's findings after you've read Kioko's final book to him."

"So it's back to 'Dr. Stanek' betwixt ye two, sad to say so, I am."

"You'll come back and read to him, like he asked?"

"Sure, and I know ye've kept close tabs on those journals since MilkEye and WonTok left 'em with us along with the rubber dingy. They mean a lot to ye. It would be a shame to come this far and leave a piece of the puzzle hangin', wouldn't it, lass?"

41 KIOKO'S JOURNAL #6, TREK NORTH TO COASTWATCHER'S STATION

Papua New Guinea, 1944–45

U.S. ARMY CENTRAL IDENTIFICATION LABORATORY (PROVISIONAL) FINDINGS, CASE NUMBER 316, EXHIBIT 3f, KIOKO TANAKYA'S SIXTH JOURNAL. DR. DEANN TOLAND'S REPORT.

STUNNED BY THE shock of my having spent a night alone with the American, Taro waited for GeeJo to leave us to attend to other matters before he unleashed the full rage of his fury. As my oldest brother, he said it was his duty to beat some sense into me for this transgression.

While Taro gathered a reed equal to the task, I dutifully slid the kimono I still wore, fresh from my honeymoon, down to my elbows exposing my shoulders. I waited. When Taro came back, I heard him raise the reed he would use as a whip and braced myself for the whisper preceding its sting. I waited some more. Then I heard Taro sobbing as he drew the kimono back over my shoulders. I cried for his gentle spirit. He could not beat his sister as custom demanded. Taro would rather live with the shame sealed in his heart. I tried to comfort him.

"GeeJo and I were not entirely alone. There was a Riami man with us, the one you saw us bring back to camp. He had warned us there were Duna in the area around Butterfly's burial site, and we best wait for pre-dawn before leaving the mountaintop."

Taro's weeping grew louder. "Jiro would've beaten you. He's always been the stronger brother, though younger than me."

I brushed my hand across his forehead. "You've got strength in other ways. My faith teaches the meek shall..."

It was the wrong choice of words. Taro turned and shook his head as if to shake off the notion. "Stop your preaching! Just tell me you did not shame our family, or if you did, beg for our forgiveness."

"Forgiveness doesn't come from man alone. God has the last word. We must all seek His forgiveness—Buddhist, Shinto and Christian alike."

He cupped his hand over his ears. "I told you. No more preaching!"

I decided it was best to change the subject. "Any sign of Lt. Mori while I was gone?" I asked.

"No, but I'm certain he has his eyes on us. He'll not hesitate to beat you, or worse, if you become too chummy with the American enemy."

*   *   *

There came a morning in late January of 1945 when we reached the Sepik River on our way to the coastwatcher's station near Mendam on the northern coast. When we came out of the mountains, GeeJo had traded with the local natives for canoes to travel the rivers flowing to the Sepik. I had seen these waters before with Lt. Mori.

I had not yet faced my brother from whom I had concealed my marriage to GeeJo. But whenever my beloved in the lead canoe turned to look at me, I yearned even more for his touch. True to his word, GeeJo did not assert his bridegroom's rights and waited to resume our "honeymoon." Nor did he give any indication to Taro we had come down from our mountaintop experience united forever. As agreed, he waited for me to break the news to Taro.

I fretted at this task, made more fearful by the knowledge that beneath the fullness of my breasts slept the child GeeJo and I, with God's blessing, had given life. Taro, nor any Japanese man, could accept or welcome a mixed blood child in the family. My parents and brothers would banish me from sight, and it would be as if I had never existed.

To make matters worse, GeeJo did not know he would be a father in almost seven months. There was no right time to tell

421

either my brother or him. One or the other would have to be given up. Although I couldn't imagine life without my Japanese family, God had placed me in this American's arms, and there I must make a new home for us.

One day as we set out from shore on the Sepik River, a heavy rain drove us back into a little cove. We took shelter under overhanging branches whose leaves offered some protection. As it happened, GeeJo in the first canoe and I in the second ended up in one cove, while Taro's paddlers, for one reason or another, headed for a cove some distance from the one in which we sought shelter.

GeeJo brought his canoe alongside mine and locked the two together. He leaned across the gunnel and pressed his lips against mine. How we hungered for each other and our passion nearly got the best of us to the delight of the two pair of oarsmen. GeeJo, in a friendly manner, directed the Chiami men to turn away. I could not see Taro, which meant he could not see us from his canoe. I did hear him call my name and ask if we were all right. I answered him, trying not to sound too cheerful at the prospect GeeJo and I could steal a moment or two alone.

GeeJo kissed me again. "Dearest love, how I've missed you and longed for you."

"I, too, my husband." And then I repeated the words spoken our first night together. "Oh, I do love you!"

He touched my breasts, ran his hand over my body and rested one of them on my mound of venus, all the while nibbling at my neck and ear. Then I could feel him break into a grin. He whispered, "No fair, Kioko. I've wasted away into skin and bones since we've been separated, and here it appears you've filled out from head to toe."

No better time to tell him than now, I decided. "Husband, the seed of our love has made me blossom. I'm carrying our child. Right there where your hand rests."

GeeJo let out a whoop, which startled Taro and must have been heard as far away as Wewak. But it was my brother who responded. "Kioko, I'm coming over there. Are you sure you're alright?"

I kissed GeeJo one more time.

In the next few minutes, the downpour let up and our convoy of canoes resumed its trek up the great river. GeeJo was ever on the lookout for a Japanese patrol boat. But the Sepik held a special fascination for my husband. At night around the campfire with

Taro and me as his audience, GeeJo spoke tirelessly of the river. Once he likened the Sepik to a 700-mile-long serpent as it slithered through the rushes and sugar cane swamps about which it coiled. My husband's enthusiasm got the best of him.

"You've got to see it from the air," he exclaimed, "as it meanders all the way to the Bismarck Sea. There the snake's tongue lashes out and kicks up the surf outside the mouth of the river about 70 miles east of Angoram."

He waved his arms as he continued. "I've heard, near Mendam to the west of the river's mouth, the coastwatcher has a rendezvous with the submarine or the Catalina flown in to ferry him and supplies back and forth from his station to Port Moresby or Brisbane harbor."

GeeJo caught himself at this point in his revelry. He confided to me, "Please, Kioko, don't translate any of this for your brother. I wouldn't want him spreading this information at Wewak after we say goodbye to him."

I gave him my promise. "But what should I tell Taro?" I asked.

"Tell him I hope your people haven't taken the coastwatcher into custody. All I seek from him is information on my comrades, or at least enough to determine if the coastwatcher sent out a distress signal that our bomber was badly damaged, and most likely crashed."

My mouth flew open. There was the word "bomber" again, possibly linking GeeJo to the bombing of Angoram! I told my husband I dare not speak the word to my brother, for we've been on the lethal end of American bombs. I was relieved GeeJo did not press me on the matter or ask for more details.

As I translated to Taro, it pained me to think I would never see him again once we reached the coastwatcher's station. How could he ever accept my decision to stay with GeeJo, especially after my husband had twice now practically admitted his crew had bombed Angoram? Yet, I was glad GeeJo's plan was to skirt Angoram on our way to the coast, since he believed it was still in Japanese hands. Neither Taro nor I would be welcome there. I remembered Mr. Hanzo's warning that it would be dangerous to return, since the Japanese soldiers had burned the village, causing far more damage than the bombs.

After many days of playing hide and seek along the Sepik, we crossed the mile wide river from south to north just below

Marienberg. We beached the canoes on the north shore. Most of the Chiami who were with us from the start stayed near this village to await our return. Six of GeeJo's loyal followers went with us as we made our way toward Mendam over swampland infested with mosquitoes and insects. Bites and blisters formed on our exposed skin. At first we wrapped ourselves in every cloth available which added to the misery in the form of heat and humidity. The Chiami men with us had a far different and more effective system. They dipped into the bogs, scooping mud from the bottom and plastered it all over their bodies. Only their eyes showed through. We followed their example, and this helped deflect the leeches as well. Insects became less ferocious, as did the heat when we awoke the next morning to a blazing sun in a cloudless sky.

After a three-hour march, we came upon a saddle of land on a hill no more than a half mile from the coast. There were no Japanese patrols in view as GeeJo feared. Instead, a tropical world opened to us. We stopped to gather papaya, bananas, coconuts and sweet potatoes. One of our Chiami natives had gone ahead and returned with shellfish he had found among huge mangrove roots on the shore. He had probably never seen the bounty of the sea before, as this was no doubt his first encounter with it.

The coastwatcher's station was the only round dwelling among a half dozen rectangular huts well hidden and situated in a small village between Aramut and Mendam on the Bismarck Sea. Like a cat stalking prey, GeeJo crept toward the round hut. When he realized the place had been abandoned, he signaled for us to gather at the door.

"Looks like nobody's been here in over a year."

"I'm sorry for you, GeeJo."

Taro must have read our body language. "Sorry for what? I'm glad if our troops ran off the Yankee or Australian devils who fought against us," he said in Japanese.

GeeJo understood, but kept quiet. Finally, he said, "I'll go inside and have a look around. Now would be a good time to say goodbye to your brother." GeeJo threw down a sack of provisions. "Tell him Wewak is 70 miles up the coast. This food and water ought to get him there, and he can keep that ridiculous sword he's been carrying."

"It's Lt. Mori's ceremonial sword."

"Fine. Then Taro can give it back to him in a ceremony at Wewak. But my guess is your bother can search until hell freezes over, but he won't find any sign of such a sadistic bastard." GeeJo parted the bamboo curtain and went inside the round hut.

Taro pulled at my arm. "What did GeeJo say to you, Kioko?"

"He says you are free to go."

"What about you?"

I looked down at the sand before I answered. "I must stay."

"I'll not let him keep you as a hostage. I'll run him through with Lt. Mori's sword."

"Taro, you must promise me. No more bloodshed!"

"I'll do no such thing if you're in danger."

"GeeJo will not harm me or his child."

"Child! You're carrying his child?"

"Yes."

"Then I'll kill him for raping you when my back was turned.'"

"No, Taro. He didn't rape me. I gave myself to him as would a bride. He is my husband in God's eyes."

Tears ran down Taro's cheeks, and his eyes were those of a man in shock and anger like Lt. Mori's the day of the bombing when he lay under the debris. My tears began to flow as well as I reached out for him, but he pulled away. "This will kill our family. I dare not tell mother or father. I'll say you're dead, like Jiro. Yes, I'll say, 'Kioko died in the bombing of Angoram'. When he gets home, Lt. Mori will back me up. He likes you and our family too much to see us shamed."

Again I reached for him. "Please, Taro, don't leave me with so much anger and hurt in your heart. I want my child to know his uncle."

Once more I said the wrong thing at the wrong time. If he had spoken, he would have told me he would never be the uncle of a mixed breed child. Instead, he grabbed the food sack GeeJo had left with him and turned his back on me. I watched him slide through the tree line and head up the beach. No words can express the sadness I felt, except to say a whole chunk of my life, much of it idyllic, gentle and benign, fashioned in the pre-war days, marched up the beach with Taro.

GeeJo came out of the hut shaking his head but smiling. "Looks like the former occupant skedaddled with no forwarding address. He left behind food, kerosene for his Electrolux

425

refrigerator and benzene for his teleradio set. I found personal items as well, like a case of whiskey and this Zippo."

He stuck the lighter in his pocket and shuffled documents he had under his arm, then continued. "Good news is, your people didn't get here before we did, or all this stuff would've been confiscated. On the down side, there's no telling where the coastwatcher hid the radio. Standard procedure calls for securing it away from the living area. If I could get my hands on a radio, we could hear how the war's going. Not from New Guinea Ginny, though. She spits propaganda from her lips like venom from a cobra."

He did not see me wince as he laid the bundle of charts he had under his arm on the ground. Then, for the first time, he rose and saw my eyes—tear stained and swollen. He rushed over to me and took me in his arms. "There, then, Kioko. No more tears. You did what's best for Taro and you. Our love in time will wash away the sadness."

"Oh, tell me it's true."

"Somewhere it's written, I'm sure, love banishes all sorrow. Or if it hasn't been put down, it should be. Maybe I'll do it now I've got some paper of my own. I can write on these charts as I've seen you do in those little tablets of yours."

He lifted my chin and kissed me. When our lips separated, I told him I needed more time to get used to my status as an orphan. He looked away for a moment. "From one orphan to another, the pain will ease a little once you've found someone to love. We're in good shape because we love each other."

"Yes, we do, GeeJo, dearest, and so it will be with our child."

"You're my girl, Kioko. Now let's see if we can find the teleradio, or a native who knows where it's located. Believe me, it takes a dozen or so men to move the speaker, transmitter and receiver from one place to another. Each component weighs 75–100 pounds, not including the storage batteries, charging engine and the benzene to run it. All add to the weight."

It was good to have something to divert my mind from poor Taro. "Where do we begin?" I asked.

"Look for a radio antenna, or as the Aussies call it, a wireless mast, camouflaged with palm fronds lashed to the top, no doubt."

"But if it's concealed..."

"Yep, it's like looking for a needle in a hay stack. Might take us the rest of the day and tomorrow as well to search for the radio. But it could be our ticket for getting help for my buddies, or maybe they're trying to send out an SOS and have gotten the aircraft radio up and working."

"You mean your missing crewmembers?"

GeeJo hung his head like a man before an altar. "Our best chance is to find a native who worked for the coastwatcher. Not just any native, mind you, but one the Aussie trusted with the whereabouts of the radio. It makes the search even more difficult. Got any ideas, beautiful?"

"Maybe there's something inside to help you."

"Good thinking. You're beautiful and bright to boot. We'll spend the night here. The coastwatcher even left his bedroll and netting behind for us. It'll be like a second honeymoon, only with more room than inside your kimono." He paused to kiss me. "You go inside, Kioko, while I round up our Chiami friends. They can help me track down one of the locals to interrogate."

The interior of the coastwatcher's hut was extremely austere for one who was supplemented from the outside by submarine and perhaps aerial drops. The only items of furniture were the bed, a refrigerator and a hand-carved table with two chairs. Against the wall, under a large window facing the sea, something else caught my attention. A wooden slab extended from the sill, forming what appeared to be a writing desk. No doubt the coastwatcher updated his daily log at this position from which he had a clear view of both the sea-lane and the sky over Wewak.

As I wondered how many of my country's ships and planes had been lost to this man's diligence, I thought, too, of his bravery. Here he kept his vigil day in and day out, surrounded by Japanese. What could possess any man to sit alone in such peril? Unlike Lt. Mori, it surely was not duty to an Emperor or allegiance to a country driving him to this outpost. If it were one or the other, he would be in uniform fighting the enemy. My husband had given me the insight. It was an obligation to his comrades and allies, some fallen, others in peril on the sea and from the air, which kept this Australian at his station. I imagined him to be older and a widower saddened by his wife's death and wanting to be alone with her memory.

Even in his haste to leave, the coastwatcher showed a great deal of fastidiousness. The one room hut was swept clean with no dirt in the rounded corners whatsoever. Someone must still come daily to keep it so clean. I reminded myself to share this observation with GeeJo when he returned.

I looked into the refrigerator for signs of recent use by the unknown custodian. Absentmindedly, I pulled open one of the drawers. Out tumbled three slips of paper. They were transmissions or messages received, written by hand in English.

The first message must have been de-coded by the coastwatcher, who was the recipient:

> Three ring circus underway on your end. Ringleader orders shut down all ops. Rescue set for next hour. Wait 30 minutes before move to beach. Do not, repeat, do not transmit from your camp. Bartender awaits to serve you at bar.

In the second message, the coastwatcher seemed to have broken radio silence. It read:

> AMC to unknown, distressed bomber. Got my marching orders. Advise if you need assistance. Time is short. Must vacate. Advise you change course and head toward sea. Can arrange off shore pickup. Reply in 15 minutes. Could stay if absolutely necessary.

The third was not written in cryptic radio text. It appeared to be a note to the coastwatcher's replacement should there be one.

> Mate, if you find these messages, you'll know I did my best in the allotted time to make contact with an American bomber which flew over this station, heading west into the interior for some unknown reason. I am not going to stay behind to mount a native-assisted search and rescue operation, which my conscience, rather than my orders to evacuate, tells me I should do. God forgive me if it turns out all weren't missing and assumed lost, as I shall put in my report. Please let me know if you find anyone. My call signal is "AMC".

At dusk GeeJo and his two Chiami companions returned from their search for the teleradio. They had with them a boy whom my husband introduced as Taipe from nearby Mendam. Taipe had led them to a radio set, but unfortunately it was in disrepair. The boy explained the coastwatcher himself had taken a club to the components to keep the radio from falling into Japanese hands intact. I learned it was Taipe who swept the hut clean each day, getting it ready for the coastwatcher's return.

"Coastwatcher *Masta*, build round house. No dust. Easy Taipe keep clean."

GeeJo said he didn't have the heart to tell the boy the white man might never come back. Instead, he invited Taipe to join us in the search for the other "good whites" the Japanese had harmed. The young man agreed to join our expedition and serve as GeeJo's house boy if the American didn't already have somebody. Before I could tell GeeJo about the notes, he and the boy had gone outside. They returned carrying a bulky receiver and storage batteries, which they laid on the coastwatcher's table.

"This is all we could salvage," GeeJo said. "There's no hope for the speaker or transmitter. But a skilled technician might be able to get this receiver up and running. At least we could listen to the news."

I thought of Taro. If only he had stayed. Repairing radios was his specialty. Yet, I doubted the *Bushido* code would allow my brother to aid the enemy, even if it contributed to our own rescue. Right now my husband needed cheering. I thought the coastwatcher's messages might do the trick. GeeJo devoured the three notes in one quick reading.

"This explains a lot, Kioko, about why the man beat it out of here, and how, in his last transmission, he broke the rules in order to help my buddies and me."

"How did you get such information from what is in the messages?" I asked.

He smiled. When we found the radio, the dial was set on seven megacycles frequency."

"I don't understand."

"Coastwatchers use this frequency to pick up aircraft traffic, including distress signals. If he had tried to reach Port Moresby to relay a message to Canberra and from there to Pearl Harbor to be broadcast all over the Pacific, the dial would've been set on the X frequency."

"I still don't understand."

"Sad to say, no search and rescue mission was initiated to find us. In other words, if I ever want to see my buddies again, we're the only ones left to find them." He paused and put his arm around the shoulder of the young man whose torso and back were marked with bumps to resemble the skin of a crocodile.

"Taipe says we're safe here at the moment, but we shouldn't dally too long, as a regular Japanese patrol boat makes its way along the coast and the Sepik River each week searching for food. Seems your people are in dire straits if they must steal from the natives. Maybe they haven't won the war after all and are under siege. If we could get the receiver going, we could find out."

I told GeeJo about Taro's skills as a radio technician.

"Wish you'd said something earlier. With a full day's start, there's no way we can catch up with your brother and persuade him to return. Maybe he'll get cold feet and come back, at least long enough to repair the receiver. The walk up the beach is longer when you're alone. We'll spend the night here and start our own long journey back to Komo in the morning."

We did not sleep together as both of us had anticipated. GeeJo's mind was on his comrades, and mine was on my family and Taro, neither of which I expected to see again. After midnight, a new danger developed.

A far away wailing pierced the still darkness, and I clung to GeeJo's arm. He patted my hand. "Go back to sleep, Kioko. It's only a *singsing*. One of the villages up the coast from us has probably gotten an early start on a funeral. Just to be sure, we'll ask Taipe."

He called the boy from his station at the door and questioned him. The moonlight shown in the coastwatcher's window, illuminating the deep lines in Taipe's brow and showing the frightened look in his eyes. I could see the *singsing* had upset him.

"*Singsing* for people who die," the boy said.

"There, Kioko, didn't I tell you. It's only a local funeral. Nothing for us to fret over."

The boy shook his head, reached in his *bilum*, produced a pair of old binoculars and slung them around his neck. "*Masta, Misis*, come with Taipe. See danger from beach."

GeeJo pointed to the binoculars. "Where'd you get these?"

"Coastwatcher *Masta*, give me before he go away. Me keep for him. Me look, see if he come back."

"What do you want us to see?" my husband asked, continuing to speak in pidgin.

The boy answered immediately. "Jap soldier kill people. You, *misis*, see patrol boat at beach. Hurry up."

We stepped from the hut and soon our hushed voices mingled with the other sounds of the night. The frogs croaked and the mosquitoes buzzed around us mercilessly. We threaded our way through trees untouched by a full moon and emerged onto a moonlit beach. It stretched wide and white to the darkened edge of the Bismarck Sea. Taipe signaled for us to kneel in the sand. The boy crept a little closer, looked through the glasses and handed the binoculars to GeeJo.

My husband muttered. "It's flying the flaming asshole all right." He stood up for a moment, and passed me the binoculars. "Rigged for plunder, don't you think so, Kioko?"

My heart skipped a beat. The Japanese battle flag indeed fluttered defiantly from the stern of the seagoing launch. In tow was a raft of split trunks from the limbom palm, latched by vines to four canoes churning through the wake made by the launch. The craft was a familiar one. Without the moonlight or binoculars, I knew a lot about this ex-army boat pressed into service in places like Angoram. The soldiers called it a floating brothel. Many, who were too anxious to wait until it reached the docks, took their pleasure from the comfort girls huddled under the awning which ran all the way aft from the wheelhouse on the 40-foot craft. The awning was there to provide a sunscreen for the almost clear deck, but in reality it hid the lust of the soldiers.

"About 12 men, including the crew are on board, wouldn't you say, Kioko?"

I did not answer my husband right away. I thought Taro might be on board. Did the crew of the motor launch discover him on the beach? Was he now leading them straight to us? GeeJo must have read my mind.

"If this is Taro's work, I'm sorry. Brother or no brother, he'll have hell to pay."

Taipe broke his long silence before I could answer.

431

"Japs come early. Need food bad. *Singsing* for people who hide food from them and die."

"GeeJo patted the lad on the shoulder. "It's too late to save the village from their murderous plunder, but if the gunboat is headed for the Sepik, our little band must prepare to stop them if they threaten the Chiami below Marienberg awaiting our return."

He said no more, but back at the coastwatcher's station, he summoned his followers and laid out a plan of attack. He poured the whiskey from eight bottles until they were left half full. He then filled the remaining space with kerosene and stuffed a rag in the neck of each bottle. He simulated the next three steps. First he dipped the wicks into the benzene, then showed how to light it with a match he provided each thrower, and, on his signal, instructed them to hurl it at the motor launch from positions in four different directions. Each man selected was allocated two of the homemade bombs. GeeJo called them Molotov cocktails to the native's delight, and they tried to repeat the word in pidgin.

"Husband, must more blood be shed in this war with no end?"

Anger flashed in his eyes. "Where was Japanese concern at Pearl Harbor? And who can assure the women and children in the village up the coast the rape and pillaging will end with this one last raid? If the Japs do their dirty deed and leave the way they came, they can get out of here without a fight. We won't start a scrap unless we have to. But we have to protect the Chiami waiting for us. If the Japs attack them and plunder our supplies there, none of your countrymen will come back this way alive."

GeeJo decided to leave immediately. Ahead of us lay a three-hour or more trek to where we had left the Chiami and hidden the canoes. While the Japanese ransacked the villages along the way, GeeJo hoped to reach the Sepik River near Marienberg.

My husband threw his hands up in the air for emphasis. "Kaboom! If the enemy continues upstream, we strike."

He then started to walk away, and as he did, he spotted movement behind the coastwatcher's hut. GeeJo motioned for the rest of us to halt and hit the ground, while he drew his gun from his shoulder holster. Then he replaced it and took out Wells' bayonet instead.

He whispered in my ear. "Sounds like one person, maybe a native. Wouldn't want to fire a shot and rouse your friends on the water. You stay here, Kioko, with Taipe and the others. I'll have a look."

He kissed my cheek and was gone, steering clear of the moonlight, crouching as he moved toward the hut. In what was a minute or two, yet seemed much longer to me, GeeJo returned with a shadowy figure he pushed in front of him at knifepoint. I did not recognize Taro until my husband shoved my brother down on his knees between Taipe and me.

I gasped in a sound unrecognizable as my own. "Taro, you've come back!"

He nodded, displaying a sheepish grin. "Only to rescue you. There's a patrol boat heading for the river, searching for us, I bet. I tried to signal the crew, but had no matches to light a fire. Don't you see what this means? Lt. Mori has come back for us like he promised."

At the mention of Mori, GeeJo did not need a translation from Japanese to English to fathom the meaning of Taro's words. "What's the chatter about Lt. Mori?"

"Taro thinks Mori's on the boat."

"Then tell your brother he's still my prisoner."

"But you freed us."

"Not to lead the enemy to our position."

"But Taro has had no contact with the soldiers on the boat."

"How do you know?"

"He told me so. We've never lied to each other even as children."

"Better hope the boat turns back at Marienberg and Taro doesn't give away our position. Otherwise, one peep and..."

"You'd kill him?"

"If I'm forced to in order to save our party or my buddies." GeeJo held the bayonet an inch from his throat and drew the blade across.

"And your wife and child, would you sacrifice us to save your buddies? Or does our survival mean more to you than finding your crewmates?"

He hesitated long enough for me to doubt whether anyone or anything, even our love, could divert him from his quest to find his lost comrades. After reflection, he made this clear. "Kioko, you must know, even if we had found the coastwatcher here, I wouldn't

433

have gone back with him without my friends, or at least an accounting of each—something to take back home with me."

Being Japanese, I should have understood. No one more than my people placed greater value on returning some part of the fallen to be enshrined in an ancestral grotto. Lt. Mori's fanatic sense of responsibility had driven him to collect relics of even the soldiers he had slain.

Nonetheless, it shattered my dream to learn now, like Lt. Mori, GeeJo placed his sense of duty above love. He was, after all, a soldier tried and true at war. Like any other combatant, his first allegiance was to the society which had spawned him and organized itself to go to war if seriously threatened. How sad one's country demands so great a sacrifice. But as great as this disappointment was, it paled in comparison to what I felt about my husband's later actions.

Near dawn, after an arduous march in a difficult terrain, replete with alligators and mosquitoes, we reached the spot GeeJo had selected for the ambush of the gunboat. But it was an ambush only to be executed if the gunboat should threaten any in our party. We found the Chiami awaiting us just below Marienberg where GeeJo expected the Japanese crew to make its intentions known after they disembarked for more pillaging in the village. Would it return to the Bismark Sea, or continue down the Sepik blocking our escape route?

I found an opportunity to brief Taro on the plan. He was shocked. He did not trust my husband and insisted he would alert the gunboat crew, at the first opportunity, that a lone American held us prisoner.

"But GeeJo promised not to attack if the boat turns around at Marienberg and heads back to the Bismarck Sea."

"We can't take a chance, Kioko. Our soldiers' lives and possibly Lt. Mori's are at stake."

"Promise me, Taro, you won't say anything until we see which way our soldiers go."

"And stay here as a prisoner? Not on your life!"

"Must I ask GeeJo to bind and gag you for your own protection?"

"You'd betray your own brother?"

I spoke out of fear. "No, I wouldn't humiliate a *samurai* and force you to commit *seppuku* afterward."

"Good sister. I promise you to do all I can to spare the American's life, knowing he means so much to you. Lt. Mori, if on board, will intercede for him since your GeeJo spared his life."

"But the child..."

"We'll take you to a midwife in Japan skilled in such matters."

"No! I won't kill our child, this gift from God."

"Then we'll hide you from the neighbors and give the child over to a white missionary, maybe one of the Germans or Italians. Our allies will care for it. There's an old *samurai* saying 'Bestow on others what you yourself are fond of.'"

"No, no! I'll go away to some neutral country and wait for GeeJo to come back to his family. I can't give up my child or my husband."

At this point Taro gave up the argument, although I could see in his boyish face he remained unconvinced mine was a feasible solution.

Perhaps all this worry was unwarranted. However, should the gunboat continue to head westward along the Sepik toward Angoram, GeeJo's contingency plan called for a dangerous rear attack by canoe. In any case, Taro and I were to stay out of sight above the shoreline for our safety. One native stayed with us as a guard, since Taipe pleaded to remain at GeeJo's side.

As fortune, or misfortune, depending on one's allegiance, would have it, the gunboat trailing its raft of stolen goods did as GeeJo had anticipated, ruling out the more dangerous option of attacking on open water by canoe. After it departed Marienberg, the craft started to head west toward Angoram, but then turned and headed back down the river toward the Bismark Sea along the northern shore. Perhaps they had pillaged enough food to fill the raft.

With the coastwatcher's binoculars, GeeJo tracked its every move, keeping those natives within earshot informed. I saw him breathe a sigh of relief when the vessel headed back toward the mouth of the great river. Nevertheless, my husband made certain the strike party, including the young boy, stayed in place.

Meanwhile, Taro and I and our guard knelt on a path above the river. As dawn broke, the gunboat reached the junction where three warriors and Taipe lay in wait with their homemade bombs. Once the armed vessel came adjacent to where we were hidden, Taro jumped up and ran along the path shouting, "Up here,

Japanese prisoners, help us!" He kept running madly and yelling hysterically until he fell down on the path out of breath.

Luckily, Taro fell when he did, for at that moment, GeeJo fired a shot at him. The report of the gun was the signal for all, including our guard, to unleash the fire bombs. In a flash the boat was ablaze. Soldiers barely had time to grab their own weapons when they were forced to jump overboard in an attempt to douse the flames engulfing their bodies.

GeeJo took the lighter from his pocket and lit the last Molotov cocktail to be thrown. It struck the gas storage area and the boat shattered into hundreds of pieces. Then my husband did what I believed unthinkable only a few moments ago. With Taipe on his heels, GeeJo walked down to the shore and shot point blank into the heads of any survivors. The corpses, whose singed bodies filled the air with the sickly odor of wet dog's hair, suffered the same humiliation. One of the wounded soldiers, perhaps an officer, fired his pistol at GeeJo, but hit Taipe in the chest instead. GeeJo shot the officer, but it was too late for Taipe. He flopped about like a fish thrown on the bank. Then he lay, still. The bullet killing Taipe was the only resistance the Japanese soldiers mounted in their defense.

Bewildered, I forgot Taro and everything except the horror, which had unfolded in front of me. I threw my hands to my face. How could the man I loved, once so tender and gentle a soul, change before my eyes into another Lt. Mori in the next? Not the cruelty of war, nor the fact of Taro's stupid act, which had initiated the action against the gunboat, nor mine in telling him the plan, could erase the sight or thought of my dear, sweet, tender GeeJo revert into the monster who must have bombed Angoram. I began to fear for my life and the safety of our child if my beloved ever discovered my secret life as New Guinea Ginny.

42 GO-BETWEEN'S BRIEFING

Goroka, Papua New Guinea, 1973

STANEK STUDIED THE *kiap's* features as the older man wiped a handkerchief across his eyes. "Splendid reading job, Roger. No need to apologize for the tender spots," Stanek said. "I felt them myself. Now, however, we need to ask ourselves, 'What did we learn from this last book in Kioko's series of journals?'"

Noble groaned. "Nothin' seems to implicate Mackelwaite in the murders under investigation. Not a word on Angus I could see."

The pathologist looked at the notepad on the stand next to his bed and indicated Noble should take it and the pen in hand. He stroked his scar with his good hand, then said, "Please note in a case like this, we can often find important clues in what's not overtly revealed."

"Call me thick-headed, but I don't follow this logic, Doc. I like things in black and white."

Stanek smiled. "I couldn't do your job, and I can't expect you to do mine. But let's take this thing from the end and see what we can deduce out of it. First, we know Kioko ended her log following the incident with the gunboat. She never took up the pen again as far as we know. Why?"

Noble groaned again. "I suppose it has somethin' to do with the cold-blooded murder of her countrymen. It's unfair since we were all at war with the Japanese then."

"Right. But we've got to think like a woman. Her heart and soul couldn't sustain the blow it took from witnessing the attack at the

Sepik. My guess is she and the American called GeeJo were silently estranged after the incident. Yet, MilkEye told us Kioko, her husband and child, and Taro spent several years with the Riami in the foothills of Mount Bosavi. Why didn't she write this down? Perhaps it was fear of detection by GeeJo of her 'New Guinea Ginny' radio broadcasts, and disappointment in the man into whose hands she had placed her heart."

The big Aussie shrugged. "I'm just glad she didn't implicate Mackelwaite in any way."

"Ah. It's one of the things left out we can't be sure of. Still, the evidence indicates at some point she must've had contact with your friend and fellow *kiap*, Angus Mackelwaite. Otherwise, how do we explain MilkEye and Wontok's discovery of her books and the raft, along with what might be Mackelwaite's remains at the Tugaru burial site?"

"Ye sound cock sure it was Angus' bones we discovered. Remember, the Tugaru wouldn't allow us to take 'em for ye to examine in detail?"

"Granted, but the lower jaw bone of the skull was missing, which might've been the token Salty Meri wore around her neck and then gave to me. We sent it off to Brisbane for analysis. Once the results are in, we'll know more. But, you're right. We can't rule out the possibility the remains found at the burial site are those of one of the ten knights, or someone else for that matter."

Noble bit down on his lower lip. "Am I supposed to jot this down?"

"No, I'm just thinking aloud. But here are the questions I'd like you to put down for follow up later by me, or DeAnn and her staff."

"Go ahead. I'm ready."

"One. Double check the source of the lighter GeeJo used for the Molotov cocktails. Was it the same one found by you in the aircraft, and did it originally belong to the coastwatcher?

"Two. Check Japanese war archives to see if they lost a gunboat on the Sepik River as described.

"Three. While we're at it, see if any members of the Tanaka family—Kioko, Kioko's son Kazuo, Taro or Jiro ever turned up in post-war Japan. Oh, yes, add Lt. Michio Mori.

"Four. Have Australian authorities at Brisbane check their files for radio traffic between their coastwatcher in Mendam and any other headquarters, so we can authenticate the messages Kioko said she found in the coastwatcher's refrigerator. Preferably we need to know what the call sign 'AMC' means, and if they have it, who it was assigned to.

"Five. Have DeAnn double check on the distance from Komo to the mouth of the Sepik River and the traveling time between the two. My calculations indicate that it was 400 miles one way and could take anywhere from 26 days to two months at a rate of 7.6 miles per day.

"Six. DeAnn might want to check out the name of the Riami warrior GeeJo and Kioko saved and whether he's still alive and available for an interview.

"Seven. Is there any trace of the binoculars taken from the boy Taipe?

"Eight. What happened to the radio equipment? Did they leave it at the coastwatcher's station, or did they bring any of it back with them?

"Nine. Inquire whether or not GeeJo was ever referred to by any other name, perhaps by MilkEye. Even a nickname might link him to a survivor of the B-24, namely, U.S., TKO, Sharpshooter, Deep, Toggle Joe or Pip Patterson."

Stanek paused, stroked the scar on his cheek again and said, "I've given you all I can think of for the moment. Wait, there's one more thing, but I'll have to check it out myself. It's a dim recollection in my memory, something the boy Taipe said about a round house being easy to sweep clean. For the life of me, I don't know where it came from. If you could make a copy of these notes for DeAnn, I'd appreciate it. Nobody has to know they came from me. I'd like to take them with me when I leave."

"Can do," said Noble. "But, mate, let me pick yer brain for a moment. If ye were to give yer best estimate of what happened to the 'Ten Knights on the Barroom Floor,' and all the other subsequent horrendous events followin' in its wake, what would ye say?"

Stanek thought for a moment. "The downed aircraft certainly has some impact on the mystery that surrounds Mount Bosavi. Something is still being concealed by whoever is behind the murders, perhaps even including the 1951 massacre, which Kioko might've believed her husband had a hand in. Right now, I'm sorry to say the leads point to your friend Mackelwaite if he's still alive. If he should be involved in illegal gold shipments, he has the best motive to keep a lid on things here and wherever the gold ends up. The murderer, whoever he is, is racing against a deadline to get as much gold out of the country as he can before the Papuans get their independence in 1975 and clamp down on their resources. Knowing this timetable is an advantage to us if this theory is correct. We know how much time is left to solve this case and can expect him to try to adjust his own schedule. A slip-up usually occurs under pressure."

Noble shook his head. "I'm sorry to hear the finger points to Angus. But I tell ye, man, if he lays a finger on DeAnn, I'll kill the bastard myself."

"With you, MilkEye and WonTok at DeAnn's side on the journey up country, I'm sure she'll be well protected. Major Yowell will be flying your group to the burial sites, with airstrips near most of them. I've got the feeling, like you, Yowell would lay down his life for DeAnn as well."

"What about ye, lad? I've seen the two of ye together. If DeAnn had her druthers, she'd just as soon have ye at her side as any of us."

"Bellicosi and other circumstances have made such a wish impossible, even if I were fit. One more thing before you go. Something else came to me when you were talking about the people who care for DeAnn. The old gardener Hanzo cared for Kioko. It'd be very beneficial to this case to see if he is still alive and living in Angoram. If Kioko kept her promise to bring a poem written with the brushes he'd given her, she might've contacted him, and thus he might be the best source to finish her story."

"Doc, I don't mean to go soft and mushy, but yer the brightest bloke I've ever met. And whatever happens, I'd like for us to be friends, even if it leads Angus to the gallows. Get well. Keep in touch."

"Thanks for the compliment, Roger. I intend to do both things. You're my main conduit to DeAnn. I wish you both well on the journey north from Mount Bosavi."

After Noble left, Stanek's mind switched to what lay ahead. The hospital stay would give him time to review his cancer research study notes and perhaps to see his adoptive mother one more time. Of course, it would mean going through Catherine again. Catherine. With all he had to work on, there was no way he could avoid his adoptive sister. She came with... no, she owned (in a sense) the territory about to swallow him up.

Oh, well, there was a bright spot on the horizon. A meeting with Lt. Dunbar was sure to bring the Haveland murder case closer to its conclusion, perhaps bringing his own unknown assailants to justice before they struck again. He knew they would never give up, nor would he until he figured out where every piece of the puzzle fit.

MEMORANDUM FOR RECORD
SUBJECT: Fraternization Fallout

The following correspondence exchange between Major
Frank Yowell and Dr. DeAnn Toland was intercepted for
General Bellicosi's file:

Frank Yowell to DeAnn Toland:

I know. I know. It was wrong to trade tobacco to
the natives for gold nuggets. I know how touchy you
and General B are about "quid pro quo." General B has
already reprimanded me, and I promised to cease and
desist. Can you forgive a sorrowful, lonely soldier?
I hope my apology will bring us back together as we
sip tea and read the love story you wished to share
with me. We had some pretty special "simpatico" going
on between us before all these interruptions.

DeAnn Toland to Frank Yowell:

You sure gave me a Texas tall tale about trading
with the natives for arrowheads for your nephew. Can
you tell me how you expect me to trust you when you
deliberately deceived me?

> Antonio Bellicosi
> Brigadier General, USA
> Casualty Operations Branch,
> Pentagon

PURSUED:
TEN KNIGHTS ON THE BARROOM FLOOR

Mel R. Jones

PART FOUR:
DANGEROUS DÉNOUEMENT

"Rise brave knights from the barroom floor
After a sortie from hell in your B-24.
Now heaven bound, ten souls doth soar,
Once the last knight out has closed the door."

43 COLE'S CONFESSION

Baltimore, Maryland, 1973

IN THE LONG DAYS and nights Emerson spent in his hospital bed in Johns Hopkins, no visitor cheered him more than Lt. Sam Dunbar of the Baltimore Police. Dunbar came three times a week to update him on progress in the Haveland murder case. Much to the chagrin of Catherine Stanek, the detective stayed more than an hour at each visit. She tried to persuade her brother to give his mind a rest along with his body. Emerson knew she really wanted to steer him toward the investigation she had conducted on her adoptive brother's origins.

After a month and two successful operations, he was able to walk on his own, and he and Dunbar, to avoid Catherine, strolled the garden overlooking Fells Point where he had played as a child. Here among the box elders and dogwood now showing their fall colors, he would encounter Jim Cole propped up in his wheelchair, soaking up sunshine, while LikLik and her new friend played nearby. As the children played among the shrubs, they brought a smile to the old reporter as they did to Emerson. Cole was in the late stages of the disease devouring him one organ after another as it metastasized throughout his system. Stanek tried to look for some hopeful signs in his friend, but none appeared. Cole's weight had dropped to below 100 pounds, and Stanek knew the trend was in a downward spiral at this point. Yet Cole tried to be cheerful as his pain increased. The two men set a date at Cole's urging for a meeting in Cole's room. Both knew it might be the last time.

"There's a matter I need to clear up before I go," Cole said. "It should help your investigation."

Stanek would've pressed Cole for more information, but Catherine arrived without calling beforehand, as was her custom. She insisted they meet in private, and she led him to a bench in the garden they had shared as children. He did promise Catherine he soon would visit his adoptive mother at Phipps. Here again, he insisted he go alone and at the time of his choosing, not Catherine's. The one concession he made to her was to hear her out on Patricia Stanek's obsession relative to the ditty on William Welch:

No one knows what Popsy eats,
No one knows where Popsy sleeps,
No one knows whom Popsy keeps, but Popsy.

Catherine threw her head back so that one of her golden ringlets almost brushed against his chin. "I know everything about Popsy, and why the ditty drives Mother up the wall."

Emerson drew back. "With so much going on in the world, you've still got this nonsense on your mind?"

"Oh, yeah? What if I told you the great pathologist, albeit great womanizer as well, Dr. William Welch, was your paternal grandfather!"

Emerson felt his jaw slacken, though he tried to conceal it by stroking the scar on his cheek. "Popsy?"

"Don't you see what this means, dear brother? Your roots are in pathology. You're already part of the dynasty mother and father, God rest his soul, wanted to create by bringing you into our family."

He tried to look disinterested, but she continued. "Remember all the stuff Mother spouted in this very garden, our special spot, about Zelda? Mother's dearest friend, Meredith Rhodes, was whom Mother really visited at Phipps, not Zelda Fitzgerald, a figment of her imagination. But get this, Meredith was secretly married, and the marriage was annulled after, rumor has it, she became pregnant. Meredith Rhodes—whatever her married name was—is your mother. And I've good reason to believe her husband, the bastard child of Welch, is your father."

Catherine held two fingers apart and went on. "I'm this close to finding out."

Emerson threw up his good arm. "How can you believe I care about this soap opera you've concocted? I liked you better when you were only after my beekeeper cancer study. Besides, what does any of this have to do with your mother's schizophrenia?"

"You doctors are dense in such matters. Listen to me. Meredith's husband, probably Welch's son, was mother's former lover. Mother's complicity in this cover-up fuels her illness."

"Have you told this to her psychiatrist?"

"No, like you, he'd brush it off as unscientific. But there's one way we could find out for sure."

"What're you suggesting?"

"Ask Mother. Ever since your visit, she's been asking about you. I think deep down she knows you're Emerson, the boy she took from the orphanage to save her friend the shame and assuage her own involvement. But whatever you do, don't mention Popsy. You've seen the response his nickname triggers. Welch, in her mind, didn't come forth and claim his own son. My father was a surrogate for both your father and grandfather. This information ought to make you see Rufus Stanek in a more kindly light."

"We both know why he threw me out."

"But Mother doesn't, nor am I willing to tell her if it could be more than she can bear. Maybe as she clings to sanity, she'll find one lucid moment to speak to you as the son she loved. I know her. She has a strong will to set things right between you."

Emerson knew there was no more for either of them to say on this matter, and he welcomed the tall, lean figure of Lt. Dunbar coming up the path. "Excuse us," he said.

The detective got right down to business. He sat in the seat Catherine had vacated, laid his briefcase across his lap and rested his elbows on it. He clasped his fingers together and touched the tip of his wide nose with the steeple he had formed. "How right you were about the *D'Albertis*. She's of Philippine registry. The vessel pulled double duty before and after the war. The Japanese shipped their American prisoners from Manila to Tokyo in her hold. After the August 15, 1945, surrender of Japan ending hostilities in the Pacific, we used her to ferry Japanese POW's captured in New Guinea and the Philippines to Japan for repatriation."

Emerson leaned forward. "Once the *D'Albertis* leaves Daru, is Tokyo her last port of call outbound?"

"Nope. Manila's her last stop. Then she turns around and heads back to the New Guinea port."

"So the ship off loads the salt in Manila? It doesn't make sense. Why New Guinea salt for the Philippines which is surrounded by salt water?"

"Sorry to say, Interpol searched her thoroughly in Manila. No sign of the salt bundles, nor was any smuggled gold discovered. We've reached a dead end."

"My informant carried the bundles on board himself."

"A native?"

"Why should it make any difference?"

"Doc, you told me yourself Papuans are prone to embellish their stories and tell you what they think the white man wants to hear."

"Except in this case, the information was passed to a trusted tribal leader, a man named MilkEye. Papuans pay a severe penalty for lying to one's chief. Besides, what did anyone have to gain by concocting a false story?"

Dunbar threw up his hands. "Beats me. You're the one who spent the last few months observing their culture. Your word is as good as gold, and if you say it was on the ship, when it left New Guinea, I believe you. But since it didn't show up in Manila, there's only one conclusion..."

"Absolutely, Sam. Now what're you thinking?"

Dunbar smiled. "Between Daru and Manila, the cargo in question must've been off loaded and transferred from the *D'Albertis* onto another vessel."

"Bound for where? Any ideas?"

"My stars! We could find out easy enough. Interpol could put one of their agents on board from the Daru to Manila leg and see what unfolds."

"Good. Then you'll get back to me ASAP?"

Dunbar's smile shifted to a wide grin. "Don't I always? My wife's beginning to complain about the time I spend here at Johns Hopkins. Now doesn't it beat all? She thinks I'm having an affair with a nurse."

Stanek grinned and the crescent-shaped scar all but disappeared in the folds of his cheek. "Want me to write you a note?"

"No. But speaking of notes, as I passed Mr. Cole's hospital room on my way to the garden, he flagged me down and asked if I would give you this paper."

"I didn't know you two knew each other."

"Oh, yeah. The reporter watches me come and go and knows we meet frequently."

Stanek excused himself and unfolded the paper the detective had handed him. It read:

```
Emerson, urgent I see you. Not much mileage left
on this old frame. Would like an update on the ten
knights case before I go. There's something I want
to tell you to shed light on your investigation of
same. Come soon. Jim
```

Stanek folded the paper with one hand and stuffed it inside the sling enfolding the other. "Anything else, Sam?"

"Yes, sir. Again, speaking of notes, yours to Mrs. Haveland paid off handsomely. I brought along the charts and dental films Dr. Haveland was studying at the pathology building right before he was murdered." Dunbar paused and reached into his briefcase. Then he continued, "Got 'em. Right here in the purple folder, just where you thought they might be."

"May I borrow the evidence for a couple of days? I'll ask the forensic dentist here to review it with me."

"Sure, Doc. We're in this case together. One more thing before I go. The wrestler with the ugly pockmarked mug who showed up at your hospital in New Guinea gave the police there the slip. He may try to get at you here at Hopkins like he did Dr. Haveland."

Stanek swallowed hard. "I'm sure the around-the-clock security you've posted will keep me safe."

"My stars, man! They aren't my people. Your sister hired them. Specially trained Pinkerton guards, I hear."

Stanek watched Dunbar retreat from the garden. "Pinkerton!" he exclaimed to himself. Every time he made headway from darkness into light, Catherine interfered. He remembered what her mother had said to him on his last visit, "We are but vanishing points in the midst of a painting of infinity." If so, Catherine and her meddling always brought him back to the world she controlled.

Perhaps the whole New Guinea experience was an insignificant occurrence. Yet, Kioko's journal and DeAnn's kiss seemed more real than any experience he had ever had with Catherine, including the singular event which had tarnished his reputation. Before the ten knights case, such psychological insights into his own nature would have been impossible. Now he feared scientific reasoning had vanished, replaced with a deeper understanding from some unknown source.

Surely these were crazy thoughts buffeting him to and fro. Catherine's injustice, hypocrisy and the wanton arrogance of her world were all he knew, and now, if she was correct about his heritage, these negative traits were in his bloodline as well. As much as he despised his adoptive sister's constant meddling and her obvious attempts to rob him of the one thing which could restore his reputation—the beekeeper cancer study—perhaps he and Catherine were shackled together by their past, marching toward the same vanishing point. If so, he must remember to treat Catherine more civilly the next time they meet. For the moment, he had to attend to Cole's request for a meeting he expected would pass for a deathbed confession of what Stanek had already uncovered.

*   *   *

Cole's room had the look, feel and smell of a death chamber, so familiar to Stanek from his residency at Johns Hopkins. The reporter's bed had been cleared of the equipment one usually finds available for an emergency resuscitation, should a cardiac infarction occur before the cancer did its job.

Instinctively, Stanek felt Cole's pulse and noticed how weak and erratic the heartbeat had become. His skin was blue and white with no pink patches whatsoever, and it felt as dry and leathery as a piece of beef jerky. The air in the room held the peculiar odor Emerson always associated with toadstools or some other decaying fungus clinging to a rotten log. Cole could expect only hours or no more than two days left in his life as his vital signs suggested.

Nonetheless, the reporter mustered a cheerful greeting in a voice higher in pitch than usual owing to the oxygen fed through his nostrils. "Emerson, thanks for coming. Wouldn't happen to have a dose of the miracle drug you gave me back in New Guinea, would you?"

"As a matter of fact, I do have enough left for one treatment, but in your condition..."

"I know I'm too far down the road. Save it for LikLik's little girlfriend, Margaret. She's trying to hang on to see her daddy safely back from Vietnam."

"We'll see, Jim. Why don't you save your voice? I know why you sent for me."

"Thought maybe you had figured it out by now. Nice of you to come and help me purify my soul by repentance, confession and communion."

"Communion?"

"In readiness for my tardy meeting with the ten knights who brought us all together. But tell me, what was the tip-off, Doc?"

"A number of things."

"I'm listening."

"First thing, the lower teeth on one side of your mouth are worn down and yellowed, sure sign of a heavy pipe smoker. Second, there was your reaction when handed the pipe smoker's Zippo lighter and the pilot's log. Remember? Seeing one or the other, or both, shocked you enough to cause fainting. And then there was the manner of your speech. On occasions you lapsed into Australian idioms.

"Fourth, and probably the most important clue of all, was the reading to me by our mutual friend, *Kiap* Noble, of a journal penned by a Japanese woman. In her last segment, she described her visit to the coastwatcher's station at Mendam where she found three messages the coastwatcher had left behind for anyone who might replace him there."

Cole's voice choked like someone close to tears. "For reasons I'll explain later, I was determined to ferret out the six-volume Japanese woman's story from someone connected with the ten knights case who was familiar with what Kioko had written. But I interrupted you. Tell me, was this the clincher?"

"Yes, my friend. The messages found at Mendam by the Japanese woman bore the call sign 'AMC.' Only yesterday, in answer to a query I had given him, I received confirmation from *Kiap* Roger Noble who checked coastwatcher records for me. The records revealed 'AMC' translates to 'Anna Marie Cole.' Noble explained that during the war it was customary for coastwatchers to use the initials of their wives or sweethearts as their teleradio call signals. Mind telling me who Anna Marie Cole was?"

The tears flowed down the reporter's cheeks and collected among the plastic tubing until Cole lifted the oxygen line and brushed them aside. "Anna Marie was my late wife. She was killed in a plane crash before I took up my post in Mendam.

"The day the crippled B-24 passed over my station heading west up the Sepik River, I had orders to vacate my post immediately for a new assignment. So I bugged out. I didn't have time to mount a rescue party before I was scheduled to evacuate; nevertheless, I always felt derelict in my duty and should not have waited so many years to follow up on any possible survivors."

Stanek patted his hand. "From what I've learned, even if you had mounted a search and rescue operation, it wouldn't have saved them. The crew flew many miles from Mendam before they reached the Southern Highlands District and crashed on Mount Bosavi. On foot, there is no way you would've been able to make contact with even one of the survivors. However, one of them did attempt to make contact with you. He accompanied, indeed led, the Japanese woman to your station at Mendam. There're still some loose ends in the story maybe you can tie up for me."

"Go ahead, Doc. I'll try my best."

"Your lighter. How do you suppose it ended up in the severed hand found by Noble when he discovered the B-24 wreckage?"

"First, tell me how you're certain it's my lighter."

"I'm not positive, but there're some clues pointing to you. First, note the initials inscribed on one side of the lighter are 'OCS' with no periods separating the letters. So it rules out 'Oscar Carlos Sanchez,' the pilot, also a graduate of the 'Officer Candidate School,' or 'OCS.' Sanchez's nickname was 'OCS', pronounced 'Ox'. Further, you'll agree neither 'OCS' or 'Ox' is a proper acronym. None of the teeth recovered from the B-24 crew show the wear and tear one expects to find from a pipe smoker. So we must search elsewhere for the owner of the lighter.

"The next logical suspect was a missing patrol officer named Angus Mackelwaite, a friend of *Kiap* Noble's, who, by the way, also smoked a pipe according to Roger. Angus and Roger served together in what was then known as the 'Officer Constabulary Service', but the insignia worn on their lapel had periods between the letters 'O.C.S.' I thought we had our suspect nailed until Noble pointed out another group used the same initials. But to distinguish it from his organization, the other group dropped the periods in between 'OCS,' indicating an 'Official in the Coastwatcher Service'.

"Here again, this all sounds confusing until one examines the message inscribed on the lighter. It is the same message as the inscription on the sundial outside this very hospital. On our first meeting, I noticed you had some sentimental attachment to the spot. Also, you wisecracked about the lack of corners for gathering dust in Billings Hall. When I read in the Japanese woman's log about the coastwatcher's round hut at Mendam, kept clean by the house boy Taipe, I later saw a possible connection. Taken together, I'd say you had more than a passing interest in the area around the sundial at Johns Hopkins. Mind filling in the blanks for me, Jim?"

"You'd make a great investigative reporter if you ever left pathology. Maybe, in turn for my cooperation, you'll publish the story I was promised by General Bellicosi. And the truth shall set us all free. As to your direct question, my father, an immigrant from Australia in the 1900's helped erect the sundial in question. He was an engineer and also worked side by side with American Army Engineer, Colonel L.J. Sverdrup, in building the airfield at Goroka where my family lived. The inscription on the sundial was a favorite of Dad's, and when I finished coastwatcher's training, he gave me the inscribed lighter as a graduation present."

"Well, I've about summed up your involvement as far as I can see, but I'm still left with the puzzle as to how exactly did the lighter end up in a severed hand? And whose hand was it, and what was the fate of the man with the severed member? We know the lighter was mentioned in Kioko's log when the American called GeeJo found it at the coastwatcher's station."

With some labor, Cole managed a smile, the first since the conversation began. "Now here's what I alluded to earlier when I inquired about what the Japanese woman wrote. You may have noticed I used the woman's name before you expressed it. I'd like to think my powers of observation and detection match yours, but I know you were just being kind in letting me think my concentration held a torch to yours. Now, Doc, I've written down the story about how I came to know the Japanese woman we all call Kioko. It's all here in this envelope on the bed."

"Jim, I think you're way out ahead of me on this matter. Help me to catch up. How in the world did you come in contact with

Kioko and her story beyond the information contained in her last log entry? "

"Which was?"

"Kioko's alleged American husband and his native followers had just blown up a Japanese patrol at Marienberg on the Sepik, southwest of your station, when Kioko saw her husband commit battle actions as cruel and ferocious as any her people had mounted. She saw him kill unarmed Japanese soldiers in cold blood, and this discovery turned love to fear for her and the American's child she was carrying. She must've been too distraught to go on, for this is where her journals end—close to where they began."

"There's much more to her story, Doc. It's all in this document. Call it my last confession. I'm afraid I'm too exhausted to even try to summarize it for you ahead of your reading of it. Please know these disclosures are a great relief to me as I wrap up my unfinished business."

"Anything else I can do for a man who saved my life?"

"My faith tells me this is not the end. We're all 'knights on the barroom floor,' hopefully to be lifted up when we close the door on this life. But if I'm allowed to split a metaphor and quote Homer and the other tragic poets regarding our worldly experience, 'Like the leaves of the forest, so are the generations of man.'

"There are two last favors I'd ask you to do for me, Doc. Both may seem trivial, but the leaves quote reminds me I promised my fellow sufferer I'd help her solve the puzzle as to why leaves fall, like the hair has fallen from her head. You're far better at this kind of thing than I'd be. Please tell Margaret your thoughts about this, but don't make it too scientific."

"I'll try. What's the other request?"

"This one's not as trivial as I thought. After I'm gone, and all the knights have been found, if per chance they're buried together, slip my old lighter into the ground with them. In this way, part of us will have come together at last. Oh, yes, wait. There's one more thing. Go easy on Bellicosi. He means well, despite his methods, and were it not for his efforts, we wouldn't be paying so much attention to the fallen. That's about it, except as we Aussies would say, 'Cherio, mate!'"

Stanek noticed Cole appeared more at peace than he had ever seen him before. Gone was the anxiety of the reporter hell bent to wrap up his story at any cost. He recalled the contempt he had felt for the man and his profession at their first encounter. He had been very annoyed and impatient when Cole had needled Tom Haveland about the ten knights case as Stanek and his colleagues stood around the sundial pondering the inscription thereon. He remembered also thinking that Cole was a fighter but his fevered quest was greatly compromised by a body which devastating cancer had rendered uncooperative.

In the closest thing to a prayer he had uttered since the age of 17, the pathologist leaned over the dying man and whispered, "Farewell, Jim. May your faith carry you to whatever destination you have in mind. And if it'll help your cause, I bear witness you were a good and courageous man, deserving of better circumstances than those you received along the road. You tried to set right what distressed you most, and to the best of my ability, I'll carry out your last wishes. I owe you as much and more."

Stanek took up the large brown envelope Cole had laid across his chest. He continued, "If this is what I think it is, Jim, you'll have brought us ever closer to identifying survivors, or at least one of them, namely, the one Kioko called her husband whom you knew about all along. And perhaps your information will help us catch up with the perpetrator, or perpetrators, of some hideous crimes. Thank you again for saving my life. I'll see to it this information is shared with DeAnn Toland. I know if she were here, she would wish you God speed."

Cole turned his head and smiled, and from some unknown source found the energy to speak. "Thanks, Doc."

"For what?"

"For the extra time. You and I, and the rest of the good guys, made one helluva team. Wish I could be around for the finale. Don't worry, though. In my report to the Man Upstairs, I expect to tell Him so, and add a word or two about your cancer research. We'd best get crackin'. One can't be late for one's own destiny."

There was nothing left to say. With head bowed, Stanek left the room, turning for a moment at the doorway to smile at the reporter. Moments later, inside his own room, he set a chair beside the bed, opened Cole's envelope, spread out its contents and began to read.

44 COLE'S MANUSCRIPT

Baltimore, Maryland, 1973

JIM COLE'S MANUSCRIPT:

THE FOLLOWING EVENTS occurred in 1953 when I returned by Catalina flying boat to the coastwatcher's station near Mendam in northeastern New Guinea, a post I had manned for over a year during the war. I had hoped to find Taipe, a native lad, who not only served as my house boy, but who had also helped me report on Japanese movements in and out of their large airdrome at Wewak. Taipe assisted me in my secondary mission as well. We searched the skies daily looking for damaged allied aircraft whose crews might need to be rescued. I had a few native scouts posted along the Sepik River east of Mendam, where it empties into the Bismarck Sea, to report on traffic moving inland as well.

To the southwest of Mendam, Taipe and his friends helped me keep tabs on a small inland Japanese "rest and recuperation" area and a small medical facility at Angoram. We knew the Japanese maintained a radio station for broadcasting propaganda at Angoram, but this had nil strategic significance. Our main focus was on the brothel and hospital. Troop numbers and their disposition at the so-called comfort station was a good barometer of how the enemy was faring in the war. Fewer battle-tested troops at the brothel meant the Japanese were hard pressed to spare time away from the island campaigns and almost daily bombardment waged against them by the Americans.

Conversely, as the casualty ratio increased at the Angoram medical facility, we found fewer soldiers able to return to combat duty. This intelligence was passed to higher headquarters along with any sightings of allied aircraft in distress. It is in the latter regard, at least in one incident, I did not fulfill my duty. Instead I left my post without obtaining further information on an American B-24 bomber that flew over my station in mid December 1943, between 1 and 2:00 p.m. Is it any excuse to say I had been called away to assist in the landings south of Hollandia where the local forces were unfamiliar with the people and terrain, and a boat was waiting to pick me up? Perhaps, but I have regretted it ever since.

My main reason for returning to my old station near Mendam ten years later was to find Taipe. I wanted to ask him if he had heard over the jungle grapevine what had happened to the damaged bomber I had failed to take action on and whether or not there had been any survivors. A man who knew Taipe gave me the following information.

Native informant's story summarized:

Just a year or so after the coastwatcher had left the area, two other whites came to the station, a *masta* and his *misis*. (Here my informant pinched the side of his eyelids to indicate a Japanese woman.) With them were five or six warriors from a far off place. Taipe came to our village and asked if any of us would help carry part of a radio from Mendam to Marienberg where they had hidden canoes. The American would pay us with shiny brass armbands he had made, Taipe said. During the night, an enemy gunboat motored past Mendam on a food foraging raid of native villages. After it passed, a third white joined up. (Here the informant pinched his eyelids together again.) This was another *masta*, but very unhappy.

Because of the sighting of the gunboat, we departed abruptly without the radio parts but with other supplies left by Taipe's *masta*, and marched toward Marienberg. The American pilot wanted to save the Chiami natives he had left there with the canoes, and he showed us how to attack the gunboat if it proceeded up river on the Sepik from Marienberg toward Angoram. We arrived before the gunboat party finished its raids. When it turned around at Marienberg and began the return down the Sepik River toward the Bismarck Sea, we knew

456

all would soon be out of danger. But the unhappy *masta* alerted the gunboat to our hidden position, forcing us to attack. Taipe was killed in the ensuing battle, and all the men from our village ran away. We came back later to get Taipe's body to take home for a *singsing*.

I thought my informant had finished, and I expressed my deep sorrow for the loss of Taipe. But, as the man shook his head furiously, I knew there was more before he told me.

"Hear me, *masta*," he said. "One week before you come this time, me see *misis* again." (He repeated the now familiar eyelid pinch.) "Same *misis* who come here time enemy kill Taipe. *Misis* at market in Angoram with old fellow who look same." (He tried to say 'Japanese', but never quite made it.)

Startled by this information, I proceeded to Angoram by seaplane to find this woman. By afternoon I was sipping tea with Miss Tanaka and an old Japanese repatriate named Hanzo. Miss Tanaka was especially interested in my quest and said so. When Hanzo's maid came to take the blind man for a stroll, Miss Tanaka quickly got on a first name basis with me, as her English was impeccable, better than mine.

I asked Kioko if I could record her story. She assented, and I wasted no time in setting a long reel on my battery-powered machine. She requested I hold my questions until she had finished, because much of what she had to impart was too painful to deal with piecemeal. Charmed by her exquisite beauty and gentle demeanor, I set aside my notebook and journalistic instincts. Instead I listened intently as words fell from her lips as soft as swan's feathers alighting on the microphone I held in front of her. What follows is my transcription of the conversation.

Kioko's dictated story:

Much of what I'm about to say, Mr. Cole, I'm sorry, Jim, augments the six journal accounts which cover my earlier experiences in New Guinea. Since this information has already been given to an Australian government official on Mount Bosavi, I'll not repeat it here. However, should anyone desire to read my complete story, they need only contact *Kiap* Angus Mackelwaite.

Please allow me to pick up the story at a point you might find of most interest. My husband, my brother and I, and a few natives brought with us from Komo, left your coastwatcher's station near Mendam to head back home to our village in the Southern Highlands District. Your native informant at Mendam must've told you about the gunboat attack, still the subject of many *singsings* in this area according to Mr. Hanzo.

The incident changed my life. Thereafter a gulf developed between my American husband and me. Like a sore which refused to heal, this chasm brought more pain and suffering the longer it was allowed to fester. The wound dug so deep, I was unable to continue my journals. But now the time has come to bring my story full circle.

The difficult trip back from the gunboat tragedy to Komo went without further incident, except to say it was more tiresome on two accounts. First, my child called to me from the womb to slacken the pace for both our sakes.

Secondly, but more importantly, as I have said, the estrangement from my beloved husband GeeJo continued to grow. We both tried to put the gunboat incident aside and rekindle the fire which had forged us into one heart beating in unison and one soul united in spirit, but we failed. We continued to sleep together openly as man and wife, about which my brother Taro had once objected. But Taro had, through his foolhardy attempt to alert the gunboat crew, forfeited any influence he might have exerted over GeeJo's actions. Like all Japanese in GeeJo's eyes, we were a race not to be trusted. I saw a fury in him reserved for a hated enemy, the same I'd seen in Lt. Mori earlier.

Back at Komo in mid-August, 1945, our son Kazuo was born. I thought his life might herald a new beginning for our little society of refugees, but I was wrong. Taro stood aloof from his nephew, not wanting to have anything to do with a mixed breed child who would only bring shame to our family in Japan. GeeJo either had similar feelings or saw Kazuo as competition for my already waning expression of affection for him. Either way, neither of the two most important men in my life came forward to bond with the child more precious to me than life itself.

When Kazuo was six, a Riami native and three other Riami warriors came to Komo. The Riami of Mount Bosavi are cousins to the Chiami who had taken us in. This native's wife had died, and he had come to her family clan with a bride's price to entice one of the dead woman's sisters to go back with him as his wife. The Riami native's chief was Situmu, the one who had sent warriors to search for Wells, whose bayonet never left the belt GeeJo wore. So, GeeJo hung on the would-be-bridegroom's every word. He became ecstatic when the native told him about the great fallen *balus* on Mount Bosavi. This giant bird, or aircraft, had to have been the size of a bomber to rate such status. GeeJo inquired whether the native had seen any white men come from the great *balus*.

"Yes," he replied. "But me 'fraid of totem on *balus*. Painted face of white spirit keep us away."

At this news my husband wanted to leave immediately for the Riami village, but he decided to wait until the man had chosen his bride, so we could accompany him and the bridal party back to Mount Bosavi.

After a march of many days, we came to the mountain and began the climb up on the north side. As we approached the Rentoul River, we saw the huge, crumpled aircraft with one broken wing laid against the mountain. My husband bounded ahead and disappeared in the wreckage. I stopped in my tracks and drew my son close to me.

"Mother, why are you shivering?" Kazuo asked. "What has frightened you so?"

I dared not say how the remnants of my heart were shattered at the sight of the grinning white skull and crossed bombs I had first seen the day the bombs were dropped on Angoram. Now this image, which had haunted my nightmares, appeared before me as something my husband cheered and I loathed. Taro put his arm around my shoulders to calm me, but I could feel he was shaken as well even before he spoke.

"Kioko, Lt. Mori was right. GeeJo was one of the bandits who struck our village. We must never reveal we know his secret, or he will have us killed to keep from having to pay for his crimes against civilians. Surely no one could label our innocuous operation in Angoram a military target. Only a madman would do such a thing."

"Who is mad, mother?" Kazuo asked.

"The whole world, but you will make it better when you are older. I named you Kazuo, 'man of peace'."

On subsequent days, my husband emerged from the wreckage carrying the remains of his comrades. Four or five times he repeated the ritual, tearfully burying the bones in a mass grave near the downed aircraft. My husband wrote a journal of his own on the backs of the charts he had taken from the coastwatcher's station. And without sharing its contents with me, he placed it in a container and buried it alongside the bones. When he had completed his task, he got us all together, including Situmu, and said all the men from his bomber were not accounted for. He wanted to know if Situmu could shed any light on the matter.

Situmu told GeeJo he and his elder son, later killed by the Tugaru, had discovered four whites after tricking the Tugaru in order to hunt near the peak of the sacred mountain. Situmu explained he had been with Jack Hides' party, the first white man to come into this area, so he could speak the language of the whites, which was pidgin. The following is Situmu's account as I remember it.

Situmu's account summarized:

My son helped me bring four sky people down the mountain, careful to avoid Tugaru eyes along the trail and in the watchtowers. Riami people had never seen white people before, so I knew I must trick them into seeing that this group, who suffered many injuries, meant my people no harm. At night I hid the sky people in the great *balus* and told them I would come for them in the morning. The next day I assembled all of my people around the great bird and sent my three-year-old son Mitu into the belly of the beast. In this way, my people could see if this three-year-old came out safely, they had nothing to fear from the sky people.

We knew the Tugaru would kill the sky people if they found out they had come down from their sacred mountain where they had fed themselves on the pig and other food sacrifices the Tugaru had left for the mountain spirit. The Tugaru had witnessed only the smoke from the cooking fires of the sky people, and thought the smoke came from the mountain spirit who was well pleased with their sacrifices.

We told the whites they did not have time to attend the dead they found inside the *balus*, but must come back for them when it was safer. I ordered all my people to keep their distance from the great *balus* in honor of how the sky people had spared my son Mitu.

But daylight was fast vanishing when I told the whites these things. So as the shadows were lengthening and the last of the people were leaving the place where the great *balus* had fallen, I told the sky people my plan. I would send them down the river in Riami canoes with six of my warriors who would take them to the government station at Nomad. But since they would be entering Giambu country, they must be careful along the Rentoul. But not even one Riami man who went with them down river ever returned.

I heard from my cousins, the Chiami, that near Komo a white man had passed their way, and I sent people to search for the one who had gone north. Only two Riami returned. One warrior found the bones of the white man in a village north of the Chiami, and he buried them at Komo. Until I heard the tales of GeeJo, there was no word of white men except the *kiap*. He made friends with the Tugaru, taking a *meri* for his wife.

Here ends the story Situmu, headman of the Riami people, told us shortly after we arrived in his village. As for the patrol officer, he was a Tugaru ally. We never saw him, until the day I sought him out before leaving on my second trip north. More about this trip later after I tell you why it was important for me to give the *kiap* my record and the events outlined in my six journals. The last was the most chilling of all.

Following the burial, our lives in the Riami village settled into a daily routine under the watchful eye of the Tugaru, proud and powerful traditional enemies of the Riami. Although the two tribes shared the same side of the mountain, the salt-well on the eastern slope belonged to the Tugaru alone. Many skirmishes were fought over this commodity. My husband worked tirelessly to get the Tugaru and the Riami to lay aside hostilities and cooperate in dissemination of the precious salt.

GeeJo met with some success when he persuaded the Riami to move the salt down the Rentoul River in the wider Riami canoes. The Riami were excellent river men and had a lot of experience in transporting cargo. Most Tugaru craft were slender and held up to sixteen warriors ready for battle. Still, there was an occasional killing. My husband was called upon as an arbitrator in extreme disputes. GeeJo tried to persuade the warring sides to accept compensation rather than more killing as was their custom under a system of payback, a ritual long engrained and practiced by both tribes.

When he wasn't holding court, my husband roamed as he pleased, except for three restrictions the Tugaru had placed on my brother Taro, my son Kazuo and myself, as well as GeeJo. Under no circumstances were we allowed to visit the sacred salt well just above the Tugaru compound. Nor were we to scale Mount Bosavi beyond the Tugaru village, or visit the burial stones on the western slope. The well, the burial stones and the higher elevations were spiritual areas of great significance to the Tugaru. Finally, our co-hosts prohibited anyone with white skin, Japanese included, to make contact with the salt train on its bi-monthly journey to Nomad. Taro and I, and my son had no interest in violating the restrictions. But my husband saw things differently. He felt a search for his lost fellows down river outweighed any risk of incurring Tugaru suspicion or anger.

Each day GeeJo grew increasingly restless, and I knew it was only a matter of time before he would once again begin searching for his lost comrades. But GeeJo did take time to participate in some of the rituals of the Riami, such as the initiation of Situmu's only male heir, Mitu, who was eleven at the time. Since he was blind in one eye due to an accident during a war game, there was some question whether he would reach headman status like his father Situmu. GeeJo nicknamed him MilkEye. It afforded him special status since it came from a white sorcerer. MilkEye became his warrior name, and after his initiation, it was the name he preferred.

Riami men were taught to wean themselves from all womanly endearments and influences before they could become warriors. My husband appeared at MilkEye's initiation ceremony when MilkEye drove the mother's blood out through his nostrils to make room for the blood of a warrior.

Nonetheless, this dear "new man" grew fond of Kazuo and me. My tenderness for MilkEye was genuine. He never treated me as inferior because I was a woman. Indeed, despite the taboos against womanly influences, I came to be like a surrogate mother for his own mother, killed during a payback raid along with his older brother. GeeJo warned me not to become too entrenched in native affairs, as it could cause harm if somebody decided to payback a murder committed by MilkEye, killing those closest to him. This advice I didn't obey, as I followed the dictates of my heart.

On one other occasion I refused to honor my husband's wishes when he decided to go down the river in search of his missing comrades. He had intended to take only a few Riami warriors, including the now new man, MilkEye. I insisted he take me, our son Kazuo and my brother Taro with him. We were all family. "Faith has bound us together," I pleaded.

"Too much danger. The Giambu still practice cannibalism. I'll not place my family in danger."

"But there's a government post in Nomad. Perhaps they'll take us in, and we can all be repatriated."

"Not on your life, Kioko. If your people are in charge in Nomad, they'd as soon kill you as me for crossing racial lines."

"Do you think, dear husband, any of us would survive at the hands of the Tugaru without your protection? The Riami themselves are in danger without you to render just decisions in their deliberations."

"Fine. I'll take you, Taro and Kazuo as far as Nomad, but no farther. We'll see whether the Australian *kiap*, who favors the Tugaru, or the Japanese instead, are there to answer our questions. Only now I'll have to take a half dozen or more Riami bow men to protect us along the way."

On the day of departure, rain constantly lashed at our convoy of small canoes, and I was reminded of our journey down and then back up the Sepik. When we marched overland to the coastwatcher's station, we might've been free of New Guinea, except for the gunboat incident and the information GeeJo had discovered there about his lost comrades. The Rentoul, swollen by the rain, was difficult to navigate. We were forced to anchor ourselves against its shoreline and wait until the rain abated in order to swerve safely around the rocks along the course.

People lived widely scattered in this wild plain. Not until our portage in a place called Lower Falls did we see a trace of other canoes or smoke from a settlement. In this land, people over the next hill or down sparse streams were in many cases unknown to each other. The Riami men paddling our canoe kept up a spirited chatter about the people over the next horizon spotted during salt train runs. For Kazuo, this was his first river trip, and MilkEye explained to him all the wonders to be encountered, including the *pukpuk*, or crocodiles, always to be avoided.

We camped near where the Riami told us there was the wreckage of a small aircraft that must have crashed during the war. My husband decided to make camp across from this spot at Lower Falls, and at dawn the next morning, he wanted to search among the debris.

At daylight, GeeJo and four Riami men set out by canoe for the northern bank of the Rentoul. He expected to spend the day searching the vegetation-covered aircraft and scattered debris and then return to our camp at dusk. Before they left, my husband cocked his head to one side and brought his shoulder up to meet it, a sure sign something about the plan weighed heavily on his mind.

"Kioko, you must promise me. Get yourself and Kazuo back to the Riami village if we do not return by sundown. You must pack up and leave immediately. Do not, I repeat, do not build any fires. The Riami men with you will be given instructions to take every measure to conceal your movements and locations."

"Can't we all turn back together?" I knew the moment I spoke it was the question of a frightened woman and mother and bore little weight.

Taro surprised me when he came to my aid. "My sister's right. This is no time to split our forces. We should all cross the river with you, or all together leave this place and turn back."

GeeJo appeared at first as astonished as I was. Then, in the next moment, my husband glared at Taro. "You're in no position to give orders. When I want a Jap prisoner's opinion,

I'll ask for it at the end of Wells' bayonet. You belong with your sister."

Eyes still burning with fire, GeeJo turned toward me. "If you won't listen to me as leader of this expedition, at least follow the instructions of your husband, like you've been taught. Or is it just more malarkey you've been feeding me?"

He did not wait for an answer. A week and a half passed, filled with tears and trepidation, before I laid eyes on my husband again. Only two of the Riami made it back with him— the young warrior MilkEye and his *age-mate* WonTok. GeeJo's eyes were wilder than when he had left us on the Rentoul River. He put down on paper the anger in his heart for my people.

(Here Kioko broke off her narrative and picked up a sheaf of papers she must have had hidden under the table.)

"You must recognize the charts from your coastwatcher's station, Mr. Cole, I mean Jim."

On seeing the tender pity she showered on my old mariner's charts by clutching them first to her bosom, then to her cheek, I could only nod.

"Thank you, Jim, for not breaking your silence."

Her voice, edged with the gold of love, had a slight tremble to it as if she were handling a love letter from the past. She caught herself and turned the charts over and began to read what she identified to me as her husband's account of a massacre.

I wanted to know immediately how she came by the documents and what significance she attached to them. But she was a step ahead of me.

As mentioned earlier, my husband, the American called GeeJo, wrote on the backs of your old charts. He began to keep his own secret journal as it were. GeeJo never confided his musings to me, nor did I ever show the contents of my scribbling to him. But one day he was out searching for his lost comrades, and I discovered quite by accident this account of what happened after GeeJo left my son, my brother and I on the Rentoul. In hindsight, I know he wanted me to find the charts and read them on my own. Since this is not my property to give away, I'll read the contents to you on your recorder so you can better understand what followed in a love that started out so beautifully, yet was reduced to the greatest extremity of distress.

GeeJo's story:

We had just completed a search of the aircraft debris, which was Japanese in origin, and finding no remains, I began to copy lettering on the engine for Kioko to translate once we reached our camp on the south bank. Suddenly, I heard someone calling in Japanese. At first I thought it was Taro disobeying my instructions, but it came from the west. I held up my hand to signal the Riami to drop down in the grass and take cover. We waited.

After about five minutes or so, we heard a new sound, the whacking away of the three-foot tall *kunai* grass growing around the wreckage site. Into the clearing stepped a native holding a machete. He wore an untidy police uniform and carried a rifle over one shoulder. He mounted the wing of the aircraft and looked around. MilkEye next to me whispered, "Bad talk man, *Masta*. No policeman. Giambu come. Better we go."

"Let's see what he's up to." The words had barely cleared my throat when several other Giambu warriors came into view followed by six Japanese in civvies. Behind them I saw two other men in western dress, but I couldn't see their faces. I assumed they were Japanese, and Kioko's people had won the war. Through a gap in the *kunai* grass, we could see how excited the Japs were at finding the wreckage. The civilians took out pad and pencil and camera. The two stragglers remained in the shadows and never joined their colleagues in the clearing. Lucky for them as it turned out.

For the first time, I noticed several of the Giambu carried the .303 Lee-Enfield small rifle, standard issue for police boys serving in the Australian Territorial Constabulary. What were they doing guiding Japs around? It didn't take long for me to get an answer.

Once the civilians had gathered in a circle, to compare their notes no doubt, the Giambu constables crept up behind them and struck each man senseless with the butt of their rifles. As he fell forward, the Jap with the camera, consciously or unconsciously, pitched it under the wreckage. The five other Japs thrashed about and moaned from their head wounds, even as the Giambu bound them head and foot and slung them onto poles like pigs carried off for slaughter. The victims were stunned and not killed outright, an ominous sign. In New Guinea, this is how cannibals insure captured meat arrives fresh in the village.

I waited, expecting the two men hiding in the bush to come to the rescue of their companions, but they turned heel, and as they did so, I saw one of the men holster the .38 revolver he must have had ready for such an emergency. As far as I could determine, none of the Japs taken captive were armed.

After the Giambu had left with their prey, I assembled my Riami followers. I asked for volunteers to help me track the cannibals, explaining my friends from the great *balus* might have suffered the same fate and at this moment were captives in a Giambu village. To a man, the Riami, armed with only bows and stone axes, said they would go with me.

The trail was easy to follow and by midday, the renegade police, as most certainly they were, stopped to make camp and cook a meal. They did not bother the six Japs whom they hung between trees like a hammock. We followed them until they made camp at dusk. We lay still in the grass and listened to the wail of the victims. But even if I was in the mind to help my enemy, there's no way I would do so and place the Riami men in jeopardy. Our biggest problem was our own hunger. One of the trussed up victims still wore his rucksack, and I was certain it contained canned food and rice cakes.

MilkEye, being the smallest in our party volunteered to pilfer the bag once the Giambu slept. He was successful. The best one-eyed thief in the world, we dubbed him. He returned with enough food to keep us going for a couple of days if rationed properly. Since the contents of the rucksack were not divided among the captors and were ignored, this raid had all the markings of a staged murder for hire. Perhaps they were given the guns as payoff. After the food ran out, we confiscated whatever else we needed from the village gardens along the way. We took turns. One man tracked the marauders so we never lost sight of them. Those not tracking cooked food for the next day, careful to build our fires in places where our pursued party couldn't detect the smoke.

As dusk fell on the third day of our pursuit, the Giambu entered a village and were greeted with shouts of joy as the people spotted the Japanese prisoners the warriors brought with them. We watched through the night as the Giambu women brought three large earthen or clay pots into the center of the village where a fire was under preparation. The next morning the whole village turned out, and the pots were made ready to receive the captives.

Nowhere in my travels through New Guinea had I seen such a horror unfold for these six tormented prisoners. Three captives were selected and set beside the pots while the others were brought front and center to see how they were to die as well. After the three victims were placed inside the pots, each was given two bamboo straws. They were ordered to place the reeds in their nostrils. They had their hands tied behind them and were made to kneel so that the bamboo straws lined up with holes in the pot. A bar was placed across the shoulders of each man so he could not stand or reach the lid of the pot as it was closed over them. The only way the victims could breathe was through the straws.

At this point I understood what was about to happen. They were going to ring the pots with fire and slowly roast the poor devils inside. As their death chamber grew hotter, the victim's screams could be heard through their breathing holes. The men seated before this execution could only look on in horror and await their own turn.

Just as the agony reached its peak and the victims inside released their straws hoping to suffocate rather than stew in their own juices, their captors opened the lid, reached in and began to cut off ears, finger joints and other members piecemeal. While they screamed in agony, pleading for an end to the torment, their cries went unheeded. Instead, the cannibals laughed as they sliced off hunks of meat and ate it.

Although they were my enemies, I could no longer stand by and see other humans suffer so. I drew my automatic and ran into the clearing and shot each of the tormented in the head, putting the poor souls out of their misery. I caught the entire village by surprise. They headed for the bush as if some demon had come from the sky and interrupted their feast.

I started to untie the binds of the prisoners made spectators, but I could see they were in no shape to escape. They pleaded with their eyes for me to do what I had done to their comrades before the cannibals came back. I shot each man in the back of the head, then dashed for cover where MilkEye and the others were waiting I could see disbelief in their eyes that I had acted on my own in such a manner. We then hastily withdrew and did not stop until we had put a day's travel between us and the village of horrors.

Still, this was not far enough. When we made camp at night, the five of us were too exhausted to post a guard, although MilkEye volunteered to awaken after a short rest and stand the first watch. Around midnight I was awakened by MilkEye, who said he heard something stirring at the edge of the clearing where we had made our camp. In the next instant a flood of warriors spilled into the clearing.

MilkEye screamed a warning to his three comrades. It was too late for two of them. I heard a sickening crash of an axe against one man's skull. A second later, another lay dead, his body shot full with Giambu arrows tough enough to pierce the fighting shield under which the Riami lay.

MilkEye was the first to react when the attack began. Hunting bow in one hand and a bundle of arrows in the other, he thrust himself in the center of the attack and brought down a number of the enemy before he was hit in the upper part of the arm. Another arrow struck MilkEye in the thigh. WonTok shielded him with his own body as he carried his friend into the bush.

By this time, I had found my automatic, which had fallen from my holster. I fired into the lead group of attackers and saw two of them fall. Those behind them turned and fled. Taking advantage of their retreat, and forgetting our own danger should they return, we sought to recover what we thought to be our wounded, but instead we were greeted with blank stares.

In a tearful ceremony, MilkEye and WonTok cut the index fingers from the corpses, wrapped them in a bark cloth and each placed one in his *bilum*. MilkEye explained in a voice almost too solemn for a boy of his tender age, "*Masta*, we take back to spirit house. All warriors see fellow he got killed in battle."

During the mayhem in the moonlight, I was certain I caught a glimpse of the white men I had seen in the background at the aircraft wreckage on the Rentoul and again at the Giambu village, but for the third time they offered no assistance and disappeared into the bush. Fearing another attack, we couldn't linger to bury our dead, but MilkEye asked if he could keep the *'thunderstick'* lying next to a Giambu slain with one of his arrows. He wanted to place it in the Riami spirit house as a token of our victory. (When we reached the Rentoul, he also asked to take the Japanese camera back to show the elders as well, the camera which had been thrown under the small aircraft wreckage during the attack on the search party.)

When I bound up MilkEye's wounds left by the arrows he had removed himself, he assured me his injuries were nothing to fret over. If the Giambu came again for payback, MilkEye said he would be ready for them. The spirit of the good Two Face had rescued us.

For whatever reason, my husband ended his log at this point after relating these horrible incidents. When I showed Taro this account and explained to him in Japanese what had been written, my brother did not believe the story. He looked at me with those sad eyes of his. "Kioko, this is a pack of lies. GeeJo killed those helpless countrymen of ours. How can we know what he has written is true? Why didn't he bring back the camera or any other evidence, like the notebook, which would show things unfolded as he has written? What good is the word of a man who hates our people? The boy MilkEye is your friend, ask him what GeeJo did to our people."

I promised Taro I would. MilkEye could only confirm the Giambu attack after leaving the village where GeeJo had killed three white men with his small *thunderstick*.

"Not six?" I asked him.

"No, *misis*. Me see *Masta* kill three. Others cook in pot. Make food for bad talk people."

No matter how much I tried to convince myself my husband had told the truth, doubt lingered in my mind about whether or not these were mercy killings. Mixed in with this was the image of GeeJo killing unarmed Japanese men in the battle with the gunboat. It's a few short steps from bombing a village to shooting unarmed soldiers to executing bound civilians.

My misgivings became more pronounced in the following days. Taro came to me and said GeeJo was trying to kill him and make it look like an accident. He feared once he had been disposed of, there would be no one to look after Kazuo and me. I set this paranoia aside until...

45 LETTER OF WARNING

Baltimore, Maryland, 1973

AROUSED FROM HIS READING by the sound of children's voices whispering outside his hospital room, Stanek set aside Cole's testimony reporting his interview with Kioko. He went over to answer a faint but urgent knock at his door. There he met LikLik and her slightly older friend, Margaret.

Each child held a bouquet of mums picked from the garden near Fells Point where he had seen them romp about almost daily whenever Jim Cole was not there to tell them stories. He was reminded of the many times he and Catherine had played pirates there and had brought flowers from the same garden to their mother.

LikLik curtseyed and offered her flowers to him. "Please, for you. Make Margaret better like you do LikLik." She patted her backside, indicating where he had administered his bee serum to her when in New Guinea.

The other girl, a full head taller, even though bald from radiation treatment, stepped forward, curtseyed and introduced herself. "I'm Margaret and my friend LikLik said you can cure people of any disease. My father will pay you well if you can help me fight cancer. Right now, all I have are these flowers. But if you like them, I can bring you more from the garden."

Stanek stroked the scar on his cheek and took some time before he lowered his hand to receive her bouquet. He looked at LikLik. "Someone's been telling tales out of school, I'm afraid, although

472

her English is much improved." He looked back at Margaret, "Where LikLik comes from, many people are thought of as miracle workers. I'm afraid I don't fit this category. I'm sure the doctors and staff here are doing all they can to help you, young lady."

"Oh, yes, sir. They are, but none of them can promise me I can live another month to see my father come home from Vietnam. LikLik and I thought maybe you could help me like you helped her."

"Who is your doctor, Margaret?"

"Dr. Susan Sinclair."

"Perhaps I can have a chat with her about your case. Now, if you young ladies will excuse me, I'm working on some very important matters myself."

Margaret dropped her head for a moment, then looked up. "Mr. Cole said you can answer any question if it is challenging enough. Tell me. Why do leaves fall?"

Stanek grasped her thin shoulders. "Ah, Mr. Cole warned me you would question me about it. But I'm sorry. I haven't had time to give it much thought."

"Perhaps you'll pray about it, and God will give you the answer." She moved over to the window and pointed to the trees in the garden. "Some leaves come twirling down like helicopters. Others come floating down like parachutes. But they never seem to land in the same spot. Then the wind comes and blows them together. I wonder if they recognize each other as falling from the same tree?"

"I can see you've given a lot of thought to this problem. Perhaps we can work on the answer together."

"Oh, I'd like to, Dr. Stanek."

She gave him her room number just as Lt. Dunbar entered the room through the open door. He smiled at the little girls and told them he had just passed the nurses' station. He had heard they were looking for both of them. As the youngsters scurried out of the room, Margaret turned back and said, "I'll tell Dr. Sinclair about you, Dr. Stanek, and, please, think about the answer to my question."

Stanek nodded and then turned to Lt. Dunbar. "Sam, what brings you back so soon?"

"Since I saw you in the garden this morning, I've gotten word from my office that Interpol hit the jackpot. They were ahead of us and had already checked out the lead you gave me before I even suggested it to them. You know, about putting an Interpol agent on the *D'Albertis* on its way from Daru to Manila to see if any salt packages were unloaded in between."

"Great work, Sam. What's the upshot?"

"Well, the bundles had salt in them all right. And they held something else as well, just as you suspected."

"Gold?"

"How did you figure it out, Doc?"

"A lot of evidence points to greed as the probable motive for a number of the murders associated with this case. For now we've got to find out the final destination of the gold smuggled out of New Guinea. Let's hope Interpol traces the illegal cargo to whomever is behind all this."

Lt. Dunbar formed the now familiar steeple with his hands, fingers placed against the tip of his nose. "Well, now, there we might've dropped the ball. Interpol took the smugglers into custody after the illegal transfer took place."

Stanek stroked the scar on his face. "Now we have another problem."

"Yeah, I know. Mr. Big, whoever he is, will know we're on to him and will tamp down his operations, or shut down completely to avoid detection."

"No, I don't think so, Sam. If gold fever and the madness of wanting to drain the last ounce out of the available source has taken hold, like I think it has, the criminal we seek has less than two years to find an alternate route to get the gold out of the country."

"Why two years?"

"Papua New Guinea becomes fully independent in 1975. Surely the new sovereignty will bring with it tighter controls than those exercised by the Australians, who only hold the territory in trust for the time being."

"What do you suggest we do, Doc?"

"Let's wait for our opponent to make the next move when he discovers what has happened to the gold and transfer vessel. I just hope it doesn't involve more murders."

"You think this guy is linked to the Haveland murder?"

"Yes, Haveland, the custodian and Filipino Freddie in this country, and who knows how many in New Guinea. I suspect

Haveland was murdered because he was thought to know something the killer couldn't risk being traced back to him. The custodian was in the wrong place at the wrong time. I believe Freddie and his hoods probably carried out the hit on Haveland. Having botched the job by not obtaining the information needed, and killing Haveland for personal reasons, Freddie was eliminated."

Stanek paused, took in a deep breath and then continued. "Now let's speculate a bit further. Suppose the guy pulling Freddie's strings didn't want Haveland killed, unless he had turned up anything in his investigation of Freddie connecting the gangster with the smuggled gold from New Guinea. Now suppose Freddie saw it differently. The assignment to ransack Haveland's office gave him the opportunity to rid himself of a star expert witness in his prosecution. But we don't know why Haveland's teeth with gold crowns were removed. Come to think of it though, in the Philippines, it's not unusual, indeed, it is considered good taste, to have all of one's teeth sheathed in gold, or as many as one can afford."

"My stars! Your description fits Freddie. He even sported gold teeth on his key chain, but it wasn't found with his body."

"Whatever the case, our killer couldn't have been too happy with Freddie's bungling. Nor did he want gold in any manner to come up as a subject, or worse, as a focus of an investigation, particularly when he's in a race with the clock."

"So Chief Gold-Tooth-in-Charge, so to speak, killed Freddie to show others in the operation not to cross him?"

"Yes, Sam, possibly you're right. But, if so, here's where our man slipped up for the third time in the early part of this case. After letting Freddie handle the job, and then coming after me as a possible replacement for Haveland on Freddie's case, he called attention to gold in the manner he disposed of Freddie. Like an ancient king whose thirst for gold never slated, Freddie had the metal which has ruined many a man funneled down his gullet with a molten lead chaser."

"My stars! You're right, and what a horrible way to die, even for a criminal like Freddie. But I'm wondering, if this operation is as far reaching and as organized as you think it is, why can't the place where the gold is smelted in New Guinea be found?"

"Ah, my friend, a good question, and there's a simple answer. Gold melts easily at 1,063 degrees Centigrade. This is well within the range of temperature of primitive cooking fires found all over New Guinea in places like Mount Bosavi from which I recently returned."

"So, they've got a simple way to smelt the gold. But let's back up a minute. I've seen prospectors pan the gold out of rushing waters, so in New Guinea, there'd have to be some sort of equipment to separate the gold from the impurities."

"For alluvial gold, all one really needs is a wool blanket. The gold dust or flakes, being heavier, are captured in the tight curls of wool, while the less heavy material is sifted through. And, believe me, since the white man has been in New Guinea, he has brought in plenty of wool blankets."

"I've got the picture. Then the gold dust or flakes are smelted into nuggets. These are sealed inside the salt balls Interpol found in its search of the transfer vessel."

"Yes, but before we leave the subject of gold, remember what's washed down rivers and streams often comes from a primary vein deposit."

"We could be talking about large vein mining operations, then."

"Indeed, all under the umbrella of a primitive environment and transported in the simplest manner so as not to draw attention over a lengthy period."

"Whoa! We're talking mega bucks! This may be too much for a local policeman to handle. Maybe we'd better call in the FBI or CIA, or somebody with a lot of resources."

"No, Sam, this is your investigation and at this point, there's too much speculation to call in the Feds. Like I said, let's wait and see what our murderer's next move is once he suspects someone is onto his operation. As soon as I get strong enough, I'm headed back to New Guinea to push him along a little faster than even he wants to go. People make mistakes, you know, when in a rush. Meantime, I'll take a look at those dental charts you brought me in the purple folder. In addition, there are a couple of favors I'd ask of you."

"All you have to do is name them."

"At Walter Reed Pathological Center, there's a severed hand found in New Guinea almost two years ago in a wrecked B-24. It should be preserved in formaldehyde, and I'm wondering if you could find out if they've traced the fingerprints. Secondly, short of having it brought here to examine, I'd like to get a photo of the hand to see where it was cut from the arm. I need to determine whether or not the wound left a jagged edge."

"Wow! I doubt if they'd let me in the door over there, much less ask for prints and take pictures of it. Seems like they'd want me to justify my need for it."

"Tell them I've got reason to believe the severed hand's tied into the Haveland murder you're investigating. I won't go into detail, but trust me, Sam. There might be a connection, flimsy as it is. It's worth following up on."

"I'll do what I can."

"Good."

"You said you have two things you wanted me to do. I hope the second is easier."

"It is. I'd like to dictate a letter for you to sign and mail today if you would. Don't worry. It's also related to the Haveland murder."

"Who gets this letter?"

"Dr. DeAnn Toland. Try to get it in the diplomatic pouch for delivery to her at Angoram, Papua New Guinea. If all goes right, she'll be there in a week or so."

Dunbar winked. "What do you want me to say to this lady of yours?"

"Sorry, nothing romantic. Just some unfinished business." Stanek began to dictate:

```
Dear Dr. Toland:
    My name is Sam Dunbar, and I'm in the homicide
division of the Baltimore Police Department. I'm
the lead investigator in the murder of Dr. Thomas
Haveland and a custodian at Johns Hopkins Medical
Center campus. Our chief suspect, a felon called
Filipino Freddie, was also killed.
    A mutual friend has asked me to contact you.
First, he wants to inform you Mr. James Cole is
near death and while still coherent, relayed
information critical to your own investigation.
Indeed, Mr. Cole has turned out to be a key player
in the matter regarding "Ten Knights on the
Barroom Floor." He gave our friend an account of
events in Kioko's life since she left the
coastwatcher's station, as mentioned in her last
journal. Mr. Cole's account not only augments
facts pertaining to the case, but offers new clues
in resolving what has been a series of murders
building one upon the other.
```

Under separate cover, our mutual friend, ever aware of constrictions placed on you by higher authority, will send you a copy of Cole's complete manuscript. Our friend noted that a check to see if the rifle and camera mentioned in the American aviator's account related by Kioko are still in the Riami spirit house would help verify her verbal account to Cole.

What I ask in return is a copy of your observations and evidence gathered on your trip from Mount Bosavi to Angoram. Similarly, I request any transcripts you might produce from your interview with a pensioner of Japanese origin known as Mr. Hanzo, if he is alive and in Angoram. I assure you both your journal notes and the insights Mr. Hanzo might have are essential in helping to solve the ten knights case as well as the three murders I'm investigating here in Baltimore. I appreciate your help in bringing the perpetrator, or perpetrators, to justice.

Finally, our office has received new evidence which, when relayed to our mutual friend, has caused him to caution you not to take a trip to the top of Mount Bosavi because of possible extreme danger. I concur with this warning. Please be so advised until further notice.

Sincerely yours,
Samuel Dunbar, Detective Lieutenant

Dunbar finished writing and looked up from his notebook. "You know, Doc, you might want to reconsider your plan to go back to New Guinea and push our murderer faster than he wants to go. Any mistake made under pressure might very well impact on you, the CIL team and their mission."

"How true, Sam. Although I want to force a head-on collision with whatever evil is afoot on Mount Bosavi, I don't want to place any colleagues in danger as they search the mountaintop for possible remains. I want to be there to help evaluate the situation before any such attempt is made, because the best way is to flush out the murderer before such a trip is attempted."

"Doc, you have to consider how close you came to losing your life in Hawaii and in New Guinea. Our murderer is playing for keeps."

"I may not be safe anywhere, Sam, until this mystery is solved. A little more legwork is needed to bring in our killer."

Dunbar stuck out his hand. "Let's hope so, Doc."

When Lt. Dunbar left the room, Stanek picked up Jim Cole's manuscript. He plunged into the narrative where he had left off when LikLik and Margaret knocked at his door. As he recalled, Kioko had written that Taro believed GeeJo was trying to kill him and make it look like an accident.

46 COLE'S MANUSCRIPT CONTINUED

Baltimore, Maryland, 1973

(Kioko's account to Cole)

...until that dreadful day. How I wish I had taken Taro's report of threats to his life by my husband seriously!

On one of those days when the clouds seemed to cling to the peak of Mount Bosavi, Taro emerged from the bush, spotlighted by a flash of sunshine, which peaked through the overcast. I noticed he was limping. I had just taken some clothes down to the Rentoul to wash them. Kazuo, still wet from playing among the rocks on the shore under the vine bridge ran forth to meet him, but my brother pushed his seven-year-old nephew aside so he would not disturb the gaping wound in Taro's thigh. I tore off a length of damp cloth and began to dress the wound.

"What happened?" I asked.

"Your husband tried to kill me!"

"GeeJo?"

"We were hunting together, and I stopped to brush off red ants attacking the back of my neck. GeeJo took a sharp plant and poked at the devils, which were not streaming up my legs. He claimed it was an accident because I had moved too quickly, but the plant dug too deep in my thigh for me to believe him.

"This is the third time in a month these so-called accidents have taken place. First there were the leeches, so bunched together on my back, I'm sure the American who was walking behind me placed them there. Then, on a narrow pathway, he brushed against me, and I found myself entangled in a cobweb looking like spun glass. Luckily, the poisonous spider had no time to strike before I got myself disentangled."

"Well, it could've been an accident."

"Then why did GeeJo laugh as if this were a joke at my expense?"

"I'm sure if he'd been aware of the danger, he would've warned you away from the web and apologized."

"Ha. Since he has learned our language, he has never offered an apology. And after what I said when he struck me with the sharp plant, I don't expect he ever will."

"Oh, Taro, please let it go."

"Never! He's the enemy and will kill us all if we don't do away with him first."

"Please, brother, don't do anything 'til I've spoken to him about your concerns."

"Ha! And let him think I'm some weak *samurai* who must hide behind his sister?"

I could see the anger and hurt in Taro's eyes and the worry, too. "Please?"

"Alright. Tell your husband what you want. But remind him I still have Lt. Mori's ceremonial sword, and if he wants to do battle man to man, I'm ready."

"You must never go so far."

As promised, I spoke to GeeJo about the three incidents involving Taro. He laughed and mocked my brother. "Poor little brother. Can't take care of himself in the wild. Maybe someone, the Tugaru perhaps, will put an end to his misery. And you can bet I won't come to his aid."

I dared not throw Taro's challenge for a duel in GeeJo's face. The threatening wrath one had for the other made me forsake my mission to bring tranquility into the relationship. In the end, all I could do was cry. After Taro had told me about these incidents, and I had spoken to GeeJo about them, they never hunted together again. Indeed they hardly spoke to one another.

One day, as they took separate paths into the steaming jungle, I noticed Taro was wearing the ceremonial sword. It was certainly not the weapon of choice for bringing down small game when he knew how to use a Riami bow and arrow. But perhaps he was going to use it to cut a path through the jungle undergrowth.

Nevertheless, I left Kazuo in the care of a Riami woman and followed Taro into the labyrinth of vines and giant trees blocking out most of what little sunlight filters through the thick jungle canopy. It had been a while since I'd been in the jungle. The choking humidity and inexplicable sounds heard so often on my long treks, first with Lt. Mori and then with GeeJo, made me turn back to the safety of the Riami village. There one could escape from the crashes, cawing, screeching and sudden rushing in the undergrowth as one type of animal or another scurried ahead.

I was foolish not to persevere. The consequences of giving in to my fears were great. It was three days before I saw Taro again, but he was not alive. MilkEye and his friend WonTok found Taro slashed to pieces in a small clearing west of the Tugaru village. My dear, sweet brother was no more! And, if I hadn't had my child, I might have killed myself rather than face the possibility my husband had killed my brother. From looking at his wounds, MilkEye and WonTok confirmed Taro had fought valiantly for his life, armed with only a ceremonial sword, which they told me was missing. I spent the night weeping over Taro's body, cut almost beyond recognition. I dressed his body for burial.

The next morning GeeJo returned with blood all over his upper torso. He said it was from the animals he had killed, but I noticed some of his wounds were puncture-type, as if inflicted by the sharp point of a sword, or by, as he explained later, sharp plants. Most damaging of all, he handed me the ceremonial sword and asked, "Where's Taro? I found his sword cast away in the bush."

I didn't expect him to mourn the loss of Taro, but I did want him to try to comfort me in my grief. Instead, he sat by himself outside our hut sharpening the bayonet. He did, however, grant me permission to bury Taro along the river a few paces from the grave of GeeJo's comrades. I gathered up everything I could find of Taro's, including Lt. Mori's ceremonial sword and his *senninbari* I had retrieved at Komo. I put it all in the ground with Taro, knowing one day I must come back and bring his remains and all he possessed back to our family plot in Japan. GeeJo knew this was the family custom and said he would honor it.

Afterward, Taro's fears became mingled with mine, and I was afraid Kazuo and I were in danger. A large stone rolled down the hill one day while I was bathing with Kazuo, and it nearly hit us. This intensified my fears, and I didn't know where to turn for help, if, as Taro suspected, this was the work of my husband. Perhaps he wished to be rid of the responsibility of Kazuo and me so he could have the freedom to go looking for his comrades.

But it didn't make sense. If he wanted to kill any of us, he need only slit our throats as we slept, or at any other time we were alone together. Perhaps he was deterred from doing away with us in this manner, however, by his own concern for what the Riami would do to him if he should kill us. The Riami treated all of us as part of the clan, and I felt MilkEye, who was to be headman someday, especially had a fondness for Kazuo and me. Indeed, when Kazuo wandered off one day, MilkEye found him caught in a trap hanging by his legs, and set him free. This was in an area where the Riami had never before placed their snares.

Whenever GeeJo went off, I still had the feeling someone was watching us from behind the grass or above from the limestone outcroppings found throughout Mount Bosavi. I could not trust my husband after he had participated in the massacre of the Japanese civilians down river. Had my husband gone mad?

The last straw came when one day GeeJo accused me of taking Well's bayonet and hiding it. After these incidents had occurred, he went off more often to search up the mountain— territory he had recently viewed with great interest despite the danger of passing the Tugaru village and salt well on the way. While GeeJo was gone, despite my fears about whether an evil presence lurked in the shadows, I let Kazuo play in a garden near our hut with his village *age-mates*. Busy sewing, I heard a terrified cry come from where the boys played.

MilkEye, who was sharpening his axe nearby and heard the scream, was the first to react. He caught Kazuo in his arms, ran a few paces, then collapsed on top of the boy, shielding him with his own body. By this time I had arrived and saw the source of the commotion. There in the middle of the clearing where the boys had gathered only a moment ago was the bayonet of Wells, which my husband had accused me of taking the night before, stuck in the ground. How close it came to striking Kazuo I cannot say, but it was near enough to frighten the poor child and his playmates. Near the bayonet, I saw what had made MilkEye move so swiftly. On either side of the bayonet there were two arrows also sticking in the ground. The arrows had come from the bows of the bad talk people, MilkEye told me later. They had never come to Mount Bosavi before, because, like everyone else, they feared the Tugaru. I thanked MilkEye for plucking my son out of the way of this attack on innocent children, unleashed by evil hands.

When I told my husband about the attack, he expressed his own concern for Kazuo and me, adding hereafter he would be more watchful to safeguard the bayonet. He also said he was sorry to have accused me of taking it. He took me in his arms, and I flinched, but he let it pass. "Kioko, a couple more trips to the mountain, and then I promise you, we'll look for a safer place for you and our son."

To test his sincerity, I asked, "Will you set us free?"

"You've always been free."

"I mean free to go back to Japan where Kazuo can be safe and reared properly."

"To fight against the Americans? No dice."

"The war will have ended, if not already, by the time he would be old enough for the army."

I saw his eyes go watery. "I suppose you're right about the war, but I can't lose both of you."

"Once our son is installed with his grandparents, I'll come back to you. Only let me take Taro's remains and his artifacts with me."

GeeJo laid his chin against his shoulder, the way he always does when he contemplates a problem and is seeking a solution. "Tell you what, Kioko, you leave your brother's remains buried here, so I know for sure you'll come back. Think of it as collateral on your promise."

For Kazuo's sake, I could do nothing other than comply, however much it hurt to return home to my aging parents without either one of my brothers they had sent me to search for in New Guinea. We kissed, and I knew my love for him would never falter. I was ashamed to have suspected him of the tragedies plaguing us.

Still, there was the matter of the Japanese gunboat and then the massacre of Japanese civilians somewhere along the Rentoul River, and perhaps Taro's death as well. I knew GeeJo must face justice for these crimes, one of which I had seen, and the other he had admitted. Because of this, I planned to give my journals, along with the information I had on the crimes committed, to someone in authority. I remembered Situmu had said a patrol officer lived with a Tugaru woman. I believed he would be the one to lift from me the burden I carried. I would have to act quickly and surreptitiously, since GeeJo had agreed to accompany his family to Angoram in two weeks' time. The next morning I sent for MilkEye and asked for his help in making contact with the *kiap*.

On an evening when my husband retired earlier than usual because of a nagging cough he didn't want to spread to Kazuo or me, I left our child in the care of one of MilkEye's young wives, and the two of us set out for the Tugaru compound. After a circuitous route only MilkEye knew how to navigate, we came to the hut of the *kiap*. Sitting in front of his hut, the patrol officer, a thickset man, disheveled and bearded, held a cap in his hand he used as a billow to fan the fire before which he squatted. He scowled at our approach, then cracked a grin, exposing teeth worn and yellowed, no doubt through lack of care and a poor diet.

"Begod, Missy, yer a pretty one and a gentle lady. Anyone can see as much. Where've ye kept yerself?'

I was sure he knew all about us, but I played his game anyway. "We live with the Riami—my husband, my son and I."

I watched his lips tighten as he stared up at me, motionless and expressionless. "Came out here lookin' for gold, eh?"

I felt a touch of regret in confiding in this man who knew very well from my note smuggled to him days earlier by MilkEye what my purpose was. "No, sir, I came to you so a proper investigation into certain events would be conducted by someone in authority."

"Why didn't yer husband come with ye?"

485

"I don't know whether he's involved or not."

"These certain events. Do they involve gold?"

"No, nothing I'm aware of."

"Good on ya. Ye see, lass, some blokes have a nose for where gold's runnin', in a stream or hid in the ground. Once they've found it, ye can't pry 'em away from their claim with dynamite. It's the God's truth."

He stood and yelled toward the hut. "Where the devil's my useless lump of coal? Salty Meri, get yer arse out here and bring a bottle and two of my tin cups."

I shook my head. "No thanks, I don't take strong spirits. Couldn't we discuss what brought me here?"

"Right ye are." Then over his shoulder he canceled the order. "Pull up a log by the fire for a stool. Ye do sit down, don't ye, Miss? Damn my manners. I don't know yer name, much less where ye come from and how ye got to this mountain. I'm Angus Mackelwaite."

I placed my six-volume journal in his outstretched hand. "Kioko's my name. My story's all there in these diaries I've kept from the beginning, except for..."

"The war crimes. Ye wrote about 'em in yer note and really want to talk to me about 'em, eh?"

He set my tablets aside, well away from the fire. MilkEye, who had been sitting motionless in the dark perimeter of the fire, made a move to retrieve the ledgers. I called him back. I never understood why, but when he watched me writing, a special childlike awe filled his face. I suppose he hated to let the books go, as I did. But if none of us were able to make it out, I wanted to leave behind some record of our lives.

Kiap Mackelwaite leaned so close I could smell the whisky on his breath, mixed with the odor of tobacco. I could see plaque had rotted his teeth. "Suppose ye tell me what's not in the books. They'll keep 'til later. Are the crimes in 'em?"

"Only one involving my husband, a gunboat incident near the Sepik River."

"Whew! Out of my jurisdiction, but I'll see the magistrate there gets an earful."

"You've got a magistrate on the Sepik? We thought my people won the war."

Mackelwaite scowled, then grinned again. "Pardon my bluntness, but our blokes drove the yella devils out and then sent 'em to hell with two big Yankee bombs. Yer boys surrendered in '45."

"But in 1951 my husband saw Japanese civilians in New Guinea."

"Whereabouts?"

"Along the Rentoul, between here and Nomad."

"Must've been one of the Nip's search parties lookin' for war dead. It wasn't 'til '51 we let 'em back in, like I said, to recover remains." He paused, then went on. "No doubt this'll be good news for yer husband. If he turns himself in to me, I'll see he is treated well and given a fair trial."

"He'll never turn himself in, no matter who won the war. Not 'til he locates the missing crewmembers from his bomber. You must've seen it along the slope near the Rentoul."

"Indeed, the great *balus* is strong medicine for both tribes in the area. It's the reason I haven't reported the sighting to my superiors yet. No sense destroying their, what ye call it?"

"Their icon?"

"Yep, or totem, of the Tugaru and Riami."

The *kiap* looked at his watch. "Enough chatter for now. Let ole Angus in on the other crimes ye want to report."

I was glad to spend as little time as possible with this creature, so I hurried through my concerns, probably saying more than I intended. I told the patrol officer about the murder of the Japanese civilians GeeJo had admitted to and of Taro's death and all the threats I had felt. My ambivalence as to whether my husband was involved in some or all was shown in my hesitation. Strange, I thought, the *kiap* took no notes, and his expression never changed even though I cried when I had finished.

He offered solace of sorts. "It's got to hurt, rough-tongin' yer own husband, but if he's kilt people like ye say, yer doin' the right thing, bringin' this to the attention of the authorities and all."

I cringed at the thought I had betrayed GeeJo. "They could find him innocent," I said.

"They could, but we won't know 'til we take him into custody. I'll deputize a couple of Tugaru, and we'll do it tonight."

"Oh, you mustn't! I've got to go back to him."

"What?"

"He's promised to take my son and me to Angoram where we're free to go back to Japan."

"Sounds like yer husband, this GeeJo bloke, is a bad devil; not that there's any other kind. Ye'll get kilt, ye will, if ye go back to him. Damn me if I let ye do it!"

I summoned my courage to bluff my way out of this dilemma with the unexpected help of MilkEye, who must have sensed the tension and moved to my side, his hand on his stone axe. "When my husband comes back from Angoram to continue his search, you can arrest him then if necessary. Once I see my son's safe in Japan, I'll come back as well. You'll need a witness. Otherwise, you've got no case, as the things I revealed just now aren't included in my ledgers. There's something else you need to consider, *Kiap* Mackelwaite."

"And what might it be, lass?"

"My husband is a beloved figure among the Riami, as are my son and I. Government or no, they won't stand by and see him hauled away like a common criminal. The people revere him as a soldier-warrior, a god-like figure, one might say, and unless you want war to break out on this mountain, I'd advise you to let him come in on his own."

Mackelwaite looked at MilkEye, then back at me. "Angoram, ye say. Why Angoram?"

"Because I have a friend who might still be there. He's old, but he'll help me secure passage to Japan."

"Angoram. A far walk, I'd say."

"I've done it several times before. It's detailed in my writings."

Mackelwaite shot another glance at the Riami warrior at my side. "Some of the white men who come out here lack the brains of a sheep caught in a snowdrift. They don't last long. But yer husband's a soldier, all right, else all of ye'd be dead by now. Trained hard for jungle fightin' I'd say. If he weren't a suspected criminal, I'd shake his hand, I would."

I made no 'reply, so he tried to elicit one with more questions. "Did ye know there was a clutch of Yankee blokes, who went down with the aeroplane, draggin' about the bush after it crashed? Suppose they're all dead by now. Yer husband hasn't come across any of 'em round about Mount Bosavi, has he, Missy?"

I shook my head, and he started to speak, but his voice died away, and he seemed resigned I'd be leaving with GeeJo. MilkEye guided me back to the Riami village shortly thereafter. All I could think of was the terrible thing I had done. The conversation with *Kiap* Mackelwaite convinced me GeeJo had one more reason to kill me. Other than my role as New Guinea Ginny, there was now this betrayal. If told, he might fly into a rage and take vengeance on Kazuo and me. I couldn't confess these transgressions until I returned to him at Mount Bosavi.

MilkEye saw me to the hut I shared with GeeJo and then left for the men's spirit house. My husband greeted me at the door. Our seven-year-old son Kazuo stood next to him rubbing his eyes. It was too dark to see GeeJo's face clearly, but he was both angry and concerned as evidenced by his tone.

"Kioko, where've you been? I found Kazuo at the hut MilkEye had built for his wives. They said you had gone off with MilkEye. Why?"

I dared not tell him the truth, nor did I outright want to lie to him. I settled on a half-truth, which is still deceit in God's eyes. "I went with MilkEye to secure my books. You know, to safeguard them until my return."

"Why not leave them with the other things in Taro's grave?"

"They're mine, not my brother's."

"I see. You didn't trust them with me. When have I ever shown any interest in reading them? You know I've treated your books with respect—off limits—except to the writer. But I hoped you'd share your thoughts with me some day."

"And I hope to do so, but for now please trust me to handle them in my own way."

"Fine. But promise me you won't go wandering off again without telling me."

"I promise."

"Good. But I've got a secret of my own I can't keep to myself any longer."

Glad for the opportunity to change the subject, I asked GeeJo to tell me. He leaned toward me, and I could see he was smiling. He whispered, "Gold, Kioko! We're rich! I found a stream loaded with it higher up on the mountain past the Tugaru salt well."

"Now you're the one who walks a dangerous path on taboo ground."

"I know, but by the looks of things, I'm not the first white man to have discovered it. Bet the renegade patrol officer living with the Tugaru *meri* got there first. Now you see one of the reasons I've steered clear of him when we found out he'd set up camp in the Tugaru village. Besides, you know I'd never let anyone take me back to civilization before I found my missing buddies. Not enough gold in the world to lure me from this, my sworn mission."

As he spoke, I saw for one brief moment the same look in his eyes Angus Mackelwaite had revealed when he spoke of gold. But in GeeJo, it quickly passed. Then he told me his plan. He wanted me to sew into my clothes and the garments of Kazuo all the gold we could carry. "Two or three more days of prospecting, and we should have enough to pay your passage from Angoram to Wewak, then on to Japan."

I pleaded with him to forget the gold and let us be on our way tomorrow. I told him I had a friend in Angoram who would help us get passage to Japan. He laughed. "Trust me. Having gold will open doors for you. Only you mustn't let anyone know how much you're carrying."

"Let's not take any," I pleaded again.

"Let's sleep on it," he replied.

GeeJo's mind was made up, however, and three days of discussion brought us no closer to resolution, only more nuggets for me to sew into our clothes. When we left the Rimai people, they pulled out their hair and gnashed their teeth as an expression of sorrow. MilkEye and a dozen warriors were our main escorts and carriers of supplies. As we passed through one village to the other, we would pick up local men to guide us to the next village and so on. The rigors of the trip were very hard on Kazuo, who sometimes had to be carried. We made our way once again through grasslands, highlands, jungle, swamp and finally by canoe on the Sepik River to the outskirts of Angoram.

When it was time for GeeJo and the Riami to turn back, MilkEye offered to cut off one of his fingers to show his grief at our parting was far greater than any other Riami. This was an act reserved for a loved one. I persuaded him to accept instead the Haiku verse I had written down for GeeJo and MilkEye had committed to memory. One last time I asked MilkEye to recite it to me. To the amazement of all the other warriors present, MilkEye held up the paper as if he were reading it and began to recite:

The lonely last leaf,
Bridging heaven and the earth.
Carry on, brave knight.

Then came the time I dreaded. I must say goodbye to my husband. I reiterated my promise to return and spoke to him the words of our nuptial night. "Oh, GeeJo, I do love you."

"Then stay," he pleaded.

"I can't. Kazuo deserves better than we can give him in a jungle home, and then there's the danger. As you said once, I couldn't bear losing both of you."

He took me in his arms, kissed my forehead, cheeks and then full on my lips. We held each other for a long time as both our bodies shook with the other's sobs. He broke free, took Kazuo up in his arms and kissed the child on the forehead. "Take good care of your mother," he said. "We'll be together again one day."

Then he slipped into the shadows, followed by the natives, and was gone. Kazuo and I stared in silence into the bush, each of us, I know, was praying he would change his mind and come back to us. We waited until dusk, then set out to search for Mr. Hanzo. Hand in hand, we consoled each other with our tears, and other than the weeping, the only sound heard was the jingle of gold sewn in our garments and the buzzing of the mosquitoes the darkness always brought with it. I felt weighed down by the precious metal, but even more by the dark shadows of fear engulfing my heart. My own transgressions were ever before my sorrowful, tear-filled eyes.

By the time Kioko had finished, we were both weeping. For if anybody could relate to the transgressions in this story it was I, Jim Cole. After we got control of ourselves, Kioko asked a favor of me. She said she was meeting someone in the evening who had agreed to help her get back to Japan. I asked if I could be of assistance. She said her contact had insisted she come alone, since it was forbidden by the trustee government to exchange gold without going through the legal ramifications. She did say, however, she had sent her son to the village of Mr. Hanzo's housekeeper several day's walk from Angoram to ensure his safety and to await her arrival, or the arrival of someone trusted she would send to get him.

She asked if I would play a role in an alternate plan if the prospect she was going to meet proved untrustworthy or unable to deliver. I asked whether her contact was credible or just some native working a scam. She replied, "No, he is white, and has connections, since he sought me out and volunteered his assistance."

I told her not all the white men in New Guinea these days could be trusted, so she shouldn't put all of her eggs in one basket. She smiled and said, "Now you see where you come in, Mr. Cole, I mean Jim. I have with me the gold Kazuo carried in his clothes. I've no idea how much it amounts to, but it must be worth 1,000 or more dollars. I'd like you to hold it for me, so if anything happens to me, Kazuo will still have enough to reach his grandparents at the Tanaka Inn set below Satta Mountain where the Takaido Road bends close to Suraga Bay. It is on the way between Tokyo and Osaka. Mr. Hanzo would need help arranging for his passage."

There is no way anyone, a man at least, could refuse such a request from such a lovely, gentle, woman, especially when one had heard this part of her story. I smiled at her and said, "I'll stay around for a couple of days to see all goes well."

"How kind of you. Thank you for your help," she said.

In hindsight I wish I had insisted on taking this woman and her child to Japan myself. For the next day, the tragic news was spread all over Angoram. A young Japanese woman named Kioko had fallen into the hands of a mob, which had stripped her of her clothing, had buried her up to her chin in a bog and had hurled stones at her head until she died. Witnesses told the authorities the natives had organized themselves to conduct this brutal murder as payback for Kioko having been part of a Japanese force that had burned Angoram during WW II.

I knew better. Her clothes were gone along with the gold sewn into them. At first I thought I should go to the authorities and tell them she had set out to meet a white man on the night she was killed to make arrangements to go to Japan. She intended to pay him in gold. But then it occurred to me I had some of her gold, and the authorities might consider me a prime suspect. I also knew the constabulary in New Guinea had its share of corrupt officials, especially among the native ranks.

So, for the second time in my life I left New Guinea by Catalina boat with unfinished business I will carry to the grave. I had abandoned my responsibility to enable Kioko's son Kazuo to go to Japan, just as I had left my duty to arrange for a search for his father GeeJo and his comrades for the sake of expedience due to personal concerns.

My one bright ray of hope is if you, Dr. Stanek, see to it Kazuo, if he has survived, gets the reward of a mother's love. You'll find the equivalent of Kioko's gold in dollars, which should have accrued a great deal of interest, in an account number 520 in the Sunshine State Bank in Honolulu, Hawaii, in the name of Kazuo Tanaka and James Cole. Enclosed is a signed withdrawal slip left for you to fill in the date and amount. If you learn the boy has perished, please give the money to his family in Japan.

It's my parting wish, Doc. If you can, help me to make amends at last.

47 POEM FOR A PATIENT

Baltimore, Maryland, 1973

S TANEK GRUNTED AND looked down at Cole's transcript spread across his bed and began to reassemble the papers. He had seen a parallel to himself in the remarkable tale spun by Kioko. He felt embarrassed, remembering how his life, too, had had its share of bumps and bruises. Nothing so tragic as those Kioko and GeeJo experienced, however.

Nonetheless, he identified more with GeeJo than any of the other ten knights. Not because he and GeeJo were so self-reliant, neither having a traditional family heritage to draw upon, but because each had embarked on a quest sidetracked at every turn. The American aviator had wanted to locate his missing comrades. Stanek desired to return to his cancer research and restore his prestige and reputation. But he knew he first had to find out who wanted him dead.

The New Guinea experience had brought other changes in his life as well. His relationship with Catherine had undergone a metamorphosis. No longer did he feel she posed a threat to his success, which was all the while in his own hands. And like GeeJo, love had stirred within him, if only the suggestion of it, through his relationship with DeAnn Toland. Yet, he had let her slip through his fingers. By now she no doubt had moved on with her own life, perhaps getting better acquainted with Frank Yowell on the trip to Angoram. Sidelined in Baltimore, he struggled to gain strength enough to return to New Guinea and resume his investigations.

"Get a hold of yourself," he chided. "You've got a number of unsolved cases to attend to. Best flush this fuzzy thinking from your mind."

Still, as he placed the last page of Cole's amazing transcript into the envelope, he caught himself in an act he had never done before. He rooted for the innocence of a suspect. If there is divine justice, he thought, perhaps Providence will exonerate GeeJo from all the murders associated with this case, including the one Stanek had witnessed the first day Mount Bosavi had appeared out of the mist. The attempts on his own life made no sense at this juncture if GeeJo was responsible, unless he had become smitten with gold fever after Kioko and Kazuo left.

For the moment, Angus Mackelwaite had surfaced as the chief suspect. Besides the physical evidence linking him to the scene, his reluctance to report the downed American B-24 bomber, as was his duty, did little to commend him. And in the former patrol officer's conversation with Kioko, he was the one who introduced the subject of gold. Of course, this was still speculation. Yet, keeping the gold strike secret served all the suspects as motive for not wanting a forensic pathologist poking around, GeeJo included.

But his earlier thought of Providence turned his mind in a direction he had not traveled since his youth. Before he was banished from the Stanek home, he had written poetry now and then. He remembered his promise to LikLik's friend Margaret, who had asked why leaves fall. So, as he lay back on the bed, he composed a poem on leaves for her. Perhaps it would satisfy Jim Cole's challenge.

WHY LEAVES FALL
I'm really not convinced at all
Nature intended for leaves to fall.
I know if I were a deciduous tree
I'd want no leaves to fall from me.
Why should a leaf turn golden brown
Only to tumble ignobly down?
Then when I look o'er fields bright green,
It's plain to see nature's clever scheme.
Millions of tiny blankets around trees enfold
To protect their roots from the coming cold.

Late the next morning when the sun warmed the crisp autumn air all around Fells Point, and the breeze off the harbor felt like medicine to the lungs, Stanek found LikLik and Margaret at play in their usual places. He approached the children tentatively. Behind his back, he held the poem on leaves a kindly nurse had committed to paper for him. She had said she liked it, but he was still uncertain. The child might disagree and be disappointed.

He remembered the day he had surprised Mrs. Patricia Stanek with a Mother's Day poem, presented at the orphanage. She had been delighted. But now as an adult, he felt silly, yet somewhat relieved. The writing of the poem for Margaret had proved a temporary catharsis, driving from his mind the horrors of Kioko's murder. She was still another victim in a bizarre case he had to solve.

Intentional, or not, the killing of the young Japanese woman and the disappearance of the gold sewn in her clothing once again pointed to the lust for gold as a probable motive for murder—hers and the others under investigation. Fine. He had the motive. Next came the task of separating the suspects until he had narrowed the field down to "Mr. Big" as Lt. Dunbar had called him. Cole was the linchpin, supplying crucial missing information. Mackelwaite was certainly involved. If not the chief suspect, he was a prime candidate as an associate. But for now, Stanek was sidetracked and must complete the task at hand he had promised Cole he would do.

Stanek did not have to call the girls over to him. As soon as they saw him on the cobblestone path, they ran up to greet him. LikLik threw her arms around his thigh and laid her head against his leg muscle. Touching was a Riami form of greeting, but LikLik held him like he had seen her do to MilkEye, her father.

The Papuan child looked up at him and then called to her playmate, "Margaret, come greet white papa."

Margaret wrapped her arms around his waist and discovered the paper he still held behind his back. "Oh, Dr. Stanek, you did remember my poem. Please, let's find a bench, and you can read it to us."

He grinned at the two girls, hanging on him like chaps on a cowboy. "You'll have to let me go so I can walk. Let me warn you, I'm not very good at this sort of thing. Poetry has very little to do with medicine."

"Dr. Sinclair says sometimes a poem, or laughter, is the best medicine," said Margaret.

"Well, I hope you won't laugh at my effort."

"Oh, I'd never do such a thing. Daddy says it's impolite to ridicule people when they've tried their best."

"What's 'ridicule'?" LikLik asked.

"You know, when you make fun of a friend."

"Well, Margaret, I can see you have a very good vocabulary. Tell me if there are any words you don't understand as I read 'Why Leaves Fall'."

Margaret asked two questions when he finished. "I'm not sure what 'deciduous' means, but it must have something to do with falling out, like my hair. Would you say the cancer made me 'deciduous'?"

"No, this falling away occurs in nature to trees losing their leaves in fall."

"I've another question. Why did you use 'nature' instead of 'God,' Who made everything?"

"Now, Margaret, you've stumped me. God is real for many people, but scientists like myself see nature at work."

"Oh, too bad—a perfect poem if only God were in it."

"Margaret, it's your poem now. Since we agreed to work on this together, you can change any words you wish."

"Oh, I will, and God bless you for such a lovely poem. I'll show it to my Daddy when he comes home. You haven't forgotten to talk to Dr. Sinclair about me, have you?"

"No, in fact I'll go into the hospital right now and consult with her about your case."

Margaret turned to face LikLik. "You're right. Dr. Stanek does have strong medicine. I feel better already and will keep this poem forever."

Back in the hospital, Stanek paged Dr. Susan Sinclair and spoke to her about Margaret's case. The woman had little hope Margaret would survive long enough for the expected rendezvous with her father. Stanek told the physician about the bee serum, but they both agreed it could not be used on Margaret on a trial basis, unless approved by the Federal Drug Administration.

"I'm afraid bee serum is a long way from approval, Dr. Sinclair. Might I suggest an alternative?"

"Yes, sir. I'm open to any and all."

"For the brief time I've observed Margaret, I've seen she has a strong faith in medical treatment."

"And an even stronger faith in God."

"Yes, well, if we were to give her a placebo administered in place of my serum, it might give her the boost she needs to hold on until her father comes home."

"You know, Dr. Stanek, I think it's worth a try. How nice of you to take time from your own rehabilitation to help this little girl. Your parents must've been very loving for you to turn out to be so sympathetic to others."

"Well, ah, one of them at least, my mother. In fact it's long past time when I should be getting over to Phipps to see her."

"Oh, I'm sorry to hear she's a patient. Let's pray the Code Blue at Phipps announced just before your call is not for her."

48 KOMO CATASTROPHES

Komo, Papua New Guinea, 1973

A LL AROUND MILKEYE were strange noises of the night which were unfamiliar to him. Each night bird, frog and even insect seemed to have its own peculiar sound. He longed for the Rentoul River valley below the Riami village. He missed the continuous murmur of the river as it flowed over the rocks, joined in the pre-dawn by the hoarse note of the bull *pukpuk*, or crocodile, barking in search of a mate.

MilkEye wondered if he would ever see his wives again. Surely, the youngest, LikLik's mother, had long since returned to her father to set a new bride price. Freed from a man who wandered off so often, the daughter could roam the gardens in search of another husband. Often a man's status diminished once a wife had deserted him, but MilkEye felt his had grown when the sky people chose him and WonTok to go up in the clouds in the small *balus*. To disguise his fear, he kept his good eye half closed so he would not appear frightened.

Situmu's silence was a bigger problem. How could he blame the Riami if they selected another leader during his absence. And who knew about LikLik? She might stay in the land of the whites, or not come home before the greatest of Riami festivals, the big *singsing*. At the festival, he expected to save face and his lineage, setting a high purchase price to be paid by LikLik's future husband.

Two Face had not allowed him sons for breaking tribal law when he substituted his sperm for WonTok's at the manhood

499

initiation rite. Without LikLik, Situmu's line would end with the life he had forfeited as future payback for killing the young Tugaru warrior at the salt well. These thoughts soared through his mind as he felt WonTok stir beside him under the wing of the small *balus*.

"You no sleep?" MilkEye's *age-mate* asked. "Chiami friend. We need no watchman."

"Me keep one eye open."

"You only got one eye."

"Enemies or evil spirits no can tell which eye to look at." They both laughed at the standard joke the two friends had shared since boyhood.

WonTok sat up and swatted at a swarm of mosquitoes on his arm, which left a large red blotch. "No enemies in Komo except mosquitoes." He held up his blood-spattered palm to MilkEye's face. "Why we no sleep in house like *misis* and *mastas* say?"

MilkEye brushed his friend's hand away from his face. "Me tell you. Tow-land put Kioko-san's books in *balus*. We watchman. No fellow steal. We find Kioko-san. Trap sorcery of evil Two Face inside her books. No more curse on me and LikLik."

WonTok, who had fallen back at the rebuke from his friend, drew himself up as the daybreak arrived and all grew quiet in the jungle. He looked toward the village. "Chiami still sleep. Me make fire. Cook food away from *balus*, like small *balus* pilot tell me. *Kiap* tell we go many places today. Look for bones of white people."

When they had landed at Komo the day before, MilkEye had nodded as he had donned the government hat with the red band *Kiap* Noble insisted he wear to identify him as a certified *luluai*. "Every *luluai* we meet will treat ye as an equal, so they'll be more apt to cooperate with us," Noble had said.

The old warrior had misgivings about the gesture until WonTok, who eagerly had accepted the red and black banded cap of a *tultul*, designating him assistant chief, drew his Riami *age-mate* aside to lecture him. "Situmu tell you, if he speak, to take honor. If *kiap* finds out you kill Tugaru boy, only put you in jail for two days because you *luluai*."

MilkEye had to admit WonTok's argument made sense. Yet if they ran into people who no longer trusted the government, he and WonTok were marked men.

The dawn began the new day and through a rift in the clouds to the east, MilkEye caught sight of the mountains. Even from his seat in the *balus* where everything appeared small, the mountains had arisen above the horizon like the spirit house does in every village of substantial size. Before arriving at Komo, he had pointed this out to WonTok.

He was about to share a new observation when the white *misis* and two *mastas* approached. The *kiap* followed MilkEye's gaze. "Bigger than Mount Bosavi, eh? Yer right. But any mountain we can't fly over, we'll walk through. Plenty of valleys ahead of us to search for bones," the *kiap* said. "Either of ye ever hear of the Huri people?"

MilkEye and WonTok nodded. Their cousins, the Chiami, had told them many stories about their feuds with the Huri.

The *misis* interrupted the *kiap*, "Roger, let me try to explain our plan. It'll give me a chance to try out my pidgin. She began by telling them the day spent in Komo had proved fruitful. "We have possibly located the bones of one of the white sky people we are looking for." She then went on to explain why she had come so early to speak to the two Riami men. "One of the..." She paused. "Roger, maybe you'd better take over. I can't muster any more pidgin right now."

Roger continued. "A man from Komo said he was there when he saw the Japanese bury a man GeeJo shot with a *thunderstick*. We wish to recover these remains. But there's a problem. The burial plot is near a Huri village, and the Chiami and the *luluai* of the Huri tribe don't speak. Each accuses the other of stealin' pigs. The Huri don't trust the government to settle this dispute, 'cause the Huri remember the *kiaps* never brought 'em the reward for their service in the war. When this GeeJo fellow was here, he kept the Chiami and Huri from tearin' each other's heads off. Now every incident, like the pig stealin', makes 'em close their villages to each other."

Noble saw MilkEye and WonTok wave fingers at each other. They had heard about the stolen pigs. "Under normal conditions," Noble continued, "we'd just march into the Huri village with a Chiami guide, but none of yer cousins will take the risk. Ye, WonTok and I must go in front of *misis* and Major Yowell to keep 'em safe."

MilkEye held his hands to his side, palms up. "How we do this, *Masta*? Huri people with wigs no friends of Riami or Chiami."

"Yes, but ye wear the government band of a *luluai*, and they might listen to ye long enough for me to speak to 'em as a *kiap*."

501

"You like WonTok and me go alone into strange village?"

"Yes. I can't use my police boys for fear the Huri will run away and not show us where to dig for the bones buried there."

"*Masta*, Huri kill WonTok and me!"

"If not for the government, then do it for Dr. Toland. She told me 'bout yer search for Kioko. The government will help her and ye find Kioko if she's still in New Guinea. It'll be yer reward. Ye and WonTok will also receive extra pay. I'll be not far behind ye, out of sight. If the Huri attack ye, I'll drive 'em away."

MilkEye huddled with his companion, then asked, "When we go to Huri village?"

"This mornin' whilst everyone is in there, before they scatter for the work of the day." The *kiap* and the two Riami warriors set off together. Behind them at a great distance came Dr. Toland, Major Yowell and three constables from the post at Komo. All went well until they came to the bend in the tract and had to cross a vine bridge spanning the Tagari River. The tract continued up an incline on the far side of the bridge.

Suddenly WonTok shouted a warning. There at the top of the rise standing astride the path stood a Huri warrior. He wore the government cap of a *luluai* perched precariously on his flowered and feathered wig. MilkEye turned to get instructions, but the *kiap* was nowhere to be seen. MilkEye could read the rage on the face of the man confronting them. It was clear he marked them as enemies from the Chiami camp. In the next instant he summoned his followers by throwing back his head and yodeling to them.

Seeing he could not retreat across the bridge and leave WonTok to face them alone, MilkEye hurried to the side of his *age-mate*. Behind the Huri chief there were now a dozen or more warriors, all yodeling as they advanced down the incline, spears at the ready. The chief broke from the group and made a sudden lunge with his spear. MilkEye and WonTok stepped to one side, and the spear missed them by a foot. The attacker reeled back, swung away and staggered up the slope to his companions who began to throw their spears at the Riami men. As boys, and now warriors, MilkEye and WonTok had trained well for this moment. They ducked and weaved to avoid the missiles.

Behind them they heard the *kiap* shout, "Fall to the ground." They had no sooner done so than two shots rang out, and the Huri scurried back up the hill, leaving their chief to make his own escape. For his age, MilkEye's conditioning was superb, and he closed the distance between himself and his adversary before the *kiap* shouted again. "Don't kill him! Take him into custody 'til I get there."

MilkEye pounded the earth with his stone axe near the squirming chief pinned under him, careful to avoid hitting the man. Far up on the hill, the yodeling increased and was joined by the rhythmic beating of a *garamut*. The drum no doubt summoned the Huri warriors to reassemble in an attempt to rescue their leader.

The *kiap* stood over MilkEye and his captive and wheezed, drawing deep breaths. *"Come a gutser!* The fat's really in the fire now!"

*   *   *

A half-mile or so from the vine bridge, DeAnn heard the yodeling, followed by two shots, then more yodeling. She listened for some sign of her colleagues, but all she heard was more yodeling joined by the beating of the *garamut*, sounding more and more frantic in tone.

Yowell pulled a .38 from his holster and sidled up next to the anthropologist. "What in the hell is all the ruckus about? Shooting, yodeling and drums weren't part of the plan. What do you say we beat a path back to Komo and get some reinforcements?"

DeAnn was surprised at the calmness in her own voice. "We can't leave Roger and the others. Get a Chiami constable up here who can speak pidgin and interpret those drum messages."

Yowell turned and half dragged the nearest man before Toland. "He'll do. They all speak gibberish. How you can make a lick of sense out of it beats me. I understand some pidgin 'til they turn motor-mouth, prating away like an outboard engine."

DeAnn took charge of the interrogation. "Hurry, constable, tell me what the drum says."

The police boy patted his rifle. *"Garamut* tell *kiap* shoot, kill Huri *luluai*. Call warriors to make payback. Me go warn Chiami people."

"Your people can read the message of the *garamut*."

The constable did not respond. Instead he and his comrades turned and fled. Yowell took DeAnn's arm. "We'd best bug out, too. Odds aren't good for a shootout at O.K. Corral. We'd be nuttier than a pecan pie to go up there."

Toland shook herself free. "Roger wouldn't kill a native short of any other way out of a scrape. The message must be false. He probably fired shots to scare them. We'll go forward and see for ourselves."

"But he told us to wait here."

"It was before the shooting. You can go back to Komo, Frank. My duty..."

"Not on your life, Sweetheart. I'm sticking with you, and you're stuck with me."

"Frank, you must realize how easy these people do an about-face. One moment they're friendly and the next at your throat. Poor Dr. Stanek. No wonder he got into so much trouble in the short time he was here."

"Wasn't short enough if you ask me, DeAnn. The fellow either had a dark cloud over him or a price on his head. What made you think of him at a time like this?"

DeAnn looked down at her boots. Better to remain silent than to reveal how often in the past weeks Emerson Stanek had been in her thoughts.

"Oh, oh. Don't move or panic, Sweetheart. We've got a bigger problem."

DeAnn looked up and saw they were surrounded by a dozen or more Huri men brandishing spears. How they managed to move so silently through the lawyer vines and other entanglements, which ripped at her clothes and lacerated her skin, she had no idea.

Yowell waved the revolver at the intruders. She urged him to put it back in the holster. "No more shooting, Frank. If the Huri wanted to kill us, they could've done so by now. I'll speak to them the best I can."

She asked for the *luluai*, but instead the *tultul* stepped forward and told her their headman was dead, killed by the *kiap*.

"It's not the government way," she insisted. She asked the *tultul* to take her and her companion to the place so they could see for themselves. "If true," she promised to make the proper restitution.

The second-in-command huddled with the other Huri and after five to ten minutes of haggling in their own language said they wanted to see what was offered for the slaying of the chief. DeAnn wished she had brought along some trade goods, or even a walkie-talkie so she could contact Noble if he were alive and find out what to do next. The main thing was to stall the Huri. For she knew if Roger was able, he, MilkEye and WonTok would find them.

The *tultul* waved his spear at her, a gesture she interpreted as "I see nothing on you to bargain with."

"Give *luluai* back or we kill."

DeAnn took in a deep breath. "First, take me to the place where this happened, and I'll show you what the *garamut* says is not true."

"No, you no talk true. You got no cargo. You like *meri*."

DeAnn realized the breast-high foliage must have made them mistake her for a *masta*. She took off her cap, unfastened her ponytail and unbuttoned her blouse, showing just enough cleavage to prove her point, as Yowell gaped.

"As you can see, I'm a *misis*, daughter of GeeJo's spirit—he who brought peace to the Huri and Chiami."

"GeeJo," the natives repeated in hushed voices.

Delighted that they had remembered the legend, DeAnn whispered to Yowell, "Go along with whatever I say and don't act surprised."

She tapped Yowell's shoulders, but addressed the Huri. "All you men hear what I have to say. This is GeeJo's son-of-the-sky. Your fathers knew him as a little boy. Though he comes from the sky and goes back whenever he likes in the small *balus* which brought us here, he is unhappy at your treatment of us."

"Why son of GeeJo no speak to us?" the *tultul* asked.

"He'll only speak to your *luluai* through the *kiap*, who will bring your chief here, if you won't take us to the place of the shooting."

The Huri huddled again, this time for a shorter period. The *tultul* replied, "Huri take you two to see if you speak true."

As they were marched away in the center of a phalanx of Huri warriors, Yowell leaned over and whispered, "Well done, Sweetie. I picked up some of what you said, and unbuttoning your blouse sure got their attention. Where'd you ever learn to tell Texas whoppers, in pidgin mind you?"

DeAnn smiled. "In the spirit of things, they weren't awful lies. Like GeeJo, I want to bring peace to these people, a shared kinship of sorts. As for you, like GeeJo, you're a second generation aviator come to this land."

"And the pidgin?"

"Thanks go to Dr. Stanek. He taught me the language at the hospital in Goroka during his convalescence."

She saw Frank Yowell's head droop. She wished she had not introduced Stanek into the conversation yet again.

A short distance from the vine bridge across the Tagari River, DeAnn saw Noble, MilkEye, WonTok and the Huri *luluai* making their way toward them. She called to the *kiap*. He did not answer, but he did quicken the pace. Then she realized Noble thought she and Yowell were in danger from the Huri warriors encircling them. After the *kiap* drew closer, the anthropologist called again.

"Things aren't as bad as they look. These men only want to verify their chief hasn't been shot."

"*Bugger it*," Noble swore. "Don't come any closer. We're faced with a dangerous situation. Could get out of hand at any moment. Be careful what ye say. Hidden in the bush are 50 or more Huri waitin' to have a go at us. I thought I had left ye protected. Why didn't ye stay put? Where are the constables?"

DeAnn quickly explained how the three constables had run off, and the natives had surrounded them. She explained how she had bought time by posing as the daughter of GeeJo's spirit and Yowell as his son from the small *balus*. She thought her actions would please Noble. After all, he had taught her how to outwit the natives.

The *kiap* pushed the Huri chief front and center. "Whether we get out of here with our skins or not depends on this fellow. He's the only one to make the Huri stand down. Doubt if he'll fall for the GeeJo line. Best try somethin' else."

DeAnn nodded and drew two fingers across her lips as if to seal them. Better to bow to Noble's experience as a patrol officer. He had the full force of the government behind him. Whatever he promised would have to be accepted unless the Huri wanted to face the consequences.

The *kiap* held up the hands of the *luluai* to show the warriors with DeAnn and Yowell and those natives whose eyes peered from the bush, the chief wore shackles. He then looked into the sea of faces. "Yer *luluai* has disgraced his office. He threw his spear at me, and I'm takin' him to the jail far away."

DeAnn bit her lip as she heard the warriors closest to her begin to chant. "No take away *luluai* to jail."

Noble drew himself up to his full height. "Then let yer chief explain why his anger makes him attack the government. And why is he ready to forget the friendship ye once had with yer neighbors, the Chiami."

DeAnn watched the chief bristle and take a stance in front of the *kiap*, no doubt to stress his authority. "Chiami no friends of Huri. Chiami no tell you come."

The *kiap* switched to English, "Slight misunderstandin' over the *garamut*, I'd say." Then to the chief in pidgin he said, "Chiami *garamut* no talk 'cause I didn't wish it to talk. I give Huri the honor. We've a long way to go to search for the bones of our brothers and sisters. Ye'll be the first to let all peoples from here to the Sepik River know we're comin' in the small *balus* to trade with 'em—knives, axes, shells and white man's food, for knowledge of where the bones are buried."

"You give cargo to Huri?" the chief asked.

"Yes. The cargo's guarded in our small *balus* in Komo. I'll give ye government paper for now. Ye can trade it for the goods later."

"No later. *Kiap* let go *luluai*. Me take you and friends to place near Huri village where white bones lay. We altogether tomorrow go to small *balus*. You give cargo to Huri."

"Fair enough."

"Good. Tonight you stay Huri village. Tomorrow you hear *garamut* talk for you."

"Splendid."

*   *   *

At the Ambuna Lodge in Tari the next evening, DeAnn sat down to dinner with *Kiap* Noble and Major Yowell. She had had her first real shower since leaving Mount Bosavi, and the dimples in her cheeks registered the way she felt about herself and her expedition thus far. Save for one or two tense moments with the Huri yesterday, the trip had produced solid gains. Her team had recovered the possible remains of Harlan Wells, the engineer on the ten knights bomber, at Komo. Of course, final identification would come back in the lab in Hawaii.

True to his word, the Huri chief had led them to the place where the Japanese garrison soldier shot by GeeJo had been buried. And the clincher came when Noble and MilkEye brought her to see the graves of the two renegade Japanese soldiers beheaded by

Lt. Mori in Tari. Nearby, where Kioko said it would be, they recovered the *samurai* sword of Lt. Mori, hidden in a hollow tree.

Yowell held DeAnn's chair out for her. "My, don't we look radiant, like a rainbow in the Texas sky."

Roger also stood. "Well put, I'd say. Ye, GeeJo, Junior, took the words right out of my mouth. She's a fetchin' lass all right."

"Thank you gentlemen, but please take your seats. I'm not used to such treatment. And, Roger, when are you going to stop teasing Frank about the story I told to the Huri?"

Noble sat down and wheezed as he let out his breath. "Not until we reach the Sepik River. His GeeJo, Junior, moniker will be useful 'til then. The natives in these parts know and respect GeeJo's legend. On the Sepik, Yowell will have to compete with Yesu."

"Yesu?" DeAnn asked.

Noble continued. "He was a one time constable sergeant at Angoram. Went berserk during the war. Killed a *kiap* and several white civilians. Thereafter, Sepik people feared him more than the *pukpuks*. Yesu went over to the Japanese side during the war and turned a lot of river people against the Allies, they say. Spread Japanese propaganda like it was gospel. Said the *kiaps* and the Yanks ran away and took the cargo promised to the natives with 'em. Yesu claimed the Japanese were tryin' to bring it back, but the Allies were bombin' the ships bringin' the cargo in."

Yowell shifted in his chair, moving closer to DeAnn. "Then why are we so keen on finding Japanese remains? They were our enemies and still may be, seeing the way they've wreaked havoc on us economically."

"Junior's got a point, lass. Japanese industrialists are getting' the money and materials to rebuild their nation from territory their soldiers used to occupy—places like New Guinea."

DeAnn broke into the conversation. "Why New Guinea?"

"For the timber and gold, mostly the gold for now, but they've got their eye on the timber for later. I've seen my share of Japanese *fossickers*, God knows I have. They're rushin' to get the gold out of the country before Papua gains independence and clamps down on 'em."

DeAnn wondered if Emerson Stanek had this information. It might prove helpful to him in his criminal investigation. She inched her chair away from Yowell's and switched the subject back to the perils awaiting them on the Sepik.

"This Yesu. Whatever happened to him?"

"Good question, lass. Far as I know, he's still terrorizin' people along the river. Never was found, dead or alive. Like Lt. Mori in Kioko's log, he just gave up the ghost and disappeared."

"Why should we pay attention to this folklore?"

"'Cause, GeeJo, Junior, me lad, we've got to come up with somethin' other than ye as a gimmick to gain native cooperation once we're on the Sepik. Many of 'em still side with the Japanese whom they expect to come back with the goods."

DeAnn laid her makeshift map on the table in front of her colleagues. "What about the two renegade soldiers who were prisoners at the former Japanese rest camp in Angoram? Do you think we'll have any trouble recovering the remains of their torsos from the burial site near Pari? The Duna there are quite fierce, I'm told."

Noble glanced at DeAnn. "Let's hope the Huri drums help introduce us as friendly to the natives."

"And the two Japanese garrison soldiers, including the doctor, laid to rest in the mountains near Porgea?"

"We'll have to make our own way there, lass."

Yowell protested and said this wasn't a topic he cared to discuss over dinner. He excused himself and headed for the bar.

"Wait, Frank, Please. Just a few more spots to go over with Roger. Then we'll let it rest for the evening."

The major settled back in his chair. "Maybe we'll get some time alone, and you can fill me in on the love story you got excited about the day I flew in with Stanek."

She patted his arm. "We'll see." DeAnn realized Yowell must have felt cut out of the general plan. Perhaps he wanted to do more than just fly the airplane from point to point. Still he had helped Roger and MilkEye recover the three sets of remains found along the Rentoul River earlier. "You've been a great help so far, Frank, and it's a comfort to have you and Roger with me as we approach the Sepik, but please, Roger, no more teasing. Now tell me, how do things look for recovering the two renegade soldiers buried at Amboin in the lowlands?"

Yowell interjected, "Can't the Japanese do this on their own? If they'd won the war, bet they wouldn't help us get our boys back.

Has General Bellicosi approved this diversion from recovering our own war dead?"

DeAnn drew a circle around several points on the map. "Until we get positive identification, we won't know for certain what their nationality was. As for the Japanese, they would've recovered our soldiers, as would any civilized nation. Now, Roger, about Amboin."

The *kiap* put his fork down. "Still far enough from Yesu's shenanigans for the natives to believe in the government system. Yesu did come up the Korosameri River where he killed several men in a minin' party whilst they were playin' a game of poker. Still, I don't foresee any problems with the natives 'til we land at Timbunke on the Sepik, thence on to Tambunam by canoe to search for the bodies of those names ye've scribbled down on yer map."

"Akatsu, the Japanese medic, and Sun-Hi, the Korean girl pressed into comfort woman service."

Noble plunked two fingers down under the names DeAnn had indicated. They might pose a challenge if Yesu's influence still permeates the place like a foul odor." Noble raised his glass. "Here's to Wordsworth's words over Rob Roy's grave:

To the good old plan
That they should take us who have the power,
And they should keep who can."

Across from their table, two middle-aged men clinked their glasses together and called out, "Here, here," in response to Noble's toast. On entering the dining room, DeAnn had paid them no notice, but she soon learned Yowell had already made their acquaintance.

"It's Clarence and Alan," the major said. "Come, join us, guys."

The one called Clarence pulled two chairs over from their table for him and his partner. "We prefer Clare and Al, if it's all the same to ye."

"Meet Dr. DeAnn Toland and *Kiap* Roger Noble. Dare I tell the *kiap* your line of work?" Yowell asked.

Clare laughed. Al, seated next to him, never looked up from the table. "We're mine inspectors. Work out of Brisbane, Al and I do. Contracted by the government to keep an eye on minin' operations in the Central Range, particularly in the Tari Valley. Frank tells us yer're out in the bush recoverin' war dead." He lifted his glass. Here's to happy huntin', if it's an appropriate toast."

Noble pushed away from the table, stood up and took DeAnn's arm. "*Come a gutser!* Word travels fast, and so must we. Come on, lass. We'll have a sandwich sent up and finish our business in yer room, or mine next door. The major's right. Ours is not a topic to discuss over dinner."

Yowell made no move to get up. "I'm staying put. Catch up with you later, DeAnn. Clare and Al, you've got to excuse the *kiap*. The way he hovers over Dr. Toland, you'd think she was his daughter."

"Can't blame him," said Clare. Al kept his eyes fixed on the table.

DeAnn gathered up her map and papers and addressed Yowell. "Don't forget we're scheduled to fly out of here tomorrow morning at 9:00 a.m."

Yowell laughed. "The way she nags me, you'd think we were married. Not that I'd object, of course."

"Just want to be sure you're in condition to fly."

"Easy, Sweetheart. How many times do I have to tell you? All the army requires is eight hours between bottle and throttle. I'll make it easily and still have time for a nightcap with you."

"We'll see."

On the way out of the dining room, DeAnn whispered to Noble, "What was our rude departure all about?"

The *kiap* jerked his thumb back toward the table they had just left. "My government closed minin' operations in New Guinea two years ago whilst we conduct an inventory for the Papuans. Ye know, to give 'em time to phase in their own inspectors once they take charge of things. Besides I'm not aware there're any minin' operations in the Tari Basin."

"Then who are they?"

"I've no idea, lass. But ye can bet I'll chat-up the district administrator first thing in the mornin'. See what he's got on two guys reluctant to render their last names."

"Shouldn't we warn Frank?"

"The major's a big boy. He can fend for himself. I just hope our GeeJo, Junior, doesn't tell 'em too much about our plans. To be on the safe side, perhaps we should plug a little diversion in our flight plan once we leave Tari. We'll tell Yowell en route."

"Sounds like you suspect foul play."

"One needs to expect the unexpected in New Guinea."

Noble left DeAnn's room about 9:30 p.m., and the excitement of the day caught up with her. She found herself too tired to undress. She kicked off her boots, slipped under the mosquito net, pulled the blanket under her chin and expected to get a full eight hours of sleep, the first since arriving in New Guinea some months ago.

Even at the hospital at Goroka where she tended Emerson, DeAnn had found it hard to sleep. First, General Bellicosi had asked her to write a letter to Erik's next of kin, expressing the sympathies of the Defense Department to the interpreter's family for their loss. This brought back memories of Daphne's drowning, and she had feared the tremor in her hand would trigger another bout of stuttering.

But of all people, it was Emerson Stanek who calmed her by asking her to read Kioko's log to him. She was moved when she saw he was touched by the love story. Unlikely circumstances had brought them together to share it. She realized how much her relationship with Stanek had matured and softened since the day he had arrived in New Guinea. The feelings she had once entertained for Yowell had been slowly transferred to Emerson and had become more than fondness for a man she could no longer ignore.

Had Emerson regained his strength? What would he make of all this? Could he find a way back to New Guinea? And dare she find a way to defy Bellicosi and get word to the pathologist about the remains they had recovered? She was anxious to tell him she had already authenticated part of Kioko's log.

She had no idea how long she lay there thinking about these matters, so she checked the time. It was 10:30 p.m., barely enough to get in the eight hours she had promised herself. Then came a knock at the door.

"Who's there?" she called.

"Frank. Brought a nightcap."

"I'm really too tired and am already in bed."

"Would it make any difference if I told you I was on a humanitarian mission?"

She got up and opened the door. "Humanitarian, my eye.

You've had too much to drink."

"Okay, no more booze, but just give me a kiss good night, and I'll be on my way to give solace to the natives."

"What in the world are you talking about?"

"Extra blankets. I've come to collect them. Poor MilkEye and WonTok, sleeping outside, don't know how cold it can get at this altitude at night."

She walked across the room and drew a blanket from the cupboard. In the next instant, Yowell had his arms around her waist and was kissing the back of her neck. "You sure do smell pretty," he said, as he slid his hands up to her breasts and pushed against her. She pulled away.

"And you smell like a brewery. Here's your blanket. Now go. And please don't try to force yourself on me. Never again."

Yowell dropped his head. "Sorry. But things used to be pretty peachy keen between us before Stanek got here. You're just upset about all the trouble he's caused, and I can respect your feelings. You're still the girl I want to take home to mama someday."

"Frank, I found out you were trading with the natives for gold in violation of our cargo cult policy. You violated the trust between us."

"Yeah, well, how do you know Stanek didn't frame me?"

"Because MilkEye told me those weren't arrowheads he traded with you for tobacco."

Yowell reached into the pocket of his flight suit and produced four gold nuggets. "Here's the extent of my dealings. Do whatever you want with them. I promise it won't ever happen again."

She lifted his chin and kissed his cheek. "This mission has been a strain on all of us. Until it's over, we dare not have dreams of our own."

He folded the blanket over his arm, and called back to her as he went out the door. "I'll add a blanket of my own. It'll take care of our little black friends."

It seemed he had not been gone more than an hour when there was a loud bang at the door. She checked the time and saw it was midnight. She thought it was Yowell returning. Since she wanted to see if he was in condition to pilot an airplane, she did not ask who was there, but opened the door.

There stood MilkEye waving his arms. *"Misis, throwim way leg. WonTok and me see two fellows kill Ma-jah Yo-well!*

513

49 FAMILY SECRETS REVEALED

Baltimore, Maryland, 1973

EMERSON STANEK EXPECTED to find his adoptive mother dead, so much so, he hurried past the code blue team in the corridor leading to Patricia Stanek's room at Phipps. One of the physicians recognized him, however. He was a cardiologist, and, like Stanek, had completed his residency at Johns Hopkins where Dr. Thomas Haveland had tutored him in pathology.

Emerson stopped and turned when the heart specialist called his name. They exchanged brief pleasantries. Stanek asked, "Were you able to save the patient?"

"Unfortunately, no. She had expired before we got there."

Stanek looked down, then straight across at the physician."Oh, she—a female?"

"Yes, a woman about 70."

"What room was she in?"

The cardiologist tapped a hand on Emerson's shoulder and smiled. "The one next to Mrs. Stanek's."

Stanek pumped the man's hand. "Thanks. My sister seems to think my mother knew the woman in the next room. Can you give me her name?"

"Sure. Meredith Rhodes-Foxhall. Your sister's right. Mrs. Rhodes-Foxhall and Patricia Stanek were close friends since childhood, I understand. I've attended both ladies for a number of years. Meredith's demise will be a blow to your mother once she learns her friend has passed away. The two used to have make-believe conversations during the day. Sometimes I'd see them strolling arm and arm in the garden."

"Was Mrs. Rhodes-Foxhall schizophrenic, too?"

"Yes. It's the psychiatrist's diagnosis, plus she had vascular disease. Your mother presents the same symptoms."

"I've been told my mother's hanging on by a thread and wants to see me."

"When I phoned your sister awhile ago, advising her of Meredith's death, she said she's on her way to see Mrs. Stanek and you."

"How about Mrs. Rhodes-Foxhall? Does she have any next-of-kin?"

"Came from a well-to-do family, I hear. Her husband was wealthy as well. Passed away some years ago—Victor Foxhall of Foxhall Furriers. I don't believe she and Victor had any children."

Stanek stroked the scar on his cheek. "Has the body been removed?"

"No. The nurses are just tidying up a bit."

"Mind if I step in to pay last respects while I wait for Catherine to arrive?"

"Go ahead, Emerson. Just tell the staff you're a doctor and you spoke to me. Did you know her?"

"Not really. Catherine bantered her name about a couple of times."

"She was a lovely woman, but no one ever came to see her, at least as far as I know. Could be what brought her into Phipps numerous times over the years."

"Someone must've been looking after her, though."

"Guess it was Mrs. Stanek. They were both troubled, but very close."

The cardiologist continued. "Come over to the old valves and pumps department later for coffee. We'll catch up on old times, and you can tell me about your beekeeper cancer research. It has this place buzzing."

The physician laughed, then turned serious. By the physician's demeanor, Stanek saw his acquaintance had remembered coffee and jokes had never been the pathologist's forte. "Got to run, Emerson. Hear you're just back from the wilds of New Guinea."

"Yes, and I'm anxious to get back to finish what I've started."

"Good luck and give my best to your sister and mother for me."

As Emerson entered the late Mrs. Rhodes-Foxhall's room, the nurses quickly covered the body with a sheet. He told them who he was, and they uncovered her face.

"You must be her son. I can see the resemblance," one of the nurses said.

"I've been told as much, but I couldn't prove it."

Emerson looked down on the woman Catherine claimed was his natural mother. Even in her later years, her skin, like his adoptive mother's, was without a blemish and not a wrinkle to be seen. He saw her as a young woman once full of vitality and exuberance, yet dignified, exhibiting the same traits he had seen in DeAnn Toland. How strange he should be here at his alleged mother's deathbed. Just a short time ago he, with the aid of DeAnn and her team, had been in the middle of murder investigations in New Guinea.

He stood frozen for a moment, and his mind wandered into yesteryear. Patricia Stanek had visited her friend, the imaginary "Zelda Fitzgerald," while he and Catherine had played in the gardens at Fells Point. Was this the "Zelda" from those times? One thing was certain. This was the woman to whom his mother had spoken through the wall on his last visit with her. As he was about to turn and leave, his sister entered the room. Catherine came over to the bed where he stood and took his hand.

"Beautiful, isn't she? So much like mother, even in appearance, except for her dark, curly hair now streaked with gray."

"How long have you known?" he asked.

"Since the New Guinea trip for certain, but even before the trip, I suspected there was a connection between mother, Meredith, H. Douglas Addison and you. I've little doubt Addison is your father."

He slipped his hand out of hers. "Catherine, please, let it go."

"I can't. We've got to face mother and let her see we share her secrets. It might jolt her back to reality long enough for her to unburden herself from the guilt she's carried all these years."

"What guilt?"

"Never telling you the truth."

"Someone else failed to tell the truth, with dire consequences for one of us."

Tears rolled down Catherine's cheeks. She reached to brush them away and asked, "Must your reproof always be so harsh?"

"Harsh? Trashing someone's reputation and ruining his life is harsh!"

"Cruel, then."

"How amusing. Come on. The real reason behind this visit and your tears is to soften me up in an attempt to get your hands on my cancer research, cruel as it may sound."

"Bet you don't talk this way to little Miss What's-Her-Name when you're in the jungle together."

"DeAnn? No. She's not after anything."

Catherine took a handkerchief from her purse and dabbed at her eyes. "Oh, I wouldn't be so sure. But, please, Emerson. We're here to help mother. Now it's my turn to ask you to let it go. Didn't you get my note saying I was sorry before you left Baltimore so abruptly after Dr. Haveland's murder?"

"I did."

"Did you read it?"

"Yes."

"So, why haven't you forgiven me?"

"If I thought you were sincere, I'd try. But your expression of sorrow fell short of our agreement of a public apology for the rape allegation."

"I never claimed you raped me."

"No, but you let everyone, including your father, think a rape had occurred."

"Father came to his own conclusions."

"He used the incident to get rid of me."

"Why, when you were ready to start college and leave us anyway, moving out into the world?"

Stanek stroked the scar on his cheek. "What better time. Perhaps it enabled Rufus to mask his real reasons for setting me adrift."

"Maybe this is something we should ask mother about."

"Agreed. But let me lead the questioning. Like I said. I don't want a soap opera to unfold, or a repeat of the Popsy business to trigger a state of comatose as occurred on my last visit with your mother."

"Of course, you're the professional in these matters, objective to the core. I'm merely the daughter whose emotions fly out of control if it involves people I love."

Stanek followed Catherine out of the room of the late Mrs. Meredith Rhodes-Foxhall and into the next room where Patricia Stanek resided. Stanek looked about him. Since his last visit to his adoptive mother's room on the day of the Haveland murder, a few things had changed. The three portraits were gone from the wall behind the easel where the unfinished painting still remained. Across the back of the chair hung the bonnet he remembered Patricia Stanek had worn when he had seen her seated at the easel. He picked up the bonnet and drew his fingers down the length of ribbon before he put the hat back in place. Catherine beckoned, and he joined her at their mother's bedside in the alcove. Patricia Stanek yawned, sat up in bed and smiled at him.

"I saw you admiring my bonnet. You know, you can tell a lot about a woman's character by the bonnet she wears."

"So I've heard," he said. "What kind of hat suits Catherine?"

"She's not wearing any, a statement in itself. Who would wear a hat with hair so golden the sun looks down with envy upon it?"

"Very poetic, I must say."

"People tell me my hair was like hers once. But never could it match Meredith's dark, swirling curls, much like yours," she said looking at Emerson. Then she addressed Catherine. "Who is this young man? Where are your manners, dear daughter? Introduce me to your beau."

"Mother, he's Emerson, the boy you and father adopted."

Catherine had ignored their agreement for him to take the lead, and Stanek started to protest, but he was thrown off guard by Patricia Stanek's response. She reached for his hand and pressed it against her cheek. He could feel the moisture of her tears on his fingers. "Dear, precious son. Why has it been so long? It broke my heart to have you leave." She kissed his fingers. "Answered prayer has brought you back. But wait a minute. You were here once before, and we talked about painting, didn't we?"

He caressed her chin. "Indeed we did. You were telling me about the portraits hanging on your wall and the painting on your easel. I see it's almost completed."

Patricia frowned, looking at her daughter. "Catherine took the portraits away. She said they were upsetting me. The one on the easel will never be finished. It was for my friend, Meredith. Did you know she no longer calls to me to complete it before one or the other of us passes away? In such a matter, I'm afraid I'm on the fast track."

"Meredith? Tell us about her." Stanek entreated.

"Oh, there's so much to tell. Where does one begin?"

"How did you come to meet her?" he prompted her.

"Why don't you pull up a chair? I'm sure you recognize the one. You squirmed and wiggled upon it when I painted you so long ago. Catherine, dear, come sit on the bed. You can fill in any bits and pieces you might recall.

"Meredith and I go way back. We grew up as next door neighbors in Ashville, North Carolina. Across the street lived Zelda Sayre, who later became Zelda Fitzgerald, wife of the famous author. Zelda intrigued us. She always had boys and young men coming to her house seeking her favor. Most of the time her father, a judge, ran them off, and then they would show interest in Meredith and me.

"My father and Meredith's were partners in a textile business until they sold out and moved our families to Baltimore. They thought we could get a better education in the northeast. We were chums all the way through Wellesley College. We were never competitive, except we both fell in love with a young doctor who called on us during our summer breaks at home."

Catherine interjected. "Was father the suitor?"

"No, Rufus came later. But like your father, this young doctor was a brilliant pathologist, a prodigy really, the likes of which Johns Hopkins has never seen. He was dashing and personable enough so everyone forgot he was labeled what my generation called illegitimate, you know, born out of wedlock.

"This didn't stop Meredith and me from falling in love with him. Of course, our families objected and our mothers, being proper scions of society, sent us away to graduate school in pursuit of masters' degrees. Our young man was persistent though, and he visited us whenever he had free time. After a while, he had to make a choice, and shocked me with his proposal. Meredith was heartbroken and got so sick she had to return home.

"When my father heard of his proposal, he forbade me to ever see my suitor again, as did Meredith's parents. Things were different in those days. Parents had more influence over their children's future. They told us to think of our own children, and how they would be stigmatized by the society in which our families moved. Partly out of concern for Meredith's health and partly out of the thought of alienating myself from parents who had only one child, I tearfully acquiesced and vowed never to see the young man again. Meredith and I formed a pact. We were like sisters, since she was an only child as well. We promised each other no matter what happened, our friendship and love would remain.

"As it turned out, Meredith was stronger than I. She was unwilling to give up the man she loved. When I refused my suitor's proposal, he turned to Meredith. When she accepted, they had a secret wedding ceremony, and as much as it hurt, I was the only witness, other than the justice of the peace. Their elopement took them to Spain, and when they returned, Meredith was pregnant.

"Her father was furious and had the marriage annulled, on what grounds I don't know, since it had certainly been consummated. When the child was born, he was placed in an orphanage here in Baltimore for adoption. Meantime, Meredith was packed off to Phipps for psychiatric treatment, which was less a stigma, I suppose, than accepting a grandchild from a bastard. Throughout her confinement, we kept our pact and vowed whoever was free and able would raise Meredith's son.

"Having lost the man I loved, I turned to another young man who was unaware of any of these incidents and had the right pedigree to be accepted by the Templetons. Catherine, this was your father, Dr. Rufus Stanek, a name his students came to fear, but he won the respect of his peers, who saw him as second in status only to Meredith's husband. Their rivalry continued for a number of years until my distraught former suitor went to Spain after his marriage to Meredith was annulled and their baby was placed in an orphanage. He served as a doctor there, although the country was in a state of political unrest.

"Before he left, he secretly professed his love for me, as well as his devotion to Meredith and his child. He vowed to come back and set us all free someday. The Spanish Civil War shattered our hopes. On a flight to treat war injured, he was reported missing when his aircraft was shot down. Witnesses saw five parachutes descend from the airplane before it crashed, one way off in the distance, but the person was never found. I learned of this through newspaper accounts and later shared the sad news with Meredith from whom there were no secrets.

"We agreed, as a means of keeping in touch with the man we both loved, I would do a painting to capture the moment of our lover's probable death in time. You've seen the painting on my easel. And the tiny dot one sees at the vanishing point represents our love throughout eternity."

Catherine stirred and started to speak, but Emerson waved her off. "I'm working on a case in which an aircraft went down in circumstances such as you describe. I won't go into it now, but something you said, coupled with the observations on falling leaves in a poem I wrote for a little girl, may have given me a clue to solve a puzzle as to how one survivor got separated from the rest of his crew. But, please, go on with your story."

"So, I'm not the only one who can turn a poetic phrase. You don't know how it pleases me, Emerson."

Stanek saw Catherine's displeasure at the digressions from her mother's story and her desire to get back to it.

"Mother, why haven't you told us the name of this lover? I'm afraid you loved him more than father."

"To be truthful, I must admit your father and I knew ours was a marriage of convenience to placate our families. I had hoped to grow to love him, but when you were born, he was extremely disappointed in me because I had not borne him a son to create the dynasty in pathology he craved. I couldn't reach him thereafter, until Meredith and I hatched a scheme to give him the son he wanted. Do I have to go on, or can you figure it out?"

Catherine rose from the bed and cupped her hands over her ears. "Stop, Mother! How could you admit you didn't marry father for love, or insinuate he was ever dissatisfied with me?"

"I didn't mean to hurt you, dear. And if it's any solace to you, your father clung to you, shutting me out, even discouraging the expression of my own love for you. So, I turned my focus elsewhere."

Catherine stomped her feet. "You needn't go any further," she said through tears. "We know what happened next. You deceived father by bringing Emerson into the family, knowing full well he's the son of your bastard lover and father's chief rival. How it would've broken his heart if he'd ever discovered the truth."

"No more than mine was broken when he robbed me of you, and then later sent Emerson away, like my father had sent away the one I loved."

"Well, it's obvious where your affection lies. Now finish your story by naming your lover."

"What does it matter now, daughter? Haven't we hurt each other enough?"

Stanek guessed Catherine was about to bring up William Welch, but he was too late to stop her.

Catherine clenched her fists. "It all started with Popsy, didn't it, Mother?"

"Catherine, don't do this!" Emerson protested.

But she pressed ahead. "Well, we know where Popsy eats and where Popsy sleeps. Now all we need to know is with whom. I'm sure Emerson would like to know who was his maternal grandmother."

Patricia Stanek blinked, but didn't lapse into a near comatose state. Emerson was astonished. In fact she answered her daughter with the same calmness in her voice he remembered had soothed his injured pride when one of the other boys at the orphanage had called him a bookworm. "The rumor with the most credibility has a well-known visiting professor from England as Dr. Welch's paramour. Of course, Hank Addison never knew her since she returned back home after his birth. But he took her last name to save Welch embarrassment. Popsy, as the students called him, discretely placed the baby with a couple who raised him, with Welch's support of course. I don't know anything more about Hank's background because of the circumstances. Is there anything else you'd like to know, dear?"

Catherine pointed to the outer room. "His was the portrait you hung on your wall beside father's and mine. How could you do such a thing?"

"I painted Hank before I married your father and kept his portrait hidden in the cellar at home. Do you remember the two of you found the painting once and inquired about it? I told you never to mention it to Rufus, but I had the feeling your father was aware of its presence, if not its significance."

"This is terrible, Mother! I don't want to hear any more!"

"Allow her to finish what you started, Catherine."

"Please, dear, bear with me a little longer. You asked why I kept it in my room here at Phipps, and I'm afraid what I have to say about it will only hurt you more."

"Impossible! What could be worse?"

"I asked you to bring Emerson's portrait from home, but you refused, and the only link I've had to him all these years was the likeness of his father, which I could share with dear Meredith. As to how it got here, after you two found it in the cellar, I gave it to our dear family friends, Tom and Lily Haveland, for safe keeping. Tom brought it here at my request on one of the days he came to tell me about Emerson's progress.

"There's more. My parents left me 500,000 dollars. I put it in a trust fund for Emerson when Rufus died, naming the Havelands as the trustees."

Catherine began to cry again and her body heaved so much she struggled to speak. "Nothing for me?"

Patricia Stanek reached up to touch her daughter's hand, but Catherine withdrew it. "Financially, your father left you millions and the great asset of Stanek Laboratories. I knew Rufus' rage was so great he cut Emerson off without a penny. He left me only enough for my upkeep and medical bills, so his legacy couldn't be distributed to Emerson, even after my death. But he didn't have control over the money my parents bequeathed, and I named Emerson the beneficiary. So now we come to the end of my story, and soon the end of my life. My wish, indeed, my prayer is for the two of you to reconcile and bury the past with me."

"Father left explicit instructions none of his money, or any of his resources, were to involve Emerson. I'm duty-bound to carry out his wishes."

"I understand you must follow the stipulation of your father's will, but I'm not bound by such a requirement. It's my own money I'm talking about."

Emerson felt he could remain silent no longer. He took the hand Catherine had eschewed. "Thank you, dear lady, but you've given me so much already. I'm on the verge of a breakthrough in cancer research. It'll not only win back my reputation, but also has the potential to help millions and earn enough for me to continue my research."

"I'm happy for you, dear, and I wouldn't trade those precious years we had together for all the gold in the world. Raising you from childhood to manhood was God's great gift to me. As for your reputation, I heard the stories told about you, but I never believed them."

"Would you believe me?" Catherine asked.

"I believe the truth is in your heart, and if I live long enough to win back a daughter's love, perhaps you'll tell me the truth, as I've tried to do to you."

Stanek laid his adoptive mother's hand to her side. "I'm afraid we've taxed you to the limit. Please get some rest, and we'll talk again later. I'll be here at Johns Hopkins for two more weeks. Let's give all of this time to sink in."

Patricia Stanek nodded and closed her eyes. As she spoke, her voice came in a whisper. "When Meredith goes, please take me home."

"Where, Mother? The house at the intersection of McElderry and North Carolina Streets was torn down long ago."

"I think she means with one of us," Stanek said.

Patricia Stanek nodded and in the next instant went to sleep.

Once out of earshot in the outer room, Emerson said, "I'm glad you didn't tell her about Meredith Rhodes-Foxhall's passing. Your scheme seems to have worked and jolted your mother back into reality. She gave us a lot to think about, and I suspect her thoughts of dying are tied up with her intuition about Meredith's condition. Actually, she may have improved enough to leave Phipps."

"Then you take her in, brother."

"You've got all the resources, and it seems to me only you can give her the healing of spirit she seeks."

"Spirit! I've never heard you talk about spirit before. Must've been some notion you picked up in New Guinea."

"True, spirit is a big part of the culture there. But let's talk about your mother's situation. If you'll take her in initially, you can have all the money placed in trust for me to use for her upkeep."

Catherine laughed. "Money? This isn't a matter of money. I could take in 100 psychiatric patients like mother and never feel a pinch."

"Then what'll it take?"

She grew serious. "There are two things I want from you. I've always wanted your love, and second, I want to share in your discoveries. How do you feel about these requests, brother?"

Stanek stroked the scar on his cheek. Your first request I can't grant. Until you tell the truth, I find it hard to speak of love, if only in a brother-sister relationship. The second wish I can grant you, but only on my terms."

"They are?"

"You keep your mother 'til I get back from New Guinea. Then I'll set up a charitable foundation where I can place my cancer research project. If Stanek Laboratories wants to get in on the action, you can negotiate a licensing of any pharmaceutical developed with the foundation's board of directors."

"I suppose you intend to be Chairman of the Board and CEO of this organization."

"No, I'd like to ask Tom Haveland's widow, Lily, to serve as its head. I've no interest in the corporation, except for the funding necessary for further research."

"Good. Then please forget New Guinea. Tony Bellicosi told me he'd relieved you of duties in the ten knight's case anyway. Get started on the new corporation instead. Of course, I'll take mother in. She'll have round-the-clock nursing care, the best available."

"No, the New Guinea case comes first. I'm almost certain it's tied into Tom's murder."

"Well, I hope you don't expect me to give you more support to continue such a dangerous venture."

"No, why should you?"

"Right. It's none of my business what you do. But remember, the whole deal falls through if you get yourself killed!"

50 ANGORAM ANSWERS

Papua New Guinea, 1973

WHEN DEANN ARRIVED on the scene with the two natives, she spotted the *kiap's* unmistakable bulk outlined against the faded moonlight. Next to Roger, half on the cobblestone pathway and half on the grass, lay the body of Frank Yowell. In silence, MilkEye and WonTok squatted in the grass near the major's head, took out their pipes and soon sent up a swirl of smoke. It caught a breeze and swept toward the Ambuna Lodge.

How can they relax at a time like this, she wondered, but then remembered the Riami believed smoke hastened the speed of the soul of a warrior fallen in battle to his final rest. Too distraught to speak, she waited for Noble to complete his examination of the body.

DeAnn felt for the gold nuggets in the pocket of her fatigue jacket. Were these to be the last exchange between her and a man she had once considered a possible prospect for marriage? She shivered at the thought of her own vulnerability, not unrelated to the way she had felt in days past whenever Yowell had taken her in his strong arms. Then his touch had made her feel secure, needed and responsive. But her last response to him was to turn away in anger over those stupid bits of gold. Even when his hands had found her breasts, and he had pressed against her earlier in the evening, as awkward as the moment had been, she had not been filled with disgust. Nor had the drunken display caused her to send him away. Her anger stemmed from his breach of contract

526

forbidding trade with the natives, a transgression for which General Bellicosi had chastised him earlier.

Now, if it were in her power to turn back the clock, she would have let him spend the night in her apartment instead of driving him away in a condition fraught with danger even under normal circumstances. But the firing on Yowell's aircraft, the killing of Erik, and the two attempts on Stanek's life were far from normal. A murderer stalked them. Now poor, dear, jovial Frank was his latest victim.

Kiap Noble finished his examination of the body and settled in beside her on the cobblestone pathway. He drew a cigarette from his pocket and, as had MilkEye and WonTok, soon sent a swirl of smoke into the crisp night air. Through a wheeze he muttered, "I really should give up cigs, ye know, but it's hard to break old habits. Our GeeJo, Junior, would say 'Amen,' if he could."

Through tears and a trembling voice, DeAnn asked, "How can you act so casual? Our friend has been killed!"

The *kiap* chuckled. "The major may wish he were dead with his hangover, but dead he isn't. Unconscious for now, he is, but wait until he wakes up and hears the wallopin' we give him for settin' back our time of departure whilst he sobers up."

"But MilkEye..."

"I know. He told me, too, he saw two men kill Yowell. He and WonTok must've stayed behind and rousted ye after tellin' me where I could find GeeJo, Junior's, body." He paused, then continued. "Jot down a note in yer anthropology papers. What natives tell ye they've seen doesn't always match reality."

"But they saw him attacked and drove away the killers."

"True. Two men jumped Yowell—probably Clare and Al. Tried to skewer him with a cassowary leg bone, like the weapon used in Erik's murder, only this time the would-be murderers wanted to insert it between the ribs into the liver and on into the heart. Death would've followed instantly, but our GeeJo, Junior, had the luck of the Irish with him. Although I'm no Dr. Stanek, mind ye, I've seen him work. He'd say the two dipsticks got their wires crossed and missed their target. Just as Yowell stumbled on a stone and fell across the pathway, they drove the weapon into the folds of the blankets Junior had over his arm and barely broke the skin. The attackers didn't know whether they'd actually succeeded, or if Yowell had passed out and bumped his head. They didn't wait around to find out. Nor would any of us if set upon by two fierce lookin' chaps wieldin' stone axes, springin' from the shadows. Our boy's unconscious but not dead."

"Still, why'd MilkEye say Yowell had been killed?"

"Anytime a warrior falls in battle, attacked by enemies who outnumber him, they assume he's been killed. The body's taken away as a trophy. Only the spirit's left behind. Yowell's lucky MilkEye and WonTok didn't bring ye one of his fingers to grieve over."

"Thank God you got here as soon as you did, Roger, or the assailants might've come back to finish the job."

"Clare and Al? They're gone to strike another day. But I'm wonderin' what made Frank the target this time."

DeAnn reached in her pocket for the four gold nuggets and handed them to Noble. "Maybe they were after these. Frank gave them to me just before he came down here with blankets for MilkEye and WonTok."

"*Come a gutser!* This complicates things. Calls for a little deception."

"Deception?"

"Let Clare and Al think they've succeeded 'til we're able to sober up the major and fly straight to Angoram."

"But we'd have to pass up the remains Kioko said were strewn between here and Angoram."

"Right so, lass. Haven't ye got enough evidence to authenticate Kioko's journals? Finding Wells' possible remains, plus those three Japanese soldiers whose bones we're taking back, as well as the *samurai* sword should do the job. Let the Japanese consulate in Sydney deal with their people. They may want to conduct a search for the chaps we've missed."

"Perhaps you're right, especially under the circumstances. But shouldn't we report this attack on Major Yowell to the District Administrator?"

"I'll have a *chin wag* with him. He's an old friend and will keep it hush-hush if I ask him to."

"But Clare and Al will come back here to search for the gold they were after."

"True, but if there's no body to search and no report of the attempted murder, ye've got to ask yerself, what'll they think?"

"They might suppose the body wasn't found, or MilkEye and WonTok dragged it into the bush, fearing they'd be blamed."

"Exactly, lass. Now all we have to do is keep Yowell out of sight 'til he's ready to fly. Then we'll slip out to the airport and on to Angoram."

"But what if we should meet the assailants?"

"It'll help our deception. We'll breakfast together and invite Clare and Al to join us, if they're there. We'll apologize for our early exit last evenin'."

"They're sure to ask about Frank."

"We'll tell 'em the truth. We'll say he's probably sleeping off his binge, and we didn't want to go to his room and disturb him. Our explanation should deter them from further inquiries. And if I know my criminals, they'll be the ones to beat a hasty exit this time, since they were the last ones, as far as they know, to see Yowell last night."

"I think we're on to something, Roger."

"Sure, lass, but if ye don't mind, I'll be beddin' down in yer room tonight, and from now on I'll stick as close to ye as yer own breath. MilkEye and WonTok can carry Yowell back into my quarters straight away and watch over him 'til we're ready to leave. Junior's not to leave his lodgin'."

"He'll be a prisoner."

"Incarcerated for his own good, ye might say."

The rest of the night DeAnn felt herself tossing and turning in bed. One thought came to the fore with the others swirling inside her head. How would this attempted murder impact her mission on Mount Bosavi? If the two men who attacked Yowell were from Brisbane and were after the gold, wouldn't this mean others knew there was treasure near the B-24 crash site? She would ask Roger in the morning what they should do to keep prospectors out until her part of the investigation of Operation Simpatico ended. If greed for gold was behind the killings and attempts on Yowell and Stanek's lives, she must find a way to warn the pathologist about the danger, and caution him to terminate his investigation, never to come back to Mount Bosavi.

Meantime, the search for Kioko was the next order of business. She wondered about the fates of Kioko and her son. Perhaps Angoram held the answer. She lay awake thinking about her meeting with Mr. Hanzo. A phone call in the morning to the

District Administrator for the Sepik River area, with a request to meet the elderly gentleman, would help in making the arrangements for their visit.

        *   *   *

As Yowell taxied the Beaver to a stop on the airstrip at Angoram, DeAnn reached over and slapped her hand against Roger Noble's. "We pulled it off just as you said we would. Congratulations!"

"And the same back to ye, lass. We'll be out of here as well before Clare and Al discover the ruse."

DeAnn looked out the window and saw the District Administrator, a short, squat man about Roger's age pacing up and down the tarmac. Yowell had barely shut down the engine before the Australian official rushed over to greet them. His face was set in a scowl as they introduced themselves. In a raspy voice, he got down to business. "Ye picked a bad time to visit Angoram. The village is rife with rumors the renegade Yesu has returned, or at least his reincarnated spirit. Yesu was a dreadful menace 30 years ago. Now Yesu's disciple's creatin' a bloody ruckus along the Sepik, kidnappin' young warriors for his uprisin' against the whites," the commissioner explained. "Perhaps ye've heard of Yesu."

Noble twirled his mustache. "Indeed we have. We've got our own legend, only GeeJo was thought of more benignly than this Yesu fellow, or any Japanese officer he might've been in league with during the war."

The administrator touched a hand to his sidearm. "Well, keep yer weapon handy, and I'd arm those two natives ye brought with ye. We could be dealin' with a Japanese straggler left over from the war. Got some of the natives believin' the Japanese still intend to drive us off, and they'll come back with the promised cargo they never received from the Allies. At any rate, one chap never knows what the other has up his sleeve in Angoram these days."

The official turned to leave, but stopped and said, "Oh, by the way, Dr. Toland, a letter in the diplomatic mail pouch from America has arrived for ye marked confidential. Also a manuscript under separate cover also marked confidential arrived with it. I'll send them up once ye've settled in at our guest quarters."

After the commissioner dropped Major Yowell off at his lodging for some more rest, he sent a constable with Dr. Toland and *Kiap* Noble to the home of Akita Hanzo. Before they went in,

Kiap Noble took DeAnn's arm. "A word in yer ear, lass. Strikes me this Yesu-type bloke the commissioner is looking for fits Lt. Mori, the nasty chap in Kioko's journals, although he'd be close to 60 by now."

"Oh, dear! Haven't we enough trouble?"

Mr. Hanzo's housekeeper met them at the door. "You no see *Masta* Hanzo today. Please come back tomorrow. He no like Yesu come back."

DeAnn clasped the housekeeper's hands, "Is there anything we can do to ease the situation? We're on a limited time schedule."

"No, *Misis*. Mister Hanzo 'fraid new Yesu is Lt. Mori. He burn Angoram in war."

"Come a gutser! Tell yer *masta*, I'm of the same mind."

DeAnn thanked the housekeeper and Noble doffed his hat, "Would nine be suitable for our return visit?" the *kiap* asked.

"Yes, Mister Hanzo get up early. Me help him take walk. He no can see."

"We won't keep him long," DeAnn promised.

The woman smiled, nodded, then disappeared through the bamboo curtain serving as a door.

After DeAnn returned to the government guest quarters, she opened the letter sent to her from a Baltimore police officer. She had already heard of Jim Cole's death in a radio phone call from General Bellicosi before they left the Ambuna Lodge in Tari. As she opened Lt. Dunbar's letter, she hoped she would not find bad news about Emerson Stanek. She paused, closed her eyes and offered a silent prayer. Then, after reading the first page, she offered another, this prayer to give thanks he was well.

The second item was a copy of Cole's manuscript that filled her in on all that Stanek had learned from reading Cole's confession. Both had suspected Cole's involvement was more personal than an opportunity for an exclusive article for his paper. But he had held secrets key to their investigation that revealed his deep involvement in the fate of the ten knights.

∗   ∗   ∗

The heat and humidity forced DeAnn and Noble to slacken their pace as they walked along the river toward the home of Mr. Hanzo. Below them, the river people were already out in the Sepik in their dugout canoes, fishing or looking for crocodiles. Clustered around the river were huts on stilts, and the women and children

MEL R. JONES

were busy climbing up and down ladders fastened to the huts.
Occasionally, at the foot of a ladder, she saw a warrior at work on a
mask especially carved for the tourist trade. The raised skin on the
back, shoulders and chests of the warriors caught her eye, and she
asked Roger the significance of the scarred torsos.

"Ye'll see the same pattern repeated among the people on the
Sepik. They're cut up at their initiation ceremonies to resemble the
pukpuk, or crocodile's skin. It's quite painful I'm told, as they rub
ashes into the wound to make the bumps. Missionaries have made
no headway in stopin' the process, 'though Lord knows they've
tried."

By the time Noble finished his explanation, they were at Mr.
Hanzo's door, five minutes early for their appointment. The
housekeeper greeted them and pointed to a table set for tea in the
center of the room. Once they were seated, she went into another
room and returned with a man so frail and stooped, the
magnificent robe of sheer purple over white with a golden stole he
wore dwarfed his body. It rustled against the planks in the floor as
he shuffled to his place at the table.

He spoke in English. "Good morning. You've come to hear the
story of Kioko. She saved my life, you know, when Angoram was
bombed during the war." His voice cracked as he continued. "But I
was unable to save her from death. The rascals buried her up to her
neck in the muck and threw stones at her head."

"I've just learned about Kioko's brutal murder in a manuscript
from a friend. I'm so sorry," DeAnn replied as she wiped tears
from her own eyes. When she regained her composure, DeAnn
turned to Noble and asked, "Rascals?"

"It's the local name for thieves, hoodlums and other
troublemakers."

The old man raised a bony finger. "Ah, but these rascals were
set on killing Kioko and her son Kazuo. Some people said they
were after the gold she carried, but they had pilfered it by stripping
her of her clothes. There was no need to kill her in such a brutal
manner. It hurts me to tell this story, so please, if you have any
questions about the incident, ask them quickly."

DeAnn reached across the table and took the old man's hand in
hers. "You were very dear to Kioko. I know this from the story she
wrote on the tablets you gave her before she left Angoram with her
brother Taro and a party of soldiers led by Lt. Mori."

She felt the old man's hand grow tense under hers. "Mori was the devil himself. He's responsible for the deaths of many people. I know little of him except I believe he was here two years ago with Kazuo."

"Did you see him, Mr. Hanzo?"

"No. I was already blind and my housekeeper had left on an errand, so I was alone when they came. He stood behind the bamboo curtain in the doorway and only Kazuo entered. The boy, now a young man, said he had come to say goodbye. Someone who had promised to come back for his mother had found him, and they were going home to his relatives in Japan. I asked who was with him and why he didn't come inside.

"Kazuo said he couldn't even give me his name, for he had done a terrible thing to Angoram during the war. If the people knew he was here, he would die like Kazuo's mother. Perhaps he would bring trouble to my household as well for harboring Kazuo all those years in the village of my housekeeper, several days walk from this place, where he grew up. Kazuo said he didn't know how the man had found him, but he had spent many years in this land. He asked me to forgive him, but he couldn't say any more."

The old man brushed tears from his eyes. "I wept at losing Kazuo and feared for his safety. Only one man could've survived so long in the bush, so I was certain the man behind the curtain was Michio Mori. Michio, 'man with the strength of 3,000'."

DeAnn patted Hanzo's hand. "The man who came to your home two years ago could've been GeeJo, Kioko's husband and the American aviator we're searching for."

"Kioko didn't tell me who Kazuo's father was. If what you say is true, I'll die with some sense of good for Kazuo coming from the horrors of war set in motion so long ago."

DeAnn reached into her backpack and took out a piece of paper and placed it in the hands of the old man. "When you gave Kioko the calligraphy brushes and tablets to give to Taro, you asked for a poem upon their return. I have brought a Haiku verse for you. Would you like me to read it?"

"Please. Is it by Taro or Kioko?"

"I'll read it, and then you'll know:

Spring blossom unfolds.
Love, the sweet nectar of life,
Eroded by fear."

"Kioko-san wrote it." His tears fell freely now. "Forgive me. I'm an actor turned gardener, filled with sentimental nostalgia for things as they used to be before the war."

The housekeeper knelt beside the old man and rubbed his shoulders. "You rest now. *Misis* and *kiap* let you go."

Hanzo nodded. "She's right. I talk too much, but I'll answer one more question as you finish your morning tea, cooler than the outside temperature, in the Japanese style."

DeAnn drew the cup to her lips, paused and asked, "Where might we find Kioko's remains or burial ground?"

"She has gone home to the inn below Satta Mountain where the Takaido Road bends close to Suraga Bay in the plot of her ancestors. Hers is the only grave bearing a cross for its marker, as we requested in her behalf."

"But, how? Did Kazuo and the man with him take her remains back with them?"

"No. The morning after her murder, my housekeeper, two strong men from her village and I dug her out of the mud, wrapped her in cloth and sent her home in a coffin. In death she never gave up her faith. Her hands were folded to form a cross. What effort she made to clasp them so, pushing against thick mud. She had left some pieces of gold with me. I used them to pay for the coffin, the preparation of her body for transport to Wewak and passage on a steamer to take her home to Japan."

Hanzo rose from his chair at the table with great effort, as DeAnn put her cup down and moved toward the old man. Her arms gently enfolded more robe than flesh. "Thank you, Mr. Hanzo. You've been of great service to Kioko and those she loved. I've a friend who'll see those responsible for her murder are brought to justice." The old man bowed and left the room.

Later that day, DeAnn hurried through lunch and skipped dinner so she could write down her experiences and observations from their journey up-country in her reply to Lt. Dunbar's letter. She knew it'd be passed on to Emerson Stanek. "I must cover every detail," she told herself. "Who knows what the brilliant mind of Emerson will deduce from any new information, deemed insignificant by an ordinary observer?"

She wished she could see his face and hear the excitement in his voice as he unfolded each clue. Surprised at how much she longed to see him, DeAnn wondered if they would ever again experience the magic created between them by the reading of Kioko's log of love.

Tomorrow they would stop in Goroka to brief General Bellicosi, and then fly back to Mount Bosavi to continue their search for remains. On the way, she intended to question MilkEye. As Stanek had said, MilkEye, of all the people involved in the case, knew more than anyone what had happened 30 years ago on Mount Bosavi. Getting the old warrior to part with this information was her next task. Still, she wondered how cooperative MilkEye might be if he found out Kioko was dead and his personal quest had ended. Then, too, General Bellicosi could pull the plug on Operation Simpatico now that his patron, President Nixon, was working feverishly to conclude the war in Vietnam.

General Bellicosi must be handled tactfully. The report to him need not be as thorough as the one she hoped to get into Stanek's hands. If nothing else, the general was unpredictable. And without Cole and Stanek in the picture, he might be inclined to place tentatively identified remains into a mass grave with those yet to be authenticated. Calling the mission accomplished, he might then send everyone packing, especially once informed of the attempt on the life of Major Frank Yowell.

51 PATHOLOGIST'S SPECULATIONS

Baltimore, Maryland, 1973

AFTER GOING OVER the dental charts with a forensic specialist, Stanek left word for Lt. Dunbar to meet with him as soon as possible. The detective appeared the same afternoon and strode into Stanek's hospital room, his face set in a grin. "Hear you've hit paydirt, Doc."

Stanek touched the scar on his cheek. "We have the dental records of three former prosecutors alleged to have been murdered by Filipino Freddie. All of the victims had one or more crowns removed after the murder. Any guess as to why, Sam?"

"To get the gold, I suppose."

"Indeed. Remember we found a gold crown missing on Dr. Haveland's body?"

"My stars! Added to the collection Freddie wore on his gold chain, no doubt."

"Yes, but there's more to this case than a few gold crowns."

"I figured as much."

"Let me go ahead," Stanek proposed, "and give you as much of the story as I've been able to piece together so far. Keep in mind what I'm about to say is speculative until all the evidence is in."

The lieutenant rested his elbows on the table and placed his chin in his hands. "Please do. And if there're parts I don't fully grasp, I'll shoot a question at you."

"Fair enough. And your insight as a homicide detective will help keep me focused."

"You've got the floor, Doc."

Stanek took in a deep breath and exhaled. "I think we both agree on some salient facts. Freddie murdered the prosecutors, not for the gold, but to get them off his case. Gold fever was a secondary motive, opportunities, you might say, in the murders committed here on Freddie's home turf. But for those attempted or carried out in Hawaii and New Guinea, gold, or rather the need to conceal it, seems a paramount concern of the mastermind."

"So there's a connection between 'Mr. Big' and your B-24 bomber case."

"Filipino Freddie is the linchpin. I initially thought he was after my cancer research, but then I realized if it were the case, Freddie could've easily burglarized one of the proposals sent to the committee in advance of my hearing for a grant. No. The night he murdered Dr. Haveland, Freddie was after something more important to the people above him. He wanted to get his hands on the documents about the ten knights case Haveland had passed on to me."

"But why?"

"'Cause the ringleader, or gang, pulling Freddie's strings wanted to know whether or not those documents mentioned the gold discovery on Mount Bosavi."

"So, Freddie and his boys murdered Dr. Haveland over something as trivial as a Pentagon report on soldiers long forgotten? It's hard to believe."

"Not exactly trivial if you're sitting on a mother lode of gold in a remote area of New Guinea and want to get as much of it out of the country as you can before anyone gets wind of the find. Factor in the primitive method our killer is forced to use to smelt and transport the material out of the highlands, so as to avoid detection before the Papuans gain independence in 1975."

"I see. There's where the salt train comes in. And don't forget the natives load the salt bundles filled with gold on the *D'Albertis* at Daru."

"Yes, but they're offloaded before the ship reaches Manila, bound for a destination we've yet to discover.

Dunbar leaned back and scratched his head. "Hard to imagine a small-time criminal like Freddie was smart enough to carry out a complex scheme."

"Complex in its global reach, Sam, but the genius lies in its simplicity. We agree Freddie isn't the mastermind."

"Then why did he kill Dr. Haveland and not just ransack his office for the documents like he did anyway?"

"And the answer is, of course, thanks to those dental records you turned up, once Freddie learned Dr. Haveland had what he called 'smoking gun' evidence against him, he did some free-lancing on his own. After they heard Haveland's comment to the custodian, Freddie and his henchmen followed him from the pathology laboratory to his office in the administration building. The killers didn't realize, however, that Hopkins protocol prescribes a process for take-home materials. They must be inserted in a purple envelope and delivered by a bonded messenger. Before he left the pathology building, Dr. Haveland dropped the evidence against Freddie in the pickup bin.

"Now, since the original intent of the gang was to search Haveland's office for Dr. Toland's report from New Guinea, Freddie decided to exceed his orders and help his own case. What better way than to destroy the new evidence—the dental records Dr. Haveland was thought to have in his possession. When Freddie came up empty-handed, on both counts I might add, he killed Haveland to keep him from testifying. He took Tom's gold crown for his macabre collection of teeth as another trophy from prosecutors he had murdered."

"Still, Freddie involved in world-wide gold smuggling? It seems hardly possible."

"Don't sell him short, Sam. The Philippines aren't far from New Guinea. Freddie might've been in or near Papua once or twice in his life, where he picked up the blade-down-the-back technique for murder, almost exclusive to the territory, I'm told. A young interpreter was killed in the same manner while I was there. Only the murder weapon was a sharpened cassowary leg meant for my back."

"And you think Freddie was responsible for the multiple attempts on your life?"

"No. Only those here when those two suspicious characters came to my hotel room door in Baltimore, and later when they showed up in Hawaii. Shortly after I reached New Guinea, you sent word Freddie was dead. His murder didn't stop the man with the pockmarked face from striking again, this time at the hospital in Goroka."

"My stars! Now I get the picture. His bosses whacked Freddie for a botched job, and they melted the gold teeth in his mouth with hot lead to shut him up for good. Then they took the gold chain and probably melted it down as well."

"You're right. And don't forget, Freddie's actions called attention to the whole enterprise. The murders on campus weren't supposed to happen. And maybe Freddie knew too much about the gold shipments. Perhaps he was getting greedy for more gold than he found in the crowns of his victims and pilfered gold from the off-loaded shipments."

"So you're saying he became a real liability, especially since he was under investigation."

"True, but whoever was behind the operation didn't count on my taking Dr. Haveland's place on the New Guinea investigation. The last thing the gold smugglers wanted was a forensic pathologist snooping around their center of operations on Mount Bosavi. They knew Haveland wouldn't take the offer to go to New Guinea because of the rigors involved and his advanced age."

"Weren't they concerned about the army body-recovery team led by your friend, Dr. Toland?

"As long as the CIL kept to the business of seeking the remains of the bomber crew, they were tolerated. But if any one tried to take gold out of there, and they knew about it, they were stopped. It happened to a Japanese woman named Kioko, and more recently, Major Frank Yowell was almost killed, as Dr. Toland reported in her letter you shared with me. I'm afraid tolerance is no longer an option for the killer. Ever since we had Interpol intercept the gold, the smugglers know their transport system has been compromised. Worse yet, they figure word is out about the gold discovery. Nobody, except the natives, is safe on Mount Bosavi any longer, especially if they venture toward the top."

"Have you anticipated the gold smugglers' next move?"

"If the top man is as greedy as I believe he is, he'll keep the operation running to drain the last ounce of gold he can get from Mount Bosavi. He's probably got a contingency plan for speedy transport out of the country."

"And where do the photos of the severed hand you asked me to get from Walter Reed fit into all of this?"

"You've got them?"

"Yep. And my stars! Did it take some doing." Dunbar handed the photos to the pathologist.

Stanek could see the detective was pleased with himself. "Great work, Sam! Another important piece of the puzzle falls into place." He drew his finger across the outline of a hand floating in a jar of formaldehyde. "See here, at the wrist where the blow was delivered. There are no jagged edges on the cut, meaning the blow was struck with a sharp, downward thrust, heavy or strong enough to slice through skin and bone."

"You mean like the meat cleaver Freddie used?"

"No, I've got something else in mind more consistent with observations made inside the wrecked aircraft with the assistance of patrol officer Noble. At that time we determined the victim had a lighter in his right hand and had laid his automatic down on the moldy jungle floor under the rusted out aircraft to dig with his left hand. Someone struck him from above probably aiming at his neck and caught his wrist instead. Judging from the probable distance from the assailant to the victim, and now these photographs, I'd say the weapon used to cut off the hand was a long, sharp instrument along the order of a *samurai* sword, carried by Japanese officers during the war."

"What was the victim looking for in the dark, digging in the ground. Have you figured it out?"

Stanek stroked the scar on his cheek again. "Gold—gold the assailant didn't want to lose, or let anyone else take out of the country. I hope to confirm this with another trip to New Guinea. I believe there's more gold hidden in the aircraft somewhere. We might have to move the wreckage to find it."

"My stars, Doc. Your brain never takes a rest. No wonder you're so good at what you do. I've got the other information you requested to run through your precision mind."

"You mean the passenger list of prisoners ferried from New Guinea to Manila and then to Tokyo after the end of the war?"

"Yep. I've got the list right here."

"Summarize it for me, Sam."

"One name doesn't check out, a prisoner of war named Hideo Yamazaki. According to Japanese authorities, the only soldier with that name was killed in 1905 during the Russian/Japanese War. Means he couldn't have been repatriated, leaving New Guinea on the *D'Albertis* at the end of WW II as the record shows. We've got an alias."

"Splendid research! We make a good team, Sam."

"Shucks. It's easy when you've got someone pointing you in the right direction. Maybe after this is over, you'll help me with a few unsolved murder cases on my docket?"

"I'll be busy for awhile on my cancer research, but after it's completed, who knows?"

"Meantime, Doc, anything else I can do for you?"

"No. We don't want to tip our hand any more than we already have. Your letter to Dr. Toland warned her against an attempt to reach the top of Mount Bosavi. But I'd like to get reinstated on the ten knights case, so I can go up the mountain and finish this investigation."

"My stars! Maybe I can help you meet this goal. The little girl you wrote the poem about leaves for..."

"Now it's my turn to ask. How does Margaret fit in?"

"She's the granddaughter of a four-star general. I made his acquaintance when he was a colonel at Fort Holabird, the former intelligence school downtown. After I tell him what you've told me, maybe he'll use his clout to get you reinstated. If this General Bellicosi doesn't like it, so what? I've observed, in a battle of stars, the man with the most always wins."

"Thanks, Sam, you're a real friend."

"Hey, Doc, you scratch my back and I scratch yours. That's how the guys in our business survive. But I hope you'll wait to go back to New Guinea 'til you get a clean bill of health."

52 REQUEST FOR REMAINS RECOVERY

Goroka, Papua New Guinea, 1973

AFTER THEY REACHED Goroka, DeAnn found a way to draw MilkEye aside. WonTok wanted to join them, as did Noble, but the anthropologist insisted she and MilkEye meet alone.

"He's more likely to open up in a one-on-one," she whispered to Noble, who stood on the veranda of her bungalow. "Give us about 30 minutes before you and WonTok rejoin us."

Noble twisted his bush hat in his hands. "This bloke isn't to be trusted no matter how friendly and helpful he appears. It'd be the same as leavin' ye alone with an untamed animal. Ye never know if the beast will come to the fore, or what he'll do. Must I remind ye of my mistake with a native? Cost me dearly, it did. My wife and daughter's lives were the horrible price paid."

She reached out and touched his hand. "I remember the terrible tale, and I'm so very sorry for your loss. Don't ever feel I don't appreciate how you look after me. But we both have jobs to do, so let's work out a compromise, shall we? Any ideas?"

"Never known an Aussie to be without one. I'll stay here on the veranda whilst ye and MilkEye ruminate out there in the clearing where I can keep an eye on ye."

"And WonTok?"

"I'll keep him here with me."

"Agreed."

"Now get along, lass, before I change me mind."

542

DeAnn led MilkEye to the open grassy area surrounded by small trees facing the mountains to the west. Their purple peaks appeared like amethyst crystals reaching for the last bit of sunlight of the day. As they walked side by side, DeAnn sensed the old warrior had instinctively picked up the reason for their separation from the others.

She told MilkEye she had news of LikLik. His daughter was well and had made many friends. In a month or so, she would be back with the Riami, relating all the stories and wonders of the white man's world.

MilkEye grunted. "Maybe LikLik like white people's place too much. No come back from sick house."

His tone was so riddled with sadness she felt obliged to ask what he thought of the white man's world.

MilkEye grunted again. "People hurry up too much. No time to look in here." He pointed to his heart. He continued, "*Balus* okay one time, but me like land, hear birds sing, river come down mountain like thunder."

DeAnn hesitated, then said, "I'm sure Kioko-san would agree with you, MilkEye. Despite its hardships, she loved this country where her son was born. Did you know the boy?"

MilkEye nodded.

"Then you know she had the same love for Kazuo you have for LikLik. And now her son will have to finish her life story, since she has gone to the spirit world."

MilkEye wailed. "*Misis*, no true! Kioko-san die? Me need Kioko-san to trap evil socery of Two Face inside her books! Take away curse on me and LikLik."

"Oh, dear, I'm sorry I've upset you."

MilkEye wailed even louder. Noble called out from the veranda, "What's he screaming about? Is everything okay?"

DeAnn waved at him to stay put. MilkEye took a knife from his girdle and laid his finger across a stone bench.

DeAnn stayed his hand. "MilkEye, listen to me! Stop! I know it's Riami custom to amputate a finger for a deep felt sorrow, but it won't help bring Kioko-san back. There're others, like her husband, GeeJo, who'll help you in your quest, if he still lives."

MilkEye withdrew the blade. "GeeJo here?"

"No, but with your assistance, we hope to find him. He's proven he's a great sorcerer. I've heard GeeJo has a place of honor in the Riami warrior's spirit house."

MilkEye squinted. "How *meri* know about taboo house?"

"In our search for our brothers' bones, we've searched everywhere. One of my soldiers saw the shrine dedicated to GeeJo in the men's spirit house."

MilkEye attempted to grin. "Ah, good. No *meri* go in spirit house."

DeAnn smiled back. "We must know other things to find GeeJo, who came to the Riami with Kioko and Kazuo."

"Me no can tell of mysteries belong in spirit house."

"No. But, can you tell me what name the Riami men called GeeJo by in the spirit house?"

"You like name GeeJo give Riami warriors in secret?"

"Yes. We can't find him without it."

"GeeJo tell me his name *one-mates* on great *balus* call him. Same name he give to Riami warriors in spirit house."

"What was it?"

MilkEye hesitated and looked up toward the setting sun, as if he were asking a silent question.

"Situmu no speak, so me tell to help you find GeeJo, MilkEye need GeeJo now Kioko-san die. GeeJo's secret name is 'Pip'. Riami warriors no speak secret name to *meris*, or to Kioko-san."

DeAnn whispered under her breath, "Phillipi I. Patterson, bombardier, identified at last!" To MilkEye she said, "You've helped us more than you know."

"Situmu cross me tell secret name. But Kioko-san is spirit now. Please help me find GeeJo, who can take away Two Face's curse on me, save LikLik and line of Situmu. Stan-neck knows no good thing me do, but he no speak to Tugaru. Give me more time to fight curse. *Misis*, me know, bears soul of Kioko-san and Stan-neck soul of GeeJo."

MilkEye turned to leave, but DeAnn grasped his arm just above the brass wristband made from cartridge shells. "GeeJo gave you this, didn't he?"

MilkEye nodded. "At initiation as Riami warrior."

"You and WonTok have been very helpful in finding the bones we're searching for. Do you know where any other bones of white men might be found?"

MilkEye pointed to the southwest beyond the purple ridge of mountains. "Small *balus* bring us back to mountain we come from."

"You mean Mount Bosavi?"

MilkEye hesitated again. "Situmu tell GeeJo about bones."

"Did your papa tell GeeJo where the bones are buried?"

"Yes. Situmu bring GeeJo to see place."

"Is it near the mountain top where evil Two Face lives?"

"Yes. But Situmu and GeeJo go up mountain before Tugaru Two Face become evil."

"Did GeeJo take the remains of his *one-mate* down the mountain?"

"No. GeeJo leave on mountain top. Like he leave three *one-mates* at Lower Falls where WonTok and me help GeeJo put white people bones in ground. But GeeJo bring *one-mate's* book back and put in ground with other *one-mates* near great *balus*."

"Thank you for showing *Kiap* Noble and Major Yowell where the remains at Lower Falls were buried. Do you know where the mountain burial site is?"

"Yes. Sky people put *one-mate* under stone by totem of Tugaru Two Face.

DeAnn realized the Tugaru totem must be the grinning skull and crossbombs from the B-24's missing stabilizer located near the mountain top. "Would you lead me to this place?" she asked.

"Me no go where evil Two Face lives. Evil Two Face kill us if *misis* look for bones there."

"Perhaps General Bellicosi will help me find a safe way to search for the bones on the mountain top."

"Evil Two Face kill Situmu. Your *luluai* no match for Two Face. Me no more speak until spirit of Situmu speak to me."

*   *   *

DeAnn tossed and turned in bed through a night she thought was her most miserable since arriving in New Guinea. She took no pleasure as the morning dawned fair, fine and clear, enhancing Goroka's eternal spring-like climate. She rehearsed over and over again what to say in her verbal report to General Bellicosi. How could she work in the attempt on Major Yowell's life without a trace of panic in her voice? The exasperated general was anxious to wrap up the ten knights case and felt her CIL team had consumed too much time away from the identification process.

The general had told her, "This is the window of opportunity we have before Congress gets wind we've diverted funds and resources to what the President's opponents would tout as a propaganda ploy."

$*$ $*$ $*$

"Had the opportunity passed?" she wondered as she sipped her coffee in the dining room where Bellicosi said they would meet. It did not bode well for her mission that he was coming to her instead of summoning her. What if Bellicosi called this meeting to order the CIL team to pack their bags and return to their home station in Thailand? To her surprise, the general greeted her with a cheerful hello and, even more oddly, a bear hug. He took the chair next to hers and lit a cigar.

"Major Yowell told me you've done a fantastic job locating the missing remains. By my calculation, you've got eight down and two more still unaccounted for. Actually, eight may be all we need to publicly launch Operation Simpatico."

He paused and continued before she could respond. "You may not have heard the news, but the President's up to his arm pits with congressional allegations very likely leading to a call for impeachment over this Watergate nonsense. Nixon will be lucky if he gets through 1973 without a trial. I don't have to tell you when he goes, with him goes all the support for this mission. So time is of the essence. Tell me, how soon can you shut down your operations on Mount Bosavi (pardon the barracks' expression) 'before the shit hits the fan'?"

In one sense, DeAnn was relieved he had not brought up the Yowell incident, which meant he had already heard about it, probably from Frank Yowell himself. The major must've admitted his assailants were after gold, and Al and Clare's bungled attempt had little to do with her investigation.

On the other hand, Emerson Stanek must've heard by now of the attempted murder in her reply to Lt. Dunbar's letter and would've plugged this information into his calculations. Stanek might upset the timetable if he could find a way to continue following the criminal leads. She looked General Bellicosi right in the eyes, the way a subordinate was supposed to face a superior whenever something important lay on the line.

"We're on the brink of identifying all the remains, and I think you'll agree, sir, completion would best fit your motto that no soldier will be left behind."

Bellicosi twirled his cigar in his fingers. "But you've got to admit, my dear, circumstances occur to make the best laid plans inoperable. Eight of ten might be the best we can do, unless you can convince me there's a probability you'll find the last two knights within the next 15 days."

"Begging your pardon, sir, but why only 15 days?"

Bellicosi puffed away on his cigar and blew the smoke out of the side of his mouth as their eyes continued to meet. "With Cole gone, I've got to find another outlet for our story, only this time it won't be an exclusive. Fifteen days from now, I plan to hold a press conference in Hawaii.

Under the table, the President has given his consent. He needs all the good news he can garner at the moment."

As the smoke swirled back toward her, DeAnn turned in the opposite direction. Bellicosi got the message, took the cigar out of his mouth and began twirling it again. "Well, the ball's in your court, my dear Dr. Toland. Tell me where you think the remains of the final crew members are, and whether you can close down this case in the time allotted."

"Of the remaining two, one was buried by his comrades on top of Mount Bosavi. The other, the survivor who was the bombardier, may be living in Japan."

"Japan! What in the hell is he doing there?"

"Living with his son."

"Lord, Almighty! Don't tell me he's a turncoat and went over to the Japanese side during the war! This information would torpedo Operation Simpatico! We'll have to keep it under wraps. What about the other one? Is he a deserter, too?"

"No, sir. Like I said, his body's buried at the top of the mountain. I'd like to go up there to retrieve it."

"I can't let you do any such thing without a whole army escorting you. Have you forgotten what Dr. Stanek said about a murderer being up there? How do you know it's not your bombardier gone berserk and dressed in armor?"

"I don't know for certain. No one can at this point. Nevertheless, I can lead a small party up there to investigate and recover the remains we know are there."

"Why not take an army and storm the place?"

"Because it'd alert whoever's up there we're on our way, and they might escape."

"Seems to me like you've crossed over into Stanek's territory. Need I remind you, we're not here, nor was it ever our mission, to track down criminals and solve crimes, real or imagined. Let the Aussies worry about the crimes."

"I could take *Kiap* Noble with me to the mountain top to satisfy Australian concerns."

"How do you know he'd go?"

"Because we discussed it."

"Behind my back?"

"No, sir. I only asked Roger last night as part of my report to you."

Bellicosi grunted. "Who else have you spoken to about this plan?"

"Major Yowell and two natives, MilkEye and WonTok."

"And they thought it could be done?"

"MilkEye has been all over the mountain as a boy with his father. He knows how to slip in and back out again without being detected. He told me about the grave site."

General Bellicosi rose an inch or two in his chair and broke wind, which he attempted to cover up with another grunt. "Damn if you don't have me over a barrel, DeAnn. Here's what we'll do. You can go up there, but you're on your own. If something happens, I didn't even know you made the attempt. Let's be clear about it."

"Yes, sir. I understand."

"Now about this traitor who went over to the Japanese side. We haven't discussed it either. In other words, this whole conversation is off the record, except you've got 15 days to complete your mission."

Relieved, DeAnn slumped back in her chair. "Understood. But there's something you should know. The bombardier you think betrayed his country did no such thing. From the evidence available to us, we believe he spent the last 28 years in New Guinea searching for his lost crewmembers, aiding his family and helping the natives. They called him 'GeeJo,' which is their way of saying 'G.I. Joe'." Most of this information was gleaned from the six journals of a Japanese woman who lived as GeeJo's wife on and around Mount Bosavi for a long period of time."

"Japanese woman! How'd she get there? Why haven't you told me about this?"

"I wanted to verify her story before I presented it to you. We uncovered credible evidence on my last journey to authenticate at least part of her journals."

"Well, you'd better hang on to them a little longer. Like I said, this conversation never took place."

"They stood up and shook hands. "Be careful, Dr. Toland. Operation Simpatico needs your expertise and credibility. I want you at my side during the press conference. If you have second thoughts about going up Mount Bosavi, remember eight sets of remains will suffice for our purposes. I'll talk to you later about the press conference."

53 KILLER'S IDENTITY DEDUCED

Baltimore, Maryland, 1973

THREE DAYS AFTER his meeting with Lt. Dunbar, Emerson looked up to see Catherine entering his room at John's Hopkins. She apologized for missing her usual every other day visit and gave as her excuse an out-of-town business trip. Since the joint meeting held with their mother when Catherine agreed to look after Patricia Stanek and continue checking on LikLik, Emerson noticed a more cordial tone in the relationship with his adoptive sister. They had buried much of the rancor between them, he thought. He was pleased Lt. Dunbar had helped him make progress on the ten knights case when Catherine was away.

On entering, Catherine threaded her way around three easels he had erected at the foot of his bed. She replaced the flowers on the nightstand with fresh ones she had brought. Glancing at the charts on the easels, she read aloud the headings on each one.

"Motive, suspects, victims/manner of death. Really, Emerson. I can see you're not working on your cancer research. Must you fill your mind with a case no longer yours to solve?"

He forced a smile. She kissed his cheek, and he could smell the jasmine perfume she favored. "Sorry to disappoint you, but the evidence suggests this case is linked to Tom Haveland's murder. However, we need to identify the murderer and bring him in."

"I hope you'll leave the apprehension part to Lt. Dunbar. What a pest he's become."

"We disagree there. Dunbar's made it possible for me to get this far. I'll have to trap this multiple murderer myself if he's to be caught."

"Not while you're still recovering."

"Every day my arm and shoulder are getting stronger. In another week, I'll be able to go back to New Guinea."

"New Guinea?"

"Yes, it's where our killer operates."

"Let Miss What's-Her-Name earn her government pay as a consultant. Why can't you turn the matter over to her or the Australian government? I'll talk to General Bellicosi."

"No! You'd spoil my plan."

"What plan?"

"If you're really interested, let me go over my findings with you. Might be good to think out loud. Like Tom used to say, 'Look for clues missed on the first, second, or third go around."

"Very well, but I can't promise I won't get bored. When father tried to discuss case histories with me, my mind wandered off to more pleasant things than murder and criminal behavior."

"Without a doubt, this case is more interesting than any Rufus Stanek ever encountered. Guarantee it."

She pushed out her lower lip. "Let's leave father out of this, shall we?"

"Gladly. You brought him up, not me."

"And I'd rather hear about your old charts than rekindle old antagonisms."

"Well, then, here goes. Under 'motive,' I've decided the overarching one is greed—the lust for gold. Other possibilities, such as revenge or betrayal, are all collateral to the driving force—gold."

"And where is this gold?"

"You saw it yourself on your visit to Mount Bosavi with Bellicosi. Remember how embarrassed Major Yowell was when the native MilkEye offered a gold nugget to the general to buy passage for his daughter? No doubt Yowell also received some gold from MilkEye."

Catherine rolled her eyes. "So who cares? One or two nuggets won't buy too much."

"No. But imagine there's a mountain teeming with gold, and you found a way to convert the nuggets into dollars and filter it through the economy. We're talking about riches beyond yours and Charles' dreams."

"Fine. Enough on motive. What about your suspects? Who are these people you've listed? I've never heard of them."

Stanek pointed to the middle chart. "Lt. Mori, *Kiap* Mackelwaite, and the surviving American aviator. None are likely to travel in your circles."

"Survivor? General Bellicosi himself told me there weren't any survivors of the bomber crash. How can you list a survivor as a suspect?"

"Good, Catherine. You've singled out the most speculative suspect of all. But here, a little girl in the hospital who asked me to write a poem about falling leaves for her, combined with your mother's comments, set me to thinking. Suppose one of the ten crew members parachuted out, like a leaf falling from a tree, perhaps by some sort of accident or miscommunication, at the vanishing point miles before the B-24 crashed. He could be the survivor written about in a Japanese woman's journals found at Mount Bosavi. From her, we learn he found gold on the mountain. If he's still living, we can't discount him as a suspect."

"You wrote a poem for a little girl? You haven't written poetry since those silly little ditties mother gushed over on Mother's Day. This is so unlike you. And this Japanese woman, who is she?"

He pointed to the end chart. "Kioko was one of the victims in this case of many murders, Tom Haveland's included."

Catherine raised an eyebrow. "Who'd have thought you'd encounter two women on your jungle excursion."

"Let me finish, and you'll see how all this fits together."

"No, thanks. I've heard enough, especially since I see you show Kioko as having been brutally murdered, as was Taro, whoever he was, on your list of 'victims and manner of death'. Spare me the details. I've no stomach for it."

"As you wish. So, what shall we talk about?"

"Anything but New Guinea. It was a horrible experience for you. You were almost killed and left me alone to handle mother. She's doing well by the way and sends you a kiss." She bent over and kissed him full on the lips.

He turned slightly. "That was no motherly kiss."

"You're right. It sprang from my pent up emotions. Oh, Emerson, how I wish we could recapture what we had before the row with father."

He pushed the button to raise the top of his bed so he was almost eye-level with Catherine. "You know what's needed. The prayer book in front of the Christ statue still awaits you."

"A young girl's promise, Emerson, but I'm a woman now. You should be able to take my word of apology without forcing me to publicly humiliate myself."

"Meaning you consider your reputation more precious than mine. Hardly a foundation to restart a relationship."

Catherine dabbed at her eyes with the jasmine-scented handkerchief. "Must you always leave me in tears? I thought we were beginning to set things right. But you've got my promise; I'll never stop trying. I'm here when you need me."

"Very good of you, Catherine, and don't think I'm unappreciative of the care you've already given, including the Pinkerton detective you've assigned as my body guard. But if you're sincere, there's something you can do for me straightaway."

"Tell me, and if it's within my power, it'll be done."

"Let me borrow one of your charter jets to fly me to New Guinea."

"Oh, no! Don't ask me such a thing. I'd never forgive myself if something happened to you. Besides, the airline went to Charles as part of our divorce settlement. I contract with him for Stanek Laboratories' corporate jets."

"I'll just have to come up with something else. A lot of people are in danger and need my help in New Guinea."

Catherine stepped back from the bed. "One, I'm sure, is your Dr. Toland. How could you ask me to help you dig deeper into the camp of a rival? She has her hooks out for you, whether you know it or not."

"If true, why should it make you so unhappy?"

"Because you know deep down I've never stopped loving you. And the thought of you being in the arms of another woman is unbearable." She moved toward the door. "I must leave before I fall to pieces altogether. Perhaps a few more days apart will give you time to reflect on our relationship, and I don't mean as brother and sister. Please give me some hope. You're all I have."

After Catherine had gone, he tried to convince himself this was one more ploy to get her hands on his cancer research project. Once the ten knights case was solved, he would transfer his cancer research to the non-profit corporation he had spoken to Catherine about. It could circumvent the curse Rufus Stanek had placed on his children to prevent any business connection between them. Only then would he be free of Catherine, except as a brother with a tainted reputation for an act she would never take responsibility for.

He looked at the charts again. It dawned on him Catherine had unknowingly made a contribution to the ten knights case. The manner of death the killer used to get rid of his victims was the key to nailing him. Why should the murders of Kioko and Taro be so brutal—the mutilation of Kioko's face with stones and Taro's body with innumerable sword slashes—unlike the other victims, as if the killer wanted to drive the two Japanese out of existence?

From his experience, this kind of destruction in a murder case signaled a great deal of passion between the killer and his prey. Domestic cases where one spouse was caught cheating on the other, or among homosexuals trying to erase errant partners from their lives, were examples.

Now he knew whom to look for. All he needed was the evidence to confirm his findings. He must leave immediately for New Guinea, because DeAnn Toland was in grave danger. He mulled over how this could be accomplished and decided he would call Charles, his former brother-in-law, and ask him to make an aircraft available for a flight the next morning.

By evening, he reached Charles, and the playboy/tycoon was surprised to hear from him. When told of the purpose of the call, he agreed to provide immediate assistance. "Anything Catherine is against, I'm always for. Just a little game we continue to play. It'll be interesting to see what she comes up with to get even with me for helping you. And, who knows, one of these days she might give up our little game and come back to me," Charles said.

Another piece of luck fell into Emerson's lap. Before he retired, he received a call from Lt. Dunbar who said he had talked to his friend, the four star general, and the way was clear for him to get back on the ten knights case. Lt. Dunbar chuckled as he relayed the conversation. "Margaret's grandfather told me to leave General Bellicosi to him, and to make things easier for you, just let him know, and he'd have an aircraft standing by in Port Moresby to fly you to Mount Bosavi." Dunbar chuckled again. "See, I told you, Doc. The guy with the most stars wins every time."

"Thanks, Sam. Your timing couldn't be better. I'm leaving for New Guinea on a chartered flight in the morning. If you could arrange things on the other end, and find a ruse to get the Pinkerton guy off my back long enough for me to slip away, I'm beholden to you."

"We'll just pull him aside and use the old ploy—check his license to carry a gun to see if it's current. It should give you the time you need."

"I'm about to close in on the killer."

"My stars! You know who he is?"

"Yes, but I'd rather not say 'til I confirm my findings."

"When I get your word, we'll have Interpol round up the accomplices."

"Thanks again, Sam. But let's just hope DeAnn Toland hasn't already headed up the mountain despite our warning."

The phone went silent for a moment, and Stanek asked, "Sam, are you still there?"

"Yes, sir, but my stars! We've got ourselves a problem. Just before I called you, I received a wire from your Dr. Toland. Here, let me read it to you:

```
    Thanks for your help. We leave in the next day
or so on a trip to the mountain peak to recover
the last set of remains. Burial site described by
MilkEye, who gave me GeeJo's secret name—Pip (the
bombardier). Can't wait as CIL recovery mission to
close down shortly. Will take precautions.
DeAnn Toland
```

555

54 ILL-ADVISED MOUNTAIN ASCENT

Mount Bosavi, Papua New Guinea, 1973

IT WAS JUST AFTER dawn when DeAnn Toland left most of her party's supplies under guard at the CIL camp and began climbing the steep range to the salt well with her small group. Though she had tried to persuade MilkEye to accompany them, he would not go near the Tugaru without Stan-neck. She was delighted when WonTok stepped forward and said he would lead them up the mountain as he knew the route MilkEye used.

Once at the salt well, *Kiap* Noble bluffed their way past the Tugaru sentries. He told them he and Dr. Stanek had gotten Salty Meri's permission to search the area around the Tugaru ceremonial burial rocks for clues related to the death of the matriarch's youngest son. But since Stan-neck had been called back to the land of the sky people, Dr. Toland had taken his place, the *kiap* explained.

The *misis*, he had added, wanted to search the area nearby for white man's bones. As for Major Yowell, he had come along in the place of a Riami constable, since the Riami weren't welcome so high on the sacred mountain.

The Tugaru crossed their spears barring WonTok's passage. "Why Riami man with you?"

Noble gently pushed the weapons aside. "This Riami man was once an accused rapist, but later acquitted and released into my custody for questioning. I must keep him at my side so he won't come to harm from others."

The guards huddled while Noble waited. "If Riami man on government business, Tugaru no stop," the senior guard reported. "You go up."

DeAnn had been holding her breath throughout these negotiations, and finally she gave a contented sigh. "Bravo, Roger," she whispered. "A virtuoso performance, and not really a lie the way you put it."

Just past the burial rocks, WonTok led them up the steeper paths lined with *pitpit* scrub. They paused at what appeared to be an abandoned sweet potato garden. "Roger, have the Tugaru pushed the limits of their village beyond the burial rocks?" asked DeAnn.

Noble laughed. "No, my dear. Any garden here was for dead spirits to eat from. But since already dead, they couldn't feast on the sweet potatoes 'til the plants had died. It's how their logic works."

WonTok was a few yards ahead of them and suddenly he turned and came back. He broke off a few stout lengths of bush and waved them over his shoulders in a fan-like motion. "You do same. Help keep leeches off. We come to swamp after limestone arch." He stamped his feet, then continued. "Keep leeches off legs, but some leeches stick. Take away at place of giant ferns and Situmu's ladder."

They were all puffing and Noble was wheezing as well when they finished the steep climb and came out into a clearing. They took turns taking the bloodsuckers off each other. Yowell paid particular attention to DeAnn, and it made her uncomfortable when his hand brushed one off of her fatigues in the area of her upper thigh. "These damn pests must be Texas Indian leeches!" Yowell exclaimed. "They've found a way to creep up on you, 'cause I can feel 'em on my back under my flight suit. Suggest we all take off our shirts to make sure we've got 'em all."

DeAnn looked to Noble. He nodded and moved the major aside. "I'll take over for ye, lad. Ye and WonTok look after each other." DeAnn removed her jacket and slipped out of her undershirt and pressed it against the front of her bra as Noble checked her back.

WonTok had kept most of the dreadful parasites off with the swaying branch technique, so he was the first to reach the vine ladder extending 30 feet or more up the escarpment. Yowell followed him and started to take hold of the ladder. WonTok brushed his hand aside with the barrel of his rifle. "Ladder no good. MilkEye say it tell mountain Two Face we come. Like *garamut* talk to far off villages."

Noble and DeAnn joined them. The *kiap* spoke to her, but in a voice loud enough for Yowell to hear. "What WonTok's trying to tell us is this damn ladder's booby trapped. Probably a cowbell, or something attached at the top, so when ye pull on it, or put yer weight on the thing, it sounds an alarm."

"What now? We didn't bring any rope." DeAnn said.

"I'll ask WonTok about MilkEye's alternate route."

WonTok told the *kiap* about another ladder 50 yards or so along the escarpment. This one had footholds carved into the rock and a rope to pull on as one climbed. "Hide rope, covered with ferns so no fellow find. But me take you there."

"Lead the way, WonTok," the *kiap* said. "Our fortune, good or bad, is in yer hands."

The climb wasn't nearly as difficult as DeAnn expected. The footholds were deep enough so one could climb the slope just using the rope for balance and leverage. Of course, it helped Noble had ascended before her, and despite his age and wheezing, practically pulled her up after he reached the top. Yowell complained about bringing up the rear, but DeAnn paid him no mind.

At the top, the foliage was thick and what path there was had been grown over. She caught up with Roger and whispered, "Did you notice the texture of the rope we used to get up here?"

"Indeed, I did, lass. Could've been manufactured in Sidney by the look and feel of it."

"Or taken from the emergency equipment stowed with the life raft on the B-24. The only item missing was a 40-foot lanyard."

"Meanin' someone had to have gotten it from the wreckage or from the hideous burial rock Emerson and I had climbed down to find Mackelwaite's possible remains."

"Yes, Roger, better mention this to Emerson if we ever see him again." She felt a tug at her heart. The thought Emerson may have vanished from her life seemed unfathomable. In her mind she said a prayer for his recovery, and added, "Why were we brought together only to have it end so soon?"

WonTok, who had been in the lead cutting a path with his machete, came back and broke her reverie. "What is it?" she asked.

"Up ahead, wide path. No need cut way through."

The *kiap* took charge. "The rest of ye wait here whilst I've a look see."

He had only been gone a few minutes when they heard a scream like someone in agony. The three of them rushed ahead, and DeAnn feared Noble had been killed. She was unarmed, but she told WonTok and Yowell to have their weapons ready.

Yowell pushed past her with his .38 caliber pistol raised. "Let me go first. Get yourself between WonTok and me."

She started to protest, but saw he was already a few yards in front of her, so she fell in step behind him with WonTok, rifle at port, last in line.

It wasn't hard to spot Noble when they came to the wider path. He was lying with his back against a tree applying a tourniquet to his upper thigh. In front of him, still swaying like a pendulum, was a log attached to a vine hung from a high branch in another pine tree, no doubt from which it had been launched. They reached him and DeAnn saw the puncture holes in his leg.

"Sorry to have screamed, but the damn catapult came out of nowhere, and the end with the prongs protrudin' out of it caught me. Had I not just turned to call out to ye to come forward, I'd have taken the business end square in the gut or head as it reached full elevation. Must've tripped the device somehow."

"You've got to turn back, Roger. Those prongs might've been poison-tipped, placing you beyond first aid, not to mention the danger of tetanus. Frank will have to get you to our medic at the CIL camp."

"By myself?" Yowell asked.

"It isn't far to the lanyard. You can let Roger down by the rope. Once down, make your way back to the vine ladder, then you can get the Tugaru sentries to help carry the government *kiap* back to the CIL camp. And, Frank, you must fly Roger from Mount Bosavi to the hospital in Goroka as soon as you can."

"*Come a gutser!* Ye can't be thinkin' of continuin' this mission, lass. I'll not leave ye here alone. Ye've got to come back with us. Whoever rigged up this damn pendulum was playin' for keeps."

"He's right, DeAnn. We can't leave you here."

"I've got WonTok. He's armed. And since no one has shown up, I think we remain undetected. This is my first and only chance to recover the remains buried at the mountain top. We'll never bluff our way past the Tugaru sentries again, especially once they see Roger's been injured. Bellicosi won't extend my deadline either. I've got to try."

DeAnn watched the two men look at each other. She saw the resistance to her plan in their eyes. Yowell put an arm around the *kiap* and helped lift him up on his uninjured right leg. "I don't like your plan, Sweetheart. It's much too dangerous. Sure, General Bellicosi made you the boss lady, and you've put months of work into this project, as all of us have. We want to accomplish the mission, too, but not at the risk of losing our leader."

"Yes, quite! We took a big risk thinkin' we could sneak up the mountain undetected, using MilkEye's alternate route. But now ye've got to see the odds are against ye, especially losin' yer real protection." He glanced at WonTok, then back at her. "Need I remind ye of my warnin' regarding the tragedy of my family? Ye don't have enough reliable backup to save ye if somethin' should go wrong."

"I assure you, we'll turn back if we run into any more trouble."

She waited for Noble to relent. "I can't stop ye if ye're intent on goin' on further, dearie, but I'm very uneasy about ye followin' a path cleared of trees. All I could see was tall sword grass and a type of wild cane a regiment could hide behind, it could. I'd feel better if ye promise to stay behind WonTok, and the two of ye get off the open trail. Bound to be more traps along the way. Even so, keep an eye out for any sentries."

DeAnn pushed back his bush hat and kissed him on the forehead. "Thanks, Roger. It'd be a shame to come this far and go back empty-handed."

She saw him try to manage a smile. "Safety first," he said.

"We were brought here for a purpose and our safety has always been in God's hands. He'll see us through."

Yowell turned to Noble. "Better if we switch sides so you can hold your left leg up and use my right arm as a crutch. Together I'll help you bunny hop out of here." He turned back to DeAnn. "I think Roger will agree. If you aren't back in camp within two hours or so, we'll bring an army up here to this leech-infested, booby-trapped mountain, whether it starts a war with the Tugaru or not."

*   *   *

Stanek tried to sleep despite the monotonous sound of the aircraft's engine, but his right arm, recently packed in a plaster cast, and the poor circulation in his injured shoulder made his right side feel numb. He kneaded his right hand with his good hand and noticed some feeling creep back ever so slowly. He wondered what help he could offer DeAnn and the others if he showed up incapacitated by his wound. Only now did he fully understand the seriousness of his injuries.

To turn back and leave the situation on Mount Bosavi for others to sort out was never an option, he decided. The viciousness of the killer on the mountain left him with a sick feeling DeAnn was in great peril. Wound or no wound, he was not ready to accept defeat in the ten knights case. The investigation had changed his life forever—a life which now included DeAnn Toland.

A few hours later, the jet landed at Port Moresby, and a light aircraft whisked him off to Goroka. But when he arrived at Goroka, he discovered he'd have to wait for a flight to Mount Bosavi. The officer of the day apologized for how slow the army had been in meeting a four-star general's request for local air transport. "Usually when so much brass gets involved, things get crackin' all along the chain of command. Sorry, but the aircraft scheduled to meet ye is still betwixt here and Lae. Best I can offer is a return flight with a med-evac mission incomin' from Mount Bosavi. Just radioed in before ye landed."

Stanek stroked the scar on his cheek. "If it's Major Yowell, radio him back and tell him about your orders, and I'd expect him to make a fast turnaround to get me to the mountain."

"Can do, sir. We'll have him off-load his casualty, then gas and go." The duty officer turned to leave, but Stanek asked him to wait.

"This casualty, any word on who it might be?"

"No, I'll get more details when I contact the Beaver."

Stanek tried to chase from his mind the thought he had arrived too late. If he were back at Johns Hopkins, this might be one of the occasions to touch the feet of the Christ statue in the rotunda at Billings Hall and ask for divine intervention. But he remembered how he had labeled such a foolish practice as superstitious claptrap. Nonetheless, his mind automatically wrapped around the phrase, "God help her." He wanted to add he needed help as well, but the scientist in him made it impossible to go so far.

After an hour, another plane landed at Goroka, but it was from Port Moresby, and when the stairway was rolled into place, out stepped General Bellicosi. He spotted Stanek and walked over to where he waited. Stanek was surprised to see the general stick out his hand, then pull it back when he realized Stanek's right arm was in a sling and in no condition for shaking hands. The general chewed off the end of a cigar and spat a plug of tobacco onto the ground.

"Well, my boy. I understand you've been given authority to proceed with your criminal investigation. Sorry we can't help you with it. Operation Simpatico is ready to stand down. I'm here to close up shop. Eight sets of remains recovered after 30 years gives us what we're looking for in order to hold my press conference in Hawaii shortly."

Stanek swatted at a bug on his bush hat. "The idea of recovering remains of our fallen heroes has considerable merit. Like you, we'd like to see it extended to cover all wars."

"We? You and your sister? It'll take some doing."

"Maybe not as much as you think. Jim Cole left resources in his will for his newspaper, the *Honolulu Advertiser*, to launch a campaign to establish an agency to bring home the soldiers from all wars in which Americans fought and died, an idea he got from you. He wrote articles ready to publish for this purpose"

"Why I never..."

"...dreamed Cole was so enamored with your ideas? He was a remarkable man none of us had time to really befriend. I think, in Cole's honor, you should cancel your press conference and give the exclusive to his newspaper as he wished."

Bellicosi crushed his cigar and threw it down on the tarmac. "It'll be the Pentagon's call. If any of these ten knights had a guardian angel, it was Jim Cole, who brought the lost B-24 to my attention. When he told me the Australians had come across the wreckage, I knew the fallen bomber and its crew were a natural platform to institute Operation Simpatico. Jim wouldn't rest 'til he got the exclusive rights to the story. But like I said, the Pentagon's..."

"It was a ruse, General, for Jim to try to find out what happened to the ten knights, part of which he already knew. I intend to finish the story."

"If this story gets bogged down in a criminal investigation, the press will swarm all over it like maggots on a sore, while the reclamation of WW II remains will take a back seat to the juicier stuff. Where does it leave me?"

"Well, Cole further stipulated his newspaper print his editorial recommending you for the position of head of the new agency dedicated to going anywhere at any time to recover lost remains from any war."

"He did? Even though he knew..."

"Yes, knowing you kept illegal secret files on all of us. Cole's last words to me were to go easy on you, but for God's sake to tell you to dump those files."

Stanek saw Bellicosi was at a loss for words. The general gripped the pathologist's left hand and muttered, "Thanks for the heads up and the tip. I'm glad to end our relationship on a friendly note."

"Who's to say it's ended? You might need a pathologist on another case someday, and I might need the work. Of course, it'd be after you let me continue our agreement to work on my cancer research with help from the National Institutes of Health, an organization, as you know, with which the Pentagon has a great deal of input these days."

"We'll honor our agreement. Well then, goodbye and good luck," Bellicosi said as he started to walk away. He stopped after a few steps and came back. "Stanek, what about Dr. Toland? What have you heard from her? I know you two have kept up correspondence through someone else, but don't worry, it won't show up in any file anywhere."

"DeAnn is in grave danger, I fear. The last word I heard was she intended to go up Mount Bosavi, where the killer operates, to find the remains of the ninth knight."

"Really? She never had my permission to do any such thing."

"Well, she's no match for the killer, who's one of the most cunning criminals I've encountered. And I'm here to bring him to justice."

"You know who it is? Tell me. We'll slap him in irons for what he did to our poor boy Erik."

"Barging up the mountain with an army would be a mistake. Even if you got past the Tugaru without a bloody skirmish, you'd find out this man has planned for a frontal attack and no doubt has a strategy for getting away in such an emergency."

"And how do you propose to bring him in?"

"Through the element of surprise. He doesn't know I've identified him, and since he's had part of his operation compromised, he's under pressure of the threat of detection. It's when he's apt to make a mistake, and I want to be there when he does."

"Good Lord, man! Tell me who he is. If anything happens to you, we'll never know who to look for."

"I don't have enough evidence to prove it yet, and I wish I had more time. But if I don't get to Mount Bosavi to stop Dr. Toland before she leads anybody up the mountain, I fear there'll be more deaths and the murderer will escape. Just as I arrived, I was told Major Yowell is expected here shortly with a casualty on board. So I may be too late already."

"Good Lord, man! Why didn't you tell me sooner? The casualty's probably someone from my CIL team. This could change everything!"

*   *   *

When the Beaver arrived, Stanek watched the general's reaction as they lifted the litter upon which *Kiap* Noble lay from the airplane. He thought he saw Bellicosi heave a sigh of relief the casualty was not CIL personnel. Bellicosi said nothing to the Australian, but addressed his questions to Major Yowell. "What in the world happened on the mountain? Have you fellows started a war? People getting killed and others injured!"

Yowell saluted. "Forgive me, sir, but I'll give you a full report when I return. Right now, I'm sorry to say, I've been instructed to make a fast turn around and to take Dr. Stanek back to Mount Bosavi."

Noble raised his hand, and beckoned Stanek to lean over the litter. "Get crackin'," he whispered, "and take my revolver with ye. Try to hold on to it this time. DeAnn insisted she continue on alone up the mountain with only WonTok. She wasn't back at camp by the time we left. Didn't want an army to come after her. I know she'd be glad to see ye, though and what help ye can muster."

Stanek nodded and slipped the weapon inside the folds of his sling. "You get better. Major Yowell and I will handle things from here on out."

Bellicosi came over to them. "What did he say?"

"Only that DeAnn may be in trouble, and we need to fly to Mount Bosavi to help her as soon as Major Yowell can refuel and clear us for takeoff."

55 RESCUE MISSION/PAYBACK

Mount Bosavi, Papua New Guinea, 1973

A S THEY APPROACHED the Tugaru burial rock, Stanek motioned to MilkEye he needed to rest. The long negotiations with Salty Meri to get her permission for the three-man expedition to go up the mountain, and the climb up from the salt well, had left him weaker than expected. MilkEye pointed to the cliff ledges above them. "Not far, *Masta*," he said reassuringly.

Stanek was concerned he might have to crawl on his one hand and knees, unless he found a way to conserve his waning strength. After a brief stop, they climbed on. But again, exhausted by the exertion and weakened by his wounded shoulder, Stanek fell far behind MilkEye and Major Yowell. The two disappeared into a wide grassy tunnel-like path walled by two towers of white-streaked limestone. Stanek thought he would never catch up, and wondered if perhaps the native and his rival for DeAnn had decided to mount the rescue on their own. He made it to the limestone and leaned against one of the walls. He turned to take another step, but fell down across the path. The Riami man turned back and extended one end of his bow to Stanek. "Take hold, *Masta*. Me and fellow pull. Two Face no like you here."

Yowell positioned himself behind Stanek as the pathologist struggled to his feet. "MilkEye will pull and I'll push, lifting you by your belt so you won't have to put so much weight on your legs. After all, you just came from a hospital bed."

565

Stanek, momentarily overcome by the kindness of his companions, didn't know what to say, so he said nothing. Furthermore, he was torn with indecision. Maybe it would have been better for them to go on ahead. He felt responsible for the slow pace they had to travel. He would never forgive himself if they got there too late to save DeAnn should she have met with trouble. Yet, without his presence, he knew MilkEye wouldn't have come. Nor could they have gotten past Salty Meri without the promise of bringing back the killer of her son.

Stanek's small group filed through the natural gateway, and as they reached the swampy area beyond the walls, he stopped to rest again before his assault on the next hill. MilkEye urged him not to linger too long in the spot he had chosen to rest, as this would only give the leeches a stationery target on which to attach themselves. Stanek sucked in great gulps of air and with Yowell's help made it through to the next obstacle, which was Situmu's ladder.

Yowell lit a cigarette and touched the fire-end against the leeches to dislodge them from Stanek's bare legs. "Can't have you losing any more blood," the pilot quipped. "Damn, I should've thought of this when I came up here at dawn with DeAnn."

Stanek listened as MilkEye explained why they couldn't use the vine ladder put in place by Situmu. Instead, he led them around the escarpment to where the 40-foot rope dangled. Stanek cocked an eye at the lanyard, then back at Yowell. "I'm too worn out to pull myself up on my own. Maybe you and MilkEye..."

"...should go on alone? No dice. We'll go up first. Then you wrap the rope around your good wing, put your feet in the holes, and we'll pull you up."

"Thanks, Frank." Stanek realized this was the first time he had addressed the pilot in so familiar a manner.

"No problem, Emerson," replied the pilot in kind. 'MilkEye's no taller than the horns on a steer, but I'll bet he's strong enough to hoist us both up if push came to shove."

At the top, Stanek rested again. Five minutes later, they were on the path Yowell told them WonTok had cut through the bush. No one spoke until they reached the clearing. Yowell pointed out the spike-tipped log hanging from a vine. "Noble almost bought the farm there."

Stanek nodded. Yowell guided them across the clearing and set them on the path through the bush taken by DeAnn and WonTok, after which he relinquished the lead to MilkEye. Yowell cupped a hand behind his ear. "By my reckoning, they should've reached the grave site, packed up the remains and headed back this way long before now, but I can't hear a thing afoot."

"Let's hope we'll see them coming back on this trail."

MilkEye shook his head. "No good three fellows go from here." He then gave a lengthy explanation to Stanek in pidgin.

"What's all the beefing about?" Yowell asked.

Stanek translated. "MilkEye thinks he should go on alone from here to see what's ahead. We're moving too slowly for him, and the spirit deity he calls Two Face takes advantage of the weak."

"So what's a mountain spirit got to do with any of us white folks?"

"Plenty," according to MilkEye. "The bad talk people, the Giambu, serve evil Two Face. MilkEye sees signs the cannibals have scoured this path, perhaps in pursuit of DeAnn and WonTok. Remember the Giambu are the ones who shot me in the shoulder, and, from an account in the Japanese woman's log, have been known to show their victims no mercy as they slow cook them."

"Ask him what the Giambu are doing up on the mountain? The last time we ran into 'em, they were on the Rentoul River in their war canoe shootin' at you."

"I'm afraid the answer lies in our attempt to rescue DeAnn if she's in trouble."

"My military mind tells me we should stay together and press on as a team."

Stanek realized Yowell had passed on to him the decision on their next move, as to whether or not to separate. It seemed incredible he had come from a laboratory, developing a bee serum as a possible cure for cancer, to a final showdown with an arch killer on a remote mountaintop in New Guinea.

But he had come too far to quit now. DeAnn needed him, and he needed her. The cancer research, avenging Haveland's murder, catching a killer of multiple murders and his own safety had all become secondary to (dare he even think it) love for a woman. The mountain top experience Kioko and GeeJo had once shared had become a personal goal. If he gave up now, the dream would shatter, as had his reputation before.

Yowell tapped him on his good shoulder. "Well, this is your call. What do you say?"

Stanek was about to reply when a rustling of the bushes in front of them, followed by the sound of yodeling in the distance, forced the trio to take cover. Stanek drew the revolver Noble had lent him from his sling and saw Yowell had already drawn his .38 from its holster. MilkEye had reacted as well. He saw the old Riami nock an arrow and pull the string of his bow taunt. Onto the path tumbled WonTok, his eyes as big as silver dollars and his rifle held high overhead. He called, "No shoot! Plenty Giambu come behind me."

"Where's Dr. Toland?" Stanek asked.

But MilkEye swooped down and pulled Stanek by his good arm into the bush, beckoning the others to follow. For what seemed ten minutes, they picked their way through the under-brush which tore at Stanek's injured arm and shoulder. Twice he nearly fainted from the pain, but each time MilkEye kept him upright. In almost total silence, they continued to thread their way through the dense brush.

Then MilkEye made a sudden stop. Stanek thought it was to take a bearing. Seconds later, the old warrior pushed him and Yowell into a small cave or shelter under a limestone outcropping. Then, after WonTok entered, MilkEye cut down a large branch and drew it over the cave's entrance, sealing it behind him. The cave, abandoned in haste by previous inhabitants, now concealed his four-man party in its narrow confines with two boxes used for sniping cassowaries.

No one dared speak. After a short time Stanek heard the Giambu closing in around them. Two warriors paused in front of the shelter and rested against their spears. He could smell the pig grease on their legs and see the tattoos on their ankles. If discovered, Stanek realized none of them had a chance to fight back. The cramped quarters had rendered their weapons useless. Stanek wondered if MilkEye had considered this when he chose this place to hide.

The big man leading the Giambu must have yodeled orders to the two warriors at the cave's entrance. One yodeled in response, and then told his leader there was a sheer drop to the jungle below beyond the ledge. "Riami government man no come here or he fall and die," the Giambu warrior shouted as he moved off with the other native to search another area.

After a half-hour when no one had come back, Stanek was the first to speak. "Looks like the Giambu have given up, at least in this area. Now tell us, WonTok, where's Dr. Toland?"

WonTok's eyes grew wide again as they carefully exited the shelter. "*Misis* find bones and put in *bilum*. WonTok watch. WonTok and *misis* go back down mountain, *Misis* fall behind WonTok. Take no good turn. WonTok no see *misis*. Go look. See same two fellows who try to kill pilot of small *balus* (he pointed to Yowell) at place of Huri."

"Clare and Al!" Yowell exclaimed.

"Where's Dr. Toland?" Stanek repeated.

"They see *misis*. Take away to cave behind Upper Falls, big cascade, like Lower Falls. Me wait, but *misis* no come out. Me go for help, but Giambu see me and try to kill me."

"Clare and Al, they're our killers," Yowell said.

"I think they only work for the man we seek, but they're still dangerous, especially now that they've captured DeAnn."

"Well, I'd like to get a crack at those two varmints while I'm sober. Let's go find the big waterfall."

Stanek glanced over the ledge some yards away and saw the 2,000-foot drop, which had scared away the Giambu. "Better check with MilkEye rather than go in there blind," he cautioned. "He seems to have covered every inch of this mountain, and he can also help us evade the Giambu."

At the mention of his name, MilkEye tapped Stanek on the back. "*Masta*, we no go under waterfall into big cave. Two Face have plenty bad talk people in there."

"Then what should we do?"

"We go up river of gold stones. Me take you secret way to other side of cave."

"What about Major Yowell and WonTok?"

"Stay near river. See if *misis* come out of cave behind waterfall."

"'Cascade'," WonTok corrected.

MilkEye shot his friend a glance meant to silence him. Then he continued, "Mah-jah and WonTok wait, then come find us."

Stanek stroked the scar on his cheek, after which he explained the plan to Yowell. "Evidently there are two entrances to the cave, one hidden by the cascade. The cave must stretch through the mountain from north to south."

"I don't like splitting our forces," Yowell said.

"It'll only be temporary. The observation of both entrances to the cave from hidden positions may give us the information we need to formulate a more effective rescue plan. Wait no more than 20 minutes before you and WonTok come to join us. Let's synchronize our watches."

"I still don't like it, but you're making the decisions. How do we get to the cave without being spotted by the Giambu, or even Clare and Al?"

"MilkEye wants us to wade upstream and split just before we get to the hidden cave, which I trust will be much larger than the one we took refuge in to avoid the Giambu."

They inched their way through the thick growth until they reached a small stream. As they waded upstream, they came to an area where wool blankets were placed about ten yards apart across the water. Stanek whispered to Yowell, "It's a primitive way to pan for gold, but effective."

Yowell moved closer. "I don't follow you."

"These blankets are strategically placed in the stream bed to trap gold and allow lighter elements like sand to sift through."

Stanek watched Yowell suck in his breath when he saw the amount of gold glittering in each of the blankets. "It's unbelievable how much has been captured. Enough to buy Dallas, if you ask me!"

"Someone interrupted the collection process, or they wouldn't have left so much. I'll ask WonTok if this is where DeAnn fell into the hands of Clare and Al."

"The four small nuggets I collected from MilkEye are a pittance next to this cache."

"Our arch criminal is probably closing down this operation, at least temporarily, to escape detection. See how some of the blankets have been removed from the stream and folded on the bank. When DeAnn stumbled upon them, Clare and Al might've been down here dismantling this part of the system so as not to leave calling cards for other prospectors."

"Part of the system? You mean there's more to it?"

"Yes, but more about it later. Now we've got to keep up with MilkEye and WonTok," Stanek said as they negotiated their way around the wool blankets.

*   *   *

After Stanek and MilkEye split off from Yowell and WonTok near the north entrance to the cave, they climbed slowly but steadily along the secret way running parallel to, but above, the cave. Stanek felt some of his strength return as they emerged from the vegetation under which they had been concealed.

One upward glance and Stanek spotted the missing B-24 vertical stabilizer. Under it was a cross marking a grave, which now lay open. Stanek stared at the skull and crossbombs on the tail fin perched so high on the mountaintop. As a youngster playing pirates with Catherine at Fells Point, he had often mused over the fantasy that someday he'd find pirate treasure beneath such a Jolly Rogers-like emblem. Never could he have imagined such a configured tail fin on such a mountain used to scare superstitious natives away, or perhaps to warn him of imminent danger.

As MilkEye shrank back from the sight of the totem, Stanek realized how much courage the Riami man had to muster to come this far up on the mountain where the evil Two Face ruled. He put his good arm around MilkEye's shoulder. "Tell me, my friend, is this Two Face, the mountain spirit?"

MilkEye covered his eyes with his hands. "Evil god of Tugaru in this place. Good Two Face stay with great *balus*, look after Riami."

"But if the Tugaru never come up this high, nor allow others to, how do they know this Two Face exists?"

"Long ago, *Bikmaus* see smoke, go up here, find. Go back. Tell Tugaru have god like Riami. Tugaru come here with sacrifices. Later, sorcerer in silver mask come here and chase Tugaru away."

"This mountain sorcerer, did he wear a shield over his body?

MilkEye nodded. "Sorcerer serve Tugaru Two Face. Same you come help Riami Two Face."

Stanek shuddered. Had he found his killer in medieval armor? If so, could MilkEye be depended upon the rest of the way, given his superstitions? He decided to test him. He pointed to the skull painted on the tail section. "MilkEye, since Two Face has two faces, how can you tell which is good and which is evil?"

MilkEye peered out from between his fingers. "Situmu tell warrior must choose good one before two faces of Two Face clash. You and mountain sorcerer fight. Me watch. Help good Two Face sorcerer win when time come for me to choose."

Not very reassuring, Stanek thought. If I falter and appear to have the weaker magic, MilkEye will no doubt turn against me. Only when they passed the skull and crossbombs emblem did MilkEye lower his hands from his face. "We come to stone ledge. See inside sorcerer's cave like you look at Tugaru burial stone," the Riami man said.

Stanek held him back. "Better we wait here out of sight 'til Major Yowell and WonTok get here. Meantime, tell me. What's the purpose of the big stone over the place where the light shines, perhaps from the cave?"

MilkEye shrugged.

"Help me climb up to the boulder. I'd like a closer look." The pathologist showed the native how to form a stirrup with his hands, and after a number of false starts he reached the craggy surface above what appeared to be the south entrance to the cave. Out of breath, he lay back against the huge rock and sucked in air through his nose, expelling it from his mouth to avoid hyperventilation. It was then he spotted the cantilever device against which the stone was balanced.

By the time Yowell and WonTok had arrived, Stanek had managed to get down from the ledge. He had hoped DeAnn Toland would be with them and hung his head until Yowell confirmed DeAnn was alive and held captive inside the cave.

"I'm almost certain sooner or later she'll show up at the south cave entrance. But tell me all you've seen, Frank."

Like two spies, he and WonTok had gotten close enough to the north entrance to the cave to see inside, Yowell explained. There were Giambu all over the place. Some mined gold from a large vein, others tended cooking fires where the gold was being smelted and others carried sacks of the gold toward the south side of the mountain. Clare and Al supervised the operation and had DeAnn tied up between them. However, when Clare and Al left the cave with several Giambu and headed toward the stream where the wool blankets with the gold were left, they had to beat a hasty retreat.

"Like a couple of bull riders bucked off a bull, WonTok and I had to hot foot it out of there."

"Good work," Stanek said. "I've thought of a plan to stop our killer when he tries to get rid of DeAnn. If he is true to form, he'll do his dirty deed on the ledge over the steep, sheer drop MilkEye says is on the south, opposite the cave entrance. Nobody would ever find a body there as it would disappear in the marsh below."

"Maybe we should rush 'em now before they get DeAnn anywhere near the ledge," Yowell suggested.

"We need to keep the element of surprise in our corner, Frank. As long as they don't know we're here and are preoccupied with the gold, the better our chances when it really counts. Right now I'd like you to play spy again and crawl around the huge boulder over the cave entrance only far enough to see what's going on inside without being seen yourself. But watch you don't trip the cantilever device at the back of the rock."

"Will do."

When Yowell returned, he threw his hands over his head. "Well hog tie me if it ain't true! Didn't believe your story when you told all of us, including General Bellicosi, you had seen a knight in armor on the mountain top. But, big as life, an hombre outfitted in armor is directing the Giambu to stack sacks of gold on pallets placed on either side of the entrance. He's wearing a visor, otherwise I could tell you what he looks like."

"Why do you suppose they're stacking gold on either side of the entrance?" Stanek asked.

"Most likely, they intend to haul it out in one fell swoop. The pallet to the far side of the cave entrance is fully loaded and packed up in a sling. On the opposite side, another is almost ready to be rigged. Looks to me like they're gonna call in a chopper or two, hover over the open space, and hoist the pallets up and away with a hook. It's what I'd do. Tricky flying though, especially with such a heavy load to maneuver."

"I believe you're on to something, Frank."

"Thanks. Now you tell me, Doc, why do you suppose they've got the boulder rigged up with a cantilever device?"

"I think our armor-clad murderer intends to seal the south entrance with the boulder when he leaves. Since the north entrance is obscured from sight by the cascade, he'll have his mother lode hidden from view by air or by land."

"We've got it figured out so far, but how do we get DeAnn out of there safely?"

Stanek stroked the scar on his cheek. "We'll have to use the big stone. If it strikes the gold stacked pallets on either side of the cave entrance, it should roll forward instead of dropping straight down to seal the entrance. You stand by the lever, and we'll ask MilkEye and WonTok to sit behind the rock. When I yell '*Shean-ee*', you push down on the lever to set the boulder in motion, while MilkEye and WonTok push against the stone with their strong, flat feet."

"And what will you be doing, Doc?"

"I'll be hidden to the side of the cave entrance, ready to spring into action once our killer moves away from the entrance, so I can trick or maneuver him into standing in the pathway of the rock."

"With all those Giambu about? You'll never make it."

"Well, a fellow named GeeJo once sent the Giambu scurrying for their lives when he appeared out of nowhere with his pistol like an avenging spirit. Maybe it'll work one more time, especially if the incident has become part of Giambu lore."

"It's a very risky plan, Emerson. And your scenario doesn't allow for the unexpected, or a fall-back position."

"Spoken like a military man, but at the moment it's our only chance to divide and conquer. There're too many of them for a frontal assault, even with our weapons. Please, let's take our positions!"

*   *   *

Stanek heard DeAnn Toland cry out from inside the cave, "Please let me go. You've no right to hold me here. I'm a representative of the government of the United States of America."

The muffled answer was difficult to hear, but Stanek heard the threat in the voice. "I'll show you how we deal with people who don't mind their own business."

DeAnn screamed, "There'll be an investigation if you kill me."

"And what will they find? Not you, nor us."

Clear of the entrance, the man in armor grabbed DeAnn by the wrists and dragged her toward the edge of the precipice. Stanek jumped out into the clearing, screamed and fired his weapon. Just as he had hoped, the Giambu ran back inside the cave, but then he saw Loud Mouth, who stood his ground. The Tugaru leader complicated matters, but it was too late to change the plan now. He switched his revolver to the hand in the sling, reached for a bag of gold and hurled it at the feet of the man in armor. "Release the woman or the next one will be tossed over the cliff."

Loud Mouth raised his spear and called to the armored man, "No afraid. Me kill for you, *Masta*."

574

Stanek threw another bag of gold at the killer's feet and swiftly ducked down behind the pallet loaded with gold just as Loud Mouth's spear whizzed by him and cracked on the side of the cave entrance.

Stanek shouted again. "Release the woman or the next one goes overboard!"

"Alright," came the muffled voice behind the visor. "But how much time do you think you've bought yourself with this tactic? You and the woman have no place to go. Inside of two minutes, you'll both be dead."

DeAnn made her way toward Stanek as he replied, "Do you really think I came here alone in this condition? The question is where will you go after you kill us?"

Stanek could hear the man behind the visor chuckling. "Put my gold down. We'll see who kills whom, Dr. Stanek. What a great jousting partner you've been!"

Tears were streaming down DeAnn's cheeks when he whispered to her, "When I say 'now', shout '*Shean-ee*' as loud as you can and run into the cave."

Stanek tossed the third bag of gold so it landed just a few feet behind and to the right of his nemesis. Then, pushing DeAnn in front of him, they reached the entrance. "'Now'," said Stanek. Together they screamed "*Shean-ee*" as they crossed the threshold into the cave.

Stanek and DeAnn heard the rumble of the heavy boulder overhead as his cohorts pushed it loose. They looked back and saw it hit the two pallets stacked with gold, rise in the air and then roll toward the precipice as it gained momentum.

The man in the armor, who had stooped to pick up the bag of gold spilled on the ground, turned to see the huge boulder bearing down upon him. Realizing his mistake, he tried to back away from the rumbling stone, but his backward thrust caused the armor to shift in the same direction. He tottered for a moment on his thin but muscular legs at the brink of the precipice, and then, without letting loose of the gold in his hand, he vanished over the edge of the cliff with the boulder rolling after him.

Loud Mouth, who had stood frozen through this episode, let out a loud wail. Then he drew a steel axe from his belt and charged toward Stanek, who fumbled in his sling for his revolver. Just then, from the ledge above the entrance, he heard MilkEye call out, "Me

Tugaru enemy. Me kill brother at salt well. Come. Take your payback."

Loud Mouth stopped and hurled his axe in the direction of the voice above him. It must've found its mark, because the next sounds Stanek heard were from a grieving *age-mate.*

Stanek pointed the barrel of the revolver at the head of Loud Mouth. He had never shot a man and though saddened by what he expected to find when they brought MilkEye down from the upper ledge, he was not about to do so now.

But WonTok had other ideas. As soon as his feet touched the ground, he leveled his rifle at Loud Mouth. "Me kill *Bikmaus* like he kill MilkEye, *Masta!"*

"Don't shoot, Constable WonTok. If you want to end the payback, end it here. You're a government man. Let the *kiap* and the government deal with your prisoner."

WonTok lowered his rifle. *"Masta,* use magic. Bring *age-mate* back, please! Please! Please!"

"I'll do what I can. You secure the prisoner."

"Please, *Masta,* you and *misis* make MilkEye plenty good."

Stanek nodded. He and DeAnn moved over to where Yowell was trying to stem the blood seeping from a gaping wound in MilkEye's chest just below the heart. DeAnn cradled his head in her lap while Stanek moved one hand over the old warrior's body. After a moment, he looked at DeAnn and shook his head. He watched as she tried to hide the tears streaming freely down her cheeks. When he looked back at MilkEye, Stanek was startled to see the old Riami smiling at him. MilkEye reached out and touched the scar on Stanek's cheek.

"You man of great spirit, Stan-neck. Me glad me no kill you. You no talk to Tugaru about MilkEye kill boy at salt well. Wait for Situmu to speak to me again. My papa help me choose you to serve spirit of good Two Face. Me go now. Sit beside papa at burial ground. Watch over Riami people. Tell WonTok, please be papa to LikLik. Get good bride price."

Those were his last words as his heart gave out. Stanek and the others took some moments to bow over the body of the man who had helped them find the remains of the B-24 crew. They needed to get MilkEye's body down the mountain, so it could be placed to rest in the Riami ancestral burial ground, a right Stanek felt

MilkEye had earned. Stanek huddled with his team and said they had to leave before Clare and Al came back with the Giambu.

"Let's go get 'em!" Yowell said.

"Hold on, Frank. Without their leader, they've got no place to go. We'll take MilkEye down the secret way we came, and let the killer's accomplices fend for themselves until the Australian government rounds them up. And we'll alert the authorities to look out for any helicopters approaching this area. Besides, I'm physically and emotionally spent. We've had enough trauma for one day. Best we get moving," he said taking DeAnn's hand.

Stanek saw more tears whelm up in DeAnn's eyes. "You've come from a hospital bed and risked your life to save mine! How can I thank you enough?"

"I didn't act alone. MilkEye and Frank deserve most of the credit. They practically carried me up this mountain."

She laid her head on his good shoulder and looked up at him with eyes made more brilliantly brown by her tears. "Thank God you came when you did."

"My injury slowed us down quite a bit. I'd never have forgiven myself if..."

DeAnn stroked Stanek's hand. "Your timing, like your brilliant mind, kicked in when it counted. The only time I was alone with this killer was just before he tried to push me off the cliff. Before then I was surrounded by Giambu, making a rescue impossible, or at least highly improbable."

Stanek cupped her face in his hand. "The important thing is you're here, and the man went over the cliff in your stead. He'll never kill again."

"Will they ever find the body and discover who's behind the armor?"

"I knew who it was before I came back for you, DeAnn. But let's wait to discuss it 'til we get to Goroka. Over a cup of your renowned tea, I can summarize this case for you, Roger, Frank and General Bellicosi, if he's still around."

"Oh, no. Is General Bellicosi back in New Guinea? He's here to shut down our CIL operation. I just know it."

"Well, let's just say he has some new developments to share with you."

"Tell me if we'll be able to finish my part of the investigation and identify all the war dead."

"All the war dead is right. In his will, Jim Cole has provided resources for his newspaper to launch a campaign for an expanded CIL, using articles he wrote before his death. In these articles, he urges Congress to create a new command structure, headquartered in Hawaii, to support CIL operations worldwide to recover our dead from all wars. There'll be plenty of other mountains for you to conquer, unless ..."

"Unless you'd like to take a much needed rest to recharge the old batteries, as the *kiap* would say."

"Yes, we both need to think of the future."

"But we've got to concentrate on getting down this mountain first. On the way, I need to make one stop at the Tugaru village. I promised Salty Meri I'd come back with her son's murderer."

"Not MilkEye?"

"Yes. You heard him admit it when he took the axe meant for me."

"But they'll desecrate his body."

"We'll insist on taking him to his own burial ground and set him beside his father like he wanted. Salty Meri will be in no position to bargain. Since Loud Mouth killed Erik, he'll be handed over to the *kiap* to face the government's payback for killing a white man." Now maybe the Tugaru and Riami can live in peace under government rule."

"I've got a stop to make, too," said DeAnn. "Down by the stream I dropped the remains of number nine knight of the ten knights crew when Clare and Al approached me."

"We'll have to be careful to pick up your *bilum* of remains without being detected. By the process of elimination, do you know the identity of the tenth knight?"

"Not for sure, but I suspect you'll enlighten us all when we get to Goroka. I only hope and pray it wasn't GeeJo who went over the cliff on the mountain!" she said.

56 MASTERMIND MURDERER REVEALED

Goroka, Papua New Guinea, 1973

STANEK SPENT THE THREE DAYS between the discovery of the killer's mining operations on Mount Bosavi and the debriefing he had promised to deliver to the interested parties getting his re-injured shoulder tended to by the doctors at Goroka. During this time, he kept the killer's identity to himself.

DeAnn, it seemed, never left his bedside. He noted, but left unstated for the moment, the emotional attachment he believed they had come to share. Not once had she pressured him to reveal the murderer before he broke the news to the others. Whenever the subject came up, she brushed it aside with the comment, "Let's get you back on your feet. Then there'll be plenty of time to discuss case histories."

On the day scheduled for the conference, DeAnn appeared in Stanek's room with her head held down and a frown on her face. He felt obliged to jokingly inquire, "Why such a gloomy Gus this morning?"

She did not look up. "Catherine's here. She flew in about a half-hour ago with LikLik. They're probably on their way over here by now. Maybe I should leave you alone with your adoptive sister."

He reached out and stroked the side of her face. "No. Catherine wants to separate us. Send word to her I'm about to conduct a briefing, and she's invited to attend. She should know how this case brought us together and..."

"And what, Emerson?"

579

"Solidified our relationship on a personal level."

She smiled. "Put a bit too scientifically, but I'll take it. Why do you think Catherine brought LikLik along?"

"To renege on her promise to send the child to school in America, and instead bring her back to the Riami. Catherine was against my coming back here. She knew why I came, and this is how she shows her pique." He paused. "But maybe I'm being too harsh on Catherine. Looking after our mother may have drained all the emotion she's capable of giving at this time in her life."

DeAnn drooped. "Oh, dear."

Stanek lifted her head and kissed her cheek. "Lying here these past few days has given me time to think about a number of things. Cheer up. We'll take LikLik back to America with us. I'll get a research position, hopefully in Hawaii, and we'll tutor LikLik in science so she can return to Papua schooled in medicine. Then she can help her fledgling country and do Situmu, MilkEye, WonTok, you and me and herself proud."

"But your cancer research..."

"I've thought a lot about the cancer study as well. With the reward money the Papuan government wants to bestow on me for helping them recover Papuan gold, together with the money my adoptive mother has given me, I'll establish the Haveland Cancer Research Fund. Tom's widow will head up their board, but without my participation on it. So, if the fund decides to deal with Catherine and Stanek Laboratories, so be it."

She smiled again and returned his kiss. "Catherine will be happy, but what about us?"

"Us?"

"Yes, us."

He chuckled. "You surprise me, Dr. Toland. A moment ago I proposed to you when I said we'll look after LikLik together." He turned serious. "Only now I ask, please, never leave me. I love you. Will you marry me?"

"Oh, Emerson, I do love you. I want nothing more than to be your partner in all of life."

He kissed her lips. "Now that we've sealed our troth, and not to sound too Shakespearean, together let's go forth from here and conclude the ten knights case for the audience who awaits, although this is by no means the final curtain."

*   *   *

After shaking hands with Noble, Yowell and General Bellicosi with his good hand, and kissing Catherine's cheek, Stanek strolled up and down in front of the chairs arranged in a semi-circle in the hospital's conference room. He paused, swung around, cleared his throat and began.

"A former mentor of mine, in fact, one of the early victims in this case, said 'if you look long and hard enough at a problem, you'll see answers you might've overlooked or thought impossible before'. With this admonition, Dr. Thomas Haveland meant for us never to give up. An unrecognized clue, however improbable, may hold the key to unlocking the truth."

General Anthony Bellicosi stood up, took a pencil from his breast pocket and broke it in half. "See here, Stanek, you brought us here to name a killer. Really, must we sit waiting while you dust off an old lecture?"

Of the five people seated in front of him, Catherine was the last one Emerson expected to rise to his defense. "Oh, for God's sake, Tony, sit down. Let my brother have his say. He's a forensic pathologist. They all carry on this way. It's part of the mystique."

The general fell back in his chair. "Alright, my dear, but I expect to ask questions."

Emerson smiled at Catherine. "By all means. I encourage questions at any time. This is a complex case. We need to think it through clearly, since all of us have, or had, a stake in its outcome. If I merely named the killer without setting the table for you to feast on my conclusions, you may or may not accept what I've offered with regard to motive, victims and suspects. But as we go through the ten knights case step by step, examining all the evidence and using logic to fill in the blanks, I'm certain you'll all agree only one person had the motive, opportunity and means to perpetrate such evil in so widespread a geographical area."

A hush descended on the room, and Stanek knew he had them in the palm of his hand. Nonetheless, he wanted their participation, so he tossed the first question to Major Yowell. "Frank, what do you suppose was the murderer's primary motive behind the mining operations we saw on Mount Bosavi?"

"Gold."

"Or should we say greed? But this killer's henchmen went beyond gold fever in committing unrelated crimes."

"Such as?" General Bellicosi asked.

"Good question. Such as the initial murders, committed on the Johns Hopkins campus, of Doctor Haveland and the custodian. These were mistakes. Neither victim had any direct relation to the gold, except the killer didn't know what Haveland knew, and whether or not gold had been mentioned in the packet sent by Dr. Toland at your request."

"I had DeAnn send the pilot's log to Haveland as a way of enticing him into joining Operation Simpatico."

"Yes, I know. Instead, you enlisted me, which further drove the killer off stride. At first I thought the burglars broke into Haveland's office to steal a copy of my cancer research, but that wasn't the main target for a nasty fellow called Filipino Freddie."

Noble caught Stanek's eye as the *kiap* shifted his crutches from one side to the other. "Go ahead, Roger. What do you have to offer?"

"Just wanted to let ye know Freddie was known throughout the Pacific rim as a small time crook, who got into big time smugglin' shortly after the war."

"Indeed, it's when Freddie no doubt met the man behind all the killings and became one of his minions. But later in the United States, Freddie had troubles of his own. A number of prosecutors were breathing down his neck, Haveland being the most prominent. Freddie saw the burglary in Haveland's office as an opportunity to get rid of his nemesis on a job orchestrated by his puppet master.

"This is where our killer lost control, albeit briefly. He didn't intend to have Haveland killed. He just wanted to prevent the possible mention of gold on Mount Bosavi in DeAnn's report from leaking out to U.S. officials. But the report wasn't on the premises. Freddie and his henchmen, having turned up empty-handed after murdering two people, figured Haveland had given the report to me, and they struck out on their own to get it back."

DeAnn sought recognition next. "You mean the threats and attacks on you in Baltimore and in Hawaii respectively were the work of this Filipino Freddie acting alone? What about the time you were shot at in New Guinea, flying over the Rentoul in the Beaver with Major Yowell? Or later outside the CIL encampment when Erik was killed by mistake in your place? And who ordered the Giambu to try to kill you on the Rentoul River trip, and again the shot fired here at the hospital in Goroka while you were recovering from your shoulder wound?"

"Thanks, DeAnn, for recounting all the attacks on my life. Let's break down the incidents geographically. The Baltimore and Hawaii attacks were on Freddie's orders, but the shootings in New Guinea had the stamp of the major killer on them. We know he didn't like an army team poking around his mountain looking for remains, but the last thing he wanted was a forensic pathologist in search of a criminal, especially so close to his gold mining operation."

"But you left out Erik, the interpreter," said General Bellicosi.

Stanek stroked his chin. "Intentionally, I might add. For you see, I believe Erik wasn't killed because he wore my hat when he left my quarters in the evening. I think he was killed for the same reason Freddie was, that is, to keep him from talking. Erik, in teaching me the local languages, told me he had studied linguistics in Tokyo. There, I believe he met the killer, who enlisted him in his organization, posing it as legitimate."

"*Come a gutser!* He was as nice a lad as ye'd ever want to meet. What service could he render the killer, being an interpreter for the CIL?"

"As a *kiap*, you know how important understanding the local languages becomes in tricky situations. Interpreting was conducted on an as needed basis for the killer. Otherwise, Erik's job was to report on CIL operations. He most likely tipped off the killer about DeAnn's report in which he thought she might've mentioned gold to General Bellicosi because of Frank's bartering for nuggets with the natives. Actually DeAnn didn't know about it then, but Erik probably did. Also, Erik was the only outsider present when we discussed the river expedition."

"But Erik was already dead the day we left to go down the Rentoul in search of remains," said DeAnn.

"Right. But he knew about it beforehand and must not have communicated the information to the killer on the mountain. The murderer either found out through Loud Mouth, or from the letter his henchmen pilfered from Cole in this very hospital. Seems somebody thought Erik and I had become too chummy. MilkEye saw Loud Mouth kill Erik. Perhaps it was Erik's reluctance to report my activities to his boss which cost him his life."

Yowell learned forward in his seat. "Damn, if this case doesn't have more twists than a Texas tornado. I want to know where Clare and Al fit in."

"Hold on, Frank. Clare and Al are bit players in this drama..."

Yowell intervened. "Maybe to you, but I'm the one they tried to kill in Tari, over four small nuggets, no less."

"Very well. As I indicated at the outset, our killer operates on a global level. It isn't unusual for him to have enlisted various nationalities, including Australians like Clare and Al to do his dirty work and clean-up operations. We know the major killer was willing to go to any lengths to keep word of the gold on Mount Bosavi from getting out. It's a fair assumption the gold nuggets you traded with MilkEye for made you a marked target for Clare and Al to hit. But we must stay focused on the main suspects, who've been narrowed down to three."

Catherine tapped her foot on the floor. "Tell them, Emerson. And let's get on to more important business."

"I know, the cancer study. It's always about the cancer research. But one thing at a time." He continued, "Our three obvious suspects are Lt. Mori, the Japanese propaganda officer during the war, Angus Mackelwaite, an Australian *kiap* who prospected for gold in his spare time, and the American bombardier on the B-24, Lt. Phillipi I. Patterson. Patterson was also known as 'Pip' to his fellow aviators and 'GeeJo' to the natives, who turned him into a legendary figure."

General Bellicosi took out a cigar, but did not light it. "I see a pattern here. Your three suspects represent all of the warring parties in the New Guinea theatre. If the American's the killer, I don't want to hear about it. Operation Simpatico would be irreparably damaged by such information. Just when I'm about to go public, pending Pentagon approval, of course."

Noble chimed in, "I feel the same way about Angus. If he's the killer, I'd just as soon have the news reach my government through a different channel than me. My colleagues would see it as one *kiap* snitchin' on another."

"We have no one here to represent the Japanese perspective. It seems unfair," said DeAnn.

Catherine stomped both feet on the ground, startling the others. "What's unfair is this waste of time. I had no idea when I agreed to listen Emerson was going to drag this thing out this long. So, if you'll excuse me, I'll wait outside before I say something I'll regret."

Stanek held up his hand like a traffic policeman. "Give me five more minutes, Catherine. We're coming to a remarkable woman whom you'll see not only represents the Japanese side, but also does it with the grace and beauty of jasmine and lilacs, two flowers of which you're fond."

"How in the world can I learn anything from this Japanese woman?" asked Catherine.

"Because through her journals she taught DeAnn and me the true meaning of love." Stanek saw his words so stunned Catherine she nearly collapsed in her chair. He went on. "Kioko Tanaka, in her interview with Jim Cole in Angoram in 1953, gave us information to break this case wide open. She was one of the killer's most tragic victims, as was her brother Taro. We need to look more closely at these brutal murders. But first, let's examine the motive, opportunity, victim and manner in which the victims died from the perspective of each of our three suspects."

General Bellicosi returned the cigar to his pocket. "We've already agreed gold, or as you said greed, was the primary motive in this case. As far as I can see, it would apply to all three of your suspects."

"Yes, General. Such a gold strike would tempt anyone, but as you'll discover later, this killer went beyond greed. Here is where we must consider clues not so obvious at first. Maybe I should attack this from a different angle. You speak for the prosecution of each suspect, and I for the defense. Roger, why don't you get the ball rolling. We'll start with Angus Mackelwaite."

Noble twisted his mustache. "I'll have to get on with it then, lad. I'm due for a pain shot for me leg soon. Much as I hate to admit it, this has all the markings of old Angus who loved gold more than he did his own life."

Stanek fingered the scar on his cheek. "Afraid so, Roger. Angus Mackelwaite was involved, but only up to a point, 'til he was murdered himself by the major killer. We found his remains with remnants of khaki shorts clinging to them in the Tugaru burial site. American aviators wore khaki, but not shorts. Although the Tugaru wouldn't let us remove the bones for further analysis, Salty Meri did give me the jawbone of her deceased white husband, who was identified by Kioko as Mackelwaite. However, the findings of dental forensics in Australia regarding the jawbone were inconclusive, but there's no doubt it's Caucasian. All but one of the B-24 crewmembers' jawbones are accounted for in the nine remains DeAnn recovered, and the tenth knight is possibly still alive."

A murmur swept through the room like a wind across a prairie.

"Furthermore," Stanek continued, "From the Tugaru burial site, MilkEye and WonTok said they recovered the rubber raft intact with emergency equipment, along with Kioko's six volumes wrapped in waterproof cloth she had given to *Kiap* Mackelwaite. Roger, you're the one who discovered the bundle the Riami men left for DeAnn near the B-24 in payment for the honey she gave them."

"*Come a gutser*! I've got mixed feelings about all this. Why do ye suppose the killer got rid of Mackelwaite?"

"With a rubber dinghy in hiding, one would suspect Mackelwaite was ready at a moment's notice to take more than his share of the gold, which he'd probably been siphoning off anyway from the salt train operation, and, as Yowell might say, 'skedaddle'. The killer probably surmised as much, took care of Mackelwaite before he could make good on his escape and buried him at the Tugaru burial rock, thinking no one would ever look for him there.

"But the killer didn't know your friend Angus had already used the burial site as a hiding place for the emergency dinghy from the B-24 bomber. Mackelwaite had the opportunity to remove the 40-foot cord for use in engineering an alternate route up to the mine in order to bypass the alarm system on Situmu's ladder.

"It's not a stretch to think Mackelwaite shared his plan with Salty Meri, whom he intended to employ as a second paddler. After the *kiap* disappeared, Salty Meri went to the burial site to see if her 'husband' had left in the dinghy without her. Instead she found his body beheaded and removed the jawbone from the head, which probably fell near the bottom of the burial site where Mackelwaite had pre-positioned the dinghy.

"By the way, I believe Angus was the first white man to discover the crashed B-24, but left it unreported, even though it was his duty as a *kiap* to do so."

Noble gasped. "I'm ashamed to admit some of those lads might've been saved if Angus had done his duty."

Stanek watched the general squirm in his chair. "General Bellicosi, perhaps you'd like to take over as prosecutor and present your suspect."

"Well, if you ask me, it has to be the Japanese lieutenant, what's his name?"

"Mori."

"Okay, Mori. The Japanese are a stubborn people. I read about a soldier who stayed in hiding in the Philippines for 30 years, or something like that, never knowing the war was over."

Stanek saw the others nod. "Yes, I think we're all familiar with the case. But the Lt. Mori in our scenario most likely perished in the jungle, alone, clutching the portrait of his beloved emperor. He was a *samurai* in his mind, and no *samurai* ever leaves his sword behind. Yet, DeAnn found it on her excursion up the Tari valley in a hollow tree where Kioko said Mori had placed it to mark the burial spot of his fallen comrades, two soldiers he had beheaded as punishment for mutiny. Lt. Mori never came back for his sword or any of the remains of those who were in his party when they left Angoram nearly 30 years ago. As you know, the Japanese place a lot of emphasis on retrieving something from their dead for proper burial at home."

The general leaned forward. "I see. Certainly the killer with so much gold had the where-with-all to set matters right for his dead comrades. Only a poor leader makes promises he doesn't intend to keep."

"You would know more about that than the rest of us. But here's something else you should know about Mori. He loved Kioko and could never have murdered her in such a brutal fashion as to have her buried up to her neck in mud and then stoned until her beautiful face was obliterated. Mori, Kioko, Taro and their party of 14 Japanese soldiers spent many months in the jungle together. Lt. Mori, if he were so inclined, had ample opportunity to kill both Kioko and her brother Taro, yet we see from Kioko's journals that Mori often went out of his way to protect her and her brother. DeAnn found Taro's remains near the B-24 at burial site X-2."

DeAnn covered her mouth with her hand. "Oh, dear, Pip is left," she murmured.

"True. Pip is the remaining suspect on our list, my dear. But let's not forget Pip, or GeeJo, loved Kioko more than Lt. Mori ever could. Kioko, in fear for their son Kazuo, who'd had his life threatened, left the mountain where they lived with the Riami to return him to his ancestral home in Japan. She promised the man she called her husband to return to him. And, like Lt. Mori, she desired to bring the remains of Taro and all of the pieces of evidence buried with him back home to Japan. GeeJo waited many years for her to return, even after he had found and buried all of his buddies. And when Kioko didn't come back, he set out to find her and their son."

Almost in unison, Stanek's audience cried out. "You've exonerated all three suspects!"

Catherine shook her head. "My, my, dear brother. It looks like you've talked yourself into a trap. So, again, why have we wasted all this time?"

"You should know better, Catherine. You're the only one here who knew Tom Haveland well and often heard his admonition to keep searching the problem no matter what. It's what your researchers do at Stanek Laboratories. Forgotten in this case is another player. He was there at the outset and at the end.

"Those of you familiar with the pilot's log will recall the bomber was attacked by a persistent Japanese pilot in a Tony fighter aircraft over Wewak. One of the crewmembers, Ingersol, or Prophet, was killed in the attack and the B-24 lost an engine. When the B-24 crew dropped two bombs on Angoram in retaliation, and then headed west following the Sepik River, the Japanese fighter pilot continued to pursue them. He dropped out of sight for a brief period, which the American pilot thought he had used to refuel. Later, he reappeared and attacked them again, wounding the copilot, Botorff, and critically injured one of the gunners, Grant. The attacker must've punctured a fuel tank as well.

"By my calculations, the Japanese pilot trailed the Americans all the way to Mount Bosavi. The B-24 bomber, almost out of fuel, barely cleared the mountain, except for part of the tail section, which hit the top, broke off and caused the aircraft to stall and crash on the north side of the mountain. All of the crewmembers in the aft section of the aircraft were thrown out when part of the tail separated from the rest of the fuselage.

"Miraculously, and the Air Force has confirmed this has happened before, they survived impact with the mountain top, except for Grant who was probably already dead. They buried him where he had fallen. From there, let's assume the crash survivors found the cave entrance behind the cascade and discovered it ran through the mountain. They hid there until Situmu found them. Initially, they subsisted off the burnt offerings left by the Tugaru at the foot of the vertical stabilizer with the skull and cross-bombs painted on it, which the Tugaru considered to be a totem of the mountain spirit."

Yowell raised his hand. "What happened to the Japanese fighter pilot?" he asked, looking to the others for approval.

Stanek continued, "Low on fuel, the Japanese fighter pilot was nevertheless able to clear the mountain, but ditched in the tall reeds along the Rentoul. The American's original plan was to return to Port Moresby by the southern route, but the fuel leak caused them to change plans. They would also have had to ditch along the Rentoul River and make it back to Port Moresby by going down the river in the rubber dinghy to the Strickland River, then over to the Fly River into the Gulf of Papua."

DeAnn leapt from her seat. "Yellowhammer!" she cried.

"*Come a gutser*! Yellowhammer!" *Kiap* Noble repeated.

General Bellicosi picked up the chorus. "Yellowhammer! Didn't the Americans nickname the pilot of the Tony 'Yellowhammer'? But how do you know his identity?"

"Yellowhammer, or our major killer, general, is Jiro Tanaka, younger brother to Taro and Kioko and second in line behind Taro to inherit the family earldom bequeathed by an emperor to one of the Tanaka ancestors. Here, then, is a motive a notch past greed.

"Earlier I mentioned Mackelwaite was beheaded. This was Yellowhammer's preferred method of killing, no doubt by the *samurai* sword, ever at his side, even when he was in the cockpit. Two of the crewman's remains found along the Rentoul had been beheaded as well, most likely by Jiro, who doomed the nearly blind copilot, Botorff, to a death by starvation as he waited hidden in the cave behind the cascade at Lower Falls."

"*Come a gutser*, lad. We still can't be sure Yellowhammer and Jiro are one and the same."

"Yes, Doctor, all this seems, to use your words, a bit of a stretch, unless you've got proof," said Bellicosi.

"I've got proof alright, but first let's consider the motive beyond greed. In all the murders committed by Jiro directly, he used his *samurai* sword to make quick work of his victims, except in the case of Kioko and Taro, where the corpses were mutilated beyond recognition. Medical examiners see this occur most often in cases where the killer feels so passionate about what he's doing, and his sense of betrayal is so heightened, he wants to obliterate the victim, as if to drive him or her out of existence. Love affairs gone awry or family disputes which get out of hand are some examples."

DeAnn moved to the edge of her seat. "But why would Jiro want to reign down such fury on his brother and sister?"

"I believe the motive beyond greed is twofold, yet anchored in pride. He couldn't accept as a *samurai* what looked like Taro's surrender to Pip. In the same vein, he was infuriated to learn Kioko had not only slept with the enemy, but also bore his child. In Jiro's mind, this made Kioko unacceptable and justified the killing of Taro as one who was unfit to wear the mantle handed down by their ancestors.

"Remember, DeAnn, Kioko opens her story with fear for her son Kazuo's life. Jiro is the one who threatened the child, Kazuo being another potential heir to the earldom even though a 'half-breed'. The husband whom Kioko thought might never forgive her for the role she played as New Guinea Ginny, spreading doubt in the form of propaganda among the American forces, was not the threat. Again, Taro and Kioko stand out as exceptions to the rule that a *samurai* never tortures his victims when a quick death shows respect.

"Ironically, Jiro, based at Wewak, started out to avenge what he thought were his brother and sister's deaths following the bombing at the radio station in Angoram. His anger drove him to pursue the ten knights so relentlessly. As it turned out, he was the one who killed Taro outright and ordered the stoning of Kioko."

Stanek paused and looked directly at Catherine. "Sometimes we destroy the one we once loved," he said. Catherine looked down and averted his gaze.

"Sorry, Doctor, I remain unconvinced until you show me tangible proof linking Yellowhammer to Jiro," said General Bellicosi. "At least give us something we can wrap our minds around."

Stanek took in a deep breath. "In Kioko's interview with Jim Cole, she told him about GeeJo's account of the murder of several Japanese citizens who came up the Rentoul in 1953. This was a search party looking for the remains of their war dead. Naturally, the Tony, overgrown with vegetation, caught their attention. One of the delegates went so far as to photograph the engine inside the cowling when they were set upon by Giambu warriors directed by two white men, whom I believe to have been Mackelwaite and Jiro. The man with the camera pitched it under the fuselage before he fell.

"MilkEye and WonTok retrieved the camera on their way back to the Riami village with GeeJo. They put it in the men's spirit house. In Lt. Dunbar's letter to DeAnn at Angoram, with which he also sent a copy of Jim Cole's manuscript under separate cover, he asked DeAnn to have Roger retrieve the camera from the Riami spirit house when they returned. Unbelievably, when the film was developed, one of the images revealed the engine number. From there we traced it to a one of a kind aircraft assigned to Jiro's squadron in Wewak."

"But Lt. Mori said Jiro was dead," said DeAnn.

"He lied to Kioko. Not the first time, as you may recall. Mori wanted to keep her dependent on him as long as possible, hoping she would grow to love him, disfigured though he was."

General Bellicosi stood up and looked at DeAnn. I'm miffed you didn't keep me informed about this Kioko woman's journals. Why wasn't I told about them?" The general shifted his gaze to Stanek. "I want to know how you can be certain this Jiro Tanaka fellow piloted the Tony pursuing the B-24. Furthermore, how did he and Mackelwaite hook up, and how did they know there was gold on Mount Bosavi?"

"All good questions, which deserve good answers. We have evidence from the manifests of ships delivering prisoners from New Guinea to be repatriated in Japan. Jiro, using the alias 'Hideo Yamazaki', had been aboard one of those ships. Interpol records show 'Hideo Yamazaki' was a soldier killed in the first Russo-Japanese war. Therefore, this information signaled to us someone else hid behind the name.

"Furthermore, since the fake 'Hideo' came from Nomad where he had lingered in jail under *Kiap* Mackelwaite's supervision for some time, there is a high probability he learned of the gold from Mackelwaite and became his partner. Before he was released in 1945, Hideo, or Jiro, and Mackelwaite most likely hatched a scheme for getting the gold from Mount Bosavi to Manila, then on to Japan without anyone knowing about it.

"We can further assume upon his repatriation, Jiro blended into Japanese society under the alias of Hideo Yamazaki. Jiro, who, according to his sister, was never interested in being an innkeeper, except for the title it carried, rejoined the circle run by corrupted merchants.

"With the business connections he solidified, he was able to set the scheme hatched by him and Mackelwaite into motion. Jiro got himself appointed, again using the alias, Hideo Yamazaki, to the main recovery team sent to New Guinea in 1953.

"Meantime, Mackelwaite had agreed to escort the Japanese search party up the Rentoul where he knew the location of Jiro's Tony aircraft wreckage. The Giambu, whom Mackelwaite had befriended, perhaps by taking a native wife, or by going easy on the cannibals he had pinched, set upon the Japanese delegation. In a betrayal of his own countrymen, Jiro allowed the natives, who still practiced cannibalism, to capture them, leaving the partners free to proceed in implementing their scheme. As we speak, Interpol is following up on this scenario to establish the veracity of the identity of the man in armor, if they can ever locate his body, and connect him to the illegal gold trail out of New Guinea to Japan. They're also going after any accomplices of Jiro still at large.

"By the way, the partial armor Jiro wore to conceal his identity when on the mountain came from the fallen B-24. The pilot's log mentions the armor was borrowed from the officer's club at Port Moresby just before their ill-fated mission.

"Note a left-handed person wrote the pilot's log. I believe the author was Pip, rather than the pilot, Oscar Sanchez, who died on impact and couldn't have been the author. Besides, Sanchez was right-handed and the copilot was left-handed. The log states each brought their predominant hands to the controls between them. The pilot sits in the left seat and the copilot in the right. Therefore, Sanchez had to be right-handed. Add to this the fact that the log was written on mariners' charts, which Kioko says in her log that GeeJo picked up at the coastwatchers' station, and we have enough evidence to surmise the true author. Why Patterson decided to assume the Sanchez persona in writing the log might've had something to do with leaving behind a record of the mission as perceived by their revered leader.

"I believe Patterson, the bombardier, inadvertently parachuted out the wheel well of the B-24 before it crashed on Mount Bosavi. He spent the rest of his days looking for his lost comrades 'til he, too, encountered the killer while digging up gold from where he'd hidden it inside the B-24 wreckage. He lost his right hand to the blade of the *samurai* sword. It's the same hand preserved in formaldehyde at Walter Reed."

General Bellicosi walked over to Stanek and pumped his good hand. "Good work, Dr. Stanek. I think we can fit the rest of the pieces of this obscure Papuan operation together from what you've already presented. I'm relieved to know it wasn't one of our lads behind all this murder and mayhem. I can go on with Operation Simpatico with what we've got, as long as you don't tell your story to the press, who'll zoom in on the sensational aspects and disregard our brave heroes altogether."

Everyone stood up and started to file out. Stanek pulled General Bellicosi aside and allowed the others to pass through. "Sir, a chapter in this episode still demands our attention."

"What could it be? Your killer's dead. If they're able to retrieve his body from under what must be smashed armor, identify him and ship his remains back to Japan for his family to deal with, the case is closed."

Stanek tightened his grip on the general's arm. "You want something from me. I want something from you."

"Go on."

"The ten knights: they lived together, fought together, and if they perished in combat together, would've wanted to be buried together. You have the power to grant them this last wish. I've discussed it with DeAnn, and we think the proper thing to do is to report the identification of individuals is at best only tentative, if indeed all the nine sets of remains recovered are actually those of the crewmembers of the crashed B-24. Therefore, we recommend the knights be buried in a common grave."

"Why, even if I agreed, we couldn't do such a thing. We've still got one missing, this Lt. Pip, or what's his name."

"As I just mentioned, we've got good reason to believe the severed hand belongs to Lt. Phillipi I. Patterson.

"Just what're you proposing, Doctor?"

"If you place the hand in the group grave with the other remains, the marker can show the names of the whole crew. If you agree, you'll have my promise the criminal side of this story will never be revealed by me or Dr. Toland."

"Why would you want to do this?"

Stanek took a crumpled sheet of paper from his pocket. Here's a poem Jim Cole had received from Kioko and handed to me before he died. One man wrote it, perhaps Pip, but I have no doubt all ten knights collaborated on it before they left on their last mission. It's the epitaph they would've wanted and comes from one source familiar to you."

Bellicosi unfolded the paper and read it. Stanek saw tears in the general's eyes as he handed it back. But the pathologist pressed the paper into his hands again and said, "No, I've made copies, so you keep this one, General."

Bellicosi tapped Stanek on his good shoulder. "You've reached the emotional Italian in me. It's a deal, Doc. I'll see to it our ten knights are interred at Jefferson Barracks National Cemetery in Missouri with full military honors. We put our group burials from World War II there."

As Stanek followed the general out of the room, he spotted Catherine, who stood by the side of the doorway. She stepped in front of him and blocked his further passage. He could see strong emotion in her flashing eyes.

"You gave some performance, Emerson," she said. "Did you intend to humiliate me? Because if you did, you succeeded."

"I thought it was the best way to avoid a scene," he said. "Humiliation wasn't my intent. I only wanted to let you down gently. You must've realized by now DeAnn and I have drawn closer together while working on this case."

"But that stuff about love shattered the dreams I had for us!"

"Those dreams are impossible under the circumstances we grew up under."

"So my love for you has been dismissed as a girlish fantasy?"

"No, I can accept your love as an adoptive sister."

Stanek reminded her of his plans for the Haveland Cancer Research Foundation, and how it would benefit Stanek Laboratories.

She forced a smile, "Well, at least we've salvaged something out of this situation, and I take it you'll release me from my promise to publicly pillar myself for the incident in the laboratory when we were young."

"I can't answer you at the moment, but one day when you're going through Billings Hall, stop at the Christ statue and look in the ledger. You'll find my answer written there."

"Must you always be so mysterious?"

"You said it yourself. It comes with being a pathologist. But before we part, I will thank you for helping me find my heritage when I didn't want to face the prospect of being unwanted in two families, yours and that of my natural parents. This doesn't mean I love your mother any less."

"And me? Did you ever love me?"

"Not in the way you wanted."

She burst into tears and cried, "What's left for me?"

"You have your mother, Stanek Laboratories and Charles, who would like to give your marriage another go."

"Charles said that?"

"Not in those exact terms. But if you want to take an older brother's advice, give him a call."

She leaned forward and kissed the crescent scar on his right cheek, then let her fingers linger where her lips had been. "Will you ever forgive me for the hurt I've caused? If I'd realized how deep this scar ran, I might've acted differently. Now, it'll always be a reminder of what could've been."

He started to answer, but Major Yowell came down the hallway and called to him. "Emerson, thanks to you, I'm being shipped back to Vietnam."

"Vietnam?"

"Yeah. Excuse me, Catherine, for busting in, but your brother needs to know I'm happy with this new assignment."

Catherine said goodbye, excused herself and left, dabbing at her eyes with a handkerchief.

Yowell followed her with his eyes as she walked down the corridor. "I take it she's not crying over my news, like some of the stewardesses with missionary airlines here have done."

"Does DeAnn know?" Stanek asked.

"Yep. And come to think of it, she shed a tear or two, but it was the kind any soldier would get, going off to war, I mean."

"Why am I responsible for your new assignment, Frank?"

"Because you wound up this case. Now I'm needed as a pilot to help with the evacuation of VIPs as we draw down U.S. forces as called for in the peace accords we negotiated with the communists.

If you ask me, the agreement isn't worth a bucket of spit, because, as we learned from Korea, the reds don't keep their side of the bargain. But I suppose we have to go through with the charade anyway.

"Hope we've left a few round-eyed women for me to chase, since you've won the heart of the only one I was really interested in here in New Guinea. It was obvious at our first meeting in Hawaii all your scientific stuff would sink my chances with DeAnn."

"Hope there's no hard feelings between us," Stanek said.

"No, Doc. Besides, you're much more likeable now than you were back then. Besides we need people like you. Who else will rid society of its criminal-type varmints like Yellowhammer. I'll be able to tell my grandchildren someday that I worked on a case with the world's foremost forensic pathologist. Of course, I'll have to have a dictionary in hand when I tell 'em."

"Good luck, Frank. And if you're in Hawaii, or the Washington D.C./Baltimore area, look us up."

"Just might do that. General Bellicosi tells me after a year in 'Nam, he'll set me up for a Pentagon job to punch my ticket on the way to lieutenant colonel."

They shook hands. Stanek left to find DeAnn. Strange, he thought, I'm about to close one chapter in my life and open another. From the cemetery in St. Louis, he, DeAnn and LikLik would go to Johns Hopkins, after which he and DeAnn would be free from both their obligations to the ten knights and from his past.

He wondered if they could talk Roger Noble into joining them at the burial site. Then there was the matter of the two mystery guests he wanted to invite. Would they be receptive to a telegram he intended to send once the burial plans were finalized?

57 LAST KNIGHT OUT SHUT THE DOOR

Jefferson Barracks National Cemetery,
St. Louis, Missouri, 1973

U.S. ARMY CENTRAL IDENTIFICATION LABORATORY
(PROVISIONAL) FINDINGS, CASE NUMBER 316. DR. DEANN
TOLAND'S FINAL REPORT.

It was the war that brought the "Ten Knights"
together and the war that tore them apart. What but
war could have caused the Americans and Japanese to
venture to New Guinea, a land that time forgot? The
war spilled into a country under Australian authority
where Papuans, bound by their native cultures, dealt
daily with personal and tribal warfare fueled by
their own payback customs. Citizens of four nations
came together in this unlikely spot with its
primitive beauty, and lethal danger.

None could forget their upbringing, the very
backbone of their identities, forged in national or
cultural homes. Despite shared experiences, family
heritage or national soul curtailed compassion
separating them, one from the other, in so many ways.

Is it the way we organize ourselves as nations
that delivers us into war, forgetting the love that
binds us together as one? Regardless of our national
or cultural perceptions, are we not all "Knights on
the Barroom Floor," hopefully to be lifted up when we
close the door on this life?

DeAnn Toland, Ph.D.
Physical Anthropologist

O N A BRIGHT, blue October day with no clouds in view, the black limousine carrying General Bellicosi and his special guests entered the main gate of Jefferson Barracks National Cemetery, St. Louis, Missouri, behind the cortege of ten hearses. Stanek, seated beside the general and across from DeAnn Toland, LikLik and *Kiap* Roger Noble, caught the sound of singing off in the distance. He opened the window. "Music's not my forte, but does anyone recognize the tune being sung?"

General Bellicosi beamed. "It's an army chorus going through rehearsal for their part in today's ceremony. The particular hymn we hear playing is my favorite, a tribute to all fighting men who face peril on air, land and sea."

DeAnn adjusted the black bonnet Emerson had bought for her. "The officially titled 'Almighty Father, Strong to Save' has been played many times at memorial services for those killed in Vietnam."

Stanek tapped his cheek below the scar. "Now I remember. I heard the hymn coming from the chapel at Tripler one evening as I passed by on my rounds. Must've been a memorial service for war dead going on."

"Thank God ye Yanks are 'bout to shut the war down. We've lost a few Aussie lads in Vietnam, too. Nobody hears 'bout 'em. My government wants it kept hush, hush."

General Bellicosi extended his hand to Noble. "Well, I'm grateful for all you've done as an ally and for the men we honor posthumously. Had you not found the aircraft, the remains of the ten knights might still be lying in the jungle unattended and without a proper send-off."

"Thanks, General. Done as a team, and a damn good one, if ye ask me, Jim Cole included."

The general studied the shine on his shoes. "Ah, yes, Jim. A pesky fellow if ever there was one."

"But with a heart of gold," said DeAnn. "I'm so glad Jim's lighter found its way back into the severed hand of the last knight, and both will be buried with the group."

"Certainly. I didn't mean to disparage the late reporter, my dear. Only wanted to point out his perseverance."

This time Stanek interjected. "From which all of us profited in our search for the truth."

DeAnn added, "None more so than the families who gather here today to bid goodbye to those they never stopped loving."

"Well put, Dr. Toland. Nice sentiment. I could've used your words in my letter of invitation sent to those who have suffered more than a quarter of a century of doubt. And let me add it took some doing to get the Chief of Staff to sign off on your status as 'four closely related persons,' thereby authorizing government travel expenses."

"I'm sure DeAnn and Roger feel the same. We'd have come here on our own if need be."

"Certainly you would, but it's much more convenient to have official status at this type of ceremony. You know what I said when the Chief of Staff asked me which of the ten knights you four represented? I said, 'Patterson, the bombardier, the last to be recognized.'"

Stanek caught DeAnn's eye. "I'm sure DeAnn feels kinship for every set of remains she's recovered."

DeAnn drew a gloved hand across her cheek. "Emerson, you're making me cry, and the funeral hasn't even started."

General Bellicosi fingered the brass buttons on his jacket. "There then, my dear. Let me finish the story of my encounter with my superiors. I say 'superiors' because the vice-chief was present when the Chief of Staff thundered, 'Patterson?!' He had the incredulous look in his eyes reserved for authority. 'You're not making this up, are you Bellicosi?' he asked. Hoisted on my own petard, I was caught, of course. I couldn't have made a case for you being bona fide representatives of one of the ten knights.

"But as it turned out, I didn't have to. The vice-chief came to my aid. He told the chief that he knew of Dr. Stanek, who had helped his daughter Margaret at Johns Hopkins when he was in Vietnam. He said he had made it home from the war before the little girl passed on (bless her soul) of cancer."

LikLik spoke up, "Margaret better like LikLik?"

DeAnn answered softly. "I'm sorry LikLik. Margaret's no longer here for you to see."

"Oh, she die!" LikLik cried. "LikLik miss Margaret."

DeAnn put her arm around MilkEye's daughter, who put her head on DeAnn's shoulder. Tears streamed down the native girl's face.

General Bellicosi tapped the little girl's knees. "I'm sorry to have upset you with the news of your friend's death. Margaret's grandfather had tears in his eyes as well at the meeting with the chief when he said, 'Margaret wanted to have a copy of a poem laid in her hand when put to rest. She said she and Dr. Stanek had collaborated on the poem weeks before the cancer reached its final stages'."

Stanek started to speak, but Bellicosi signaled him with his eyes he desired to continue. "Let me finish, please, Emerson. The vice-chief then said Margaret told him Dr. Stanek was a sensitive, caring man. He added that he was only too glad to assist in getting you to a mountaintop in New Guinea to finish your casework. 'My recommendation,' the vice-chief said, 'is to allow Dr. Stanek and his colleagues to represent Lt. Patterson at the interment, especially since records show Patterson was an orphan. Otherwise, there'll be no one to stand in for the bombardier along with family representatives for the other nine crewmembers'."

General Bellicosi took a cigar from his breast pocket, looked around and quickly put it back. "After all this banter, the Chief of Staff said, 'Done.' End of my story. So here we are, grateful to have friends in high places."

DeAnn glanced at Stanek as she spoke to the general, "How thoughtful of you to enclose in your invitation to the surviving representatives of the ten knights, the copilot's letters of condolence addressed to them from New Guinea as he lay dying."

"Credit goes to Dr. Stanek, my dear. And it was his idea, too, to put Cole's lighter back into the severed hand and bury the two together in Lt. Patterson's coffin."

Stanek twisted in his seat as DeAnn's warm smile bridged the space between them. "Why do I feel our busy little bee has another surprise in store?" she asked. "I suspect it has something to do with Kioko's original journals you asked me to bring along."

Stoplights on the hearses in front of them glowed bright red, and Stanek looked out the window to see an army band raising their instruments. Beside the band, drawn up in three ranks stood an honor guard platoon.

Bellicosi leaned across Stanek, "They're from nearby Fort Leonard Wood and will act as pall bearers and render a salute fired just before taps. Each family has had a personal escort assigned to them. When we leave the limousine, I think it would be appropriate for the four of you to walk behind the casket designated for Lt. Patterson, so the military escort can seat you under the canopy over there with the families of the fallen. All told, we expect about 100 guests, including immediate family members, aunts, uncles and friends. Any questions?"

"How long will the ceremony last?" Stanek asked. "After we see Roger off at the airport, DeAnn, LikLik and I are headed for Baltimore this afternoon."

"Oh, these things usually run 30–45 minutes or so. We'll hear the band play *America the Beautiful.* Then I'll say a few words, followed by the chorus. The chaplain will lead us in prayer. Thanks to our friend Noble and the Australian consulate, we'll hear *Amazing Grace* on the bagpipes. We'll fire a salute and finally a bugler will sound taps.

"We allow families to take as long as they want at the gravesite after the soldiers have been dismissed. Folks like to leave mementos of their loved ones beside the grave. Later, to protect them from the elements, we collect and place the items in a museum on the grounds where they're available for viewing in perpetuity."

"What a wonderful gesture," said DeAnn. "I'd like to stay for it, only we've nothing to leave behind for Pip, except for Kioko's logs."

Stanek waved a finger at her, but addressed Bellicosi.

"Sure we do. General, did you bring the poem on the ten knights I gave you?"

"Indeed I did. I've even had it framed and intend to use it in my remarks."

"Good. DeAnn and I will place it at the grave and later you can collect it for the museum."

"An aide opened the door on General Bellicosi's side of the car. He hesitated before he alighted. "Oh, by the way folks, as a family you'll be presented with the American flag draped over Lt. Patterson's designated coffin. Do you want me to put it in the museum as well?"

"No, thank you, we have a special place for it," Stanek replied.

       *   *   *

The honor guard came to attention as the band played *America the Beautiful.* Stanek noticed those under the canopy not in uniform put a hand over their hearts. General Bellicosi welcomed relatives and friends and outlined the sequence of events. He closed his remarks with an invitation for the families to stay as long as they liked after the bugler renders taps. "I'm sure," he said, "many of you will feel the need to bid a final farewell in your own manner." He then told them about the arrangements made for any relics they should desire to leave behind. "We'll see they're cared for," he said. "And the next time you come to Jefferson Barracks National Cemetery, they'll be there for anyone to see that you want to bring with you not represented here today."

Near the conclusion of his speech, General Bellicosi read the poem the ten knights had composed together as revealed in the copilot's log:

Rise brave knights from the barroom floor
After a sortie through hell in your B-24.
Now heaven-bound, ten souls doth soar,
Once the last knight out has closed the door.

General Bellicosi stepped back from the podium, and the chaplain took his place. He read passages from both the Old and New Testaments, then concluded his inspirational message with the reading of the names of the fallen. During the playing of taps, Stanek gripped DeAnn's arm as she was on the brink of pouring out her emotions as the family representatives had already done. She held it well, he thought, until the sergeant in charge presented her with the American flag from Pip's designated coffin. At this point the floodgates opened, and he, too, found himself choking back tears.

Once the military officials had left, family members came forth one by one along with their escorts, to bow over the coffin of their loved one. As if by prearranged signal, they followed a certain order. First, came an elderly gentleman aided by a middle-aged woman. Together they placed a model airplane beside the coffin of Lt. Oscar Sanchez. Next came the copilot's sister identified by the brand new fishing reel still boxed she laid down beside the coffin of Toggle Joe.

Then, as soon as she departed to rejoin her family, a middle-aged man, carrying something under his arm Stanek did not recognize at first, stopped at the bier of "Admiral", the navigator.

"Who is he?" DeAnn asked as the stranger took a sextant from under his arm.

"It's got to be 'Skipper,' the friend Nelson encouraged to go on to become a navigator, like himself, after his friend washed out of pilot's training," he whispered.

DeAnn cupped her hand over Emerson's ear. "The representatives of the officers are going first. Does this mean we're up next as the bombardier's representatives?"

"No. We're to go last," he said softly.

In front of them, a stout woman made her way to Timothy O' Leary's coffin. Noble, who had been silent, spoke up in a voice Stanek thought almost too loud for a funeral. "I know an Aussie lass when I see one. She's got to be the bird Sgt. O'Leary was chalkin' up in Sydney." The *kiap's* observation was confirmed when the woman in question set a stack of letters tied with a red ribbon at the head of O'Leary's flag draped casket. A man about the same age as she stepped forward and helped her back to her seat under the canopy.

"Looks like she went on with her life and found another bloke, as it should be, if ye ask me."

From under the canopy, a man wearing a skullcap and shawl over his shoulders stood as the Australian woman took her seat. He carried in his hand a yarmulke.

"Ingersol's rabbi," Stanek whispered. "Perhaps he's surrendering the old yarmulke 'Prophet' wore to the services in his synagogue." He watched Rabbi Rosenberg bow and heard him say Kaddish.

A woman in her 50s accompanied by a young man in his mid-30s passed by Stanek, DeAnn, Noble and LikLik. Stanek caught a glimpse of their memento. It was a framed picture of the two of them seated outside the Peedee Café.

"It's the wife and son of Sgt. Wells, wouldn't you say, Emerson?"

Stanek squeezed DeAnn's hand and LikLik's. "Think of it. The boy was much younger than LikLik when he lost his father."

Retracing the steps of Wells' family came a man in his 50s bearing a stack of comic books held together with what looked like a dog collar. "I suppose "Signals'" grandparents have gone to their reward, and are represented by Alexander's cousin Danny, and if only in spirit, his dog Teddy," said Stanek.

Two well-dressed elderly men rose from their seats, picked up their canes and leaned on each other for support. After some confusion, they were led to the coffin containing the remains of Sgt. Douglas Shipley by one of the military escorts. They had their arms linked and in their free hands carried a four-in-hand tie and an old Dodger's baseball cap. With a great deal of effort, one knelt down and placed the baseball cap on the grass with its bill face down. The other gentleman knelt as well and laid the tie over the cap. They helped each other up, made the sign of the cross and went back to their seats.

"Thanks for coming, Uncle John and Uncle William," Stanek murmured under his breath. Then he said to the others, "There's one more and then it's our turn. As we all know, the ninth knight located was the hardest to recover, considering his remains were buried so close to the center of Yellowhammer's global gold mining and smuggling operation. I know Alfred Grant detested war the most and was the only one buried with his dog tags so we could get full identification. Yet, his brother consented to have U.S. placed beside his buddies, even though Grant discouraged his younger brother from glorifying combat and wanted him to go into medicine instead. Looks like he took his older brother's advice. If I'm not mistaken, Dr. Norman Grant is making his way to the coffin with a stethoscope in his hand to leave behind."

When the doctor returned to his seat, Stanek stood up and indicated DeAnn, Noble and LikLik should follow his lead. "Now it's our turn," he said. "Pip's casket is number ten in the second row. We'll leave the poem General Bellicosi read, and after a moment of silence, if you like, come back here and greet the other representatives."

Since the four of them had been seated in the front row with the other families, Stanek was unable to see who stood behind them under the canopy overflowing with people, some of whom had already dispersed. But after he bent over to place the poem by the side of the grave, he looked up and saw two men looking intently at him as they stood silently in the shade of the canopy. LikLik, who had knelt down beside him, followed his gaze. She jumped up and pointed to the tallest of the two men and cried, "GeeJo!" Before DeAnn or Emerson could stop her, she raced across the lawn and threw her arms around the legs of the stranger. Keeping one hand in his pocket, he embraced her with the other.

The younger man and shorter of the two appeared startled as did DeAnn. "Good," Stanek said. "They got my invitation in time and decided to come."

Emerson took her by the hand, "DeAnn, come with me and bring Kioko's tablets with you. Roger, you come, too. I want you to meet Pip and his son Kazuo. They came all the way from Japan, Suraga Bay below Satta Mountain, as a matter of fact."

Together they joined LikLik who kept repeating, "GeeJo here. Me tell Papa's spirit next time he speak. Me see GeeJo. Papa glad."

"Gentlemen," said Stanek. "MilkEye would've been here with his daughter, who's now in our care, but he rests beside Situmu, guarding the Riami village from the ceremonial burial ground. I'm Dr. Emerson Stanek who sent you the telegram. With me is Dr. DeAnn Toland, whose search for remains helped make this moment possible, and *Kiap* Roger Noble who discovered 'Ten Knights on the Barroom Floor' on Mount Bosavi in 1972. I'm aware you want to keep your identity secret so you can live out your days in peace at the Tanaka Inn where Kioko is buried in the gardens of their ancestors. We've arranged for the remains of Kioko's brother Taro to be returned there as well. But Dr. Toland has something to present to the husband and son of Kioko Tanaka."

The tall man put his arm around DeAnn as she attempted to hand him six tablets bound together with Jim Cole's manuscript in a bundle, along with the U.S. flag memorial. When Stanek shook his head, DeAnn caught the signal. Pip had but one hand, and it was draped over her shoulder. She turned slightly and gave them to the young man. "Kazuo, take these for your father. They belong to both of you."

Stanek added. "Included with Kioko's journals is an interview of the coastwatcher, Jim Cole, with Kioko in 1953. You'll see Kioko left another legacy as well, this time in Cole's care. It has been held for Kazuo in a bank in Hawaii, collecting interest all these years. The coastwatcher passed away recently and left instructions in his will to forward the money to the rightful heir when found. Now this legacy can finally be bestowed."

The tall man hugged each in turn. Pip kissed DeAnn's cheek and bent down to do the same to LikLik. "Thanks to all of you for all you've done for my buddies and my family," he said. He and his son took a step back and both bowed before they departed. For a long time the four watched in silence as the two men made their way across the field and out of sight.

DeAnn squeezed Stanek's arm. "Now they'll know Kioko never stopped loving them, and I'll never stop loving you, although you could've prepared me for this surprise after a day when almost all my emotions have been drained."

"Hold tight, dear. There's one more thing I must do at John's Hopkins, besides seeing mother, before we stop in Chicago to see your parents and then head back to Hawaii."

"Another surprise?"

"More for someone else than for you, although I'm sure you'll approve."

PURSUED:
TEN KNIGHTS ON THE BARROOM FLOOR

Mel R. Jones

EPILOGUE:

"Love comes to those who seek it, uniting them,
whatever the hour."

EPILOGUE

T HE NEXT DAY at Johns Hopkins, Stanek left DeAnn and LikLik outside Billings Hall to study the sundial Jim Cole's father had helped build while he went inside the rotunda. He crossed the threshold and stood at the feet of the Christ statue. And, as he had seen so many of his colleagues do over the years, he placed a hand on the feet worn smooth by so much touching. He inclined his head and then moved over to the ledger against the wall. He found a blank space, wrote in the date, then inscribed the following message:

To Catherine Stanek and her family and to my natural parents:
"All is forgiven!"
Signed: "Emerson Addison Stanek"

Stanek found DeAnn and LikLik at the sundial. "Thanks for your patience," he said as he took each by the hand. They turned to leave, but Stanek hesitated, came back and read the inscription on the sundial's brass plate aloud:

One hour alone is in thy hands,
The hour on which the shadow stands.

Stanek stroked his beard. "You know, this ten knights case, and all that has happened since the day Tom Haveland, my colleagues and I tried to address the riddle, have given me an answer which escaped me before."

DeAnn squeezed his hand. "And what is it, dearest?"

Now the message reminds me that 'love comes to those who seek it, uniting them, whatever the hour.'"

ABOUT THE AUTHOR

Mel R. Jones's diverse military career included serving several years as an enlisted soldier in the U.S. Army. Later he became an artillery officer and a public information specialist attaining the rank of Lieutenant Colonel. His public affairs duties included serving as press aide and speech writer for the Secretary of the Army.

Jones's other notable assignments included two tours of duty in Vietnam, the first of which in 1962-1963, as an advisor, he created and edited the MAAG/MACV (Military Assistance Advisory Group / Military Assistance Command, Vietnam) Observer, the first official U.S. Armed Forces Publication in Southeast Asia.

A second Vietnam tour in 1969-1970 as public affairs officer for the 1st Air Calvary Division, required Jones to accompany his unit into Cambodia, where he established a press center in a hostile area of operation and provided support to international media as spokesperson for the spearhead division.

As the first public affairs officer for all recruiters during the startup for the Volunteer Army, Jones authored the U.S. Army Recruiting Command's Public Affairs Handbook for Commanders and PAOs. He was inducted into the U.S. Army Public Affairs Hall of Fame in 2001. During his Army career he earned the Air Medal, Bronze Star and Legion of Merit among other awards.

After his Army career, Jones worked as public relations director for several firms including the Experimental Aircraft Association. Later he established his own public relations firm. He graduated from Florida Southern College with a B.A. degree in international relations and a minor in journalism and later earned two masters degrees, the first in international relations at Boston University and the second in mass communications at Marquette University in Milwaukee, Wisconsin.

Jones's published works include a book of poetry and two non-fiction books as well as numerous magazine and newspaper articles. The late Mel R. Jones is survived by his wife, Marian, his children Beth, Grace, Mark and Matthew, seven grandchildren and four great grandchildren.

OTHER TITLES BY MEL R. JONES

Other titles written by Mel R. Jones include a book of poetry entitled, *In the Eye of the Storm*, 1965, a non-fiction book *Above and Beyond: Eight Great American Aerobatic Champions*, Tab Books, Inc., 1984, and co-author of *A Silent Siren Song, the Aitken Brothers Hollywood Odyssey 1905–1926* with father-in-law Al P. Nelson, Cooper Square Press (an imprint of Rowman Littlefield Publishing Group), New York, 2000. The co-authors of *A Silent Siren Song* won a Distinguished Service to History Award of Merit from the Wisconsin Historical Society in June 2001. An inspirational article, "Candle in the Dark", based on Jones' first tour of duty in Vietnam, was published in *This Week* magazine in December 26, 1965.

Jones also wrote numerous magazine and newspaper articles, including magazines such as *Proceedings, Amphibious Warfare Review, Sea Power, Army, Guardsman, Infantry, Armor, Aviation Week & Space Technology, Family (Army, Navy, Air Force Times), TWA Ambassador, The Flying A, Catholic Digest, Wisconsin Trails* and others. In addition, he wrote a museum guide, *Putting Wings on Dreams* for the Experimental Aircraft Association.

IMAGE ATTRIBUTION